His hand roamed. Down h̲͟_͟_͟_͟_͟_͟_͟_͟_͟_͟_͟ ̲͟_͟_͟_͟_͟_͟_͟_͟_͟_͟ leaving fire in its wake.

Megan broke away, gasping for air. With each rapid breath, reason rushed in. They lived in different centuries. The universe was playing with them like pawns on a chessboard. She feared losing her heart to a man already dead.

She rested her forehead on his. "Seth. Stop."

He sat back, his arms releasing her as his eyes searched her face.

She said softly, "You're ruining everything."

Seth ran a hand down her arm, sending a shiver through her. "What am I ruinin'?"

"Our friendship. Everyone knows the surest way to ruin a friendship is to have sex. So we're not going to."

"I agree. We won't have sex."

Surprise and disappointment warred inside her.

He took her hand. "We'll make love."

She yanked her hand free. "No, we're not!"

"We're not?"

She shook her head.

He tilted his. "Ever?"

She shook her head again.

"Never ever?"

She shook her head so hard her curls bounced.

One corner of his mouth twitched, then the other corner curved upward, and a full-blown smile spread across his face. He laughed.

The sound of it annoyed her. She drew away. "What's so funny?"

"You. Because you're wrong, Miss Megan." The way he said *Miss Megan* sounded like an endearment. He reached out and stroked her cheek with his knuckles. "You are so very wrong." He cupped her face. "You and I *will* make love." His hazel eyes turned serious. "Often." He leaned closer. "Very often." His mouth covered hers.

Seth's Door

Linda L. Carlow

KenLin Enterprises

This book is a work of fiction. Names, characters, places, events, and incidents are either products of the author's imagination or are used fictitiously.

Copyright © 2018 by Linda L. Carlow

All rights reserved.

No part of this book may be reproduced, or stored in a retrieval system, or transmitted in any form or by any means, electronic, mechanical, photocopying, recording, or otherwise, without the written permission of the publisher.

Published by KenLin Enterprises
Alvarado, Texas
kenlinent@gmail.com

Cover design by Yael Pardess

Photo credits:
Door: 123RF © Texelart
Girl: 123RF © Robert Nystrom

ISBN-13: 978-1-7323264-0-8
ISBN-10: 1-7323264-0-1

Library of Congress Control Number: 2018909366

Available from Amazon.com and other online stores

Printed in the United States of America

10 9 8 7 6 5 4 3 2 1

To the cowboy who rode his motorcycle into my work place in Fort Worth, Texas, in 1981, and changed my life forever. Who believed in me, pushed me, and knew I could do it—if I just persisted. Who signed me up for a writing critique group without telling me, and insisted I go. Who is my best friend, biggest fan, and the smartest choice I ever made. This is for you, Ken, from your little Yankee gal.

Dedicated to the library,

Happy reading!

LL Carlow

Chapter 1

Bang!

Megan McClure ignored the sound of the backfire from the old Chevy on the street below as she relaxed on the bed in the B&B, looking over her notes.

The locked door on the outside wall slammed open, and in ran a cowboy, dripping blood on the hardwood floor.

Megan shot off the bed.

He came to a sliding halt. His chest heaved. Blood coated his right hand, clasped to his upper left arm, and soaked the sleeve of his blue shirt. "Who the hell are you an' where's my sister?"

"Get out of here!" Megan grabbed the nearest thing she could get her hands on—a tall blue vase from the nightstand beside the bed. Yellow and white daisies whipped to one side as she swung the vase over her shoulder and held it like a baseball bat. "I said get out!"

He walked toward her as if he owned the place, confident and unafraid, and entered the circle of light thrown by the lamp on the nightstand. He was in his late teens, she guessed. Well built, around six feet tall, and appealing in that not-a-boy-but-not-quite-a-man way. The brim of his black cowboy hat shadowed his eyes. His brown trousers, worn and dirty, had seen better days, as had the cracked leather vest. He looked like he'd just stepped out of a John Wayne western. It seemed fitting, since she was in Fort Worth, Texas, *Where the West Begins*, as it said on the masthead of the local paper. The only thing John Wayne Jr. lacked was a six-shooter strapped to his thigh.

He came closer his steps slow but determined. Gun or no gun, he looked a lot tougher, bigger, and madder than he had just a second ago. An icy chill slid down Megan's spine. She was alone in a strange city, threatened by a hoodlum/burglar/who-knew-what. Her grip tightened on the vase.

"I asked ya, where's my sister? This is her room." His eyes scanned the room, a puzzled look moving across his face like a cloud. "Though it don't look a'tall like it oughta."

"It's been my room for the last two days, so I guess you missed her. Now get out of he—"

"Look, lady. I don't know who you are or what you're doing here but this is my sister Lottie's room an' I need t' see her somethin' fierce." His voice cracked on the last word. "If you'd kindly go fetch her I'd be much obliged."

"And I'd be much obliged if you got the hell out of my room!"

"Lottie! Lottie!"

"Shout louder. Wake everybody up."

The cowboy gave her a strange look. He snorted. "Ain't much sleepin' goin' on in a whorehouse."

Megan's jaw dropped. *What on earth? Surely, this beautiful and expensive place doesn't rent rooms by the hour.*

The room was on the second floor of the B&B. It was furnished Western style with antique furniture and brass fixtures and lamps. Framed pictures of vibrant sunsets blending into fields of wildflowers hung on the walls. The bed was so high Megan used a stool to climb on top of the mattress. Six tall windows, stretching from waist-high almost to the ceiling, covered with lace curtains, lined the outside wall. The room contained the sitting area, sleeping area, a small dining area, and a bathroom off to one side. And a supposedly locked door on the same wall as the windows. He'd slammed it open so hard it had bounced shut behind him.

What did the owner tell me about this place?

"I reckon you're a new gal," the cowboy said, "an' maybe you ain't met Lottie yet. But I really need t' find her."

"New gal?"

"Wellll," he drawled in a way she was familiar with after being in Texas only two days, "maybe *gal* ain't the right word seein' as you're gittin' to be a bit long in the tooth."

Megan huffed indignantly. *Long in the tooth? Isn't that a quaint way of saying old?* "I'm only twenty-seven," she snapped.

"I gotta tell ya," his gaze drifted lazily down to her toes and slowly back up, "you're still easy on the eye despite your years."

Beneath his perusal, that of a man's not a boy's, Megan felt naked despite her nightclothes, a pink and white flowered tank top, and pink shorts. She'd been relaxing in bed minding her own business when the cowboy showed up. Now he insinuated she was a whore.

An *old* whore.

She closed her eyes. "I must be dreaming," she muttered. "I'll pinch myself, wake up, and the cowboy will be gone." She pinched herself then opened her eyes. The cowboy still stood there. Blood leaked between his fingers and dripped on the floor near his scruffy boots.

Curiosity got the better of her. "How did that happen?" She nodded to his arm.

His eyes widened. "You didn't hear that gunshot right before I came up?"

"All I heard was that old Chevy backfiring when it left the house next door."

He cocked his head. "Old what?"

She made a dismissive gesture with one hand. "Look. I don't know who or where your sister is but, as you can see, she's not here. You have three choices. You can either go back the way you came, or I can bash your head in with this—this vase—"

He snickered.

She hefted the vase menacingly "—and I'll call the police. Or I can look at your arm. Which will it be?"

He glanced at his arm, pursed his lips then looked at her. "What do you know 'bout doctorin'?"

"My mother was a nurse. I helped her sometimes."

"You can dig out a bullet?"

Shit. It's still in there. He didn't need to know how little she knew. No point in both of them being scared witless. "I've never done it, no, but I can do it." She muttered, "I'm pretty sure."

He cocked an eyebrow.

She lifted her chin. "Or you can bleed to death. I don't care."

He looked her up and down. "All right. Dig it out."

"Before I put this vase down I want you to know that if you try to hurt me or attack me or anything like that I'll kick you where it counts, scream bloody murder, and wake up the whole house."

He looked down his nose at her. It was crooked, as if it had been broken a time or two. "I would never harm a woman."

"Oh yeah, the code of the west, right?"

"Huh?"

"Never mind." She placed the vase back on the nightstand. The daisies bobbed cheerfully. They reminded her of her mother, having been her favorite flower. She could almost hear her mother say, *What have you stuck your nose in now, Megan?* Any woman in her right mind wouldn't be offering aid to her would-be assailant.

Megan's instincts told her the cowboy was harmless. And intriguing. She could smell a story.

She wrinkled her nose. She could also smell him. Sweat and horses and an earthy smell she couldn't place.

She pointed to a spindly-legged wooden chair with ornate carvings on the back and thin curving arms. It was beside a small table near one of the tall windows framing the darkness outside. "Sit over there. I'll be right back." She went to the bathroom barely big enough to turn around in, grabbed a washcloth, wetted it, and found her first aid kit. She rummaged through it, checking the contents while she walked back and put it on the table.

The cowboy stood in front of a calendar hanging on the wall beside a beautiful antique armoire in the far corner of the room. He turned when she walked up behind him. His face deathly pale, he pointed a blood-coated finger at the calendar.

"Is that right?"

Megan leaned closer. "Yep. It's Wednesday, April 1."

"Not the day," he said in a strangled voice. "Though that ain't right neither. I mean the year."

"1981? Of course. Why?"

He put his blood-soaked hand on the edge of the armoire.

"Holy moly, don't do that!" She jerked his arm away. "They'll charge me for damages. Here." She slapped the washcloth in his hand. "Hold that over your wound so you quit bleeding all over." Fuming, she bent over for a closer look of the bloody handprint. In the corner of her eye, she saw him stumble and belatedly realized he'd clutched the armoire to support himself. Maybe he was weak from loss of blood.

"You said you was twenty-seven." His voice shook. "What year was you born?"

Fretting over the mess he'd made she said, "1954." A preposterous thought made her straighten and turn to him. "What year were you born?"

"1860."

She almost believed him. He looked so sincere and confused and, well, scared. Then she burst out laughing. "Oh, that's a good one. A real good one."

He stared at her, white-faced and wide-eyed.

"Look, buddy." She put her hands on her hips. "I don't know who you are or where you came from but—"

"I came through that there door yonder." He waved the washcloth at the door on the outside wall. "Just like I have a hundred times before."

"My point exactly. That there door yonder," she mocked him, "is locked, there's no key. It won't open. I asked. The owner said there used to be a stairway to the street there, but it was removed years ago, and the doorway bricked up."

He walked to the door in a couple long strides, holding the washcloth against his wound.

She hurried after him. "It's locked. I tried it."

He grabbed the glass doorknob and yanked open the door.

Megan stopped in her tracks. "Well, what do you know. At least I was right about it being bricked up."

The cowboy glared at her. "Are you plumb blind? It ain't bricked up!"

"Of course, it is."

"You don't see those stairs?" He flung his bloodied hand *through* the brick wall.

As if it wasn't there.

His hand had disappeared.

Megan felt like the world she knew had fallen away beneath her feet.

"Whoa now." He gripped her arm. "Don't faint on me. Here" He propelled her to the spindly-legged wooden chair. "Sit down."

She sat and put her head between her knees, her long curls falling forward.

After a couple deep breaths, she sat up, and flipped back her hair. She stood and marched over to the brick wall, the cowboy hot on her heels. "Let's get this straight, pal. This is a brick wall." She pounded her fist on it. "A solid brick wall."

He stared at her fist, then at her. "Are you joshin' me?"

"No, I'm not *joshin'* you. Bricks and mortar, buddy. Bricks and mortar."

"I see a stairway. It's dark but there's a stairway to the street. This is my sister's room. At least it was minutes ago when I was in 1877."

Unconvinced, Megan pounded on the bricks.

He took a step. His leg went through the bricks and disappeared.

Megan gasped, grabbed his wounded arm, and jerked him back.

He howled and whirled on her, knocking her hand away. "What the hell do you think you're doin'?" He towered over her.

She waved her hands. "Shh! You'll wake everyone." She gestured to the brick wall. "Your leg disappeared!"

"Disappeared?"

"Yes! What do you see when I do this?" She pounded on the bricks again.

"You beatin' your fist in the air. Considerin' some of the things you been sayin', that don't surprise me none." He frowned at the brick wall he said he couldn't see. He thrust his hand through it. "What do you see when I do that?"

"Your arm goes through the bricks up to here." She placed a finger near the middle of his forearm, right up against the wall. She could feel the wall, real and solid. Feel his arm, just as real and solid. Through her head ran the theme song from *The Twilight Zone. Do-do-do-do, do-do-do-do.* "I don't see anything beyond it. Not your hand, wrist, nothing."

"Truly?"

"Truly." She chewed her lower lip then snapped her fingers. Waving at him to follow, she ran across the room to the door leading to the hallway. "Open it."

He grabbed the glass doorknob. "It won't turn." He struggled with the knob. "It's locked."

Megan brushed him aside, grasped the knob, and opened the door. A hallway lit by antique light fixtures high on the walls stretched before her. "What do you see?"

"A—a brick wall."

"Beat your fist on it."

He scowled at her.

She made a go-ahead motion with her hands then watched him beat his fist in the air. "Watch this." She stepped out into the hallway.

"Hey!" he cried, and she stepped back into the room. He grabbed her arm and pulled her away from the door, putting himself between it and her, glaring at it then her. "Where'd you go just then?"

"Out in the hallway. What did you see?"

"You disappeared! Just walked right into the wall an' disappeared!"

She ran back across the room and slammed the door to nowhere shut then tried to open it. "Just what I thought. I can't open it." She spun around. "But *you* can."

He could. She couldn't no matter how hard she tried. He couldn't open the other door no matter how hard he tried. But she could. Another idea came to her. She got one of her socks and threw it out into the hallway. When he threw the sock, it stopped in mid-air and fell to the floor, which is what it did when she threw it at the brick wall on the other door. He threw it right through the bricks and *poof* it was gone.

"What the hell's goin' on?" He glared at her as though it was all her fault.

"I have a crazy hunch. But first," she touched his arm, "let me tend to your wound, okay?"

He scowled then jerked his head in a nod.

"Sit down. I'll have to cut off your shirtsleeve."

"Just git it over with." He sat on the chair, removed his hat, placed it on the table, then clapped his hand to the washcloth on his arm again and looked stoically ahead. His sandy hair was short and unevenly cropped.

Megan crossed the room to a low-seated vanity. She took the dried flower arrangement out of a big glass bowl and carried the bowl to the bathroom where she washed it out in the claw-footed tub then filled it with hot water. She tossed several washcloths and a towel over her shoulder, grabbed a bar of soap then carried the bowl back to the table. Despite walking with great care water sloshed on the floor. *Great. More damages.* Her gaze slid to the bloody splotches on the floor. She sighed. *More damn damages.* After putting the bowl of water, washcloths, and soap on the table, she turned on a lamp with a frilly shade and dangling crystal teardrops and moved it closer for better lighting. She sat beside the cowboy and went to work. She tried to be gentle as she cut off his sleeve, but he bit his lip a couple of times as she pulled the blood-soaked material away from his skin. Other than that, he was as still as a statue.

"I suppose we should introduce ourselves. I'm Megan McClure."

"Seth O'Connor." He sucked in his breath.

"Sorry," she muttered.

"Ya got any whiskey?"

"No. Aren't you a little young to be drinking whiskey?"

He sent her a sharp glance. "Had my first drink when I was ten."

"Drinking laws in Texas must be pretty lenient."

"Ain't no law against drinkin'." He stiffened as she dabbed his wound with a wet washcloth.

A shot of whiskey sounded good to Megan too. She wasn't normally squeamish, but she hadn't seen so much blood and raw flesh since the accident that had killed her parents. From the looks of the cowboy, he wasn't kidding about needing some whiskey, either. To distract him, she said, "Tell me about yourself, Seth." When he remained silent and pale, the muscles in his jaw working overtime, she said, "All right, I'll go first. I'm a freelance writer. Mostly articles, some short stories. I came to Fort Worth to write about the opening of The Tejas Honky-Tonk."

"Never heard of it," Seth replied through clenched teeth.

"Really? It's been all over the news. Seems to be a big deal about a big bar. Anyway, my parents are dead, no siblings. I grew up in a small town in Illinois and live in an apartment in Chicago now. Not that I'm home all that much." She felt him stiffen.

"I figgered ya for a damn Yankee from your accent."

"I'm not a Yankee," she said not for the first time since coming to Texas. "I'm from the Midwest. We're not Yankees. That's New York and all those states over there. I don't have an accent. You do."

"Anyone north o' the Red River is a damn Yankee. Ouch!" He shot her a glare over his shoulder.

"Sorry." She smiled innocently and resumed cleaning his wound as gently as she had before his Yankee remark. His arm was tanned and muscular. Her gaze drifted upward to his profile. Crooked nose, square chin dusted with peach fuzz, high cheekbones. All in all, a handsome guy. *From the 1800s? Impossible!* She looked at his clothes, dirty and worn, definitely not the current style, and recalled all he'd said. "The Civil War—or, as you maybe call it, the War Between the States—ended over a hundred years ago, Seth."

"To me it was twelve years ago." His voice cracked. "My two oldest brothers died in it. I hardly 'member anythin' about 'em. We was livin' in Georgia an' after the war Pa moved the rest of us here to Texas then he up an' drowned a year later. A fever took Ma an' my two little sisters when I was 'bout ten. Since then it's just been me an' Lottie. She's three years older 'an me an' did whatever she had t' do t' take care of me. The last few years she's had this room here in Miss Matilda's. I don't like her sellin' herself like she does, but she claims she makes a good bit, enough to keep the two of us fed anyways."

Megan rinsed soap off his wound. She felt him watching her.

"I ain't never seen someone with purple eyes."

"Actually, they're a deep, dark blue."

"Lemme see. Look at me."

She paused with the washcloth on his arm and met his gaze.

He had beautiful eyes. Hazel with flecks of green.

Her heart skipped a beat.

He shook his head. "Nope. Not blue. Purple."

She concentrated on his wound. "I prefer violet, not purple. With my violet eyes and black hair, some people say I look a little like Liz Taylor, although," she gave a small laugh, "I don't see it."

"Who?"

Her hands, her breath, everything within her stilled. It had been a test. He had failed. *What red-blooded twentieth century man hasn't heard of Liz Taylor? He really is from the past.*

Holy moly!

He can't be!

Can he?

That quick, between one heartbeat and the next, the world she had known shifted to something else, somewhere new.

Where the improbability of time travel was possible, and a time-traveler had happened upon her.

She sucked in a breath and blew it out. "Never mind."

"You said you had an idear 'bout what was goin' on. You gonna tell me what it is or just say n*ever mind* again?"

"All right." She dunked the washcloth in the bowl then wrung it out. A thin layer of red spread throughout the water. "The year is 1981 and this is Miss Fleeda's Bed and Breakfast, which is like a hotel. According to historical records this used to be a brothel during Fort Worth's Wild West days back in the late 1800s." She draped the wet cloth over his wound. "What I'm thinking is that somehow, I don't know how, that door is a portal, an opening between my time and your time. When you came up those stairs tonight and stepped through that door, you stepped into my time—the year 1981."

His jaw dropped. His eyes bulged. "Does that happen a lot?"

Of all his possible responses, she hadn't expected that one. She chuckled. "As far as I know it's never happened. Except in the movies and on TV."

"Movies? TV?"

There wasn't a television in the room and it seemed too complicated to explain. "It's moving pictures on a screen but never mind that for now. You've used those stairs before?" He nodded. "And this never happened before?" He shook his head, looking a little frightened and younger than his seventeen years. Her heart went out to him—a stranger lost in time. A wounded stranger. "Did you notice anything different about the stairs or the doorway this time? Anything odd?" She opened her first aid kit, took out a penknife and a pair of long-nosed tweezers, and put them on a towel on the table.

The cowboy's eyes followed her every movement. Creases formed in his brow. "It felt mighty cold near the top. 'Specially for a hot summer's eve. An' it was dark. The lamp Lottie always keeps burnin' at the top was out. She never lets it go out. An' it was quiet as a tomb." He straightened. "I gotta find her. Make sure she's all right." He started to stand.

"Whoa there, cowboy." Megan put her hand on his shoulder and pushed him back down. "I'm not done here. Brace yourself. I'm going to disinfect your wound."

"You're gonna do wh—godawmighty!" He jumped a foot off the chair when she poured alcohol on his arm.

"I told you to brace yourself. Now," she picked up the penknife, held it over the bowl and poured alcohol over it, "sit perfectly still while I get that bullet out." She put the alcohol down, held up the knife, and looked at him. "Ready?"

He grew a shade paler as his gaze went from the knife to his arm to her eyes. His Adam's apple bobbed. He nodded then took a deep breath.

She gave him what she hoped was a reassuring smile and took a couple of deep breaths herself. She made an incision through the wound with the knife. She glanced at Seth. "Doing okay?"

He nodded.

She put down the knife, poured alcohol over the tweezers, told her pounding heart to calm down, and poked around in the wound with the tweezers. Still and silent, he stared straight ahead. Long agonizing moments later, she exclaimed, "Got it!" and triumphantly held up a bullet clamped between the tweezers.

Sweat beading his ashen face, Seth released a breath, slumped in the chair like a rag doll, and closed his eyes.

"I need to clean the wound and pack it. Can you handle all that?"

Eyes still closed, he nodded.

Megan put down the bullet, cleaned the wound, and packed it with gauze. She layered padding on the wound then wrapped it with more gauze. She got a glass of water and a couple aspirins then touched him gently on his shoulder. His eyes blinked open. "Here." She held out the aspirins. "Take these to ease the pain and prevent fever."

"What are those?"

"Aspirin. You know it as willow bark. Swallow them down with this." She gave him the pills and the water. "You'll feel better soon."

Seth did so, then inspected his bandaged arm. "You saved my life, Miss Megan. I'm much obliged." He pushed himself off the chair and struggled to his feet, swaying a little.

"Sit down." She pushed him back down on the chair. "You just had surgery. You're not going anywhere for a bit. Keep pressure on that arm." She cleaned the blood off his other hand, then pressed it against the gauze covering the wound. "Now listen to me. This is important." Her gaze held his. "You need to change that packing every day and disinfect the wound with something. Whiskey, I guess. Pour it on the wound. Then repack it with clean ... rags and wrap it up. Do not, I repeat, do not forget to change the packing, and clean it every day.

Hopefully it won't turn red or ooze pus and you'll avoid any infection. You got all that?"

He nodded. "Thank you, Miss Megan." He braced himself, as if to stand. "I gotta find Lottie. I gotta warn her."

"You're pale as milk. I know you're in pain. You won't be any use to her if you pass out so sit there and rest." He started to speak. "Don't argue."

With a sigh, he slumped in the chair, head down, eyes closed. Megan grabbed a washcloth, got down on her hands and knees, and scrubbed the bloody spots on the floor.

"Sorry 'bout that," he muttered after a moment.

Glancing up, she found him watching her. Glancing down, she realized what part of her he was probably watching. She sat up a little straighter, adjusting her top. He cleared his throat and shifted in the chair. She tsked. *Boys will be boys no matter when they're from.* She resumed scrubbing, being careful to not bend over too far. Lamplight gleamed on the floor, turning the wood a rich mahogany color. Maybe it was mahogany. She clicked her tongue against her teeth. *Is that used for floors? Isn't it expensive wood? Just my luck!* She scrubbed a little gentler. "Why were you shot?" She glanced at Seth. "What do you need to warn your sister about?"

"Lottie's got some regular customers an' one has taken a shine to her an' wants her all to hisself. Fella named Johnny Bingo. He owns the fanciest saloon in town an' is one o' the richest men 'round these parts. He don't take no for an answer."

"And Lottie told him no," Megan guessed.

"Worse." Seth sighed. "She done fell in love with Billy Hicklesten."

Megan sat back on her heels. She meant to go clean up that bloody handprint on the armoire but stayed where she was, caught up in the story. "Does Billy love her?"

"He surely did," Seth replied glumly. "But it don't matter none now."

"Why not?"

Seth heaved a longer sigh. "While we was walkin' t' the livery Bingo shot him."

"*What?*"

"The bullet went clean through Billy an' hit me. Billy fell down dead, I reckon, an' Bingo came runnin' up, shoutin' he was gonna kill Lottie. I punched Bingo a good one an' hightailed it to Lottie's t' warn her. I ran up the stairs, him followin' me an' shootin' at me—an' here I am." Seth straightened, planted his feet on the floor and slowly stood, swaying a little. "I gotta find her." He stared at the bricks he'd come through then looked at Megan as she scrambled to her feet. He started to say something.

Bang!

"Lottie!" he shouted.

"It's just that old Chevy," Megan insisted.

Bang! Bang!

Seth snatched his hat off the table, ran to the door, yanked it open, and disappeared through the brick wall. The door slammed shut behind him.

She ran over and tried the doorknob. It wouldn't budge.

Two more bangs came from the old Chevy.

Is it that old Chevy?

Megan stepped to a window and scanned the street below bathed in the streetlights.

The Chevy wasn't anywhere in sight.

Chapter 2

The alarm clock jangled. Megan flung out a hand to hit the off button then stretched, yawning, warm and cozy beneath the covers. She rolled onto her side and faced a window with hazy sunlight behind the lace curtain. Her sleepy gaze drifted along the windows lining the wall, then stopped when it came to the locked door.

Holy moly. What a weird dream.

She flung back the covers, bolted from the bed, ran to the door, and grabbed the doorknob. Locked.

Seconds later, she was back in bed, sitting cross-legged, a notebook on her lap, writing down her dream from beginning to end. It had been so vivid, almost real. Her pen moved quickly. It slowed then stopped when she reached the part about the cowboy putting his bloodied hand on the armoire. Her gaze went to the armoire in the far corner of the room. The handprint would have been on the side near the wall. She had meant to clean it up but didn't. *Or did I?*

Megan tapped the pen on the notebook. She remembered cleaning up after the cowboy left. *Or was it all a dream?* She'd emptied the big bowl and replaced the dried flowers, repacked her first aid kit. It all seemed so real. She remembered cleaning the floor and leaned forward. Her gaze moved over the area of the floor where she thought the blood had been. The wood gleamed in the morning light. Unblemished. She sat back and continued writing while the details were fresh.

Finished, she read it over then clutched the notebook to her chest.

This is it! The book I always knew I'd write—one day. Her published writings were articles or short stories. She had started a couple of novels that lay unfinished in her bottom desk drawer at home.

But *this* one seemed ... alive.

She read it over again, adding a word here, taking one out there, hearing Seth's words echo in her mind. *Seth. Where did that name come from?* She'd never known anyone named Seth. She liked it. No surprise the story involved time travel. She'd grown up watching *The*

Twilight Zone, One Step Beyond, and *The Outer Limits,* all of which had episodes that dealt with time travel. Those TV shows had instilled in her young mind that anything was possible. Maybe not probable but possible.

The quest of the possible had sent her on wild goose chases after the weird and strange. Articles and short stories about noteworthy people, places or events were her bread and butter. Searching for and writing about the improbable but possible were her passion.

Now, she'd dreamed up a time-traveling cowboy. She could hardly wait until bedtime when she could pick up where she left off and find out what happened next.

She glanced at the clock. "Oh no!"

She jumped out of bed. Forty minutes until her interview.

Minutes later, she checked herself in the mirror as she tucked a multi-colored long-sleeved blouse into the waist of a slim black skirt. She slipped on a pair of black heels then ran the hairbrush once more through her hair, wondering if she should cut it. Although she did like those curls cascading halfway down her back. She stuffed her notebook into her purse and headed for the door. She paused with her hand on the doorknob and glanced at the armoire.

Of course, there's no bloody handprint.

Something compelled her to look.

She went to the armoire. And clapped a hand over her mouth.

***

She took the wrong bus and arrived twenty-five minutes late for her appointment with the owner of The Tejas, Derrick Traynor. When she entered his office out of breath and apologetic, he scowled at her from behind his desk and glanced at his watch. He half-rose from his chair as she sat down. Framed documents hung on the wall behind him. She made a mental note of them. Diploma from Texas A&M University. Award for Texas A&M Basketball.

Mr. Traynor cleared his throat.

Megan's attention snapped back to him. She began the interview.

Derrick Traynor was in his mid-thirties, with blond hair and a thin mustache. Tall and thin, six-six maybe, he wore jeans and a light blue shirt beneath a leather vest. He scowled at her often, clearly displeased with her lateness and unimpressed by her. He answered her questions brusquely and cut the interview short.

"I'm a busy man, Miss McClure. I'm sure you understand. Opening night and all."

Megan stood and thanked him. She gathered her notebook, pen, and dignity, and left. Outside on the sidewalk she paused to put her things into her purse, mentally kicking herself. She had worked hard to land that interview only to have it turn out to be one of the worst of her career. Not only had she been unprofessionally and rudely late, her mind had been on that bloody handprint the whole time.

Is it real? Had Seth really been there? Is time travel possible?

She'd lost her train of thought several times and stumbled through her questions like a greenhorn reporter.

No wonder he practically threw me out on my ear.

She crossed the road for a better look at The Tejas Honky-Tonk. Her statistics stated it had 100,000 square feet including almost 12 acres of parking. The building had originally been a big hay barn built in 1900. Enclosed in 1920, it had housed numerous businesses, including a speakeasy, a general store, and a roller-skating rink. It stood vacant for a decade then Derrick Traynor's grandfather bought it. The ink had barely dried on the contract when he died. The building went to his grandson, a banker, who decided to turn it into a Texas-sized honky-tonk and saloon. The grand opening was two nights away. However, tomorrow night was VIP preview night, by invitation only.

Megan had hoped to get an invitation after dazzling Mr. Traynor during the interview.

Fat chance of that.

Megan wandered down Main Street to Exchange Street. Lining the streets were souvenir shops full of items made in the shape of Texas, bars with country western songs twanging out the doors, a sidewalk shoe/boot shiner, barbecue joints, and Mexican restaurants. People strolled along the sidewalk, window-shopping and reading pamphlets. After a look around the historic stockyards, Megan headed back to Main Street. The sky opened, drenching her before she could duck beneath an awning.

"Good ol' Texas cloudburst," a man standing beside her said as he lit a cigar. He was a big man wearing a big cowboy hat with a big stomach hanging over a big belt buckle emblazoned with the shape of Texas.

Wet as a drowned rat, her hair plastered to her scalp, her blouse stuck to her skin, she couldn't even manage a smile. The rain quit. The sun came out.

The man puffed out a cloud of smoke. "Gonna be humid now." He nodded to her and stepped out from beneath the awning, bending low to keep from knocking his big hat off his big head.

Sweat beaded Megan's face in no time. Her stomach rumbled. Up ahead a sign advertized *Barbecue*. She paused outside the hole-in-a-wall restaurant and fussed with her hair but soon gave up on the wet mess. Nobody knew her there anyway.

Inside, the lunch crowd packed the small place. It had beer signs and pictures of country western singers on the panelled walls and a dozen tables beneath slow-turning ceiling fans. The tables held a hodgepodge of crumpled napkins, glasses of drinks and bottles of beer, and red plastic baskets full of sandwiches and French fries. Megan waited her turn in line, ordered a number two to go, and stepped aside to wait for her food.

"Megan?"

Megan turned. Her eyes widened in surprise. "Lori? What are you doing here?"

"Same as you. Making a living."

Lori Rinsky was a tall statuesque blonde with deceivingly innocent blue eyes. She and Megan were the same age and had grown up in the same town, gone to the same schools all the way through high school, and both had worked on the school paper. They were cordial to each other, but they weren't friends and never had been even when they were little. Megan went away to college to earn a degree in journalism and moved to Chicago where she got a job as an entertainment reporter at *The Chicago Tribune*. A year later, she couldn't believe it when Lori started working there too. From then on, a mild rivalry existed between them that at times caused disharmony at work. After a year, Megan struck out on her own, freelancing. She'd run into Lori a few times since then, always on a story for *The Trib*, where Lori still worked in Megan's old job.

Aware of her own bedraggled appearance, Megan sighed.

Lori looked like a model in her crisp white blouse and long flowing hair framing a perfect oval face.

"Join us." Lori waved a hand with bright red fingernails to the empty chair at the table she shared with two other women. "This is Marvella, a local reporter, and this is Susie, my assistant. Girls, meet Megan McClure, former entertainment writer for *The Trib*."

The women exchanged greetings.

Megan remained standing. "Thanks for the invite but I can't stay long." She glanced at Susie, probably fresh out of college. "Assistant, huh?"

Lori beamed. "After you left I was doing the work of two, sometimes three. I told Ed I'd had enough. Either hire me an assistant or I quit. Susie started soon after."

"Lucky you," Megan muttered just loud enough for Susie to hear.

Susie's eager smile turned to puzzlement.

Lori took a swig of beer. "What'd you do? Take a shower with your clothes on?"

"I got caught in the rain."

"Rain? It didn't rain here."

"Welcome t' Texas, y'all," Marvella, the Texan, drawled. "Where it'll rain on one side of th' street but not th' other."

"Don't you just love her accent?" Lori's gaze swept the room. "Look at all these cowboys in their tight jeans. Mmmm. I can't wait to see them on the dance floor on opening night at The Tejas." Lori grinned at Megan. "That's right! You landed an interview with Derrick Traynor for *Country Music Now*."

Megan nodded. "I just came from there."

"I hope it was before the rain." Lori smiled sweetly. "Did it go well?"

"Splendidly," Megan lied. Not even under torture would she admit to Lori that it had been a disaster. "He's a very nice man. Southern gentleman deluxe." She heard her number called and, excusing herself, went to get her order.

Bag of food in hand, Megan paused beside Lori's table on the way out.

Lori said, "I was just telling the girls about some of your escapades since you lit out on your own. Like your piece on that frog man in New Mexico."

Megan hiked her purse up on her shoulder. "It was a lizard man, near Winslow, Arizona."

"Lizard man?" Susie asked.

"Half man, half lizard," Megan replied.

Susie's jaw dropped. "Did you see him?"

"No. But I spent a month in the wilderness with two hunky guides and made more on that article than I did working three months at the paper."

"You're kiddin'," Marvella said. "Y'all didn't even see him an' you made that much?" When Megan nodded, Marvella whistled. "How'd ya get interested in stuff like that?"

Lori said, *"The Twilight Zone."* The girls looked at her. "She watched that show all the time. She'd come to school reciting the latest episode almost word for word. Her mom used to holler at her to turn that TV off, go outside and play. I bet you still know some of those shows. Why don't you recite one for us?" Lori smiled at Megan.

"Sorry. I need to go. Deadlines, you know."

The girls nodded understandingly.

"You'll be at the VIP preview tomorrow night, right?" Lori asked.

"Of course," Megan lied again.

"Great!" Lori said. "You can introduce me to your buddy Derrick."

"Oh, sure, of-of course. Gotta run."

Megan left the restaurant, mentally kicking herself again for being trapped in her own lies. *Somehow, I have to go tomorrow night.* The smell of barbecue wafted up from the bag. She hurried to the B&B.

Entering her room, Megan kicked off her shoes and set the bag of food on the table. On it was something she hadn't noticed earlier.

A bullet.

The bullet she'd removed from Seth's arm.

The sight of it sent a shiver through her. She checked the armoire.

The handprint was still there.

Megan dropped to her hands and knees and studied the floor until she found them. Dull spots amid the gleaming richness of the rest of the floor. The places where she had cleaned up Seth's blood.

Megan sat on her heels. *Seth is real. He was here, in my room. A man from the 1800s.*

She ate at the same table where she'd dug the bullet out of Seth's arm. As much as she enjoyed the old TV shows about anything weird, she knew things like that never happened in real life. Stories about the unusual and bizarre—like the lizard man in Arizona, and a big hairy monster that lurked in a Louisiana bayou she had searched for futilely—usually had a logical explanation, or were hoaxes, lies, or at the very least, products of very active imaginations. But she wasn't imagining those dull spots on the floor, the bullet, or the bloody handprint on the armoire. Or the washcloths she'd hung up to dry on the towel rack in the bathroom.

She sprang up and tried the door.

Locked.

She gazed out the adjacent window. The Tarrant County Courthouse stood in the distance along the skyline of Fort Worth. She liked looking off into the distance at the view. She refused to look down. She had done that only twice; the first time she'd been in the room, and last night. Down below, a garden of irises blooming purple and white stood tall against the building. A strip of grass just big enough for a lawn mower lay between the irises and the fence around the property. The wrought iron fence had pointed tips. The first time she had seen them, an image of her father in the last moments of his life flashed through her mind, the memory chilling her with a coldness that sliced all the way through her soul. She had not looked at those pointed tips again. Until last night. She hoped she never had to rely upon the windows as an exit because she didn't know if she could jump out of them. Not with those spears down there, a couple of yards away from the building, maybe too far out to jump clear of.

Megan sat at the table to finish eating. A ton of work and a deadline awaited her. She put the previous night's events from her mind and went to work trying to salvage something useful from her disastrous interview.

Immersed in her article, she heard a knock on her door and went to answer it.

The owner of the B&B, an older woman with silver hair named Mrs. Powell, smiled. "You have a phone call downstairs, Miss McClure."

"Thanks." Megan ran down the stairs to the first-floor hallway. She picked up the house phone in a small alcove near the front door. From the sitting room down the hall on her right came the sound of the TV. On her left was the front door leading outside.

"Hello?" Megan said, and heard her best friend's voice. "Donna! It's good to hear from you. Yeah, everything's okay. Yeah, had it today. Oh Donna, it was awful. I got there late. Real late. Pissed him off, and, well, the whole interview sucked. What? No, no, I can do it. I can get enough words out of it somehow. Guess who I ran into. Lori. Yes, *that* Lori."

Megan laughed. "Yeah, I remember that night. Hey, Donna. I gotta problem. I need to go to that private opening tomorrow night. No, I didn't get invited. But I need to go. Do you think you can pull a couple strings and get me in? You know I hate to ask and I rarely do but this is important. Besides, what good is having a friend who works for the Chicago Chamber of Commerce if I can't take advantage of it every now and then?"

Megan listened a moment then grinned. "You're the best, Donna. I owe you one." Megan laughed. "Okay, two. Thanks so much. I'll call you in a couple of days and let you know how it went. I love you too. 'Bye."

She hung up the phone and did a little jig, punching her fists in the air, then danced her way up the stairs to her room. She settled down to work on her article. Words flowed easily, the results pleasing her. Every so often, she glanced at the locked door, half-expecting to see Seth come through it.

He never did.

It was late when she finally went to bed. She didn't think about work, as she should. She thought about Seth. *Is his wound healing? What had happened to Lottie? Is Billy dead? What about Bingo the bad guy? Will Seth ever come through that door again? What did it all mean? Why him? Why me?* And try as she might she wasn't able to return to the dream to continue her novel because it hadn't been a dream at all.

Instead it was the story of a lifetime. Of the century. Of all time.

The improbable was possible. Time travel was real.

She could make a fortune.

Who would believe me?

No one.

Unless she exposed Seth. Subjected him to endless scrutiny. Made him a lab rat for doctors and scientists and God knew who else.

She couldn't do that. Best to keep him a secret.

Besides, he might never come through that door again.

***

The next morning Megan talked on the phone with the editor at *Country Music Now*, discussing The Tejas articles and some upcoming work. Megan hung up, letting out a breath of relief. She made a good living and saved a lot of money by not owning a car since she used Chicago's public transportation, but she was by no means rich and knowing there were paychecks in the future eased her money worries.

After eating a hearty breakfast of eggs, sausage, and hash browns Megan took a cup of coffee to her room and sat down to work on her article. Around noon, she received a special delivery and let out a joyful yip when she saw the ticket for The Tejas private opening that night. *Good old Donna.* Humming to herself, Megan searched through her clothes looking for an outfit for that night. Nothing she'd brought with her seemed right. She grabbed her purse and went shopping.

That night, a searchlight swept the dark sky above The Tejas. In front of it, a line of limousines slowly moved along the driveway, depositing the rich and famous at the front door. For a couple of hours Megan stood on the sidewalk making notes of the elite attending the opening. She jotted down the names of the mayor of Fort Worth, the state senators, and several television stars. A brisk breeze tossed her hair and, despite a jacket, made her shiver in her new clothes. The skin-tight jeans had a nice neat crease down the front and the cherry-red blouse had puffy sleeves and a low neckline.

Inside, she flashed her VIP ticket then squeezed her way through the crowd up to the bar. She snatched an empty barstool before another girl could. The girl flipped the bird and turned away. Megan removed her jacket and draped it over her purse on the bar then sat and ordered a beer. The place was packed. Elbows to assholes, as they used to say during her college days. Megan counted twenty bar stations for the waitresses, who wore jeans, western shirts, and cowboy hats. Beer flowed freely, and the noise was deafening. One of the senators gave a speech. The mayor gave a speech. Derrick Traynor gave a speech.

Megan yawned while she made notes. Through a cloud of cigarette smoke, she spied Lori Rinsky at the other end of the bar, chatting with three cowboys. The first performers were Alabama. They had the place hopping and Megan tapping her foot. Several men asked her to dance and she finally followed one onto the crowded floor and let loose for a while. She waved at Lori on the dance floor. She saw Derrick Traynor and waved at him, then made her way to him and shouted, "Thank you for the interview!" in his ear. She made sure Lori saw her with Derrick Traynor. She visited one of the huge restrooms, then checked out the gift shop. She ate a hamburger while watching several men take a wild ride on a mechanical bull. She shook her head, baffled by the activity, then wandered around, people-watching and taking notes.

Around midnight, Megan downed the last of her beer and stuffed some dollar bills in the tip jar on the bar. The bartender bobbed her blonde head in Megan's direction. Megan put on her jacket, gathered her things, then threaded her way through the crowd and out of The Tejas.

Back at the B&B, Megan entered her dark room. She tossed her purse on the sofa then kicked off her shoes. Bare feet padding on the floor she turned on the lamp on the nightstand, the soft light falling across the bed. Humming a country western song, she stood before one of the tall windows and drew back the lace curtain to gaze out. She had a pleasant beer buzz. She wasn't much of a drinker anymore, unlike during her college days, and knew when to stop. The bed beckoned her, but she lingered at the window. All was quiet on the streets below. All was quiet in the room except for an occasional groan from the old house.

A door creaked. The locked door.

She caught her breath.

Ever so slowly, the door opened. She couldn't see who was behind it. *Is it someone else? A whore with her customer? A customer looking for a whore? An outlaw? Lottie?* Megan's heart pounded. She wished she had a weapon. Something besides that stupid vase.

A boot tip appeared. Then the brim of a black hat.

"Miss Megan? You there?" a voice asked softly.

"Seth?"

He stepped out from behind the door. "Howdy, Miss Megan." He grinned. He was dressed much the same way he'd been the other night. Trousers, boots, dark shirt, vest, and hat, which he removed and held in his hand.

She hurried toward him, glad to see his friendly face. "How's your arm? Is it healing?"

He tilted his head. "My arm?"

"Your gunshot wound, silly. How is it?"

"Why, that was three months ago, Miss Megan."

She took a step back. "It was two days ago."

"What?" He spun around, took a couple of long strides, and stopped before the calendar. "It's the same month here? We're headin' into fall."

"So, there's not only a difference in years but in the lengths of time, too. It's been just two days for me but three months for you. And there's something else I noticed." She hurried to the nightstand where she picked up her notebook. Seth tossed his hat on the table then stood beside her as she thumbed through the notebook. "The next morning, I wrote down everything that happened, thinking I'd dreamed it all and not wanting to forget any of it. I remembered you saying—here it is. You were describing the stairs." She read aloud. *"He said it was mighty cold at the top, especially for a hot summer's eve."* Megan looked at him. "I guess it wasn't April in your time when you came here."

He shook his head. "August. I tried to come back an' see you a lotta times but the stairs was never dark an' cold like it was that night. Until tonight. I saw the light was out an' crept up the stairs an' suddenly it was freezin' cold an' dark as sin an' I opened the door an' there you were." He touched Megan's arm and grinned shyly. "For the longest time I was beginnin' to doubt you was real. I wasn't sure if I'd really come here, to your time, or if I'd imagined the whole thing."

"Me too. I thought it was a dream until I saw your bloody handprint on the armoire. That's when I knew it had been real. You're real. I'm real." She shrugged. "Who knows why this is happening. Sit down and tell me everything. How is your arm?"

"Just dandy." He flexed it. "You done a fine job an' I thank ya."

"You're welcome." They sat on the sofa. Megan shoved her purse aside. She drew her legs up under her. "How's Lottie? Last I knew Billy had just been shot. And you ran out of here when you heard what you thought was gunfire."

"It *was* gunfire. As I was goin' down the stairs, Lottie was runnin' up 'em followed by Bingo's bullets. I dang near ran her down but managed to grab her arm, yank her back into the room, *her* room, not this one, an' slam an' bolt the door. We hit the floor an' Bingo shot her door fulla holes. Finally, the sheriff came an' hauled Bingo off to jail. 'Course, he bought his way out faster than a body can spit."

Megan glanced at the door, solid and sound.

"Lottie had it replaced." Seth went on. "She's still workin' here. She was mighty upset when Billy died an' won't have a thing to do with Bingo these days. Said she's sockin' away money so's she can quit an' we can leave here. That reminds me." He leaned to one side and reached into his trouser pocket. "I been waitin' t' return this." He gave her back her sock. "I been carryin' it with me all these months hopin' to return it to you an' see your time. I was so worried 'bout Lottie last time I didn't pay much mind t' anything around me. Now, I wanna see what the world is like in your time." He grinned boyishly.

She smiled and showed him her world.

He marveled at the electric light. Turn it on, turn it off with the flick of a switch. He turned it on and off, on and off, on and off until she stopped him with her hand on his. The ink pen fascinated him. He took it apart and studied each piece then put it back together and scribbled in her notebook. The electric typewriter made him scratch his head. Megan refused to let him take *it* apart. He smacked the side of his head when he saw the toilet, exclaiming what a grand idea it was. But what made him whoop and holler was the shower. Hot water on demand. He didn't even have to ask. Megan showed him what to do, handed him a clean towel, and left him alone in the bathroom after telling him to toss his clothes out the bathroom door.

While he showered, she grabbed his clothes and ran down the stairs to a 24-hour Laundromat across the street. She had learned that in Texas it was called a *washateria*. She'd never heard that word before. She threw his clothes and some detergent in a washer, fed it coins, then returned to her room. The shower still ran. It was still running when she returned from putting his clothes in the dryer.

She knocked on the door. "Seth? Seth? You done yet?"

"What?" he hollered over the sound of the shower.

"That's long enough. Dry yourself off and come out of there."

The water quit. Minutes later, the door opened, and Seth stepped out in a cloud of steam, wearing only a towel wrapped around his waist.

Megan caught her breath. *Wow.*

He was lean, without an ounce of fat. He had broad shoulders and muscular arms ribbed with veins. His sculptured chest had a smattering of sandy hair. His flat, tight stomach rivaled that of a Grecian statue. The towel covered little of his long legs.

Holy moly.

She gave herself a shake. For heaven's sake, she was acting like a teenager. She was no prude, she'd seen her share of naked men, she'd gone to college during the seventies, when streaking was popular, and the sexual rebellion was in full force. She'd had a couple of serious relationships, but she wasn't promiscuous by any stretch of the word. Besides, no matter how good-looking or nice he was, he was much too young for her. And, he lived in the past.

She held out an opened can of pop. "Have you ever had a carbonated drink?"

He nodded and took it from her with his free hand. He took a sip then wrinkled his nose. "Tickles."

She laughed. "I've missed you." And realized she meant it.

"I've missed you too." They smiled at each other. He glanced around. "Where's my clothes?"

"In the dryer."

"The what?"

She explained washing machines and dryers, and he expressed amazement at how easy everything was in her time. They stood side by side and looked out the window at the twentieth century night. He stared openmouthed at all the lights and asked how anyone could ever see the stars. A car drove slowly down the street, passing in and out of the patches of light from the streetlights then disappeared around the corner. Megan gave him a rudimentary explanation about cars.

Seth scratched his chest. "That's the godawfullest thing I ever seen. What the hell is wrong with ridin' a horse?" He shook his head. "So many buildin's crowded so close together an' stretchin' as far as the eye can see. Sure looks mighty different. 'Specially with all them trees. Ain't many trees in my time."

A full moon rode high in the clear night sky.

Seth leaned one shoulder against the side of the window, his head tilted up. "At least that big ol' Texas moon is pretty as ever an' still the same."

"Well ... not exactly."

His head jerked around. He stared at Megan, his expression almost fearful. "What's been done to the moon?"

"There are footprints on it."

His Adam's apple bobbed. "F—footprints?"

Megan nodded.

"Human?"

She nodded again.

His eyes widened. "Men have walked on the *moon*?" Disbelief and awe filled his voice.

"On July 20, 1969, Neil Armstrong became the first man to walk on the moon. I watched it on TV. The whole world did. He's an American hero."

Seth raised his face to the moon. "Gosh." Again, more passionately, "Go-o-o-sshh."

Once he was dressed again, marveling over his clothes still warm from the dryer, they sat on the rawhide sofa.

Megan had some questions of her own. "Is this whole room Lottie's room?"

"Shucks no. Lottie's got this here part where we sittin'. There's a wall right there," Seth drew a line in the air with his finger, "and Corabell's room is on the other side, in your bedroom area. Trixie's room is where your privy is, only a little bigger but not by much." His face softened. "I've a certain fondness for Trixie. She was my first."

"Your first?"

Seth nodded. "A birthday gift from some of the fellas when I was fourteen."

"Wait a minute. You had sex for the first time with a whore for your fourteenth birthday?" *Holy moly!*

Seth nodded. "Lottie was hoppin' mad. Said she'd horsewhip the men who set it up iffen she ever found out who they was. She weren't too pleased with Trixie, either, but she was just doin' her job."

Megan decided to drop that subject. "Tell me about your time."

Seth settled back on the sofa and described Fort Worth, circa 1877. Wooden buildings and sidewalks, dirt roads dotted with horse dung, the bellows and smells of cattle from the slaughterhouse, the various townspeople, endless fields of long grass and wildflowers.

He told her about a part of town called Hell's Half Acre with its saloons, brothels, and cribs. The brothel/B&B was on the edge of the Acre. It sounded like a notorious place, full of outlaws, cowboys, and gunfights. Megan hung on every word until dawn brightened sky.

"I better git." Seth stood. "Thanks for everythin', Miss Megan. My clothes ain't never been so clean. Or me, either, I reckon."

She stood also. "Will you come back?"

"I hope so."

"Tonight. Try it again tonight in your time."

He nodded as he reached for his hat and put it on. He stared at her for a moment. Megan sensed he wanted to say something else, but he just smiled, touched a hand to her cheek then went to the door, opened it, and stepped through the brick wall.

She got in bed and wrote down everything that had happened. When she came to the part where he returned her sock, she paused, realizing what it meant: objects could go from her time to his and come back.

Can people?
Can I?

***

The next morning, she woke up late and groggy. Several cups of coffee later she was typing her piece about Derrick Traynor when she looked up, fingers poised over the keyboard, and said, "Damn." Tonight was the opening of The Tejas. She'd asked Seth to come back tonight. He usually showed up late. If he could come at all. She'd make it a point to be home early just the same. She didn't want to miss him.

Around mid-afternoon, she put on jeans and a t-shirt, slipped on a pair of sandals, and went for a walk. She strolled around, enjoying the breezy day, and a couple tacos. Walking down the street, she ran into Lori.

"Hi Megan. All set for the big night tonight?" Lori wore tight dark jeans, a gauzy turquoise blouse, gold hoop earrings and high heels. Next to her, Megan felt like a peasant.

"It's just a bar, Lori."

"A bar that is going to be wall to wall cowboys and I plan on finding a good stud to ride."

Megan made a face. "Is that all you think about? Getting laid?"

"Only if the cowboy owns a big ranch or his daddy does. Gotta run. See you tonight!"

***

Beneath the searchlight, a line of people stretched all the way around The Tejas. Inside it was wall-to-wall people. A haze of cigarette smoke hung over the crowd and drifted throughout the vast building. Couples jammed the dance floor to the music of Charlie Daniels, then Janie Fricke. Waitresses hurried back and forth filling drink orders. The building capacity was 5,000. The fire marshal arrived and locked down the building due to the massive crowd. With the noise, the crowd, the loud music, mass chaos reigned.

Megan wrote it all down from her seat at the bar where she sipped a beer. Out in the crowd, Lori sat at a table with two girls and a half-dozen men dressed in jeans, cowboy shirts and hats. Lori saw Megan and waved. Megan waved back and resumed writing, taking a sip of her beer every now and then. Her second beer in hand, she walked around, people-watching and taking notes, then left.

She walked into the B&B just as the ten o'clock news ended on the TV in the sitting room. Passing by, she nodded to a middle-aged couple sitting on a flowered sofa then hurried up the stairs to her room. Inside, she dropped her purse on the couch, turned on the light beside her bed, then sat down and read over her notes about the evening. All the while, she kept one eye on the locked door.

It never opened.

She slept late and woke to a cool day with gray clouds covering the sun. A perfect day to play hooky. She snuggled under the covers and went back to sleep. Awaking again around noon she threw on some sweats and a sweater and went downstairs in search of food. A cup of coffee in one hand and a sweet roll in the other, she sat in an easy chair in the sitting room to watch the noonday news, followed by an old Cary Grant/Deborah Kerr movie. Outside, a light rain fell. That evening she relaxed on her bed, writing in her notebook while waiting for a pizza delivery. Silence filled the old house and she immediately heard the doorknob turn. She sat up, grinning.

Chapter 3

"You missed a night," Megan chided Seth, smiling.

"Shucks, Miss Megan, I been checkin' those stairs ever' night for two months. Tonight's the first time it was ... different." He glanced at the bathroom. "Can I wash up?"

"Of course. By the time you finish, the pizza should be here."

"The what?"

"Pizza." She laughed at his puzzled look. "You're gonna love it."

While Seth showered, Megan put two paper plates on the table. She hummed a country western song as she tore two paper towels off the roll, folded them in half and placed them just so beside the plates. She gave the room a quick tidying up then checked the six-pack of beer on ice in the Styrofoam cooler she'd bought the day before. She stood by the bathroom door and hollered, "Hurry up, Seth." Someone knocked on the door. Megan answered it, figuring someone downstairs had let in the pizza delivery person.

"Hi!" Lori grinned. "I met the pizza boy downstairs. Paid him too."

"What are you doing here?" Megan dug in her pocket for money to repay Lori. The smell of the pizza made her stomach growl around the knots it had developed upon Lori's appearance. Megan had to get rid of Lori before she saw Seth.

"You left early last night. I didn't see you anywhere today and, well, I was worried about you, so I thought I'd stop by and see if you're all right."

Megan rolled her eyes. *Nosy is more like it.* "I'm fine. How'd you know where I'm staying?"

Lori smirked. "I have my ways."

"Thanks for the pizza." Megan reached out to take the pizza box, but Lori held on to it and stepped across the threshold. She wore tight blue jeans and a hot pink tank top that molded her breasts like skin on grapes. Her white-sandaled feet displayed shocking pink toenails.

The shower still ran in the bathroom. Megan hoped Lori wouldn't notice it.

"Why did you leave so early last night?" Lori's gaze darted around the room.

Megan shrugged. "It was noisy and smoky, and I'd seen all I needed to see. I'll take that." She tried again to take the box, but Lori brushed past and walked further into the room.

"This place is fabulous!" Lori gushed. "A lot nicer than that dump I'm in." The delighted look on her face dissolved into bafflement when the shower quit. Her gaze darted to the bathroom door then to Megan then, like a nail drawn to a magnet, to the table set for two. Her dancing eyes met Megan's. "Why Megan McClure, you sly dog. That's why you left early. You picked somebody up and he's still here."

Megan snatched the pizza box and put it on the table. "For heaven's sake, Lori. Grow up." She put her hands on her hips. "And get out."

Lori wagged a pink-nailed finger. "Oh no. I'm not leaving until I meet your mystery man. Is he a cowboy? Is he—?"

The bathroom door opened, and Seth stepped out. He wore a pair of brown trousers—and nothing else. Beneath the wet spikes of his hair, his eyebrows shot up and his jaw dropped when he saw Lori.

"H-howdy, m-ma'am." His gaze went from Lori to Megan and back to Lori.

"Howdy yourself, cowboy." Lori turned to Megan, scrunched her face and whispered, "Ooo, he's hot! And so young!" She swung back around to Seth.

"Lori—" Megan began.

Lori, hips swaying, approached Seth. "I'm Lori. Please don't call me ma'am. I've about been ma'amed to death since coming to Texas, haven't you, Megan?" Lori kept her full attention on Seth, who continued to stare at her bug-eyed. She stepped closer to him. "And you are ... ?"

Before Seth could answer—if he was even capable of answering, which Megan doubted from the way he looked at Lori—Megan quickly replied, "Seth. My cousin."

Lori spun around, her eyes wide. "Your *cousin*?"

Megan nodded. "On my mom's side."

"I don't remember you having any relatives in Texas." Lori turned back to Seth and peppered him with questions. Where did he live? What did he do? What did he think about The Tejas? Tongue-tied, bug-eyed Seth could hardly speak, giving Megan the chance to answer the questions, making them up as she went. Until Lori turned with a huff and snapped, "Why don't you let Seth say something?"

"He's shy." Megan patted Seth's back. "Aren't you?"

His gaze glued to Lori's breasts, he swallowed hard and nodded.

Bang!

Seth jumped and looked around, his face etched with concern.

Megan squeezed his arm, saying softly, "It's just that old Chevy."

"Bit jumpy, aren't you?" Lori batted her eyes.

"I don't like that old Chevy," Seth muttered.

Megan bit back a laugh. He didn't even know what a Chevy was.

He looked at Megan. "Somethin' smells good."

"The pizza," Lori squealed. She opened the box. "It's getting cold." She looked squarely at Megan. "Do you have an extra plate?"

Megan's mother had drilled manners into her so thoroughly that Megan opened her mouth to say, reluctantly, *yes,* but out came, "Yes, I do—but this is *our* meal. Seth has to leave soon, and we have a lot to talk about. I'd really prefer that you leave, Lori."

Lori lifted one thin eyebrow. "Quite the gracious host, aren't you?" The two of them locked eyes for a moment then Lori turned to Seth and held out her hand. "It was nice meeting you. And seeing you." Her appreciative gaze swept over him as they shook hands. She headed for the door, saying to Megan, "Have fun with your *cousin.*" Her blue eyes shone with malice as she tilted her head slightly toward the bed.

"Good Lordy," Seth said when the door closed behind Lori. "Do all the gals in your time dress like your friend?"

"For the most part." Megan sat at the table. "Although some flaunt themselves more than others. Like Lori. And she's not my friend. I wish she hadn't seen you. She's a busy body. Always sticking her nose where it doesn't belong." Shrugging, she put Lori from her mind and smiled at Seth. "Have some pizza. Pepperoni and green peppers."

He sat across from her.

She took two beers from the cooler and handed one to Seth.

"It's cold!" He stared at the can in amazement then looked it over. "How do ya open it?"

She reached over, popped the top then did the same to hers and lifted it high. "Cheers."

He took a drink then grinned like a boy on Christmas morning. "Boy howdy, that's good!" He took a longer drink. "Never had *cold* beer."

"You drink it warm?" She wrinkled her nose. "Yuck."

"We chill it in the creek but it's never this cold." He let loose a belch that made Megan laugh and him mutter, "Sorry."

The hot pizza was almost as big a hit as the cold beer. They ate every morsel and drank another beer. Seth sat back in his chair, one hand on his stomach.

"That was mighty fine grub, Miss Megan. I'm full as a tick on a hound dog."

She laughed. "I'm glad you liked it. Pizza's one of my favorites." She started cleaning up the table. "How's Lottie?"

Seth shrugged. "Still ignorin' Bingo. Still whorin'. An' still claimin' she's gonna quit it one day just as soon as she has enough money." He frowned, his young face serious. "Truth is, Miss Megan, I don't think she's ever gonna stop whorin'."

Holding the empty pizza box and crumbled paper towels, Megan paused. "I'm sorry, Seth. Maybe she thinks there's no other way for her to make it in the world."

He grunted, looking glum. "She's no dummy. She knows her letters an' numbers, she can read an' write. She can sew some right pretty dresses. But all she does is whorin'." His face tightened. "I think she likes it."

Megan squeezed his shoulder then resumed cleaning up. When she was done, she said, "Come sit with me. There's something I have to tell you." Seth looked at her curiously as he settled his lanky frame on the rawhide sofa. The light falling on his hair brought out the red in it. "Tomorrow night is my last night here. I'm leaving the next day."

"Leavin'?" His eyes widened. "Whaddaya mean?"

"I'm checking out the day after tomorrow and going home."

He frowned. "You mean next time I come to your time you won't be here?"

She nodded.

His frown deepened. "I never reckoned on that. I just figured you'd always be here."

"You know I don't live here."

"Yeah. But ..." His voice trailed away as he glanced around the room. One side of his mouth lifted in a half smile. "Won't the next people I walk in on be surprised?" He looked at her. "If there is a next time."

"What do you mean?"

"Maybe I won't be able to come back if you're not here."

Megan hadn't thought of that.

"It's possible, you know," he went on. "This never happened until you came here. I been up those stairs plenty of times before I met you. Maybe when you leave that door will stay shut for good an' I'll never come back to your time again."

"Oh, I hope not, Seth."

His eyes searched hers. "Why do you think I been able to come here? Why has this happened?"

"I don't know. Maybe I was here to stop you from bleeding to death and save your life. Maybe you're going to go on to do great things."

Seth barked a laugh. "That's plumb foolishness. I'm nobody." He took a drink of beer. After a moment, he looked Megan in the eye. "Why'd you say that? You know somethin' 'bout me? 'Bout my future?"

"I thought about looking you up in the historical records but ..." Her gaze dropped from his.

"But?" he prodded.

Her eyes met his again. "But then I'd find out when and where you died, and I don't want to know that. Not yet."

He laughed humorlessly. "I don't wanna know that either."

"It's also possible that there wouldn't be any records of you. That would mean that you're a figment of my imagination, and I'm crazy."

"You ain't crazy, Miss Megan. No crazier than me."

She laughed.

He grinned then took a swig of beer. "Maybe my comin' here has more to do with you than me. Like I said, this ain't never happened until you showed up. Maybe I was supposed to meet you for some reason."

"I can't imagine what that would be. Or why."

"Nothin' strange has happened to you since you been here?"

She shook her head then paused, thinking.

"What?" He turned sideways to face her and propped his elbow on the back of the sofa.

"I just remembered the first time I saw this place."

"What happened?"

"I arrived in Fort Worth about noon Monday. After checking into my hotel room, I decided to walk around and get a feel of the city. I've never been here before. Never been in Texas. I walked down this street, and saw this beautiful old house, which happened to be a Bed & Breakfast."

"Like a hotel."

"Exactly. On a whim, I walked inside to see if they had a vacancy."

"I'm right glad they did."

"Actually, they didn't."

Seth raised an eyebrow.

"I remember hearing the phone ring the minute I stepped inside. A woman stood beside a table in the hallway, going through the mail. She was the owner, Mrs. Powell. I asked if she had a vacancy and she said they were all booked up. Just then, a man, her husband, stuck his head out of a doorway down the hall and said someone had just cancelled. The woman said this must be my lucky day and asked if I wanted to see the room that just that second had become available."

She took a drink. "When I entered this room, the first thing I saw wasn't the beautiful antiques or the view out the windows. It was that door." She pointed to the door on the outside wall. "I walked right over to it and tried the doorknob. It was locked, of course. Mrs. Powell told me the story about the door, showed me around the room, told me the price, and I said I'd take it. When I introduced myself, she said, *Megan McClure? That's really your name?* She looked shocked. Almost ... unbelieving. Like she'd seen a ghost."

"Why?"

Megan slowly shook her head. "I have no idea. She asked if I had people in Texas. I said no. She asked if I had any past family members who had lived in Texas at one time or another. I said no. She gave me the key and explained the rules and has been very nice to me ever since. Her husband too." She shrugged. "That's my strange experience here. Nowhere near as strange as yours."

Seth ran his hand around the back of his neck. "I reckon not." His brow furrowed. "So, what're we gonna do?"

"I guess I'll go home and you'll return to your time. And we'll both wonder for the rest of our lives what this was all about."

Seth scowled. "That don't sound right. Not right a'tall."

Megan shrugged, agreeing, feeling helpless.

"I'm gonna miss you somethin' fierce, Miss Megan."

"I'm going to miss you, too. Do you think you can come tomorrow night?"

"I dunno. I ain't got no control over it." After a moment he said, "So—so this might be goodbye?"

"I'm afraid so."

He set his beer on the floor, put his elbows on his knees, clasped his hands, and looked around the room. "I can't believe I'll never see you again," he said with a catch in his voice and a glance at her.

"Me neither." Megan blinked back unexpected tears. She had come to care for him more than she had realized.

"You can't stay a few more nights?"

"I can't afford it. I splurged on this place in the first place and just can't afford to stay any longer."

He sat up. "I'll find a way to help you pay for it."

"I can't let you do that."

"I want to."

"It costs a lot to stay here. Where are you going to get that kind of money?"

The muscles in his jaw tightened. "I'll find a way. Don't leave yet. There's still so much I wanna know about your time."

"And so much I want to know about yours. And you. But Seth—"

"Don't leave, Miss Megan. Please don't leave." He stood and headed for the door.

She shot to her feet and followed him. "You're leaving now?"

"I gotta git busy. Gotta git you that money."

"Seth—"

He paused and turned to look at her, his hazel eyes searching her face. "I'll be back in two shakes of a cow's tail with some money for you. I promise. Don't leave." He touched her cheek, his fingertips lingering like a butterfly on a blossom. Then he stepped through the bricks.

***

The following night, her last night there, he did not come.

The next morning Megan went down to breakfast and was helping herself to a cup of coffee and a chocolate donut when Mrs. Powell, the owner, walked up.

"I hope you've enjoyed your stay, Miss McClure. I'll arrange a taxi to take you to the airport whenever you're ready."

"I was wondering if I could have the room for another night?"

"Extending your stay? That's wonderful."

Megan worked on a couple articles that night, keeping one eye on the locked door. Seth never came. The next morning Megan once again found Mrs. Powell and asked for another night.

"I'm sorry, but it's already rented out for the next three nights to newlyweds from up north. But I have a room on the other side that's available."

"No," Megan said quickly, "it has to be *my* room." The owner gave Megan an odd look. Megan went on. "It's the-the atmosphere of it."

"Atmosphere?"

"I'm a writer, you know, and that room has been very good for me. I've accomplished a lot since I've been here, and I want to stay in it a few more days. Maybe a week. Maybe longer."

"Well, I'm plumb flattered you've found the room so inspirational and I'd love to accommodate you. But I simply can't let you stay there any longer with that young couple—"

"I'll pay double the rate."

Mrs. Powell's eyes widened but she continued with hardly missing a beat. "I'll bring you some fresh towels, sugar."

Almost in a daze Megan tried to eat scrambled eggs and hash browns but her stomach reeled and rolled. *What the hell was I thinking?* The food stuck in her throat. Megan went up to her room and sat at the table with pen and paper to figure out her finances.

She dropped her head in her hands. *I can't afford to stay. But how can I leave?*

She played with the numbers again. Several times.

She threw down the pen and flopped back in the chair. "Shit. I have to get a job."

Chapter 4

Three days later Megan limped into The Tejas. She paused to let her eyes adjust to the dimness then hobbled to the bar, climbed on a stool, and ordered a beer. The bar held a couple of dozen people, more than Megan had expected for late afternoon on a weekday. Most of them wore the customary boots, jeans, and cowboy hats. In her blue dress and matching heels, Megan felt out of place.

She ordered a beer then leaned her elbows on the bar.

"I remember you." The blonde behind the bar set a bottle of beer in front of Megan. The bartender was a tall, pretty girl with shoulder-length hair and blue eyes. In the V of her white blouse an acorn-sized chunk of turquoise dangled just above her cleavage. "You were here at the VIP and opening nights. I saw you takin' notes." She tapped a cigarette out of a pack lying on the bar, lit it and took a drag. "You a reporter?"

"Freelance writer." Megan lifted the bottle and took a drink. It went down easy and she took another one. "I wrote an article about The Tejas for *Country Music Now*."

"No kiddin'? I read that all the time." The bartender grinned. She put her cigarette in an ashtray and went to wait on a customer further down the bar. A bar rag hanging out of a back pocket of her jeans swayed with her movements. A country western song about beer, a pickup and lost love played on the jukebox. Several couples two-stepped around the dance floor.

Megan tossed down another swig then slipped off a shoe and rubbed her foot. Smoke drifted and curled, filling her nose. Grimacing, she pushed away the ashtray just as the bartender returned.

"Sorry 'bout that." The bartender picked up her cigarette for a drag, then blew the smoke to the ceiling. She took the rag from her back pocket and started wiping down the bar. "You're lookin' kinda glum there, girl. Somethin' the matter?"

"I've been pounding the pavement looking for a job and my feet hurt. Oh, and no job."

The blonde paused, bar rag in hand, and took another drag off her cigarette before stubbing it out in the ashtray. "I thought you writers made a lot of money."

Megan rolled her eyes. "We're not all Stephen King."

"What kinda work you lookin' for?"

"At this point—anything."

The blonde gave Megan the once over. "We can always use another waitress."

Megan thought of what her room at the B&B was costing her and her unsuccessful attempts to find a job. She'd been offered the opportunity to submit articles to the local paper, the Fort Worth *Star-Telegram*, but it wasn't guaranteed, or steady. She'd never been a waitress. *How hard can it be?* "Who can I talk to about the job?"

The blonde grinned. "I'll see if Joe can interview you right now." She walked out from behind the bar and disappeared down a hallway. Minutes later, she waved to Megan, and led the way to the office, saying over her shoulder, "I'm Bonnie."

Twenty minutes later, Megan left The Tejas. She started her new job that night.

***

"You're doin' a great job," Bonnie said six nights later. She took a tray of empty beer bottles and glasses from Megan.

Megan brushed a lock of hair from her brow. "I'm glad you think so. I've never worked so hard in my life."

Bonnie laughed as she tossed the empty bottles, glass clinking, into the trashcan. "Wiggle your ass like I showed you and it won't seem so hard when the tips come pourin' in."

Megan returned Bonnie's smirk then waited for her to fill the next order. The place was filling up for Willie Nelson's performance later. It was his second appearance at The Tejas and if it went the way Megan had heard his first appearance had, it was sure to be a crowd-pleaser. Her order ready, Megan picked up the tray, smiled at Bonnie then turned and walked away, adding a little wiggle to her walk.

"Atta girl," Bonnie encouraged. "Now you're gittin' it."

Megan laughed, shaking her head. *Wiggle my ass, wear low-cut blouses and skintight jeans. Holy moly. The things I'll do for money.* She delivered the tray of drinks to a table of rowdy cowboys, all of them clean-cut and cute, then went to a nearby table to empty ashtrays and collect empty beer bottles. Guitars twanged a country western song on the jukebox as couples shuffled around the dance floor. After wiping the table clean, she picked up the loaded tray, turned around, and rammed the tray into Lori Rinsky's stomach. Two bottles toppled over and fell on the floor. Susie, Lori's assistant, squealed and jumped out of the way.

"Hey! Watch out—Megan?" Lori stared wide-eyed at Megan. "What are you doing?"

"Working." Megan picked up one of the bottles, relieved it hadn't broken. She couldn't find the other one. "What are you still doing in Fort Worth?"

"I've been writing about the local entertainment all week. Tonight, it's Willie." Lori wore tight jeans and a low-cut orange blouse showing more cleavage than any of the waitresses did. "Did you just say you *work* here?"

"Yup."

Lori tilted her head. "I thought you were doing so well chasing after lizard man and Bigfoot with hunky men."

"A little spending money never hurts. And I've never looked for Bigfoot. I gotta get back to work. Have fun." Megan smiled at Susie and started to leave, then paused when Lori spoke.

"Did you just clean this table?"

Megan faced Lori. "Yup."

Lori bent down and studied the table. She pointed one long red fingernail. "I think you missed a spot."

Biting back some choice words, Megan set the tray on another table, took out her rag and gave the table top a thorough cleaning. She smiled sweetly at Lori then picked up the tray.

Marvella, the local reporter, walked up, holding three bottles of beer. "Hey, Megan, how's it goin'? I didn't know you'd be here too."

"She's working." Lori pulled out a chair and sat at the clean table. Susie and Marvella sat too. "The adventurous reporter is our waitress tonight." Lori smiled at Megan. "Keep 'em coming."

Megan smiled back. "Sure." She turned to leave.

"Oh, Megan."

With a sigh, Megan turned back around.

Lori's sandaled foot rolled out the second fallen beer bottle from under the table.

Megan snatched up the bottle then moved on to the next table. *At least I didn't hit her over the head with it.*

Soon Willie had the place hopping, and the customers had Megan hopping. During a brief lull, she dashed to the restroom. On her way out, she ran into Lori.

"I talked to my mom the other day," Lori said.

Megan feigned interest. Their mothers had been close friends.

"I asked her about your mother's relatives. Mom said your mom didn't have any brothers or sisters, so you couldn't have any cousins on that side of the family. Same with your dad's side. So who's Seth?"

"It's none of your business, Lori. And what do you care?" Megan turned and walked away.

Near closing time, Megan cleaned up Lori's table, and found her tip. "Bitch."

Lori had left a penny.

***

"Miss Megan? You awake? Miss Megan?"

Megan jerked awake. Light from the streetlights seeped through the curtains, and in the dimness, Seth leaned over her. She sat up. "Seth? Where have you been? It's been over two weeks since you were here."

"That all? Been over a year for me."

"A year!" She leaned sideways to turn on the lamp then studied him in the soft light. His face had matured and filled out. His peach fuzz had grown into a sandy beard and mustache. His voice had deepened. He seemed taller, broader in the shoulders. Older.

Almost twenty, she guessed.

"You were sleepin' so soundly I hated to wake ya but this is the first chance I got to see you an' have I gotta surprise for you." He picked up a bag off the floor and dumped it upside down on the bed.

Megan stared dumbstruck as bills tumbled out. "Is that money?"

Seth grinned from ear to ear. "Yep. An' it's all yours."

Megan picked up one of the bills. It looked strange but was definitely a hundred. So was the next one, the next one, and all the rest. "Seth," she breathed, "where did you get all this?" Her gaze darted to his. "You made this much in a year?"

He laughed. "Shucks no, Miss Megan. I tried makin' money. God's witness, I tried."

"Tell me all about it." Megan scooted over, shoving money out of the way to make room for him.

He tossed his hat on a chair and sat on the edge of the bed. It dipped beneath his weight. "After I saw you I gotta job in a saloon cleanin' up at night. Wasn't much money so I started cleanin' out the livery, too. Then I clerked for a spell at the general store but waitin' on all those old biddies 'bout drove me crazy. So did the owner's kid." He rolled his eyes.

"She pestered me like a fly that wouldn't shoo. Then I hired on a trail drive headin' to Abilene, Kansas."

"That must have been exciting."

He laughed. His laugh was deeper than she remembered. He wore a tan shirt with bone buttons, and brown trousers. His hair was longer than it had been the last time she'd seen him. "It was long days of eatin' trail dust an' chasing after beeves. Downright borin' at times, just ridin' along, 'cept for when we rode through some hellacious storms. But I sure saw some purty country."

"Beeves?"

"Cattle."

"And you made all this money doing that?"

"Nah." He shook his head, looking a little abashed. "Spent most o' my earnin's in Abilene whoopin' it up with my pardners."

"Then where did you get it?"

He dropped his gaze from hers. "Ah hell, Miss Megan ..."

"Seth?"

He stood and walked around the room. "What difference does it make?" His long strides ate up the floor. "You needed money." He stopped and faced her. "I got you some."

"But how?"

He spread his hands wide. "Does it matter?"

"Yes. Especially since you're being so evasive."

He crossed his arms. "I won it playin' poker."

She regarded him through narrowed eyes.

He drew his arms in tighter. A muscle jumped in his cheek, then his gaze drifted from hers.

"You're lying."

He glanced at her then away.

"You're not a very good liar, either." She patted the bed. "Sit down and tell me."

He ran a hand through his hair.

"Come on, Seth."

A resigned look on his face, he plopped on the bed. It sank beneath him. Feet on the floor, he leaned forward, elbows on his knees, and dropped his head in his hands. "I did somethin' awful," he muttered.

Concerned, she leaned closer to him. "What did you do?"

He mumbled something into his hands.

"What?"

He mumbled again.

"You rubbed a back?"

He pulled his hands away from his face and stared at her. "I what?"

"That's what I'm wondering. You rubbed a back?"

"I robbed a bank."

Her eyes bulged. "You *what*?"

"I. Robbed. A. Bank."

Her mouth fell open.

"It wasn't hard. Heck," he sat up and held his hands shoulder-high, "I didn't even have a gun. Just said I did an' the clerk handed the money over an' I lit out o' there."

"Oh, Seth. You shouldn't have done that."

He looked away.

"Besides," she picked up several bills, "these aren't any good. They're worthless in my time."

He stared at the money. His broad shoulders slumped. "I never thought of that. Gosh, Miss Megan, I just never thought of that. So, I did it all for nothin'."

Megan squeezed his arm. "At least nobody got hurt."

"I sure scared the daylights outta that clerk," Seth admitted in a low voice. "I feel 'bout as low as a snake's belly for doin' that to that poor old woman." He raised his gaze to Megan. "I ain't never done nothin' like that in my life, Miss Megan. I ain't no thief. I swear. I want you to know that. But I didn't know how else to help you."

She leaned back against the pillows. "Actually, it's one of the nicest things anybody's ever done for me."

Seth chuckled. "I've missed you, Miss Megan."

"I've missed you, too. We have to figure out a way for you to return the money."

Seth knitted his brow. "How'm I gonna do that?"

"Is it a bank in Fort Worth where people know you?"

He shook his head. "I was goin' southwest through the countryside to deliver some supplies for Mr. Mead. He owns the General Store I worked at. I still help him out sometimes. On the way, I passed through a town called Cleburne. There was a bank on the corner of two streets I heard someone say were called Main an' Wardville."

"And on a whim, you decided to rob it?" Megan flipped back a curl that had fallen over her shoulder. She wondered if her hair was a mess then shrugged it off.

"Not then." Seth shifted positions, jostling the bed. "I went on to Glen Rose an' made the delivery then stayed there a day or so. I looked for work, somethin' that'd pay more'n what I could get in Fort Worth. But I didn't find anythin' promisin' an' finally headed home. I was feelin' pretty low, knowin' I wasn't gonna get you any money like I promised. While comin' back through Cleburne again, I saw the bank an' thought of all that money just sittin' in there. I thought of Bingo an' all his money. An' other men like him with so much money they couldn't spend it if they lived to a hundred." Seth's eyebrows drew together in a frown and the light from the bedside lamp threw his features in sharp relief. "I just about choked on the unfairness of it all, Miss Megan. So many folks with next to nothin' an' those few folks with ever'thin'. Just ain't fair. With nary a twinge of feelin' it was wrong, I pulled my bandana up over my face, stuck my hand in my pocket like it was a gun, walked in, an' robbed 'em."

"Holy moly." Megan shook her head in disbelief.

"It was plumb easy."

"We have to give it back, Seth. You know that." She leaned forward and put her hand on his. "Right?"

He pursed his lips then nodded. "But how?"

They ran through several possibilities then Megan reached for her pen and notebook and flipped it open to a blank page.

"I'll write a note to the sheriff explaining that I'm the robber's wife. Widow, actually." She wrote while she spoke. "My no-good husband came home with a sack full of money and was dancing around the yard with it when he tripped on something, fell and hit his head on a rock, killing him. I'm returning the money to clear my conscience." She signed her name, tore the sheet out of the notebook and handed it to Seth, who stared at it, a frown beetling his forehead. She wondered if he could read but before she could ask, he looked at her.

"You reckon this'll work?"

"I don't see why not. The thief is dead, the money returned. End of story."

His expression still doubtful, Seth folded the letter and stuck it in his shirt pocket.

"Maybe you shouldn't deliver it. That might implicate you and—"

"I'll do it," he said quietly. "It's the least I can do." His eyes, so serious, met hers. "But that still leaves you needin' money."

"Don't worry about me. I found a job. I'm doing fine." What a lie. The rent was killing her. Her feet were killing her.

"So, you'll be stayin' here a spell?"

He sounded so hopeful she forgot about her sore feet and dwindling finances and smiled. "I'll be here a spell."

"Good. 'Cause I been thinkin' 'bout you an' me an' why all this is happenin'."

Megan twisted around to fluff up her pillow then leaned back on it. "What's your idea?"

"I can't leave this room—I can't even open a window. The only place I can go is back to my time. Maybe you're supposed to come back with me."

"I can't go through that brick wall."

"Maybe you can go with me. I carried that sock of yours to my time an' back."

"I'm a little bigger than a sock."

Seth glanced around. "I'll try it with that lamp." He rose from the bed, walked to the sofa, and picked up a metal floor lamp. It was about five feet tall and had longhorn steers and roping cowboys pictured on the lampshade. Seth glanced at Megan, wiggled his eyebrows, then faced the brick wall and walked through it, lamp included.

Megan sat up straight in bed, the blankets pooling around her waist. "Holy moly."

Seth came back through the bricks, still holding the floor lamp. "I knew it would work." He put the lamp back at the end of the sofa then turned to Megan and held out his hand. "Your turn."

Megan pushed back the covers and swung her legs over the side of the bed. One foot touched the stool then she stood on the floor. She approached Seth, the wood floor cool beneath her feet.

"Scared?" he asked.

She tossed her head. "Of course not." She put her hand in his. Then snatched it back. "I can't go like this." She had on her nightclothes—a sleeveless blue top with white geometric designs all over it and light blue shorts.

"We'll come right back an' you can change. Come on."

Megan looked around at her twentieth century room—*For the last time?* —then placed her hand in Seth's. He squeezed it, smiling at her, then faced the wall and stepped through it, pulling her along.

She watched his shoulder disappear into the bricks. Then his elbow. Her heart pounded. Her mouth felt dry. Time seemed to slow, and her legs moved as if in a dream as the bricks consumed his forearm. His wrist. The base of his thumb. She felt the force of his pull cease, stopped by the brick wall that scraped her knuckles. All she could see of Seth were his fingers wrapped around her hand, his thumb curled around hers.

"Seth! Seth! It didn't work."

He came back through, scowling. "I was sure it would work. Let's try this." He picked her up in his arms. She let out a surprised yelp. "Hang on." She clasped her hands around his neck and held on. He walked to the bricks. Megan resisted the urge to close her eyes. Seconds later, she was squished between the bricks and Seth's broad chest.

"Ish not working," her distorted mouth mumbled.

"Damn it." He turned backwards and tried to pull her through, but the brick wall stood solid and unyielding.

Back in her room, still holding her in his arms, he repeated more forcefully, "Damn it."

"Maybe you can only take inanimate objects back with you." At his puzzled look, she explained, "Things that aren't alive. The sock. The lamp. But not people."

He grunted, scowling again.

"Could you hear me when you were ... over there?"

"Faintly." Seth tilted his head. "What's the point of all this? Why am I here, with you?"

His face was inches from Megan's, his breath warm on her face, his green-flecked hazel eyes intelligent and questioning. His strong arms held her easily, securely, and her naked thigh felt warm beneath his hand. Warmer than warm. Hot.

He was hot.
Hot and handsome and kissably close.

She almost gave in. She came *that* close. But the brick wall stopped her just as surely as it had stopped her entrance into his world. He belonged on that side of the wall. She belonged on this side. No matter how much she longed to kiss him he was still too young, and she refused to lose her heart to someone who, literally, lived in the past.

Megan squirmed until Seth released her and set her on her feet. She straightened her nightclothes. "I don't know why this is happening. I wish I had some twentieth century wisdom to impart." She looked up at him. "But I don't."

He stared at her, his face dark and glum, his hands in his pockets. "Reckon I better git." He crossed to the bed where he stuffed the hundred-dollar bills into the bag. He slung the bag over his shoulder then grabbed his hat off the chair.

Surprised and disappointed that he was leaving so soon, she touched his arm. "You'll let me know what happens with the robbery money, won't you?"

"'Course I will. If this is the only place we can see each other, well, I reckon I'll keep comin' back until the day you ain't here no more." He settled his hat on his head then reached out and touched her cheek. "See ya soon, Miss Megan."

Megan lay awake a long time, wondering
What if we kiss?
What if we have sex?
What if we fall in love?
What if?

Chapter 5

The locked door opened.

Megan put her pen on the table and looked up expectantly.

Seth walked into the room. "Howdy, Miss Megan."

"Howdy yourself."

He ambled over to where she sat at the table and angled his head, looking down at her notebook. "What cha doin'?"

"Writing an article. Having a beer." She closed her notebook. "Want one?"

"Sure." He sat on the other spindly-legged chair.

She handed him a beer from the cooler near her feet.

"Been writin' all night?"

"Just since I got off work a couple hours ago." She still wore her work clothes—skintight jeans and a low-cut red blouse with short sleeves.

"Did you have any trouble returning the money?" She'd last seen him two nights ago.

"No problem a'tall. The banker looked inside the bag an' 'bout fell over when he saw the money. He read your note, read it again, then said he was fixin' to ride over an' thank you hisself an' see how you was gittin' by. I told him right fast you'd moved back East. He was disappointed at that, I could tell, an' he just about shook my arm off when I left. Last I heard, he'd put your letter in a frame an' hung it on the wall in the bank for ever'one to see."

Megan laughed. "That's going a bit far but I'm glad it worked. And that you didn't get into any trouble. Please, *please,* don't do anything like that again."

He looked away and took a swig of beer. He licked his lips then met her gaze. He seemed to have a hard time doing so. "Wellll," he drawled, "I mighta done somethin' even dumber."

Megan lowered her beer. "What did you do now?"

He pursed his lips. "I told someone about you. About ... here."

"Holy moly. Who?"

"My friend Tim. Tim Summerfield."

"How on earth ..."

"We was horsin' around an' he grabbed my saddlebags an' all that money come tumblin' out." Seth chuckled, shaking his head. "You shoulda seen Tim's face. He was bug-eyed as a bullfrog. When he could finally string some words together, he asked me where'd I get that money. I couldn't think fast enough to lie so I just told him the truth." Seth's steady gaze rested on Megan. "I told him ever'thin'."

Megan digested that a moment. "Do you think he believed you?"

Seth shrugged. "Don't rightly know. Said he did, after a while, but he sure gave me some funny looks. Still does. But tell you true, Miss Megan." He leaned back in the chair, grinning. "It sure felt good, tellin' someone. I feel like I been livin' a-a secret life, comin' here to see you, an' it's a relief to have someone to talk to 'bout it."

"I can understand that. There are times I want to tell someone about *you.* But I don't think they'd believe me any more than Tim probably believes you. Instead of talking about it, I've been writing everything down."

"You're not mad at me?" Seth asked hesitantly.

She said with a shrug, "You're the one who has to deal with a friend who thinks you're crazy."

"He said I should bring somethin' back from here to prove it." Seth shot her a smile. "Guess I shoulda kept that sock of yours."

Take something back? The idea gave her a chill. *What would be the consequences?*

"Reckon you don't think that's a good idea." Disappointment laced Seth's voice.

Headlights from a car outside flashed through the lace curtains, throwing fleeting light and shadows on the walls and the side of Seth's face. Megan drained her beer then wiped her mouth with the back of her hand. "Did you show him my letter to the bank?"

Seth nodded. "Tim studied it real hard—he's sharp as a spine on a prickly pear. He turned the paper over an' over an' rubbed it between his fingers. He even wet his finger an' touched the ink to taste it. He agreed it looked different than anythin' he's ever seen but it's just paper." Seth shrugged. "Guess he needs somethin' more to convince him."

"I'll think about it." *What could I send? A pen? A sock? A coin? All too tangible. Too easy for someone else to see.* She bent down to grab another beer from the cooler. Straightening, she found Seth's gaze glued to her gaping low-cut blouse. She cleared her throat. His gaze slowly rose until it met hers. Heat smoldered in those hazel eyes. Sudden heat flamed her cheeks. Something even hotter blazed inside her, low, below her belly, a place untouched far too long.

"You look real pretty in red, with your black hair."

His soft-spoken words flowed over her like warm honey. She found she couldn't look away from him, so handsome in a faded blue shirt, red bandana around his neck, and those beautiful eyes. The room suddenly felt too warm. Her cheeks still burned. And that blaze inside ... She blurted, "How old are you?"

Surprise flashed across his lean face. He lifted his beer for a drink, regarding her over the rim of the can. He set the can on the table. "I turned twenty months ago."

She raised her beer. "Happy belated birthday." Twenty. She still thought of him as a seventeen-year-old boy. "Tell me about Tim."

Seth looked at her for a moment then sat back and stretched out his legs. "I met him when we first moved here. Been pardners ever since. He's a couple years older than me, an' a couple inches shorter. Husky fella. Has a dimple that sets the gals all aflutter. He went with me on the trail drive an' now he an' me are helpin' out on a ranch." Seth smiled. "He's a prankster and keeps me an' the boys on our toes. Never can tell when Tim's gonna drop a handful of burrs in your boot or stick a gob of lard, or worse, inside your hat." He chuckled. "I remember one time—"

While Seth told tales about Tim, Megan rested the beer can against her cheek. The cold aluminum lessened the heat of her skin. That blaze deep inside her finally cooled to the controlled burn she was becoming used to whenever Seth was near.

After another beer, she excused herself and went to the bathroom, aware of him watching her. She returned to him with one hand behind her back, saying, "I've got it."

"What?"

"Proof for Tim. Granted, it's just paper. But I bet it's something he's never seen before." She tossed Seth a roll of toilet paper. "It'll fit in your pocket, it's useful, and once it's used up, it's gone. No evidence. Nothing left to influence the future. Let's see what Tim has to say about that."

Seth chuckled. "I can't wait to see Tim's face when he gets a gander of this."

***

"Tim told me to tell you howdy, Miss Megan," Seth said in greeting the next time he opened what she now called Seth's door.

Smiling, Megan put aside the newspaper she'd been reading and rose from the rawhide sofa. It was Sunday, her night off. She'd finished writing one article, had it all typed up and ready to be mailed, and had started writing another. She'd ordered a small pizza then caught up her notebook about Seth. All in all, a good day, which had suddenly gotten better.

Seth wore a long gray coat dripping water on the floor, and muddy boots. He closed the door and paused, looking down. "I'm makin' a mess."

"Give me your coat and leave your boots by the door."

She took the coat and shook off the water over the tub, sending droplets everywhere. They dotted her navy-blue shirt. Droplets of water that just seconds ago had fallen from the sky in the late 1800s. *Mind boggling.* She hung the coat on the back of the bathroom door then grabbed a towel and tossed it to Seth.

He caught it and rubbed his hair and face dry. He wore a dark shirt, black trousers, and black stockings.

She dried her hands on her jeans. "I guess it's raining in your time."

"Like a dozen drunks pissin' in the street." His face reddened. "Pardon my language, Miss Megan."

"I've heard—and said—worse. So, Tim is a believer now?"

"That toilet paper had him plumb amazed. Said he'd read about it but since he had the Sears and Roebuck catalogue to use he didn't see the need to buy somethin' else. But after usin' that toilet paper, he claimed it was a sight better than those catalogue pages and the best idea he'd ever heard of. I told him it weren't nothin' next to a hot shower." Seth looked longingly toward the bathroom.

Megan laughed and waved a hand. "Go ahead." *Imagine, wiping with catalogue pages!* She shook her head, chuckling.

His shower done, Seth joined her at the table. If he noticed she had moved from the cozy, comfortable sofa to the table he didn't let on. She said, "I have a surprise for you." From the table she picked up the last two days' copies of the local newspaper and handed them to him. "The daily paper."

He held the newspapers as if they were priceless treasures and stared at them a moment. Then his gaze, somewhat hesitant, met hers. "I can't read real good."

"I'll help you."

He was a quick learner, she discovered as they read newspapers together that night and during his next few visits. He was intelligent, inquisitive, passionate. Meant for more than cleaning saloons or riding trail drives or wrangling horses.

One night he wore tight black trousers, and a crisp white shirt beneath a shiny green and canary yellow vest that molded his chest and torso. He looked divine. "I'm dealin' Faro in one of the saloons," he said.

"Johnny Bingo's?"

A scowl darkened his face. "Hell, no. I'm hopin' we put that bastard out of business."

Another night, Seth's door opened and a blast of nineteenth century snow blew in, followed by Seth. At least she hoped the figure in the sheepskin coat, scarf-wrapped face, snow-covered black hat, and boots was Seth.

"Lordy, Miss Megan, it's colder 'an a dog's nose pokin' through ice."

She helped him out of his coat and unwrapped his face, which was red and cold. Ice crystals clung to his eyelashes, mustache, and beard. He stood on one foot then the other, stumbling a little, while she tugged and yanked and pulled his boots until they came off.

"You g-got any h-heat in here?" Seth asked through chattering teeth. He was shivering and rubbing his hands together, blowing on them.

She wore blue jean shorts and a t-shirt. "It's 80 something degrees outside. You're lucky I don't have the air on. Go sit on the sofa." She ran to the bed, grabbed a blanket, and wrapped him in it. He continued shivering. She wrapped him in another blanket then sat beside him and took his cold big hands between hers to warm them. "What were you doing out in a blizzard?"

"H-helping Mr. T-Toby get his h-herd to shelter. Been s-snowin' all day an' gettin' c-colder by the minute. I been at it since before n-noon. Must be after midnight by now." He sneezed twice.

"I hope you're not getting sick." Megan rubbed his hands. He still shivered. She rose, tugging his hand. "Get up."

"Where we goin?"

"You're going to get in bed and warm up. Come on."

He pulled his hand free. "I ain't g-gettin' in your bed."

"Seth—"

"I'm dirty. I ain't washed lately. I st-stink."

"I don't care."

He pulled the blankets tighter around him. "I do. I ain't dirtyin' your bed." He yawned. His face was tight and lined. "I just need a bit of shuteye." He leaned his head back against the sofa and closed his eyes, looking dead tired.

She got a pillow and another blanket then touched his shoulder, rousing him. "Stretch out. Here's a pillow. There you go." He had to curl on his side to fit on the sofa. She tucked the blankets around him. He smiled at her sleepily. "Feeling warmer?" she asked.

He nodded. "'Cept my feet."

She felt them. "They're freezing!"

"You could sit on 'em to warm 'em up."

She wondered if he was teasing. But his feet were very cold. She sat on them. "Better?"

"Feelin' warmer already." He wiggled his toes against her butt.

She snorted a laugh. "I still think you should be in bed."

Her heart skipped a beat when he murmured, "Only if you're in it with me," before falling asleep.

***

A couple nights later, Seth looked up from the newspaper he'd been reading on the sofa. Rain pelted the windows and lightning flashed, followed by rumbles of thunder that shook the old house. "Miss Megan? Why ain't people here in your time found a way to end war?"

Surprised by his question she stared at him a moment then burst out laughing. "End it? Hardly. War is big business. Keeps the economy going. But we *have* gotten better at it. Bigger guns. Better bombs. We can blow the planet to smithereens a couple times over with the weapons we have now. All the deadly sins are alive and well, Seth. We still have hatred, bigotry, greed. Murder is rampant. Rape. Robbery. You name it. Evil still thrives. Why, some nut tried to assassinate the President a couple days before we met."

Seth frowned. "Folks still talk 'bout President Lincoln's murder."

He had told her all he could remember about the war and his brothers and she knew their young deaths had affected him greatly, their absences leaving him bitter about the reasons behind their deaths. He didn't like guns either, although he owned one but never carried it. She said, "There have been other presidents killed. John F. Kennedy was assassinated in 1963. I was in fourth grade and remember it like yesterday." She shrugged. "We may have more conveniences and gadgets in our time, but, when you get right down to it, humanity hasn't really come all that far from the cave."

His frown deepened, creating furrows in his handsome face. "I would think by your time people woulda learned." His voice trailed off and he stared down at the headlines screaming of war, violence, death.

He looked distressed and disillusioned, and she had no answer for him. Changing the subject, she asked him something she'd been meaning to ask him for a while. "What do you want to do with your life, Seth?"

Rain poured down the windowpanes while he stared at the paper, but Megan doubted he saw the print. Down on the street a car honked, tires squealed.

Seth finally lifted his head and his eyes, so serious, met hers. He said quietly, "I want to end war. I want to change the world."

***

Megan recalled his stunning words the next day when she stood in a used bookstore holding a book about the history of the United States up to its bicentennial in 1976. She considered the many consequences of someone from the past knowing the future. *What could he do with the knowledge? What changes could he possibly cause?* She walked to the counter, reaching for her wallet, thinking the world could stand a little changing. Off the top of her head, she could think of several people that should be eliminated from history, with Hitler and Stalin at the top of the list. Her purchase in hand she left, imagining the look on Seth's face.

It was priceless. He thanked her over and over then they sat down to read it together. A few days later, she bought a book on the history of the world since 1900, and one on the history of Fort Worth. The latter made him scoff, "It ain't nuthin' like that."

One night in early May, Megan learned two things about Seth: he now wore a gun, and he had a new friend.

***

"—and Tim said there's no telling where that horse ended up after he tied those ribbons all over it and it lit out." Seth laughed and slapped his knee.

Megan wiped tears from her eyes. Her stomach hurt from laughing. "You and Tim. What a pair of kooks."

Seth smiled. He stretched his arm across the back of the sofa and crossed a knee with an ankle. "He's the best fella a body can have for a friend. I know I can count on him and he'll do whatever he can to help."

"I'm glad you have a friend like that."

"Like your friend Donna."

"Yeah. She's the best." Megan drew a leg up beneath her on the sofa. She was barefoot and wore blue jean shorts and a white tank top. Seth looked as handsome as always in tight brown trousers and a beige shirt with white stitching. She had noticed the gun belt around his trim waist the minute he entered the room. "Why are you wearing a gun now?"

He drummed his fingers on the rawhide. "I was wondering when you'd bring that up. You've said yourself enough times over the years that I live in the Wild West."

Years.

Megan sometimes still found it hard to fathom the time difference. For her, it had barely been a month. "Is Bingo causing trouble again?"

"When ain't-isn't he. And he's not the only one. There's been a string of questionable characters passin'—passing through lately."

"That's something else I've noticed about you."

Seth raised an eyebrow.

"There's a vast improvement in your speech. I don't hear as many ain'ts and you're not dropping as many g's like you used to. Are you going to school or something?"

"I've been gettin'-getting help from a friend."

"That's wonderful."

"Her name's Susannah."

Megan's stomach dropped to her toes.

"Her daddy owns the general store," Seth continued. "I knew her when she was in pigtails and pesterin' me while I was working there. She went back East to some fancy school for a couple years, an'-and now she's home. She's nice and real smart. When I asked her to help me, she agreed on the spot."

No shit, what red-blooded woman wouldn't? Megan held up a long curl of her hair and studied it as she asked casually, "Is she pretty?"

"Pretty enough. Whiskey-colored hair an' eyes. A mite taller than you."

"Is she your girl?" She glanced at Seth, found him regarding her with a slight smile.

"Jealous, Miss Megan?"

"Of course not," she scoffed. She shot to her feet. "I hope you two are happy as peas in a—"

"Come 'ere." Seth grabbed her hand and pulled her on his lap.

She landed awkwardly, one leg flying up in the air then her foot hitting the floor with a thud. He chuckled. His arm slid around her, cradling her. The smells of horses and dust from long ago rose from his shirt. His heart beat beneath her shoulder. He ran his free hand lightly over her hair. Heat flared in his eyes. His arm tightened around her and pulled her closer as he lowered his head.

A battle erupted inside Megan.

He's too young.
He's older every visit.
He's still too young.
He might be 21 by now.
He's still—
I don't care!

Megan rose to meet him. Her eyes closed. Her lips puckered. Her heart pounded like a herd of wild stallions running across the Texas plains.

Bang!

Seth jerked back.

Bang!

Her eyes shot open. Seth stared at his door, his expression troubled, his hold on her loosened. Disappointment sliced through her. She reached up to turn his face toward her. "It's just that old Chevy."

The muscles in his jaw tightened beneath her fingers. "I don't think so."

Her eyes widened. "Sometimes those bangs *are* from *your* time?"

He nodded and glanced at the door again. His chest moved with a deep breath. His eyes met hers. "I gotta go. Lottie—"

"Go." Megan pushed herself away from him and found her footing, then reached back to take his hand as he rose from the sofa. Hand in hand, they walked to Seth's door. He grabbed his hat off the table then turned to her when they reached the door.

"I'm sorry." He squeezed her hand before releasing it.

"Me too." She smiled. "Be safe."

"I like whiskey. But I like midnight black more." His fingers touched her cheek while his gaze rested on her lips. "We'll finish this next time."

"Promise?"

"Promise."

Then he was gone.

The Chevy backfired again.

Or is it gunfire?

Is Seth all right?

What about Oh! Susannah?

***

Seth did not follow through on his promise when he showed up three nights later. He seemed distracted and restless as he roamed the room. He gave the light switch a couple of flips before moving on to inspect the electric typewriter sitting on a small table near the armoire.

He glanced at the armoire. "It's still there."

Megan knew he meant his handprint, now crusty and dried to a reddish brown. "I keep meaning to clean it off. But sometimes I need to look at it to reassure myself that I'm not crazy."

He looked at her, a frown creasing his forehead.

She shrugged and gave a little smile.

He continued wandering around the room. He paused before a painting of a longhorn steer standing amidst a field of wildflowers. He didn't even glance at the history books piled on the floor beside the sofa, no talk of ending war or changing the world. He had little to say about Tim, no funny stories to share. He mentioned dancing with Susannah at a barn-raising, then at a wedding. He didn't touch Megan except with his eyes, and even that wasn't very often.

She swallowed her disappointment when several minutes later he said he had to leave.

He stepped through the bricks, and Megan pictured him stepping into Susannah's arms. As much as she hated it, she couldn't blame him. He was a man, after all, and a handsome one at that. One such as he wouldn't be without a woman for long. Susannah lived in his time, was of his world, part of his everyday life. Megan didn't blame Seth, or whiskey-haired Susannah. But she didn't like it.

Almost a week later, Megan walked out of the bathroom, ready for bed in her nightclothes when Seth's door slammed open.

He ran in with his gun drawn and murder in his eyes. When he saw her, he came to a sliding halt, breathing heavily.

"Seth! What's the matter?"

His hair was a mess, his clothes dirty, and his right cheek bore a bloody cut.

"God damn Bingo! I'm gonna kill him!" He looked wildly around the room, as if expecting to find Bingo there.

Megan approached him cautiously. "He's not here, Seth. Put the gun away. Please."

He sent one more menacing look around the room then shoved the gun into its holster. He scowled at Megan. "I don't want to be here. I never even noticed the changes—the cold and the dark at the top of the stairs as I ran up here. I gotta go down the stairs an' come back up, hopin' I'm back in my time. I gotta find him. He's somewhere in this whorehouse."

"What happened?"

"He beat Lottie. Bad."

"Oh no!"

"She's got a black eye, busted lip, bruises all over, shoulder out of whack, couple of broken ribs."

"Holy moly."

"He gave it to her good this time, and it's the last time. I swear, Miss Megan, it's the last damn time that bastard will lay a hand my sister." He stared down at Megan, as if finally seeing her through his haze of anger. "I can't stay. I'm sorry."

She stepped closer and touched his arm. She could feel the coiled tension in his muscles. "Please be careful. Don't get yourself shot."

"If I do, I know where to come get fixed up." A brief smile crossed his hard face. Then he turned and headed for the door.

Halfway there, he spun around and stared at her across the room. He took two long strides, grabbed her by the shoulders and pulled her up against him, his gaze searing into hers. His mouth came down hard on hers and he kissed her hungrily, his fingers digging into her shoulders, his tongue deep in her surprised mouth. Abruptly, he released her and stepped back, his breathing heavy, his eyes full of heat and passion. He touched a hand to her cheek then turned, drew his gun, and ran through the bricks.

Megan stared after him, shaken, breathless, wanting more. She ran to the brick wall and pressed an ear against it. *Is that gunfire? The old Chevy? Or my imagination?* She honestly could not tell.

She threw on some clothes, hurried to a drugstore, and bought some rolls of gauze, a box of Band-aids, a bottle of alcohol, a bottle of aspirin, and some ointment. She hurried home and waited, expecting Seth to come staggering through his door, shot all to hell.

He never came.

Nights passed. Megan went to work and came home. She wrote two more articles, cashed a much-needed check from a previous article, and wondered when, if, Seth would return.

Although she missed him and worried about him, in a way she was glad for some time alone. Between working past midnight many nights then sitting up with Seth until daybreak then writing down everything they had said and done—she had started a second notebook—plus writing every day she was getting little sleep. Waitressing was wearing her out. She'd never worked so hard. Or for such low pay. Granted, the tips were good, some nights excellent, but the money wasn't steady and no matter how much she scrimped, her funds were in the red.

Fortune smiled on Megan one sunny Friday afternoon when she handed Mrs. Powell the weekly rent money.

"Sugar, you don't need to pay me any extra anymore. And you can stay in that room as long as you want and pay a lower weekly rate. In fact, you can have this week for free."

Megan threw her arms around Mrs. Powell. "Thank you! Oh, thank you!" She drew away, her grin fading to confusion. "But why would you do all of that for me?"

"I've been feeling mighty guilty, making you pay extra."

"Why?" Megan asked in surprise.

"I guess I never told you how I got this place—" Mrs. Powell broke off when her husband stuck his head out of the office and said the plumber was on the phone. "I'll be right there, dear," Mrs. Powell said to him then turned back to Megan. "Excuse me, but I have to get that. Plumbing problems. It's never ending in this old house." She patted Megan's arm. "Remind me to tell you later."

Although her financial problems had eased, Megan kept her job at The Tejas. It gave her a reason to go out every day, gave her new ideas to write about, and the money came in handy. Plus, she met a vast array of people. One of them was Barton Crone.

Chapter 6

The Saturday night crowd crammed The Tejas. Country western music blared. Couples two-stepped around the packed dance floor. The tables were filling up and crowds lined the bars beneath a thick haze of cigarette smoke. Huge amounts of alcohol were being consumed all around. The mechanical bull had a steady stream of victims.

Megan stood beside a table, delivering drinks as she chatted with the customers when she noticed a man weaving his way between the tables leading five people behind him. Husky, tall, six-three maybe, with jet-black hair, he was movie star handsome in a black suit, tie, and white shirt. He stopped beside a table, held out a chair for a thin blonde in a floor-length slinky pale pink dress, then sat beside her. The rest of the group, two other couples, also formally dressed, took their seats.

Megan foresaw a nice tip. She adjusted her low-cut turquoise blouse, pulled a curl of hair forward over her shoulder, and headed for their table. The man looked up when she approached. His gaze swept her from head to toe then his blue eyes met hers.

Holy moly, what a hunk. She smiled. "Hi. Welcome to The Tejas. How are you guys doing?"

He smiled back and looked even handsomer, as impossible as that seemed. "Evenin', darlin'. Bring us a couple pitchers of beer and keep 'em comin'." He winked at her then gave her the once over again before leaning forward to say something to one of the other men, draping his arm around the blonde's shoulders.

Megan kept their drinks coming along with drinks for several other tables. A couple of hours later she stepped out a side door for a quick break. She stood on a small concrete pad at the top of several steps leading down to the parking lot in back. She took out a cigarette from the pack in the back pocket of her jeans then leaned her elbows on the handrail and took a deep breath of the cool night air. A steady breeze stirred her hair. Insects buzzed around the security light over the door. A chorus of crickets chirped in the darkness beyond. Above the haze of city lights and pollution a few stars shone. The door opened, letting out the music, and the hunk.

"Mind if I join you for some fresh air?" he asked.

"Not at all," she replied.

He shut the door, blocking out the music. He lit a cigarette then held out the lighter for the unlit cigarette between her fingers.

"No thanks. I'm just holding it."

"They do last longer that way." He put the lighter in his pocket.

She faced him, leaning back against the handrail. "I just pretend to smoke."

He took a drag. "Why?"

"It didn't take me long to realize that waitresses who smoke get more breaks. No one bats an eye when someone says, *I'm stepping outside for a smoke.* So, after working here a couple of days I bought my first pack in two years, two months and twenty-four days and take as many smoke breaks as the rest of the girls."

"But you don't really smoke them." He leaned back against the door, his hand still in his trouser pocket, and crossed one ankle over the other. His loosened tie hung a little lopsided against his white shirt. The security light shone down on him, accentuating the planes and angles of his face and his long straight nose.

"If someone else is out here I pretend." She wrinkled her nose. "Nasty habit."

"Ah. Nothing worse than an ex-smoker."

"It was a gift to myself for my twenty-fifth birthday. And look at all the money I've saved."

"Rest assured your secret's safe with me, Miss ... ?"

"Megan."

He tipped his head. "I'm Barton. This is quite a place."

Megan chuckled. "It's certainly an interesting job."

"Have you been working here since the opening?"

Megan swatted a mosquito on her arm. "I started a week or so after it. Figured I'd earn a little extra money while I work on other projects."

"Such as?"

"I'm a writer."

"Really? I've never met an actual writer. Books?"

"Articles mostly. I just wrote one about The Tejas' opening night for *Country Music Now*."

He whistled. "That's a big-name magazine. You freelance and work here too?"

She nodded, waiting for the usual comment—*I thought all writers made a lot of money.*

He surprised her by saying, "It must be tough. Having to hustle for work all the time. Never knowing what's coming up next. You've got a lot of guts." He took another drag then blew it out. Smoke curled and drifted in the breeze.

Megan pushed wind-blown hair off her face. "What do you do?"

"I'm in land acquisitions for a major home-builder in the area."

"Construction seems to be booming around here."

"It's an exciting time."

Profitable, too, judging from the big diamond ring on his pinkie finger twinkling in the light. She'd bet next month's rent the watch she'd glimpsed was a Rolex. "Are you from here?"

"Born and raised. You?"

"Born and raised in rural Illinois, live in Chicago now."

"A Yankee." He flicked his cigarette away. It burned an arc in the darkness. "I figured as much when you asked how we were doing. A Texan would have said, *How are y'all doin'*. And you have that accent." She huffed a sigh at his comment. He laughed, a rich baritone. "I reckon you've heard that more than once since you've been here."

"Oh yeah."

Silence fell between them. Crickets chirped. A car door slammed somewhere out in the dark parking lot. Flashing lights in the black sky depicted the path of an airplane. Megan ran a hand through her hair, feeling Barton's eyes upon her. Sirens wailed in the distance.

Megan looked toward the sound. "Holy moly, I hope they're not coming here."

"Cops come here a lot?"

"Actually, there was only one time that I know of. The crowds can get pretty rowdy but not out of hand. So far anyway."

He uncrossed his ankles and stood straight. "You're lucky. There's a bar here called The Wagon Wheel that has at least one fight a night. Guys bashing beer bottles over each other's head, glasses and chairs flying everywhere. It gets pretty wild."

"Jeez, how juvenile." She asked with a smile, "How many of those beer bottle bashes have you been in?"

He laughed. "Just one. Back when I was young and dumb." He laughed again. "Beer bottle bash. That's a good one."

"It sounds like the name of a country western song."

"It does!"

They laughed, the sound rivaling the chirping crickets.

Barton asked, "When's your article going to be in that magazine?"

"Probably in the next couple weeks. Keep it current, you know."

"Maybe you'll autograph my copy—if you're still here, that is."

She recognized a come-on when she heard one. And him with his girl waiting inside. She shrugged. "I may be here. I may not. I don't know."

"Footloose and fancy free, huh?"

"That's me."

"So, all your family and friends live in Yankeeland? And you don't know anyone around here?"

"Yup." She got out the pack of cigarettes from her back pocket.

"Sounds like a lonely life."

"Not at all." She stuffed the cigarette back into the pack. "I make new friends everywhere I go." She smiled at him. "Like you." In the overhead lighting, she saw him smile back. *There oughta be a law against a man looking that good.* "I'd better get back to work." She stuck the pack in the pocket of her jeans. "It was nice meeting you, Barton."

"The pleasure was entirely mine, Megan." He opened the door then held it for her and followed her inside. He went back to his table and his blonde while Megan went back to work. Every now and then, she saw him out on the dance floor. He danced the way she had known he would—smoothly, effortlessly, gracefully. The blonde looked at him like he had hung the moon, as they said in Texas.

When Megan got a chance, she threaded her way through the crowd to the restroom. She sat on the toilet for a few extra moments because it felt so good just to sit. She could almost feel her veins forming rope-like bulges in her legs. With a sigh, she left the stall then washed and dried her hands. A couple of quick fluffs to her hair and she was ready for the home stretch to closing time.

Several guys wearing jeans and cowboy hats and holding bottles of beer stood near the restroom, talking and laughing, a couple of them stumbling, slurring drunk. As Megan walked by, one of them grabbed her ass. It happened all the time. She'd learned to ignore it, accept it as part of the job. But she was tired and cranky, and her feet hurt.

She whirled around and glared at the cowboys. "Keep your hands to yourselves, boys."

"Howdy, schweeheart," one of them slurred, flinging his arm around her shoulders. "Hows 'bout I buy ya a beer an' we git friendly." His beer breath hit her in the face.

She squirmed out from under his arm. "Let me go!"

He made a grab for her and caught the neckline of her blouse, pulling one side off her shoulder. "Aw, come on, sugar—"

"You heard the lady, bucko. Let her go." Barton appeared out of the crowd.

The drunk kept his grip on Megan's lopsided neckline. He wavered a little on his feet as he snarled, "Who the fuck are you?"

His face hard, his eyes cold, Barton stepped closer. His arms hung loosely at his sides, but his hands clenched. He towered over the drunk and his friends. "I'm the guy who's gonna rearrange your face if you don't let her go and leave her alone."

The drunk's grip on her blouse loosened. She yanked free and moved out of the way. The drunk, despite his friends' attempts to stop him, started towards Barton, who looked ready for a fight.

"Hey, what's going on?" Another man hurried up. He took one look at the drunk and gave him a shove. "Ah hell, Pete. You causing trouble again?" He turned to Barton. "I'm sorry, man. He gets mouthy when he's had too much." He looked at Megan. "Sorry, miss, for whatever he did. Real sorry." He turned back to his drunk friend and, waving his hands, started giving him hell.

Barton turned to Megan. He reached over and pulled her blouse straight then took her arm and steered her away.

"Thanks," she said. "That was very gallant of you."

They paused near the dance floor where couples shuffled around in a circle to a song on the jukebox while the band took a break. Barton released her arm. "I'm just glad I happened by. You okay?"

She waved her hand in a dismissive gesture. "Just another night at work." She looked toward the bar. "Speaking of which—"

"Dance with me."

Megan's gaze snapped back to Barton. "What?"

"Dance with me." He held out his hand, palm up.

She glanced at the dance floor. "I don't know how to Two-Step."

"Just follow me." He wiggled his fingers.

After a moment of indecision, Megan placed her hand in his and followed him into the crowd. Just then, the song ended. Seconds later, Anne Murray started singing *Could I Have This Dance*. Barton took Megan in his arms and guided her around the floor. She felt clumsy and awkward and stepped on his toes.

"Relax." His breath stirred the hair on her forehead.

She gave into the moment. He smiled down at her as they glided and spun, weaving between the other couples, his strong arm holding her securely, the faces around her a blur as she gazed at his handsome face. When the song ended, he dipped her low. Laughing, she held on until he pulled her upright.

As he did so, her gaze collided with Barton's blonde standing beside their table, hands on her hips, lips pressed tightly together, her eyes shooting daggers at Megan.

Megan quickly lowered her hands and stepped away from Barton. "That was fun. Thanks. I better get back to work." He nodded. She felt him watching her as she walked through the crowd to the bar. *I bet the blonde gives him hell!*

Hours later the crowd started thinning out and Megan noticed Barton and his friends leaving. Their gazes met. He tipped his head. She smiled and watched him walk away, the blonde stuck to his side like a piece of tape. Megan went to clean their table. Her jaw dropped when she saw the tip.

Holy moly. He made a mistake.

She snatched up the bill and ran through the bar, dodging the few remaining customers, then shoved open the front door. She paused and scanned the parking lot until she saw his tall figure and the blonde walking in the glow from one of the light poles. She ran after him as he stopped beside a car and opened the passenger side door for the blonde.

"Mister! Barton! Wait!"

He looked up as he shut the door on the blonde inside the car.

She stopped, gasping for air. "I think—you made a mistake." She held out the bill, aware of the blonde glaring at her through the car's window.

"It's not a mistake, Megan. I'm just helping out a new friend."

He walked around the car and got in on the driver's side. He drove off, leaving her standing there clutching a fifty-dollar bill.

***

The following Friday afternoon Megan, wearing jeans, a sleeveless green top, and sandals, walked out of the bank after cashing her paycheck and ran into Barton as he was walking by on the sidewalk. After greetings and small talk, he asked, "You off today?"

She shook her head then slipped on her sunglasses, a necessity in Texas, in her opinion. "I go in at seven tonight."

"You have any plans for this afternoon?"

She shook her head again.

"I'm going to a gun show. Want to come? It'll just take an hour or so to look around. We can grab something to eat afterwards."

"Won't your girlfriend mind?"

His dark brows drew together. "My girlfriend?"

"The blonde? From the other night at The Tejas?"

"Oh. Her. She's not my girlfriend."

Megan adjusted her sunglasses. "Does she know that? She looked ready to kill me after you and I danced."

Barton chuckled. "Tammy's the kid sister of my best friend. We were in his wedding that day. She's always had a thing for me, but she's too much like a little sister for me to mess with her. I'm not dating anyone at the moment. Are you?"

She thought of Seth. Whatever they had, she wouldn't call it dating. She shook her head.

"How 'bout it? The gun show, and barbeque?"

A line of cars streamed by on the street. One honked. Another car honked. A motorcycle rumbled by, followed by a pickup with Mexican music blaring.

Megan chewed her lower lip. Between waitressing, writing, and Seth, she had little time for socializing. Except for Bonnie and the other people at work, Megan did not know anyone else in town. She thought of her lonely room at the B&B. She'd been in Fort Worth over a month and had hardly seen any of it because she spent most of her free time waiting for Seth. He hadn't been to see her in almost two weeks. For all she knew he could be dead. Well, actually, he *was* dead. *Holy moly, sometimes dealing with Seth is so confusing. His time. My time. Never our time.*

Resentment welled up inside her. While Seth dealt cards in the saloon and caroused with his buddy Tim and danced with Susannah, Megan sat in her room and waited and waited and waited. She had never been one for just sitting around. She liked adventures, challenges, seeking out the impossible. Just last fall she'd slogged through a Louisiana bayou in search of a hairy two-legged monster the locals claimed to have seen. She'd once spent three nights in Salem in a house haunted by witches burned at the stake, although they never made their presence known to her. A year ago, she'd climbed a high hill and spent an afternoon interviewing a shaman in South Dakota.

"I didn't think it was that hard of a decision."

Her attention snapped to Barton. His black hair stirred in the wind as he waited for her answer. He wore sneakers, jeans, and a short-sleeved shirt with vertical stripes of varying shades of blue on it. His broad shoulders and chest filled out the shirt. His biceps bulged like a construction worker's. He had close-set eyes. Bright blue, like the sky behind him. It had been a long time since a handsome guy had asked her out.

"I'd love to go."

"Great." Barton grinned. "My car's right here."

"Your car?" She gulped. "Can't we walk there?"

"Walk?" He laughed. "Too far."

He led her to a cherry red Corvette parked at the curb and opened the door for her. She stopped, assaulted by anxiety and a sick feeling curling in her stomach. She couldn't move her left leg to put her foot on the floorboard of the car and climb in. Despite the warm April sun on her skin, a chilling coldness permeated her soul.

"Problem?" Barton asked.

Her gaze darted up and caught his questioning look. She swallowed back the vomit threatening to spew from her mouth and formed her lips into a tremulous smile. She shook her head. She took a few steadying breaths then with concentrated effort forced her leg to lift into the car and plant her foot on the floorboard. With the slowness of an old woman, the rest of her body followed until she sat on the oyster-colored leather seat.

He closed the door then went around to his side and got in. "Pretty day isn't it?"

She nodded, controlling her nervousness and breathing.

He turned the ignition key. The car roared to life.

She sat stiff and anxious. Except for taxis, she hadn't been in a car in several months. Even longer since she'd ridden shotgun. While Barton chatted, and she tried to contribute to the conversation, she watched his driving with a critical eye. He seemed to be a good driver. Attentive, observant, in control. Her shoulder blades relaxed against the back of the seat and she breathed a little easier.

She glanced around the interior of the car. It looked almost new and was very clean. "Nice car."

He ran a loving hand over the dashboard. "A '78 model. Got her about eight months ago. She's my baby."

At the gun show at the Amon Carter Exhibit Hall, a steady line of people filed past the booths displaying just about every type of gun and weapon imaginable. Megan and Barton walked together for a while then he said he wanted to check on something in a booth they'd already passed.

"I'll catch up with you in a bit," he said.

"I'm going to check out the coin show across the hall," she said.

He nodded and disappeared into the crowd. Megan left that room and crossed the hall to a much smaller room with fewer tables and less people. She wandered down the aisles, stopping occasionally for a closer look at something or other. Halfway down an aisle she paused at a table, and looked at an assortment of old bills, commemorative coins, and coins encased in protective white squares of cardboard. The old bills made her smile, reminding her of Seth, the bank robber. Near the back of the table, she spotted a big ceramic bowl full of loose, old, dull coins of every size from smaller than a penny to silver dollar size. Idly, she picked up one and turned it over. She looked at the date. 1883.

A jolt shot through her. A coin from Seth's time.

She looked at another coin. 1878. And another. 1880. After checking each coin, she ended up with about three dozen dated between 1867 and 1900. Seth's money. He might have even held one or more of them at one time or another. Just holding them, she felt closer to him.

"Can I help you, miss?"

She looked up. A gray-bearded man in bib overalls watched her.

"I'll take these." She pushed the pile toward him.

He glanced at it. "Five dollars."

She paid and walked away, clutching a small felt bag of old coins. Seth's coins.

"What'd you get?" Barton asked when he met up with her.

"Some old coins." She opened the bag to show him.

He took the bag from her and jingled some coins out on his palm. "What'd you pay for these?"

"Five dollars."

His head snapped up and he laughed. "I hate to tell you this, darlin', but you got ripped off."

"I don't care." She took the bag and coins back. "I like them."

He raised an eyebrow then shrugged. "You done here? I'm ready to go if you are."

"Sure. Did you find anything interesting?"

He flashed a satisfied grin. "Got a nice little piece I've been looking for." He patted his trouser pocket. "I collect guns."

Memories swept over her. Digging that bullet out of Seth's arm. Hearing the backfires of the old Chevy that Seth said was gunfire. Seeing Seth run into her room, gun drawn with murder in his eyes. She wrinkled her nose. "I'm not a fan of them." Her stomach growled.

Barton chuckled and took her hand. "Sounds like you're hungry. I know a little place down the street."

They talked and laughed over barbecued ribs and iced teas. He told her his last name was Crone, he was thirty, he had a business degree, and a house on the west side of Fort Worth. He'd been married briefly in his early twenties, no kids. His parents and younger sister, a teacher, lived in east Fort Worth. Megan shared some of her history, finding him easy to talk to.

Back at the B&B, standing outside the front door, Barton asked, "You gonna ask me up?"

"I have to go to work." She made a face.

"Not for over an hour." He stepped closer to her. "I'll get you to work in plenty of time. I promise."

Megan never let anyone in her room anymore. Seth could show up at any time and after that fiasco with Lori, she'd rather not go through that again. Megan had even arranged with Mrs. Powell that Megan would change her own bedding and linens for the reduced cost of the room. That way no one had a reason to go in it.

When she remained silent, Barton stepped even closer and placed his hands on her shoulders. "Megan—"

"I'd better not." She shook her head. "I'm sorry. I've got to get ready for work."

He smiled an easy smile. "Maybe next time." He squeezed her shoulders, said goodbye, got in his Corvette then sped away.

Late that night, when work was over, and she was in bed, she held the small bag of old coins. They made her feel closer to Seth since he couldn't seem to make it back to her in person.

***

Three days later Megan got a call on the house phone at the B&B. When she answered, Barton greeted her then said, "I'm fixin' to deliver some paperwork to a builder out in the country. Want to ride along?"

The article she was writing could wait a little longer. "Sure."

Thirty minutes later, he opened the passenger side door of his Corvette. He bowed low and waved his hand. "Your carriage awaits, Madame."

Megan laughed. "You're quite the character."

Barton gave her ponytail a playful tug as she tossed her purse on the floorboard where it landed with a thud. She got in the car with a little less anxiety than the last time. Once he was behind the wheel, off they sped.

In no time, she learned how much he loved his Corvette. He talked about its great features all the way to the interstate. As he merged onto the freeway, he said, "Here I am talking your ear off and you can't get a word in with a wedge."

"That's okay. I know plenty of guys who are car crazy." She crossed one leg over the other and rested her arm on the armrest. "I don't have a car."

His head snapped around and he stared at her open-mouthed.

Vehicles crowded the highway, everyone driving ninety to nothing. An 18-wheeler barreled by on the left. A pickup cut right in front of them.

Megan gripped the armrest. Her heart leapt into her throat. Her foot slammed an invisible brake pedal. "Watch out!"

Barton's attention shot back to the road and he swerved, just missing the back end of the pickup. A car behind them laid on the horn. Megan gulped in air, unaware she'd been holding her breath. She eased her death-grip on the armrest.

"Sorry about that. But you threw me for a loop." Barton glanced at her as they sped south on I-35W out of Fort Worth. "I don't think I know anyone—any adult—who doesn't have a car." He pulled a cigarette from a pack in his denim shirt pocket and lit it. After exhaling, he asked, "Do you *know* how to drive?"

Megan forced herself to relax. She replied in a voice that sounded almost like her own, "Of course."

"Then why no car?"

She gave the memorized answer she'd been using for a couple of years. "After living in Chicago a few months and dealing with traffic and parking and all that, having a car just became too much of a hassle. So, I sold it. Don't miss it a bit. Just think—no car insurance, no monthly payments, no yearly plates." She waved a hand at a gas station on the access road. "No buying gas."

"A dollar twenty-five a gallon! Can you believe it?" Barton shook his head then took another drag on his cigarette. One hand on the steering wheel, he changed lanes. "Can you drive a stick?"

"I did once. An old pickup. The thing was on the column."

"So, you're saying you don't really know how to drive one."

"Well, it's been a while. But I think I could handle it." *I hope it never comes to that.* "Just follow the diagram on the knob. You could teach me." The idea of her behind the wheel of his precious baby must have rattled him because he sent her a wide-eyed look of something akin to horror. She chuckled and reached over to pat his shoulder. "Forget I mentioned it. I don't need to know how to drive your car anyway unless you have a heart attack or something." Her gaze swept over his hale and healthy form. "I seriously doubt that'll happen."

He looked at her and made a face, wrinkling his nose and wiggling his eyebrows. He lowered his voice and said, "I guess that means while you're in my car you're at my mercy."

She laughed at his goofy expression and sinister-sounding tone, but a sudden chill slid down her spine. Unbidden, something an old neighbor lady used to say popped into Megan's head: *I felt like someone just walked over my grave.*

"How do you get around without a car?" Barton stubbed out his cigarette in the ashtray then brushed ashes off his shirt.

She shrugged off the weird feeling. "Bus, taxi, friends, the L—that's the Elevated Train to you non-Chicagoans. If I really need a car, I'll rent one. Since I've been here, I've been taking the bus and walking a lot. Sometimes one of the girls from work gives me a ride."

Barton's gaze scanned the length of her from her sandaled feet to her crossed bare legs to her blue jean shorts then up over her yellow tank top. His eyes met hers. "All that walking is paying off."

She smiled in response to his admiring gaze. They chatted while the scenery sped past and they left the city behind. Megan rolled down the window, enjoying the wind on her face, the sun warm on her skin, the fresh country air. Puffy white clouds dotted the sky. A flock of black birds took flight from a field in perfect synchronization, rising, twisting, and turning as one. The sight made her smile. She watched until they flew out of view. A hawk perched on top of a telephone pole. In the distance, several kids played with a dog in a fenced yard around a farmhouse. Cows grazed in the greening fields.

I've missed this. Fresh air and sunshine. The room at the B&B suddenly seemed like a prison. One she had been stuck in, by choice, far too long. She was tired of sitting around, waiting for a man who may or may not show up ever again. *What's Seth doing right now? Will he ever walk into my room again? Is he even still alive in his time? How long should I wait?*

Why *should I wait?*

"Too bad the bluebonnets are already gone." Barton interrupted her thoughts. He had one hand on the top of the steering wheel, the other on the gearshift. The radio played softly. "A couple weeks ago they stretched as far as the eye can see along here. A beautiful blue blanket."

"I'm sorry I missed it." Familiar resentment stirred inside her. *What else have I missed while I wait night after night for Seth?* She lifted her face to the wind rushing in the car window and tossing her ponytail. Perhaps the wind cleared cobwebs from her mind because for the first time in weeks she thought, *Maybe I should go home.*

Barton turned off the freeway and drove west for several miles on a narrow winding road lined with greening trees interspersed with splashes of pink and white blossoms of flowering trees. Patches of daffodils and wildflowers dotted the green grass. They passed a mixture of houses—brick, wood frame, mobile homes, old farmhouses in the middle of a pasture. He made several turns, swerved to miss a dog sleeping in a sunny patch on the road, then passed beneath a canopy of trees. A few miles later, he pulled onto a rutted dirt driveway leading up to a rust-spotted, doublewide trailer with the skirting missing and a broken window held together with a big X made of duct tape. Rusting cars and pieces of cars cluttered the yard that was mostly brown dirt spotted with patches of weeds and dandelions. A mesquite tree stood beside the driveway and purple clusters of wisteria draped the falling down fence along the road.

Staring at the dilapidated trailer and junk-filled yard, Megan said incredulously, "This guy is a builder?"

"It's his son's place." Barton turned off his Corvette and reached behind his seat for a briefcase. "I'm just dropping the paperwork off here. I'll be back in a minute." He got out of the car, closed the door, and headed for the trailer. Megan noticed how his jeans fit his nice butt. His hair shone blue-black in the sunshine. He mounted the steps and knocked. A skinny, longhaired man wearing ragged jeans and nothing else opened the door. Barton went inside, closing the door behind him.

A slight breeze scented with wisteria blew through the open windows of the car. Megan took a deep breath ... then wrinkled her nose. *Ew! What's that other smell?* Something sickening sweet overpowered the fragrant wisteria. She looked around the yard, but she didn't see anything else blooming that could account for that strange smell. It stuck in the back of her throat. Not at all pleasant.

The trailer door opened, Barton appeared and hurried down the steps. Whistling, he crossed the yard, opened the car door, and got in.

"You forgot your briefcase," Megan said as the Corvette roared to life.

"The guy has to sign the papers in it. I'll get it back when he's done."

As he drove down the road, Megan asked, "What was that awful smell?"

"What smell?"

She looked at him. "You didn't smell it?"

"What?" He glanced at her then back at the road.

"The smell outside that trailer. First, I smelled the wisteria but then that other odor hit me and *whew!* Nasty." Barton shrugged so she let it go. But she knew if she ever smelled that smell again she'd recognize it.

Barton drove back a different way through the country. "I'll show you the sights," he said with a smile. Miles later they headed into a city. "Welcome to the big city of Cleburne." Barton turned right onto a busy street and stopped at a stoplight on the courthouse square.

Megan admired the beautiful old courthouse then noticed the street sign on the corner. Main and E. Chambers Streets.

Seth's words suddenly came back to her. *I came to a town called Cleburne ... The bank was a brick building at the corner of Main an' Wardville.*

She glanced around, wondering which way Wardville Street was.

Barton looked at her. "What's wrong?"

"Can we stop at a bank? I have some quarters I want to exchange."

"Sure thing. There's one right here." He turned right, pulled into a parking lot, and went inside with her. "I need to check out the facilities."

While he was in the restroom, Megan went to the teller window and exchanged the rolls of quarters. She stuffed the bills into her purse and asked the teller, "Do you happen to know where Wardville Street is?"

The older woman flashed a friendly smile. "Sure do. It's two blocks north."

"Is there a bank on the corner there?"

The woman shook her head. "Used to be, a long time ago. That's where the city's first bank was way back when."

Megan's heart beat a little faster.

"But it's been gone for years now," the teller continued. "There's a picture over there on the wall of one of the early banks." She pointed to her left. "Also, some other old documents from those days, if you're interested."

"Thank you." Megan approached the half dozen framed documents and pictures hanging on the wall. The first one on the left, the biggest one, was picture of an old building.

"Hello," a woman said behind Megan.

Megan turned and saw a smiling silver-haired woman wearing a gray jacket over a white blouse, a dark blue skirt, and sensible shoes.

"I'm Mrs. Cuffee. I hear you're interested in our banks?"

Megan smiled. "I'm curious about the first ones in town."

"You're looking at one of the earliest." The woman pointed to the black-and-white photo of a corner two-story building. It had an arched doorway made of stone with a round corner room directly above it, a sign with BANK in big bold letters, and two horse-drawn buggies waiting at the curb. "That's the Farmers and Merchants National Bank. It opened in 1890. Over here," she moved to the next frame, "is a ledger from the Bank of Cleburne, which opened in 1877. It's in surprisingly good condition, wouldn't you say?"

Megan followed along as the older woman explained the next three documents. Clouds dimmed the sunshine outside.

"*This* one," Mrs. Cuffee stopped in front of the last frame near the front windows, "is my favorite."

Megan stood rooted to the floor. There it was.

Her writing.

Her signature.

Her letter.

Mrs. Cuffee told the story of a letter written by a bank robber's widow who returned the stolen money. A story Megan knew all too well and barely heard.

She sucked in a breath. *Holy moly, it's true. It's all true.*

She expected shock and surprise to overwhelm her, leave her feeling faint and weak-kneed. She expected a shaft of sunlight to part the clouds outside and stream through the plate glass windows to fall upon the letter, bathing it in glorious light while music swelled majestically, and cooing doves flew heavenward.

It was that kind of a moment.

Or a *Twilight Zone* moment.

None of that happened, though. No shaft of light. No swelling music. No cooing doves. Not even *The Twilight Zone* theme music.

Megan didn't feel any of the emotions she had expected either.

Instead, as she slowly let out her breath, she felt a great burden she didn't even realize she had been bearing lift from her shoulders. Because that letter, more than the sight of Seth stepping through a brick wall, more than his bloody handprint, more than even his hard, hungry kiss and gripping fingers that had left faint bruises on her shoulders, that letter proved beyond the shadow of a doubt that all that had happened had truly happened. Irrefutable, undeniable, historical proof stared back at her.

An unexpected wave of sweet relief mixed with joy swept over Megan when she realized, *I'm not crazy. I'm not crazy. Oh, thank God! I'm not crazy!*

Ever since Seth's first appearance, there had lived, deep down, in the darkest place of her soul, the tiny, terrible, unspeakable, unthinkable fear that she was, in fact, crazy. That she'd somehow conjured up the whole thing in her mind. Even Lori's meeting with Seth. All of it the product of a sick, crazed mind. Maybe a flashback from that one time she'd taken acid back in college. Maybe the workings of an overactive imagination. Or a psychotic nut.

I'm not crazy, she thought again. *It all really happened.*

As Megan stood there, she felt something inexplicable fall upon her like a blessing, and a distinct feeling of peace settled deep inside her where that fear of insanity had so recently dwelt. She smiled.

She stepped closer and touched a finger to the glass protecting her letter. Written mere weeks ago, the passage of a hundred years had yellowed the paper and faded the ink, although it was darker than the ink she'd seen on the other framed documents. The creases made when Seth had folded it were a darker yellow than the rest of the paper, the ink in those creases fainter than ink elsewhere in the letter.

Mrs. Cuffee stood beside Megan. "Do you notice anything odd about the paper?"

Megan lowered her hand, feeling a little guilty for touching it, as if it was a museum piece, and shook her head.

Mrs. Cuffee moved closer. "It looks old, because of the color. But if you look closely, you can see that it looks remarkably like our modern-day paper."

"In what way?" Megan's voice was surprisingly steady.

The older woman said, "The spacing between the lines doesn't match the typical lined paper of that era. However, it matches today's college-ruled notebook paper. Then there's the ink. You probably noticed it's darker than the ink on the other documents. It's not the same kind that was used back then." Mrs. Cuffee reached out to adjust the frame, moving one side up a little then back down, then up just a hair. She took a step back, tilted her head. "It's not only a fascinating story but a fascinating document, too. I hope someday we can afford to have it properly studied."

Megan bit back a grin. *Won't that blow someone's mind!*

"Sorry I took so long." Barton walked up beside her. "I had to use the pay phone." He backed up and ran his gaze down the wall, scanning the documents. "What's this? Some interesting stuff?" He leaned closer to Megan's letter. "Whoa!" His head jerked around, and he stared at Megan, pointing a finger. "That's you!" He barked a laugh, turned back, and leaned in for another look.

Mrs. Cuffee asked Megan, "What does he mean, *That's you?*"

Megan saw no way around it. "My name is Megan McClure."

Mrs. Cuffee's eyes widened and she clapped a hand to her chest. "You're kidding. Is the writer of the letter one of your ancestors?"

"I doubt it. My family never made it as far as Texas."

"Extraordinary." Mrs. Cuffee grinned. "Wait here, please." She hurried across the floor, passed the teller window, and turned down a hallway.

"Boy, this sure is weird, huh, Megan?" Barton looked from the letter to her.

She smiled and nodded.

Mrs. Cuffee returned, carrying a Polaroid camera. "Do you mind if I get a picture of you standing beside it?"

"Oh, I don't know—"

"Come on, Megan." Barton put an arm around her shoulders and pulled her against him as they stood beside her framed letter. He said to Mrs. Cuffee, "Would you mind taking one of us for me, too, ma'am?"

She took two pictures of Megan and Barton. "What a handsome couple y'all make. Both with that black hair." Then she took two shots of just Megan beside the letter. As the camera spit out each picture, Mrs. Cuffee carefully placed the wet prints on a nearby counter to dry.

Barton slid his arm around Megan again. "What's the story behind the letter?"

Mrs. Cuffee told the story once again. This time, Megan listened. It went exactly the way Seth had said it did. The teller called for Mrs. Cuffee, who excused herself and went behind the counter.

Barton gave Megan a squeeze then released her to go look at the other documents.

Megan frowned when she realized one vital piece of information was missing from the older woman's story.

Mrs. Cuffee hurried back and checked the prints to make sure they had dried then handed Megan and Barton each a copy of the one of the two of them and gave Megan one of just her alone. "It has been a pleasure meeting y'all. Come back any time." She smiled and turned away.

"I have a question," Megan said, making the older woman turn back. "What was the name of the man who returned the money and delivered the letter?"

"Did I forget that part? According to the bank manager, the young man only gave his first name. Seth."

***

The radio played softly as the Corvette sped east then north to Fort Worth. The picture of the two of them stared back at Megan from the dashboard where Barton had placed it.

Barton glanced at Megan. "You're awful quiet."

"It's been a strange day."

"Seeing your name on that wall was pretty freaky, huh? At least it wasn't on a wanted poster." Barton shot her a grin.

Megan studied his profile. One chance meeting with him had led her to today's revelation. Gratitude welled up inside her. She placed her hand on his on the gearshift. He glanced at her. "Thank you for today, Barton. It's been ... wonderful."

He eyed her with confusion. Then he smiled and turned over his hand to hold hers. "I'm glad you're havin' a good time, darlin'. I reckon a city gal like you without a car doesn't take a lot of afternoon drives through the countryside."

"It's been a long time." She uncrossed her legs and turned more toward him. "I'm not really much of a city girl either. I grew up in a small farming town in Illinois. When my friends and I started driving, we used to tear up those dirt roads and do donuts in the cornfields. There are times I miss not having a car."

Their hands remained linked until traffic thickened and Barton needed two hands. "You want to eat before you go to work?"

Megan glanced at her watch. "I better not." She yawned, covering her mouth. "Sorry. I think I need a nap."

"Those late nights are catching up with you."

"Yeah. Plus, I've been working some extra shifts for another girl and, holy moly, that's getting old."

He laughed. "You and your holy moly. Where'd you come up with that?"

"Blame my mom. When I came home for Christmas break the first year in college, I said holy shit a lot, and worse. A lot worse. Mom sat me down one day and said she'd heard enough and she didn't want to hear anymore, and I'd better find another way to express myself. She suggested holy moly. I've been holy molying ever since."

"I think it's adorable."

They chatted until he pulled up in front of the B&B and turned off the car. He turned toward Megan, resting his wrist on the steering wheel. "Thanks for going with me. Made the drive a lot more fun." He reached over with his other hand to brush wisps of windblown hair off her forehead then rested his hand on the back of her seat. "You want to get together again? Lunch or something? Unless," he frowned, "you're going back to Yankeeland soon."

The minute Megan had seen her framed letter she'd known she wasn't going anywhere anytime soon. "I'll be here awhile longer. And yes," she smiled, "I'd like to see you again."

His blue eyes lit up and he grinned. He got out of the car then helped her out. "I'll call you soon." He put his hands on her shoulders, lowered his head, and kissed her. Lightly. Tenderly.

Seconds later, his Corvette roared down the street. She stared after him, frowning. For all his good looks and charm, his kiss left her ... disappointed.

Late that night when she finally crawled into bed, exhausted, she thought of her letter and Seth and the reality of it all. Her last thought before falling asleep was one small but gigantic word—*Why?*

Chapter 7

The next day Megan left early for work so she could stop at the main library, a big rectangular building in downtown Fort Worth. Inside, she followed the signs to the archive section on the lower level. With help from the librarian, Megan found the microfiche of the Federal Census of 1870 of Tarrant County, Texas. When the librarian left Megan alone with the reader, she scrolled down the list of scribbled, at times almost illegible, names. Her heart skipped a beat when she read *Mary O'Connor, seamstress, aged 42. Charlotte O'Connor aged 13. Seth O'Connor aged 10. Catherine O'Connor aged 7. Mary Ellen O'Connor aged 6.*

Megan pictured Seth as a sandy-haired boy of ten, running wild around the frontier town with his buddy Tim, trailed by two little sisters pestering him to play with them. The image made her smile.

Next, she scrolled through the Census of 1880 and found *Charlotte O'Connor aged 23* followed by *Seth O'Connor, ranch hand, aged 20.* Tears stung her eyes when she saw in black and white his once-large family dwindled to just one sister and him. How awful it must have been for him to lose his parents and four siblings—two older brothers to the war, two little sisters to a fever—before he even hit his teens. So much grief for one so young.

When she couldn't find the next census, she went to the woman seated behind the desk. "Excuse me. I can't find the census of 1890. Can you help me?"

The woman looked up over the top of her glasses. "That census was damaged in a fire at the Commerce Department in Washington, D. C. in early 1921. Only fragments remain, none of them from Tarrant County. We do have the tax records, if that will help."

Megan glanced at her watch. "I've got to get to work. I'll come back. Thanks."

She left the library in a hurry, running late for work, but glad that she had gotten up the nerve to look for Seth's name in the historical records. To know he had actually lived. Gladder still that she hadn't yet discovered when and how he would die.

***

"Have lunch with me," Barton said over the phone to her at the B&B the next afternoon.

"Aren't you at work?"

"I'm in between clients and hungry for a steak. How about you? Pick you up in about twenty minutes?"

Megan toyed with the phone cord. It had been awhile since she'd had a steak. A free one, at that. "Okay. I'll be waiting outside."

She hung up and dashed up the stairs to her room where she flung open the armoire. Inside hung three dresses, two skirts, a pair of jeans, and five tops, all bought during a recent shopping spree. She usually traveled light and hadn't planned on being in Fort Worth this long. Megan shoved aside several hangers, drew out a sleeveless lavender dress, and held it up against her. It was pretty and springy, like the sunny day outside. She stripped off her clothes, slid the dress over her head and pulled it down, smoothing it over her hips. The hem swished just above her knees as she walked to the vanity, picked up the hairbrush and swept it through her hair. The picture of her next to the letter in the bank and the one of her and Barton were propped against the corner of the mirror. Keeping an eye on the time, she applied mascara and a dab of lipstick then slipped on a pair of white sandals. She grabbed her purse and left the room.

The Corvette pulled up right on time. Barton jumped out and opened the passenger side door for her. He looked like a typical businessman in a grey suit, white shirt, and a charcoal tie. They chatted until he pulled up to the front door of Steak 'N Ale. He put the car in neutral, set the brake, then got out, came around to her side, and opened her door. "Why don't you wait for me here while I go park?"

"Okay." She took his outstretched hand and got out.

He closed her door, then snapped his fingers. "I almost forgot." He went around to his side, climbed in, sat down, reached behind the seat, and pulled out a briefcase. He leaned over the passenger seat and looked up at her through the open window. "Could you hang on to this?" He passed the briefcase to her through the window. "My partner forgot it and I told him I'd meet him outside here to give it to him." Barton glanced at his watch. "He should be here any minute. If he comes before I get back, just give it to him, okay?"

"What does he look like?"

"Older guy. Short and thin with glasses. Graying brown hair. Walks with a limp. His name's Jim."

"If he comes and you're not here yet, how will he know me?"

"I told him I'd be waiting on that bench over there with a pretty gal with long black hair. Besides, he'll recognize his briefcase."

One side had a big faded yellow smiley face on it.

"His son put that decal there when he was just a kid. I'll hurry." Barton settled back in his seat and the Corvette roared off.

Carrying the briefcase, Megan walked over and sat on the bench he had indicated beneath a big oak tree. Birds twittered above her. She put the briefcase on her lap so the smiley face showed and watched people entering and leaving the restaurant. Traffic rushed by. A slight breeze stirred her hair. She crossed her legs and swung her sandaled foot. Minutes later a short, thin man with graying brown hair and glasses limped up the sidewalk. He paused, looked her way, then headed to her.

"You Barton's friend, miss?"

"Yes. I'm Megan. You must be Jim. I believe this is yours." She held up the briefcase.

"Thanks." He took it from her. "Barton ain't around?"

"He's parking the car."

"Well, tell him thanks for me, miss. It was nice meeting you." He limped back down the sidewalk, carrying his briefcase.

Not long after, Barton walked down the sidewalk on the other side of the street. He crossed at the light then walked up to her. "I see Jim showed up."

Megan uncrossed her legs and stood. "Yup."

He dropped a kiss on her forehead. "Thanks, darlin'. Let's go eat."

Inside, the hostess led them to a secluded table in a corner and handed them menus. After placing their orders, Barton's gaze rested warmly on Megan. "You look real pretty in that dress. It brings out the color of your eyes." He tilted his head. "I just realized something. You look like Liz Taylor with your black hair and purple eyes."

"Violet," she corrected. She barely heard the sweet nothings spill from Barton's lips because his comment reminded her of the Liz Taylor test she had given Seth. Over three weeks since she'd seen him. *How much time has passed in his time? Is he coming back?*

***

"What's wrong with Julia?" Megan asked Bonnie the next evening while waiting for her drink order. "I'm getting tired of filling in for her on my nights off." Megan flicked a piece of lint off the front of her yellow blouse. It had a V-neck that showed a bit of cleavage.

Bonnie finished putting a perfect head on a draft and placed the mug on Megan's tray, then turned to the counter behind her and grabbed a bottle of tequila in one hand and a bottle of triple sec in the other. She poured a generous amount of both into a shaker filled with ice cubes. "Julia better watch her ps an' qs or she'll be lookin' for another job."

"What's her problem?"

Bonnie righted the bottles, put them back on the counter and put the lid on the shaker. She wiped her hands on her jeans then swiped the back of one hand across her forehead, shoving her blonde bangs to one side. She wore a short sleeve white blouse, unbuttoned down to just above her bra. "Crank." Bonnie picked up the shaker and shook it. Ice rattled.

"What?"

"Crank. Speed. Methamphetamine. Bad shit. You never heard of it?"

Megan shook her head. "I wasn't ever into drugs very much. Smoked pot in college. Tried coke a couple of times. Acid once." She shrugged. "Not my scene. You tried crank?"

"Couple times. Kept me awake but I didn't like how it made me feel. All jittery and nervous. And major dry mouth—Whew!" Bonnie gave the shaker an extra hard shake before putting it on the counter. "I snorted it, but I heard tell that shootin' it up gives a gal an orgasm." She picked up a glass, ran a wedge of lime around the rim then dipped it in salt.

"You're kidding."

Bonnie shook her head. "That's what I heard." She emptied the contents of the shaker into the glass, stuck a lime wedge on the rim and put the margarita on Megan's tray. "Check out Julia's arms next chance you get. Tracks all up an' down 'em. She's an addict, and fixin' to lose her job."

Megan picked up her tray then paused to watch Bonnie behind the bar. It was like watching a dance. Step back to reach for a bottle, step forward to pour, step back to replace the bottle, step forward to draw a beer. Ring up the sale, wipe down the bar, wash the glasses. She was constantly moving and made it look effortless. She had bartended elsewhere for five years before starting at The Tejas and was a favorite among the locals. By the end of most nights, her tip jar overflowed with bills.

Megan delivered the drinks, took more orders, then returned to the bar. Couples danced around the floor to Willie Nelson's *On the Road Again* playing on the jukebox. The live show didn't start until nine.

A group of cowboys had Bonnie laughing at the other end of the bar as she drew beers for them. Finished with the cowboys, she headed back to Megan. "I got an idea for somethin' you can write about."

"Lay it on me."

"Crank."

"Hmmm."

"I know it's not as exciting as staying overnight in a haunted hotel or looking for Bigfoot but—"

"I never looked for Bigfoot."

"—it's timely. You could probably get a lot of information from my cousin Bubba. He could at least tell you who to talk to."

Cousin Bubba was a Fort Worth police officer who had The Tejas on his beat. He often stopped in during the night, keeping an eye on things. Megan had never met anyone named Bubba before. Since coming to Texas, she had met three. Bubba's real name was Ronald. "But he won't answer to it," Bonnie had said.

"That's not a bad idea. Maybe I can interview Julia, too. Get the addict's side of the story." Megan's mind whirled with the beginnings of an article.

"Yeah. I like that. Maybe you could—Oh my God." Bonnie looked past Megan. "There's that hunk again."

Megan turned and saw Barton zigzagging around the tables through the crowd. He wore dark blue jeans, a denim shirt, and a smile when he saw her. Megan turned back to Bonnie. "We've been out a couple of times."

Bonnie's eyes widened. "You have? Lucky girl! I wanna hear all about it on the way home. After we talk about your crank article." She picked up a mug and drew a beer, smiling at Barton when he walked up.

"Howdy, darlin'." His gaze swept over Megan before he looked at Bonnie. "You must be Bonnie. Megan's told me about you. I'm Barton."

"Nice to meet cha."

On the jukebox, Anne Murray started singing *Could I Have This Dance*.

"Mind if I take Megan for a spin around the dance floor?" Barton said to Bonnie. "They're playin' our song." He took Megan's hand.

"Sure," Bonnie said, surprised. Then she leaned over the bar and whispered to Megan, "Y'all have a *song* already?"

Megan shrugged and followed Barton onto the floor where he took her in his arms and waltzed her around. He guided her expertly through the other couples, whirling her around, smiling down at her. She only stepped on his toes twice. When the song ended, he pulled her close and kissed her.

His tongue danced with hers as expertly as the rest of him had danced to the music. A hint of woodsy cologne clung to him. His strong arms circled her. His kiss deepened.

Megan felt nothing. *Nothing!*

When they drew apart, he cupped her cheek. "I wanted to do that after our first dance."

"I wouldn't have let you. You were with that blonde."

His thumb traced gentle circles on her skin. "A gal with scruples. I like that. How about I give you a ride home after work?"

"Thanks, but Bonnie's giving me a ride. She has a great idea for an article and I want to pick her brain a little."

"I reckon I'd better not interfere with a gal trying to make a livin'. But I hope you'll save your next night off for me."

"It's a date."

Hand in hand, they walked back to the bar. Barton released her hand, gave her a quick kiss, nodded to Bonnie, then disappeared into the crowd.

After closing time, Megan and Bonnie walked across the dark parking lot to Bonnie's beat up green pick-up. The rattle of cicadas punctuated the warm night air. Megan pulled open the passenger side door. The hinges screeched. She climbed in and sat on the seat striped with duct tape over torn vinyl. The door clunked when she slammed it shut. The interior stunk from the overflowing ashtray.

Bonnie got behind the steering wheel and turned the key. The engine coughed twice then sputtered to life. She patted the dashboard. It had a long horizontal crack across the front. She drove across the parking lot then pulled out onto the street. They rolled down their windows. "God's air conditioner," Bonnie had said more than once while sweat dripped down her face as she drove.

"It'll be a week or so before you can talk to Bubba. He's out of town," Bonnie said.

"Boy, you work fast." Megan gripped the torn and tattered armrest as the pick-up sped around a corner.

"I called my mom, she called my aunt, an' my aunt said Bubba's gone fishin' at the coast. I got his number for you."

"Thank you." They stopped at a red light. Megan asked, "How's school going?"

"I'm lovin' it but it sure is hard. Between this job and my other job, it's hell findin' time to study. Much less spend time with Penny." For the last year, Bonnie had been taking classes at the local junior college and hoped to be a physical therapist one day. She also cleaned houses a couple days a week. The light turned green and the truck shot forward. "You serious about talkin' to Julia?"

"I'd like to get her viewpoint."

"Well, I don't reckon you'll have much of an intelligent conversation with her, but I can take you over to her place tomorrow when I get done cleanin', if you want." Bonnie lit a cigarette.

"You're a sweetheart."

She really was.

"White trash," Megan's mother would have said. Her mother had been a snob. Megan took after her dad, who had been more tolerant and forgiving and believed that everybody deserved respect until proven otherwise.

Born on the wrong side of the tracks, and still living there, Bonnie Hudson was twenty-nine, a single mother with a toddler named Penny, living with her mom and two younger brothers. She had two older sisters, and numerous aunts, uncles, and cousins who all lived near each other. The kind of big family that Megan would have given her right arm for. Bonnie was down-to-earth, fun-loving, generous, and ambitious.

"Now, I wanna hear all about you and the hunk."

Megan shrugged. The rushing wind blew back her hair and swept away the cigarette smoke. "Not a whole lot to tell. We went to a gun and coin show, had lunch afterwards. Then I went for a ride with him through the countryside when he had to deliver some paperwork. We had lunch the other day. No big deal."

"No big deal?" Bonnie laughed. "It is to him."

"Oh, I don't think so. It's nothing serious."

Bonnie snorted. "Your *nothin' serious* sure staked his claim on you out there on the dance floor tonight."

"Don't be ridiculous."

"I'm tellin' you, with that kiss he was lettin' every Tom, Dick, and Bubba in there know you're off-limits."

Megan stared out the window then muttered, "Holy moly."

"What?" Bonnie stubbed out her cigarette in the ashtray. "Don't you like him?"

"He's all right." Megan shrugged. "But I don't want anything serious. I don't even live here."

Bonnie came to a four-way stop. "I've been wonderin' 'bout that." She glanced at Megan. "Why are you still here?" Bonnie looked both ways then turned left. "Why are you workin' your tail off for peanuts when you could be somewhere excitin' writin' about excitin' stuff an' makin' a helluva lot more than tips?"

Megan stared at Bonnie's profile, lit by the lights of an oncoming car. She hesitated, not knowing what to say, knowing full well what she *wanted* to say. In that instant, Megan understood why Seth had told his friend Tim about her and her time and could appreciate the relief Seth must have felt afterward, because with every atom in her body Megan longed to tell someone about him. Bonnie seemed open-minded and level-headed, but Megan didn't really know her that well, and she would probably think Megan was crazy.

"I thought I'd stay awhile to check out the area," Megan replied. The answer sounded lame even to her ears.

"You do that often?"

"Sometimes. Two years ago, I spent several weeks in Reno, Nevada. After that, I spent part of the winter in the Florida Keys. It's one of the perks of working for myself."

Bonnie pulled up in front of the B&B and stopped. "Sounds kinda lonely to me."

Megan frowned. Barton had said the same thing the first night they met.

"No offense," Bonnie quickly added.

"None taken." Megan slung her purse strap over her shoulder and pulled on the door handle. The hinges screeched as she opened the door.

"So, you wanna visit Julia tomorrow?"

"Sure. If you don't mind."

"I'll pick you up about noon. 'Night, Megan."

Up in her room, Megan changed into her nightclothes then climbed into bed. She picked up her notebook from the nightstand and looked over her notes on her latest article. Ghosts in the historic Swift Armor Meat Packing Plant in the Fort Worth Stockyards. Some of the locals she'd met at work had told her about various weird happenings associated with the old building. She wasn't fond of writing about ghosts, but it was a huge market, and she knew a couple of editors who always needed articles. She wrote, crossed out words, then wrote some more. She chewed on the end of the pen, thinking, then wrote some more.

Bang!

Her head snapped up at the sound of the old Chevy's backfire.

Bang!

Is it the Chevy?

Bang!

She jumped out of bed and ran to look out the window. No Chevy. She went to press her ear against Seth's door, and listened.

She heard, or thought she heard, two more bangs, very faint, very far away

She tried the knob. It didn't budge. She knocked on the door. "Seth." She knocked harder. "Seth!" she said as loud as she dared, then pressed her ear against the door again, and listened, but heard nothing more.

She stepped back, hands on her hips, and glared at the door. Then she went back to bed, crawled beneath the covers, and turned off the nightstand light. She lay awake, wondering what was happening to Seth on the other side of that door.

***

Bonnie's truck pulled up in front of the B&B promptly at noon and Megan climbed in. The sun shone brightly in a cloudless sky. They chatted for several miles until Bonnie stopped in front of a small, one-story house with peeling yellow paint. A row of red roses in full bloom lined the driveway. On the porch, a weathered wooden swing swayed gently in the breeze that ruffled the leaves of a philodendron in a big green pot near the door. One corner of the porch roof sagged. Bonnie and Megan got out of the truck and walked up the sidewalk of cracked and heaving concrete then up the porch steps. Morning glories twined around the handrail.

Bonnie knocked on the screen door, saying to Megan, "Don't get your hopes up for a big, detailed interview like you're probably used to. You'll be lucky if Julia's even coherent."

The door opened. Rock and roll music blared as a short, thin girl peered at them through the screen.

"Hey, Julia, how're you doin'?" Bonnie asked. "We were nearby and thought we'd stop by and say hi."

Smiling, Julia pushed the door open. "Hiy'all. Whatasurprise! Comeonin. Awfulhot outain'tit?"

All Megan heard was a garbled mess of slurred together words spoken very quickly. "Pardon me?" She looked at Bonnie. "What did she say?"

"Come on in." Bonnie walked inside.

Megan followed, and looked around in surprise. It was one of the cleanest, neatest homes she'd ever seen. The floral couch and matching chair were shabby but clean. Not a speck of dust touched the gleaming wood surface of the end tables or the low oval table in front of the couch. The oval table held a vase of roses, a cigarette lighter shaped like the head of a panther, a spotless ceramic ashtray, all sitting on lace doilies, and a neat stack of magazines, with *Better Homes and Gardens* on top. The noonday sun streamed through the front windows framed by crisp white curtains decorated with colorful wildflowers. An entertainment center covered one wall. Its compartments housed a TV, VCR, turntable, stacks of albums and cassettes, and the stereo playing loudly. The kitchen was straight ahead, and a hallway on the left led to other rooms. The smells of Pine Sol and furniture polish lingered in the air.

"Y'allsit yourselvesdown. Si'down." Julia gestured to the couch as she hurried over to turn down the music. She was the one messy thing in the room. Her dull brown hair hung in tangles to her shoulders, her eyes were dilated, and sweat beaded her forehead and flushed thin face, and ran down her neck. She wore holey blue jean shorts with ragged hems, and a t-shirt. She was in her early twenties but looked much younger. She grabbed a long-sleeved faded denim shirt off the back of a chair and pulled it on, even though the temperature was in the mid-eighties.

Megan and Bonnie sat on the couch. Bonnie looked around. "Seems funny, not seeing your grandma here." She said to Megan, "I used to date Julia's brother back in high school. Julia was just a kid then. Their grandma left her the house when she died last year."

"Isuremissher." Julia sat on the matching chair. "Shewasthebest grannyever. I wishshe couldalived forever,you know?" Julia bobbed her head to Reo Speedwagon playing on the radio. She tapped her foot and drummed her fingers on the armrest. She constantly licked her lips and worked her mouth like a toothless old man chewing something.

"What cha been doin?" Bonnie asked.

"I'mfixin'to rearrangethe furniture. Thought I'dmovethe chair over there and the couch overhere an'seehow Ilikeit. Whatdoyou think?" She jumped out of the chair. "Y'allwantsome icetea? Ijust madesome." She hurried into the kitchen.

Megan turned to Bonnie. "She talks so fast I can't understand a thing she's saying. All her words run together. And what's with all the mouth work?" Megan moved her mouth the way Julia did.

"Crankers do that 'cause of dry mouth and 'cause they're jittery as a June bug in a fryin' pan. The fast talkin' is part of it, too. Just like the furniture rearrangin'. I bet she just moved it all around yesterday, and the day before that, and the day before that."

Megan scoffed, "Come on."

"It's true. She's got nothin' else to do all day but clean an' rearrange her stuff. Lotta cranker women do that. Hell, most of 'em can't hold a job. They gotta do somethin' all day while they're all hyped up. So, they clean an' rearrange. You see her arms before she pulled on that shirt?"

Megan nodded. Track marks dotted Julia's arms.

Julia returned, carrying three large plastic glasses of iced tea. She passed them out then sat down in the chair again. She bounced one knee to Aerosmith while she worked her mouth in between sips of tea and looked around the room with a vague look on her face.

Bonnie took a drink, then asked, "How's your brother doin'?"

"He'sinAustin workin'inabar. Somenights he getstoplay hisguitar withtheband an'youknow howmuchhe's enjoyin'that. He'slivin' witha girlwho worksina tattoplace an' hasalittleboy—"

Julia babbled on at the speed of light, tapping her foot, drumming her fingers, bouncing her knees, bobbing her head, and fidgeting on the chair. Bonnie tried to carry on a conversation with her. Megan drank tea, listened, and smiled. She glanced at her watch. They had been there twenty minutes. Felt like hours. She caught Bonnie's eye and jerked her head toward the door.

Bonnie gave a small nod. "We'd better get goin', Julia. But I think Megan has something to ask you." She nudged Megan with her elbow.

Knowing any formal interview questions were out of the question, Megan asked the most obvious one. "Are you going to be able to work tonight, Julia?"

"Ohyeah,I'llbe atwork. Thanks somuch forcovering forme, Megan. I'll makeitup toyou."

Megan stood and handed her glass to Julia. "You have a nice place, Julia. Thanks for the tea."

"See you at work." Bonnie gave Julia a hug then followed Megan out the door.

They were almost to the pick-up when Megan said, "That was awful. How on earth is she going to be able to work tonight? She's in bad shape."

"She'll probably take a downer. You think you can use any of it in your article?"

Megan glanced at the house. "I think someone should be told about this."

Bonnie stopped and grabbed Megan's arm. "You're not gonna call the cops on her, are you?" Bonnie's tone was hard.

"She needs help, Bonnie."

"She sure as shit won't get any in jail."

Megan yanked her arm free. "For someone who claims she only snorted that stuff a couple times, you sure seem to know a lot about it."

Bonnie pressed her lips together and looked away for a moment. "Git in the truck. I'll tell ya about it."

They got in. Megan leaned back against the door and waited.

Bonnie lit a cigarette and took a couple of drags before saying, "Several years back I took off for California. Went to go *find myself*. I started hangin' around with some bikers. They were all doin' crank. Like I said, I snorted it a couple times an' that's it, I swear on a stack of

Bibles." She held up her right hand. "The guys were cookin' it an' dealin' it while their old ladies stayed home an' cleaned an' rearranged the furniture. You think listenin' to Julia was annoyin'? You should be in a roomful of 'em. Everyone babblin' like idiots, talkin' faster than a slick-haired Yankee tryin' to sell you a piece a shit car, no one listenin' to anyone else. Felt like I was livin' inside the Tower of Babel itself. I remember one fella. He'd sit in a corner an' talk about space ships an' aliens all night long. Just talkin' away, not carin' if anyone was listenin' or not. Buncha strange people, *pitiful* people, all messed up on that shit. I left after a few months." She gazed out the windshield, smoking, then looked at Megan. "I was pregnant with Penny an' knew I didn't want to raise my kid around all that. So, I came back here to have her an' been here ever since."

"What happened to Penny's father?"

Bonnie smiled. She draped a wrist over the steering wheel. "He followed me here an' for a spell everythin' was hunky dory. We were a happy little family." Her smile faded. "Then one of his buddies from California showed up. He brought some crank with him. One night, they got all fucked up an' decided to stick a gun in a clerk's face in a store. They both ended up in Huntsville."

"What's in Huntsville?"

A car sped past them on the narrow street. Bonnie turned her head toward it. "Prison."

"I'm sorry, Bonnie."

"I sure loved that no-good son of a bitch. Don't miss him a bit now."

They sat silently for a moment. Bonnie finished her cigarette and stubbed it in the ashtray.

Megan waved away the smoke. "When did crank hit this area?"

"First I heard of it here was about six months ago. I ran into some bikers I know here an' they were doin' it. Since then, I've heard more an' more about it. This is just the beginnin', I'm tellin' you." Bonnie looked Megan in the eye. "You wanna help Julia?"

"Of course."

"The best help she could get is to cut off her supply. You could do that."

"Me?"

"You write that article an' maybe it'll shake people up around here. Make them aware of what's goin' on right beneath their noses. Maybe it'll flush out the cooks an' the head guy. The one financing it an' collectin' all the money while his flunkies get hooked on the shit an' ruin their lives."

Megan stared in amazement at Bonnie, the crusader. "You have a vested interest in this."

"Huh?"

"It's personal for you."

"Yeah." Bonnie nodded. "It's real personal."

"Cut off the supply. Bring down the kingpin. That's a pretty tall order for one measly article."

"I heard a saying somewhere: *The pen is mightier than the sword.*" Bonnie started the truck, checked the rearview mirror, then looked at Megan. "Is it?"

"Well, it has been, and it can be, so I guess, yes."

"You really wanna help Julia and all the other Julias out there? Write somethin' that'll knock people's socks off. I know you can do it." Bonnie pulled out into the street. "I was studyin' at the library the other day an' read some of your stuff."

"You did?"

"Sure did. You write real good. Not as good as Stephen King—"

Megan laughed, and swatted Bonnie's arm. "You said *flush out the cooks.* I take it the cooks are the people making it?"

"Yeah."

"Tell me all you know."

They talked until Bonnie stopped in front of the B&B. Megan started to climb out when Bonnie said, "Hey, we're both off tomorrow night. Wanna go out with me and some friends? We eat then go to a movie or bowlin' or somethin'. Just us girls."

Megan couldn't remember the last time she'd been out with *just us girls.* "I'd love to."

***

The following evening as Megan put on mascara for girls' night out, her gaze fell upon the picture of her and Barton propped against the mirror.

"Oh shit," she muttered, remembering her words to him concerning her next night off—*It's a date.* She shrugged it off and left to have a good time with Bonnie and her friends.

There were six of them, counting Megan. They had Mexican food and margaritas, then went bowling. They drank beer, talked, and laughed, and welcomed Megan like a long-lost member of the group. They left the bowling alley, went to a corner bar, and closed it down.

The next morning, Megan woke up with a hangover. She staggered to the bathroom, swallowed a couple of aspirins, and went back to bed. She was up and around by noon, feeling more like herself but still headachy and sluggish. *No writing today,* she decided as she squeezed and squeezed the toothpaste tube, trying to get that last little dab out of it. The shampoo was almost gone, too. She finished up in the bathroom then sat down at the table and wrote a shopping list. A walk in the sunshine and fresh air sounded like the perfect tonic for a hangover. She put on a pair of shorts and a sleeveless top. Barton watched her from the picture while she stood in front of the mirror and brushed her hair. His smile seemed more like a sneer. She reached out and flipped the picture face down on the vanity.

She turned away, then spun back, studying the vanity. Something was wrong.

Her gaze swept over the top of the vanity. Something was missing. *My picture!*

She moved the brush, picked up a comb, shoved aside the curling iron, the make-up bag, a stack of notes for an article.

No picture.

She liked that picture. It was a good one of her.

She got on her knees and searched the floor all around the vanity and underneath it, in case the picture had fallen or gotten knocked off.

"Where is it?" she muttered, pressing the side of her head against the wall so she could see behind the vanity.

She sat back on her heels, hands on her hips, frowning, looking around. She stood and shoved everything around on the top of the vanity again, then started taking everything off one by one. She picked up the picture of her and Barton and turned it over. In the sudden glare of sunlight falling upon it, she noticed something. A crease on the right side. She knew it hadn't been there before. Before this morning, she hadn't touched the picture since placing it against the corner of the mirror the day it was taken. She put her thumb near the crease and realized that a thumb had made that crease.

She whirled around and stared at Seth's door.

Damn it! Seth came last night while I was out with the girls. While waiting for me, he probably wandered around the room, and saw the pictures.

She imagined Seth picking up the picture of her with the arm of a smiling, handsome man around her, and thinking, feeling something that made him squish that side of the picture with his thumb. Then he'd taken the picture of her and left.

Just to be sure, she searched everywhere all over again. No picture. It was gone. The only person who could have taken it was Seth. She slowly walked around the room, looking for any other sign that he had been there. Nothing else seemed disturbed or out of place.

She checked the bathroom.

Two towels hung on the towel rack. She had used the same one last night and this morning, so there should not be two. She must not have noticed the second one when showering earlier. No surprise, with her befuddled brain.

She put her hands on her hips. He had finally come. And she hadn't been there. All those nights she sat here, waiting for him, and he picked the one night she went out to have a little fun.

Men!

Disgusted, disappointed, she found her sandals, shoved them on, grabbed her purse, and left the room. She went down a couple of steps, then paused. *Has Seth come other times when I wasn't here? Has he taken a shower and left, without me ever knowing? How many times has he been here? Is he avoiding me? Why?* She met the owner of the B&B heading up the stairs.

"You have a phone call, dear."

"Thanks, Mrs. Powell." Megan hoped the caller was an editor she was waiting to hear from. Maybe Donna. It had been too long since they had talked. She went down to the ground floor, walked to the phone near the front door and picked up the receiver. "Hello?"

"Hello, Megan," she heard Barton say.

"Oh. Hi. Look, I was just running out the door and—"

"I was in The Tejas last night. You weren't there."

"I had the night off so I—"

"I thought you and I had a date on your next night off."

Megan's eyes widened. He sounded like a petulant child who didn't get his way. "I didn't think it was set in stone."

Silence from his end.

"Barton? You still there?"

"I had plans for us, Megan. You should have told me."

She rubbed her forehead. She had a headache and a hangover. She'd missed Seth's visit after waiting and wanting for so long to see him again. She didn't need any shit from Barton.

"I don't have to tell you anything." Megan slammed down the phone, muttered, "Asshole," and stalked out the door into blinding sunlight that shot daggers into her hungover brain. She put on her sunglasses and went on about her errands.

Two hours later, she was back in bed, taking a nap. She woke up refreshed, took a hot shower, and got ready for work. She glanced at her watch. "Holy moly!" She grabbed her purse, locked the door behind her and ran down the stairs. She pulled the front door open and ran into Barton.

Chapter 8

"Whoa there, darlin', where's the fire?" Barton grabbed her shoulders before she could mow him down the steps.

Megan squirmed to be free. He released her and backed down a step. She looked at him through narrowed eyes. "What are you doing here?" She straightened her top and hiked her purse strap up on her shoulder.

Barton held a yellow rose and a purple iris. "To say I'm sorry. I acted like an ass earlier and don't blame you for being pissed at me. I'm sorry, Megan." He offered her the flowers.

She took them and buried her nose in the sweet-smelling rose.

"The yellow rose of Texas." Barton gave a lopsided smile. "I know it's corny, but—" he shrugged. "The iris matches your pretty eyes."

"They're beautiful. But I have to get to work." She glanced at her watch. "The bus stop is two blocks away and—" The bus passed by on the street behind him. "Great. There it goes." Disgusted, she waved a hand at the rear end of the bus belching black smoke. "I'll never make it to the bus stop in time."

Barton looked down the street then back to her. "I'm sorry. On top of everything else, I've made you miss your ride." He placed one foot on the step she stood on. "Let me take you. It's the least I can do."

She reached inside her purse for her sunglasses and put them on while considering her options—taxi, hitchhiking, or running.

Barton added, "My fare is cheaper than the bus."

"What is it?" *A kiss? Cop a feel? Sex?*

"Forgiveness."

Megan blinked in surprise. He looked sincere. He was also the most logical option. "You're forgiven. Let's go. I don't like being late."

Barton took her elbow as they ran to his car. Seconds later, the car merged into the traffic and zipped down the street. "Don't worry. I'll have you there on time. I know short cuts. We'll probably beat the bus." After several blocks, Barton turned left onto a side street lined with older two-story houses surrounded by small yards bursting with roses, wildflowers, and flowering shrubs. "Hey, Megan? I'm sorry for acting like such an ass."

She kept her purse on her lap and held the flowers in one hand. "It wasn't your best moment."

"I was just so disappointed." He came to a stop sign. Traffic crowded the cross street. A semi rumbled by. Exhaust fumes followed in its wake and blew through the car's open windows. "I wanted to take you out to dinner in Dallas. Make a night of it. Maybe go dancing." He shot her a smile. "We dance so well together."

She did not smile back. "You sounded very controlling. I don't like that. I've been on my own for a long time and—"

"You're an independent career woman. I get it." A break came in the line of vehicles. Barton pulled out, turning right. "It's one of the things I like about you. That fierce independence."

Megan didn't consider herself fierce and wondered where he got that idea. He was probably just saying things he thought she'd like to hear. She stared out the windshield.

Downtown office buildings rose around them, the lowering sun reflecting off the many windows. People heading home after work crowded the sidewalks and gathered, waiting, at the crosswalks. Traffic thickened and slowed. Barton swerved around a concrete truck chugging through its gears and shot through a yellow light. A car honked. Two blocks later, he pulled up beside the curb and stopped.

"I need to make one quick stop." He leaned forward to see around Megan, who glanced at her watch. "It'll just take a second. Jim's inside that car rental place. He's going out of town and forgot his briefcase."

"Again? What's his problem?"

"He's a busy guy. Has a lot of irons in the fire." Barton reached behind the seat and grabbed the briefcase.

Megan looked to her right. Inside the nearest building, Jim stood at a counter, looking at a pamphlet. "Is he coming out?"

"I'll run it in to him." Barton twisted in his seat and looked over his left shoulder to see behind him. He had one hand on the door handle, his other on the handle of the briefcase with the smiley face decal on its side. A stream of traffic drove by with gaps between vehicles here and there. Sirens wailed somewhere down the street then faded into the distance.

Seconds ticked away. Megan scowled at Barton. He had missed several opportunities to open his door and get out. The smiley face grinned up at her as if it knew something she didn't know. She resisted the urge to stick her tongue out at it. She glanced at her watch again. She looked at Jim, still standing at the counter, his nose buried in whatever he was reading. "Give it to me." She yanked the briefcase from Barton.

He said, "I'll do—"

She got out of the car, briefcase in hand, and ran into the car rental place. She shoved the briefcase at Jim. "Here."

She didn't wait for a reply. She ran out, yanked open the car door, got in, and slammed it shut. "Let's go."

"Yes, ma'am." Barton nosed his car into the traffic then drove like a madman. He passed slower cars, cut through an alley, took side streets, ran three yellow lights and one red light. The whole way, Megan gripped the armrest, braced for an accident. He pulled up in front of The Tejas, put the car in neutral, set the brake, and turned to Megan with a smile. "I think we did beat the bus."

"Thanks for the ride." Megan pulled the door handle and started to get out.

"I know I screwed up today. Will you give me another chance?"

She paused with one foot outside on the concrete, one still on the floorboard, and the flowers clutched in her hand. She regarded Barton over her shoulder. "Tell me something. You could have any girl you want. Why me?"

"You're intelligent, interesting, attractive. I'd like to get to know you better."

What a line of crap. I bet he's said that to plenty of girls.

He held up his hand. "I know you're just here temporarily. But that doesn't mean you can't have a little fun, does it?"

"I had a lot of fun last night with some girls. Today, you act like a pissed off, controlling boyfriend. I don't need that."

"I know, I know."

"I also don't like you checking up on me. If I'm not at work, it's none of your business where I am."

He hung his head then his eyes met hers. "I'm sorry. Like I said, I was disappointed. and I let it get the best of me." His face softened. "I'm glad you went out, made some friends. I worry about you being all alone in the world."

She frowned. "I'm not all alone in the world."

"I meant here, in Fort Worth. You don't know anyone."

She turned more towards him. "Did you quit smoking? You haven't had one yet."

"I know you don't like them, so I decided not to smoke around you. But believe me, I'm lighting up the minute you're gone." He smiled.

She blinked in surprise. "That's very nice of you."

"What can I say? I'm a nice guy." He rested his hand on the back of her seat. "So, what do you say? Will you go out with me again? See a movie maybe?"

His eyes had a pleading look in them. A lock of windblown black hair curled on his forehead. A five o'clock shadow darkened the lean features of his lower face. He had acted like an ass. But she *had* blown him off. Perhaps he was *a tad* justified in his anger. "It would have to be a matinee. I'm never sure what night I'll be off. There's a girl I'm always filling in for." Megan tilted her head. "She's a local girl, maybe you know her? Julia Whitson. She's short, thin, shoulder-length brown hair."

"Doesn't ring a bell. A matinee sounds great. This weekend? How about Sunday? I'll pick you up at noon."

Megan smiled at his persistence. "All right. I gotta run. Thanks again for the ride. And the flowers."

"Thanks for giving me another chance, darlin'. I'm looking forward to Sunday."

***

Later that night, at the end of their shift, Bonnie washed the last of the beer glasses. "I been meaning to tell you, Bubba's back from the coast."

Megan looked up from the table she was cleaning. "Already? That wasn't a week."

"His girlfriend got sunburned, so they came home early. Bubba called an' gave me the name and number of the cop you should talk to." Bonnie dried her hands on a towel, dug into a front pocket of her skin-tight jeans, pulled out a scrap of paper, and put it on the bar. Spots of water dotted her low-cut black blouse. "Detective Sullivan."

"Thanks." Megan picked up the paper, looked it over, then shoved it into her back pocket. "Tell Bubba thanks for me."

"He's havin' a fish fry Sunday afternoon. Go with me an' tell him yourself."

"I'd love to. But I already have plans." Megan gave the table one last swipe then moved to the next one. She picked up the dirty ashtray and put it on top of a stack of them on the bar. "Barton and I are going to a movie." Although the fish fry sounded more fun.

"Ooo." Bonnie made goo-goo eyes. "You two gonna sit in the back row an' make out?"

Megan laughed as she scrubbed a glob of dried ketchup on a table. "No."

Bonnie paused while putting away glasses behind the bar. "Don't tell me you haven't jumped his bones yet."

"Okay. I won't tell you."

"Oh my God." Bonnie's blue eyes grew as large and round as dinner plates. "You haven't."

A couple of quick swipes and Megan finished with that table. "I thought I wasn't supposed to tell you."

"There's not a girl workin' here who'd turn down a roll in the hay with that hunk. Including me." Bonnie put up the rest of the glasses then began straightening the liquor bottles. "I get the feelin' you're not too excited about him."

Megan carried the stack of stinking, dirty ashtrays behind the bar, dumped them into the lukewarm water in the sink, and started washing them. "He's nice enough. He even said he wouldn't smoke around me. No one's ever done that before."

"So, let's see." Bonnie leaned against the bar and counted on her fingers. "He's nice, considerate. Good lookin'. Wears diamond rings an' leaves generous tips. Gives you flowers." She jutted her chin towards the rose and iris in a tall glass of water near the register.

"Those are I'm-sorry-I'm-such-an-ass flowers. I don't think that counts."

Bonnie had heard the story. She went on without missing beat. "He drives a flashy expensive car. He obviously has money. Did I mention he's *damn* good lookin'? And you aren't attracted to him because ... ?" She looked at Megan with raised eyebrows. "Unless ... you're not a virgin, are you?"

Megan laughed as she rinsed an ashtray, shook off the excess water, and set it aside to dry. "Hardly." She rested her hands on the edge of the sink and realized it had been awhile since she'd had sex. The last time was with one of the hunky guides in Arizona, almost a year ago. He'd had long brown hair, warm brown eyes, and muscles everywhere. *The soft sand beneath our blanket, a star-studded sky overhead, the desert wind blowing over our naked bodies ...* She sighed. *It has been way too long.*

***

Sex was on her mind while she got ready for the movie with Barton on Sunday. She leaned closer to the mirror and applied mascara to her eyelashes. *Should I?* She did the other lashes. *Or shouldn't I?* She straightened and backed up to see the results. *I did shave my legs.* Her gaze fell on their picture, propped against the corner of the mirror. Barton's smile seemed to say, *Hell yes, darlin'!* Her gaze moved to the empty spot beside it where her picture had been. She turned to glance at Seth's door, heaved a sigh, then turned back to the mirror, picked up the brush and ran it through her hair several times. "Face it," she said to her reflection, "you're horny." She put on a yellow sundress with a scooped neck, slipped on a pair of white sandals, grabbed her purse and a sweater, and left the room.

She walked out of the B&B and up to Barton's Corvette parked at the curb. The passenger side window was open. She leaned down and peered inside. Papers covered the passenger seat. Barton sat behind the wheel with an open briefcase on his lap, studying a piece of paper in his hand. The radio played softly.

"Why are you working? It's Sunday."

Barton looked up when she spoke. A grin creased his handsome face. "Howdy, darlin'. I'm fixin' to finish up here. Jim has to deliver some papers in Austin tomorrow and I'm just checkin' things over." He returned his attention to the paper he held. "Makin' sure all the *i*'s are dotted, and all the *t*'s are crossed. I'll just be a sec."

"Take your time." She leaned both elbows on the door and watched him. He bobbed his head to the music as he read. His hair was shiny black and looked as thick as an animal's winter pelt. The smell of his woodsy cologne drifted on the breeze flowing through the open windows. The papers looked like a mixture of invoices and bills, a big-sheeted land plat, and official-looking forms with fancy printing and inked stamps on them. Barton sorted the papers and put them all in a neat stack. The diamond on his pinky finger sparkled in the sunlight that warmed her head and back. He placed the papers inside the briefcase and closed it with two snaps. The smiley face flashed its irritating smile at Megan as Barton lifted the briefcase then shoved it behind his seat.

Megan opened the door and climbed in. "I guess we're going to meet up with Jim again?"

"At the theater, on his way out of town to Austin." Barton leaned over to kiss her cheek. "Thanks for being so patient." He leaned back, his gaze warm and inviting. "You look as pretty as a sunflower."

"You don't look so bad yourself." He wore jeans and a long-sleeved light blue shirt that made his eyes even bluer.

He started the car, checked the rearview mirror then pulled out into the street. "I thought we'd see *The Jazz Singer.*" He glanced at Megan. "Sound good?"

"I love Neil Diamond."

They chatted during the drive beneath a cloudless sky. Traffic was light. On the radio, Alabama sang *Feel So Right.* They pulled into the theater parking lot and Barton parked up near the entrance.

He looked around. "There's Jim." Barton pointed to a silver sedan parked three rows away. They got out of the car, and he did a double-take behind him. "Oh man, there's a guy I need to talk to." He checked his watch. "The movie starts in a few minutes." He looked at Jim, looked at the man he said he needed to talk to, then his gaze met Megan's on the other side of the Corvette. "Could you take Jim his briefcase while I try to catch up with that guy?"

"Sure."

"Thanks, darlin'." Barton got back in the car, reached behind the seat, pulled out the briefcase, and put it on the passenger seat.

She grabbed the briefcase handle and hurried over to Jim's sedan. She handed him the briefcase. "Have a safe trip." Jim thanked her and drove off. Megan headed back to the Corvette where Barton stood, smoking a cigarette. "Did you catch that guy?" She reached inside the car for her sweater, put it on, then closed the car door.

"Wrong guy." Barton dropped his cigarette and crushed it with his foot. "Sure looked like him but it wasn't."

He locked his car and held her hand as they walked into the theater. He paid for the tickets then bought a jumbo box of popcorn and two soft drinks. Snacks in hand, they entered the semi-dark, almost empty theater where Barton chose their seats. Not the last row, but near it.

They sat down just as the theater darkened and the previews began. Soon, the theater darkened even more. The movie started. While the story unfolded up on the screen, Barton and Megan munched on the popcorn until only pieces and seeds rolled around the bottom of the box. He put it on the floor.

Megan shivered and tugged her sweater tighter. Barton put his arm around her shoulders and pulled her close, rubbing his hand up and down her arm. He radiated heat. Megan snuggled up against him. He kissed the top of her head then rested his cheek there. Eventually, she stopped shivering.

He leaned forward to look at her. "Feelin' warmer?" he whispered.

She nodded.

In the light from the movie, she saw him smile. He kissed her forehead then put his arm around her again and held her close while the movie played on. They both laughed during a funny part.

Barton whispered, "You want more popcorn or anything?"

Megan looked at him and shook her head.

He bent his head and kissed her.

She closed her eyes and opened her mouth.

His tongue slid inside as he turned towards her more, the seat creaking beneath his movements. His other hand stroked the side of her face, her hair, her neck as his mouth moved with hers. He twisted around more and leaned over the armrest, pressing her back against the seat, deepening their kiss.

Megan ran her fingers through his thick, soft hair. The smell of his cologne filled her nose. She heard his breathing quicken as their tongues twined. Her own was none to steady. Up on the screen, Neil Diamond sang *Love On the Rocks*. Barton's hand slid down her neck to her breast where he hesitated a second before covering it, cupping it, gently squeezing it.

Holy moly that feels good.
But it should feel wonderful.

Barton broke their kiss to whisper in her ear, "Remember the song on the radio on the way here? The one by Alabama? *You* feel so right."

"Barton—"

He silenced her with his mouth and busy tongue. He brushed aside the sweater and settled his hand upon her breast again where it stayed and played. His thumb found her nipple.

Megan drew in a sharp breath as something stirred deep inside her. Something sweet and aching, something too long ignored. She closed her eyes and gave herself up to the moment. Her thoughts wandered. Straight to Seth. She let her imagination and longings run wild. It was Seth kissing her so thoroughly. Seth's hand caressing her breast, toying with her nipple. His sandy hair her fingers ran through. His hand that found its way down the front of her sundress, inside her bra, to stroke her naked skin while he leaned over her in the theater seats and kissed her until she was breathless and panting for something wonderful.

"Oh, darlin', you feel damn good."

The raspy voice in her ear jerked Megan right out of her fantasies.

Barton was practically on top of her as much as the seats allowed.

The lights came on as the credits rolled onscreen.

She pushed him off, sat up, and quickly adjusted her breasts inside her bra. She tugged her sundress and sweater straight. Her face felt flushed, and her heart pounded as if she'd run a mile. She was mortified that she'd let herself get so carried away. *But it's been so long*. And it had felt good. She looked at Barton out of the corner of her eye. He was sitting back in his seat, one hand wrapped around his drink in the cup holder, while his other hand ran through his hair a couple of times. He blew out a big breath, puffing his cheeks, then picked up his drink and shook it, rattling the ice. He took a sip from the straw, making that slurping sound. The dozen or so other people in the theater left.

Megan slung her purse strap over her shoulder, and perched on the edge of the seat, ready to leave. When he didn't move, she sent him a questioning look.

"Give me a minute, darlin'. I can't walk yet."

After they left the theater, they ate at Whataburger. Barton dunked a couple of fries in a glob of ketchup on the hamburger wrapper. "What have you been writing about lately?"

Megan wiped her mouth with a napkin. "I'm about done with the article about the ghosts in the Swift Armor Meat Packing Plant. I think

I told you about that. I'm also working on a promotional piece about the B&B. The owner has been so nice to me, giving me a cheaper rate and all, I figured it's the least I can do." She took a drink of water. "I have an interview tomorrow about another article." She'd called Detective Sullivan and had an appointment for the next morning at eleven.

"What's this one about?"

She took a bite of her burger and chewed a moment. "I'm not too sure of my angle yet so I'd rather not say. It may not even pan out. I'll know more after tomorrow."

Barton drove back to the B&B and parked in front. He turned to Megan. "You gonna take me upstairs and show me some of your writings?" He wiggled his eyebrows.

Megan laughed at his silly expression. "I have to work tonight."

"Not until seven. It's not even five yet." He reached out to play with a long curl of her hair that lay along her upper arm. His knuckles grazed her breast. "I can think of a few ways to while away a couple hours." He slid his other hand around the back of her neck to pull her closer and kiss her, his fingers massaging her neck.

She pulled away. "I need to prepare for that interview tomorrow."

"Are you sure, darlin'? I promise you, it'll be delightful."

She felt that stirring begin again deep inside. Her emotions were still too close to the surface. She drew away from him, not wanting to use him as a substitute for something—someone—else. "I'm sorry. But I need to work before I go to work."

He gave her a disappointed look, released her, then got out of the car and came around to open her door. When she was out, he closed the door and backed her against the car. He put one hand on the roof beside her shoulder while the knuckles of his other hand stroked the side of her face. "When can I see you again? One afternoon this week?"

She rested her hands on his waist, where she felt not an ounce of fat. "How can you take so many afternoons off? What about your job?"

"I work my own schedule." He leaned closer. "Sometimes it's busier than others. Gives me lots of flexibility." He kissed her forehead. His body pressed against hers. "Do you like picnics?"

"Picnics? Sure."

"Have you been to the botanic garden here in town?" He kissed her temple. His lower body pressed harder against her. "It's beautiful in the spring."

"Not yet." His weight on her felt so good.

"How about we have a picnic there on Wednesday? I'll pick you up about eleven."

She drew back and, squinting against the sun behind him, looked into his eyes. "You're an unpredictable guy, you know that? I never would have guessed you'd be the type who'd want to go on a picnic."

"I like the outdoors. Hiking, fishing, picnics." He brushed a lock of hair off her face. "I like you." He pinned her against the car and kissed her.

Her arms went around his strong, broad back. She could feel his muscles bunch.

A car honked, and someone hollered, "Give it to her, buddy!"

A giggle surged up inside her but by the time it got past their active tongues it sounded more like a groan. He groaned in response. His knee nudged her legs apart and he settled completely against her. Through their clothes, she could feel his erection.

He tore his mouth from hers and rasped in her ear, "You're killin' me, Megan. Killin' me." His hand slid down her side then slipped around to squeeze her butt. "You sure you don't want to make some sweet lovin' on this pretty afternoon?"

Tempting. *He* was tempting. Fit, strong, handsome, successful. Her resistance ebbed beneath his soft Texas drawl and grinding hips.

He felt good. Not wonderful. Maybe, sometimes, good was good enough. *It's been so long.*

She ran her fingernails lightly down his back, drawing a low moan out of him. "Let's go in—" she broke off, hearing a familiar-sounding engine. A green pickup drove up and parked behind the Corvette. "There's Bonnie."

Barton nuzzled behind her ear. "Who?"

"My friend Bonnie. The bartender from work."

"What's she want?"

"I don't know. She's still sitting in her truck."

Barton kissed the side of her neck. "Maybe if we ignore her she'll go away. Now, what were you saying?"

Megan tsked. "There might be something wrong." She waved a hand at Bonnie, who waved back through the windshield, then held up her palms in a helpless gesture. Megan waved Bonnie over then squirmed out from between Barton and the Corvette. She heard Barton heave a monstrous sigh and mutter, "Fuck," as he let her go. Megan walked to the back of the car. "Hi, Bonnie. What's up?"

Bonnie smiled as she climbed out of her truck and walked around the front of it, her ponytail swinging from side to side. Her gaze moved behind Megan, and her smile faltered, her steps slowed. She fidgeted with the hem of her top. "I'm sorry for bargin' in on you two. Maybe I should just go—"

"Don't be silly. You remember Barton?"

"Sure do. Hey there." Bonnie waved.

He leaned against the car, his elbows on the roof, a cigarette between his fingers, a scowl on his face. He flipped his hand in the semblance of a wave, then took a drag, and blew a stream of smoke out of his nostrils, like a dragon.

"How was the fish fry?" Megan asked Bonnie.

"A lotta fun. I was on my way home an' thought of some questions you could ask tomorrow an' didn't wanna wait until we got to work." Bonnie shot a look at Barton. "Or are you two ... busy?"

"Wait here." Megan turned and went to Barton. "I'm sorry, Barton, but Bonnie has some ideas for my interview tomorrow. I'd really like to hear them."

"Humph." His mouth set in a firm line, he looked at Bonnie then back at Megan. He dropped his cigarette on the pavement and ground it out with a quick twist of his foot. "It must be an important article."

"They're all important."

He blew out a breath then pushed himself away from the car. "We're still on for a picnic Wednesday, right?"

"Sounds lovely. Thanks for today. It was fun."

A slight smile smoothed away the scowl on his face. He stepped closer and put his hands on her shoulders. "It was, wasn't it." He lowered his head and gave her a tongue-filled kiss, as if to let her know what she was turning down.

She could taste his cigarette as she waved at him driving away.

Bonnie watched after him. "Boy, was he pissed at me. The look he gave me when I got out of the truck almost made me jump back in it an' haul ass." She turned to Megan. "I'm sorry I barged in on your date."

"Bonnie, my friend, you arrived in the nick of time to stop me from doing something I'm pretty sure I would have regretted later. Thank you."

"Oh." Bonnie smiled knowingly. "No wonder he's pissed I showed up. I reckon he damn near poked a hole in the side of his fancy car, standin' there the way he was."

Megan chuckled. A car drove by, blaring rock and roll music out its windows. A gust of wind swirled dust and scraps of paper down the street and blew her hair across her face. "Do you think I'm leading him on?" Brushing her hair out of the way, she turned to Bonnie, who leaned back against the front of her pickup, elbows on the hood, ankles crossed.

"Seems to me if a gal's wonderin' if she's leadin' a fella on, she is."

"I don't mean to." Megan frowned. "I was tired of just going to work and coming back here. Then Barton came along." She held up her hands in a helpless gesture. "Suddenly I have a boyfriend I don't know what to do with or am even sure I want."

"Why not just have a little fun? Nothin' wrong with a little sex for the sake of sex."

"God knows, I've done that before. But now, I want something more. I want," she paused and thought of Barton, how he felt, how he made her feel, and decided that good wasn't good enough after all. "I want something wonderful."

Bonnie laughed. "Good luck findin' that."

Megan sighed. "Well, enough about my love life." She dug in her purse for her keys. "Let's go in."

She led Bonnie inside and upstairs to her room. She unlocked the door, opened it, and peeked inside to make sure Seth wasn't there. She walked in, tossing her sweater on the back of the sofa. "Make yourself at home." Nothing seemed out of place. She checked the bathroom. No extra towel on the rack or water on the floor. Or Seth, hiding behind the door.

Megan grabbed two beers from the Styrofoam cooler. Bonnie walked around the room, oohing and ahhing over the antique furniture. She marveled over the view out the windows. "What's this door for?"

Megan held her breath as Bonnie grabbed the doorknob of Seth's door. *Open! Open!* screamed in her head.

"Huh. Won't budge." Bonnie released the doorknob and stepped back, hands on her hips. "Must've been a stairway here goin' down to the street."

"There was." Megan swallowed her disappointment and walked up beside Bonnie, handing her a beer. "The place used to be a brothel in the late 1800s. *This* room had stairs to the street. I don't know if any of the other rooms did." She made a mental note to herself to ask Mrs. Powell about that.

"Must've been a special whore livin' here." Bonnie popped the top on the beer and took a drink. "Some rich guy's favorite."

Maybe Bingo built it for easy access to Lottie. I'll have to ask Seth. If I ever see him again.

Bonnie said, "We'd better get to work before we have to go to work."

Megan gestured to the sofa. "Tell me your ideas."

***

The next morning, Megan walked into the main office of the Fort Worth Police Department. After a short wait in line, she gave her name at the front desk then sat down on one of the few vacant straight-backed hard chairs along a wall. She put her purse on her lap and straightened her red blouse. She smoothed her black skirt along her thighs and tugged the hem to her knees while she looked around.

On her right, a man slouched in the chair, his cowboy hat pulled low over his eyes, his arms crossed. There were holes in the knees of his blue jeans. On her left, a woman in a flowered housedress softly scolded a teen-aged boy with a sullen look on his pimple-spotted face sitting beside her. The large room bustled with uniformed police officers milling around, many carrying cups of coffee, some carrying clipboards or small spiral notebooks. Some carried briefcases. Megan didn't see any smiley faces plastered on any of them, to her relief. Briefcases seemed to be haunting her lately. An officer walked by escorting a longhaired, bearded man in dirty jeans and handcuffs. Telephones rang. Radios squawked. A door slammed somewhere down the hallway. The front door opened, and several police officers walked in, talking, and laughing.

A man in a dark suit and tie approached Megan. He was middle-aged, average size and build, with slicked back brown hair. He wore dark-rimmed glasses. "Miss McClure? I'm Detective Sullivan."

Megan stood and held out her hand. "Thank you for seeing me, Detective." She thought she saw a flash of recognition on his otherwise poker face and thought it odd. She'd never met him before, yet he seemed to recognize her. Perhaps he'd seen her waitressing at work.

After shaking her hand, Detective Sullivan said, "Would you follow me, please?" He led her down a hallway to a small windowless office and gestured to one of two chairs. She sat while he closed the door then went to sit behind the desk. Shelves full of books lined one wall. On one of the upper shelves was a framed picture of the detective with a dark-haired woman and three teen-aged girls. File cabinets lined another wall. A potted ivy sat atop one cabinet and draped down one side. A black cowboy hat rested on top of another cabinet. On the desk were a phone, a shiny brass nameplate, a brass penholder full of pens and pencils, a Rolodex, and several stacks of papers in an organized mess Megan recognized. She used the same system.

"What can I do for you, Miss McClure?"

"I would like some information about methamphetamine. I'm writing an article about it."

Surprise flickered across his face. "Because ... ?"

"Because it seems to be a problem in Fort Worth. One that could turn into a big problem. I think people need to know about it. About the effects, the signs of usage, the consequences and dangers."

"Why you?"

She paused while taking her notebook out of her purse. "Pardon me?"

"Why are *you* writing about methamphetamine? It seems to be a bit outside the realm of your usual writings. Which, I believe, is called fluff."

Megan took no offense at the comment. She had heard her writing pursuits called worse. "I write about many things. Whatever catches my fancy."

The detective reached into his shirt pocket and pulled out a small spiral notebook. He flipped it open and thumbed through several pages, then stopped and read. "In 1978 you wrote about the Serpent Mound in southwestern Ohio." He looked at Megan.

"It's a sacred place. Beautiful. Brimming with energy. No one is exactly sure when it was built, who built it, or why. It may be the largest serpent effigy in the world."

"Hmmm." He studied her a moment then glanced at his notes. "You wrote about rocks in Death Valley that supposedly move on their own."

"Not just rocks. Boulders." She spread her hands wide to indicate the size. "Nobody knows how they move, whether on their own or some other way. But you can see their trails in the sand."

"But you didn't see any move?"

She shook her head. "I sat up for six nights with my camera, waiting. None of the rocks I was watching moved. However, others did. I saw rocks in places where they hadn't been the day or days before, with the trail behind them. Very weird." She smiled.

He looked at his notes again. "You wrote about the Hopi Indians in Arizona."

"They're a wise and noble people. Fascinating."

"Your topic was a two-headed spirit dog revered by them."

"Like I said, fascinating." Megan guessed that he recognized her from her picture that accompanied some of her articles he'd obviously read.

Detective Sullivan put the notebook back in his pocket. "And now methamphetamine has *caught your fancy*." A crease formed between his eyes. "It just seems a little odd to me, you choosing to write about meth. If you don't mind my asking, what brought this on?"

"I have some friends here whose lives have been adversely affected by the drug. It's because of them."

"Where do you plan on publishing it?"

"I'm meeting with an editor at the *Star-Telegram* tomorrow. I hope they run it."

Detective Sullivan sat back in his chair and studied her a moment. "May I read it before you submit it?"

"Of course."

"So, what do you want to know? I'll tell you what I can."

Megan opened her notebook and clicked her ballpoint pen. "Let's start at the beginning. Where did methamphetamine come from? And when?"

"I believe it was first made in Japan, around the early 1900s. Both the Axis and Allied forces used it during World War II to fight fatigue and increase focus. Truckers started using it in the fifties, then college students. It became popular among motorcycle gangs in California during the seventies, and it's now made its way here."

"So, it's spreading like a virus across the country." Megan kept writing. "What is it made from? I know it's not a plant like marijuana or opium."

"It's man-made. Its ingredients are ether, iodine, hydrochloric acid, red phosphorus, sodium hydroxide, methanol, and pseudoephedrine, which is found in Sudafed pills."

Megan looked up from her notebook. "People actually snort all that stuff? Or inject it into their bodies?" She shook her head then continued writing. "Sounds like some volatile stuff."

"It is. Meth labs blow up quite often."

"Where are these labs typically located? In houses?"

"Houses, mobile homes, motel rooms, storage buildings, you name it. Most of the labs are in rural areas because of the smell."

"The smell?"

"Methamphetamine has a distinct odor. A sickening sweet smell. You can walk by a meth house and smell it from the sidewalk. A lot of users reek of it."

Sickening sweet smell rang a bell in Megan's memory but she was too busy writing to think about it now. "What are the effects of the drug?"

"Let's see." He put his elbows on the armrests, and brought his hands together, tenting his fingers. "Some physical effects are dilated pupils, flushed skin, dry mouth, excessive sweating, twitching, restlessness, hyperactivity—"

As Megan wrote, she thought of Julia.

"—accelerated heartbeat, rotten teeth, known as meth mouth, insomnia, numbness, tremors, convulsions, heart attack, stroke, death."

Holy moly! "And the psychological effects?"

"Euphoria, anxiety, increased libido, alertness, increased concentration, increased energy, self-esteem, and self-confidence. Sociability, irritability, aggressiveness, paranoia. The intensity of all of those depends upon how much it's been stepped on."

Megan looked at him. "Stepped on?"

"Diluted. Cut with something else."

"Such as?"

"Sugar. Powdered sugar. Baking soda. Baking powder. Baby powder. Salt."

"So, meth is sold in powder form?"

"Correct." He reached up to adjust his glasses.

"How is it sold? Like marijuana, a quarter, half, or whole ounce? And what are the going prices?"

"On the street, it's usually sold by the gram for a hundred bucks. An eight ball is a popular buy. It's three and a half grams, or one-eighth of an ounce. Sells for two hundred fifty or so. An ounce is a thousand dollars. Wholesale, a pound goes for ten thousand."

"Big money," Megan muttered as she wrote it all down. She chewed her lower lip for a moment. "How much would fit in, say, a briefcase?" She waited for his answer, her pen poised on the paper. When he didn't say anything, she looked up at him, and caught a fleeting mix of surprise and puzzlement on his face before it settled into its usual stoic features.

Detective Sullivan uncrossed his legs and sat straight. "A briefcase, huh?"

"A briefcase is pretty much standard sized." She had briefcases on her mind. She'd had a dream about them last night. There had been dozens of them, opening and snapping shut, chasing after her like Pac-

Man. All of them wore a sinister-looking smiley face that sneered at her as she ran. She had awakened in the dark of night with a pounding heart, cold chills, and an irrational fear of she didn't know what. Sleep had not come easily after that.

Megan shifted on the chair. "I guess we could use a bread bag. How much would fit in a bread bag? Not a small loaf. A regular sized loaf."

"No. We'll use a briefcase. It would hold a lot. At least a pound. Ten thousand dollars-worth. If it's still wet. The wetter it is, the heavier it is. Dry, you could probably get two pounds in a briefcase."

"Twenty thousand dollars-worth. Wow. Can you tell me how it's made? The process?"

Thirty minutes later, Megan left the police station pleased with the interview. The detective had been a font of information. He'd given her his card in case she had any further questions.

At work that night, Megan told Bonnie all about the interview. Bonnie's face lit with excitement when she heard it had gone well. The next day, Megan met with an editor from the *Star-Telegram*, pitched her idea, and was given the go-ahead. She promised to deliver the article in two weeks. She hurried home and sat down to write. She had the night off, so she ordered a pizza then wrote all evening. She went to bed before midnight, exhausted. Hopefully too exhausted to dream about snapping briefcases.

***

Something soft brushed her lips. Megan blinked her eyes open. In the darkness, she saw a shadowy figure in a cowboy hat bending over her. Her first instinct was to scream. She went with her second instinct. "Seth?" She sat up. "Is that you?"

The figure quickly backed away then turned.

"Seth?"

Footsteps hurried across the room, heading for Seth's door.

"Seth!" Megan scrambled off the bed and ran after him, her bare feet slapping the wood floor. She caught an arm and yanked so hard the cowboy hat fell off. "Seth!"

He stopped and turned. Faint light from the streetlights seeping through the curtains bathed the contours of his face. "I'm sorry, Miss Megan. I didn't mean to wake you."

Still clutching his arm, she stepped closer to him. "You didn't mean to wake me? I haven't seen you in over a month and *you didn't mean to wake me?* What's going on? Why are you avoiding me? Why do you come here when I'm gone? Why did you kiss me just now then run away when I woke up?"

He remained silent.

She tugged his shirtsleeve. "Well?" When he still didn't answer, she released him and stepped back, crossing her arms. "I never imagined you a coward."

He jerked back slightly, as if she'd hit him, then bent down to retrieve his hat and held it in one hand. He replied in a low voice, "I was kissing you goodbye."

Chapter 9

"Goodbye? *Goodbye?* Why?"

"Things have changed," he replied in the same low voice.

"What things?"

In the dimness, the shoulders of his shadowy figure lifted in a shrug. "Everything."

She took a couple of steps back and pulled the chain on the floor lamp—the same lamp he had taken through the brick wall weeks ago. In the light, she got her first good look at Seth. His clean-shaven face was leaner than she remembered, the cheekbones more pronounced. His right cheek bore an inch-long vertical scar of puckered white skin. His sandy hair was trimmed short and neat. He wore a black overcoat over a shiny black waistcoat. Satin, she guessed. His white shirt was crisp and clean, and a black string tie circled his neck. He wore tight black trousers. She had read somewhere that men didn't wear belts back then and instead wore their trousers very tight. *No lie there.* He looked like he was going to a wedding or a funeral.

A bolt of dread struck Megan.

It's his wedding day.

She held out her hand to him. "Sit down and tell me what's changed."

He didn't take her hand, but he slowly walked to the sofa then waited for her to sit before he sat on the other end. He hung his hat on his knee.

She jumped up. "Want a beer? I think there's a couple left in the cooler." Not waiting for his answer, she crossed the room to the cooler, feeling his eyes on her. On the way, she grabbed her robe from where it hung on the bedpost and slipped it on over her flowered tank top and shorts. For some reason, she felt oddly uncomfortable sitting around in her nightclothes with him. Not that the robe covered much. It was flimsy and hit her mid-thigh. She went to the cooler, got two beers then went back to the sofa. Seth's gaze swept over her and he gave her a curious look but said nothing as he took the can of beer she offered. He popped the top and took a drink.

Megan sat on the other end of the sofa, pulled her robe closed, then opened her beer and drank a generous amount of liquid courage before turning to him. "Tell me what's going on." She steeled herself for the news of his wedding.

"I went to a funeral today."

Relief swept over her. Shame at that relief quickly followed. Then concern took over. She hoped it wasn't Lottie. She stretched her hand along the back of the sofa to touch his shoulder. "I'm sorry. Whose was it?"

"Mr. Toby. Doc said it was his heart."

The name sounded familiar. "He's the man whose cattle you helped round up during a blizzard."

Seth looked surprised. "You remember."

"It was just a few weeks ago."

"It was a couple years ago for me."

The time difference always amazed her. Weeks for her were years for him. She drew her hand back. "You two were close?"

Seth nodded, his face somber. He rested his beer on the sofa's armrest. "He was like a father to me. He took in me an' Lottie when our ma died an' took care of us until Lottie moved in here. I still live with him. Off an' on anyway."

"Off and on?"

"I stay with Tim a lot. He's got a place here in town."

"What's Tim doing these days?"

"He's workin' in a bank. He never was partial to gettin' his hands dirty." Seth stared at his beer can, frowning. "Mr. Toby left me his ranch."

"That's wonderful!" Puzzled by his frown, she asked, "Isn't it?"

He nodded slowly. "Damn generous of him. I wasn't expectin' it. It's not a very big spread. Only a thousand or so acres but—"

Megan almost spewed the beer she'd just drunk. "A thousand acres? Not very big?" She wiped her mouth with the back of her hand. "Are you kidding?"

A slight grin touched Seth's mouth. "A thousand acres ain't nothin'. But it's a start. It's real pretty land, hilly with a creek runnin' through it and lots of wildflowers in the spring. There's a small house, a barn, corral, and a couple hundred head of cattle."

"It sounds beautiful. What's the problem?"

"It's about fifteen miles from town."

"So?" She shrugged. "Fifteen miles is nothing."

He leaned forward and shrugged off his overcoat then twisted around to lay it over the armrest. His satin waistcoat stretched across his broad back. He turned back to her and said, "It is on a horse."

"Oh yeah. Forgot about that."

"An' there's a lot of work to do on the ranch. I won't have much spare time for comin' to town very often. I don't know when I'd be able to come see you again, an' I don't want you just sittin' here waitin' for me anymore."

Megan looked away from his intent gaze, afraid he would see the sadness in her eyes. She understood the logic in his thinking but couldn't imagine never seeing him again.

"It's not like you've been around much lately anyway." She kept her voice steady. "The last time I saw you, you ran in here waving your gun around, looking to kill Bingo. Your clothes were dirty, and you had a cut on your face that's now a scar." She looked at him. "You kissed me like there was no tomorrow then left. Tonight, you sneak in here like a thief in the night to kiss me—not even *tell* me—goodbye."

"I left a note on the table."

"Gee, thanks." She rolled her eyes. "I was worried about you. I didn't know if you were dead or alive." The absurdity of her statement hit her.

"I didn't mean to worry you. I'm sorry."

"So, did you ... kill Bingo that night?" It was the first time she'd ever asked anyone if they had killed somebody. It gave her a chill.

Seth shook his head. "But he hasn't laid a hand on Lottie since then, although he still threatens to all the time. I'll tell you true, Miss Megan, the time will come when him an' me are gonna have it out."

"I know you've been here while I was gone. You took showers, and you took my picture."

His gaze went to the dresser by the bed where the picture of her and Barton was propped against the corner of the mirror. Seth asked with a jut of his chin, "Who's the fella?"

"A friend." She waved a dismissive hand. No need to discuss Barton with Seth.

Seth stared at the picture a moment longer. A muscle worked in his cheek. He took his hat off his knee and put it on top of his overcoat on the armrest then turned towards her more. "Is that really the letter you wrote to the banker?"

"It sure is. Shocked me to see it. But it finally convinced me I wasn't crazy."

Seth chuckled.

She frowned. "What if someone else sees that picture? How will you explain it?"

"No one will see it. Except Tim. I showed it to him. Mr. Toby knew about you, too."

"He did?" His surprises kept on coming.

Seth nodded. "Not many details. Just that there was a girl I met somewhere far away. He figured it was in Kansas while I was on the cattle drive. I never told him any different." He reached up, crooked a forefinger over his string tie and loosened it with a tug then let out a sigh of relief. He tipped his beer up for a swig. Headlight beams from a car on the street below swept over the walls.

"Why didn't you ever wait for me any of those times you were here?"

"I couldn't. I'd wait as long as I could. But when it's time to go, it's time to go."

"What do you mean by that?"

A frown beetled his forehead. He ran a hand through his sandy hair, leaving it in attractive waves. "It's hard to explain. I feel it."

"Feel what?"

"Like I'm ... comin' apart. That's when I know it's time to leave."

She pictured the transporter on *Star Trek* disassembling someone's atoms then reassembling them in another place. "Is it painful?"

"Not exactly. More uncomfortable than anything. Might be painful if I waited longer."

"Hmmm. Coming apart. Interesting." She drew her leg up beneath her on the sofa, smoothing her robe on her thighs. "Another thing I've been wondering. If you're here for, say, an hour, is it an hour in your time?"

He nodded. "Thereabouts. Although the time of day can be different. It might be night in my time, and maybe afternoon here. I never know till I come through the door."

Megan remembered something Bonnie had said. "Is this the only room that has its own outside stairs?"

"Sure is. They were Bingo's idea. He paid for 'em. I built 'em."

"You did?"

He nodded again. "Finished 'em about a year before we met."

"Only you and Bingo use the stairs?"

"Far as I know."

"I've wondered a time or two if anyone else could come through that door."

Seth tilted his head, looking thoughtful. "I think it's just me that can. A year or so back, Tim asked me to come get him the next time it felt cold when I went up the stairs. When I did, he followed me up to the door. He said he didn't feel the cold like I did, although he said the light Lottie always leaves on was off and it was black as night. I opened the door and stepped through. Real faint like, I heard Tim hollering for me, so I went back through the door. He was holding a match and had the strangest look on his face. I asked him what he'd seen, and he said a brick wall then saw me come back through."

"He sees a wall too."

Seth nodded. "He pounded on it a couple times. Said it was the damndest thing he'd ever seen."

Megan propped her elbow on the armrest and idly ran her fingers through her hair. She suddenly realized it must be a mess from sleeping and ran her fingers through it several more times until she noticed Seth watching her. She rested her cheek on her knuckles. "At least I don't have to worry about walking in here and finding Tim prowling around my room."

Seth laughed.

"What did you do all the times you've been here while I wasn't?" Megan envisioned him pawing through her underwear drawer.

"I've been reading. I'm up to 1950 in the history book of America."

Megan looked at him in surprise, impressed.

"Sure are a lot of wars." He shook his head. "And those camps where those Nazis"—he pronounced it with a long *a* and a short *i* —"killed all those people is just horrible. Then those two cities were destroyed with those bombs, and, my God, Miss Megan, the bloodshed never ends."

"It still hasn't. Probably never will. They're called Not-zees, by the way."

"Not-zees," he repeated.

"Remember that word and tell your kids—" she smacked her palm on her forehead. "What am I thinking? You can't tell your kids—or anybody—anything."

He looked away from her, rubbing one hand on the top of his thigh. "It's a lot to keep to myself."

She reached along the back of the sofa to tap him on the shoulder until he looked at her. "You have to. You understand that, don't you?" She gave him a pointed look.

After a long silence, he drew his brows together and heaved a heavy sigh. "Yeah. But—"

"No buts about it, Seth. Don't go changing history. Who knows what the consequences could be? You change one thing and God only knows what could happen. I hope you haven't taken anything else back with you besides my picture. Not even more toilet paper for Tim."

"He has asked."

"No, Seth. Nothing else goes back to your time. Promise me."

He twisted his mouth to one side and scowled at her. "All right, all right."

They sat in silence a moment. Then Seth said, "I've read some of your writings, too."

Her eyebrows rose. "You have?"

"You don't mind, do you? I mean, writing is supposed to be read, isn't it?"

He was just brimming with logic tonight. "I guess it's all right since it's after the fact."

He finished his beer then stood and walked to the trash container near the table to throw the can away. The waistcoat hugged his lean torso and trim waist. The tight black trousers delineated his butt and long legs. A fine specimen of a man. One beyond her reach. She sighed in resignation.

He went to one of the windows framing a lace-curtained black night and looked out. She drained her beer then rose to her feet. She tossed away the empty can as she crossed the room to his side.

He said, "Sometimes I'll stand here, or pull up a chair an' sit here, an' watch the world outside. I'll watch the cars pass, an' wonder what it's like to be inside one. I'll watch people walking by, an' wonder about their clothing, where they're going, what they're doing. I'll see an airplane up in the sky an' try to imagine what everything down here looks like from up there. What it would feel like to fly like a bird. I'll look at that courthouse, knowin' it's the same one that people in my time are just now talking about building. I'll watch the trees bend in a wind I can't feel. See people wiping sweat off their foreheads from a heat I can't feel except through the window pane." He rested his hand on the window frame. "There's been moments when I wanted to smash the glass, so I could find out what your world feels like. The wind. The heat. The smell of the air. The sound of the birds, the cars, whatever else there is to hear. I spend a lot of time looking out these windows at a world I can only see but not feel. Not be a part of. An' I wonder. About everything."

He turned his back to the window and stared about the room. "I've been enjoyin' my time in this room. It's peaceful. Not at all like it is in my time when Lottie an' all the other whores are livin' here. No fights or stabbings or gun battles. No stink of human waste. It's kind of been like a-a-" he frowned. "What's the word?"

"Refuge?" She pictured him sitting on the rawhide sofa, one leg crossed over the other, reading by the light of the floor lamp in the quiet of the old house.

"Yeah. A refuge. I'm gonna miss it," he added softly. He looked at her. "I haven't been avoiding you. We just weren't ever here at the same time."

"Why has inheriting Mr. Toby's farm prompted you to tell me goodbye?"

"I told you. It's fifteen miles from town. I won't be—"

"Bullshit. Tell me the real reason."

He frowned and pressed his lips in a firm line then said, "Because it's time I settled down. I want to run the ranch the way Mr. Toby taught me, an' make it a success. I want to buy more cattle. I want it to be my home an' raise my family there. I want a wife an' kids." He looked down at the floor, shifting his weight from one foot to the other, then met her gaze. "You want kids?"

"Someday. More than one. I always wished I had a sister or a brother. So two at least. Three would be more interesting. Four, even better. Five must be chaos. Joyous chaos." She smiled, and he smiled back.

"I want a passel of 'em." His smile faded. "I can't have any of that if I keep running up those stairs to see you." His expression softened, and his eyes searched her face. "It ain't fair to you, either, Miss Megan. Maybe it's time you go home."

Stunned by his words, in her heart she knew he was right. *Home.* She laughed suddenly, humorlessly. "Just today I wrote a check for next month's rent on my apartment and realized I couldn't remember what color the carpet was. Or the sofa. Or the curtains. I can hardly recall anything about it. This place," she gazed around the room, "has come to feel more like home than any other place I've lived since my parents died."

"You've never told me how they died."

She sent him a sharp look.

He shrugged. "You know just about everything about me."

"Hardly!" she scoffed and looked at him as if he was crazy. "Until tonight, I didn't know where you lived. Or that Mr. Toby had been like a father to you. Or that you have the skills to build a stairway. I don't even know how old you are."

"I turned 25 this month. March."

It took her a moment to absorb that. "A spring birthday. See?" She held up her hands, palms up. "I don't know *anything* about you."

"Well," he chuckled, scratching his chin. "I wouldn't say *anything*, but I reckon *everything* isn't right neither. Guess it just seems like it, being's I've known you so long."

Megan burst out laughing at the absurdity of his statement. The absurdity of the whole situation. "Known me so long!" Shaking her head, she walked to the vanity, muttering, "Known me so long. Holy moly." She looked in the mirror. *Yikes!*

She picked up the brush from the top of the vanity and ran it through her hair several times, wincing when it hit a tangle. She worked out the tangle then brushed all the way to the end of a long curl then started at the top again. On the right side of the mirror, she saw Seth's reflection.

He stood by the window, his hands in his trouser pockets. The tie hung in crooked, uneven black strings against his white shirt. His gaze traveled down her back to her bare feet then back up and did the same to the front of her reflection where her robe gaped open. His gaze lifted, met hers in the mirror. The brush moved slower through her hair as they shared a long silent stare until she felt heat climb up her neck to her cheeks. Her gaze skittered away, only to land on Barton's smiling face and watchful eyes. With the end of the brush, she tipped the picture face down on the vanity then resumed brushing. She didn't need two men staring at her.

"So," Seth said. "About your folks?"

Her hand stilled then slowly lowered the brush to the top of the vanity. She kept her eyes downcast. "I never talk about that night."

Silence fell, disturbed only by the hum of the air conditioner kicking on.

"I reckon I'll go first, then, an' tell you something about my pa's death that I never talk about."

Her gaze darted up to Seth's reflection. He leaned back against the wall beside the window, ankles crossed, regarding her steadily in the mirror.

"Your father drowned, right?"

Seth nodded. "It was my fault."

To Megan's ears, the words fell like a bomb in the quiet room. His admission shocked her almost as much as the ease with which he said it. "You were just a boy."

"Nine years old. It was early spring an' had been rainin' a couple days. The nearby creek was swollen an' rushin' like a river, overflowin' its banks. Churnin', muddy water. Wasn't long before we saw debris from floodin' upstream rush by. Furniture, live animals, dead animals, pots an' pan, wagons, whole houses, barns." Seth shook his head. "I was in our house, kneelin' on a chair, lookin' out a window. I'd never seen nothin' like it before." His drawl had become more pronounced, his speech less refined. "Pa an' some other men were out there pullin' people off floatin' rooftops an' logs an' many of 'em straight out of the water. A lot of 'em were dead. The rain finally let up and Ma kept my two little sisters inside but let me an' Lottie go out. I ran over to the creek to watch all those things float by. Pa kept yelling at me to stay away from the edge of the creek 'cause the ground was soft. I'd back away from the water when he hollered at me, then wait until he wasn't lookin' and I'd go right back to standin' beside the creek. Suddenly, the ground gave way and I fell in the water."

"Oh no!"

"It was cold an' fast an' before I knew it I was swallowin' water an' being swept downriver. I heard Lottie screamin' my name. Pa jumped in an' managed to get to me and grab me an' haul me to the bank. He pushed me out of the water." His voice roughened with emotion. "I grabbed a tree root an' pulled myself out then turned around—an' Pa was gone."

Megan turned to face him. "Oh, Seth. How awful."

He looked away and stared across the room. A muscle worked in his cheek. "I was gonna jump back in to find him, but Lottie grabbed me, stoppin' me. She meant to jump in instead, but Ma ran up an' grabbed us both an' the three of us stood there hangin' on to each other, searchin' the water for some sign of Pa." He lowered his head. After a moment, he said in a low voice, "They found his body the next day a couple miles downstream."

"I'm so sorry."

He raised his head and looked at her, his eyes bright with a telltale shine. "You don't know how many times I've thought, If only I'd listened to him. If only I'd stayed in the house. If only ..."

Megan crossed the room and placed a hand on his arm. "It wasn't your fault. Your father did what any parent would do. He gave his life for yours."

He ran his other hand over his face a couple of times then plowed his fingers through his hair. "Try tellin' that to a nine-year-old. Ma was never the same after that. She an' Pa had been married forever an' it was a good marriage. They'd laugh together all the time an' were real happy. After that, she didn't laugh much anymore. Things got bad. If

Mr. Toby hadn't helped us, I don't know what would have happened to us. He was sweet on her, an' she was right fond of him, grateful, too, an' I think he would have convinced her to marry him sooner or later. Then the fever hit, an' when my two little sisters died, well, I think it was just too much for Ma. She caught the fever an' went real fast. Mr. Toby said she just gave up. He took care of me an' Lottie after that to honor my ma more than anythin', I think. Oh, he thought the world of us, but he did it for her."

"You were lucky to have him." Megan squeezed his arm before releasing it. "And you shouldn't blame yourself for your father's death."

"Yeah. Well ..." He shrugged and turned his head away from her to look out a window. After a moment, his gaze came back to her. "Tell me about your folks. Not just their dyin' but their livin' too."

Megan crossed her arms and stepped away from him. "I feel like we're trying to cram a lifetime of discoveries about each other into a couple of hours."

"I reckon we are." He leaned a shoulder against the wall and looked at her expectantly.

He wasn't going to let it rest. She crossed her arms tighter, hugging herself. He wanted her to speak of the unspeakable. A chill not caused by the air conditioner skittered over her skin. She wasn't sure if she could bring herself to tell it all. The grief, the heartache went deep, almost as deep as the guilt. Yet he was no stranger to grief, or guilt. She looked down at the floor then said softly, "There's one beer left. Wanna split it?"

"Sure. I'll get it an' meet you on the sofa."

He pushed away from the wall and headed for the cooler near her bed while she went to sit on the sofa and took a moment to collect herself. Seth handed her the beer then sat on the other end of the sofa. She popped the top and took a long drink. She grimaced. The beer wasn't very cold since the ice in the cooler had almost melted. She took another swig before handing it to Seth, who took a drink then rested the can on the armrest. He shifted a little sideways, facing her, and waited.

After a deep, steadying breath, Megan began, "My parents were an oddball couple. They grew up next door to each other, went to the same schools all through the years, and married shortly after high school. No one thought it would last because they were as different as night and day. Total opposites. My dad was loud and boisterous. A joker. The life of the party. He never met a stranger. He was the manager of a grocery store and knew every customer and their kids, their families, knew everything about them. Everyone loved him. My friends called him Mr. MC." Megan chuckled. "Dad loved it. Made him feel like part of the gang. In many ways, he was just a big kid. My mom, on the other hand, was quiet and reserved. She was cool to everyone but dad, me, and her few friends. She was nice to my friends. Maybe polite is a better word. The only one she ever really liked was Donna. Well, Lori, too, because her mother was Mom's closest friend. No one ever called Mom Mrs. MC. It was always Mrs. McClure."

Megan shook her head, smiling. "Such an odd couple. Dad would wear ratty old jeans and a torn t-shirt splattered with paint or oil or spaghetti sauce, his curly hair going every which way. And there'd be Mom in a nice dress, high heels, her hair perfect, makeup impeccable. She was a nurse, a damn good one, very conscientious and professional, but she viewed her job more as a problem to be solved than a person to be helped. I loved her, but I didn't always understand her. I was Daddy's little girl, and more like him than her. But they adored each other and were very happy. He'd do something goofy and she'd just roll her eyes and say with a tsk *Heavens to Betsy, Harvey*." Megan hadn't thought of that in a long time. It made her smile.

"Dad said they were destined to be together because they both came from dying lines." At Seth's questioning look, she explained, "Neither of them had any siblings. Nor did any of my grandparents. Or great-grandparents. It was always just one child in all those families. Weird, huh? And here I am, the last of a long line of only children."

He lifted the beer for a drink then passed it to her. She tipped it up, grimacing again, and wished she had a cold six-pack. She handed the beer to Seth then wiped the back of her hand across her mouth. She blew out a big breath then summoned all her courage to continue.

"During the fall when I was 23, I was visiting my parents for a weekend. We spent that Saturday night with friends of my parents and it was late when we headed home. It was raining. The roads were slick. We were driving along the river, went around a curve and hit a slippery spot. Suddenly we were airborne." She absently overlapped the corners of the hem of her robe on the top of her thighs and smoothed them repeatedly. "I don't remember much about it, it all happened so fast. Later, I was told that when the car landed it rolled several times before a tree stopped it from rolling all the way to the river."

She licked her suddenly dry lips. "I remember the sudden silence when the car finally stopped. So quiet. Just the ticking of the engine, the rain on the roof. There was glass everywhere, all the windows busted out. M-mom had gone through the—the windshield." Her voice trembled. She cleared her throat, swallowed hard, then glanced at Seth. "That's the glass across the front of the car that people see out of."

Seth nodded. His eyes never left her face.

Megan looked down at her lap. Her hands continued smoothing the robe. "The doctors said she probably died on impact. God, I hope so." She shuddered at the memory of the mangled bloody mess that had been her mother. Her staring dead eyes so surprised. "Dad had been sitting in back, but he wasn't there anymore. I crawled out through the broken window and called his name then looked for him in the dark and the rain. There were trees all around. I heard someone calling my name ... my mom's name. I looked and looked, calling him. Not far from the car was a drop-off down to the river. I heard dad's voice again, but I couldn't see him in the dark. I walked to the edge of the drop-off and looked all around. Then lightning lit up the night. I was looking straight across in front of me and saw him. He was a couple of yards away. Face up. Arms and legs spread wide and hanging down. With the pointed tip of a-a tr-tree com-coming out of his—his t-torso." Her voice shook. She heard Seth draw a sharp breath. Tears burned her eyes. Some spilled over and rolled down her cheeks. Her hands kept smoothing the robe on her thighs, over and over. "He was im-impaled on it. Like a-like a b-bug on a p-pin."

Seth's hand covered one of hers, stilling it, gripping it, hard. She hadn't even noticed him scoot closer to her on the sofa. "I'm so sorry. How bad were *you* hurt?"

She laughed a little wildly, dashing away tears on her face with her free hand. "Me? I barely had a scratch. Had some bruises the next day and I was sore for a while but ... but it was nothing. Not at all like ... like them. The doctors said it was a-a miracle." She drew in a shaky breath then slowly released it just as shakily.

Seth's warm, strong hand wrapped around hers. She clung to it. "I kept waiting for the car to explode. From the gasoline. They always explode in the movies. When I saw Dad, I-I wished the car *would* blow up. And kill me too."

Seth's grip tightened on her hand. "Don't say that."

She continued as if he hadn't spoken, "Dad asked about M-mom. Telling him she was dead was the h-hardest thing I've ever had to do. And he said, so typical of him, that she'd gone ahead to fix up their new place for him." She laughed again, brokenly. "I told him I was going to get help. I ran up the hill to the road. It was pouring down rain. I kept sl-slipping and sliding back down in the mud. Finally, I crawled up to the road. Not one car came by. It was late, two, three in the morning. I went back down to Dad and stayed there with him through that long horrible night. We talked. About everything. I was unhappy at work. Lori was working there by then and making my life miserable. For a while, I'd been thinking about freelancing, but I was too scared to give up the steady paycheck. Dad told me to go for it. Said he and Mom had put a little money aside and he wanted me to use it to give freelancing a try. We talked and talked. Childhood memories. Funny stories. A lot of *Do you remember* ... ? At some point," she heaved a trembling sigh, "he quit talking. Eventually, I realized he was dead."

Seth's thumb slowly rubbed the back of her hand.

She picked at the material on the armrest with a fingernail on her other hand. "You know the fence down below outside? With the pointed tips, like spears? I can't look at them. Whenever I look out the windows, I don't look down. I can't. When I do, I see Dad ... stuck on one of them." She brushed hair off her face. "I hope to God there's not a fire here or an emergency of some kind where the only way out is that window.

Because I don't know if I could jump out it with that fence down there. I'm too afraid I'd ... I'd end up like Dad. That fence is the only thing I don't like about this place."

Seth crossed his legs, leaning a little closer to her. "How long were you there before anyone helped you?"

"It was hours after daybreak. They had to cut the tree off below Dad's—Dad's b-body to carry him out of there. I insisted he and Mom be buried in the same coffin. They'd been together all their lives ... Their funeral was one of the biggest our town had ever seen. The church was so packed people stood outside. A year or so later, I quit my job and started working for myself. I couldn't have done it without the money Mom and Dad left me. Any beer left?"

Seth handed her the beer can.

She downed it then made a face. "That beer *sucked*." She burst into tears.

"Hey, hey." Seth took the can from her then put his arm around her, and pulled her, sobbing, to him. "I'm sorry I even brought it up. I'm so sorry."

Her voice muffled by his shirt, she wailed, "You don't understand!"

He stroked her hair. "Tell me."

"*I* was dr-driving. *I* had control of the car. I lo-lost control and k-killed my parents."

His arm tightened. "It was an accident. A terrible accident."

"It was my fault!" she blubbered She cried while he held her. He tucked her head beneath his chin and stroked her hair, rubbed her back. His body was hard and warm, and he smelled of horses and a faint scent of tobacco that had been smoked 100 years ago. Eyes closed, her ear pressed against his chest, she accepted his quiet comfort, more grateful for it than she'd thought possible. And wished she could stay in his strong arms forever.

After she had cried herself out, he asked, "Is that why you don't own a car?"

She nodded her head against his chest. "Although all the other reasons are true, too." She sniffled. "The expense. The hassle with parking. But mainly, I'm afraid to drive."

"Have you? Since then?"

"Did I get back on that horse? Donna made me. A week after the funeral. I did okay. That time. The next time, a couple days later, it was raining. I was with another friend. I made it about a block then pulled over and told her she had to drive. I couldn't do it. Not in the rain. That was the last time I tried, rain or shine. I rented a car once when I was out of town. Had it for a week and never even got behind the wheel. I just couldn't bring myself to do it. I hardly ever ride in a car even as a passenger unless it's in a taxi. But there are times when I miss it." She thought of the day she had ridden through the countryside with Barton to that trailer. She had enjoyed that. Something about the trailer jogged her memory. Ignoring it, she snuggled closer to Seth, savoring the moment.

His fingers brushed back hair from her temple. "I know it was hard for you tellin' me all that. I'm sorry I put you through it."

"It was hard for you too, talking about your father, wasn't it?"

"Yeah."

She drew away enough to look up at him. "His death wasn't your fault, Seth."

"Your parents' deaths weren't yours."

"You'll never convince me of that even if we had a lifetime."

A lifetime.

The words hung between them. One of the many things they would never have together.

His Adam's apple bobbed with a swallow. There was a sad droop to his mouth, so close to hers. So near yet so far.

Megan felt fresh tears well. She pushed away from him. "I have to go ... powder my nose." She rose, pulling her robe tight around her, and went to the bathroom. She flipped on the light and shut the door. She looked in the mirror. Puffy reddened eyes stared back at her. Her face felt tight and salty from dried tears. She blew her nose, sounding like a honking goose. She turned on the tap and splashed cold water on her face. She used the toilet then washed and dried her hands while looking at herself in the mirror. She felt drained and sad. She looked drained and sad. *Is this how you want him to remember you?* She smiled. It looked fake, forced. She smiled bigger. Worse. She made a face then left the bathroom.

He stood looking out the window, hands clasped behind his back. She approached him, stopping a few feet away. The Fort Worth skyline lit the black sky. A quarter moon peeked through blowing tree limbs. He turned around. His shirt had wet splotches on it.

"I'm sorry. I got your nice shirt all wet."

"Did you hear me complainin'?"

She shook her head. "You've always been a gentleman."

He looked surprised at her assessment of him. Surprised, and a little pleased. "Will you be leavin' soon? Headin' back up north?"

She shrugged. "There's nothing here for me."

Seth's gaze went beyond her. "What about him?"

She knew where he was looking. "Barton? I doubt he'll give me a second thought the day after I'm gone."

"What a fool," he muttered. Then his gaze shifted and stayed.

She glanced over her shoulder to see what had caught his attention. The bed.

Her heartbeat accelerated. Her gaze jumped to him. He stared at her with the same intensity he had given the bed. Her entire body pulsed. For the first time that night, his eyes reflected all she felt—pain at their separation, longing for what could never be, regret for all they'd never have.

"Miss Megan, I—" he frowned, and looked away. He ran a hand through his hair. His chest heaved with a sigh. He finally looked at her, only to say the words she had been dreading. "I reckon I better go."

As he walked to the sofa and put on his overcoat, she wondered if he was leaving because he felt like he was *coming apart,* or because he just wanted to get out of there.

He reached for his hat and settled it on his head. His eyes met hers. "I'll never forget you, Miss Megan."

She slowly walked toward him. "I'll never forget you either."

"Thanks for—for everything."

She forced a smile, willing herself not to cry. "My pleasure."

"I'm gonna miss our talks."

She swallowed back a lump of sobs. "I'm going to miss you."

He looked at her for a long moment then looked around the room, as if taking it all in one last time, until his gaze came to rest on her again. He stepped closer, raised his hand, and touched her cheek, a simple gesture he had made since their second meeting. It was her undoing. An ache seared her heart and tears filled her eyes.

"Don't cry, Miss Megan. Please don't."

"I can't help it."

Then she did what she had dreamed of doing, had imagined doing countless times.

She flung her arms around his neck, knocking his hat off, and kissed him the way she'd always wanted to kiss him. Openmouthed, her body pressed against his, her fingers in his thick hair. His arms circled her, and they clung together, kissing wildly, cramming a lifetime into a few precious moments.

He tore his mouth from hers and rasped in her ear, "You're makin' leavin' you harder."

"Is it Susannah?" she wailed.

He drew back enough to look at her. "What?"

"Is it Susannah you're dumping me for?"

He didn't know the term but seemed to understand the concept. "She's a good friend. Nothin' serious. There's another girl. Patsy. She has black hair like you. But not your pretty purple eyes."

"Vi-violet."

He gave a sad little laugh then kissed her again until they were both breathless and their hands started to roam. He took her by the upper arms and held her away from him. "I gotta go, Miss Megan." His hazel eyes searched her face. His palms slid down her arms to clasp her hands. He squeezed them, hard. "I-I gotta go." He released her, bent down to pick up his hat and settled it on his head. He gave her one last look then turned and headed for the door.

"Seth."

He paused and looked over his shoulder.

"That land Mr. Toby left you. Keep it. Don't sell it or divide or anything. Keep it. Someday it'll be worth a lot of money. Maybe not in your lifetime but someday."

He nodded then turned to leave.

"Seth!"

He stopped again, lowered his head a moment then looked at her.

"Buy a Model T when they start making them. Sometime in the early 1900s."

"I read about them. Henry Ford."

"Buy one and take good care of it. Buy two. One to drive and one to keep in pristine condition. Someday it'll probably be worth more than those thousand acres. Your children and grandchildren will thank you. I wish I could think of something you could buy or invest in that'll help you during *your* lifetime. Some stock or—"

"You shouldn't be tellin' me all this."

"—company. There's a depression sometime during the 1890s. Get your money out of the bank—"

"Miss Megan, don't tell me any of this."

She wrung her hands to keep herself from reaching for him and clinging to him and begging him not to go. "I want you to be happy." Her voice broke on the last word. She blinked tears from her eyes. "I want you to live a long, full life. I w-wish you ... love."

He stared at her from across the room. "I'll think of you and miss you every day of the rest of my life. I wish—" he broke off and glanced away from her, then back. His eyes glistened in the light. "Be happy, Miss Megan."

He turned and walked through the brick wall. The door shut behind him with a soft yet deafening click. He was gone.

Chapter 10

Loud knocking on the door jerked Megan awake. She pushed herself up on one elbow and squinted at the clock. 11:00 a.m. Any other morning, she would have shrieked at the lateness and jumped out of bed. Instead, she pulled the covers up, flopped down on her stomach, and shut her eyes. More knocking. Megan put a pillow over her head.

"Miss McClure? Miss McClure, you in there?"

Mrs. Powell. Shit. Megan shoved off the pillow and blankets then flung out her hand, anchored it over the side of the bed, and pulled herself to the edge. One leg slid off, then the other. Facing the bed, feet on the stool, she put her palms on the mattress and pushed herself upright. She put a hand on her throbbing head. Her mouth tasted like last week's garbage. She glanced around for her robe, looked down, and saw she had slept in it. Pulling it closed, she walked barefoot to the door and opened it.

"There you are." Mrs. Powell's bright smile faltered. "Are you feelin' poorly?"

"A little." Megan ran a hand over her unruly hair. "What can I do for you?"

"There's a young man waiting for you outside. Quite a handsome young man. Looks like one of those models in the Sears summer catalog." Mrs. Powell struck a pose in her tailored pants and summery blouse then gave Megan the once over. "I'll tell him you'll be down shortly. Give you some time to ... freshen up."

"Thanks." Megan shut the door, wishing whoever was downstairs would go away. The bathroom mirror showed her she looked the way she felt—like hell. It took several minutes to get her hair under control. The bed looked inviting. She turned her back to it and changed clothes. Foregoing a bra, she slipped on a t-shirt, grabbed a pair of shorts off the top of the dirty laundry pile and pulled them on, then, barefoot, left the room.

Downstairs, Mrs. Powell stood outside her office, shuffling through the mail. She glanced up. "That young man is not only handsome but polite and very nice. You should have put on some lipstick, dear."

Megan opened the front door.

"Mornin', darlin'." Barton flashed a cheery smile. His eyes narrowed. That smile disappeared. "You're not ready?"

She shaded her eyes from the sunlight and squinted at him. He had acquired a tan since she'd last seen him. He wore a short-sleeved tan shirt opened at the throat, displaying a tuft of black chest hair. He had one hand in the pocket of his shorts. He really did look like a magazine model. "Ready?"

"For our picnic today."

"Oh yeah. A picnic." She bit her lower lip. She'd forgotten all about it.

Barton pulled his hand out of his pocket to glance at his watch. "I'll wait while you get ready." He smiled. "I have the perfect spot. A nice secluded place in the shade. Just you and me and nature, darlin'."

The idea of spending a hot afternoon fighting off mosquitoes and Barton made her stomach roll. "I can't go. Not today."

He scowled. "Why not?"

"I received some bad news last night and I don't feel up to it."

His features softened. "I'm sorry, darlin'. Anything I can do?"

"No. Thanks."

He stepped closer. "Maybe you need to get out in the fresh air. Relax among some beautiful flowers." He trailed a finger down her arm. His voice took on a husky tone. "Maybe I can help take your mind off things a while."

His touch made her shiver, and not in a good way. She backed away from him. "Not today. I can't. I just c-can't." Tears welled up and from out of nowhere, a sob escaped her.

"Hey, hey," he said, the same way Seth had said the night before, and the memories and heartache sent tears rolling down her cheeks.

"I'm—I'm sorry." She turned and fled back inside the B&B, the door shutting behind her. Her head down, she hurried by Mrs. Powell, who said something, but Megan ran up to her room. She crawled back into bed and burrowed beneath the covers.

It wasn't until weeks later she recalled what Mrs. Powell had said. *I don't know what you said to him, but he looks mad enough to spit nails at a kitten.*

***

Late afternoon sunlight streamed through the windows when Megan finally dragged herself out of bed. After a long hot shower, she stood in a t-shirt and panties in the middle of the room, combing her long, wet hair. She looked around her very lived-in room. *I might as well start packing. There's no reason to stay any more.*

The mound of dirty laundry looked like the best place to start. She got a garbage bag and stuffed it with dirty clothes, followed by towels and washcloths from the bathroom. The leg of a pair of jeans stuck out from beneath the bed. She pulled it out then got down on her hands and knees and looked under the bed. She fished out a tank top and two panties. *How on earth did those get under there?* She tossed back the covers on the bed and pulled off the top sheet.

A piece of paper fluttered to the floor. Seth's note, which was long enough to be a letter. He had left it folded in half beneath the lamp on the table. She had read it after he left and cried her eyes out. She had read it again in bed and cried herself to sleep with it clutched in her hand.

Megan stripped the bed then stuffed the sheets and pillowcases into the dirty clothes bag. She picked up the paper and sat on one of the spindly-legged chairs by the table. Before, she had concentrated on the words. Now, she took a moment to study the paper itself. She rubbed it between her fingers. It felt heavier than present-day paper. Thicker, too. It wasn't exactly white, more a dingy white. She thought of her framed letter in the bank, yellowed with the passage of almost a century, yet she had written it just weeks ago. Seth's letter looked almost as fresh as present-day paper. It boggled her mind that just yesterday the paper had existed in 1885. The ink was blotchy and thinly applied in some places, thicker in others. She imagined Seth bent over the paper, carefully printing his thoughts, occasionally dipping the quill in the inkwell. Either he didn't know about the use of apostrophes in contractions, or he didn't care. He spelled *I'll* as *Ill*. *We're* as *were*. He also didn't use any commas. He had some misspelled words, many of them because he left off the *g* in all the *ing* words.

Megan laid the paper on top of the table and smoothed it with her hands. Sunlight shining through the windows warmed the back of her wet head. She crossed her ankles and leaned her elbows on the table as she reread Seth's letter.

Dear Miss Megan   20th March 1885

I wont be comin to see you no more. It pains me somethin fierce to rite those words but we cant go on like this. It aint fare to you or me. Were both stuck. You waitin for me to come thru that door. Me runnin up those stairs hopin to see you. Pointles. Crazy. Why did this happen, Miss Megan? Sure wish I new. But we gotta end this, for both our sakes. The man who took me an Lottie in when ma died left me his ranch. He died yesterday. His name was Toby Harcort. Mr. Toby I always cal him. I aint cried in a long time but I sure been sobbin like a babe since I found him in his bed. He looked mighty peacful. I reckon he went easy an Im glad for that but Im sure gonna miss him. It got me to thinkin how short life is. How it can change quick like. You lay down one night an never wake up. Thats it. End of the trail. Im 25 and I aint done nuthin. Aint seen nuthin. Dont have nuthin much to speak of. Now I got Mr. Tobys ranch. It aint big but its a start. Real pretty country. Youd like it. Sure wish you could see it. I want to make somethin of it. By more cattle. Grow some crops. I want a wife and young uns. I cant have any of that if I keep runnin up the stairs to see you. I met a girl named Patsy. She works in the saloon servin drinks playin piano an singin. She makes me laugh. I like her better than Susanah. Shes to serious. But so smart. She told me how to rite this note. First one I ever rote. I no you met a fella. I seen the piture. Reckon I shouldna took your piture but you look so pretty. I wanted somethin to member you. Not that Ill ever ever forget. I keep your piture in my shirt pocket near my heart. Itll stay there forever. When I die someone maybe my children will find it an wont they wonder at the pretty woman wearin such odd clothes. Wont they wonder. Its time you go home Miss Megan. Time you git on with your life. I hope your happy. I hope you do great things. Im gonna try to. Maybe youll read about me in the books an Ill make you proud. I probly wont change the world but maybe I can make it better for some folks, an change there world at least. Thanks for patchin me up. For everythin. Ive wondered if I love you. I dont no. I never been in love. But I sure like you heaps an will miss talkin to you. Ill think of you every day an never forget you as long as I draw breath. Mr Toby talked about somethin called well I dont know how to spel it but part of it sounds like tarnation. Means you come back in a later life. If there is such a thing as a later life maybe well meet again. Maybe well git another chance an thingsll be diffent. I sure hope so. You take care Miss Megan. Have a long good happy life. Ill never forget you.

Respectfuly yours　　　　　　　　　　　　*Seth O'Connor*

Megan traced his name with her finger. She felt sorry for smart, serious Susannah, replaced by party-girl Patsy. Megan hoped Seth came to his senses and chose the smart one. She ran her palm over the letter, slowly, lovingly. Someday someone, maybe one of her children if she ever got around to having any, would find it tucked among her precious things. "And won't they wonder," she murmured, smiling through a mist of tears. "Won't they wonder."

She went to the nightstand and picked up the notebook where she recorded her visits with Seth. Nearing the end of the second notebook. She sat down at the table and flipped to the back. Pen in hand, she wrote down the events of the night before. The last entry. *The end of our story.*

She folded Seth's letter and stuck it between the pages she'd just written then closed the notebook. Resting her hand on the cover, Megan whispered, "Goodbye, Seth."

Chapter 11

Bonnie looked up from the cash register till where she was counting change. Her eyes narrowed. "You look like someone ran over your dog then backed up an' ran over you. What's the matter?" She wrote down a figure on a tablet then counted dimes.

Megan pushed a barstool up to the bar. "Rough day."

"I reckon." Bonnie finished counting, wrote down the number then started on the nickels.

"I got some bad news last night."

Bonnie paused with her hands full of nickels. "I'm sorry. No one died I hope?"

Megan shook her head. She waited for Bonnie to finish counting all the change and add it up. "I'm going back to Chicago pretty soon."

Bonnie's head snapped up, her blue eyes wide. "You are?"

Megan nodded.

"I sure hate to hear that. I'll miss you. It won't be the same in this ol' place without you." Bonnie tapped the pen on the bar. She wiped her other hand on her jeans. Her brow knitted, she looked Megan in the eye. "You're gonna write the article before you leave, right?"

Megan hadn't given her writing projects a thought all day. Despite her good intentions of cleaning and packing, she'd only managed to put clean sheets on the bed and fill the garbage bag for a trip to the Laundromat, which meant hauling the bag all the way downstairs and across the street. The bag still sat by the door. It wasn't until she had walked into work and seen Bonnie that she even remembered the meth article, and realized she had a reason to stay around a little longer after all, whether she wanted to or not. "Of course. Please don't say anything to anybody else about my leaving. I'll give plenty of notice."

The pen quit tapping. Bonnie put the tablet in the register drawer and shut it. "Mum's the word. You wouldn't want to leave now anyway. Not with the big weekend comin' up."

"What weekend?"

"Memorial Day, silly. This place'll be hoppin'. You know what that means."

Good tips. I have to get that laundry done. And write that article so I can go home. Then what?

***

During a lull Sunday night, Megan slipped out the side door of The Tejas for a break on the concrete pad at the top of the stairs leading down to the parking lot. Another waitress named Sarah said she might be out soon too. Megan put one foot on the bottom rail of the handrail, rested her elbows on the top rail, and lifted her face to a slight breeze that stirred the warm, muggy air. She plucked at the front of her blouse to free it from her sweaty chest, and wished she had on shorts instead of skintight jeans. Cicadas and crickets sang their summer songs, and frogs croaked somewhere out in the darkness. She reached up both hands to lift her hair off her neck. She clasped her hands on the back of her head then, fingers still linked, stretched her hands high. It felt so good she moaned. Her feet and back ached.

The door opened, spilling the sound of twanging guitars into the quiet night.

"I was wondering if you were still coming out, Sarah," she said over her shoulder as the door shut, silencing the music. "I swear, if one more guy grabs my ass I'm going to deck him."

"Can't say as I blame them."

She turned at the sound of Barton's voice. "Oh, hi. I thought you were one of the girls."

He stood beneath the security light where a multitude of insects flittered. He wore jeans and a white shirt that emphasized his tanned skin and dark hair. "Mind if I join you?"

"Not at all."

He stood beside her at the handrail. "No unlit cigarette?"

"I stopped doing that. It was a dumb idea anyway."

"Been busy this weekend?"

She nodded. "Crazy. I'm glad the weekend is almost over."

"It was packed Friday night when I was here."

She looked at him in surprise. "I didn't see you."

"You were busy." He leaned one elbow on the handrail. "We sat over on the other side. Only place we could find a table." He waved a bug away. "Have there been any beer bottle bashes here this weekend?"

"Not yet. But it's bound to happen sooner or later."

"Beer bottle bash." He nudged her with his elbow. "Hell of a name for a country western song."

They laughed then stood together in silence as the sounds of the insects and frogs filled the night. A siren wailed nearby then faded into the distance.

"I'm sorry about the picnic." She brushed hair off her face. "It was a bad day."

"I hope things are better now."

"I'll live."

"Hey." He tilted his head toward the building. "They're playing our song."

"How can you hear that?"

"Good ears." He held out his hand. "Dance with me."

"I can't hear the music."

Barton looked down as if he was looking for something then glanced over the handrail and sprinted down the stairs.

She leaned over. "Where are you going?"

"Hang on." He stooped down and picked up a rock then hurried back up the stairs. He propped the door open with the rock. Anne Murray's voice floated out into the night. Barton stood and held out his hand.

Megan laughed. "You're persistent; I'll say that much for you."

He wiggled his fingers.

Megan placed her hand in his. He took her in his arms. And they danced.

Barton smiled at her as they waltzed beneath the glare of the security light. After a couple of spins around the concrete pad, he wrapped his arms around her while they did a slow back-and-forth. Megan rested her cheek against his chest and closed her eyes. He was warm and strong, like Seth had been on their last night together when he held her on the sofa. Unlike Seth, Barton was here and now. A Stephen Stills' song came to mind. *Love the One You're With.*

"I've missed you," Barton said as they swayed back and forth. When she didn't reply right away, he said in a disappointed tone, "I reckon you didn't give me a thought."

"Actually, I've been thinking about you quite a bit."

He drew away, his face in shadows. "Good thoughts, I hope?"

"Hmmm. A mix of good and not so good."

He snorted softly. "At least you're honest."

She tilted her head. "Aren't you?"

"Of course." He bent his head and kissed her.

She kissed him back as they slowly swayed from side to side while insects buzzed, and cicadas rattled.

His mouth left hers to feather kisses across her cheek then down the side of her neck. "Can I see you this week?" he murmured. When she nodded, he asked, "Try a picnic again? Tuesday? The holiday will be over, the crowds gone."

"I can't Tuesday." She had another appointment with Detective Sullivan. "Wednesday?"

"Great." He kissed her. "Pick you up about 11?"

"Okay. I better get back to work."

Barton's hand slid down her back to squeeze her ass. "Anyone in there ever gives you any trouble let me know, okay?"

Her hands linked around his waist, she leaned back, looking up at him. She remembered the night they had met and how he came to her rescue from the obnoxious drunk. "You going to rearrange his face?"

"If I have to."

"Bit of a temper, huh?"

"Just protecting what's mine, darlin'."

***

On Tuesday, Megan interviewed Detective Sullivan again. She finished her second page of notes, flipped to a new page, and asked her next question, "What are some ways meth dealers distribute their product?"

"Sometimes they hire people and pay them in cash, jewelry, electronics or other items taken in trade. Or pay them with meth. Sometimes they give someone meth for free, get the person hooked on it, and in exchange for more make the person deliver as needed. Sometimes they use blackmail, threats, even violence and force. Sometimes they use someone who unknowingly transports the drug. Say, in a briefcase, using the example you mentioned the last time we met."

She stopped writing as an image of Jim's briefcase popped into her head. Aware of the sudden silence, she looked up to find the detective regarding her with his usual bland expression.

His eyes locked with hers, he added, "And that person becomes an unwitting partner in organized criminal activity. A felony. Four to twenty years."

Beneath his steady gaze, she felt her cheeks flame, and had no idea why. Except that he made her feel uncomfortable and ... guilty. She ended their meeting shortly after that.

***

A steady breeze carrying the scent of new-mown grass swept through the Fort Worth Botanic Gardens. The temperature hovered near 90 but it felt about ten degrees cooler in the shade where Megan lay on her back on a blanket. Birds twittered in the branches overhead. She had her eyes closed, one hand laying on the blanket above her head, her ankles crossed while she thought about her interview with Detective Sullivan the day before, and about the briefcase with the smiley face beside her.

Megan recalled each incident with Jim's briefcase. The first time had been outside that restaurant. Barton parked the car while she waited for him with the briefcase, then Jim showed up before Barton returned. No big deal. The second time, Barton had waited and waited for an opportunity to open his car door until she finally grabbed the briefcase and took it to Jim inside some business. That time had been *her* choice. The next time she'd seen Barton in his car with the briefcase propped open against the steering wheel while he went through the paperwork. They had gone to the movies where she'd given the briefcase to Jim in the parking lot.

Separately, each incident seemed innocent enough. Putting them all together, however, the pattern seemed suspicious.

Or am I overreacting? Reading more into it than is there. Maybe I'm so immersed in methamphetamine from writing the article that my imagination is running wild. Maybe it's all just a coincidence.

Barton certainly didn't seem like the type of person who would be a drug dealer. Not that she'd ever known any drug dealers, but he didn't seem to fit the sleazy, shifty-eyed character she pictured as a dealer. *But what do I know?*

She ran through the three occasions again, looking at them from all angles. She found nothing odd about the first time. The second time, she had grabbed the briefcase from Barton because he was taking too long to get out and give Jim the briefcase and making her late for work. Unless that had been his intention all along. She frowned. The next time, she'd seen the paperwork in the briefcase with her own eyes. Unless Barton had had *two* briefcases behind his car seat. One with the paperwork in it, one with ... something else.

Someone made a throat-clearing sound then a man said, "Uh, excuse me, miss?"

Megan opened her eyes. "Hi, Jim. What's up?"

Barton's partner stood looking down at her. "Um, just here to get my briefcase."

"Forgot it again, huh?"

He gave a little laugh. "Sure did."

She felt something crawling on her leg and brushed it off. "Barton isn't here. He went to the john."

Jim glanced at his watch.

"What's in the briefcase, Jim?"

His gaze snapped to hers. His Adam's apple bobbed. "Wh-what?"

She rolled onto her side and propped herself up with her elbow. "What's in the briefcase? I tried to open it. It's locked."

He shifted from one foot to the other. "Paperwork. Contracts. Legal stuff." He glanced over his shoulder then held out his hand. "Can I have it, miss?"

Barton had given her the same answer when she'd asked him in the car on the way to the park. He'd shot her a look of surprise then quickly looked back at the road but not before she saw him scowl. Then he was his usual charming self, telling stories about his golf buddies.

"How come you keep forgetting such important papers? Doesn't make a lot of sense. What's *really* in the briefcase?"

He held out a hand. "I'll open it and show you."

Now we're talking. Megan sat up and picked up the briefcase with both hands. She held it for a moment. *One pound? Two pounds?*

"Miss?" Jim wiggled his fingers.

She handed him the briefcase.

Jim held it by the handle while he fished in his pocket with his other hand. "No key." He patted both shirt pockets. "Must be in the car. I'll fetch it and be right back." He turned and walked away with his limping gait, saying over his shoulder, "You wait there, miss. Be right back."

Shit. I walked right into that one.

***

"How was your picnic with the Hunk?" Bonnie asked that evening as she straightened the liquor bottles. A smattering of people sat at the tables, and half a dozen regulars congregated in their usual spot at one end of the bar, swapping lies, smoking cigarettes, and flirting with the waitresses. Two couples had the floor to themselves as they danced to the music playing on the jukebox.

Megan brushed hair back from her sweaty brow. The cool air inside was a relief after just coming in from the heat outside. "I fell asleep."

Bonnie laughed. "Fun date you are."

"I feel terrible about it. When I woke up, Barton was sitting beside me, reading a magazine. This one." Megan pulled a rolled-up magazine from the back pocket of her jeans and tossed it on the bar.

"Ooh, *Country Music Now.*" Bonnie grabbed it. She squealed, "Oh man, we're on the cover! The Tejas is on the cover!"

Megan laughed. "Check out page ten."

Bonnie found the page. "Lookee there. Your article."

Julia hurried over. "What'rey'all hollerin''bout?"

"Look!" Bonnie held up the magazine. "We're on the cover!"

"Farout! Lemme seethat." Julia took the magazine and held it in her hands. Hands that shook like an old person's, Megan noticed. She also noticed the long sleeves Julia wore.

Bonnie leaned her elbows on the bar. "Megan wrote the article in there about The Tejas. Page ten."

"Nokiddin'?" Julia looked at Megan with dilated eyes. "That'socool. Ican't believeIknow arealwriter." Julia turned to the regulars, waving the magazine. "Heyy'all, yagotta seethis." She scurried down the length of the bar.

"Great." Bonnie propped her chin on her hand. "I didn't even get to read it."

"I have one for you," Megan said. "Barton gave me several copies."

"That was sweet of him. What'd he say about your article?"

"He seemed surprised, impressed." *Damn good article,* he'd said. *I had no idea you wrote this well.* After that, she'd caught him giving her a funny look several times during their afternoon together, almost as if he was seeing her with new eyes and didn't quite know what to make of her. At the end of the bar, Julia babbled away with the regulars as they passed the magazine around. Megan asked Bonnie, "Julia's not doing well, is she?"

"She's been havin' trouble gettin' meth from her dealer. I think he's fixin' to go big time and doesn't want to deal with small potatoes like her."

"She told you that?"

Bonnie nodded. "The other night. She was sittin' out in the parking lot, cryin'. I sat down with her and we talked for a little bit. Well, she talked, and I tried to listen. She hadn't had any meth in a couple days and was in pretty bad shape. She's actually a lot better tonight, believe it or not. Poor kid." Bonnie grabbed a damp rag and swiped it across the top of the bar. "I'd like to find her dealer and kick him in the nuts for gettin' her hooked on that shit."

"Hey Megan!" hollered one of the regulars, a burly, bearded truck driver. "Come here, gorgeous." As Megan joined the group, Bonnie trailing behind, he added, "Maybe we should call you Barbara Walters."

Megan laughed and gave him a playful swat on the arm.

The men crowded around her, one of them holding the magazine. He said, "Great job!"

A gray-haired man in a business suit, asked, "Since you can write like that, what are you doing here?"

Another man with a big belly leaned in to say, "She's probably takin' notes about us for her next piece called *The Handsome Cowboys of Cowtown*."

The men roared with laughter, holding their beers high and slapping each other on the back. Other customers and waitresses drifted over to join the group and look at the magazine.

Megan soon found herself surrounded by adoring fans, as well as a slender man in his early thirties. The manager. Her boss.

Bonnie grabbed the magazine from someone and stuck it under his nose. "Look, Joe!"

Joe's eyes widened, and he grinned. "The cover of *County Music Now*? That's fan*tas*tic."

Bonnie flipped to page ten and put her finger on the byline. "Look."

He leaned closer. "Megan McClure?" He looked up. "*Our* Megan?" Grinning, he put his arm around Megan's shoulders. "This is great advertisement. Could increase business ten, fifteen percent. Maybe more. I could kiss you."

"Kiss her. Kiss her," the regulars chanted, pounding their beers on the bar. Soon everyone joined in.

Megan and Joe looked at each other, laughing. They shrugged, and he gave her a loud smacking kiss on the lips.

The crowd cheered.

Joe shouted, "Drinks on the house!"

The crowd went wild. Bonnie hurried back behind the bar.

"I want you to autograph it," Joe said to Megan. "Then I'm gonna frame it and hang it on the wall."

Megan thought of her framed letter hanging on a wall in a town south of Fort Worth. It seemed she was leaving her mark all over the North Texas area one way or the other.

Through the loud, boisterous crowd, Megan noticed Barton standing near the doorway, watching them. She stood on tiptoe and waved to him at the exact moment he turned and left.

"I'll be right back," she told Joe and anyone else within earshot. She pushed her way through the people and hurried after Barton. She shoved open the front doors and ran out into the warm night air. The usual chorus of crickets and cicadas greeted her. A half-moon hung amidst the fading pinks and oranges of a dying sunset. In the glow of the parking lot lights, she saw he had almost reached his car. She ran after him. "Barton! Barton!"

He turned around, flipped a cigarette away, and started back to her.

"Why are you leaving?" she asked breathlessly.

"Looks like y'all are having a good time in there." He put his hands in the pockets of his jeans. The overhead lights cast his face in shadows.

"Oh, they're all in a tizzy over the magazine. Holy moly." She laughed and flipped back her hair. "I felt like a celebrity. That was fun." She glanced toward The Tejas and said a bit wistfully, "I've missed that."

"Being a celebrity?"

She chuckled. "No, silly. I miss the camaraderie of coworkers. You don't have that with freelancing." *Our Megan.* When Joe said that, she had felt a rush of affection for him, Bonnie, her coworkers, even the regulars. "Were you just out and about?"

"I was sitting around the house doing nothing. Done with work. Nothing on the tube. And ... well, I got to thinking about you and ..." Barton looked down and kicked a stone with the toe of his sandal then looked back at her. "I missed you." Emotion roughened his voice.

She blinked in surprise. "That's so sweet." She touched his arm. "Why don't you come back inside? Joe's probably still buying rounds."

"He kissed you. I didn't like it."

Megan stepped back, crossing her arms. "Don't start that again."

"No, no," he held out his hand, "it's not that, it's—shit." He ran his hand through his hair. "This is coming out all wrong. Not at all like I imagined it on the way here." He stared at the ground, kicked the pavement a couple of times with his foot. He raised his head. "Megan, there's something I want to tell you. I'm not what I—"

A car tore into the parking lot and roared across the pavement. Teenagers hung out the windows, whooping and hollering, waving their arms. The car swerved back and forth and drove close to a row of cars before it straightened, tires squealing, and raced out another exit.

"Stupid kids," he muttered, staring after them.

"You were saying?"

Barton looked at her. "Never mind. This isn't the time or the place. You go on back and enjoy your camaraderie. I'll see you soon and we'll talk then."

"You're clearly struggling with something."

"Just my feelings for you."

He said the words solemnly, quietly, yet to Megan they sounded louder than the noisy insects. "Barton—"

"Not here. Not now." He cupped her cheek and leaned down to give her a quick kiss. "Go back to work and have fun."

She put her hand on his chest. "Thanks again for the magazines. Especially the extra copies. They've about pawed one to pieces."

She ran back across the parking lot to The Tejas. She paused with her hand on the front door and looked back.

Barton stood beneath the parking lot lights, hands in his pockets, watching her.

He looked lonely.

She recalled his words. *I'm not what I—*

What had he been about to say?

***

Megan finished her article on methamphetamine several days later. She let Detective Sullivan read it. Then Bonnie. Megan edited it using their suggestions. On Monday, she delivered it to the editor of the Star-Telegram. Upon leaving the building, she practically skipped down the steps, buoyant with relief. That afternoon she and Barton went to a movie and necked like teenagers in the back row. Two days later, they went to the Kimbell Art Museum and the Amon Carter Museum. Afterwards, they made out in his car in a park, the air conditioner running full blast. They went bowling one afternoon, miniature golfing another. Barton was funny, affectionate, and treated her like a queen. But he never brought up what he'd wanted to talk about that night.

Every now and then, the briefcase with the smiley face accompanied them, to Megan's annoyance, until Jim came to reclaim it.

***

One evening in early June, while waiting for her drink order, Megan said to Bonnie, "I saw the flyer in the break room."

"About the Chisholm Trail Round-Up this month?"

Megan nodded. "Sounds like a big deal."

"It is." Bonnie's dangling earrings danced with her movements as she made a margarita. "There's a parade, chuckwagon cook-offs, Indian powwows, mock gunfights, music, tons of food, arts and crafts. Plenty of beer. What's a festival without beer?"

"I saw what Joe wrote on the bottom about wearing a costume that weekend. Where am I going to find something like that? In a week?"

"Check the thrift stores, second-hand shops, Goodwill. You never know what you'll find. There's a church having a basement sale this Thursday through Sunday. I'm fixin' to check it out Thursday morning. Wanna go? I'll pick you up around ten."

***

On Thursday, Megan and Bonnie went to a church basement where rows of tables lined the concrete floor. Some tables held kitchenware, appliances, and gadgets. Knickknacks, picture frames, lamps, and floral arrangements made of plastic flowers crowded another table. Some had dolls, board games, roller skates, toy soldiers, stuffed animals, and all sorts of toys. Rows of books filled two tables. One table had a jumbled pile of cowboy boots of all sizes, many with rundown heels. Racks of clothing stood along one wall. A small crowd of mostly women pawed through the clothes, working their way down the racks. Megan and Bonnie joined them.

After several minutes, Bonnie said, "Wow. Look at this one." She pulled out a hanger holding a floor-length bright blue dress. It had a scooped neck and short puffed sleeves, all edged with black lace, and a black lace bow in the back. Bonnie tried it on in a makeshift fitting room, which consisted of blankets thrown over clothesline strung in rectangles in one corner of the basement. The dress flattered her slim figure and fell in graceful folds around her curves. The color made her eyes even bluer.

"Bonnie, you look beautiful." Megan smiled. "Get it. My treat."

"Don't be sil—"

"I'm buying," Megan insisted. "Since you won't take any gas money for all the times you haul me around."

Bonnie hugged Megan. "Thanks so much. Now we have to find something for you."

Megan pushed one hanger after another down the rack, finding nothing she liked and growing more discouraged.

Until halfway down the last rack.

Chapter 12

The color caught her eye. Megan held the floor-length dress against her front.

Bonnie walked around the end of the rack with her blue dress draped over one arm. She whistled. "That's some dress." She reached out and rubbed the material between her fingers. "Feels like silk."

"You think so?"

Bonnie shrugged. "I'm no expert when it comes to fabric and sewing and stuff. I can sew on a button or hem something but that's about it."

"Same here."

Bonnie bent closer. "What's that?"

"What?"

"There's something on the inside of the neckline."

Megan looked at the lining around the neck. "It's a piece of paper safety pinned to the lining."

Bonnie craned her neck. "What's it say?"

"CH."

"Huh?"

"Just the initials CH."

"Let me see." Bonnie held the neckline with the small square piece of paper attached to it. "CH. Maybe it's someone's name." She looked at Megan and grinned. "Celeste Holm."

"Celeste Holm?"

"You know, the movie star? She was in *All About Eve, High Society*. Maybe this is one of her dresses."

Megan eyed Bonnie doubtfully. "I don't think—"

"Charlton Heston!" With a look of delight, Bonnie gave Megan a little shove. "Maybe someone wore it in one of his movies. Wouldn't that be cool?"

Megan laughed. "I don't remember seeing anything like this in *Ben Hur* or *The Ten Commandments*."

"Try it on," Bonnie said, "before I do."

Megan went inside the dressing room, hung the hanger on a hook, and took off her clothes. Turning to the dress, she grinned. *I love the color!* A rich purple. She held out one side of the dress and saw panels of an even deeper purple. She flipped the hanger and the dress around and started unbuttoning from the top. Her hands shook with excitement, making her fumble with many of the buttons. They were about the size of a nickel and looked like they were made of bone.

"Finally," she muttered, finishing the last button.

She took the dress off the hanger and pulled it over her head. A faint scent of mothballs enveloped her as the purple material slid down around her body. She tugged everything into place and smoothed her hands down her hips. She reached behind and buttoned as many of the buttons as she could.

When she stepped out from behind the dressing room curtain, Bonnie's eyes widened. "Whoa. You look like a million bucks."

"Would you button it up for me?"

"Turn around."

Megan did so, holding her long hair to one side.

"Jeeze Louise, there's about two dozen damn buttons," Bonnie muttered. "Let's see how it looks." She stepped back and gave Megan the once over as she spun around. "Boy howdy, Megan, it looks like it was made for you."

Megan ran a light finger across the lace on her chest. "It's gorgeous." The same cream-colored lace circled the puffed sleeves. The bodice hugged her torso. She held the full skirt out to one side.

"I bet if you had on a petticoat that skirt would really flare," Bonnie said, "and show off the colors on those pleats."

"Those are called godets," a woman behind them said.

Megan and Bonnie turned around.

An older woman, late-fifties maybe, smiled. "Sorry. I overheard your conversation."

"What'd ya call those pleats?" Bonnie asked.

"Godets."

"Never heard that high fallutin' word before."

"It's a sewing term for an extra piece of fabric set into a garment that adds width and volume. Or flare, as I heard you mention." The woman smiled at Bonnie then looked at Megan. "Hold the dress out on each side and I'll show you."

Megan did so.

"See here?" The woman pointed to the pleats. "The full skirt has two godets of deep purple inserted on either side of this lighter purple panel in the center. A striking contrast. And look at those adorable satin bows."

Megan looked down at the bows. There were four on each godet. They were the same color as the bodice and skirt. They were small at the hipline, gradually increasing in size as they neared the hemline.

Bonnie nudged Megan. "Here's your expert."

Megan said to the woman, "You seem to know a lot about sewing."

"Been sewing all my life. You curious about this dress?"

"Yes. But only if you have the time."

The woman shrugged. "I'm just here looking at stuff I don't need but will probably end up buying anyway. What do you want to know?"

"Is the dress made of silk?"

"Most definitely. Many old dresses were."

"How old do you think this one is?" Megan asked.

The woman tilted her head. She had short gray hair and wore a blue pantsuit. "My guess is before the 1900s."

Megan's eyes widened. Seth's time.

"It looks like it was hardly worn," Bonnie said.

"It's in remarkably good shape for its age." The woman reached out to touch the dress then hesitated. She looked at Megan. "May I?"

"Of course."

"I'm curious about the stitching." The woman stepped behind Megan and lightly touched the waistline. She bent closer to study it. She straightened and ran her finger along the neckline, pausing at the spot where the cream-colored lace attached to it. She pulled it out a little bit and looked at it through squinted eyes, running her thumb over it.

"I love this lace across my chest." Megan touched the lace that went from just below one shoulder to just below her other shoulder and formed a V below her bust line. It was edged with a light purple ribbon and cream-colored lace.

"It's called a yolk," the woman replied.

"And this ribbon?" Megan drew her finger down the purple ribbon in her cleavage.

"That's called shirring, which is a gathering made by drawing up parallel lines of stitches. Very elegant." The woman bent over to pick up the hem and looked it over as she drew several inches of material through her hands. "Amazing. It's hand-stitched." She dropped the hem and straightened. "Beautiful workmanship. They don't make clothes like this anymore. It's a beautiful dress. Hardly worn at all, from the looks of it. And it doesn't smell like so many old clothes do. They're either moldy and musty or reek of cleaning chemicals." The woman patted Megan's shoulder. "Buy it, dear. With your hair and eyes, it was meant for you."

"Thank you for all the information," Megan said.

"My pleasure." With a smile, the woman walked away.

"Wow," Bonnie said. "That was impressive."

"Would you unbutton me, Bonnie?"

Bonnie stepped behind Megan and went to work. "You gonna get it?"

"You bet." Megan stepped into the dressing room and changed back into her clothes. She put the dress back on the hanger then ran her hand down the purple silk. A dress possibly from Seth's time. *I wonder if he'd like it on me.* It didn't seem fair to find it now, after Seth had told her goodbye.

She grabbed the hanger and left the dressing room. She and Bonnie carried their dresses to a table near the main door to pay for their purchases.

"Hey Bonnie!" a girl hollered from a couple of aisles over.

Bonnie waved. She said to Megan, "I'll be right back."

"Give me your dress. I'll meet you outside."

Megan carried the dresses to the checkout table.

"How lovely," the woman standing behind the table said as she held up the purple dress. She gave it a shake then looked at the inside of the collar.

"What does that piece of paper mean?" Megan asked.

"It was donated." At Megan's questioning look the woman explained as she folded the dress, "We often receive vintage clothes from many of Fort Worth's oldest families for our sales. Draws a bigger crowd." She put the folded dress on the table and gave it a pat then opened an index box. She peered through glasses perched on her nose as she flipped through index cards. "Ah, here it is." She pulled out a card. "It was donated by Candace Huntington. It's been in her family since the late 1800s. Says there's a petticoat, too." Her brow furrowed. "How odd. There's a question."

"A question?"

"What color are your eyes?" The woman looked at Megan. "Deep, deep blue? Purple?"

"Violet," Megan said without thinking.

The woman grinned. "It appears you answered correctly. I'll get the petticoat. It's on the rack back here."

"May I see that card please?"

"You can have it." The woman handed Megan the index card then turned to a rack of clothes behind her.

Megan took the card and read the words written in an elegant, flowing script. *Before selling this dress, ask the buyer, What color are your eyes? Then say, Deep deep blue? Purple? If she answers violet, sell her the dress. Otherwise, make some excuse and say it's not for sale. Dear Buyer of this purple dress, please call me at your earliest convenience to learn about its history. Candace Huntington.* A local phone number followed.

Megan read it again. *What the hell?*

Suddenly the theme song from *The Twilight Zone* played. It sounded so real. It grew louder and louder until it seemed to fill the church basement. The hair rose on the back of her neck when Rod Serling said just as clearly as if he were standing near her, "You have just entered *The Twilight Zone*."

"What a voice that man had," someone said next to Megan.

Megan's head whipped around. "You hear him too?" she asked a heavy-set woman, who gave Megan a startled look before backing away.

"Johnny, what did I tell you about touching things? Turn that TV off and get over here."

Megan spun the other way and saw a harried-looking woman grab a little boy's arm and drag him away from a table cluttered with clock radios, alarm clocks, transistor radios, two turntables, and a small TV showing *The Twilight Zone* blinking off the screen. Megan felt like a fool. Although it certainly seemed appropriate after reading that card.

She stuffed the index card in her purse.

"Here you go." The woman behind the checkout table returned with her arms full of petticoat. She and Megan stuffed it into a big plastic bag along with the purple dress. Bonnie's dress went into its own bag. Megan paid with the fifty-dollar tip from Barton.

"Thanks for buyin' my dress." Bonnie started her truck.

Megan rolled down the window to let the breeze into the hot cab. "I'm buying lunch, too. Barbeque sound good?"

They chatted and laughed over barbeque sandwiches, fries, and drinks while the index card with a phone number on it loomed in the back of Megan's mind. A couple times she came close to telling Bonnie about it, but that would ultimately lead to telling her about Seth, and Megan couldn't do that. She took a bite of her sandwich and wished she could talk to Donna, tell her everything. But she was a thousand miles away.

Back at the B&B, her arms full of the bulky plastic bag containing the dress and petticoat, Megan hurried up the front steps and struggled to open the door. Inside, she put the plastic bag on the floor then dug in her purse for the index card. She picked up the house phone and dialed the number on the card.

"Hola?" a Spanish-speaking woman answered.

"Hello. I would like to speak to Candace Huntington, please?"

"Meesis Huntington ees not able to come to thee phone right now. But I weel geeve her a message, por favor?"

"My name is Megan McClure. I bought a purple dress today and—"

"*You* bought the purple dress?" the woman's voice rose with excitement. She sounded breathless.

Megan's hand tightened on the phone. "Y-yes."

"Geeve me your name again and spell eet, por favor?"

Megan did so, followed by the phone number of the B&B.

The woman carefully repeated it. "She weel be so pleased. I weel tell her when she ees up and about. She has good days and bad days."

"I'm sorry to hear that." Megan had the phone in a death grip. *She will be so pleased?*

"What can one expect at her age, no?"

"If you don't mind my asking, how old is Mrs. Huntington?" Megan listened, and a chill skittered over her skin. She said thank you and hung up, then rubbed goose bumps on her arms.

Candace Huntington was 100 years old.

***

After work that night, Megan put on her new old dress and stared at herself in the oval mirror on the vanity. Running a hand down her side, she marveled at how well the cut of the dress accentuated her bust and waist. The color could not be more flattering. The whole dress was ... perfect.

She tilted her head to one side as she gazed at her image. *Too perfect to be a coincidence? It looks like it was made for you,* Bonnie had said. *It was meant for you,* that other woman had said. You *bought the purple dress?* the Spanish-speaking woman had asked. *She weel be so pleased.* Questions and a wild possibility whirled through Megan's mind until she put a hand to her forehead and muttered, "Stop it."

She reached up behind her to unbutton the top buttons. Her gaze landed on Seth's door reflected in the mirror. She slowly lowered her arms. Maybe the dress was the key. She marched across the room, grasped the doorknob and ... it wouldn't budge. She snapped her fingers and went to put on the petticoat. It was flouncy, made of silk. Once she had on the whole ensemble, she stood before the mirror. *Holy moly, all I need is a big fancy purple hat and I'm Scarlett O'Hara.*

The door still would not open. Dejected, she once again reached behind to unbutton the top buttons when she saw a flash of something on the dresser reflected in the lamplight. The old coins. She went and picked them up, held them on her palm.

She had the clothes. She had the money.

She marched across the room, her hand reaching for the doorknob of the door that would not open.

But it will. It will.

She had confidence. She had the trappings of the time. Most of all, she had desire. She wanted to go there. She wanted to see Seth. She wanted that more than anything. Even if he didn't want to see her.

Her hand closed around the glass knob cool to her touch.

She turned it.

Nothing.

She twisted it harder.

It didn't budge.

"Damn it!" She beat her fist on the door. "What more do you want?" she hollered at it. She kicked it. Kicked it again, harder.

It did not open.

She pressed her ear against it, listening.

Silence.

She took off the dress and petticoat and went to bed. She lay awake for hours, staring at the dark shape of the purple dress hanging on a hook on the outside of the bathroom door. On the dresser, the old coins glinted in the light seeping through the curtains. On the nightstand lay the index card bearing words written by a 100-year-old woman. A woman from Seth's time. Who owned a dress from his time. Who might have even known him.

A woman who will be so pleased about—what?

Chapter 13

Megan shut the front door of the B&B with one foot while juggling a 12-pack of beer, a bag of ice, and three bags, one with toiletries in it, one full of snacks, and one containing her lunch—hamburger and fries from a burger joint down the street.

Mrs. Powell stood in the hallway, talking on the phone. She saw Megan and waved. "She just walked in." She handed Megan the phone. "It's for you, dear."

Megan put the 12-pack on the floor and laid the bag of ice on it. She set the bags on a chair in the hallway. The smell of the burger wafted up. Her stomach growled. "Thanks." She took the phone from Mrs. Powell, who smiled and went into her office. Hoping the caller was Candace Huntington, Megan put the phone to her ear. "Hello, this is Megan." She heard the voice of the editor at the *Star-Telegram* she'd been working with. She listened a moment. "I'm glad you like it. Two Sundays? Of course." Her eyes widened at the mention of more money. "I'll bring it to you on Thursday. Thank you very much." She hung up and punched her fist in the air. "All *right*." She dialed Bonnie's number.

"Bonnie? I just got a call from the editor at the *Star-Telegram*. They're going to run the meth article in two parts. The first part will be in the paper two weeks from this Sunday. The second will be in the next Sunday paper. They want seven hundred more words. Isn't that great?" She held the phone away for a second while Bonnie screamed then put it back to her ear and laughed. She listened a moment. "Yeah, I was thinking of adding that part. And remember when you said—yes, that too. I'll call you if I have any questions. I'd better get writing. See you later at work."

Megan hung up, feeling a mix of emotions. She was proud of her article, glad they liked it, thrilled they were making it a two-part series, jubilant over the extra money, and disappointed the caller hadn't been Candace Huntington. "Damn," Megan muttered. She had planned to do some research on Candace Huntington. That would have to wait. She gathered all her purchases and headed to her room. The bag of ice bumped against her leg with each step. In her room, she dumped a variety of snacks—bags of chips, packages of cookies, and some fresh fruit—into the bottom drawer of the vanity, put the rest of the groceries away, then sat down to write.

The next few days passed in a blur as Megan wrote feverishly during the day and waitressed at night. She declined two afternoon dates with Barton and begged off a night at work to finish the addition to the meth article. After dropping it off at the office of the *Star-Telegram* on Thursday morning, Megan finally went in search of information about Candace Huntington.

***

Megan closed the book *Oil Barons of Fort Worth* and put it on top of *Who's Who in Fort Worth, First 25 Years of the 20st Century*. A stack of four other books sat on her left. She leaned back in the chair and stretched her aching back. She covered a yawn and glanced at the clock on the wall of the Fort Worth Main Public Library. Three hours had passed since her arrival from the courthouse, where she'd spent two hours searching old records. She pulled over her notebook and read the notes she had gathered from microfiche, history books, and public records about Candace Huntington.

Candace Pryor—born January 1, 1881, to Hiram and Addie Pryor. One sister, Cordelia, 3 years older. Father owned several businesses in FW, including livery and blacksmith shop, cigar emporium, cooper shop, plus lumber mills in E. TX. Later made fortune in oil. 1890s, family lived in mansion in Quality Hill. Age 19, 1900, Candace married Thomas Hume, banker, eldest son of local banker. Active in church, charity work. He died in house fire 1905. She survived. Age 26, 1907, Candace married Montgomery St. John, of law firm St. John, Haslett, & St. John. Lived in FW, summer homes in CO and upstate NY. Supported the arts, child labor laws, prison conditions, women's rights. Active suffragette. Active with church. St. John died in train crash in 1923. She survived. Age 45, 1926, Candace married Freddie Stacy. Occupation unknown, professional gambler? Moved to Europe 1927, lived in Paris, London, Brussels, left before WWII, back to FW. After war, went to Far East, Tibet, Jerusalem, Africa. Freddie died, cause unknown, 1947. Age 68, 1949, Candace married John Dorlaw, doctor, 17 years younger, in Cairo. 2 years later he died of fever. Age 75, 1956, Candace married Joseph Huntington, childhood friend. Lived in FW. She ran for city council, lost. He died 1969; she was 88. Last marriage. Sister Cordelia died in 1974, age 96. Unmarried, no children. Worked in financing then publishing. Parents died in plane crash in 1948. Candace survived.

Megan propped her elbows on the table and read her summation. *Candace Pryor Hume St. John Stacy Dorlaw Huntington Wealthy, educated, active in church, community, local government. Raised millions for charities, gave away personal millions. Traveled the world. Survived 2 plane crashes, 1 train crash, 1 fire. Searched for spiritual enlightenment. Ran for public office in her 70s, lost. Married 5 times. No children.*

Megan picked up her pen and added, *Lived life to the fullest.*

I can't wait to meet her.

***

Back at the B&B, Megan used the phone in the hallway. "Hello. This is Megan McClure again. I was just wondering—"

"Oh, Mees Megan—do you mind eef I call you Mees Megan por favor?"

"Of course not."

"Mees Megan, Meesis Huntington ees een the hospeetal."

"I'm sorry to hear that." Megan gripped the phone. "Is it ... is it serious?"

"I don't know. They are geeving her tests. I hope she ees home soon. I weel call you then."

"Yes, please do. Thank you. Give Mrs. Huntington my best regards."

Megan hung up then closed her eyes. *Please get well. Don't die yet.*

***

"Boy, am I glad it's Sunday night. Finally," Bonnie said as she made a tequila sunrise.

"I'll say." Megan put her elbows on the bar and propped her chin on her knuckles while waiting for her order. "What a weekend. I'm beat."

"Joe said Chisholm Trail Round-Up Days was the best weekend we've had since opening night. He also said several people mentioned they read about The Tejas in that magazine. He seemed pretty pleased about the extra exposure." She finished the tequila sunrise then picked up a bottle of vodka and splashed a generous amount into a glass. She grabbed a quart of orange juice and added it to the vodka, filling the glass to the brim, then stirred it up. "Maybe you'll get a little bonus out of that."

Megan laughed. "That'd be nice." Money seemed to be flowing her way lately. The extra pay for the meth article addition, a recent check from a previous article, and the generous tips from the three previous nights.

"How many marriage proposals are you up to now?"

"Five."

Bonnie frowned. "Damn. You're one ahead of me." She glanced at her watch. "There's still time for me to catch up." She carried the drinks to a customer on the other side of the bar.

"Megan?"

She turned around. Barton stood a few feet behind her. Unexpected pleasure surged through her at the sight of him. They hadn't seen each other in over a week. *I've missed him,* she realized, a little stunned by the revelation. She smiled at him. "Hi. How've you been?"

"Busy." His appreciative gaze slowly traveled down the length of her and back up before he stepped closer. "You look stunning."

She struck a pose in the purple dress. "Quite a dress, isn't it?"

"Darn tootin'. I like your hair that way."

She had the top and sides pulled back and hanging in long ringlets down her back.

"But the shoes are the real kicker."

She lifted the silk skirt and petticoat and stuck out one tennis-shoed foot. They both laughed. "Comfort before looks. What have you been up to?"

His eyes twinkled in the smoky light. "I had a good week. Made a very good deal."

"Here're your drinks, Megan," Bonnie said.

Megan turned back to the bar to pick up her order.

Bonnie shot a glance Barton's way then made big eyes at Megan.

"Stop it," Megan hissed.

"What a hunk," Bonnie said in a low voice.

Megan silently agreed as she looked sideways at Barton. His coal-black hair lay in attractive waves. His clean-shaven face was tan and rugged. He wore a shirt with brightly colored geometric designs all over it, tight dark jeans, and black cowboy boots. Megan wrinkled her nose at Bonnie, picked up her tray, told Barton she'd be right back and walked off to deliver the drinks. The dress swayed like a bell around her. She felt Barton watching her and looked over her shoulder. He was leaning back against the bar, ankles crossed, a bottle of beer in one hand. He tipped the bottle towards her and smiled a smile that seemed just for her, sexy and tempting. A flush of warmth rushed over Megan, and desire blossomed deep inside her.

Tonight, we're going to have sex.

The thought popped unexpectedly into her head and sent a blast of heat through her.

Yes. Tonight, her answering smile promised him before she turned away, carrying the tray of drinks. She squeezed between two chairs, squashing the dress. It popped back into shape until the next tight spot.

When she returned to the bar, Barton said, "The gorgeous girl in blue," he dipped his head towards Bonnie, "said I could steal you for a dance if you're willin'. How 'bout it, darlin'?"

Bonnie did look gorgeous in the floor-length blue dress with her blonde hair piled high on her head. She shrugged.

Megan held out her hand to Barton. "I'd love to."

He took her hand and pulled her close for a kiss. "I don't think I could have gone another minute without kissing you. Seems ages since I've seen you."

She pressed herself against him. Her dress ballooned out on each side of her. "Maybe you should kiss me again, to make up for lost time." He chuckled before lowering his mouth to hers for a more thorough kiss. Beneath the cover of the wide dress, Megan placed her hand on Barton's thigh and slowly stroked it. She heard his sharp intake of breath. He raised his head and looked in her eyes while her hand rested on his thigh.

He lifted one eyebrow.

"Are you two going to dance?" Bonnie asked from behind the bar. "Or what?"

Megan pushed away from him and took his hand. "Come on." She led him to the dance floor, saying over her shoulder, "We can *or what* later. At my place."

Barton's other eyebrow shot up. He grinned. "Yes, ma'am."

They walked out onto the floor just as the first notes of the next song played on the jukebox.

"Hear that?" Barton put his arm around her waist and linked his other hand with hers. "They're playing our song." They waltzed away to Anne Murray's voice.

He maneuvered her between the dozen or so couples on the floor. Most of them, male and female, wore blue jeans and western shirts, and most of the men wore cowboy hats, mainly black. They all gave Barton and Megan plenty of room because of her wide skirt. Barton's arm was warm and strong around her as they glided and spun and twirled. They danced together effortlessly, gracefully, and Megan wondered if he was as good in bed as he was on the dance floor. She'd know soon enough.

The other couples gave Barton and Megan more room, and the next thing she knew they were the only couple dancing.

She said breathlessly, "Everybody's watching us."

"Of course, they are. You're the most beautiful woman here." He pulled her close. "Shall we give them something to look at?"

She shot a nervous glance at the crowd standing at the edge of the dance floor. "Oh, no, no. I'm not—"

"Relax and follow me." He dropped a kiss on her forehead. "You're the belle of the ball."

His hand on her back, Barton pushed her away. He twirled her around then pulled her back. They glided across the floor, moving as one, stepping one way then the other. He dipped her, pulled her to him, and dipped her again then danced her to the other side of the floor and back again. Megan half expected him to lift her up in the air. They spun around and around, her dress swaying and billowing, her ringlets flying. The faces of the crowd became a blur. Barton smiled at her.

She managed a weak grin, feeling dizzy.

He whirled her and twirled her around the dance floor. The people surrounding them spun by faster and faster. The blue of their jeans and the black of the cowboy hats formed a smear of color circling the room.

Then everything changed.

Megan blinked. Blinked again.

She saw women in beautiful, bell-shaped ball gowns in every color of the rainbow, their upswept hair sporting ringlets and fancy combs. She saw with men with beards and mustaches, wearing black coats and trousers with white shirts and black string ties. Lanterns strung high circled the dance floor, and instead of a ceiling with recessed lighting, she saw a sky of black velvet speckled with twinkling stars. Everything spun around and around, the women's gowns a kaleidoscope of color, the stars glittering like a disco ball.

Megan tore her gaze from the bizarre vision and looked up at her partner. She gasped.

Seth smiled at her, his hazel eyes warm and inviting, the strong lines of his lean face softened by the glow of the lanterns. His big, rough hand held hers as they waltzed to the music of fiddles beneath the brilliant stars.

Everything spun, the people, the lanterns, the stars.

Megan tripped over his foot and felt herself falling.

Strong hands gripped her upper arms.

"Don't worry. I've got you," Seth said. "I'll never let you go."

"Whoa there, darlin', guess I got a little carried away."

Dizzy, dazed, held upright by two strong hands, Megan lifted her gaze and saw—

"Darlin'? You all right?"

She blinked several times then looked into Barton's troubled eyes. Concern furrowed his brow. She glanced beyond him. No lantern lights. No multitude of stars overhead. No people dressed in old-fashioned clothes. No fiddle music. No Seth. Everything was normal again. A smattering of applause and whistles came from the blue-jean clad crowd watching from the edge of the floor. Several couples returned to the dance floor when the next song blared from the jukebox.

Megan managed a shaky laugh as she leaned against Barton, real and solid. "I tripped. Clumsy me."

I'll never let you go, imaginary Seth had said.

Liar. You already did. She wrapped her arms around Barton's waist and held on, anchoring herself to here and now.

He held her close. "I think I overdid the spinning."

"I did get a little dizzy. Plus, I'm starving. I haven't had a decent meal in days." She gave him a quick hug. "I'd better get back to work. Thanks for the dance."

His hand cupped her cheek. "You sure you're okay? You're awful pale."

"I'm fine. Just hungry and tired."

He led her off the dance floor. Several people stopped to compliment them on their dancing as they walked hand in hand to the bar where Bonnie was drawing a draft.

"You two looked like Fred Astaire and Ginger Rogers out there."

Barton reached into his jean's pocket with his free hand and pulled out some bills. "Thanks for letting us dance." He stuck two twenties in the tip jar.

Bonnie's eyes widened. "Any time, sugar." She looked at Megan with raised eyebrows as she nodded to a tray of drinks. "There's your order."

Barton said to Megan, "What time do you get off?"

"I should be out of here by eleven or so."

"You need to eat. I'll take you wherever you want to go."

"Actually," she said as she looked over the drinks on her tray, making sure the order was correct, "what I'd really like is a thick juicy steak, medium rare. A baked potato with butter and sour cream and a sprinkle of chives on top. Some fresh vegetables. And a salad with cucumbers, peppers, tomatoes, the works. With French dressing." She looked at Barton. "But I suppose that late on a Sunday night there's not much chance of all that." She shrugged, picked up her tray and went to deliver the drinks.

When she returned Barton said, "I've got an idea. I'll be back for you around eleven."

***

He leaned against his Corvette, smoking a cigarette, when she walked out after work.

"Where are we going?" she asked when they were seated in his car.

"It's a surprise." He drove south down the dark, empty streets of downtown Fort Worth then parked near the Convention Center.

Megan gave Barton a puzzled look as he helped her out of the car.

"Have you heard of the Water Gardens?" he asked.

"Yes. I've been meaning to see it."

He took her hand. "You're gonna love it."

Hand in hand, they walked into a shadowy landscape of concrete and shrubbery. An empty moonlit sidewalk lined by dark shapes of ledges, walls, and trees, where birds twittered and rustled in the overhead branches, stretched before them.

Megan gave Barton's hand a tug. "There's nobody else here. Are you sure it's okay for us to be here?"

"I'm sure. I reserved it for us."

She glanced up at his shadowed face. "Reserved it?"

"I know someone who works for the city. He chased everybody out. It was a slow night." He shrugged. "Money talks."

"I'll say," Megan muttered.

The trees and concrete walls muffled the sounds of the city, creating an oasis of quiet, broken only by the raucous calls of birds congregating in the trees.

They came to a wall about as high as Megan's chest. The top of the wall had a silvery sheen.

Barton nudged her. "Touch it."

Megan did so. "It's water." She dangled her fingers in a trough of cool water stretching in either direction. Water flowed over the lower, rounded inner edge. She stood on her tiptoes and looked down. "It's a wall of water. All the way around. Wow."

"Come on." Barton led her down a stairway with water running down the walls. At the bottom stretched a long rectangular pool of still water reflecting the moonlight. Four walls of water etched with shadows cast by a row of bald cypress trees enclosed the area. "This is the Quiet Pool."

"It's lovely. Soothing." The water fell all around with a soft whisper.

Next, they came to a pool full of fountains a foot or so high that sprayed in an unusual wide spiral. "This is called the Aerating Pool," Barton said. "This was all built in the '70s. Actually, you've probably seen some of it before."

"How so?" Megan asked, entranced by the fountains that looked like they belonged in fairyland.

"It's been used as a setting in a few movies, most notably *Logan's Run.*"

They walked into a large open area. A single light atop a pole came on, shedding light upon the pavement and the concrete walls and ledges all around the perimeter.

Megan cocked her head. "The water's getting louder."

Barton smiled. "Come on." They came to the edge of the pavement. "This is the Active Pool."

Megan stared down in amazement. Water flowed continuously down terraced concrete all around to a small pool at the bottom. Staggered steps of big, concrete slabs curved down to the pool. Barton led her down the steps. Water sparkling in the moonlight rushed beneath them. Megan held her skirt high with one hand, relieved that she wasn't wearing heels. There weren't any handrails on the steps.

"Careful." His grip tightened on her hand. "It might be slippery. Some people get vertigo from these steps."

At the bottom, big blocks with gaps between them creating waterfalls bordered the pool. Megan and Barton stood in the heart of the water feature. Water splashed and rolled and tumbled into the pool. Mist dampened her hair and face.

"This is wonderful." She had to shout over the roar of the cascading water.

He squeezed her hand. "I thought you'd like it."

When she'd had her fill, they climbed up the big steps to the top. Megan gasped when Barton said with a wave of his hand and a slight bow, "Your table is ready, Miss McClure."

A couple of feet from the top of the stairway were a square table and two folding chairs. White linen covered the table bearing a long, tapered candle topped by a dancing flame, and crystal place settings for two.

"You're just full of surprises," she said as he pulled out a chair for her and she sat.

He sat in the chair opposite her. "I try, darlin'."

Seconds later, a young man in jeans and a white jacket with his hair pulled back in a ponytail and an earring in his left ear greeted them. He placed a bowl of salad in front of each of them then melted back into the darkness. Megan took a moment to admire the salad—cherry tomatoes, sliced cucumbers, chopped peppers, and broccoli florets on a bed of crisp lettuce, covered with French dressing—before picking up her fork and stabbing a tomato. The ponytailed waiter returned with a bottle of wine and two glasses and stood quietly while Barton went through the wine ritual. Swirl the wine, inhale its aroma, sip it, and gravely nod his approval.

Megan giggled.

The waiter filled their glasses and left.

Barton held up his wineglass. "A toast."

Megan lifted hers.

"To a beautiful night in a beautiful place," he touched his glass to hers, "with a beautiful woman."

"Oh, Barton—"

"You are." His eyes shone in the candlelight over the rim of his wineglass as he took a sip. "Especially in that dress."

"Thank you. I bought it with your tip."

He grinned. "Well spent, darlin'."

She tasted the wine, found it very good. Almost as good as the meal the waiter delivered. A thick juicy steak, medium rare, accompanied by a baked potato oozing butter and topped with a dollop of sour cream sprinkled with chives, and a serving of mixed vegetables, crunchy and colorful. The meal was exactly what she had wished for back at The Tejas.

"If you're trying to impress me, Barton Crone, you're doing one hell of a job."

He laughed, his teeth white against his tanned face.

When the table held only the burning candle, two wine glasses, and a half-full wine bottle, Megan sat back, one hand on her silk-covered stomach, and groaned. "I'll never eat again."

"Room for more wine?" He held up the bottle.

She slid her glass over. "Can't let it go to waste." Glass clinked on glass. She sat back and took a sip. "You mentioned earlier you made a good deal this week."

"Sure did." Barton smiled a self-satisfied smile. "A damn good one."

It must have been, the way he was throwing money around. "Buying land for development, right?"

"Yeah." He shifted in his chair and looked down at the wineglass in his hand. "Closed a big deal north of town." He waved his other hand in the direction that must be north. "There's going to be a lot of growth in that area."

She crossed her legs, smoothing the dress over her knee. "Isn't that farmland up there?"

He nodded. "That's progress."

"Hmph. Progress may not always be a good thing."

"It usually is." He rested one arm on the back of his chair. "Take, for example, where we are now. The Water Gardens and the Convention Center across the street used to be part of Fort Worth's most infamous area. Hell's Half Acre."

"This was part of the Acre?" Seth had talked about Hell's Half Acre. The B&B, a brothel in his time, was supposedly on the edge of it.

"Sure was. It started around Twelfth Street and Commerce Street, which was called Rusk Street back then. Over the years, it expanded to about two and a half acres. Main Street was for drinking and gambling. Rusk was for whoring. This whole area"—he swept his arm in a half circle— "was saloons, boarding houses, and brothels. The Wild West at its wildest. The Acre was known far and wide, and anyone who was anyone passed through it sometime or other. The Earp brothers, Doc Holiday, Bat Masterson, all the legends came here."

"Including Butch Cassidy and the Sundance Kid." Megan loved the movie with Paul Newman and Robert Redford.

Barton nodded. "The infamous picture that caused their capture was taken right around here by a local photographer." He took a sip of wine. The diamond on his finger flashed in the soft moonlight.

"How do you know so much about Hell's Half Acre?"

"My great-grandfather owned a saloon there. No kidding." He grinned in response to Megan's surprised look. "Some pretty wild tales about him have been passed down through the family."

"Such as?"

"Oh, let's see." Barton shifted in the chair and crossed his legs. "He killed about a half-dozen men. Supposedly shot two in cold blood. Guess he had a temper. He had a wife and two kids back East and a string of whores out here. Some say he was involved in the opium trade. I've learned to take the stories with a grain of salt. As a youngster, though, I couldn't get enough of them and learned a lot about the local history."

Megan propped an elbow on the table and gazed around at the expanse of pavement bordered by concrete ledges and walls. She tried to imagine how it used to be and thought of all the people who had lived there through the decades. "It's sad."

"What is?" Barton asked.

"All that history buried beneath concrete."

"It was a notorious place."

"It was filled with people who had lives and hopes and dreams, just like you and me." Chin in her hand she looked around. "I wonder what they would say if they saw it now."

"They'd say it was a vast improvement."

"Hmm. I wonder what Seth would say," she mused, and immediately wished she could take the words back.

"Seth?" Barton cocked his head, frowning.

She reached for her wine and took a sip, avoiding Barton's narrowed gaze. "He's a friend. He's into history."

"Friend from home?"

She shook her head. "From here."

Somewhere out on the street tires screeched and a car honked. After a moment, Barton asked, "Do I have a rival?"

Megan's gaze shot to his. "A rival?"

Barton reached across the table to take her hand. "I like you, Megan. A lot. I'd like to keep seeing you. More often, too. Do I need to worry about this Seth character?"

I'll never let you go, Seth's words rang through her head.

Go away! Leave me alone!

"He's just a friend." She said the words a little sharper than she had intended, hoping to silence his voice in her head.

From the look of relief on Barton's face, he didn't hear her tone, only the words. "That's good to know."

"You know I don't live here—"

"I know you have to go back to Yankeeland sooner or later. But I'm hoping you'll find a reason to stay." His eyes, dark and serious, never left hers.

She wondered if he could see her surprise in the dimness. *Holy moly. He wants a relationship. I just want to get laid.* "Barton, I can't make any promises—"

"I'm not asking for any. Yet." He stood, took her hand, and drew her to her feet. "Dance with me."

"There isn't any music," she said with a smile as he took her in his arms.

"I'll hum something. I just want to hold you."

They danced in a slow circle while he hummed a Willie Nelson ballad. She rested her cheek against his chest and closed her eyes, enjoying the feel of his hard body against hers, his strong arms around her.

"Remember earlier you said we can do *or what* later, at your place?"

She drew back and looked up at him. "I remember."

His eyes searched her face. "You sure?"

"I'm sure." Megan lifted her mouth to his and they kissed as they slowly moved back and forth on the concrete to the music of tumbling water and twittering birds.

He ran his hand down her back. "Lots of buttons," he muttered against her mouth. "I'm going to savor unbuttoning each one of them."

"I hope you don't take *too* long on those buttons. I think we've waited long enough."

"By golly, I think you're right."

His kiss deepened. His tongue played with hers while his fingers tangled in her ringlets. They stopped dancing as their kissing grew more heated, and their hands explored, and his knee pressed between her thighs.

Megan tore her mouth away for a breath. "The waiter just brought out another course."

Barton feathered kisses down the side of her neck. "That must be dessert."

"Dessert! If I keep hanging around with you I'm going to get fat."

He chuckled and kissed her forehead. "Don't worry. You're fixin' to get plenty of exercise real soon." He winked at her and put an arm around her as they walked back to the table. "It's cobbler. I didn't know what you like so I ordered peach and apple. Take your pick."

"Apple."

He held out her chair for her then sat down in his chair. "Good. Peach is my favorite."

They washed down the cobblers with the rest of the wine while they chatted.

Barton drained his glass and set it on the table. He pushed back his chair and stood. "If you don't mind, I'm going to step over there and water the plants."

Megan watched him walk away, climb up one of the ledges, and disappear into the shadowy shapes of the shrubbery. He was confident, handsome, successful, and interested in her. A definite catch. She wasn't sure she wanted to catch him, but she did like him, and he certainly knew how to get her juices going. She could still feel the press of his knee against her. She squirmed on the chair. She could hardly wait until they were in bed.

It's been way too long!

Feeling restless, she stood, and stepped to the edge of the concrete. She looked down at the cascading water. Moonlight rippled down the terraces. The sight was hypnotizing, the sound deafening. It seemed to grow louder and louder. Down at the bottom, the pool beckoned.

The next thing she knew, she was standing on the big blocks around the pool and staring into it. She tasted the mist on her lips. It clung to her lashes. Dampened her forehead. The sound of water roared all around her. Water splashed, tumbled, swirled, roared.

From the depths, over the roar, she heard something. She leaned over the pool, head turned to one side, listening.

A whinny.

A horse? She frowned, perplexed.

Another whinny, louder. And voices. People talking, the words faint, indistinguishable. Another whinny. Laughter. Male laughter. More voices.

She leaned over farther, listening closer.

The voices grew louder, louder. A familiar voice.

The water swirled, swirled, swirled.

Her knees bent slightly as she got ready to—

"Megan!" A strong hand grabbed her arm, pulled her back. "Megan!"

Dazed, she looked up at Barton. Concern etched his shadowed face. Her knees turned to jelly while the moon spun crazily overhead. He swept her up in his arms in a rustle of silk. Her head bobbed against his chest as he carried her up the big steps, away from the sounds of horses and voices down there in the water.

Barton lowered her onto her chair and gave her a glass of water. "Are you all right?"

"Give me a minute." The water in the glass jiggled and jumped as she lifted it in her shaking hand for a sip. Her teeth clinked against the glass she couldn't hold still.

Barton paced back and forth, pausing occasionally to stare down at the water. He stopped in front of her. "What the hell was that all about? Too much wine?"

"No." She pushed herself upright in the chair. "No. It wasn't the wine. I got up to stretch my legs, walked down there, and felt ... felt dizzy. I-I don't know why." The swirling water, the whinny of horses, the voices. She shivered in the warm night air. She passed a shaky hand over her face then looked up at Barton. "I hate to ruin this lovely night but—"

He was at her side immediately. "I'll take you home." He took her arm and helped her stand. "Do you want me to carry you?"

"No, no. I'm fine."

"You sure? For a second there, I thought you were going to jump in the water."

Megan stared at him, stunned. In the second before he grabbed her, she *had* felt a powerful urge to jump into that swirling pool full of voices. *Seth's voice.*

The waiter appeared. "Is everything all right, sir?"

Barton smiled. "Everything was perfect, young man. Thank you."

The waiter looked at Megan. "Are you all right, miss? I saw you—"

"She's fine," Barton said. "Just a case of vertigo I think." He reached in his pocket and pulled out a wad of bills. He peeled off two and handed them to the waiter.

The waiter grinned. "Thank *you*, sir."

Barton helped Megan into his car. She pushed her ballooning skirt down and leaned her head back on the headrest.

Someone shook her shoulder.

"Megan, wake up. We're here."

Her eyes shot open and she sat up, confused. "Where are we?"

"The B&B," Barton replied. "You fell asleep on the ride back."

"I did?" She stared at him, aghast. "I'm the worst date *ever!*"

He laughed. "Hardly. Maybe the most tired." He got out of the car then came around to open her door. Taking her hand, he helped her out then shoved her dress out of the way, so he could close the door. He walked her to the front steps. "Are you feeling better?"

"I'm fine. Just tired." She put her hand on his chest. "I'm sorry about tonight."

"Don't be." He brushed a lock of hair off her cheek. "There'll be other nights." He kissed her forehead. "And mornings." He kissed her nose. "And afternoons."

He was so sweet she didn't have the heart to tell him her days in Fort Worth were numbered. "Thank you for a delicious meal. It was the best one I've had in a while."

A frown crossed his handsome face. "You work too hard. Those two jobs are wearing you out. You don't get enough sleep. You don't eat right."

She laughed. "You sound like my mother."

"I'm serious. I worry about you." His voice turned husky. "You're very special to me."

There he goes getting serious again. Something popped into her mind. "Remember the last time we saw each other? Outside work? The night everyone saw my article about The Tejas in the magazine?"

A long pause. "I remember."

"You were going to tell me something. Something that was troubling you. But you never did. You said, *I'm not what I—* then you stopped. What were you going to say?"

He ran a hand through his hair. "I wanted to talk to you about it tonight but ..." He shrugged. "Some other time."

"What's it about?"

After a long moment, Barton replied in a low voice, "Me."

"What about you? What's the matter?"

He blew out a breath and looked away for a moment. "Not tonight, darlin'." His gaze met hers. "We'll talk soon, okay?"

"We could go upstairs now and talk."

He chuckled. "We go up there, there won't be any talkin' goin' on so not tonight. You need a good night's sleep. I want you wide awake the first time we make love."

"Oh, I will be." Megan smoothed down his collar. "I had a wonderful time. Thank you. It was very romantic. *You* are very romantic."

He pulled her to him. "It's because of you. You bring out the best in me." They kissed until he gently pushed her away. "Go on upstairs. Before I change my mind."

"I'll see you soon."

"You can bet on that."

She turned and, holding up her skirt with one hand, climbed the steps illuminated by the light above the door of the B&B. At the top of the steps, she paused with the key in the lock and looked back at Barton.

He stood with his hands in his pockets, watching her from the bottom of the stairs, the light bathing his upturned face.

"Barton, your great-grandfather, the saloon owner, what was his name?"

Barton looked mystified at the question but answered, "John Bingo."

***

John Bingo.

As she climbed the stairs to her room, that name was one of three things whirling around in her head, the other two being the strange visions while she and Barton danced, and the voices in the water. It was like a puzzle whose picture she hadn't seen beforehand and was slowly piecing together. Her steps quickened. She suddenly felt wide awake. So much to write in her journal. The pool in the water gardens must be another portal. She entered her darkened room, closed, and locked the door behind her, then leaned back against it a moment, thinking back over the long, strange night. It had ended disappointingly. No sex again. Just frustration. At least the tiredness was gone.

She pushed away from the door and walked across the room. Her dress swished with each step. She kicked off her tennis shoes then stood on one foot and pulled off a sock. She did the same with the other foot and wiggled her toes. She went to the nightstand beside the bed and pulled the chain on the lamp, turning it on.

"It's about damn time you got here."

Chapter 14

Megan whirled around in a swirl of purple at the sound of the deep voice she thought she would never hear again. Lamplight spread to the end of the bed and spilled across the floor.

In the shadows across the room, the silhouette of a tall figure in a cowboy hat leaned against one side of the farthest window.

She clenched her fists. "Oh my God, stop haunting me."

The cowboy hat tilted. "Haunting you?"

"Why are you doing this? Leave me alone!" She heard the hysteria in her voice and bit her bottom lip, turning away.

"What the hell—"

"You're not here, you're not here," she muttered as she marched to the vanity. "I'm hallucinating. No one's here. Just me." She stopped in front of the mirror and began yanking hairpins out of her hair and tossing them in a porcelain dish on the vanity.

Ping. Ping. Ping. Hairpins hit the porcelain like hail.

"Miss Megan? What's the matter?"

She slammed her palms on top of the vanity, making the dish and the hairbrush jump. Bottles of perfume and make-up wobbled. Barton's picture tipped forward slightly then settled back against the mirror. She glared at the reflection of the shadowy apparition in the mirror. "You know damn well what's the matter! Earlier tonight, you appeared out of nowhere and started dancing with me. Then I heard voices in the water. One of them was yours."

"I don't know what you're talking about."

She covered her face with her hands. "I'm cracking up. I'm talking to a figment of my imagination. Or a ghost. I'm actually cracking up." She heard footsteps behind her and spun around.

The figure crossed the room, tossing the hat on the table as he passed it. He emerged from the shadows into the light.

Megan caught her breath.

Seth stopped about a foot away from her. He had a beard and a mustache, both neatly trimmed and redder than his short, sandy hair. He looked older, more mature, and very real.

"You're not ... cracking up." He reached out to take her hand. She flinched at his touch, bringing a frown to his face. "I'm not a figment of your imagination." His grip tightened. "I'm real. I'm here."

She stared at his hand enveloping hers. It looked real. A sprinkling of light hair near the knuckles. Short, clean nails. It felt real. Warm as a campfire on a chilly night, strong as iron. She wanted to believe him. But it had looked and felt real earlier when they danced beneath the stars while fiddles played. Her gaze slowly rose to his.

He must have seen the doubt in her eyes. He placed her hand on his chest and held it there. "Does a ghost have a heartbeat?"

Beneath the rough material of his gray shirt, his heart beat strong and rhythmic. Her own pounded like a bass drum at a rock concert. She drew a steadying breath and inhaled the smells of him—horses and leather and that earthy scent that belonged to only Seth. Her fingers gripped the front of his shirt as she looked up at him. "You're really here?" she whispered hoarsely.

"Yeah. Been here a couple hours." Seth lifted his other hand and touched one of her unraveling ringlets. "Waiting for you."

She released her grip and pushed him away. "What are you doing here?"

He stumbled a bit from the force of her push, or maybe surprised by it, then backed up a couple of steps and crossed his arms. "I was gonna ask you the same thing. Why are you still here? I figured you'd gone back up north."

"I had commitments to fulfill. Loose ends to tie up. I certainly wasn't waiting around for you to show up after *you*," she jabbed a finger at him, "said goodbye to *me*."

He scowled. "I don't know what you're all riled up about. I thought you'd be happy to see me."

A humorless laugh escaped her. "Isn't that just like a man. Last time I saw you, you gave a big speech about wanting to get your ranch going and start a family. You wrapped it up with a dramatic goodbye." She put her hands on her hips. "Now you come waltzing back in here like nothing happened and expect me to welcome you with open arms. Be happy to see you," she mimicked him. "Well, think again, cowboy. For all I know, you have a couple of kids by now."

"Well, I don't."

"Are you married?"

His scowl deepened. "No."

Relief rushed through her, irritating her. She didn't *want* to care about his marital status. Caring would only lead to heartache. "What happened to Patsy?"

He looked away. "She left town," he said in a low voice. "Ran off with a milk-faced gambler."

She stared at his profile through narrowed eyes. *Party-girl Patsy broke his heart and he comes crawling back to me. The nerve!* "Pity," she said, without an ounce of pity in her voice. She faced the mirror and reached up to yank out more hairpins.

His gaze snapped to her reflection. "Who put a bee in your bonnet?"

"You." *Ping. Ping.*

"How? I haven't been here in a while."

Ping. Ping. Ping. "No kidding." She ran her fingers through her hair a couple of times, separating the ringlets while Seth watched in the mirror. She glared at his reflection and picked up the hairbrush. "You still haven't told me why you're here." After several brushings of her hair, she saw Seth staring at her dress with an odd expression on his face. "What's the matter?"

"You look like a woman from my time in that dress." He pursed his lips. A crease appeared between his brows. "That dress—" He shook his head.

She faced him. "What about it?"

"My sister sews. She's made dresses for just about all the womenfolk, especially among the important people. Everyone in the area knows that Lottie O'Connor is the one to see if you need a dress. 'Course it's all real quiet like. Lottie'll meet some woman in an alley or at night behind a building, never in broad daylight or out in the open for anyone to see them. No one talks about where the women get their dresses, but everyone knows a whore made them. The women pay a goodly sum for those dresses."

"You think your sister made this dress?"

He shrugged. "I've seen her make dozens of dresses, and this looks like her work. She's partial to that cream-colored lace. She likes combining different shades of the same color." He gestured to the panels of light purple and dark purple. "There's one way I can be sure. Mind if I take a looksee at the hem?"

Megan waved the hairbrush. "Go ahead."

Seth knelt on one knee in front of her and picked up the hem. He slowly ran it through his hands. After studying about two feet of the hem, he paused. "There it is."

"What?"

"Her initials. She always sews them somewhere on the hem. See?" He held it up.

Megan bent over to look. "I don't see anything that looks like an L."

"Not L. COC. Charlotte O'Connor. Right here."

Megan studied where his thumb was. Then her eyes widened. Along a seam, very small, purple thread spelled out *COC*. A shiver ran over her. "Lottie made this dress." Her voice sounded far away to her own ears.

"You all right? You're a might pale."

She shook her head to clear it. "It's been a long, strange night that keeps getting stranger."

Seth unfolded his lean frame and rose to his feet. "I reckon we got a lot to talk about. Why don't we sit down?" He gestured to the rawhide sofa.

Megan brushed her hair a couple of times then put the brush on top of the vanity. "All right." She went to the sofa and sat on one end. Her skirt and petticoat ballooned up into her face. She pushed them down and slid to the end of the cushion. "I'm going to change clothes." She started to rise just as Seth sat at the other end.

"Don't. Please. You look so pretty."

Her gaze darted up and collided with his. He smiled that smile she had missed more than she realized. Her cheeks suddenly burned beneath his admiring gaze. The sofa suddenly seemed too cozy, the meager lighting too intimate. She suddenly could not trust herself to sit too close to him.

She stood. "Want a beer? I could use one." She remembered the warm beer they had shared during his last visit. "It's cold."

"Sure."

Her dress swished and rustled as she walked to the Styrofoam cooler beside the dresser, aware of Seth watching her. She bent down to open the cooler and dug two cans of beer out of the cold water thick with melting ice cubes. She gently shook off the water, closed the lid, and straightened. With nonchalance she didn't feel, she took him a beer then went to the table and pulled the chain on the lamp. The room brightened. She sat on one of the spindly-legged chairs, arranged her skirt and petticoat then opened the beer with a *whoosh*. It tasted good going down.

Across the room, Seth silently regarded her from the sofa. He glanced at the other end of it then back at her. He popped the tab on his beer and took a drink, then stretched his arm along the back of the sofa and crossed a knee with an ankle. "Tell me about the dress. Where you got it, and why."

"I had to get a costume for work for the Chisholm Trail Round-Up. That's a weekend festival with a parade, lots of food, arts and crafts, music, make believe gunfights. Western stuff. Oh, and beer."

"Folks in your time have heard of the Chisholm Trail?"

"Holy moly, yes." Megan rolled her eyes. "This town celebrates its history every chance it gets. I bought the dress at a sale. A woman named Candace Huntington, from one of Fort Worth's oldest families, donated it. Her maiden name was Candace Pryor."

Surprise spread across Seth's face. "Candy Pryor?"

Megan leaned forward. "You know her?"

"Sure. Sweet kid. About seven or so. She has an older sister, Corrie."

"Cordelia."

Seth nodded. "So that's one of Candy's old dresses?"

"Maybe. I'm not sure." Megan stood and went to the nightstand. She picked up the index card with the information about the dress on it and handed it to Seth. "Read this." She returned to her chair and sat.

Seth set his beer on the floor. He stroked his bearded chin with one hand while he read the index card. The sound of sirens rose up from the street below outside. Flashing red lights briefly danced on the walls around the room then the sirens faded away. Seth looked up, his eyes wide with amazement. "Candy is still *alive?*"

"She's one hundred years old."

"A hundred!" His shocked gaze dropped back down to the index card. "Well, I'll be hogtied to a fence post. Little Candy. Tarnation." He stared at the card for a moment. A frown beetled his forehead. He looked at Megan. "How'd she know the color of your eyes? Or that you'd be buying that dress on that day at that place?"

"I have no idea. Freaky, huh?" She raised her hand, palm up. "See why I often wonder if I'm going crazy?"

Seth snorted softly. "You're not going crazy. There's just crazy things happenin' to you."

"I'll drink to that." She did so.

"Have you talked to Candy?"

"Not yet. I've tried, twice. Last I heard she was in the hospital having tests done."

"Hospital." Seth had a look of horror on his face. "Lordy, I hope she survives being in there. I'd sure like to hear what she has to say."

"Me too. I can't wait to meet her. Have you seen this dress before?"

He shook his head. "Lottie must not have made it yet. I know I'd remember it. It would have reminded me of your purple eyes."

"Violet. Didn't you read the index card?"

Seth laughed. He lifted his beer for a drink then rested the can on the armrest. "Speaking of crazy things, you said something earlier about us dancing. Want to tell me about it?"

For a moment, the only sound was the hum of the air conditioner.

"I was at work tonight and Barton came in. It wasn't very busy, so we danced one dance. He was spinning me around and around and I got a little dizzy, and suddenly ... suddenly everything changed."

"What do you mean?"

"Like I said, everything changed. The other people there suddenly looked like people from your time. The women wore dresses like mine. The men had on their Sunday best, black trousers, black coats, black string ties. There were lanterns strung around the dance floor, which I think was the ground because we were outside. There were a million stars overhead. And it wasn't Barton I was dancing with. It was you."

Seth uncrossed his legs and leaned forward on the sofa. "Then what happened?"

"I tripped or stumbled or something and you caught me. You said, *I've got you. I'll never—*" She clamped her mouth shut and dropped her gaze from his.

"I'll never what?"

I'll never let you go.

Afraid she'd say something she didn't want to say, Megan turned on her chair, picked up a stack of typewritten papers off the table and tapped them straight. "Never mind. It wasn't important."

Seconds slid by then Seth said, "So we're back to *never minds* again, huh?"

She shot him a glance, which skittered away from his probing gaze. She put the stack of papers aside. "I told you, it wasn't important."

"All right," he said, his tone implying, *We'll come back to that later.* "Did we keep dancing?"

"No. Everything was suddenly normal again. The people. The place. I was dancing with Barton. The rest of the night was fine until we went to the Water Gardens." She saw Seth's puzzled look and explained, "It's not really a garden with flowers. In fact, I don't know if there are even any flowers there. It's mainly manmade water features. Very pretty and different. Anyway, there's one big area with terraced sides all around running down to a small pool in the middle. There's a staircase of big blocks leading down to the pool. After we had dinner, I got up to stretch my legs and suddenly I found myself at the bottom of the staircase, standing beside the pool. I have no memory of walking down there."

Seth raised an eyebrow.

"I'm serious. One minute I was at the top of the stairs, looking down. The next thing I knew, I was at the bottom, beside the pool. The water tumbled and splashed, the sound deafening, and suddenly I heard a horse whinny."

"A horse whinny?"

She nodded. "Then I heard voices. Male voices. And laughter. More whinnies. And I heard your voice."

"Mine?" He touched a hand to his chest, his expression shocked.

She nodded and took a drink to wet her dry mouth. "I leaned closer, trying to hear better. Suddenly Barton yanked me back. I felt dizzy and almost fainted, and Barton swept me up in his arms and carried me out of there."

"Of course, he did."

Megan heard Seth's muttered words and glared at him. He had told her goodbye and left her. He had no right to say anything about Barton. "He was very gallant. He's also nice, successful, and handsome."

Seth made a derisive sound. "I reckon he's one of those *loose ends* you mentioned earlier."

"Do you want to talk about Barton or hear the rest of my story?"

Seth motioned with his beer. "Go on."

Megan shifted on the chair. "When I was staring into the pool, just before Barton grabbed me, I had a fleeting but strong urge to jump into the water where the voices were. I think it's another portal."

His eyes widened. "Like the door?"

She nodded. "Either that or this dress is special." She looked down at herself. "Like a—a magic dress."

"A magic dress?" His eyes widened more. "Christ A'mighty."

Megan frowned. "Although I've worn it to work the last few nights and tonight is the only night anything strange happened."

Seth propped his elbow on the armrest and smoothed his mustache with his thumb and forefinger. Footsteps in the room above made the ceiling creak while he stared off thoughtfully. He lowered his hand and looked at Megan. "Then how could it be just the dress? Something else must have been different about tonight."

She thought for a moment. "The only other difference is that Barton was there tonight."

"Ah, Mr. Gallant."

Megan made a sour look. "Are you going to start that again?"

Seth waved a hand. "Sorry." He didn't look at all sorry. "What did Barton do to trigger the ... What would you call it? Visions?"

She sat quietly, twisting the beer can around and around on the table. "Maybe it isn't what Barton did but what I was thinking when I looked at him," she said slowly, recalling how she had glanced over her shoulder and seen Barton leaning against the bar, ankles crossed, beer in one hand, watching her walk away to deliver an order. He had tipped his bottle to her and smiled that tempting, sexy smile. She had decided then and there—

"What were you thinking?" Seth's question broke into her memory.

"That tonight I was finally going to have sex with him."

Her spoken thought fell like a ton of bricks in the quiet room.

Heat burned her cheeks when she realized what she'd said, and to whom. Her mortified gaze darted to Seth. "Oh God, I didn't mean to say that! I—"

"Don't fret so, Miss Megan." A slight smile curved his mouth. "I know ... things ... are different in your time. Very different. While I was waitin' tonight, I read about the sixties. Peace and love." Seth held up one hand with two fingers splayed in a V.

A mad giggle welled up in Megan at the sight of a nineteenth century cowboy displaying the peace sign.

"I also read about your president's assassination, riots between white folks and Negroes, protests against a war somewhere I never heard of, the sexual revolution, birth control pills, womenfolk burning their undergarments, and sex, drugs, and rock and roll." He scratched his head. "I'm still ponderin' that rock and roll part."

Megan laughed.

"After readin' all that and thinkin' about it while standin' here in the dark and lookin' out the window, well, I'm not surprised you're ..." He tipped his head to one side, frowning. "How'd the book say it? Sexually active."

Megan had just taken a drink and almost choked on it. She sputtered then coughed several times, feeling her face heat up again. She couldn't believe they were sitting there, drinking beer, and discussing her sex life as casually as if it were the weather.

"You all right?" Seth leaned forward on the sofa.

Hand to her chest, she cleared her throat and managed to croak, "I'm fine."

He settled back. "I reckon your fella Barton wouldn't be your first lover."

She shook her head then ventured, "Disappointed?"

He looked surprised. "At what?"

"That I'm not a virgin?"

He shrugged. "I can't expect you to live any other way than the time you live in. Your time has its own rules, beliefs, habits. It's different from my time. Better or worse, who's to say? I reckon we oughta just accept the differences and move on. Besides, I'm no monk," he added nonchalantly.

Megan snorted. *Braggart.* He was probably a favorite among the whores in this very house. Maybe got a family discount.

He went on, "So after you thought about beddin' your fella you and he danced and everythin' changed to my time?"

She nodded.

"Were you thinking along the same lines when you heard the voices in the water?"

Megan thought back to the Water Garden just hours before. Barton had disappeared into the shrubs to answer nature's call. She had realized she could hardly wait to get him into bed. Restless with desire, she'd stood, walked to the edge to look down at the pool, and an instant later, she was beside the pool, hearing horses and voices. She nodded again.

Seth took a couple of swigs of beer. "Maybe it isn't the dress that triggers the visions." His gaze went to Barton's picture on the dresser. "Maybe it's your fella."

"He's not my *fella*. I wish you'd quit calling him that," Megan said, although she had a feeling that Seth was on the right track, except it wasn't necessarily Barton who caused the visions. Or the dress. She decided not to share her idea with Seth just yet. It was too personal. Too strange. Instead, she leaned over the table to grab a stack of papers. "I'm curious as to where the portal in the Water Gardens comes out in your time. If there really *is* a portal." She flipped through the papers until finding the ones she wanted. "Take a look at these."

Seth rose from the sofa and joined her at the table, sitting on the chair she pulled beside her. She spread out two maps on the table then pointed to the one on the right. "This is a map of Fort Worth today. Here's the Water Gardens." She showed him the area then put the other map below the first one. "This is Fort Worth in 1886. Here's where the Water Gardens would be." She traced her finger around the area. "It used to be Hell's Half Acre. Is there any water in there?"

Seth leaned in for a closer look. His thigh pressed against hers. She shifted, breaking the contact. He glanced at her then looked back down at the maps. "There's saloons all along here." He ran his finger down a street then ran it down another. "And over here. Mostly brothels here and here." He pointed them out then shook his head. "But no water."

"Are you sure? No ponds or fountains? The river? A well? A cistern?"

He shook his head. "It's saloons, gambling dens, and whorehouses."

She sat back in the chair, disappointed. "No water? Anywhere?"

"Just watering troughs." His gaze met hers. "Sorry, Miss Megan."

"Watering troughs?" Excitement propelled her upright on her chair. "That would explain the horse whinnies."

"Well, yeah, I reckon it would," he said slowly as he straightened. He bent his leg and hooked the heel of his boot over the chair rung. "So, if someone from your time jumps in the pool in that water garden place they might climb out of a trough in my time."

Megan laughed. "Wouldn't that freak people out."

"Freak?"

"Umm, surprise, and not necessarily in a good way."

"Oh yeah, it'd surprise 'em all right." He chuckled. "It'd be the talk of the town. Whoever uses that portal won't have the same problem I have here."

She put her elbow on the table. "What problem?"

He waved the beer can around the room. "I'm trapped. I can't leave this room except through that door."

"That's true. No one could be trapped in a watering trough because they'd drown, making it useless as a portal."

He nodded. "Whoever comes through might be able to move freely in my time."

"Seth." Megan put her hand on his arm. "If you came through the pool you might be free here, too. You might not be stuck in this room." She squeezed his arm. "You could walk around the future Fort Worth."

He stared off across the room, as if pondering the possibility while taking a couple drinks of beer. Megan studied his profile. The straight line of his forehead. His crooked nose. The way the light hit his hair, highlighting the red in it. Yes, definitely a favorite among the whores. He set his beer on the table and his eyes met hers.

"To get here I'd have to jump in every waterin' trough in Hell's Half Acre to find the right one. I'd for certain sure be jailed for drunkenness or some such."

They shared a smile. A warm look settled in his eyes. Her hand still rested on his arm. He covered her hand with his.

"Would you?" he asked.

"Would I what?"

"Jump in that pool and come through the portal to my time?"

He looked so earnest, maybe even hopeful.

But he had left her.

She remembered crying herself to sleep that night. Remembered his goodbye letter. Remembered the hurt and sadness he had left behind when he closed that door supposedly for good.

Her hand slid free of his. "You still haven't told me what you're doing here. Why you came back tonight."

The warm look in his eyes cooled as he leaned back in the chair, crossing his arms. "I was out celebratin' this evenin'. I bought a saloon."

"Why on earth did you buy a saloon? Where'd you get the money?" Megan put a hand to her chest. "You didn't rob another bank, did you?"

He burst out laughing. "I reckon one bank robbery in my life is enough. I've been savin' my money, got a loan from Tim and a couple other fellas. Some from Lottie."

"What about your ranch? Isn't it doing well?"

"It's doing fine. I got two good hands helpin' me. They both worked for Mr. Toby for a coon's age and I asked 'em to stay on when I took over. I don't know what I'd do without 'em." He shook his head. "I got more cattle a year or so back. Sold a couple dozen calves last fall and made a tidy sum. Wasn't much rain this past summer and we had to dig a deeper well. Got awful dry. There were cracks in the ground wide enough to swaller an armadillo." He smiled. "It's pretty in springtime. Wildflowers as far as the eye can see. Bluebonnets everywhere. Mighty fine sight. Peaceful, too. Quiet. Sometimes too quiet."

Megan propped her chin on her hand. "It must have been a big change for you after living in town."

He nodded. "I go to town every chance I get."

She suddenly understood. "You're a city boy stuck out in the country and wishing you were back in the city."

He gave a little laugh. "I reckon so. I miss Tim and the other fellas. And Lottie. I'm used to seein' her all the time and, well, it don't feel right being so far from her. She's all the kin I got." He picked up his beer, drained it, and put the empty can on the table.

"Is Lottie doing all right?"

The corners of his mouth drew down as he shrugged. "If bein' a whore is doin' all right then I reckon she's just dandy." He shoved his chair back, scraping the floor, and stood. "Mind if I have another beer if you got any?"

"There's plenty. Go ahead."

"Thanks." He walked over to the cooler, leaned over to open it, and fished out a beer.

Megan watched his black trousers pull taut across his butt. It put Barton's to shame. Her gaze traveled down his long legs in those tight trousers that left little to the imagination then back up over his lean hips to the homespun gray shirt stretching across his back as he closed the cooler.

He straightened and caught her studying him. He held up a beer. "Want one?"

"Not yet, thanks." She crossed her legs, pushing down her skirt and petticoat as they bobbed up and thinking for the umpteenth time what a beautiful dress it was. When he sat down at the table, she said, "Lottie should open a dressmaking shop. She has a real talent."

Seth grunted as he popped the top on the beer. "No way in hell would anyone rent her a place, much less lend her any money to start out."

"I didn't think of that. I was just thinking of her beautiful work. It's too bad people are so narrow-minded and unforgiving in your time."

"Not everyone. You're not the first person to suggest that Lottie open a shop. Susannah said the same thing not too long ago when she got a new dress from Lottie."

"Susannah is still around?"

"Oh sure. She's a schoolteacher and helps her father at his store."

Megan picked up a long curl of her hair. She toyed with it a moment then held up the ends, studying them for split ends. She asked casually, "She married?"

"Nah. Couple fellas are sweet on her, but she won't bat an eye at 'em. Thought for a while she and Tim might get hitched but nothin' ever come of it. Damn shame. They make a fine couple."

Megan looked at Seth and shook her head. *Idiot. She wants* you. "What happened with Patsy?"

"She left over a year ago. Just as well." At Megan's questioning look, he explained, "Oh, she was a pretty little thing and could liven up a room with her laughin' and jokin' but she didn't have the brains God gave a stump. She couldn't read, wasn't much good with numbers. Hell, she didn't even know who's the governor of Texas." He shook his head. "Dumb as a pile of rocks. She ran off in the middle of the night with a no good, cheatin' gambler. No tellin' where she's at now but I'd bet my horse she's already moved on to some other man. She's like a bee buzzin' from flower to flower, never staying anywheres for long. She wasn't the gal for me." He lifted his beer in a toast. "Hallelujah."

"You didn't love her?"

"Nah." He propped an elbow on the back of the chair. "Thought I did for a while there but soon she just became annoyin', like a pesky fly that won't leave you be. A dumb fly at that."

Megan laughed. "Are you dating—I mean courting anyone these days?"

He cocked his head to one side and sent her a lazy grin. "You seem mighty curious about my love life, Miss Megan."

"You know about mine." She shrugged. "Fair is fair."

His gaze went to Barton's picture and stayed there a moment. He opened his mouth then closed it, as if he meant to say something then changed his mind. He shifted on the chair as he looked at Megan. "There've been other women, no one in particular. No one right now. Kinda hard with me at the ranch so much. Sure ain't no women out there. Gets mighty lonesome with just us three men swappin' lies night after night."

"Is that why you bought the saloon? To be in town more?" She lifted her beer for a drink.

"It's a good investment. Busy place. Good location. The price was right." His jaw tightened, and his eyes narrowed. "I'm gonna spruce it up and have the best damn saloon in Fort Worth and run Bingo outta town. If I don't kill him first."

The beer suddenly tasted flat in Megan's mouth as Barton's words rang through her mind. *He killed a half-dozen men* ... "I found out tonight that Barton's great-grandfather was named John Bingo, a saloon owner in Hell's Half Acre in the late 1800s."

"You think it's the same John Bingo?"

"Are there any other John Bingos living in Fort Worth?"

Seth shook his head.

"It must be the same man. Barton said Bingo killed six men."

Seth laughed scornfully. "More like three. An' that was probably just luck."

His cavalier attitude towards shootings and killing, even though he *did* live in the Wild West, suddenly made her see red.

"I don't know how you can laugh about it. One of those three was Billy, your friend and the man Lottie loved. The same bullet that killed him I dug out of your arm on this very table." She jabbed her finger on the table. "Your dried blood is still on that armoire." She jabbed her finger in the general direction. "If not for me you could have bled to death or died from an infection." She jabbed her finger at him. "*You* might be number four, or five, or six, Mr. Smarty Pants."

"Hey, hey." Seth held up a hand. "Settle down. I ain't worried about Bingo."

She flopped back in her chair, arms across her chest. "I suppose you're the fastest gun in the west."

"Ah, no." He gave her an odd look.

She looked him over. "You're not even wearing a gun."

"It's hangin' on the doorknob over there."

"Have you ever been in a gunfight?"

"No."

"Have you ever shot anyone? Killed anyone?"

"No and no."

"Oh my God, you're screwed." Megan dropped her head into her hands. "Bingo will slaughter you." She heard Seth's chair creak and felt a hand settle on her shoulder, his skin warm on her exposed flesh. She raised her head.

Seth looked intently at her as he leaned closer. "I'm not a fightin' man by nature but I will fight if need be. I'm not afraid of any man, includin' John Bingo. I can, and I will, kill him if he forces my hand." His features softened. "I can take care of myself. I'm not overly fond of guns but I won't hesitate to use one. I'm a good shot. Don't worry about me."

She searched his face, from his hazel eyes to his mustache and beard and the lips between them. Those lips held her attention for a moment before moving back to his eyes. "Before, when we saw each other regularly, I used to lay awake at night, wondering if you were dead. Which is ridiculous, because in *my* time, you *are* dead. Still, I worried." A humorless laugh escaped her. "And you called *Patsy* dumb."

"You're not at all dumb. It's one of the many things I like about you." His warm breath, carrying a hint of beer, fanned her face. "I'm sorry you worried about me. On the other hand," he smiled ever so slightly, "it's kinda nice knowin' you were thinkin' of me." His hand slid down her arm to her elbow then slowly back up. Every nerve ending tingled beneath his touch. When his gaze dropped to her lips, her entire body pulsed. The temperature in the room seemed to leap ten degrees. He leaned towards her, his hand cupping her shoulder, his thumb rubbing small circles on her skin.

The water pipes in the walls of the old house rattled with the flush of a toilet somewhere in a nearby room. Megan squirmed on her chair. *Damn the power of suggestion.* She leaned away from Seth. "I need to use the bathroom."

His hand dropped away. "Oh. Sure." If he was disappointed, he hid it well as he scooted back his chair and stood while she rose and went to the bathroom, shutting the door behind her.

After using the toilet, she washed her hands in the sink then dashed cold water on her flushed face. She turned off the faucet then reached for a towel. Two towels hung on the rack. She touched the one that hadn't been there when she'd left for work and found it still damp. She looked at the claw-footed tub ringed by the shower curtain and pictured him there, his sandy hair a shade darker and plastered to his head, water gliding over his muscles, down his long lean naked body, water dripping off his nipples and the tip of his—

She spun to the sink, twisted on the cold-water faucet, and splashed her hot face again and again. She grabbed her towel and patted her skin dry, aware of her pounding heart and the raw desire thrumming her nerves. *He was going to kiss me. Then what? Sex?* She looked in the mirror. *Is that all I want? A roll in the hay? Is that all he wants? How can we have more?* She fluffed her hair. *Another portal. Can I use it? Will I?* She shook her head, her fingers busy in her hair. *No phones. No a/c. No indoor plumbing. No cars or planes. Primitive medicine. No job. Cowboys and Indians. Warm beer. No pizza or burgers. I can't cook!*

The mirror reflected her anxious face beneath the semi-Afro her nervous fingers had created.

She broke into laughter at the sight of herself, clapping a hand over her mouth to muffle the sound. She took a couple of deep breaths to calm down. She grimaced at her over-fluffed hair then went to work patting it flat. *If I go, can I come back? Would I want to? Would he want me to stay? Would I want to? Live in the past the rest of my life? If I can't go to his time, what's the point? There's no future for us. All we will be to each other is a roll in the hay. Is that all I want? Is it enough?*

Megan looked herself in the eye.

Is it?

She whispered, "I don't know."

Barton would be a roll in the hay.

Is Seth?

She grabbed hold of the sink with both hands and dropped her head, closing her eyes. Several heartbeats later, she opened her eyes and raised her head. She looked in the mirror and whispered, "I don't think so."

When she left the bathroom, Seth looked up from the maps spread open on the table and smiled at her as he stood. That smile made her heart skip a beat, but she stiffened her spine as she walked back to the table. Seth held her chair for her when she sat.

"Need a beer?" he asked.

"No thanks. I still have one." *Holy moly, I've been drinking a lot lately.*

He pulled his chair near hers and sat down.

Megan fussed with her skirt and petticoat and, trying not to be too obvious, slid her chair away from his. She reached for her beer. After a fortifying slug, she looked at Seth.

He sat with his arms crossed, one leg stretched beneath the table, the other bent at the knee, and no smile. She regretted its absence. He was obviously disappointed that they didn't pick up where they had left off. *Tough,* she thought as she smoothed a wrinkle out of the silk. They still had things to discuss. "I just remembered something else Barton said about Bingo."

Seth sent a malicious glance at Barton's picture.

Megan wondered if he thought she'd spent her time in the bathroom wishing Barton were with her instead, which would explain, in Seth's mind, her sudden coolness towards him. *If he only knew!* "He said Bingo was involved with the opium trade. Do you know anything about that?"

"Not about Bingo, no, but I know of a couple men who sell it in their dens."

"Well, you might keep an eye out for any of the symptoms. Loss of appetite. Sleepiness. Unfocused eyes—"

Confusion wrinkled Seth's brow. "In Bingo?"

She hesitated, knowing her next words would hurt. "In—in Lottie."

He sat up straight. "Are you accusin' my sister of being an addict?"

"I'm just saying you should watch for the signs in her in case ... well, just in case."

He crossed his arms tight against his chest. "Lottie wouldn't take opium." He glared at Megan. "She wouldn't go to one of those nasty dens. I know she wouldn't."

"I hope not. It depends upon how much influence Bingo has over her." *And how much she hates her life.*

His shoulders suddenly slumped as if she had popped him with a pin and let the air out. He hung his head and rubbed a hand over his face, muttering, "Surely she isn't that stupid. Oh God, surely not."

"I'm sorry." Megan reached out to touch his arm then stopped herself. She put her hand around the beer can instead. "I just wanted to warn you. Hopefully, there's nothing to worry about. But I thought you should know."

Seth scraped his chair back and stood. His long legs quickly took him to the bathroom where he closed the door behind him.

Megan crossed her legs and drank her beer. The pipes rattled with the flush of the toilet. Then silence. Minutes passed. She supposed he was having his own moment in there.

When he finally came out of the bathroom, he walked across the room to one of the tall windows and looked out at the night.

She shifted on her chair to face him. "Why did you come here tonight? Was it the first night the portal was open?"

He gave a harsh laugh. "No." He turned around and leaned back against the wall, crossing his arms. "No, it sure as hell wasn't the first night. Those first couple months after I last saw you it was open more than it was closed. Got to be I finally just quit tryin' to go see Lottie and put my mind to movin' out to the ranch house. I'd been at the ranch two, three days when Lottie came ridin' into the yard in a cloud of dust, hair all wild, the poor horse all lathered. Hell, I thought the town was afire or somethin'. Her fancy boots no sooner hit the ground and she lit into me. Wanted to know why I hadn't been to see her much lately, and why I left town without a by-your-leave. Tarnation, she was madder than a mother hen guardin' her chicks. I had to stand there, red-faced, listenin' to her while Jack and Sly stood over yonder, slappin' their knees and cacklin' like a couple old women." He chuckled at the memory. Then his serious eyes looked at Megan. "But what could I say to her? Not the truth." He shook his head. "I still don't see her much 'cause of that damn portal. Whenever I'm in town, it's open almost every time I come up those stairs. It's almost like—" He stopped and ran a hand through his hair.

"Like what?"

He suddenly laughed and spread his arms wide. "Now you're gonna think *I'm* crazy."

"Try me. What is it almost like?"

Hands on his hips, Seth looked down at the floor. His shoulders lifted with a deep breath then lowered with the exhale. After a moment, he said, "Like-like ... somethin'," he looked at Megan, "*wants* me to go through that door."

Megan half-expected to hear the *The Twilight Zone* music swell in the background. "What *something?* God? Fate? The universe?"

"I dunno." He shook his head, frowning, then ventured, "God?"

She grunted. "I haven't had much use for God since my parents died. I'm not a firm believer in fate either. That leaves the universe." She laughed humorlessly. "Just my luck, the whole universe is screwing with me. With us."

"Whatever it is, somethin' is keeping that door open almost all the time now when before it only opened every now and then. Seems the more I ignore it the more it's there."

She lifted her beer in a toast to him. "Welcome to the Crazy Club." She drained the beer and set the empty on the table.

"Then there's your dress."

"What about it?" she asked, although she knew in her bones what he was going to say.

"Lottie made it. Well, Lottie *will* make it, sometime in my future. And I'm beginnin' to think she makes it for you."

It looks like it was made for you, Bonnie had said. *With your hair and eyes, it was meant for you,* the sewing expert woman had said. Megan looked down at the dress. *Holy moly.*

Seth went to the cooler and got out a beer. He brought it to Megan, popping the top before handing it to her. "Now there's another portal."

"Maybe." She took the beer she didn't really want but thought he was sweet for getting it for her. "Thanks." *I'll quit drinking tomorrow.*

"You're welcome." He sat beside her. "*Maybe* there's another portal. And *maybe* it's for you."

Megan rubbed her forehead. It was all becoming too much.

"And there's another thing."

"Now what?" she mumbled.

"Remember earlier when you were tellin' me about you and Barton dancin' and suddenly everything changed, and you were dancin' with me? You said I said somethin' but you won't tell me what. I think it must be somethin' ... important ... and you don't want to tell me because you want to see if I say it sometime in the future." His gaze bore into hers. "Am I right?"

She dropped her head into her hand. *I'll never let you go,* imaginary Seth had said. An instant later, she had been back dancing with Barton.

She nodded.

Suddenly she jerked upright. "I almost brought Barton up here tonight. Thank God I didn't! What a mess that would have been."

Seth looked at Barton's picture then looked down at the table. He picked up his beer and took a drink. Took another drink. He stared at the can as though reading the label then set it down. "Do you love him?" He looked at her.

Megan held his gaze. "No. It's just as well because I'll be leaving soon."

He turned toward her. "You're not going anywhere."

She said softly, "I can't stay here forever. I can't afford it. And I can't just sit here the rest of my life waiting for you to pop in." He started to say something, but she went on, "Which reminds me," she tilted her head. "Why did you pop in tonight after ignoring the portal all those other times?"

He propped his elbow on the back of his chair, his hand hanging down. "I was curious." He shrugged. "It's been over two years since I was here—I don't know how long it's been in your time, and—"

"Twenty-six days." She blushed. She had known exactly how many days.

He didn't quite smile, but the corners of his mouth lifted slightly. "I didn't think you'd still be here." He moved his hand closer to her arm. His forefinger flicked the lace edging on the puffy sleeve of her dress. "Figured you'd left long before this. I was wonderin' who was stayin' in the room now. Then I saw your things and reckoned I'd wait a spell."

"You were *curious? That's* why you decided to come here tonight?"

"That's one reason."

"What's the other one?"

"There's somethin' I been hankerin' to do for some time now." His arm slid around her and he kissed her.

For a moment or three, she kissed him back, until his arm pulled her closer and his mouth grew more demanding. She pushed him away, averting her face. "Don't."

He nuzzled her neck. "I missed you." His breath warmed her skin and shot a thrill along every nerve in her body. Despite herself, she closed her eyes and tilted her head just a bit to give him better access. "That damn portal is always open, tauntin' me. Temptin' me." He brushed her hair aside and kissed her ear. "I couldn't stay away any longer." He feathered kisses along her jaw line. "And you look mighty fetchin' in that dress." His mouth found hers again.

Her head reeled from his startling words, his husky voice, his busy tongue. Megan kissed him back. He turned in his chair until his thigh pressed against hers. He wrapped both arms around her and pulled her as close as her dress and petticoat allowed and kept kissing her, turning his head the other way. Their tongues danced. Megan's hand touched the side of his face then slid up to grip his coarse hair. One of them moaned. She didn't know which of them it was.

One roll in the hay ... maybe just once ...

His hand roamed. Down her back ... up her sides ... leaving fire in its wake.

Megan broke away, gasping for air. With each rapid breath, reason rushed in. They lived in different centuries. The universe was playing with them like pawns on a chessboard. She feared losing her heart to a man already dead.

She rested her forehead on his. "Seth. Stop."

He sat back, his arms releasing her as his eyes searched her face.

She said softly, "You're ruining everything."

Seth ran a hand down her arm, sending a shiver through her. "What am I ruinin'?"

"Our friendship. Everyone knows the surest way to ruin a friendship is to have sex. So we're not going to."

"I agree. We won't have sex."

Surprise and disappointment warred inside her.

He took her hand. "We'll make love."

She yanked her hand free. "No, we're not!"

"We're not?"

She shook her head.

He tilted his. "Ever?"

She shook her head again.

"Never ever?"

She shook her head so hard her curls bounced.

One corner of his mouth twitched, then the other corner curved upward, and a full-blown smile spread across his face. He laughed.

The sound of it annoyed her. She drew away. "What's so funny?"

"You. Because you're wrong, Miss Megan." The way he said *Miss Megan* sounded like an endearment. He stroked her cheek with his knuckles. "You are so very wrong." He cupped her face. "You and I *will* make love." His hazel eyes turned serious. "Often." He leaned closer. "Very often." His mouth covered hers.

Chapter 15

A hickey! Megan glared at the big red splotch on the right side of her neck. "Damn you, Seth," she muttered. The mirror reflected her naked body, rosy and damp from a hot morning shower. Sunlight brightened the room. She spent the next several minutes trying different ways to arrange her long hair to hide the hickey. She threw up her hands in disgust. Taping the hair in place or wearing a turtleneck seemed the only answers. It was going to be near 90 that day.

"*Damn* you, Seth!"

She stomped over to the armoire and yanked open the doors. She pawed through the clothes, pushing hangers along the metal rod. All her blouses were summery, with short sleeves and low necklines. No turtlenecks. She dug through the dresser drawers, and pulled out a long, narrow, gauzy scarf. It had been in the Lost and Found box at work. She liked the color. Light purple. She stood before the mirror, tied the scarf around her neck and arranged it to cover the hickey. She draped the short end down her front. The long end hung down her back. She smiled, pleased with the look. Her gaze slid to the reflection of the bed where she and Seth had lain together so briefly just hours ago before everything went to hell. Her smile ebbed.

He was gone for good. It was over. She eyed herself ruefully as she raised one arm and applied deodorant, then did the other. He wouldn't be back. Not after last night.

It's just as well.

Liar, her reflection said.

"What's done is done. It's over."

She turned away from the mocking reflection and went to put together an outfit to go with the scarf. She finally settled on a yellow sleeveless top, blue jean shorts, and sandals.

Thirty minutes later, Megan locked the door to her room. She descended the stairs and headed for the front door. The voices of Mrs. Powell and her husband drifted out of the office as Megan passed by and went outside, squinting in the sunshine. She paused on the top step, got her sunglasses out of her purse, and put them on, thinking there wouldn't be any sunglasses in the late 1800s. Not that it mattered now.

A taxi pulled up in front and stopped at the curb. The back door opened. A black high heel touched the pavement then a young woman climbed out. She took a moment to straighten her short-sleeved pink blouse and smooth a hand down her grey slacks. She hiked a purse the size of a briefcase up on her shoulder then looked toward the B&B, shading her eyes with one hand as the taxi drove away.

Megan screamed, "Donna!" and ran down the steps into her best friend's arms. They hugged, laughing, broke apart and looked at each other, then laughed and hugged again.

Megan drew away. "What are you doing here?"

Donna brushed a lock of shoulder-length straight brown hair out of her face. "I hadn't heard from you in a while and was thinking of taking a couple of days off to come see you. Then Bob, my co-worker, you met him, broke his leg and couldn't make this convention. So here I am." She had brown eyes and a light dusting of freckles on her cheeks. She stood six inches taller than Megan, two inches of that from the black heels. She had broad shoulders and curvy hips. Megan's mother had called Donna big-boned.

"I'm so glad." Megan grinned. "I can't believe you're here."

"Are you busy right now? Should I come back later?"

"I was going out to run some errands. Don't you have to go to the convention?"

Donna shook her head. "There's a meet and greet later today that I don't *have* to attend. I have to be there all day tomorrow and most of Wednesday. I have a six-p.m. flight that night. I'm staying at a hotel downtown."

"Don't be ridiculous. You can stay here. I have tonight and tomorrow night off."

Donna's face lit up. "Are you sure it's all right?"

"I'll ask the owner. She's in her office. Come on."

They went inside the B&B just as Mrs. Powell was leaving the office.

"Mrs. Powell, this is my friend, Donna Miller. Donna, Mrs. Powell owns the B&B"

The two women exchanged greetings.

"Donna's in town for a convention. Would it be all right if she stays here tonight and tomorrow night?"

"Of course." Mrs. Powell smiled. "What a grand time y'all will have."

"Thank you. I'll pay extra for those two nights—"

Mrs. Powell waved a hand. "Pshaw. Don't worry about it, dear. You can have over anyone you want." She leaned closer to Megan and added in a low voice, "Even that handsome young man of yours." She winked and gave Megan a knowing smile.

Megan started in surprise, at first thinking Mrs. Powell meant Seth. Then realized it had to be Barton. "Ah, thank you." She tilted her head. "But ... why?"

"Why what?" Mrs. Powell asked. The phone rang in her office.

"Why are you always so ... well, generous? I mean, you're charging me next to nothing for my room, and haven't I overstayed my welcome by now?"

Mrs. Powell put a hand to her cheek. "Why, I do believe I haven't told you yet how I came to own this place. You see, back in—"

"Honey?" Her husband stuck his head out of the office. "Excuse me, ladies." He looked at his wife. "Phone. Your sister. Doesn't sound good."

"I'll be right there." Mrs. Powell looked at Megan. "My sister has cancer."

"I'm so sorry."

"Thank you. Remind me next time I see you to tell you the story of how I got this place." She smiled at Donna. "Y'all have a good visit." She hurried into her office.

"That's nice of her." Donna linked her arm with Megan's. "What shall we do on this beautiful day? Whatever it is, it's my treat."

"Oh Donna—"

"I'm buying. Subject closed. What's with the scarf? That's a new look for you."

"Just trying something different." Megan tugged the scarf down a bit, hoping it was doing its job. "I'll show you around town then we'll get your things from the hotel. You'd better call and cancel your room. Use the house phone over there."

Donna made the call and arranged to pick up her suitcase later that afternoon then they headed downtown and walked around, chatting all the while. They had hamburgers, fries, and a couple of beers at Billy Miner's, then caught a bus to Exchange Street and walked around the Fort Worth Stockyards, checking out the stores. Donna bought a Texas souvenir spoon for her collection and a shot glass with bluebonnets painted on it.

Afternoon shadows stretched across the sidewalk as they headed to The Tejas where Megan proudly pointed out the framed article about opening night hanging on the wall. She introduced Donna to the manager and a couple of the waitresses. Megan saw Bonnie behind the bar and hurried over, Donna following behind.

"I thought you were off today," Megan said as she and Donna pulled up stools to the bar and sat.

"Someone called in sick." Bonnie had her blonde hair in a ponytail and wore a red-and-white-checkered blouse. She eyed the scarf around Megan's neck but didn't comment on it. She smiled at Donna. "Howdy."

Donna grinned. "Howdy yourself."

"This is my friend Donna, from Chicago," Megan said. "Donna, meet Bonnie, the best bartender around and the inspiration for my article about methamphetamine."

"So, you're the one." Donna plopped her big purse on the bar. "I've heard a lot about you today."

Bonnie leaned against the counter. "Heard about you, too. Nice to meet cha."

The three of them chatted awhile then Donna excused herself and went to the bathroom.

Dolly Parton sang *Nine to Five* on the jukebox while two couples kicked up their heels on the dance floor. Bonnie emptied the ashtray then whipped the rag out of the back pocket of her blue jeans and started wiping off the bar. "Did you and Barton have a nice dinner?"

"It was lovely," Megan replied. "We ate at the Water Gardens." She briefly described the night.

"Wow." Bonnie looked impressed. "I didn't know you could reserve the place. How romantic. Did he spend the night?"

Megan shook her head.

Bonnie's eyes widened. "You're kidding. He did all that for you and gave you whatever that scarf is hiding, and you sent him home?"

Megan self-consciously touched the scarf and shrugged.

"No sex yet?"

"Nope."

Bonnie straightened beer mugs then stacked some glasses. "You and Barton been seein' each other how long? Month and a half or so? And you still haven't slept with him? No offense, but I wonder why he's still hangin' around."

Megan propped her chin on her hand. "I wonder the same thing."

Donna walked up to the bar. "I hate to be a wet blanket, but I have to pick up my suitcase."

"I forgot about that." Megan pushed her stool back and stood. "I'll see you Wednesday night, Bonnie."

"Y'all have fun."

They stopped by the hotel and collected Donna's suitcase then caught a taxi back to the B&B. On the way, Megan said to Donna, "There's someplace I want to show you." Megan leaned towards the driver. "Could you take us to the Water Gardens please?"

The driver parked near an entrance to the Water Gardens and agreed to wait.

Megan and Donna joined the stream of people enjoying the cool oasis on a hot June evening. It looked different in the light of day. More trees and greenery than Megan had thought the night before. The chirping and rustle of birds settling down to roost in the trees rivaled the muffled sound of traffic on the city streets a stone's throw away. A continuous bench of concrete lined the walkways and other paths further up the terraced landscape. Megan saw little of it as she led Donna through the crowd of business men and women, families, couples young and old, and kids riding skateboards down the walkways.

"What a fabulous place." Donna stopped to look at the four walls of water. Several people strolled by. A warm breeze stirred the trees alive with noisy birds.

"I knew you'd like it. Come on. There's more." Megan kept walking.

"Jeez, where's the fire? Slow down." Donna hurried after Megan.

They came to the pool with the spiral-spraying fountains. Kids played in the water, squealing and laughing as they splashed and ran around. Megan barely gave Donna a chance to look before hurrying on to the open span of concrete with the steps leading down to the small pool.

"This is beautiful. Just beautiful," Donna said, following behind Megan down the big steps with water rushing beneath and all around. "Hey! Wait up! I'm wearing heels."

Megan reached the bottom and joined several people milling around on the concrete blocks bordering the pool. She pushed her way to the inside edge and stared intently into the tumbling, swirling water. The deafening sound of the water overwhelmed conversations around her. Ignoring the jostling crowd, she leaned over the water and listened, turning her head to hear better, and waited. Eyes closed, she wished.

"Wow. I love it!" Donna said. "Megs? What's the matter?"

Megan straightened, opening her eyes, disappointed to her core. "Nothing," she answered. Nothing was exactly what she had heard. She pasted a smile on her face and turned to Donna. "Cool, huh?"

Donna gave Megan a long look. She brushed hair off her face. "Yeah. I'm glad we came."

"Me too. Ready to go?"

Back inside the taxi, Donna said, "I've talked your ear off all day. Tell me about you."

Megan picked at a loose thread on the hem of her shorts as the taxi pulled away from the Water Gardens and headed for the B&B. "There's not much to say. I write during the day and work at night."

"Megs." Donna touched Megan's arm. "I know there's more than that going on. Something you're not telling me."

Megan bit her lip and looked out her window at people passing by on the sidewalk. It would be such a relief to tell Donna everything. *She'll think I'm nuts! Who wouldn't? Hell, I thought I was crazy! Some moments still do. How can I convince her?*

Seth's friend Tim had wanted proof when told about Seth's time traveling. The roll of toilet paper she'd sent back with Seth seemed to convince Tim. Maybe if Donna saw something from the past related to

Megan, belief might come easier. Megan glanced at her watch. A little past four. They probably had time. "There's something else I want to show you. If you don't mind paying a hefty cab fare."

"I told you. Today's my treat."

Megan leaned forward to give the cabbie new directions.

Donna rummaged around in the big purse covering her lap. Megan would bet her next paycheck that there were a couple Harlequin Romances in that purse. Donna loved those books almost as much as she loved rock and roll, jazz, and old movies. Donna pulled out a hairbrush. "Where are we going?"

"You'll see. Sit back and enjoy the ride. There's some pretty country down here."

"It looks a lot like home." Donna brushed her hair, damp with sweat near her temples. "I expected desert, tumble weeds rolling down dirt roads, and an oil well in every yard." She dropped the brush into the purse and put it on the floor of the car. She shifted sideways to face Megan. "If you don't want to talk about what's wrong right now, and I know there's something wrong so don't give me that look, tell me about your methamphetamine article."

Forty minutes later, the taxi drove around the square in downtown Cleburne then pulled into a parking lot and stopped. Megan climbed out. She hiked her purse over her shoulder. "Hurry up. It'll be closing soon."

"We're going to a bank?" Donna got out, grabbed her purse, and walked around the back of the cab. "Feels like an oven out here. Wait up!" Her high heels clicked a rapid cadence on the sidewalk. "My God, you walk fast. No wonder you're in such great shape."

"You would be too if you stepped it up a little," Megan said over her shoulder.

"Nag, nag, nag," Donna muttered.

Inside the bank, Megan walked past the few people waiting in line and went to the historical pictures on the other side of the lobby.

Donna staggered up on her heels, wiping sweat off her face. "Jeez, it's hot down here. How do people stand it? Feels good in here." She blew out a breath then looked around. "What was so important we rode an hour to see it?"

"There's some cool historical stuff here." Megan gestured to the row of six framed documents hanging on the wall. A tall potted plant with big oval leaves stood in the middle of the wall. "You like that sort of thing."

"Well, yeah." Donna sent Megan a confused look then stepped up to the black and white photo of the Farmers and Merchants National Bank in 1890. Next, Donna looked over the 1877 ledger from the Bank of Cleburne.

Megan trailed along behind. Her pulse steadily sped up as Donna stopped in front of each of the next three framed documents. Then

Donna walked to the last document closest to the big front windows where late afternoon sunlight slanted in.

For several heart-thumping seconds, Megan considered grabbing Donna's arm and getting out of there and spending the night together talking about anything, *anything* but a time-traveling cowboy named Seth.

She'll think I'm crazy.

I'll go crazy if I don't tell someone. She loves me. I have no one else to tell.

The last thought jolted Megan. She *didn't* have anyone else to tell. No parents or siblings. No relatives. No boyfriend. No other friend as close as Donna. *Sounds like a lonely life,* both Barton and Bonnie had said about Megan's lifestyle. Suddenly, she felt lonely. And shocked that they were right. She had no one else to tell except Donna.

It was now or never.

Now or forever keep her secret.

Her hand gripping the shoulder strap of her purse, Megan stayed to one side as Donna approached the frame displaying Megan's letter to the banker.

Donna leaned in for a better look then gave a small gasp. Her gaze shot to Megan. "Is this some kind of joke?"

"Joke?" Megan's heart lurched at the sight of Donna's scowl.

Donna dug in her purse. She pulled out an envelope and held it next to the framed letter. "That's your handwriting. Your signature." She waved the envelope bearing Megan's name and address written by Megan in her face. "*You* wrote that let—"

"Miss McClure, how nice to see you again." The manager walked up to join them.

Megan snatched the envelope from Donna and stuffed it in her purse then turned to greet the silver-haired woman wearing a beige blouse and brown skirt. "Hi, Mrs. Cuffee. I was showing my friend Donna the letter."

Mrs. Cuffee smiled at Donna. "Nice to meet you."

"You, too," Donna replied, arranging her scowl into a tight smile.

Megan asked, "Would you please tell Donna about this letter?"

"Of course." Mrs. Cuffee clasped her hands at her waist. "Back in 1879, a lone man robbed a bank that used to be a couple blocks down on the corner. No shots were fired, no one was hurt, in fact, it's not even mentioned if the robber had a gun. But he got away with quite a bit of money. About a week after the robbery, a young man named Seth walked in the bank and handed the banker the bag of stolen money and that letter. The banker was, naturally, amazed. Said he'd never heard of such a thing. Neither have I." She laughed. "Imagine, the robber's wife *returning* stolen money. All of it, according to the banker. He tried to find the widow McClure, but she went back East and was never heard from again. He framed the letter and hung it in the bank for everyone to see." Mrs. Cuffee touched the side of the frame.

Donna said, "That's quite a story. But the handwri—"

"Tell her about the paper and the ink," Megan urged.

"Oh yes. It's fascinating." Mrs. Cuffee pointed to the letter. "You see how yellowed the paper is? It looks old. But it's not like other paper from that time."

"It's not?" Donna leaned closer to the letter.

The woman shook her head. "The line spacing is more like today's college-ruled paper. It doesn't match any of the lined paper from its time that I've seen. And I've seen quite a few. I volunteer at the Layland Museum here in town and love to peruse old documents. Which is why I also noticed the ink in this letter is different from what was used back then."

"It is?" Donna's nose almost touched the glass in the frame.

"It's darker, and it's applied very evenly and smoothly, no difference in width or depth, no blots or smudges. Not at all like the ink out of an inkwell. I've put this letter beside documents from the same year or thereabouts, and this ink looks nothing like the ink on other old papers. Personally, I think it looks like the ink from a modern-day ballpoint pen."

Megan gasped softly, surprised by the woman's astuteness.

Donna must have heard because she sent Megan a sharp glance.

Mrs. Cuffee continued, "Which, of course, is impossible, since the letter is over one hundred years old."

"Have you had an expert look at it?" Donna straightened.

"Oh, no, no. We have a small historical society here. There aren't any funds for something like that. Truth be told, I'm the only person in the group who is so fascinated by the letter."

"Maybe it's a hoax."

Donna's comment made Megan sigh inwardly. As much as she loved her friend, sometimes Donna could be a little pushy. She was smart, analytical, argumentative, and blunt. *That girl should be a lawyer,* Megan's mother had often said.

Mrs. Cuffee arched her eyebrows then shrugged. "To what end? Besides, it's been hanging right here," she waved at the wall, "for the 15 years I've been here. I've seen old pictures of the lobby and in a few of them you can see the letter in the background. Another bank in town had it on display before this one. In the museum, there's a picture of the banker, Mr. Reynolds, standing beside the letter a year or so after he hung it up in his bank." She ran a finger along the top of the frame then flicked off dust. "Its provenance is unquestionable. The letter is part of our banking lore."

She turned to Megan. "I just remembered something. I recently met a man who studies names. I forget what that area of study is called. He read that letter then told me a most peculiar thing. He said the name

Megan wasn't used in the United States until earlier this century and he was *very* surprised to see the author's name was Megan. A name that wasn't in use any time near 1879. Odd, isn't it? I thought you'd find that interesting since you have the same name."

"Have you checked for Megan McClure in the historical records?" Donna asked.

Megan rolled her eyes. *There she goes again.*

"Of course," Mrs. Cuffee said. "Years ago. Never found anything about Megan McClure or her husband. I searched the surrounding counties looking for some mention of the mysterious McClure couple. I didn't find anything anywhere. Not one speck of evidence of their existence. Except this letter. Fascinating." Mrs. Cuffee beamed.

***

"Well, that was interesting," Donna said as she sat in the back of the cab with her big purse beside her.

Megan leaned forward to tell the driver to take them to the B&B then sat back. She dreaded the ride, dying to Donna everything but not sure how to go about it.

Donna held out her hand and wiggled her fingers. "Can I have my envelope back now?"

Megan handed it over.

Donna looked at it, then looked at Megan, frowning. "Why is there a letter that's over 100 years old written in your handwriting hanging on the wall of a bank in a small country town in Texas? Explain that to me." Donna plopped back and folded her arms, the envelope still clasped in her hand.

Megan looked away from Donna's probing gaze and stared out the window at the various stores around the town square. After a moment, she said, "We've known each other a long time." Her eyes met Donna's. "Since that first day in the dorm at college."

"You were the first one I met on the floor."

"We ate dinner together in the cafeteria. Sat in the corner."

Donna unfolded her arms and placed the envelope on the seat between them. "Two scared little freshmen." She smiled slightly. "Boy, were we dumb. Then junior year we moved to Adams Street."

"That was a great house."

"Actually," Donna laughed, "it was a dump. The big *yard* was great."

"Great for parties," Megan added. They both laughed. Good old college days. "You ever hear anything about Greg?"

"He's a lawyer in Boston or Baltimore. Can't remember which. Married. Two kids." She shrugged. "I hope he's happy." She looked out the side window. Sunlight shining in the cab's windows added a hint of gold to her brown hair. "Thought he was The One. Instead he's the one that got away," she said softly, sadly.

Megan touched Donna's arm. "I know he broke your heart, but I was so glad you moved back from D. C. I really missed you those two years."

"I missed you too." Affection replaced the sadness in Donna's eyes. "Wasn't much fun without you there. Then, as soon as I got home, Mom and Dad started their divorce. What a circus that was." Donna shook her head. "Thank God you were there to keep me sane."

"As you were for me when my mom and dad died."

Donna smiled sympathetically. "We've been through a lot together. Which is as it should be since we made that vow that day during Happy Hour sophomore year."

"Friends to the ends," they said at the same time, and made a motion of clicking beers.

"No secrets." Donna picked up the envelope and waved it under Megan's nose.

A semi rumbled past them as the taxi headed north among the thickening traffic on I-35W.

"No secrets," Megan repeated softly. She took a deep breath. "I'm going to tell you something that will make you think I'm crazy."

Donna snorted. "Won't be the first time. I often wonder about your sanity when you tell me about your next jaunt. Death Valley to see boulders that move on their own. A deep cave in Missouri to see some phosphorescence purple and orange slime the size of half a football field that pulses like a heart." She shook her head. "Your whole life is a bit crazy."

"What I'm about to tell you is ... different from all that. Very different. It involves—" Megan bit her lower lip before she could say *time travel*. She fidgeted with the scarf, wanting desperately to finally tell someone, but afraid to say the words that could change everything between her and the person she loved more than anyone else.

Her notebooks came to her mind.

Filled with the words she was afraid to speak.

"Megs?" Donna touched Megan's arm, worry in her eyes. "You can tell me anything. You know that."

"I will. Once we get back to the B&B. Can we just drop it until then?"

Donna's eyes searched Megan's face. "If you answer one question for me."

"All right," Megan agreed reluctantly.

"*Did* you write that letter in the bank?"

Megan hesitated. One nod would change everything. *No secrets.*

She nodded.

Chapter 16

Back at the B&B, Donna changed into blue jean shorts and a t-shirt with a picture of the Beatles on it then strolled around the room, admiring the furnishings and the view of the courthouse against the evening sky. She paused before the vanity. "Who's the stud?"

"Barton."

"My, he's fine. Is it serious?" Donna glanced at Megan. "Do you love him?"

"God no."

Donna picked up the picture and looked closer. "You're in the bank. Beside that letter. That same damn letter." She flung the picture on the vanity and turned to Megan. "Cut the crap and tell me what's going on ... Widow McClure."

Megan took a deep breath. "The widow McClure the banker looked for never existed."

Donna crossed her arms.

Megan opened the top drawer of the nightstand and took out the first notebook about Seth's visits. Then, remembering that Donna had taken the *Evelyn Woods Speed Reading Course,* she picked up the second notebook and gave them to Donna. "Read these while I do my laundry across the street." She held up a hand when Donna started to speak. "It's all there. I promise. Read. Then we'll talk."

Megan gathered her dirty clothes and her notebook and went to the washeteria. A woman and her two little boys were the only other people there. The boys sat on the dingy tiled floor dotted with cigarette burns and played with toy cars and trucks, making motor noises as they pushed them around. While her clothes washed, Megan sat on a plastic chair and tried to write but couldn't concentrate. She picked up an old issue of *Better Homes and Gardens* off the folding table. She flipped through pictures of beautifully decorated and immaculate homes that looked more like movie sets than residences. She tossed the magazine on the table. The washing machines finally quit. She filled the dryers and fed them coins. The woman and her boys hauled several baskets of clean laundry out to a car and drove away, leaving Megan alone in the brightly lit room with peeling puke green paint on the walls, half a dozen empty laundry carts, and a steady hum from the dryers.

She stepped outside into the muggy June night and stood on the sidewalk, watching the last streaks and smears of a pink and magenta sunset fade in the darkening sky. The sound of distant traffic and the chirp of crickets filled the still air. A tantalizing smell came from a small Mexican restaurant on the next corner down the street. Above the restaurant was a big neon sign in the shape of a sombrero, a landmark Megan used to find the B&B. Her room was around the corner. She walked to the end of the block and looked up at her second-floor windows, five long rectangles of light, the sixth one shortened by the air conditioner unit in the bottom part of the window.

What's Donna thinking? Megan picked her fingernails. *I can't imagine.* She looked at her ragged nails and stuffed her hands in her pockets. The streetlights blinked on. The light shone on the faint outline of the remnants of Seth's door on the outside wall. She imagined what it would have looked like with the staircase there. And wondered if the portal was still open. It probably didn't matter anymore to Seth if it was.

Megan took her time folding her clothes and putting them neatly in the laundry basket then carried it to her room. She paused outside the door and took a deep breath, squared her shoulders. Then opened the door.

Donna sat cross-legged on the couch, one of the notebooks open on her lap. She held a beer balanced on one knee. She looked up. "This is quite a story. Great idea for a novel." A furrow appeared between her dark eyebrows. "But it's not a novel, is it."

Megan pushed the door shut and leaned back on it. The laundry basket rested against her stomach. "No."

The furrow deepened. "It was one thing to see that old letter written in your handwriting. But this," she spread her hand over the open pages of the notebook, "is mind-blowing." Her gaze narrowed. "If it's true."

"It's true. Every word."

The air conditioner kicked on and rumbled softly while Donna stared at Megan. "You've met a time-traveling cowboy from the days of the Wild West. You really met him."

Megan nodded.

"Here. In this room. He visits you."

"Yes. Since the first of April. Just like you read."

"H-how?" Donna's face turned pale. "How can that be?"

"I have no idea how. Or why."

"But it's impossible. *Impossible.* Shit like that just doesn't happen!"

Megan shrugged. "It did."

"But it-it—"

"Donna." Megan shifted her grip on the basket, so she could hold up one hand. "I swear that everything you've read is true. It happened just the way I wrote it. It really, truly happened. I swear it on my parents' grave."

Donna's face whitened until her freckles stood out like dots made by a brown marker. "Fucking mind-blowing." Her voice was barely above a whisper.

"Tell me about it. You okay?"

Donna's hand shook as she lifted it to rub her forehead. "Yes. No. I'm-I'm not sure." She lowered her hand and leaned forward, her expression worried. "Are you having problems? Are you homesick? Lonely? Feeling iso—"

"You're wondering if I had a breakdown or something? Gone off the deep end?"

Donna raised her eyebrows. "Do you blame me?"

"I told you you'd think I'm crazy." Megan put the basket on the bed. "You don't know how many times I've questioned my sanity since Seth first came through that door." She opened a dresser drawer and started putting away clothes. "The day I saw that letter in the bank I knew I wasn't crazy. Although there have still been plenty of crazy things happening."

"Oh God," Donna moaned, "I'm afraid to ask."

Megan took several blouses out of the basket and draped them over her arm. She went to the armoire and hung them up. "It's all written there. What part are you at?"

"Seth is telling you goodbye."

"There's not much after that. You hungry?" Megan straightened a blouse on a hanger. "Thought I'd get some tacos while you finish reading. Then we'll talk." She closed the door of the armoire. "Did you check out Seth's handprint here on the edge?"

"Yeah. Bizarre. Tacos sound great. With extra cheese. Better grab more beer. I have a feeling I'm gonna need it."

About thirty minutes later, Megan returned with a bag containing half a dozen tacos with extra cheese and some packets of hot sauce. She also had a six-pack, and an iced tea to go.

Donna stood before the mirror, holding the purple dress against her. "This is gorgeous." She turned and held out the dress. "Put it on."

Megan put the food on the table. "Oh for—"

"Put it on."

Donna wouldn't take no for an answer and helped Megan change into the petticoat and dress. After buttoning up the back, Donna stepped away and clasped her hands to her chest as Megan did a slow turn. "Oh, Megs, that dress looks fabulous on you."

Megan looked down at herself for a moment then back up at her friend. "Like it was made for me?"

Donna's jaw dropped. "You don't think ...?"

"Frankly, Donna," Megan held up her hands, "I don't know what to think anymore."

Somewhere on the floor above, a door slammed. Heavy footsteps pounded down the stairs then gradually faded away. The old house moaned and groaned as if injured by the abuse.

Donna rubbed her arms. "This place gives me the creeps."

Megan smiled. "I've grown rather fond of it."

"You would." Donna made a face. "All this weirdness is right up your alley. You should be ecstatic. You're living your own personal *Twilight Zone* episode. Look at you." Donna waved a hand at Megan. "Standing there in a 100-year-old dress you think was made for you. Which is ridiculous. Granted, the color could not be more flattering. And it does fit you amazingly well. But for it to have been made just for you, you would have to be the exact same size you are now. How do you explain that?"

"I can't." Megan shrugged. *Unless it's made for me soon.* A shiver zipped down her spine. "Did you read the index card?"

"Oh yeah. That's pretty weird, too. How did the writer know your eye color? And that you would buy that dress at that sale on that day?"

"I don't know. Seth asked the same thing."

Donna sent Megan a sharp look. "You've seen him since he said goodbye?"

"Last night."

Donna put a hand to her chest. "Last night? He was here last night?" She glanced around as though expecting him to reappear. "He gave you that hickey?"

Megan had forgotten all about the hickey. She hadn't even thought of it when she removed the scarf to change into the dress. She nodded.

"What happened?"

"I'll tell you while we eat. But first," Megan stuck a seductive pose, "I'm going to slip into something more comfortable." Donna laughed her loud full-throated laugh, the sound of it reassuring. Megan turned around and held up her hair. "Would you unbutton me?" While Donna did so, Megan said, "You have no idea what a relief it is to finally tell someone all this."

"I can imagine. Well actually, I *can't* imagine. I guess all this is why I haven't heard much from you."

Megan hesitated then asked softly, "Do you believe me? About Seth and ... everything?" She glanced over her shoulder at Donna, who pressed her lips together while her fingers worked their way down the buttons.

"I've never known you to be a liar," Donna said after a moment. "Frankly, you're not a very good one. You have a wild imagination, but I don't think you'd make up something like this and try to pass it off as real. You're not a deceptive person and have always been up front with me. You have some, well, evidence. The letter in the bank is the most concrete. There's the goodbye letter from Seth. Very touching, by the way. That's not your printing so I know you didn't write it. I seriously doubt you had someone else do it as a lark. The paper is different enough from ours to be convincing. Then there's the index card with its strange questions."

"And the dress," Megan added.

"I'm still not sure about the dress but there is definitely something strange about it, too." Donna sighed. "So as much as I hate to admit it and as weird and impossible and totally far out as all this is, yes, I believe you."

Megan whirled around and hugged Donna. "Thank you!" Relief surged through her, the same intense relief Seth must have felt when he told Tim about his travels. "Oh, thank you. I love you."

"I love you too." Donna gave Megan a hard squeeze. "Go change. Let's eat."

While they sat at the table and ate tacos, Megan told Donna about the previous night. Donna almost choked on a swig of beer when she heard about the visions Megan had while dancing with Barton. When Megan mentioned hearing the voices in the Water Gardens, Donna said, "That's why you were acting so strange when we were there today. You were listening. Did you hear anything?"

Megan shook her head then told about Seth's visit.

"He actually said that? You and he will make love? Very often?"

Megan nodded as she picked up pieces of lettuce off the wrapper and put them back on the taco. She took a bite. Meat, cheese, tomatoes, and lettuce spilled out. Grease trickled down the side of her hand.

"Then what happened?"

"He kissed me." Megan wiped her mouth and hand with a napkin. "Holy moly, did he kiss me. He hauled me to my feet, wrapped his arms around me, and kissed me until my knees buckled. They actually buckled. Like in those romances you read." She stared at the taco a moment then looked at Donna. "I've never had that happen before, Donna."

"Me neither." Donna looked wistful as she slowly chewed.

"Not even with Greg?" Megan asked, surprised.

Donna slowly shook her head. "If knee-buckling kisses are a criterion I guess he really wasn't The One. Go on about Seth."

"He picked me up in his arms and carried me to bed—"

"Just like in the movies!"

"—and we started making out. It was-it was wonderful. I've never *ever* wanted someone as much as I wanted him. I practically ripped his shirt off him. It all happened so fast. He had all those buttons on my dress undone before I even realized it." Barton had said he would savor unbuttoning all those buttons. Seth had them undone in seconds. Just as quickly, he had her out of her dress, petticoat, and underwear. She remembered the rush of cold air across her breasts, followed by the heat of Seth's hungry mouth. "And then-then ..."

"What? What?" Donna demanded when Megan paused and frowned at her half-eaten taco.

"He said he was 28. I—"

"What?"

"He said he was 28. I pushed him off me and told him to stop—"

"Wait a minute, wait a minute." Donna held up a hand. "You stopped because he said he was 28?"

Megan nodded.

"Big deal." Donna shrugged, confusion on her face. She opened a packet of hot sauce with her teeth and squeezed it over a taco.

"That's what I said. Big deal. He said, *'I'm finally older than you.'* He looked so pleased. I said so what? In a few days you'll be a couple of years older than me. A few weeks you'll be a lot older than me. In five, six months you'll be an old man. You'll probably be dead by spring. Or maybe you won't come back at all. Maybe I'll sit here waiting and waiting, never knowing if you moved away or married or died." Megan paused to breathe. She'd been talking so fast she'd run out of air.

"His age was really enough to change your mind about having sex with him?"

"Donna, he was 17 when I met him two and half months ago. In that time, he aged 11 years. Yeah, it changed my mind. We were *that* close." Megan held her thumb and forefinger almost together. "Then he had to open his mouth. If he'd just kept silent I wouldn't be so damn frustrated now."

"Been awhile, huh?" Donna smiled sympathetically.

"Oh yeah."

"Why didn't you have sex *then* fight?"

Megan took a bite of her taco and washed it down with a sip of iced tea. "Because when he said he was 28, it was like someone flipped a switch and I went from hot to cold like that." She snapped her fingers. "I shoved him off the bed. Boy was he surprised. He stood there with his mouth open, naked as a jaybird. Lean and muscular with a washboard stomach. A smattering of sandy hair on his chest. All the right equipment." Megan sighed. "*Damn* he was gorgeous. It made me even madder that he had ruined the moment by opening his big mouth. So, I lit into him about buying that saloon."

"What's wrong with that? He's the entrepreneurial type. I like that."

"I do too. He's ambitious. But he could have chosen more wisely than owning a saloon."

"Hmmm." Donna wiped hot sauce off her mouth, studying Megan. "Does this have something to do with your waitressing job? Tired of all those obnoxious drunks grabbing your ass and boobs all night long?" She jutted her chin at Megan's drink. "I notice you're drinking iced tea. Not beer."

"I've been drinking a lot lately," Megan admitted. "Last night I drank a bottle of wine with Barton then had a couple of beers here with Seth. Thought I'd take tonight off." Megan sipped her tea. "And yes, I am tired of the obnoxious drunks. Working in a bar has been a revelation of inebriated human behavior. But I have nothing against bars or saloons or even drinking. It's just that Seth is made for better things. He could be so much more than just a saloon owner. That's what I told him. Well, I yelled at him. I told him he should be part of the solution not the problem. He said, '*What do you mean by that?*' I said he could get a job working for the city or the government. He could study law or business.

Or return to his ranch and make a go of it. He could do so much. He knows so much. Hell, he sat here I don't know how many times reading those history books." Megan pointed to the books on the floor beside the sofa. Her eyes widened. She muttered, "Oh no," and quickly wiped her hands with a napkin then jumped up and ran over to the sofa. She dropped to her knees beside the two books stacked one atop the other.

"What's the matter?" Donna turned in her chair.

Megan picked up *From the Prairie Grew a City: The History of Fort Worth* and *200 Years: A Bicentennial of the United States of America*. "He took one. The son of a bitch took the book of world history from 1900. Holy moly." She tossed the books down and stood, so mad she was shaking. "I told him time and again he couldn't take anything back with him. I worried about giving him toilet paper as proof about his time traveling for his buddy Tim." She paced back and forth while Donna looked on with a frown on her face. "Then Seth took my picture back. I worried about that. Who's going to see it? How would he explain it? Now he takes a damn history book. *World* history. If someone sees that or reads it." She plopped down in her chair, put her elbows on the table and covered her face with her hands. "Oh my God."

"Brilliant idea on his part. But awful," Donna quickly added when Megan lifted her head and scowled. "Simply awful. He, or someone, could really screw things up." Donna took a drink of beer. "But if he, or anyone had changed anything since he was here last night wouldn't we have noticed? Or maybe we wouldn't."

"I've got a headache just thinking about the consequences and now you point that out." Megan propped her chin on her hand and shook her head. She looked around the room. "I wonder what else he might have taken all those times he was here alone."

"Maybe you can go to his time and get the book back."

Shocked, Megan stared at Donna. "I can't believe you just said that."

"I can't believe I just said that," Donna said at the same time.

They giggled a little, pondering the impossible. Or maybe just the improbable.

"But how would I get there?" Megan almost whispered. "I can't open that door." They both looked at Seth's door.

"I can't either," Donna admitted. "I tried. But there's that other portal."

Megan rolled her eyes. "You sound like Seth. He brought up that portal in the Water Gardens. I said we don't even know if it's real. He said I need to try it. Go there and jump in the damn water and see what happens. Can you believe it?" Megan threw up her hand. "I said if, *if* there is a portal, who knows where it goes? It may go to my future. Or back to ancient Rome. Or one million years B. C. Who fucking knows? He said I should throw something in the pool, something from my time, and see if and where he finds it in his time and discovers where the portal is. I said, what, like a message in a bottle? He said that was a great idea. Write a message just for him so he'd know it was from me. I said what if someone else in his time finds it? Or maybe I'll get arrested for littering. I'd probably end up in jail or the nuthouse if I jump in the water and thrash around in it looking for a portal that doesn't exist. He called me a coward. I said he was a fool. We had a horrible fight. Said terrible things to each other. It was awful." Megan covered her face with her hands again. "Just awful."

A gentle hand rested on her shoulder, warm and comforting.

"Do you love him?" Donna asked gently.

"I don't know," Megan moaned. "I think so." She raised her head, pushing hair out of her eyes. "So what? He lives a hundred years in the past. He's dead."

"How and when did he die?"

"I don't know," Megan admitted.

Donna sat back, surprise on her face. "You mean you haven't looked him up in the historical records?"

"Partly. He and his family were listed on the 1870 census. Just he and his sister were on the 1880 one."

"So, you know he actually existed. But you never looked up when and how he died?"

Megan looked down at the table. "I don't want to know. Not yet. On the day I leave here, I'll stop by the library on the way to the airport. I'll find out what happened to him, then go home and get on with my life." The thought of going back to Chicago depressed her.

"If you had the chance, would you tell him how he dies?"

Megan rubbed sudden goose bumps on her upper arms. "We talked about that once. He said he didn't want to know. Would you?"

"Yes," Donna replied immediately. "Especially if it was years and years away."

"What if it's Wednesday? On the plane?"

"I'd take another plane." Donna grinned.

Megan did not grin back. "I don't think you can cheat death."

"I take it you wouldn't want to know?"

"No way."

They ate tacos in silence. The air conditioner went off and made that ticking sound for a minute or so.

"What do you think those so-called visions you had were all about?" Donna asked.

"Seth thought that the dress was causing the visions. Then he said that maybe it's Barton. My fella, Seth called him." Megan made a face. "Although I don't think either of them is the cause."

"What's your theory?" Donna unwrapped the last taco and took a bite.

"It's pretty off-the-wall."

Donna burst out laughing, spewing bits of food everywhere. "Ooh, sorry." She quickly covered her mouth and swallowed then leaned over to flick a chunk of food off the front of Megan's shirt. "This entire conversation is pretty off-the-wall."

Megan wadded up the taco wrapping and stuffed it into the paper bag from the restaurant then wiped crumbs off the table with a napkin into her palm and dumped them into the bag. "It seems that every time I get close to having sex with Barton, something intervenes. One afternoon we went to a movie and made out like teenagers. He brought me back here and we were standing outside his car, kissing. It felt good. It'd been so long. I hadn't seen Seth in a while and—" Megan shrugged.

Donna cleaned up after her meal. "What happened?"

"Just as I was about to invite Barton up here for the first time, Bonnie drove up and wanted to talk about the meth article. So, I sent him on his way."

"Bet that pissed him off."

Megan nodded. "Then last night—I can't believe it was just last night—Barton showed up at work. He looked good. Exceptionally good. I was delivering drinks and I glanced back and saw him watching me walk away. He smiled the sexiest smile I've ever seen and that instant I decided that tonight was the night. Seth was gone, he'd told me goodbye. Barton was here. And handsome. And seems to like me. And I wanted him. Maybe I just wanted someone who wanted me," she added softly, looking at the armoire bearing the remnants of Seth's blood. "We danced. He whirled me around the floor and I wondered if he was as good a lover as he is a dancer. The next instant, well, you know what happened. I was dancing with Seth. Then I snapped out of it and was back with Barton. Later, at the Water Gardens, I told him I wanted him to spend the night with me. We danced and kissed. Then he went to pee in the bushes and I ended up down beside the pool, hearing horses and voices and feeling dizzy. Barton brought me back here then left."

"So, you think *something* is purposely keeping you from, what? Forming a relationship with someone else besides Seth?" Donna shook her head. "Pretty weird, Megs. As all of this is. Pretty weird."

Megan leaned back in her chair and stretched out her legs, scratching a mosquito bite on her thigh. "Welcome to my world."

"I know you don't think this *something* is God. Or destiny since you don't believe in that either."

"For lack of a better term, I'm going to call it the universe."

"Hmmm. The universe. Heavy shit." Donna downed her beer and wiped the back of her hand across her mouth. "Why do you think the universe is interested in you? Why are you so important? I mean, I love you and think you're great but why does the universe?"

"I have no idea. Maybe Seth is the important one. Maybe I save his life, so he could do great things."

"Maybe it's not him but one of his kids. A kid he has with you."

Megan sent Donna a sharp look and saw she was kidding. At least partially.

"You could test your theory. Pick up some random guy at the bar one night and see what happens. If you're right, something will intervene. If you're wrong," Donna shrugged. "You'll either have sex with a stranger or run like hell." She laughed. "Other girls talk about their jobs or their guys or their kids. Not us. Nothing that mundane for the two of us. Tell me about Barton."

Megan yawned again. "Not tonight. I don't know about you, but I'm beat. I was up late last night and now it's midnight. You have to get up early for your conference. Let's go to bed."

After their nightly rituals, Donna got into the bed from one side while Megan used the stool to climb up on her side. Once they were both under the covers, Megan turned off the light on the nightstand. Darkness settled over the room.

Donna said, "Maybe Seth will show up. I'd love to meet him."

"He won't be back."

Donna rolled onto her side, facing Megan. "You sound so sure."

"I told him to get out and never come back."

"Doesn't mean he won't. He said goodbye then came back anyway."

"I told him if he had any sense at all he'd marry Susannah."

"*What?*"

"I told him he should marry Susannah. He said, *What do you know about her? You've never met her.* I said I know she loves you. Why do you think she's remained single all this time? So, marry her. He pulled on his shirt—he'd put on his trousers long before this—then reached into his pocket and took out the picture of me. He looked at it a long moment then looked at me. *Maybe I will,* he said. He ripped the picture into pieces and threw them at me. He glared at me and repeated with a snarl, *Maybe I will.* He grabbed his hat and gun and, I guess, the book, although I didn't see that, stomped out of here and slammed the door so hard the wall shook. End of story."

***

The next day while Donna attended the conference Megan worked on an article. She took a break and went downstairs to find Mrs. Powell and hear about how she had obtained the B&B.

"Sorry, miss," said one of the girls who helped with the cleaning and laundry. "Mr. and Mrs. Powell went to Lubbock to arrange her sister's funeral."

Megan used the house phone to call Candace Huntington's number. The Mexican woman answered and said Mrs. Huntington was still in the hospital and not doing well. Disappointed, Megan hung up. The universe wasn't cooperating today.

That night she and Donna had pizza and beer in the room while Barton's story unfolded. When Megan finished with the news of Barton's relationship to Johnny Bingo from Seth's time, Donna said, "Except for that part Barton sounds too good to be true. Handsome. Charming. Seemingly well off." Donna counted his attributes on her fingers. "Tips well. Drives a Vette. Not pushy when it comes to sex?" She glanced at Megan, who shrugged. "He says he likes you. He sounds perfect." Donna picked up a piece of pizza. "Which is impossible so what's his flaw?"

"He's bossy, possessive, and a hot head."

"Now we're getting somewhere."

"He has one odd behavior. He has this friend. Business associate, maybe, is more correct. His name is Jim and he's always forgetting his briefcase and Barton is always returning it to him. When I'm with him Barton has me carry the briefcase then he's never around when Jim comes to get it. This has happened seven, eight times or so."

"Always in a public place?"

Megan nodded.

"What's Jim like?"

"Older guy, around forty maybe. Has a limp. Nervous type. Never says much. Just mumbles thanks and off he goes with his briefcase."

"What's in the briefcase?"

Megan shrugged. "I assume paperwork. Barton's in real estate so it's probably deeds, forms, legal stuff." She picked a piece of pepperoni off a pizza slice and ate it.

"You never opened it?"

"It's always locked. But one time, Barton was waiting for me in his car and he had the briefcase open and was going over paperwork. It looked like any other briefcase full of papers. Nothing special or odd about it."

"And you gave that briefcase to Jim?"

Megan nodded.

Donna ate a piece of pizza. After a moment she said, "Maybe Barton let you see all of that on purpose then pulled the old switcheroo on you."

Megan bit her lower lip, frowning. "The same thought has crossed my mind. I guess there *could* have been another briefcase behind his seat."

Donna licked tomato sauce off her fingers. "It might behoove you to find out what's in that briefcase. Might be something illegal. Drugs. Counterfeit money. Guns."

Detective Sullivan's words came back to Megan. *A suitcase that size could hold $20,000 worth of meth.* Six times $20,000. $120,000. *Holy moly.* "I've had my suspicions. But it doesn't make any sense. He seems to have a pretty good life."

"He might not be all he *seems to* be."

"The other night he was real serious and wanted to talk to me. He said, *I'm not what I*—and never finished the sentence. When I asked him about it last night, he said we'll talk soon. Weird, huh?"

Donna tilted her head. "You don't really care for him, do you?"

Megan shook her head. "I think he's falling for me, Donna. What am I going to do about that?"

"Poor guy doesn't stand a chance if the universe has plans for you."

***

"I've got some great news for you," Donna said the next afternoon when she returned to the B&B after the conference. "One of my colleagues who is also a freelance writer mentioned he's part of a group that's starting the NWU. The National Writers Union."

Megan's eyes widened. "A writer's union?"

Donna nodded. "The only labor union that will represent freelance writers."

"Holy moly." Megan sank down on the sofa. "I can't believe it. I never thought it would happen. A union."

"They're having meetings in major cities all over the country about starting a chapter in each area. They'll be in Chicago July 11 and 12." Donna sat beside Megan. "I told him about you, how you've been freelancing for almost three years. He wants you to come to the meeting in Chicago and give a talk."

Megan started in surprise. "A talk? Me?" She frowned. "Oh, I don't know—"

"You'd be great." Excitement danced in Donna's brown eyes. "You've been living the freelancer's life. You know the ropes. The pitfalls, the problems, the satisfaction, the freedom. Plus, who knows who you'll meet? What connections you'll make?" Donna touched Megan's arm. "You need to do this, Megs. He wants to talk to you. His name is Brian Stevens. I have his phone number at the hotel. He said he'll be there until around three." Donna glanced at her watch. "Let's call him."

Megan stared at Donna in amazement. It was all happening so fast.

Donna tugged Megan to her feet. "Come on."

Downstairs, Donna dialed the number on the house phone. "Hi, Brian? This is Donna Miller. I'm glad I caught you. My friend Megan is right here. Sure." She handed Megan the phone.

Five minutes later, Megan and Donna headed back upstairs. Donna almost skipped up them. "This is just great! What a brilliant idea I had."

Megan followed slowly behind. It was great and a brilliant idea. A wonderful opportunity for her. Good exposure. For a cause she believed in. Yet her feet dragged. She had to be in Chicago by July 10. She had to leave Fort Worth, leave this house, leave Seth.

Back in the room, Donna put her suitcase on the bed.

"You're leaving already? Your plane doesn't leave until six."

"You know I like to be early. I heard the traffic is bad. I want to get going." Donna shuffled clothes around in the suitcase. "Did you get a lot done today?"

Megan sat on the end of the bed. "Finished my article. Got a check in the mail for another one. Oh yeah, I forgot to tell you that yesterday I found out Mrs. Powell is out of town and Candace Huntington is still in the hospital."

"You'll let me know what each one of them says, right?"

"Of course. I'm so glad you came, Donna."

Donna paused with a blouse in her hands. "Me too. I was worried about you when I didn't hear from you." She shook out the blouse then put it in the suitcase. "What day are you coming home? I'll pick you up." Donna pinned Megan with her eyes. "You *are* coming home for the meeting, right?"

"Of course. I'm glad it's still a couple weeks away. The first part of my meth article will be in the paper a week from this Sunday. The second half will be the next Sunday, the fourth of July weekend. I'll head home sometime that next week. Wednesday or Thursday. Plenty of time before the meeting on Saturday." She looked around the room and said in a louder voice, "You hear that, universe? Seth? Three weeks. That's all the time I'm giving you. Three weeks. After that, don't screw with me anymore."

Thirty minutes later the taxi driver loaded Donna's suitcase into the idling cab while Donna and Megan hugged each other.

"I wish you didn't have to go." Megan's voice shook with emotion. "You're the only thing I miss about Chicago."

"I can't wait for you to come home." Donna drew away. "If you need me, call anytime, okay? Even if it's just to talk. I don't know how you kept such a big secret all this time without going nuts. I want to hear everything that happens. Every vision, every suitcase incident. Everything." Donna got in the back seat of the cab and shut the door. She rolled down the window and motioned Megan closer. "You're not alone in this now. And don't you dare go back in time without calling me first." Donna shook her head and laughed. "Now that's something I never thought I would say." With a wave, she rode away.

Chapter 17

"Is your friend headed home?" Bonnie asked that night as she put four bottles of beer on Megan's tray.

Megan nodded. "She should be on the plane right now. Bonnie, I turned in my notice tonight. My last day here will be July fifth."

"Oh man, you're really gonna leave us?" Bonnie stuck out her lower lip. "I sure hate to hear that, but I guess you gotta go home sometime."

"I've been gone long enough." Now that Megan had a deadline, leaving didn't seem such a hard decision.

"What did Barton say when you told him?"

"I haven't told him yet. I haven't even seen or heard from him since Sunday night. Please don't say a word. I'll tell him ... soon."

Bonnie made a motion of zipping her mouth. She shook her head. "Gonna break his little ol' heart."

"I doubt it." Megan laughed.

Couples filled the dance floor as Dottie West and Kenny Rogers sang *What Are We Doin' in Love* on the jukebox. The regulars at the end of the bar were raising hell and pounding their beers about something.

"At least you'll be here to see both of the meth articles in the Sunday papers. First part is next weekend. Then you'll be baskin' in the glory, girl."

"Glory that is partly yours. Without your idea, information, and motivation, it wouldn't have happened. Thank you." From the back pocket of her jeans, Megan took out a folded check and slid it across the bar.

Bonnie eyed the check. "What's that for?"

"The article. You were the heart and soul of it."

"But you did all the work."

"I was just the voice." Megan pushed the check closer to Bonnie.

Bonnie wiped her hands, picked up the check, and unfolded it. She blinked a couple times. "Thanks, Megan. You're the best." She flashed a trembling smile, stuck the check in her back pocket, then quickly turned around and moved some bottles of liquor from one shelf to another.

Megan delivered her drinks on feet as light as her heart.

Hours later, she went to the restroom. A slender young woman stood in front of the mirror brushing her long blonde hair. She was still there when Megan left the stall and washed her hands in the sink. The woman took a tube of mascara out of a small plastic purse the same bright red as her sleeveless blouse and leaned towards the mirror. She applied a layer of mascara to lashes already thick with it. She was pretty, with a golden tan, and long thin legs in tight jeans. She looked familiar. Her pale blue eyes met Megan's in the mirror.

"I remember you," Megan said. "You're Barton's friend Tammy. I'm—"

"I know who you are." The woman straightened. She closed the tube and dropped it in her purse. "And I'm not Barton's *friend*." She snapped the purse shut.

Megan dried her hands on some paper towels. "Sorry. Thought you were."

The woman looked at Megan with disdain in her eyes and a sneer on her red lips. "You don't know anything," she paused for a heartbeat then added with venom, "bitch." She stalked out of the restroom.

***

"Want to go out tonight?" Barton asked Megan over the house phone at the B&B.

"I have to work."

"Call in sick."

"I can't. It's Friday. Busy night." Megan swung the phone cord back and forth.

"Your dedication is admirable but frustrating, darlin'. I haven't seen you in a coon's age." He added gruffly, "I miss you."

The phone cord stilled. Telling Barton she would be leaving soon suddenly seemed more complicated than she had anticipated. *Am I gonna break his little ol' heart?*

"Megan? You there?"

"Yes."

"I'd take you out to lunch or a movie this afternoon, but I have a meeting. Don't know how long it'll last. Can I give you a ride home after work tonight?"

"I'd like that. Hey, I ran into your friend Tammy the other night at work." She repeated the brief, unfriendly conversation. "What's her problem?"

Barton's sigh came over the phone. "She's jealous, even though she's nothing more than a friend. I'm sorry she was rude to you, darlin'. I'll have a talk with her." His voice took on a hard edge. "She shouldn't be bothering you at work. Or anywhere."

"It's not like she's harassing me or anything. It's no big deal."

"Yes. It is."

He sounded pissed. She almost felt sorry for Tammy. "I gotta go. My writing is calling me. I'll see you tonight."

"Should I bring my toothbrush?"

She chuckled. "Bring it and whatever else you need."

"My toothbrush and you is all I'll need."

***

A couple hours later Megan turned off her typewriter and sat back in the chair. She stretched her arms overhead and arched her back until it popped. Warm sunshine streamed in the windows framing a blue sky. She needed a break. A brisk walk seemed just the thing. She changed out of a t-shirt and baggy shorts into a light green tank top and white shorts that weren't at all baggy. She stepped out of the B&B and into an oven.

She paused on the steps. *What was I thinking?* In a couple of weeks, she wouldn't have to deal with the Texas heat. Just Chicago humidity. She put on her sunglasses and went for a not-very-brisk walk.

At the Mexican restaurant beneath the big sombrero, she turned left and headed south. A sign on a bank flashed a temperature of 94. Just knowing the actual degree made a few more beads of sweat pop out on her forehead.

Traffic thinned and quieted as businesses gave way to residences. She strolled through a neighborhood of small wood-framed houses with one-car garages and gardens of straggly flowers trying to survive in the oppressive heat. She could empathize. She felt a little straggly herself. The merry tune of an ice cream truck cut through the heat. She followed the song and three blocks away found the truck surrounded by half a dozen kids. She waited her turn then stood on the sidewalk in the shade of a big tree, licking an orange Popsicle, savoring the coldness. The last bite plopped on the ground before her tongue could catch it. She threw the trash in an empty garbage can on the curb then licked her sticky fingers. She glanced at her watch. Time to head back and eat, clean up, maybe write a little before work.

Megan didn't know exactly where she was but knew enough to head north. She paused at a corner as a truck drove by and glanced down the street then did a double take. Parked in the middle of the block on the other side of the street was a cherry red Corvette.

It looked totally out of place for the neighborhood.

It looked like Barton's.

Megan walked toward it and recognized his license plate.

She stopped beside the car and looked at the house. Small, with weathered wood, a porch across the front bordered by rose bushes missing most of their leaves. A pot of wilted purple and white petunias draped over the porch railing. On the left side of the house, a driveway of broken concrete with weeds growing in the cracks led to a garage in back. An old pickup sat in the driveway. *What's Barton doing here? He's supposed to be in a meeting. Surely, he doesn't live here.*

The rumble of a motorcycle split the quiet neighborhood. The roar grew louder as the bike came down the street then pulled into the driveway. Silence returned when the engine quit. A young man with shaggy, wind-blown hair got off the bike, carrying a six-pack of pop cans. He gave Megan the once over and grinned as he swaggered across the browning grass toward her.

"Howdy, sweet cheeks. You just move in the neighborhood?" He looked around twenty, wearing worn jeans with holes in the knees and a black muscle shirt that lived up to its name.

Megan bit back a grin. *Sweet cheeks. Holy moly.* She shook her head. "Just out for a walk."

"Nice day for a ride." He jutted his chin towards the bike, a shiny black and chrome machine almost as big as a cow that looked like certain death to Megan. It also looked as out of place as the Corvette. "Wanna go for a ride? Snuggle up close?" He wiggled his eyebrows and lifted the six-pack as if it were a barbell, flexing the muscles in his arm.

"No thanks." She hesitated, figured what the hell, and asked, "Is Barton here?"

"You a friend of his?"

Megan nodded.

"He's inside with my dad. Come on." He jerked his head for her to follow and walked to the front door. He looked back at her. "Sure you don't wanna go ridin'?"

"I'm sure."

He shoved open the door, hollering, "Hey y'all, I'm back. Barton, there's a good lookin' chick here to see ya." He said over his shoulder to Megan, "Everyone's probably in the kitchen. That's where the fun is." He winked at her then headed down a dimly lit hallway to a room at the end.

She hesitated. *What fun?* Entering the house of a stranger made her leery but curiosity won. She stepped inside and paused to shove her sunglasses up on her head, enjoying the cool relief of air conditioning. She closed the door and followed the young man, passing the living room. Couch, recliner, TV, stereo, coffee table with magazines and an over-flowing ashtray on it, dingy beige carpet. Nothing looked new or even close to new except the TV and stereo. The house reeked of cigarette smoke mixed with a smell of something else that made her nose wrinkle. A nasty odor she recognized but from where eluded her. Talking and laughter came from a room behind a closed door at the end of the hallway.

The young man pushed open the door and put the six-pack on a counter along a wall. "All right. I got here just in time."

Megan entered the kitchen and stopped. A sickening sweet smell hit her like a slap in the face. The same smell as that trailer in the country. The smell Detective Sullivan had described. *Methamphetamine has a distinct odor. A sickening sweet smell.* The smell, its associated memories, and the truth of its origin—meth—hit her with almost as much force as what she saw.

A guy in his early twenties stood beside a table that held four cans of pop, two tall glasses with varying levels of iced tea in them, another over-flowing ashtray, a red Bic lighter and a blue one, a pack of Marlboros, a pack of Winstons, two spoons, two syringes, and a small baggie containing white powder. Megan caught her breath at the sight of the powder. A guy with a bad case of acne sat with his arm extended on top of the table, palm up, his hand made into a fist. Megan recalled a cruel high school nickname used for kids with acne—Pizza Face. Next to him sat a girl with messy hair and a goofy smile, tearing bits of paper into tinier and tinier pieces while she jabbered away at ninety miles an hour seemingly to herself. They ignored Megan in the doorway.

The young man she had followed inside pulled out a chair and sat at the table. "Barton's here somewhere. I'll get him for you as soon as I've had my turn."

The guy standing beside the table was short and skinny and had wild red hair like Bozo the clown. He asked Pizza Face with the clenched fist, "You ready?"

"Fuckin' A." Pizza Face grinned.

Bozo picked up a syringe. He held it at eye level and squirted liquid out of the end of it. He leaned down and pressed the needle to Pizza Face's inner arm near the bend.

Megan took a step forward. "What the h—"

"Megan?"

She whirled around.

Barton stood behind her, shocked surprise on his face. "What are you doing here?"

"What are *you* doing here? Shooting up like *them*?" She jabbed her finger at the table.

He looked beyond her. His eyes widened. "Oh fuck." He grabbed her shoulders. "Go wait outside."

She knocked his hands away. "Are you next?"

His lips pressed into a thin line. He said with anger in his voice, "Stay here." He pushed past her and charged into the room, hollering, "What the fuck are you kids doing?" He yanked the syringe out of Bozo's hand, making Pizza Face scream like a teenage girl in a horror movie, and threw it in the garbage can near the sink. The girl quit jabbering and watched with wide-eyed fascination, her mouth making weird motions.

The young man Megan had followed inside jumped to his feet, ran to the garbage can and reached in it.

"You touch that, I'll break your arm," Barton snarled.

The young man withdrew his hand from the garbage can, staring at Barton as if he'd gone crazy.

"Hey man, what the fuck?" Bozo yelled then backed away when Barton turned on him.

"What'd Jim tell you kids about bringing that shit into his house?" Barton, his face furious, towered over Bozo. "Huh?" Barton poked Bozo in the chest. "What'd he say?"

"Uh, uh." Bozo backed up again.

Barton slapped Bozo upside his head. "Asshole. I can't believe you're doing that shit."

"Jeez, man." Bozo rubbed his head. "What's your problem?"

"You ripped me open when you yanked that rig out," Pizza Face whined. "Look! I'm bleedin'!" He held up his arm streaked with a thin line of blood.

"You're lucky I don't rip your damn head off for shooting that shit in your arm." Barton yanked Pizza Face out of his chair by the back of his t-shirt and shoved him toward the sink. "Wash that before it gets infected. And use soap, for God's sake." Barton leaned over the table, grabbed the girl's chin, and stared at her. "Man, are you fucked up." He released her and turned to Bozo. "Take your sister and get out."

Bozo stepped around Barton, keeping his distance, and pulled the girl to her feet. "Come on, Sue, let's blow this fuckin' place."

Barton looked at Pizza Face holding his arm beneath the running faucet. "You too. Finish up and get out." Barton jabbed his finger at the doorway where Megan stood.

"Oh damn," someone said behind Megan.

She glanced over her shoulder and met Jim's eyes. She'd been so caught up in the commotion in the kitchen she hadn't noticed his presence.

"Sorry 'bout all this, miss." Jim had a miserable expression on his lined face. "Damn drugs."

"Bad scene." Megan realized the young man who had led her inside must be Jim's son. She returned her attention to the kitchen where Barton was saying, "I told you to get out of here."

"All right, man, cool it. Just let me get my shit." Bozo made a move toward the table.

Barton grabbed the edge of the table with both hands and flipped it over.

Megan's jaw dropped.

All four kids erupted into shouts of surprise and protest.

The glasses shattered against the wall. Cans of pop crashed to the floor, spilling pop everywhere. The ashtray went flying, scattering butts and ashes. Cigarette packs, lighters, spoons, the syringe, and the baggie ended up on the liquid-covered floor.

"Shit, Barton, look what you did!" Jim's son fished the baggie out of the gooey mess and held it up. Sugary dark liquid mixed with ashes dripped from the baggie. "What the fuck's the matter with you!"

Barton snatched the baggie out of the outstretched hand, tore it open and dumped the white powder on top of everything else on the floor.

"Are you fuckin' nuts?" Jim's son hollered, throwing his hands up. Veins stuck out on his forehead. "That was a fresh batch you just—"

"You dumb shit." Barton took two steps, crunching glass beneath his sandals, grabbed Jim's son, slammed him against the wall next to a splotch of coke, and pinned him there with a forearm across his neck. Bozo and Pizza Face started toward Barton.

Jim quickly limped into the kitchen and grabbed an arm of each boy. "Time you leave, boys."

Bozo said, "God damn it Jim, let me get my cigarettes and—"

"Now. Before Barton starts on you." Jim jerked the boys around. "Maybe I should let him. You got some balls bringing that crap into my home." He shoved the boys toward the doorway. "Get out and don't come back. You too, Sue."

Pizza Face and Bozo, dragging the girl by the arm, stormed past Megan and went out the front door, one of them shouting, "Fuck you, Barton!" before slamming it shut behind them.

Hands on his hips, Jim stared at the mess on the floor then looked at Barton, who still had the struggling young man pinned by the throat and was talking to him.

Megan strained to hear what Barton said to the young man but all she heard was the anger in Barton's low voice. Whatever he said must have scared the bejesus out of the young man because he quit struggling, his eyes widened, and his face turned pale. Barton talked a moment longer then released Jim's son, who nodded while swallowing and rubbing his throat. Barton gave the young man a slap on the back, the friendly, man-to-man kind. Then Barton put his hand on the back of the young man's neck and propelled him toward Jim, saying, "Now apologize to your father." Barton released the young man and stepped aside. He took a cigarette out of the pack in his t-shirt pocket, a lighter out of the pocket of his jeans, and lit up.

The young man looked at the floor and mumbled something.

Barton slapped the back of the young man's head. "Speak up, Tony."

Tony glared at Barton then looked at Jim. "Sorry, dad." Sullenness and insincerity dripped from the words.

Jim put a hand on his son's shoulder. "I know things have been hard for you, son. But drugs aren't the answer." Jim pushed Tony toward a door at the back of the house. "Why don't you go out in the backyard and—"

"Hold on there, Jim," said Barton, who stood puffing away on the cigarette. "Tony needs to clean up that mess, don't you think?"

The three of them looked at the overturned table, pop cans and broken glass in the syrupy puddle on the floor. The meth was slowly congealing and resembled lumpy flour.

Jim rubbed a hand on the back of his neck, frowning. His gaze shot to Barton before darting away. "Reckon you'd better get busy, son."

Tony grimaced then said with an exaggerated sigh, "Sure."

"Before you start, you need to apologize to Barton's girlfriend Megan." Jim nodded toward Megan, standing in the doorway.

"Girlfriend?" Tony repeated, his face suddenly as red as Bozo's hair. His gaze went from Barton to Megan. "Sorry 'bout everything, ma'am," Tony mumbled. He bent over and started picking up the debris on the floor.

She wondered if he was regretting his *sweet cheeks* comment upon finding out she was Bad Ass Barton's girlfriend.

Barton looked at Megan as if he'd forgotten she was there. He dropped his cigarette into an empty pop can in the garbage then hurried to her side. "I'm sorry you had to see all that, darlin'." He slid his arm around her, but she moved away, putting distance between them.

"So am I." *That was either a family in crisis over drugs or a performance—for my benefit. Not sure which, but I'm leaning towards the latter.* Whatever it was, Barton was clearly in charge. "I never expected to walk into a meth house." She crossed her arms. "Much less find you in one."

"This isn't a meth house. It's Jim's place. He's lived here four, five years since his divorce."

She threw caution to the wind. "Is he your partner in crime?"

Barton jerked back as if slapped. "What are you talking about? Are you nuts?"

"When his son picked up the baggie out of the mess on the floor he said, *That was the fresh batch you just*. Then you slammed him into the wall. Sounds like he got that meth from *you* and *you* wanted to shut him up."

A muscle jumped in Barton's cheek as he stared at her.

"*Hugh* just got," Tony said.

Megan looked at Tony, who was squatting on the floor picking up pieces of glass. "Who?"

"The guy with red hair."

Bozo.

"His name's Hugh," Tony continued. "It was his crank. He just got it last night. Barton had nothin' to do with it."

Hugh. You. They did sound alike. Perhaps she had heard wrong.

She turned to Barton. "Show me your arms."

"What?"

"Show me your arms to prove to me you haven't been shooting up with the kids."

"Oh, for—"

She headed for the front door.

"Okay, okay. Here."

Barton held out his arms, palms up. She drew him into the kitchen for better lighting then inspected the skin on the inside of each arm from wrist to shoulder, pushing up the short sleeves of his t-shirt. Detective Sullivan had shown her pictures of needle tracks and she'd glimpsed Julia's track-riddled arms a couple times, so she had an idea of what to look for. Barton's arms were tanned and muscular, ridged with tendons and veins. No needle marks.

"Satisfied?" he asked a bit sarcastically.

She met his gaze. "You could have injected it somewhere else. Your leg. Your neck. You could have snorted it."

"Good Lord, you're a suspicious little thing. I did not inject anything anywhere or snort anything. I did have a couple beers." He raised an eyebrow. "Is that allowed?"

His eyes were clear, the pupils normal. He wasn't doing any weird meth-mouth motions. He didn't seem hyped up. Apparently, he was clean.

He must have seen her conclusion on her face because he said, "I'm glad you finally believe me. I don't blame you for thinking what you're thinking. Walking in and seeing something like that." He shook his head. He drew her back to the hallway and said in a low tone, "A few months back Tony moved in with Jim. He's Jim's youngest and has been a problem since he got here. He was going to junior college, but he hasn't attended any classes in weeks. He sits home and does dope all day. Now his friends show up at all hours. Like today."

Jim stood nearby. He threw up his hands. "I'm at my wit's end with that boy."

"Where's his mother?" she asked.

"She died several months ago. Car wreck," Jim said.

Megan's heart went out to Tony, who was wiping the floor with a wad of paper towels. She asked Barton, "What are you doing here?"

"Jim called me. He needed a friend to talk to. I stopped by to see him after my meeting, which was shorter than I had anticipated. I got here in the middle of a fight between Jim and Tony. I took Jim to the back room and sent Tony to the store for some sodas to give them a chance to cool off. That other kid, I forget his name, was here too. He must have let Hugh and his sister in while we were in back. I was just as surprised as you to see them doing that. Stupid kids." He raised his voice and said, "You're doing a great job there, Tony."

Tony shot Barton a dirty look and kept on cleaning. Wadded up paper towels filled the garbage can. The smell of meth still lingered in the air, potent and clinging.

Megan said to Jim, "What will you do about Tony?"

Jim avoided her gaze and ran a hand through his thinning hair. Before he could say anything, Barton said, "I know a doctor at one of the hospitals. I'll see if he knows what resources are available."

"I appreciate that," Jim replied.

"You two have known each other a long time?" Megan asked.

Jim looked up at Barton. "Since you were what, 13 or so?"

Barton nodded. "Jim lived down the block from us. I mowed his yard after he came back from Vietnam."

Jim tapped his bad leg. "Damn gooks."

"We've been working together a couple of years now."

"Best boss I ever had." Jim grinned at Barton. "Do you want to sit down, miss? It'd be more comfortable while we talk." Jim limped in the direction of the living room off the hallway.

Megan glanced at her watch. "No thanks. I'd better go. I have to get to work soon."

Jim stopped behind her in the hallway.

Barton stepped closer to her and rested his left hand on the wall above her head. "You never did say what you're doing here."

"It's a nice day. I went for a walk."

"You *walked* here?"

She nodded. "So?"

"It's six, seven miles from your place."

"That far? No wonder I'm hot and sweaty and need a nap." She smiled.

Barton did not smile. "And you just happened to end up here?"

"I saw your car. It seemed an odd place for your meeting. Then I ran into Tony. He said you were here and invited me in. Now I'm going to walk back."

Barton's eyes searched hers. His hand stayed on the wall above her head on her right. His bulging biceps formed a barricade on that side.

Tony sat back on his heels on the kitchen floor holding a big piece of jagged glass, watching them.

Jim stood in the hallway between her and the front door.

For a brief, awful moment, Megan had a feeling they weren't going to let her leave.

Don't be ridiculous.

"I can't let you just walk out of here."

Fear shot through her veins at Barton's words. She saw a dark look in his eyes. The blood drained from her face. Her heart pounded. Every limb of her body tensed. They had her trapped. Her fingers gripped the strap of her purse, heavy with rolls of quarters she'd meant to exchange at a bank. *Heavy enough to knock him out?* He stood so close her back pressed against the wall. There wasn't enough room to maneuver a swing, or a way to escape. The smell of meth curled around her like a choking vine. She struggled to breathe, then to speak, but could only manage, "Y-you c-can't?"

The slightest of smiles touched his mouth, as if he knew she was scared, and he enjoyed it.

"Of course not." His hand left the wall to stroke her hair. It took all her willpower not to cringe beneath his touch. "I'd be worried sick about you. This isn't the kind of neighborhood you should go walking around in. I'll take you home." He turned and walked into the kitchen. "Tony, you're going to keep your nose clean, right?"

Megan sagged against the wall, weak with relief and questioning her sanity. Something she'd been doing a lot since coming to Fort Worth. She jumped when Jim spoke.

"I apologize for all this, miss."

"Good luck with Tony. Tell Barton I'm outside." She brushed past Jim, made a beeline for the front door, and went outside. She didn't stop until she was on the sidewalk beside the Corvette. She pulled her sunglasses off her head and shoved them on her face. She took several deep breaths. Never had the hot Texas sun felt so good, the muggy air so refreshing. It cleared her head. That meth smell in the house had been getting to her. It put strange ideas in her head. It made her see strange things, like that sinister look in Barton's eyes. Made her feel strange things. Trapped. Threatened.

"Bad shit," she muttered. She grabbed a handful of her hair and sniffed it, grimacing at the smell of meth clinging to it. She fluffed her hair, hoping the smell would dissipate in the slight breeze. She couldn't wait to take a shower.

Barton came outside and hurried toward her. "You all right? You looked mighty pale in there."

"I'm fine. It's just that smell." She shuddered.

"I'm sorry about all that, Megan. I feel awful, you walking in on that. Jim feels bad too." Barton smiled slightly. "My partner in crime."

She frowned. "Considering all that happened, can you blame me for thinking that?"

"No. I just hate having you think the worst of me."

It was difficult to think badly of Barton as he stood there in the sunshine, oozing charm and good looks, his eyes, blue as the Texas sky, filled with concern. She felt foolish now about her suspicions and imaginings. Still, everything she'd seen and heard made her uneasy. She hiked her purse higher up on her shoulder. "I'm going home. I'll see you later." She turned and walked down the sidewalk.

"If you're headed to the B&B you're going the wrong way," Barton said with a hint of humor in his voice.

She stopped and looked around. "Thanks." She started back the other way.

Arms crossed, Barton blocked the sidewalk. "You don't even know where you're at, do you."

She lifted her chin. "I have a pretty good idea."

"I meant it when I said this isn't the kind of neighborhood to go walking around in."

As if on cue, a low-riding Buick with a loud muffler drove by. The men inside let loose a chorus of whistles and comments in Spanish. Megan suddenly felt conspicuous in her tank top and tight shorts.

"Let me take you home." Barton gestured to his car.

Just the thought of the long walk home in the heat made her tired. She had to work in a couple of hours. "All right."

Minutes later, they sped off in his car. She made a mental note of the names on the street signs. Just in case.

"I hope Tony gets help. Those other kids too." Megan crossed her legs. "I wish I could find out who their dealer is."

The Corvette jerked to a stop at an intersection. Barton stared at her. "What? Why on earth—?"

"For my article. If I could name some names it'd be so much better. More like investigative journalism rather than my usual stuff."

"What article?"

"I recently wrote an article about meth."

Surprise flittered across his face. "You did? What about it?"

"How it's becoming a big problem here in Fort Worth. How it affects people physically and psychologically. Even economically, since users have a hard time keeping a job. I interviewed a detective with the Fort Worth police department, and a waitress at work who's a user. Well, it wasn't really an interview. More an observation. She's usually pretty messed up when I see her. The whole thing was Bonnie's idea."

"Bonnie?"

Megan nodded. "She's been around meth before. In California. I'd never even heard of it until I came here."

Barton drove forward, shifting gears. "You still have to find a publisher. It could be months before it's published."

"Actually, it'll be in the *Star-Telegram* in two editions of the Sunday paper."

His head whipped her way, his eyes wide. "*What?*"

"I know!" She laughed. "Isn't that great? Two Sundays. Writers would *kill* to be in the Sunday paper. I'm going to be in it two weeks in a row. Maybe on the front page of a section."

Barton's attention snapped back to the road. His fingers tapped the steering wheel until they pulled a cigarette from his shirt pocket. He lit up. Cigarette smoke filled the car. Megan cracked the window and looked at him curiously. Except for that cigarette he'd smoked in Jim's kitchen, this was the first time in a while he'd smoked around her.

He also didn't seem impressed with her pending publications nor congratulate her. Quite the contrary. His mouth was set in a grim line, and when he wasn't holding the cigarette to his lips, he held it between his fingers as they tapped a mad dance on the steering wheel.

After several blocks had passed, she asked, "What's wrong?"

"Huh? Oh, just worried about Jim and Tony." He took a drag then stubbed out the cigarette in the ashtray with quick, jerky motions. "I hope they can work things out." He stared ahead at the road, looking worried. Maybe even angry.

They rode in silence the last few blocks. Barton pulled up in front of the B&B. He turned off the car and looked at Megan. "You need to go talk to the editor at the paper and tell him you don't want your article published."

His words threw her for a loop and she could only stare at him, speechless, for a moment. "Are you out of your mind?" she said when words finally came to her. "I'm not going to do that."

"Publishing that could be dangerous. Drugs are big business. Lots of money involved. You piss off the wrong people, affect their suppliers or users, cause heat from the cops, stir up the public, they'll be looking for your ass."

"Don't be ridiculous."

He leaned towards her. His eyes bore into hers. "Drop it, Megan. You're messing with big bad guys and they don't like being messed with."

She stared right back at him. "I guess you'd know all about big bad drug dealers."

"Don't start that again." He heaved a sigh and rubbed his hand on his forehead. "Look. I'll admit I know some dealers. Old buddies from high school. Guys I knew working construction. Some of them are the kind you don't want anything to do with. Mean mother fuckers."

"Well, I'm not dropping it. I worked too hard on it. Besides, I'm doing a public service. The public needs to be made aware of what's going on right under their noses. If they know what to look for, maybe they can help stop the spread of meth."

"Please." He took her hand. The look in his eyes softened. "I don't want you getting hurt. I'm falling for you, Megan. Falling hard."

He pulled her to him and kissed her until the gearshift sticking in her stomach hurt too much and she pulled away. He released her and sat up, smiling at her with warm eyes and sexy lips.

She didn't fall for them. She had some thinking to do. She picked her purse up off the floorboard. "Thanks for the ride." Her fingers curled around the door handle.

If he noticed she hadn't replied to his *I'm falling for you* statement, he didn't let on. "I'll pick you up after work." He winked. "I'll bring my toothbrush."

She opened the door. "Not tonight."

His smile quickly changed to a surprised scowl. "What do you mean not tonight? We made plans—"

"It's going to be a busy night. And after today ..." She shook her head. "Not tonight, Barton." She got out of the car, shut the door, and walked into the B&B without a backward glance.

Upstairs in her room, she looked around to see if anything was out of place or different. *Did Seth come while I'm gone?* She doubted it. She still checked to see how many towels hung in the bathroom and how damp they were. All seemed normal.

She went to the bed and dropped her purse on the floor. It landed sideways, spilling change out of the side pocket onto the floor. A few coins rolled beneath the bed. She got down on her hands and knees and fished them out, along with the four pieces of her ripped up picture. She put everything back in the side pocket of the purse then stood, holding the photo pieces. She went to the vanity, dug around until she found a roll of tape, and carefully taped the picture back together. She leaned it against the mirror and put Barton's picture facedown.

Chapter 18

The manager of The Tejas walked up to Megan during her shift and handed her a vase of red roses, white lilies, and baby's breath.

"Why, thanks, Joe."

"They're not from me." He smiled and walked away.

"They're gorgeous." Bonnie stuck her nose in a rose then, like a bee, moved on to a lily. "From Barton?"

Megan nodded as she read the card. *Love B.*

"I reckon you haven't told him you're leaving?"

"Not yet."

"Are these more I'm-sorry-I'm-such-an-ass flowers?"

Megan stuck the card in her back pocket. "Possible. He *is* male." Bonnie snickered then went to wait on a customer. Megan hadn't seen any reason to tell Bonnie what had happened at Jim's house that afternoon. She didn't want to sully Barton's name if her suspicions were wrong. Although Donna had certainly gotten an earful over the phone. She and Megan decided that Detective Sullivan should be told. Just in case.

Love B. Holy moly.

She half-expected Barton to show up at The Tejas that night. He never did, to her relief. She took home half of the bouquet and left the rest on the bar.

The next night, near closing time, Bonnie asked, "Megan, do you think you can find another ride home?" Bonnie glanced at the good-looking cowboy seated at the bar that she had been flirting with most of the night. He had brown hair, a short beard, and a deep ready laugh.

Megan remembered Bonnie mentioning that her daughter was spending the weekend with her cousins. "Of course. I'll call a cab."

After closing, she stood outside waiting for the cab and waved goodbye as Bonnie drove off behind the cowboy's pickup. Megan exchanged goodnights with other employees as they filed out and headed to the parking lot. Several couples arm in arm passed by. Unexpected envy filled Megan as she watched them go off two by two. When the cab arrived, she climbed in and tried not to think about Bonnie and her night ahead with the cowboy. Or the couples going home together. Or couples all over the world who had somebody on a Saturday night. Or Seth and whoever he ended up with.

At the B&B, she opened the door to her room, greeted by the dim light of the lamp on the nightstand. She left it on now when she was gone to avoid walking into any more surprises. The sweet smell of the roses and lilies in a glass on the table scented the air. She closed the door, and her gaze automatically went to Seth's door. Closed, as always. *He won't be back.*

The arms on the alarm clock pointed out two a.m. She was wide awake. Papers strewn across the table and the typewriter in the corner waited for her, but work held no interest. She could start packing, but she wasn't leaving for over two weeks, so packing seemed pointless. For the first time in a long time, she wished she had a TV. Watching some mindless drivel for a couple of hours seemed just the thing.

I wish I could talk to Donna. Just to hear a friendly voice. But it's so late.

I wish I could talk to dad.

The thought hit her like a fist to her stomach. She sank onto the bed, overwhelmed by a wave of sadness. What she'd give to hear her dad's calm, reassuring voice. He had always been the voice of reason, the rock in her life. Tonight, she missed him more than she'd missed him in a while.

"My life sucks," she said to the quiet room.

She was alone and lonely and suddenly dissatisfied with her rootless, solitary life. She was returning soon to an apartment that was no longer home, just a place to store stuff she didn't seem to need since she'd lived without it for almost three months now. She gazed around the room she had grown fond of, but it wasn't home either. She had no home. A long sigh escaped her. Her gaze landed on the typewriter.

She had ideas to research, articles to write, money to make, but suddenly wild goose chases didn't fill her with excitement and a sense of adventure. She no longer wanted to be footloose and fancy free.

I want a home. I want someone to come home to. I want ... more.

Perhaps this was how Seth felt when he told her about the ranch and wanting a home, a family. He too wanted more. She finally understood why he had told her goodbye.

She pushed herself off the bed and went to the vanity. She picked up the taped-together picture of herself. *How old is he now? What's he doing? Running the saloon? Did he ever marry?*

Their last words to each other rang in her mind.

If you had any sense at all you'd marry Susannah!

Maybe I will, he had snarled before storming out of her time, out of her life.

"I hope you did," she murmured, staring at her picture, wishing it was one of him. Memories and a letter were all that remained of him. "I hope you're happy." Her life had never seemed empty until she had met him. He had somehow filled all the cracks and crevices within her that she hadn't even known were there. Now emptiness stretched endlessly before her.

She asked his memory, "Do you ever think of me?"

***

"Can you work tonight, Megan?" her manager asked her over the B&B's house phone Sunday afternoon.

"Sure. Someone call in sick?"

A disgusted sigh came over the phone. "Julia."

That girl. "When do you want me to come in?"

"Five or so. If it's not busy you can leave early."

Megan hung up and hurried to her room, elated that she had something to do to fill her evening. Her melancholy mood from the night before had stretched into today and she hadn't written a single word. Instead, she'd spent the day watching TV in the downstairs sitting room. She had seen a Doris Day/Rock Hudson comedy that cheered her up, then made the mistake of watching a John Wayne western. All the way through it, she could almost hear Seth scoffing at Hollywood's version of the Wild West. She had missed him more than ever and wished she had a carton of ice cream to drown her sorrows in.

Good thing I didn't have any ice cream, she thought as she pulled on a pair of skintight jeans and a low-cut blouse.

***

"Is Julia really sick?" Megan asked Bonnie at work.

Bonnie put two bottles of beer on Megan's tray. "I reckon she's either too high to work or not high at all and lookin' for more. Joe's really pissed. I think he's gonna fire her this time."

"Too bad. But I don't blame him." Megan watched Bonnie draw a draft with a perfect head. Bonnie looked exceptionally pretty with her long hair loose and a healthy glow on her face. She wore blue jeans, a turquoise gauze blouse, and gold hoop earrings. "Well?"

"Well what?" Bonnie put the draft on the tray.

"You're really going to make me ask? How was last night?"

Bonnie leaned across the bar and said softly, "It was the best night *ever.*"

Megan laughed. "So that's what put the roses in your cheeks."

"Man, am I in lust." Grinning, Bonnie straightened and picked up a glass. She poured vodka into it followed by orange juice. "If I happen to go home with him again tonight could you find another ride home?"

"Have fun and don't worry about me." Megan looked around at the sparse crowd in the bar. "Pretty slow night."

"Maybe we'll get to leave early."

It stayed slow the rest of the night. Bonnie's cowboy showed up and sat down at the bar. Megan learned his name was Sam, he was the manager of a feed store, and he had eyes only for Bonnie. When told she could leave early, Bonnie and Sam didn't waste any time getting out of there. Megan wiped down tables and chairs, filled saltshakers, and kept busy doing whatever she could to avoid returning to her quiet, empty room. Eventually, though, she too was told to leave. She got her purse from behind the bar, slung it over her shoulder, and headed toward a pay phone near the restrooms to call a cab. A man using the phone hung up, turned around, and Barton's eyes met hers.

His widened with surprise. "Megan? What are you doing here? I thought you were off on Sundays."

"Someone called in sick. Thank you for the beautiful flowers."

"I'm glad you like them." He stepped closer. "I'm really sorry about the other day." He looked properly contrite. "Could we talk when you get off work?"

"I'm off now. Slow night. I was just going to call a cab."

"Want to go somewhere and get a drink?"

"Aren't you here with someone?"

"Just havin' a drink with a buddy. I'd rather be with you."

Megan bit her lower lip. *He might be a drug dealer. Or not. He might want more from me than I have to give him. Love, B. Maybe he simply wants what I want—sex.* He looked handsome as all get out with his wavy black hair and deep tan. He wore blue jeans and a gray t-shirt that defined the muscles of his broad chest. As she looked him over, the Bellamy Brothers sang on the jukebox *Do You Love As Good As You Look*.

It took all her willpower not to laugh aloud at the coincidence. But a smile escaped her, and she sent it his way. "Why go somewhere else? Buy me a drink here."

A furrow appeared between his eyebrows. "Here?" He glanced around as though looking for someone. "You sure?"

She shrugged. "Why not? Just not over there." She pointed to the area where she worked. "I'm there enough. Maybe over there." She pointed to the other side of The Tejas. "I never go there."

"How about over here?" He took her arm and propelled her to a nearby table in a darkened corner. "It's quiet. We can talk." He pulled out a chair for her. "What's your poison?"

"Anything but beer. Surprise me."

He went to the bar then returned shortly and handed her a Tequila Sunrise. He sat in a chair beside her, a whiskey on the rocks in his hand. He had his back to the room, all his attention on her.

She took a drink, savoring the mix. "Shouldn't you tell your friend you're over here?"

"I will in a bit. I'm glad I ran into you. I felt awful all weekend. Thought about calling you a dozen times or stopping by but—" He looked down at his drink. He slowly twirled the glass on the table with one hand.

"But?"

The twirling stopped. His serious eyes met hers. "I was afraid you'd tell me to go to hell and don't come back."

"I might have. I was pretty freaked out by what I saw. I've never been around anything like that. Heard about it. Read about it. But never actually saw someone stick a needle full of drugs into his arm. And to find you there, well, it seemed like you were next in line."

He shook his head. "Never. I snorted it a couple times but that's it. Swear to God." He held up his right hand. "As for sticking a needle in my arm—" he shuddered. "No way."

"What's the deal with Jim's briefcase?" She took a drink, watching Barton over the rim of the glass.

"What about it?" He shrugged.

"Sometimes when we're together you make me deliver it to him and—"

"Whoa now, wait a minute." He held up his hand again. "I don't *make* you. I ask you if you'd mind holding it while I'm parking the car or in the john or something and if Jim shows up would you give it to him. It's not like I've got a gun to your head, saying *Do this or else.* I mean, jeez, Megan." He shook his head, propping his chin on his knuckles. "If it bothers you that much it won't happen again." He eyed her curiously. "Why would I be *making* you do that anyway? What do you think is in it?"

They were in a public place. She laid it on him. "Meth."

His eyebrows shot up almost to his hairline and he stared at her for a moment then threw his head back and burst out laughing. When he could speak again he said, "You're kidding. Right?" He put a hand on his chest. "Me? Making you, what, deliver meth for me?"

"I guess I was your mule." She took a sip of the Tequila Sunrise.

He laughed again, shaking his head. "Darlin', darlin', what a wild imagination you have. No wonder you're a writer."

She leaned back in her chair and crossed her arms. "I don't know what you find so amusing. After what I saw Friday at Jim's house—"

"I'm really sorry about that." All amusement left Barton's face. "So is Jim. It was just a messed-up deal, you walking in at the wrong time. Those kids had the drugs, not Jim, not me. I make a good living at a job I enjoy. I don't need to deal drugs. As for the briefcase, it's full of legal papers. Jim's forgetful. Since 'Nam his memory hasn't been worth a damn. And it's not getting any better. Half the time he can't find his car keys. But he's a wiz with numbers and we make a good team. I think—"

"Well, isn't this a fine howdy do."

Megan and Barton looked up at a skinny blonde who stood a few feet from the table, hands on her hips and a scowl on her face.

Barton smiled at the young woman. "Hey Tammy, how's it going?" He stretched his arm across the back of Megan's chair. "Did you see your brother over there?" He jutted his chin towards the other side of the room.

"No." She glared at Barton. "I didn't see him." She turned her glare on Megan.

"When you do," Barton continued, "tell him I'll see him later. I'm having a drink with my girl before I take her home." His hand cupped Megan's shoulder. "Megan, you remember Tammy?"

"Hi." Megan smiled at the scowling woman in blue shorts and a halter-top.

Tammy started to say something then cut her gaze to Barton and snapped her mouth shut.

Megan glanced at Barton, wondering what Tammy had seen on his face to shut her up. But he looked calm and collected as he lifted his glass for a drink.

Tammy shoved the empty chair next to Barton against the table, making Megan's drink wobble. "Tell him yourself." She turned and took a couple of steps then said over her shoulder, "You left your cigarettes and lighter on the table."

"Would you be a sweetheart and bring them to me?"

Megan shot Barton an incredulous look at his request.

Tammy flipped him the finger as she stomped off.

"Well, it didn't hurt to ask. Reckon I'll go get 'em myself. Excuse me, Megan." He pushed back his chair and stood.

"Barton? If Tammy just arrived how did she know your cigarettes and lighter are on some table over there?"

He shrugged. "Her brother Tom and I have our usual place and I guess she checked that table out first. He was probably getting a drink or something. He's my best friend."

It occurred to Megan that she'd never met any of Barton's family or friends, except Jim. "I'll go with you. I'd like to meet him." She started to rise but stopped when Barton spoke.

"Uh, probably not a good idea. If Tammy's over there, there's no telling what kind of scene she could make. I'll bring Tom over here. You need another drink?"

Megan shook her head. As he made his way through the tables, she went to the restroom.

When she came out, Barton stood beside the table, smoking a cigarette, and looking around. He spotted her, and relief replaced his troubled look. "I wondered where you went." He put out the half-smoked cigarette in an ashtray then held her chair for her until she sat then joined her. "Had me worried for a minute. Thought I scared you off."

She put her purse on the chair beside her then rested her forearms on the table. "I don't scare that easily. Where's Tom?"

"He just left. He has to work in the morning. He has a concrete crew and they start at four or some ungodly hour. He told me to tell you he hopes to meet you soon." Barton's hand covered hers. "So, are we okay? I hate it when we fight."

"So do I." The jukebox switched to another song and Megan did an internal eye roll when she heard it. *Another coincidence? Or the universe's idea of a joke?*

He tilted his head. "Hear that? The Bellamy Brothers. *Do You Love As Good As You Look.*" His thumb made circles on the back of her hand as his gaze met hers. He asked in his soft, sexy drawl, "Wanna find out?"

She studied his blue eyes and handsome face.

She was tired of being alone. Tired of mooning over a dead man. Tired of the universe screwing with her. She recalled Bonnie's earlier comment *Man, am I in lust.* Megan knew the feeling.

She squeezed Barton's hand. "Let's go back to my place."

Take that, universe.

***

They held hands on the drive to the B&B, their entwined fingers shifting the gears together. A country western station played softly on the radio. Nervous excitement skittered through Megan. *It's been so long!* To fill the silence between them, she said, "The other night one of the regulars mentioned something about a goat man of Greer Island. Do you know anything about that?"

"It's a local legend. Also called the Lake Worth Monster. Half man, half goat, with fur and scales. It was first seen in 1969, I think. You fixin' to write about that?"

"Maybe. I'd like to check out the area."

"It's not far. Northwest side of Fort Worth. I'll take you." Barton flashed a smile as the lights from an oncoming car illuminated his face. "We'll make a day of it."

"Sounds great. Thanks."

They stopped at a light and Barton said, "Got a question for you. If money was no object, where would you want to live? The mountains? The beach? Somewhere overseas? An island in the Caribbean? I've read about entire islands for sale."

"Oh, I don't know. I like the mountains and the beach." She tilted her head. "Are you fixin' to come into some money or something?" Her eyes widened. "Holy moly!" She clapped her hand over her mouth. "I just said fixin'. I've been here too long."

Barton laughed. "I reckon Texas is growing on you. I'm glad." He squeezed her hand beneath his on the gearshift. "Like I said, I'm just curious about where you'd like to go."

She studied his profile as they shifted gears when the light changed. *As in go somewhere together? Is that what he's implying?* A warning voice screamed in her head, *Tell him you're leaving soon. Tell him!*

But that would put a damper on the night. She kept her mouth shut.

After entering the B&B, Megan gently closed the door behind them then, hand in hand, they ran up the stairs as quietly as possible. She had a hard time manipulating the key to her room what with Barton kissing her ear and the back of her neck while his hand slipped beneath her blouse to stroke her side. Her breathing quickened, every inch of her felt sensitive, and she feared they would do it right there in the hallway if she didn't get the damned door open.

Finally, the key slid in, the lock clicked, and she led him into her dimly lit room where the faint scent of the fading flowers still lingered. He closed the door behind them, locked it, then took her in his arms.

"At last," he murmured then kissed her.

Her purse hit the floor as her arms went around him. His busy tongue filled her mouth. His erection pressed against her. His hands slid up her sides, taking her blouse with them. She raised her arms high and he pulled off the blouse then tossed it aside. Her hair tumbled down around her shoulders. Shadows hid his face as she leaned back against the door, aware of his gaze on her. He bent his head and placed a kiss just above the bow in the middle of her bra.

"You're so beautiful." He straightened and cupped her breasts with his hands. "It's like unwrapping a present." His thumbs swept over her nipples.

She caught her breath.

He grinned. "It's gonna be good between us, darlin'."

Megan grabbed the hem of his t-shirt and tugged it up. Barton crossed his arms, pulled the shirt over his head, and tossed it on the floor. She ran her hands over the thick black hair covering his chest. She wasn't usually attracted to hairy chests but his would do for the night. She did like those muscles though. Her fingers toyed with his nipples. He sucked in a breath and pulled her to him. They embraced and kissed, and their hands explored until Megan wanted to push him to the floor and straddle him right there. *What is he waiting for?*

He pulled away and took her hand. "Come on." He led her to the bed with the lamp shining softly beside it. She went eagerly. He stopped, not at the side of the bed or near the head but at the foot. "Sit down."

She sat, looking up at him in confusion. Her mouth fell open when he knelt on one knee in front of her. *Oh God is he going to propose?!*

"Do your feet hurt?"

"What?"

"You often complain about your feet hurting. Do they?"

"Well, yeah."

"We can't have that." He knelt on both knees and she watched with growing amazement as he leaned over and untied the laces on her right tennis shoe. He slipped off the shoe and sock, put them aside, then picked up her foot. He placed his thumbs on top, fingers on the bottom, and proceeded to massage her foot. It jerked back. He glanced up. "Ticklish?"

"A little. What are you doing?"

"Easing your aches." His strong fingers kneaded her foot. "Feel good?"

"Ecstasy." A different kind of ecstasy than she had anticipated but wonderful all the same. She leaned back on her palms and let him work his magic, imagining other magic those fingers could work.

"Have you talked to your editor about dropping your meth story?" Barton asked casually.

Megan scowled. He certainly knew how to ruin a moment. "No. And I'm not going to."

He glanced up. "You're not?"

"It's my livelihood, Barton. It's what I do."

He didn't reply. She relaxed back on her hands again while his hands resumed their magic. "Ow!" She jerked her foot back and glared at him.

He raised an eyebrow. "Problem?"

"You got a little rough there."

"You don't like it rough?"

Megan knew he had a mean streak. Apparently, it extended to his sexual activities. Maybe he was pissed about her meth article for some obscure reason. "No."

If he heard her angry tone, he ignored it. "I'll keep that in mind."

"You do that."

He motioned to her foot. "Can I continue?"

"You'll play nice?"

"Promise." He held up his right hand. "Okay?"

When she nodded and relaxed back again, he propped the heel of her foot against his thigh and with both hands massaged her toes. After a moment he said, "Know what I'm gonna do when I get done with your feet? I'm gonna peel those tight-ass jeans off your pretty legs. Then I'm gonna run my tongue all along here." He placed one forefinger on the hem of her jean leg and slowly ran it up the inside seam to her crotch. Her breath caught in her throat as her legs spread open of their own accord. His finger ran just as slowly down the other inside seam to the hem of that leg. As he concentrated on her toes again, he asked softly, "How long has it been, Megan?"

"Since what?" Even though she knew what he meant.

His gaze met hers. "Since you had sex."

"Last summer. How about you?"

A crooked grin lifted one side of his mouth. "It hasn't been *that* long." Holding her heel in one hand, he ran the knuckles of his other hand on the bottom of her foot.

"Oh, that feels good," she moaned, leaning her head back and briefly closing her eyes.

An echoing moan, soft and low, rolled through the room like a distant rumble of thunder until the hum of the air conditioner starting up drowned out the sound. She wondered if it was from a summer storm. She glanced at Barton. He showed no sign of hearing anything. She put it from her mind and gave into the pure pleasure of the massage.

"We're just getting started, darlin'. When I get through licking my way up and down your pretty legs I'm gonna take that bra off and massage your breasts. I'm gonna massage 'em *real* good. They need massaging, don't they?"

"God yes." He had her practically squirming with his actions and words.

He ran his knuckles back and forth on the bottom of her foot. "You could massage 'em yourself, right now. You ever done that? Hmmm?"

She sat up a little straighter. "That's what you're for."

He chuckled and gave her a lazy smile. "Maybe another time." He put that foot down then started untying the laces on her left shoe. "I feel like a kid unwrapping a present on Christmas morning."

"You don't act like one. Any kid I've ever seen on Christmas morning is totally out of control, tearing into the presents." *Which is what you should be doing,* she thought as she leaned back on her elbows.

He glanced at her. "I'm *always* in control." His eyes glittered in the lamplight that turned his hair blue black. Her left tennis shoe and sock came off and his fingers went to work on that foot. "Now, where was I? Oh yeah, your beautiful breasts. I'm gonna take my time with them. I'm gonna massage 'em and kiss 'em. I'm gonna play with those nipples and suck on 'em until they're as peaked as the Grand Tetons. Think you'll like that?"

"*When* are you going to do that? You're driving me crazy."

"Am I?" He tilted his head, looking at her while his fingers started on her toes. "Payback."

She blinked. "Payback?"

"For teasing me all these weeks. Playing hard to get while all I get is hard." He placed her foot on the bulge in his crotch and held it there. "I've had that since the first night I met you. You've been driving me crazy for weeks. Now it's my turn to torture you."

She pushed herself upright. "T-torture me? I thought we agreed on nice."

"Teasing torture. Sweet agony. In a couple hours you'll be beg—"

"A couple hours!" She stared at him, aghast. *That's not nice!*

He pressed her foot against him. "Weeks. That's what you put me through."

She rubbed her foot up and down, and smiled to herself when Mr. In Control sucked in a breath and tightened his grip on her foot. "How about we first play *Wham Bam Thank You Ma'am* then play your little game?"

His massage continued. "Nope. I'm gonna take my time unwrapping your lovely body and learning every inch of it. You might as well just lean back and enjoy some sweet agony. Now, where was I?" He manipulated her toes one by one. "Ah yes. After I'm done with your breasts there's just one more part of you to unwrap. I'm gonna pull your panties down inch by inch and—"

While Barton went on about all he was going to do to her—eventually—Megan leaned back on her elbows to enjoy his attentions. She'd never had a foot massage. It felt wonderful. And the view was superb. Muscular chest, corded arms, washboard stomach. The sight of his fine physique and the memory of his hard length beneath her foot made her blood run hot. She sighed in frustrated impatience.

Quit playing around and let's do it, Barton!

She tore her gaze from him and let it wander around the shadowed room behind him. The dark shape of the armoire stood in the far corner.

The rawhide sofa stretched lengthwise about five feet behind Barton. Her gaze drifted left, to Seth's door.

Her heart stopped.

She jerked upright.

It's open!

"Did I hit a tickle spot? Megan?"

Her gaze shot to Barton. "What?"

"Did I hit a tickle spot?"

"Yeah. It tickles." She forced a giggle. "But it feels so good."

He gave her a quizzical look then smiled. "Like that, huh? I thought you would. You'll like everything I have planned for you. Imagine my tongue running up your thigh and—"

Megan leaned back on her palms while he droned on. She tried to act natural as her gaze returned to Seth's door. It stood open maybe a foot. Shadows gathered in the door. *The one time I don't check to see if it's open. The one night,* one night *I bring someone here.* The universe had a perverse sense of humor. The door was opened just enough she could see that no one stood in it. She looked around the room. The bathroom door was wide open the way she'd left it. Darkness filled the interior. *Is he in there? Watching? Listening?* She felt her face redden with more than the flush of sexual arousal. But she saw no movement or evidence of anyone lurking in the bathroom. *Where is he? Behind the armoire? Under the bed?* She looked down at the mattress. *Oh God I hope not!*

"What's wrong?"

Her head snapped up and her gaze collided with Barton's. "Wr-rong? Nothing. Why?"

His hands cradled her foot. "You had a look of almost ... horror on your face."

She mustered up a laugh that came out a little shrill. "Because I'm horrified that I've gone all these years without a foot massage. It's wonderful." She batted her eyelashes and said in a sexy tone, *"You're wonderful for giving me one."*

"Darlin', I've got a lot more than that to give you. It's time I unwrap your pretty legs." He started to put her foot down.

She leaned forward and stopped him with a hand on his arm. "Could you massage it here a little bit more? Please?" She indicated the instep of her left foot. "It's always sore."

He chuckled as he reached for her foot. "I hope you're this insatiable after I've unwrapped you. I don't plan on us sleeping much tonight."

"Oh, don't stop." She leaned back again and murmured sounds of enjoyment while she scanned the room. Everything looked the way she had left it. Makeup and toiletries scattered across the vanity. Papers strewn on the table. One sandal lay upside down near a table leg. A pair of cowboy boots, lying on their sides, toe-to-toe and heels splayed, stuck out from behind the end of the sofa near the outer wall. The history books were on the—her gaze snapped back to the cowboy boots.

I don't own any cowboy boots.

Seth! Or someone is behind the sofa.

Her gaze swept the length of the sofa and stopped just to the right behind Barton. Her eyes widened. A dark stain spread out from just beneath the front of the sofa like spilled wine.

Blood! She recalled that soft, low echoing moan. Whoever lay behind the sofa was injured.

I have to get rid of Barton. Claim a headache? How lame! My period started? Little late to bring that up. Think, Megan, think!

"I reckon your legs are next." Barton put her foot down and slid his hands up her legs.

A low, soft moan moved through the quiet room like the rumble of a passing truck.

Barton looked over his shoulder. "What the—"

Megan shot up straight, clutched her stomach and doubled over, moaning loud and long.

Barton jerked his hands back. "What's the matter?"

"Ohhh, my stomach—" Head to her knees, she moaned loudly again.

"Your stomach?"

"It's been feeling funny for a while now. Rolling and churning." Her voice was muffled against her leg. She strained to hear that other moan but thankfully didn't. "I kept hoping it would go away. Must be that hamburger I had earlier."

"You think you might have food poisoning?" His tone said, *Are you shitting me?*

She bumped her head against her knee in a nod. She took a deep breath, prayed for more acting ability than she'd demonstrated in a high school play, and struggled to sit up. She pushed her hair off her face with a shaking hand and met Barton's narrowed gaze.

He looked confused, concerned, skeptical, and angry all at the same time. His gaze dropped to her bra-covered breasts. She could almost feel the frustration emanating from him.

It was his own fault for insisting to play his little game.

She held her arm tight against her stomach and grimaced. "It-it must have been some bad meat. It tasted funny. I'm so sorry." She hoped her expression showed genuine disappointment. "But I-I feel awful."

Anger flashed in his eyes. "Funny. Your feet didn't feel cold."

"What?"

"Cold feet. That your problem?"

"No!" She shook her head. "Oh no. Not cold at all. But the rest of me feels terrible."

He leaned forward and placed the back of his hand on her forehead, then on a cheek. "You are warm and awful flushed." He sat back on his heels. "My sister had food poisoning once. She was sick as a dog. My parents almost took her to the emergency room. She was that bad." His expression softened. "I hope you're not that sick."

He looked so worried she felt like a heel.

Behind him, splayed cowboy boots stuck out from behind the sofa, and blood pooled on the floor. She had no choice.

She covered her mouth and mumbled, "I think I'm going to puke."

Barton shot to his feet. "Where's a trash can?"

She grabbed his hand before he could go anywhere or see something he shouldn't. She made a show of swallowing hard then uncovered her mouth, making a face. "Ugg. Awful." Her gaze met his and she squeezed his hand. "I'm really sorry. I—"

"Hey, you can't help it if you're sick." He stroked her hair with a gentleness that surprised her, all trace of his anger gone. "We've waited this long. What's another night or so? I just want you to get well. Is there anything I can do or get for you?"

He was being so nice she felt worse by the moment for deceiving him. "No thanks, but you're sweet for offering. Could you help me up?" Once she was on her feet, she led him to the door, bending down to grab his t-shirt off the floor on the way. At the door, she made sure he kept his back to the room and the puddle of blood seeping out from beneath the sofa.

He put on the t-shirt. "Maybe I should stay. You shouldn't be alone."

Afraid he'd linger while someone bled to death behind the sofa, Megan said the crudest thing she could think of. "I think I'm going to have a blow-out from both ends. I'd prefer you weren't here for it."

He smiled slightly. "I get it."

"Thanks for being so understanding. I'm really sorry."

"I am too." His gaze swept over her. "Real damn sorry. Take care of yourself. Call if you need me." He kissed her forehead and left.

Megan closed and locked the door then ran behind the sofa.

Seth lay on his stomach in a blood-soaked shirt, his face turned to the wall.

She fell to her knees beside him. "Oh, Seth, what happened to you?"

He was unconscious. What she could see of the left side of his face was bruised and bloody, his lip split, his eye swelling shut. She gently ran her hands over him. The blood soaking his shirt came from a stab wound in his left side and a bullet hole in his right shoulder. His ragged, shallow breathing filled the silence.

Beaten, stabbed, shot. The sight of him tore a hole in her heart. Her hands red with his blood, Megan whispered raggedly, "Oh, Seth, Seth."

Somewhere in the air around her, the universe sneered, *Take **that**.*

Chapter 19

Megan entered the dining room and stopped abruptly, blinking her tired eyes in the sudden brightness. It was a sunlit, cheery room with daffodil yellow walls trimmed in white and lace curtains on the tall windows. White lace table clothes and vases of white and yellow daisies graced each of the several small dining tables. The tables and chairs were a rich dark wood that matched a china cabinet full of glassware. Everything looked pretty and perfect. Megan grimaced, thinking of her room, which was currently a disaster.

At a counter along one wall, she poured a cup of lukewarm coffee. She gulped it down, needing a jolt to wake her up after a long night with little sleep. She refilled the cup and put the empty pot down. Her gaze swept over the platters on the counter bearing the remains of breakfast. Three pieces of shriveled sausage links, four small strips of bacon, a glob of scrambled eggs, a scoop of hash browns. She piled it all on a plate. Seth would be hungry when he woke up. If he woke up. *He doesn't look good.* She shoved the dark thought away as Mrs. Powell walked in.

"Good morning, Miss Megan." Mrs. Powell smiled. She wore a short-sleeved blue blouse, and navy slacks. Dangling silver earrings matched the color of her hair, cut short and hugging her head.

"It's good to have you back, Mrs. Powell." Megan put the plate, coffee cup and silverware on a tray. "I'm sorry about your sister."

"Thank you. It was a beautiful funeral." Mrs. Powell stopped beside the counter and looked at the empty platters then Megan's plate. "Mighty slim pickin's."

"My fault. I came down late." She picked up her tray, ready to head upstairs to Seth.

"Probably cold too. I can whip up some more for you."

"Thanks, but that's not necessary." She looked at the empty coffee pot. "Maybe some fresh coffee."

"Certainly. If you change your mind about breakfast let me know." Mrs. Powell ran her hand over the lace tablecloth, smoothing out a wrinkle then brushed some crumbs off. In a corner behind her, the spear-like leaves of a tall potted plant trembled in the currents from the air conditioner. She looked up with a small crease between her brows. "Excuse me for asking, but is everything all right?"

Megan adjusted her hold on the tray. *Do I look that bad?* She'd thrown on a tank top and shorts, ran a brush through her messy hair, dashed cold water on her face, then pressed the wet washcloth to her tired puffy eyes, holding it there while she counted to ten. It hadn't done much good. "Yes. Thanks for asking."

She started to leave, but Mrs. Powell stopped her by asking, "Are you sure?"

"Umm. Yes."

Mrs. Powell clasped her hands together and looked troubled.

Megan asked, "Why?"

"Well, this old house doesn't have very thick walls."

"I'm not sure I follow you."

"Earlier this morning, the couple in the room below you mentioned that late last night they heard ... disturbances coming from your room."

"Disturbances?" The word sent a more powerful jolt to Megan's system than a whole gallon of coffee could as all that had happened the last few hours flashed through her mind.

"Loud noises. Like something crashed on the floor."

Megan bit her lower lip. *That could be the curtain rod falling when I pulled down the plastic shower curtain to cover the bed, so Seth wouldn't bleed all over it. Or when I knocked over that chair while running to the bathroom for more towels. Or when Seth slid off the plastic on the bed and hit the floor like a ton of bricks.*

"Someone sobbing."

When I was trying to stop the bleeding. So much blood.

"Grunting and groaning and the sound of something being dragged across the floor."

I half-carried, half-dragged him to the bed then tugged and pulled and pushed him on top of it. Had to get him up there again after he slid off. Damn bed is so high! I did a lot of grunting and groaning.

"Shouting."

I shouted at the ceiling, I'm a writer not a doctor! Maybe more than once.

"They said it went on quite a while. I assured them I'd talk to you about it."

"I'm sorry. I didn't realize I was bothering anyone. I'm a writer, you know, and sometimes I act out the parts to get everything right. I guess I got a little carried away last night."

Mrs. Powell blinked. "You writers are an eccentric sort, aren't you? I never would have imagined ... If you could keep it down a bit—"

"I will. Please give them my apologies and tell them it won't happen again."

"I will, dear."

A miniature grandfather's clock on the fireplace mantel chimed the tenth hour. Mrs. Powell glanced at it over her shoulder. She tsked and muttered, "That girl." She went to the fireplace on the far wall. She reached up and switched around an old coffee grinder and the clock, centering the clock in the middle of the shelf. She stood back, arms crossed, and regarded the mantel, which also displayed a white-speckled blue coffee pot, a dented metal mixing bowl, a four-legged copper pot with a lid and a ladle, an old iron, and a kerosene lantern. She reached up and moved the clock just a bit to the right then turned around with a satisfied, "There."

Megan bit back a grin. *What a perfectionist. She'd faint if she saw my room.* She adjusted her grip on her tray.

Mrs. Powell walked back toward Megan. "I feel like I was gone a month instead of not quite a week. I missed this old place."

Megan smiled. "It's a beautiful house. I love it."

"Me too." Mrs. Powell gazed around the room with a look of pride and almost reverence. "It has a certain ... something about it, doesn't it?"

Megan chuckled. "It certainly does."

"I like to think it's the spirit of Megan McClure."

The tray slipped from Megan's hands and clattered on the table. A sausage rolled off the plate into the coffee that had sloshed onto the tray. She stared wide-eyed at Mrs. Powell. "Wh-what did you say?"

Mrs. Powell stepped closer, frowning. "Are you all right, dear?"

"Yes, yes, the tray just ... slipped. Sorry. What did you just say?"

"That it's the spirit of—Lord a mercy." Mrs. Powell put a hand to her cheek. "I still haven't told you how I ended up owning this place, have I?"

"No. You started to a couple times."

"Do you have a moment? Or do you need to get back to your writing?"

Megan thought of Seth. She'd finally stopped the bleeding, then tended his wounds, cleaned him up, forced two aspirin down him when he roused briefly, and left him warm and snug in her bed. He hadn't looked good.

He's been beaten, stabbed, and shot. Of course, he doesn't look good.

He was probably still asleep. "I have time."

"I fell in love with this old house years ago," Mrs. Powell began. "It was a boarding house for decades then sat empty a year or so and, well," she spread her hands, "you know what happens to a house when it's not a home. It falls apart. One day I saw it was for sale. And my heart leapt inside me. I *knew* this place was meant for me. It was in mighty poor condition by then and I was shocked at the asking price. It was much more than I could afford on a teacher's salary."

"I'm surprised the historical society wasn't interested in it," Megan said.

"They had bigger fish to catch than an old brothel turned into a boarding house." Mrs. Powell began stacking the empty platters and cleaning up as she talked. "Nobody else wanted it either and it was slated for demolition on April 1, 1974. The thought of that broke my heart but I just couldn't come up with enough money to buy it plus fix it up. On March 30, two days before the wrecking ball was to come, I received a phone call from a bank here in Fort Worth. I was told to come to their trust office as soon as possible to discuss an important legal matter. I had no idea what they were talking about and went there immediately. The banker said that a trust fund had been established earlier that year in my name with instructions to contact me on that day. He showed me a portfolio of stocks initially purchased in the first two decades of the 1900s. Coca Cola, Hallmark, U. S. Steel, IBM, GM, Birdseye, among several others. Even some from overseas. All mine, supposedly. I was flabbergasted."

"I imagine! Who bought all those shares?"

"A woman I'd never met or even heard of named Cordelia Pryor."

Megan gasped. *Candace Huntington's sister!* "But ... why did she do that?"

Mrs. Powell shrugged. "I have no idea. I found out she was a spinster from a prominent family here in Fort Worth. I tried to contact her but was told she was very sick. She was in her 90s. She died a month after I bought the house."

"That's awful," Megan said in all sincerity. She hoped the same thing wouldn't happen to her—Candace dying before they could meet. And what a coincidence that Cordelia had picked those stocks—all of them long-term winners. *As if she knew ... Oh my God—she read about them in that history book Seth took back!*

"I was so disappointed. I wanted more than anything to meet her and ask her why," Mrs. Powell interrupted Megan's thoughts. "And thank her from the bottom of my heart because when I cashed in those stocks it was enough money to buy this place free and clear with some left over to fix it up."

"What a great story." Megan grinned.

"Oh, it gets better." Mrs. Powell's eyes twinkled in the midmorning light flooding the room. "The person who gave Cordelia Pryor the initial $25 to invest along with instructions about managing the money and how to contact me was a woman named Megan McClure."

Megan's grin froze on her face.

The room started to spin around her.

Not again!

She gripped the edge of the table with one hand to anchor herself to the here and now. She called upon all her willpower to resist spinning visions of yesteryear—a dark paneled, smoky room with red velvet curtains covering the windows, oil lamps burning on tables, a spittoon near a table leg, several plump chairs, and a rose-colored sofa, where scantily clad females lounged with cigar-smoking men—until they scattered like ashes in the wind. The room that for several seconds had looked vaguely like a brothel returned to daffodil yellow.

"Oh my." Mrs. Powell laughed as she clapped a hand to her chest. "You look as surprised as I must have looked the day I showed you the room and you told me your name."

"You looked like you'd seen a ghost," Megan whispered, forcing the words through her numb lips as three impossible little words whirled around in her mind. *Was it me?*

Mrs. Powell nodded. "The ghost of a woman who was just a name to me. A woman I have wanted to thank ever since I first held that money in my hands."

Understanding dawned on Megan. "That's why you've been so nice to me. And generous. Letting me stay in that room so long, charging me next to nothing for it. Because of my name."

"It's the least I can do to finally be able to show my gratitude to that long-ago Megan for all she did for me. Although I do feel awful for taking double the rate from you those weeks. Reckon I got a little greedy. The plumbing here always needs fixin'." Mrs. Powell rolled her eyes as she poured water into the coffee machine. She said over her shoulder, "I'm still trying to make that up to you."

"Nonsense." Megan eased her grip on the table as she returned to normal much slower than the room had. "I made an offer and you took it. That's business."

Mrs. Powell bent over to open a door in the cabinet beneath the counter and took out a coffee can. She set it on the counter and opened it. "Your name is also why I asked if you had any people who had lived in Texas at one time. Maybe your grandmother or great-grandmother."

Megan shook her head. "I never knew any of my grandparents but as far as I know none of them ever lived in Texas and no one was named Megan. Did you look for her in the local records?"

"Of course. Never found a thing. Not one mention of a Megan McClure." Mrs. Powell poured coffee into the top of the machine. "It's almost as if the woman dropped out of the sky, did her wonderful good deed, and disappeared. How and why she chose me, well, I just can't imagine. It's like she picked a name out of the blue and came up with Florence Henderson. And no," she glanced over her shoulder, "no relation to that Florence Henderson."

That's easy enough to remember. The next instant Megan wondered why she'd thought that. *Why would I need to remember her name? Unless ...* A shiver ran over her skin like little mice feet.

"How that woman chose that specific date in 1974 and connected them to this house and to me, well, it's baffling." Mrs. Powell shrugged.

"You said you first learned about the money on March 30? That's the date I came here."

"I noticed that too. Exactly seven years later a woman named Megan McClure shows up at my door asking for a room." Mrs. Powell tilted her head. "Odd, isn't it?"

Megan recalled that day.

The minute she'd stepped inside the B&B the phone started to ring. A silver-haired woman—Mrs. Powell—had said there wasn't a vacancy. Suddenly there was a last-minute cancellation on the phone and an available room. A room with a door that would not open. Two days later, on April 1, seven years after the planned demolition day, Seth came through that door.

Holy moly.

Mrs. Powell put the coffee can back beneath the counter. "And why someone so long ago would know or care about what happened to this old house decades in the future is just another part of the mystery, another piece of a puzzle I doubt I will ever put together."

"It was all to save Seth's door."

Mrs. Powell sent Megan a sharp look. "What did you say?"

Megan hadn't realized she'd muttered the words aloud. "N-nothing." She quickly changed the subject. "Why is the name Miss Fleeda's B&B? Who's Fleeda?"

"My aunt. She offered me some money when I first talked about buying the house. She said it was a gift with one stipulation—I had to name it after her. I would have promised her the moon for that money, so I agreed. When Aunt Fleeda found out I had other resources she said she wouldn't hold me to it. But she's been a good aunt, she still gave me her money, and I love her, so I named it after her. But in my heart, it's Miss Megan's B&B. Maybe someday I'll change the name."

Mrs. Powell checked the sugar bowl and put it beside the creamer along the back of the counter. "You said something about saving a door?" She looked at Megan, who kept her face blank and stayed silent. "Funny you would say that. I had to promise I would leave that locked door in your room exactly the way it is. I couldn't remove it or cover it up with a piece of furniture. Odd request, don't you think?"

It took all Megan had not to laugh out loud. *Boy can I tell you about odd!* She merely shrugged. "This entire story is very odd. What year did ... Megan," those mice feet skittered over her skin again when she said the name, "give Cordelia Pryor the $25?"

Regret on her face, Mrs. Powell spread her hands. "I can't tell you."

Megan blinked in surprise. "What do you mean you can't tell me?"

"Before I could receive the money I had to sign a statement promising three things. I would only use the money to restore a house at a specific address, this one. I would leave that door alone. And I would never tell anyone when Cordelia Pryor received the money from Megan McClure. I never have. Not even my husband."

Mrs. Powell stepped closer. "But I will say—" She broke off and quickly glanced around as if making sure no one was listening then leaned toward Megan and said softly, "It was before the turn of the century." She straightened. "And that's all I'll say. Sorry. I promised." She turned on the coffee pot. "I'll have this ready in a jiffy. I'll make you breakfast too. That floating sausage doesn't look very appetizing."

***

"—and that's all she would tell me. I swear, Donna, I could almost hear *The Twilight Zone* music playing in the background," Megan spoke softly on the house phone so no one else could hear her. After her conversation with Mrs. Powell, Megan had run upstairs to check on Seth, found him still sleeping, then had run back down and called Donna while waiting for breakfast. Megan had skimmed over the night before with Barton, saving the details for another time, focusing mainly on Seth and the news about the B&B. The aroma of brewing coffee wafted from the dining room.

"I wonder why she had to promise not to reveal the initial date," Donna said.

"I don't think the date is important. The act itself is."

"What do you mean?"

"Without that money, the house would have been destroyed, along with the door."

"So, you're saying the whole point was to preserve Seth's door," Donna said. She was silent a moment. "Why did she wait so long to tell you all this? You've been there a couple of months."

"She tried to several times but kept getting interrupted. The same way something always interrupts Barton and me." The smell of frying bacon drifted down the hallway. Her stomach rumbled.

"Poor Barton." Donna laughed. "But it's his own fault for taking his sweet time last night."

"I don't think it would have mattered one way or the other. The universe would have probably interfered somehow to get its way. And maybe if Mrs. Powell had told me that first day about that other Megan McClure I wouldn't have thought anything about it besides wow, what a coincidence. Even a couple of weeks ago I wouldn't have given it much thought."

"And now?"

"Now I see it in a whole different light."

A longer moment of silence came before Donna said, "Oh my God—you think that Megan is *you*! That does it. I'm flying down tomorrow and—"

"No. You're up for that promotion. Don't you dare screw it up over me. Although if you were a nurse or a doctor I'd be singing a different song."

"He needs to go to the hospital, Megs."

"He can't leave the room. Remember? I'm doing all I can. I learned a lot from my mom. You know that. He has a slight fever and lost a lot of blood but he's strong and healthy, he'll be okay." *Oh, please be okay.*

"I hope so. It'd be even harder to explain his dead body in your room." Donna paused then asked in her most serious tone, "Do you really think you're that other Megan?"

"You know everything that's been happening to me. What do you think?"

"I hate it when you answer my question with a question. It usually means you're not going to answer. You'd better call me before you do anything rash. I mean it. And you'd better come home. You are coming home, aren't you?" Donna asked sharply.

"Two weeks from this Thursday. I already turned in my notice at work and bought my plane ticket." Megan sounded more confident about her plans than she felt. She mainly said that to placate Donna and dissuade her from coming to Texas when she had so much at stake at her job. *If I am that other Megan I won't be going to Chicago anytime soon.* "I've got to go, Donna. My breakfast is getting cold. I'll call you soon."

Megan hung up, dialed work, and called in sick for that night. Then she called Bonnie, explained she had food poisoning, and she'd see her in a couple of days. She hung up again and hurried down the hallway. In the dining room, she looked at the generous helpings of scrambled eggs, bacon, hash browns, toast, and a cup of coffee on a tray ready to go and frowned, thinking of Seth.

"Something wrong, Miss Megan?" Mrs. Powell asked.

"Do you think I could also have a bowl of soup?"

"Soup?" Mrs. Powell's expression said *It's 100 degrees in the shade and you want soup?* "Of course. I believe I have tomato."

Minutes later Megan headed upstairs with a hot breakfast and a bowl of soup for Seth. She hoped he woke up before it grew cold. She hoped he woke up period.

***

A thin film formed on the tomato soup long before Seth awakened. The hours dragged by. Megan sat on a chair beside the bed staring at a magazine she couldn't concentrate on when she heard a raspy voice whisper, "Miss Megan."

Her head snapped up. Seth looked at her with his one good eye. She shot out of the chair, the magazine falling on the floor. She stood on the stool beside the bed and leaned over him, relieved he was awake and alert. His left eye was black and blue, and swollen shut. More bruises marred his otherwise pale face.

"Welcome back." Megan placed her hand on his forehead, her spirits lifting upon finding it cool. His fever had broken. "How do you feel?"

"Like a coyote chewed me up and spit me out then trampled on me for good measure," he rasped. He licked his cracked lips.

She slipped her arm beneath his shoulders and held him up while he drank water from a glass she held to his lips. She eased him back down and put the glass on the nightstand. The plastic shower curtain between the sheet and the mattress crackled with the movements.

"How long ... have I been ... out?" he asked, his voice sounding rusty from disuse.

"I found you here last night. It's now late afternoon."

He lifted his right hand a few inches then gasped, grimacing, and quickly lowered it back to the bed. His eye closed. "Christ A'mighty, I hurt."

She straightened the covers over him. "I imagine."

"Reckon I got a black eye, huh?"

"You reckon right."

He gave a small snort. His eye opened and looked at her drowsily. "What else do I have?"

"A bullet hole in your right shoulder. I cleaned it, packed it, and wrapped it. That arm is going to hurt for a while." She gently smoothed his hair off his forehead. His hair was longer than the last time she'd seen him just a week ago. He had a mustache and a stubble of sandy beard. She tried to give him a reassuring smile, but her lips trembled. "You were stabbed in the left side. I cleaned that up too and doctored it the best I could. It wasn't very deep, and I don't think anything vital was damaged, but I'm not a doctor. I don't know if I did everything right." She swallowed, overwhelmed anew by her inadequacies. "I took off your boots and socks. I had to cut off your shirt. It's ruined. It was soaked with blood. I left your trousers on. There's not much blood on them. You lost a lot of blood. You should be in a hospital or at least see a doctor but—"

"You did good," he whispered, interrupting her anxious babbling. "Thought for sure ... I was headin' for that," he drew a ragged breath, "big ranch ... in the sky." His eye fluttered closed and he promptly fell asleep.

"Damn." She had meant to give him more aspirin while he was awake. She needed to clean his wounds again, and he should eat something. He looked so peaceful though. She decided to let him be. His left hand lay on top of the blanket on his stomach. No wedding band circled the ring finger. She didn't know if men in his time wore a wedding ring. She drank in the sight of him, thinking about all that Mrs. Powell had said, and wondering just what the hell it was all about.

She sat on the sofa to work on her writing.

Grunts, groans, and crackling plastic woke her. She jerked upright on the sofa.

Evening light and shadows fell upon Seth seated on the side of the bed, struggling to stand. She hurried to him and caught his left arm as he pushed himself, wobbling, to his feet.

She held him steady. "Are you nuts? What are you doing out of bed?"

"Gotta piss," he gasped, his ashen face tight with pain. He dropped his chin to his chest and stood there trembling and breathing hard.

She glanced at the bathroom. It looked miles away. "You think you can walk that far?"

He lifted his head and stared across the room at the bathroom. She wondered how far away it looked to him. His jaw tightened. He nodded.

"Okay," she said. "We'll take it slow and easy."

"Not too slow ... or it'll be runnin' down my leg."

"Put your arm around my shoulders." He did so, and she wedged her shoulder in his armpit. She wrapped her right arm around his waist, over the gauze binding the wound in his side, and held him tightly but carefully due to his injuries. His skin was warm and firm, ribbed with muscles. "Take it easy now."

They took baby steps across the room, his weight heavy upon her smaller frame, his grip on her left arm almost painful as he held on, his breathing labored. They finally made it to the bathroom.

"You need any help in there?"

He grunted and pulled free of her. He staggered into the bathroom and shut the door. She stood outside a moment, listening anxiously in case he fell or something. She heard him urinate and then a long moan. She grabbed the doorknob then paused, realizing it was a moan of release. She went to the bed, stripped off the sheets, pulled the plastic straight on the mattress, then put on clean sheets. She straightened the blankets and fluffed the pillows. His warmth and scent lingered on the bedding. She gathered up the dirty sheets and stuffed them into a garbage bag full of blood-soaked towels then hauled it near the door for a trip to the Laundromat. With enough bleach, she hoped they'd turn white again. Otherwise, she'd buy replacements.

She shot a worried glance at the bathroom. He'd been in there a while. She knocked on the door. "You okay?"

"Yeah," his weak voice answered.

Minutes later, he opened the bathroom door and leaned against the doorjamb. She hurried over to help him back across the room. When she eased him down on the bed, he asked, "What's that cracklin' noise under the sheet?"

"The shower curtain." At his questioning look, she explained, "To protect the mattress."

His eyebrows drew together as he looked at the bed then at her. "Did I soil your bed?"

"Don't worry about it. Here. Take these." She gave him two aspirin. He took them obediently and chased them down with a drink of water. He crawled beneath the covers and rested his head on the pillow. He heaved a deep sigh, his face drawn. She perched on the side of the bed. "Feel better?"

"Think I'm gonna live."

"I should clean your wounds. Change the bandages."

He yawned widely. "Could you do it later? I'm awful tired."

"Of course." She smoothed the blanket, tugged it straight. "Go to sleep."

He caught her hand and gave it a squeeze. "You saved me again. I thank you, Miss Megan." He fell asleep.

Megan tried to write but kept yawning and nodding off and finally gave in to exhaustion. She changed into her nightclothes, curled up on the sofa beneath a blanket, and slept.

Hours later, Seth woke up needing to use the bathroom again. Megan helped him, following a path of moonlight across the floor. He walked easier, with less help. When he was back in bed, he said, "I feel heaps better. 'Cept I could probably eat a whole cow raw."

"Holy moly, you must be starving." She went to the vanity and opened the bottom drawer where she kept a stash of snacks and stuck her hand inside to feel around in the dark. "I have a banana." She held up a package and brought it closer to her face for a good look. "A few chocolate chip cookies." She held up a small bag, gave it a shake. "And half a bag of potato chips. Any of it sound good?"

"All of it."

She gathered up the snacks and put them on the bed. She handed him the banana. "Have you ever had a banana?"

"Once." He peeled it and ate it in three bites.

She picked up the magazine she'd read earlier and put it on his lap. "So you don't get crumbs everywhere." She went to fill the glass of water in the bathroom. When she returned, the cookie package was empty. Seth took the glass from her and drained it then handed it back. She went to refill it. Soon the potato chips were gone.

She looked at the empty packages in dismay. "I wish I had more. You need to build up your strength after losing all that blood. I should have gotten you some food. But I was afraid to leave you a—"

"Don't fret so. I'm fine. I feel much better."

"I'll get a big breakfast for you in a couple of hours." Megan threw away the trash, brushed crumbs off the magazine into the trashcan then sat on the side of his bed, facing him. The shower curtain crackled. She adjusted her robe, fiddling with a corner where it lay on her thigh. She peered at him through the dimness. Shadows pooled in the hollows of his face. "Do you feel like talking?"

"Reckon I can manage it for a bit."

"Who did this to you? What happened?"

He was quiet for so long she thought he'd fallen asleep. Then he muttered, "You were right. About Lottie. Using opium."

"Oh, Seth, I'm so sorry."

"I didn't know for sure until a few days ago. I been real busy at the ranch and runnin' the saloon. Hadn't seen Lottie in months. Almost as long since I last saw you. I went lookin' for her the other day but couldn't find her. I figured the other girls knew where she was. Took some badgerin' but one of 'em finally told me." He ran his left hand over his face then rested his hand on his chest. His voice took on a lower timbre when he said, "I found her limp and staring blankly at nothin' in the corner of a filthy, rat-infested room."

Megan shuddered. "How awful."

Seth shook his head. "It was bad. Terrible bad. I carried her back to her room, told the girls to help her all they could, and went to find Bingo. Can I have some water?"

After he drank, she said, "I guess you found Bingo."

"I went in his saloon, walked up to him, and slammed my fist into his face." Seth made a small motion of jabbing the air. "He went flyin' backwards over the bar, arms spread wide like a pair of wings. He smashed into the mirror, shattering it to kingdom come. He slid to the floor and slumped there like a rag doll with blood pourin' out of his nose."

"Holy moly." She sensed him looking at her.

"I'm not a violent man, Miss Megan. I do all I can to avoid a fight. But I gotta tell ya, it felt good. It felt damn good hittin' that slick-haired, shifty-eyed son of a bitch. Felt so good I high-tailed it around the bar to hit him again. I lit into him until his men pulled me off him and held me until the marshal came. I let every man there know right quick why I'd done what I did. Told 'em Bingo was an opium sellin' piece of horse shit among other things. Not that it mattered to anyone. Hell, lots of 'em smoke it."

"But they're not your sister."

"No. They're not." He sighed. "I still can't believe she's doin' it."

"Were you arrested for assaulting Bingo?"

Seth shook his head. "Spent the night in the jail, got out the next day. "Course, the marshal is Bingo's man."

"Was Bingo hurt very badly?"

"Had some cuts and bruises. Broke his nose. His face looked almost as bad as mine."

She rolled her eyes at the pride and satisfaction in his voice. *Men.* "Who did this to you?"

"'Couple nights after that Bingo's men jumped me in the dark. Think there were four of 'em. They left me for dead behind the livery." He rose up a little off the bed, saying angrily, "Those bastards probably stole my horse!"

"Take it easy." Megan gently pushed him back down with her hand on his chest. "You can reclaim him when you go back."

"They probably stole my gun too," he snapped.

"It's over there." She pointed to the gun holstered in the gun belt draped over the doorknob on Seth's door.

"Oh. Good." He muttered, "Bastards."

"So, they left you for dead and you managed to make it up the stairs? To get help from *Lottie?*" Megan couldn't keep the surprise out of her voice. Seeking help from Lottie the drug addict seemed ridiculous.

He turned his head away from her, pulling the covers up to his chin. "I don't recollect. I'm mighty tired."

She rose from the bed and stood. "Of course. Holler if you need me."

He looked up at her. "I hate to put you out of your bed. You could sleep here, too. It's big enough. Though the cracklin' is annoyin'."

"The sofa's fine. You need your rest."

"We'd both get plenty of rest. It's not like I could do anything else. Unless you want to do all the work."

A blush warmed her face. "Go to sleep." She resisted the urge to kiss him goodnight, whether on the forehead or the cheek or ... everywhere. She lay on the sofa, pulled the blanket up, and wiggled around until she found a comfortable position. After a moment, the darkness gave her the courage to ask, "Seth?"

"Hmmm?"

"Are you married?"

A long pause.

She held her breath.

"No."

She thought she heard a smile in his voice.

A smile spread across her heart.

***

In the morning, Seth wolfed down a plateful of scrambled eggs, sausage, bacon, hash browns, and toast. Mrs. Powell had raised her eyebrows at the pile of food Megan had but said nothing. Seth wrinkled his nose after tasting the coffee but drank it anyway, along with a glass of orange juice. After breakfast, he washed up then sat on a chair while Megan knelt on the floor beside him and carefully removed the dressing on his wounds. She cleaned and disinfected them, pleased that they seemed to be healing well. No sight or smell of infection.

"You'd make a good doctor," Seth said, his arms raised, his right one just a little, so she could wrap fresh gauze around him just above the waistband of his trousers.

"No thanks. And I wish you'd quit forcing me to practice medicine. You're lucky I had all these medical supplies on hand."

"Why did you?"

"Remember that night you came running in here waving your gun around looking for Bingo because he'd beat up Lottie? The night you got that scar on your cheek?" Her face was inches from the side of his waist as she leaned forward to pass the roll of gauze from one hand to the other on the opposite side of him. She sat on her heels as she rolled the gauze to her side.

"I remember."

"I went out after you left and stocked up on bandages, gauze, alcohol, and other things. Just in case." She glanced up at him. "Good thing I did, huh?"

"That was right smart of you and I'm mighty grateful you did, Miss Megan." The warmth in his smile reflected in his eye.

She turned her attention to cutting the gauze with a scissors and taping the end to the gauze wrapped around him. "There." She stood and stepped back to look him over. The white bindings around his middle and running diagonally across his chest from his right shoulder to his waist stood out starkly against his sun-browned skin. He didn't have Barton's bulk and bulging muscles. Seth was sinewy and narrow-hipped, with a flat stomach and compact muscles. His chest had a smattering of sandy hair. His swollen eye looked a little better, but the bruises were still violently colored, black and blue mixed with purple.

"I changed the sheets again. And removed the shower curtain."

"I appreciate that." He scratched his chest just above the dressing.

"I have to go out today and run some errands, do the laundry. I'll be gone a few hours. Will you be okay?"

He nodded. "I'll probably sleep."

She went to the vanity and rummaged through her purse, making sure she had enough change for the laundry and enough money for the items on her shopping list. Behind her, Seth's bare feet padded across the floor. The bed creaked when he sat on it.

"Could you wash my britches?"

"Sure. Take them off and ... whatever else you're wearing." She stuffed the shopping list in the pocket of her shorts. She took her purse, dropped it beside the bag full of laundry, and went to the bathroom. When she came out, Seth was in bed, propped up against the pillows, the blanket pulled up to his waist.

"I put my clothes in the bag." He jutted his chin to the garbage bag.

She picked up her purse. "You need anything?" He shook his head. "I'll be back in a couple hours. Get some rest. I'll bring back something to eat." She grabbed the top of the garbage bag and tried to lift it. Holy moly it was heavy.

"Squirrel stew or roasted rabbit?"

She paused and looked at him. "What?"

"For supper." He shrugged. "Just some suggestions." A smile played around his mouth.

"Very funny." She made a face at him. "Those don't even sound good."

"They're delicious. I'm partial to rabbit. Especially the way I cook it." He stretched his good arm up and put his hand behind his head. His elbow pointed to the ceiling. "I bet my boots you'd like it."

Her gaze followed the line from his bent elbow down his arm to the tuft of hair in his armpit down his side to the edge of the blanket at his waist then traveled over his bandaged chest. *Does he have any idea what a picture he makes? Lying there in my bed, posed like a piece of eye-candy in Playgirl. Does he know what he does to me? And he cooks!*

She tore her gaze from him and picked up the garbage bag. "Don't get your hopes up. Unless you see a rabbit down in the yard and shoot it through the window, we won't be having rabbit." Leaning lopsided from carrying the heavy bag, she went to the door then paused with her hand on the doorknob and glanced at him. "If someone happens to knock, please don't answer the door." She smiled. "See you later." She left, locking the door behind her.

She did the laundry first. Despite a lot of bleach and the cold-water cycle, the towels came out with rust-colored blotches. The worst ended up in the trashcan. The rest she kept for future use. Just in case. The sheets came out cleaner, the few bloodstains gone. His trousers cleaned up, too. She took the laundry back to her room. Seth snored softly, his face turned toward the windows. She put the bag of laundry at the foot of the bed and left.

Hours later, Megan unlocked her door while juggling a twelve pack of pop, a grocery bag holding a bunch of bananas, some apples, a bottle of orange juice, a big bag of potato chips, some cookies, several rolls of gauze, four new towels, along with other items, and a bag of food from the restaurant beneath the big sombrero sign. A bag of ice bumped against her leg with each movement. She entered her room and shut the door with her hip.

Seth looked up from where he sat in bed with pillows behind him and a book spread open on the blanket on his lap. "Howdy." He grinned. "How was your day?"

She paused, struck by how nice it was to have someone to come home to, someone to ask about her day. "Productive. Yours?"

"Restful." He closed the book and put it on the nightstand. "I feel a lot better."

She smiled. "That's great." The bag of ice hanging against her thigh had made it numb. Holding the bag away from her leg, she walked to the vanity and unloaded her arms. She put four cans of pop and the bottle of orange juice in the cooler, opened the bag of ice and dumped it over the beverages. She ran her hand over the ice cubes, spreading them evenly, then closed the cooler. She straightened and wiped her hand on her shorts, glancing at the book on the nightstand. The title reminded her of a bone she had to pick with him. She gathered up the remaining two cans of pop and the bag of food and put them on the table.

"Dinner is served." She turned to him, saying, "Your trousers are in the—" she broke off, seeing he had gotten out of bed and was wearing his trousers. She glanced at the end of the bed where she'd put the garbage bag of clean clothes earlier. "Where's the bag?"

"I wanted my britches. I put everything else away while I was at it. I didn't know where to put the sheets and towels, so I put 'em over there." He nodded to the sofa.

Megan's eyes widened when she saw the stacks of neatly folded towels and sheets on the sofa. She added to her list how nice it was to have someone help do things. "Thank you."

He shrugged. "It's the least I can do." He walked to the table as Megan took the food out of the bag and unwrapped it. "What's this?" He pulled out a chair and sat, wincing a little and holding his side.

"Mexican food. Tacos and burritos." She put two of each and a can of pop in front of him then sat down across from him.

Seth stared at the food. "That doesn't look like any kind of Mexican food I've ever seen."

"Well, that's what they call it." She opened the cans. "The store was fresh out of rabbit and squirrel. Sorry."

He chuckled then looked dubiously at the food. He poked a finger at the mound of shredded lettuce spilling over the top of the taco shell. He leaned down and took a sniff of it, then straightened. He picked a taco up with one hand and held it sideways like a sandwich. Cheese and lettuce fell on the paper wrapper.

Megan giggled. "Like this." She picked up a taco with both hands and showed him how to hold and eat it. A few of the fillings fell out. Seth held his taco the way she did and took a bite. A whole mess of cheese, lettuce, tomatoes, and meat fell out.

"Oh damn," he said. "Messy." He chewed a moment then added, "But tasty."

Megan laughed, enjoying his discovery of new things. They ate in companionable silence accompanied by the hum of the air conditioner. Once Seth got the hang of eating tacos, he ate them in no time then picked up a burrito.

"I see you were reading the book of American history. Are you going to take that one back with you too?" She gave him a pointed look.

He paused with the burrito almost in his mouth then lowered it. His one-eyed gaze held hers. "I reckon I shouldn't have done that. Don't even know why I did 'cept I was mad as a riled-up grizzly when I left."

"I was pretty damn mad too. And you gave me a hickey. I hate hickeys."

"A what?"

"Hickey. On my neck." She touched the spot.

His gaze rested on her neck. "Oh. A love mark."

Her face warmed at his term for a hickey. Her blush deepened when his gaze briefly dropped to her breasts before meeting her eyes again.

"I don't recollect you complainin' when I gave it to you."

The conversation wasn't going the way Megan wanted it to go. She looked down and brushed crumbs off her tank top. "I just wish you hadn't taken that book back with you. The possible consequences—"

"No one else will see it. I promise."

Megan thought of Cordelia Pryor and wondered.

Seth finished his burritos and eyed the two in front of Megan.

She pushed them across the table. "Here."

He glanced at her as he reached for them. "You sure?"

She nodded then pursed her lips and said with a tsk, "I should have gotten you steak and potatoes or chicken or—"

"This is fine, Miss Megan. My belly's not picky." He looked down at the burrito a moment then back at her, his expression serious. "You've been awful good to me. Savin' my life. Fixin' me up. 'Specially after the way we parted."

"Seth—"

"I said some things I shouldn't have." Regret showed in his eye. "Things I didn't mean and I—well, I feel mighty bad about it all. It's been eatin' at me for a while and—"

"We both said things we didn't mean. Ultimately, it was my fault though. I overreacted. I'm sorry."

A small smile touched his lips. "You and your frettin' about my age."

"Since you brought it up, how old are you now?"

"Forty-eight."

"*What?*"

He burst out laughing. "I knew that would get you riled up." He laughed again, his good eye twinkling. "You should see your face."

"Very funny." She tried to sound mad but couldn't help smiling at his hearty laughter.

Still chuckling, he said, "It's been almost five months since I was last here. I'm still 28 for a month or so."

"It's been a week for me." She sat back in her chair. "Wow. Donna was here just a week ago. Seems longer than that."

"Your friend came visitin'?"

Smiling, Megan nodded. "She surprised me last Monday. She stayed for three days. We had a great time. I didn't realize how much I've missed her until I saw her again." She picked up some pieces of cheese off the wrapper and ate them. "I showed her my letter in the bank in Cleburne."

Seth raised his eyebrows. "You did?"

She nodded. "I told her about you."

His jaw dropped. "You *did?* Lordy." He gave her a knowing look. "Felt good, didn't it."

"Liberating. What a relief to finally tell someone and have someone to talk to about it."

Seth didn't say *I told you so,* but his expression did. "Think she believes you?"

Megan shrugged. "Probably as much as Tim believes you."

"Tell me 'bout her visit."

Megan did so while they finished eating. They moved to the sofa and told each other about their respective lives since they'd seen each other. Seth did most of the talking since Megan didn't mention how Mrs. Powell got the B&B. Or about finding Barton in a possible drug house. Or that Barton had been in the room two nights ago. She didn't want to talk about Barton at all. They talked long into the night until Seth went to bed. She curled up on the sofa. Her cheek pillowed on her hand, she sighed contentedly. *What a wonderful evening.*

Through the darkness came an echoing sigh.

Of contentment? Frustration? Exhaustion? Or just a plain old sigh? What is he thinking? What will tomorrow bring?

She could hardly wait to find out.

Chapter 20

Megan snuggled against a firm, warm pillow pressed all along the front of her body as she lay on her side. Her arm tightened around it, pulling it closer. *So warm. Solid. Smells so—*

It snored and mumbled something.

Her eyes shot open. She stared at a back crossed by a swath of white gauze. *Seth? How on earth?* She eased her arm off him and put her hand behind her on the mattress to brace herself as she rose up on her other elbow and stared around the room in confusion. The tall windows framed the soft rosy glow of early morning. She glanced down and saw she was still in her nightclothes. She lifted the covers an inch or so then quickly lowered them. Seth still had on his trousers. *How did I get here?*

Seth rolled onto his back and opened his good eye to look at her. "Mornin'." He yawned. His hair stuck up every which way.

"I-I'm sorry." She inched towards the edge of the bed.

He raised his head, his one eye squinting at her. "For what?"

"I don't remember getting in bed. I must have sleepwalked or—"

"I put you here."

She looked at him in surprise. "You did?"

"I got up to relieve myself. You looked mighty uncomfortable on that sofa. I picked you up and put you in your bed where you belong."

She let his *where you belong* comment slide and said incredulously, "You carried me? In your condition? Are you crazy?"

He chuckled. "Shucks. You don't weigh much more than a sack of taters." He yawned again. "Once you hit the mattress you stretched like a cat, arms and legs going straight out, archin' your back. Thought you might start purrin' any minute."

A blush crept over her face, knowing he had watched her sleep. Although she had done the same with him to make sure he was still breathing, and to store up images for when he was gone.

He gazed down as if noticing for the first time the distance she had put between them. His eye met hers. "You gettin' up already?"

"I should."

"You have errands to run today?"

"Not really." She ran a hand through her hair, wincing when she hit a snarl. *I must look like a witch!* "Just get us breakfast."

"That's awhile yet."

"Probably."

"So why get up? I'm not." His head hit the pillow and he rolled on his side again.

Megan climbed out of bed and went to the bathroom. When she came out, fluffing her just-brushed hair, she paused and looked at Seth lying in her bed. He would be leaving soon. Tomorrow, maybe the next day. Soon. They hadn't talked about it. Neither of them had mentioned it. But it loomed over them. Over her anyway. *Too soon.* A week, a month, a year would be too soon. She threw caution to the wind and followed her heart back into bed beside him.

She lay on her side, stiff and still, staring at his back. Warmth radiated from him. She inhaled his scent and longed to touch him. Lying beside him but apart was agony and ecstasy.

Seth reached behind him and fished around until he found her hand. He pulled it back over his side, making her scoot closer and press the front of her body against his back. He laced his fingers with hers and held their joined hands against his chest. His warmth enveloped her, mingling his scent with hers. She closed her eyes, her toes curling from the thrill of being so close to him. She fell asleep with her arm around him.

Megan opened her eyes and saw the hands on the alarm clock pointing out nine o'clock. She sat up and put her hand on the empty space beside her. Dread shot through her. *He's gone!*

"Mornin', sleepyhead."

Her head whipped around.

Seth, wearing his trousers, stood near the vanity eating a banana. "Woke up hungry." He pulled the peel further down and took a bite.

Dread quickly gave way to relief and turned into joy that brought a smile to her face. At least she still had today with him. She threw back the covers and stretched her leg over the side of the bed to touch the stool.

"You sure look pretty in the mornin'."

Her foot on the stool, she glanced up and saw him looking at her bare leg as if he hadn't seen it many times before. His gaze slowly rose up the rest of her, pausing briefly at her breasts covered by the thin material of her nightclothes, until meeting her gaze. She reached up self-consciously to run a hand over her messy hair. He watched her every move.

"'Course you look pretty any time." He reached into the bottom drawer of the vanity and pulled out another banana. "Want one?"

With you watching me? I don't think so! She shook her head. "Not right now." She got out of bed and went to the bathroom.

She took a shower, threw on a pair of shorts and a sleeveless top then went downstairs. Luckily, the dining room was empty. No one saw the two heaping plates she took upstairs.

After they ate, she changed the dressing on Seth's injuries. "You must be a quick healer," she said as she knelt beside him and wound clean gauze around his waist. "Everything is healing nicely. Even your face looks much better. The swelling around your eye is almost gone. The bruises are fading and have a tinge of green."

"I can finally see out of it a little."

"Amazing. It's hard to believe you were at death's door two nights ago." She finished his dressing and sat back on her heels. She looked him over then tilted her head. "What's the matter?"

He had grown quiet and still and stared intently at the door she had named after him, his lips pressed together. "It's just ... that first time I came here?" His gaze met hers. "With that bullet in my arm? When I got back to my time, that wound healed awful quick it seemed. Couple days maybe. I didn't give it much thought then. But now that you mention how well I'm mendin', and we both know I shouldn't be, not this quick, I'm wonderin' ..." he paused, as if gathering his thoughts, "well, I'm wonderin' if maybe that door has somethin' to do with it."

Megan stared at him. "You think that door has curative qualities? You cross the threshold and bam! Let the healing begin?"

Seth shrugged. "I know men who've been shot like me. They take to their bed for a week or so. I was stabbed and beaten too and certain sure I was gonna die. I swear, Miss Megan, as I dragged myself up those stairs I was prepared to meet my Maker. Look at me now," he spread his hands, "just two days later. It ain't natural."

Supernatural.

She shook her head. "Holy moly, what next? Well," she rose to her feet, "we know it won't work on me since I can't go through it." A chill rushed over her. She glanced at Seth's door. It looked too innocent to house so much mystery.

"Miss Megan? What's wrong?"

Her gaze darted to Seth's. "Nothing. I'm just glad you're recovering so well no matter what the reason is."

"Me too. I'm not fond of feelin' like coyote vomit." He stood and pushed the chair back up to the table. "Do you have to go to your work today?"

She shook her head. "I called in sick again. I didn't want to leave you alone."

"I feel fine."

"You could have a relapse. You might need me."

His gaze traveled the length of her. "Yeah. I reckon I might at that."

Her face heating up, she gathered up the roll of gauze and everything else and went to put it all away in the bathroom. When she came out, she asked, "What do you want to do today? I know your options are very limited but—" she shrugged.

"Tell me what you've been writin' about."

Pleased with his interest in her livelihood, she told him about the methamphetamine article, due to be published in the upcoming Sunday paper. She let him read her article about the B&B. She'd sent it to a friend who worked at a travel magazine and hoped for the best. He read her article about the ghosts in the Swift Armor Meat Packing Plant she was waiting to hear back from an editor about. The business didn't exist in his time yet. They talked the morning away.

For lunch, they had apples, cookies, and potato chips washed down with pop. Then he took a nap while Megan wrote. Although she spent more time watching him sleep than she did writing. When he woke up, she broke out a deck of cards and they played poker with Megan's tips. He won all the coins. They hung the shower curtain back up on the rod circling the claw-footed bathtub.

For dinner, he suggested pizza. They sat at the table eating a large pizza with everything while light from the evening sun stretched into the room and brought out the red in his hair. As night fell, they sat on the sofa and she answered his questions about what he was reading in the book of American history up to 1976.

The first moon landing. Woodstock. Watergate. Skylab. Abortion laws. The Vietnam War. Kent State. The resignation of President Nixon.

Seth thought legalized abortion was a grand idea, having known several women who had done it to themselves, some of them suffering terrible consequences, some of them dying. His upper lip curled in disgust at the war and he was sympathetic to the protesters. He decided President Nixon deserved a horsewhipping. He seemed most interested in space travel and NASA. Woodstock made him scratch his head and look baffled.

The floor lamp behind the sofa cast a cozy circle of light around them. The air conditioner hummed valiantly along, keeping at bay the hot June night beyond the sheltering walls of the old house.

Hours later, Megan changed into her nightclothes. She spread a blanket over the sofa then put her pillow at one end.

Seth came out of the bathroom. "I don't know why you're fussin' with that. Once you fall asleep I'm just gonna pick you up and put you in your bed. You don't want me strainin' anythin', do you?"

She laughed. He had his hand clasped to his bandaged side, his face twisted with exaggerated pain. "No, that wouldn't be good. Although you'll probably be asleep in minutes. You were falling asleep sitting on the sofa."

"I'm almost seein' cross-eyed. So, it's best you just get in bed and spare me from havin' to tote you over there."

She picked up her pillow and with a casualness she didn't feel walked across the room and climbed in bed. It dipped and creaked when Seth got in on the other side. She turned off the nightstand light. Darkness settled over the room. They each lay on their side of the bed.

She stared at the ceiling, every cell in her body aware of him mere inches away.

What now? Will he? Should I?

She wavered between waiting for him to make the first move or making it herself. Although he had been yawning a lot, and his face looked drawn and tired.

"Miss Megan?"

She turned her head toward him. "Yes?" she asked, maybe a little too eagerly, and added, "Something wrong?" Her eyes had adjusted to the dark and she could see his profile. He also lay on his back, staring at the ceiling.

"I just wanted to tell you," he paused, "I've never been able to talk to anyone the way I can talk to you. I've missed that. Today was a mighty special day." He rolled his head toward her. "You're a mighty special woman."

Pleased by his comment, she replied, "You're the time traveler. I'd say that's pretty darn special."

He snorted softly. "Some time traveler I am. I can come here but I can't do anythin'." He yawned then asked, "What's the point?"

"There are big things in store for you, Seth. I just know it."

"I don't know why you keep sayin' that. I'm nobody. Just a dumb ol' cowboy."

She put her hand on the bed between them. "You are much more than that. You're a rancher, a businessman, a landowner. You can build things. You're ambitious. Smart. Kind. You can do anything you want. One of my teachers used to say it's never too late to be the person you were meant to be. You'll figure it out. Follow your heart."

After a moment, he asked, "You really think all that 'bout me?"

"I said it, didn't I?"

Seth rose up on his elbow, facing her. "You think we'll ever know why this is happening to us? What it's all about?"

She thought of the purple dress, the index card with the question about her eyes, her visions of the past, Mrs. Powell's story about the B&B. They all pointed to something Megan was slowly coming to terms with: *I'm going to go back to his time.*

It was the first time she fully acknowledged it. It left her stunned. Scared. Curious.

How? When? What portal? Why?

She hadn't told Seth about Mrs. Powell yet and opened her mouth to do so. Then paused. He was yawning again. No matter how much he had seemingly recovered, he was still healing and needed rest. She replied, "I believe we will. Hopefully before you turn forty-eight."

He laughed. Then he leaned over and kissed her. A soft, quick kiss placed with surprisingly good aim in the dimness. He drew back slightly and hovered over her. "If I wasn't so damn tired," he muttered. He yawned again then shook his head, muttering, "Damn it."

"Get some rest." She kept the disappointment out of her voice. She knew he was tired.

He kissed her again, more thoroughly this time, with a sweep of his tongue inside her mouth, then drew away. She sensed his reluctance. Heard it in his voice when he said, "'Night, Miss Megan."

She turned on her side, away from him. This time, she was the one to reach behind and fish for his hand. She drew it over her side, laced her fingers with his, and held their joined hands just below her breasts. His long warm body curved around her. His breath stirred her hair. She closed her eyes, savoring his nearness, his warmth, him.

Moments later, he snored softly, the sound comforting, peaceful. It made her smile. She recalled his comment about the day being mighty special. Nothing special had happened. Just simple, mundane things. Talking, eating, playing games, laughing, teasing, comfortable silences. Having someone to share all those little things that made up a life had turned the simple and mundane into something wonderful.

She wanted that every day. With him. She wanted to sleep beside him like this every night. She wanted a life with him so badly it sent her heart racing and made her catch her breath in surprise at its intensity. It didn't matter if it was back in his time or here in her time or even in a time neither of them had been in before. As long as it was their time, together, the rest was just background.

Megan knew of only one way they would ever have their time.

She stared into the darkness. *Okay, universe, you win. Do with me what you will. On one condition—when whatever you have planned for me, for Seth, is over, let us be together. That's all I ask. Because,* she pressed their joined hands against her chest, over her heart, *because I love him.* She squeezed her eyes shut.

God help me. I love him.

Chapter 21

Megan sat on the back seat of a taxi with a bag of groceries beside her. A smaller bag containing hamburgers and fries warmed her lap. A 12-pack of pop on the floor bumped against her calf as the taxi drove to the B&B. Her early morning walk to the grocery store had been pleasant and invigorating, but she wasn't up to walking back with her arms full. Not with the temperature already climbing. The sign on a bank on a street corner flashed *86 degrees* then *11:39*. The refreshing cool air blowing out of the vents in the front of the taxi stirred the hair around her face, and she wondered, *How am I going to survive in Texas without air conditioning?*

It was the latest of numerous *How am I going to survive without* questions she'd been asking herself since she'd awakened with Seth's arm still around her. He'd slept soundly while she dressed. She left him a note before leaving the room. She'd needed to get away from him, get outside in the sunshine and fresh air. Get a new perspective on things. Last night had been a big night. Accepting the fact that she had fallen in love and she might/will/could possibly actually time travel had been a double whammy.

She had spent an inordinate amount of time in the grocery store browsing the aisles full of modern day conveniences. Canned pop. Cold beer. Processed cheese. Minute Rice. Tabloids. Tampons. Electric can openers. Pot pies. Fritos. Deodorant. Toothbrushes. Cold medications.

Her favorite shampoo. The list of things she would have to learn to live without seemed endless. People had done so since time began, but she hadn't. *I'm going to miss those tampons.* Her stomach rumbled from the smell of hamburgers and fries filling the cab. *And fast food.*

The whole idea of her time traveling was fucking mind-blowing, as Donna would say.

Donna.

Megan stared out the window of the taxi at the passing pedestrians. *How am I going to survive without Donna?* The thought of life without her dearest friend tore a hole in her heart.

How can I go? Give up everything? Give up Donna? If I go, can I come back?

Doubts and questions plagued her as she got out of the cab, gathered her groceries, and carried them into the B&B. The sound of *Hollywood Squares* came from the TV in the sitting room off the hallway. A middle-aged woman sat in a chair, watching the show. A white-haired man sat in another chair, his hands folded across his round stomach, his eyes closed. The woman and Megan exchanged a smile. Megan hefted the grocery bag for a better grip and climbed the stairs, wondering if they were the couple who had complained about her.

Inside her room, she shut the door with her hip.

Seth stood in front of a window, looking out. He turned. "There you are."

One look at him and all her doubts and worries vanished. For him, she would give it all up. Gladly. She had been in love before, thought she had been anyway. What she had felt those couple times paled in comparison to all she felt for this time-traveling cowboy. He wore his trousers and, she noted with surprise, he had a blanket wrapped around him. "You're cold?" she asked, wiping sweat off her forehead.

He tugged the edges of the blanket closed across his chest. "Felt as cold as a blue-tailed 'Norther in here." He took the 12-pack and bag of groceries from her. He set the bag on the table and went to the cooler, squatting down to fill it with the pop. The blanket spread out like a cape around him.

"I guess you figured out how to control the air conditioner?"

"Sure did. Turned that big knob to *off.*" He stood, wiping his hands on his trousers, then pulled the slipping blanket around his shoulders again. "Damn blanket," he muttered. "Wish I had a shirt." He glanced at her. "Been feelin' kinda funny, sittin' around here bare-chested all this time. Feels disrespectful."

Megan recalled how in old westerns the men always pulled on a shirt when a lady arrived on the scene. "I haven't minded it a bit."

He cocked an eyebrow.

She smiled. "Hungry?" She held up the bag of food. He grabbed two cans out of the cooler then joined her at the table, popping the tabs on the cans. She pulled the hamburgers and fries out of the bag and gave him his. He watched her a moment as she ate her burger then picked up his.

After he had a couple bites, she asked, "You like it?"

He shrugged, nodded, and took another bite. "Though I've sure got a hankerin' for a hot home-cooked meal."

"Like some of your famous roasted rabbit?"

He chuckled. "Just mentionin' it makes my mouth water. Now Tim, he makes a tasty squirrel stew. He's a fair cook. Most of the men are. Have to be or they'd starve."

Holy moly, I'm going to starve! Not only did Megan not cook very much, it didn't even interest her. "Does Lottie cook?"

"She can, but she doesn't. Not in years. One of the best cooks in town is Susannah. Her chicken 'n dumplin's are my favorite. Her pies and cobblers are the best this side of the Mississippi."

Susannah. It was the first time her name had come up. The sound of it grated on Megan's nerves like fingernails on a chalkboard. *She's still in the picture.* The hamburger suddenly tasting like cardboard. *It's my own fault. I screamed at him that he should marry her.* She could still hear him snarl, *Maybe I will.* She squeezed more ketchup onto the Styrofoam carton, asking casually, "Do you eat with her often?"

"Couple times a week maybe, if I'm in town. She helps me with the books for the saloon. Don't know what I'd do without her."

Megan frowned at the French fry she swirled in the ketchup. She had never considered herself the jealous type but that green-eyed monster roared to life upon learning that Susannah appeared to be making herself indispensable to Seth. She'd been hanging in there a long time, trying to win his affections. A decade or so.

How long will he resist her? How quickly can I get back there?
How can I get back there? The portal in the Water Gardens?

They ate quietly for several minutes then Seth put down his half-eaten hamburger. "I'm feelin' poorly."

Alarmed, Megan shot to her feet. "Is it your wounds? Let me see."

He waved away her reaching hands. "They're fine. I did like you told me and washed 'em when I got up then put that ointment on 'em and wrapped 'em back up. It's more like," he pursed his lips, "I feel awful tired and ... outta sorts. I kept thinkin' it'd go away, but it ain't. Instead it's gettin' worse."

She put her hand on his forehead. "You don't have a fever." Her hand slid down to gently cup his uninjured cheek. The bruises on the other side of his face had faded to a light purple tinged with green giving way to yellow. "Your eye looks much better." His hazel eyes flecked with green stared back at her. She had always liked his eyes. She thought of him at 28 what she had thought of him when he was 17 just months ago. *Hot and handsome and kissably close.* He had been too young then. But now ...

She leaned down and kissed him softly with barely parted lips. *Has Susannah kissed him? Has he kissed her? Do I really want to know?* The thoughts raced through her head while her lips lingered on his and her hand cupped his cheek. She finally broke away and looked in his eyes. "You feel just fine to me."

"You feel mighty fine too." He smiled slightly, then his gaze turned troubled. "But I think I better go lay down before I fall down."

"You feel that bad?"

"Reckon I'm havin' that relapse you mentioned." He started to rise, and abruptly sat back down. His brow beetled, he braced his palms on the table and pushed himself up but didn't make it very far before sitting again. The blanket slid off his shoulders. He made no move to replace it but just sat there a moment, his head hanging down, his hands gripping the edge of the table.

His obvious weakness and its sudden onslaught alarmed her even more. "Maybe it's the food. Your stomach isn't used to anything you've been eating. All that pop can't be good for your system either." *Is this my fault?* She felt awful.

"I don't know what it is. But I'm weak as a new-born calf." He looked at her with something close to shame in his eyes. "I hate to be more of a burden to you, but can you help me to bed? I-I can't make it myself."

Her shoulder wedged in his armpit, her arm around his waist, she got him to the bed where he sank with a groan. She helped him get beneath the covers and pulled them up to his chin. "Are you warm enough? Need another blanket?"

"Quit fussin' over me," he snapped, then muttered, "sorry. I'm just so tired. Feel like there's rocks sittin' on my eyelids." He looked at her drowsily. "I don't know what's wrong with me."

"You need rest. You're still healing. I'll let you sleep and go do laundry. Will you be all right?"

He nodded.

She gathered her dirty clothes, then went into the bathroom and got the dirty towels and the new ones she'd bought. When she came out, Seth's trousers lay on the floor. She put them in the garbage bag with the rest of the laundry.

He was asleep.

She watched him a moment, worried about his sudden setback. He had been doing so well. She kissed his forehead, picked up the bag of laundry, and left.

When she returned to the B&B a couple of hours later, Mrs. Powell stopped Megan in the hall. "I have a letter for you. It looks important." Mrs. Powell shuffled through a handful of envelopes she held. "It must be in my office somewhere. I'll bring it up when I find it."

"I'll come down later and get it," Megan said quickly.

"It's no problem for me to bring it to you."

"I'll come get it. Save you another trip up those stairs."

Mrs. Powell beamed. "You're such a dear."

Megan hurried up to her room. Inside, Seth still slept. She quietly closed the door, put away the clean clothes and linens, and draped Seth's trousers over the back of a chair. She sat at the table to write.

A while later, someone knocked on the door. Megan swore softly. Mrs. Powell must have decided to bring up the envelope after all. Megan hurried to the bed, tossed the covers over Seth's head, and bunched up the pillows and blankets along the length of him. She went to the door then glanced at the bed. It was visible from where she stood but it just looked like a messy, unmade bed. She opened the door just enough to look out.

"Special delivery." Barton, smiling, bowed slightly. He flattened his hand on the door and shoved it open, then handed her an envelope.

"What are you doing here?" Megan stared in shocked surprise. She grabbed the envelope while holding the door, so it wouldn't open any further.

"I stopped by The Tejas last night. They told me you're still sick, so I thought I'd stop by and see how you're doing. The landlady let me in and asked if I'd bring you your mail since I was coming to see you anyway." He raised an eyebrow. "You gonna let me in?"

"This isn't a good time, Barton. I—"

He shoved the door wide and pushed past her, then closed the door behind him. "I haven't seen my girl in over two days. I'm not taking no for an answer." He turned his back to the room and studied her. "You must be feeling better. You don't look sick at all. In fact, you look pretty damn good."

He reached for her, but she sidestepped his hands and placed the envelope on the sofa. She had to make sure he kept his back to the room, and she had to keep him near the door, away from the rest of the room, away from her bed where Seth lay sleeping. She had to get rid of him. "I'm busy right now, Barton, and—"

"You don't seem happy to see me." He frowned.

"I'm in the middle of something. I have a deadline to meet today. So, if you don't mind." She reached for the doorknob. A hard grip on her upper arm stopped her. Her gaze flew to Barton's.

"You givin' me the brush-off, Megan?"

"Take your hand off me."

His grip tightened. "What's with you? I thought we had something special." He studied her a moment. "Something's different about you."

"Let go!" She yanked her arm, but he held on and dragged her closer to him.

"You're mighty feisty for someone who's been so sick the last couple days." His eyes narrowed. "Were you even sick?" He shook her. "Were you?"

"Let go, damn you!" She kicked him in the shin.

"Ow!" He looked at her in surprise. "You bitch! I oughta—"

"You heard the lady. Let her go."

Barton and Megan whirled around at the sound of Seth's voice. Seth stood beside the bed with its covers thrown back. One of his hands clutched the sheet wrapped around his waist. His other hand was a fist held at hip level. Surprise lit Barton's face, quickly replaced by anger.

"Who the hell are you?" Barton pinned his furious eyes on Megan. He pointed at Seth. "Who the hell is he?"

"None of your business."

"It is when he's naked in your bed," Barton said through clenched teeth.

"Who I have in my bed is my damn business," Megan shot back.

His face twisted with rage. "You lying little tease. Stringing me along all this time while you're fucking this asshole."

"I said, let her go." Seth's voice was soft, calm, deadly. "Before I do somethin' you'll regret, and I reckon I'll enjoy."

Barton swept his gaze over Seth's bruised face and bandaged body. He laughed scornfully. "You and what army? You look like a piss poor fighter if I ever saw one."

"Seth was shot, stabbed, and beaten," Megan snapped. "By four so-called men. I wonder how well you would fare in such a fight."

"Yet he was able enough to crawl into your bed." Barton's eyes were cold as ice.

"You're such an ass. I'm taking care of him." She struggled again but Barton squeezed her arm so hard a cry escaped her. She knew there would be bruises.

"I bet you are." He glowered at her.

She glowered right back.

The click of a gun being cocked swung their attention to Seth standing beside the bed with his gun trained on Barton. "I'm not tellin' you again, mister. Let her go or I'll put a bullet between your eyes."

Barton released her and backed away.

Seth smiled coldly. "That's good. Megan. Come here."

Megan had quickly moved near Seth before he'd finished speaking.

Seth motioned to the door with the gun. "Why don't you skedaddle?"

Barton stood his ground, his chest puffed out, his hands fisted at his side. "Aren't you the big man. Hiding behind a gun while wearing a sheet."

"Give me another day, and I'll wipe your face all over this floor with my bare hands. In the meantime, be on your way like a good little boy."

Barton took a step closer, his right fist raised slightly. "Who the hell are you to tell me to leave?"

"I'll tell you," Megan said. "Get out."

Barton stared at her. A muscle worked in his jaw. "I walk out of here and we're through. You hear me? *Through.*"

"Oh, we're through all right." She crossed her arms.

His eyes hard and piercing, Barton snarled, "I bet that nice lady downstairs wouldn't be too happy to hear there's a freeloader in one of her rooms."

Megan gasped. "You wouldn't dare."

A cruel smile distorted his lips. "I most certainly would, my lying little darlin'. And I reckon I'd enjoy it." He glanced at Seth when he repeated Seth's words.

She clenched her fists, wanting to hit him. "Get out of here, Barton." Her voice shook with rage. "Get out before I take that gun and shoot you myself."

A vein throbbed in one of Barton's temples as his gaze raked her.

"You heard her, mister. Unless you want me to give her my gun and let her have a go at cha."

"Fuck you, asshole." Barton jabbed his finger at Seth then turned his ice-cold gaze back to Megan. "And fuck you too." He spun around, yanked open the door and slammed it shut behind him so hard the walls shook, and picture frames bounced against the paneling.

Seth sat down heavily on the bed, his face white as the sheet he wore. Megan hurried to his side as he hung his head down, elbows braced on his knees, the gun held loosely in his hand.

"Are you all right? And would you put that thing down?"

His hand shook as he laid the gun on the nightstand.

"Where did you have it?"

"Under my pillow. Good thing, huh?" He slanted a glance at her. "Nice fella you got there. I can see why you're sweet on him."

"Very funny. He's history now. I'm done with him."

Seth slowly shook his head. "He's trouble, Megan. Mark my words. He's gonna cause you trouble." He looked at the door. "I sure liked his shirt. Wish I'd told him to leave it."

Megan couldn't remember what Barton's shirt looked like. Denim maybe. Short-sleeved. An image of shirtless Barton giving her a foot massage flashed through her mind.

She blurted, "He was here that night." At Seth's questioning look, she said, "The night you were injured, I brought him here for the first time."

Seth slowly sat up. "I thought I heard voices. I recognized yours, then figured I imagined it all when I heard another one. So, I ruined your big night together, huh?"

Megan detected a hint of amusement in his tone. "You definitely changed its course. For the better. You look awful. Lie down."

"Hand me my britches, would you? I'd rather have 'em on in case he comes back."

"God, I hope he doesn't." Megan handed him his trousers off the back of the chair. "Need any help?"

Seth gave his trousers a shake. "I'll manage."

She went to look out a window at the sunny afternoon and blue sky. She kept her back to Seth to give him some privacy but stayed nearby in case he fell over or passed out or something. The bed squeaked with his movements. Several cars and a bus passed by on the street below. An old man walked a little dog on the sidewalk. After a moment, she asked over her shoulder, "You decent?"

"Yeah."

She sat on the side of the bed. "Are you feeling any better?"

He shook his head. "Worse. But that little excitement just now had me feelin' better there for a moment." His gaze turned serious. "Megan, you need to—"

Someone knocked on the door.

"That didn't take long," Seth said.

"Miss Megan? Are you in there, dear?"

"It's Mrs. Powell," Megan whispered. She shot to her feet.

Seth rose more slowly.

Another knock followed by loud pounding. "Open up, Megan."

"Barton!" Megan whispered. "*Shit!*"

Seth picked up his gun off the nightstand.

Megan grabbed his arm. "You can't shoot him. You might hit Mrs. Powell."

"I'm not shootin' anyone," he whispered back. "I'm gonna skedaddle so you don't get in trouble. Where're my boots?"

"Behind the sofa."

More beating on the door. "Open the damn door, Megan!"

Seth quietly but quickly crossed to the sofa and shoved his feet into his boots. He grabbed his gun belt off the doorknob on his door.

Megan hurried to his side. She whispered, "Are you coming back?"

"Of course." He looked surprised that she had even asked.

"What if you can't? What if your door closes and that's it?"

"I'm comin' back. I want to find out what happens."

Harder, more rapid pounding on the door made Megan jump.

Seth put a steadying hand on her shoulder. "If he raises a hand to you or threatens you in any manner, holler. I'll come take care of him." He touched her cheek, then opened his door, and stepped through the brick wall. The door closed with a soft click.

Megan tiptoed to the bathroom and flushed the toilet. She took a couple of deep breaths to calm her hammering heart. Squaring her shoulders, she walked to the other door and opened it, smiling at Mrs. Powell, who had a frown on her usually cheerful face. "Sorry it took me so long. I was in the bathroom." Megan did not smile at Barton. "What are you doing here? I told you to get out."

"Cut the crap, Megan." Barton shouldered her aside and barged into the room, looking around. "Where is he?" He went into the bathroom.

"Where's who?" Megan looked at Mrs. Powell, who stepped to the middle of the room, her gaze darting here and there. "What's he talking about?" Megan heard Barton yank back the shower curtain.

"Mr. Crone claims you're caring for an injured man in here." Mrs. Powell folded her arms across the front of her blouse. "Are you?"

Megan raised her eyebrows in surprise. "Why on earth would he say a thing like that?"

Mrs. Powell stepped closer, her frown smoothing away. "So you're not?"

Megan swept out her arm. "Do you see anyone else in here? Well, besides him." She nodded to Barton coming out of the bathroom, his expression murderous.

"Where are you hiding him, Megan?"

"Who?"

"You know damn well who."

She looked at him innocently.

He turned away, muttering, "Bitch," and headed for the bed.

Megan leaned toward Mrs. Powell, saying softly, "I just broke up with him. He's not taking it very well."

"Apparently." Mrs. Powell watched with interest as Barton jerked back the bed covers. He got down on his hands and knees and looked underneath the bed from one end to the other.

Megan stifled a laugh at the sight of him on all fours in his jeans and denim shirt, which looked a little big for Seth.

Barton stood, sending her a malicious look. "Where is that son of a bitch?"

"Really, Mr. Crone. Such language." Mrs. Powell's mouth pinched with disapproval. "I believe it's obvious no one else is here. It's time we leave."

Barton stalked across the room, swinging his head left and right, searching. "He's here. I saw him." He looked behind the sofa, then spied the armoire and hurried to it. He yanked both doors wide open then reached in to shove aside the clothes. Metal hangers scraped across the metal rod.

"Young man," Mrs. Powell put her hands on her hips, "you have no business pawing through Miss Megan's possessions."

"I've nothing to hide," Megan said.

"Still." Mrs. Powell's eyebrows drew together.

He slammed the doors shut and ran a hand through his hair as his gaze searched the room. "He's hiding here somewhere. I *know* it." Barton looked at the windows. "Unless ..." He hurried to a window and looked outside and down, turning his head both ways, then stepped back and tried to open it.

"They haven't been opened in years, as far as I know," Mrs. Powell told him. She looked at Megan. "Have you opened any?"

Megan shook her head. "I tried to. I think they're all stuck."

"Probably painted shut. I'll have my husband look at them. Maybe this weekend or the next. Until then, if, God forbid, there's a fire or something, just go ahead and break one."

"I'll keep that in mind," Megan replied dryly.

Barton ignored them as he checked all the windows. He stopped at Seth's door.

Mrs. Powell muttered, "Want to bet he tries to open it?"

Megan shrugged. "I did."

"Everyone does. I've tried hundreds of times."

Barton grabbed the glass doorknob.

Megan imagined him opening the door and finding Seth on the other side. She wondered who would be more surprised—Barton, Seth, Mrs. Powell, or herself.

The doorknob didn't budge despite Barton twisting it and yanking on it. He stepped back and looked the door up and down. "What's this door doing here?" he snapped.

"There used to be a stairway there to the street below back when this was a brothel," Mrs. Powell replied.

"A brothel." He turned and sneered at Megan, "No wonder you feel so at home here, you lyin' Yankee whore."

Megan almost laughed. He thought his words could hurt her.

Mrs. Powell gasped. "That's enough talk like that!"

"Sorry, ma'am," he muttered, not looking or sounding at all sorry. He sent Megan another murderous glare then looked beyond her. His eyes suddenly lit up, and he practically ran across the room.

Megan's gaze got there before he did. She quickly scanned the area around the vanity, wondering what had caught his attention.

Between the vanity and the dresser on the adjacent wall was a gap in the corner. Something was wedged in that gap.

Barton made a beeline for that corner. He bent down, then turned around, grinning triumphantly as he held high a black cowboy hat.

Megan caught her breath. She'd forgotten all about Seth's hat. She had put it on the vanity Sunday night and it must have somehow fallen off or been knocked off into the corner.

Barton came toward her, holding the hat. "I told you he's here. This isn't yours." He plopped it on her head. It slid down over her eyes. She pushed it up with one finger.

"Of course it's not mine." Then she told her first lie since Barton's return. "It belonged to one of the regulars at work. He gave it to me a week or so ago."

"It wasn't here the other night when I was here."

"You were too busy giving me a foot massage to notice anything else."

He clenched his teeth. "God, you are such a lying little—" Making a noise between a snarl and a moan, he spun away from her, both hands to his hair as if he wanted to tear it out. He stopped a few feet away, planted his hands on his hips, and stood there a moment, his shoulders rapidly rising and falling.

Megan pushed the hat further back, tipped her head toward Mrs. Powell and whispered, "He gives a great foot massage. I think that's the only thing I'll miss about him."

Mrs. Powell whispered back, "There's nothing like a good massage. Foot or otherwise." She winked at Megan, who had to wipe her grin off when Barton spun back around, his expression furious. He stomped across the floor, snatched the hat off her head, and shook it in her face.

"You know damn well this hat belongs to that man you're hiding in here somewhere. What's his name? Seth?"

"I don't know what you're talking about. Yes, I have a friend named Seth. But he's not here." She waved her hand around. "As you can see for yourself."

Barton threw the hat on the floor. He pinned her with his hard gaze. "Are you enjoying making me look like a fool? I don't know what kind of game you're playing but you and I both know this is bullshit. Pure fucking bullshit."

Mrs. Powell had started toward the door. "I'm fixin' to call my husband up here. He'll throw you out on your ear, Mr. Crone."

"Ma'am." Barton held out a hand to her, making her pause. "I swear on a stack of Bibles that when I came in this room just minutes ago, there was a naked man in that bed." He pointed to the bed.

"Naked!" Eyebrows raised and a slight smile playing around her mouth, Mrs. Powell looked at Megan.

"There's no one else in this room," Megan assured Mrs. Powell.

"I can see that, dear."

"He was here, ma'am" Barton insisted, his voice tight with anger and frustration. "His trousers were draped over that chair." Barton pointed to the chair. "He's around my age maybe. Sandy hair. Bruises on his face, a fading black eye. He had bandages across his chest and around his waist. She," he glared at Megan, "said he'd been beaten, shot, and stabbed and she was taking care of him. He pointed a gun at me."

"A gun!" Mrs. Powell's shocked gaze darted to Megan.

"A gun!" Megan echoed. She hoped she looked as shocked as Mrs. Powell.

A vein stood out in Barton's neck. He looked ready to strangle Megan and maybe Mrs. Powell too. He stepped closer to Megan, towering over her. "I bet you never reported to the authorities that *your friend* was shot and stabbed like you're supposed to. My buddies on the police force might be interested in that little tidbit."

"Go ahead and call them." She lifted her chin. "There's a few things I might want to tell them about *you,* and your friend Jim, and his son."

His gaze narrowed. His nostrils flared. One side of his upper lip curled. His right hand rose ever so slightly before lowering again.

A shiver skittered up Megan's spine. He would have hit her if not for Mrs. Powell, who stood tense and still, watching them, her face creased with worry.

"You don't know anything," he growled.

"You don't know when you're not welcome anymore," she growled back.

Mrs. Powell stepped between them. "Let's go, Mr. Crone. There's no one here despite what you claim you saw. We've bothered Miss Megan long enough." She nodded toward to the door. "Will you come with me please?"

Barton pointed his finger at Megan. "This isn't over. Not by a long shot."

She crossed her arms. "Goodbye, Barton."

Mrs. Powell said more forcefully, "I'll see you out, Mr. Crone. Or should I call my husband? The police?"

Barton turned to Mrs. Powell. "I just want you to know I'm not lying and I'm not crazy. There is, or was, a man in here and Megan is lying about it. You'll have to ask her why. I'm sorry for bothering you, ma'am. I'm sorry for using such language in front of you. I'll see myself out." He inclined his head. He shot Megan one more glare then headed to the door. On the way, he stomped on Seth's hat, flattening the crown. He kicked it across the floor to Megan. "Tell him that's from me."

Mrs. Powell watched Barton leave then said to Megan, "My word, he has a temper. He was mad as a hornet's nest when he stormed into my office claiming there was a man staying with you. He also said you'd been sick. But you look fine and you've been eating like a horse lately. I didn't know what to think. He sounded very convincing."

"A few days ago, I *did* tell him I was sick. I just didn't tell him I was sick of *him*. Until today."

"Bruised that male pride, did you?" Mrs. Powell chuckled. "So, he came up with that cockamamie story about you caring for some injured man. Then he acts like a fool." She tsked. "Pity. He seemed like such a nice young man. Too handsome for his own good. Did he give you your letter?"

"I forgot all about it." Megan picked up the letter off the sofa. She recognized the return address and tore the envelope open.

"Now that all the excitement's over, I'll leave you be, Miss Megan."

"Wait a minute, Mrs. Powell."

Megan unfolded a sheet of paper. Inside it was a check. She quickly read the letter. A smile spread across her face. She stuck the check in the pocket of her shorts and handed Mrs. Powell the letter, saying, "I wrote an article about Miss Fleeda's B&B and sent it to a friend who works at a travel magazine called—"

"*Travel Holiday*," Mrs. Powell gasped as she read the letter. "I read that religiously." She raised her startled gaze to Megan. "You mean to tell me *my* bed and breakfast is going to be in *Travel Holiday*?"

Megan nodded, smiling. "Maybe the November issue. December for sure."

"The holidays. Saints and angels." Mrs. Powell looked even more stunned, as impossible as that seemed. "I'm going to be in *Travel Holiday* for the holidays. I can't believe it."

"It's not the cover article. Or even very long. I wish I'd submitted it sooner, so it could have come out earlier in the fall but—"

"This is a dream come true. My place has never been written about." Mrs. Powell gave Megan a quick hug. "I don't know what to say ... how to thank you."

"You've been very good to me. It's my way of thanking you."

Mrs. Powell smiled fondly. She handed back the letter. "I can't wait to tell my husband. He won't believe it." A look of horror suddenly spread across her face. "Goodness gracious. The holidays. I might be busier than ever. I'll need to hire another girl. Make more food. Something special. For the holidays. Heavens, I have a lot to do the next few months." She headed for the door, then paused on the threshold. "Don't you worry about Mr. Crone darkening your door anymore. He will not be allowed inside again."

"Thank you. I'm sorry you had to see all of that." As Megan closed the door, she heard Mrs. Powell muttering, "*Travel Holiday*. Goodness gracious."

Megan smiled as she hurried to Seth's door and knocked on it. "Seth? Open up." She knocked again, tried the doorknob. Nothing. She pressed her ear against the wood. Not a sound. She knocked again, harder, then stepped back. "Come on, Seth," she muttered, fearing he couldn't come back.

The door cracked open. "M-M-Megan?"

"Seth!"

The door opened wider and he stumbled in, shirtless and shivering. He shut the door and slumped back against it, rubbing his hands up and down his arms. "L-Lordy, it's c-c-cold." He could barely speak through his chattering teeth.

Megan grabbed a blanket off the bed and wrapped it around him. He clutched it closed at his throat as he shook uncontrollably. She rubbed her hands briskly on his arms. "You're freezing. Get in bed."

He pushed away from the door then sagged back against it, his head hanging down. "Damn. I hate f-feelin' this weak." He asked with resignation in his voice, "C-can you help me again? I d-don't think ... I can m-make it on my own."

She helped him to the bed and covered him up, then sat on the edge of it. His face had a tinge of gray to it and he continued to shiver. "You look worse than before. I was hoping you'd feel better ... over there."

"I d-did."

"Yet you still came back?" she asked in surprise.

He shrugged. "Said I would. Although I wasn't sure if the d-door would open again right away. I have no c-control over it, you know. Sometimes it opens. Sometimes it won't. T-tell me what happened. I c-couldn't hear anything through the door until I heard a loud kn-knock."

Megan related the whole scene with Barton and Mrs. Powell. Seth gradually stopped shivering as he listened. She handed him his crushed hat, relaying Barton's message that this was from him. Seth popped out the crown with his fist then brushed off the brim.

"I thought of it the moment I left but it was too late to come back and get it." He put the hat on the nightstand then gave Megan a worried look. "Do you think he'll send the law?"

Megan snorted. "I doubt he's that big a fool. He knows I have a thing or two to tell them about him."

"What do you mean by that?"

She was silent a moment, then told Seth all about Barton. The trailer in the country, the drug house in town, the briefcase with the smiley face on it, the way he flashed money around.

Seth shook his head. "You need to stay away from him."

"Oh, I intend to."

"Megan." Seth reached his hand over and covered hers resting on her thigh. "He's trouble. You need to get far away from him. You need to go home."

She caught her breath. "But Seth—"

"I gotta leave too. Soon."

Her heart lurched. "But you're still healing. You're still—"

"'Member me tellin' you how I start feelin' when it's time I leave here?"

She thought back. "Like you're ... coming apart?" Her eyes widened with understanding. "Is that what's wrong with you?"

"I reckon it's gotta be. I've never been here this long. I didn't start feelin' poorly until today. Worn out and weak and outta sorts. The minute I went through that door I felt better. 'Cept it was so damn cold. I went almost all the way to the bottom of those stairs and felt a whole lot better. Warmer, too. I almost," he pressed his lips together, "I almost got off the stairs and went back to my time because I felt so much better. Like my old self. But I wanted to find out what happened here. And I'm ... I'm not ready to leave yet. But I'll have to soon 'cause I'm feelin' mighty bad. I don't think I have the strength right now to crawl to that door much less walk to it. Much as I hate to," his hand squeezed hers as his serious eyes gazed into hers, "I gotta leave." He paused, then said the word she dreaded hearing the most, "Today."

Megan blinked back threatening tears. She bit her lower lip to still its trembling.

"I don't want to, Megan. But I'm afraid if I don't go I'll really, well ... I'll really come apart." He scrunched up his face. "I don't even know what that means but I don't wanna find out."

She stood. "Get up."

"I just told you. I can't. Not right now."

She tossed back the covers and grabbed his arm.

"What are you doin'?"

"I'm going to drag you across the floor. Don't look so surprised. It won't be the first time. Hopefully, you can reach the doorknob to open the door. I'll push you through the brick wall down the stairs to your time. And you won't come apart anymore."

His features softened. "Come here."

"But—"

He tugged her hand. "It's not that dire yet. I just need a little time to get my strength back. Lay down beside me while I rest my eyes."

Reluctantly, worried about his state of being, literally, she crawled into bed beside him and put her arms around him. He nestled his head on her shoulder.

She asked, "Does anyone else know you were injured that night?"

"Nope. Just the four men who jumped me. It was late. I don't think anyone else saw me. Why?"

"I was wondering how you were going to explain being so badly hurt one minute then showing up the next minute almost healed."

"Probably a sight more than a minute has passed since I left."

She drew away and looked at him. "You once said that when you returned to your time mere minutes had passed."

"Used to be." He yawned. "But things have been different the last couple times. Once, I was here several hours and almost an hour had passed when I got back. The last time I was here, I was gone a few hours in my time. No tellin' how long I'll have been gone this time. Could be a day or so has passed." He yawned again. "Anyone says anythin' I'll just tell 'em I was holed up somewhere, healin'. No lie there."

He fell asleep within minutes. She lay with her cheek on his hair, warmed by his body pressed against hers, wondering about portals, and what it felt like to time travel, and life at the turn of the century. *Will I eventually feel like I'm coming apart? What does that mean?*

Dust motes danced in the evening sunlight slanting through the windows when he woke up. He got right out of bed.

Megan sat up, amazed at the change in him. "You seem a lot better." She couldn't hide the hope that leapt within her.

"I always feel better when I first wake up." He frowned, running a hand through his hair. "It might not last long. I need to get a move on while I still can. I have one more favor to ask of you."

"Anything."

"Can I take one last shower?"

Megan smiled despite her breaking heart. "Of course." She gestured with her hand. "Go ahead."

He looked at her a moment, his eyes full of regret. He bent down and kissed her then went to the bathroom and closed the door.

While the shower ran, Megan threw the bed together. She gathered some scattered papers on the table into a stack then straightened her makeup on top of the vanity, finding anything to do to keep busy and control her tears until he was gone.

Gone.

She closed her eyes. *I'm going to miss him. When will I see him again? Will I ever see him again?*

She opened her eyes and looked at herself in the mirror. *Who am I kidding? I know where I want to be.*

She yanked off her clothes then paused, remembering wet t-shirt contests in college, and how the guys hollered, yelled, and applauded. She put on a t-shirt. Her hand on the bathroom doorknob, she paused. The sound of the shower continued. Her heart raced erratically.

She opened the door.

Chapter 22

Steam filled the bathroom and fogged the mirror. The shower curtain showed Seth's silhouette with both hands raised to his head thrown back. The shower ran full blast.

Megan reached up to pull back the curtain.

It jerked out of her hand and Seth's face popped out from behind it. Water darkened his sandy hair plastered it to his head.

"Somethin' wrong?"

"I thought I'd check on your wounds before you leave." She pulled the curtain further back with no resistance from Seth. He made no move to cover himself as water showered down upon his naked body. She caught her breath. He was beautiful, and obviously happy to see her.

She swallowed hard before saying, "Turn to the left so I can see that wound." Without a word, he did as she asked. The tub's clawed feet added maybe six inches to Seth's height, putting the stab wound above his waist almost level with her chest. Her gentle touch on his injury made his stomach muscles, and other muscles, tighten. He was healing nicely. She placed a light kiss on his wet skin, then smiled up at him, blinking from the water spraying her face and the front of her shirt.

His gaze dropped to her chest. "Your shirt's gettin' all wet."

She pulled the hem down on both sides, stretching the wet material over her breasts as she looked down at herself. "Hmmm. So, it is." Aware of his intense gaze and loving it, she pulled the hem down a little tighter to give him a more graphic hint of what lay beneath. Her breasts rose and fell with her quickened breathing as anticipation thrummed every nerve. "Awful wet."

"Sure is. Might ruin it."

"Can't have that." She pulled off the t-shirt and tossed it on the floor. Sudden shyness heated her face as his gaze traveled the length of her body.

"How brazen of you, Miss Megan."

He said it teasingly but the look in his eyes said she was beautiful. She stood a little straighter and prouder. His perusal sent a flush over her so hot she was surprised the water hitting her skin didn't sizzle.

"You're back to calling me Miss Megan?"

"I could call you darlin'."

"Please don't ever *ever* call me darlin'."

Chuckling, he held out his hand. "Come here, Miss Megan."

No endearment could ever sound sweeter than the way he said *Miss Megan*. She put her hand in his and he helped her into the tub. She yanked the curtain closed. He pulled her into his arms beneath the spray of hot water. She was instantly soaked as she wrapped her arms around him, flattening her hands on his back. Their lips met, their bodies pressed together with only water between them.

There was no foot massage or teasing torture or droning talk of what was going to happen.

There was urgency and impatience. Tongue-filled kisses and roving hands gliding over slick, wet skin. She strained against him, wanting more, wanting all. Water ran in her eyes, streamed down her face, turned his muscled flesh to silk beneath her eager fingers. He kissed her cheek, the side of her neck, then blazed a trail downward. Her knees turned to jelly. She leaned back and met no resistance from the flimsy shower curtain. She lost her balance and slipped on the slick enamel, making her yelp.

Seth grabbed her before she fell. He almost slipped himself before clasping her to him. "You all right?" He smoothed hair off her forehead.

She nodded. "We should get out of here before we crack our heads open."

He turned off the water and stepped out of the tub. He helped her out then took a towel from the rack and started drying her off. Her hair hung in long wet ropes dripping water on the floor. She grabbed the other towel and did the same to him until the towels fell at their feet as they kissed.

He picked her up in his arms and carried her to the bed.

"Wait." She pushed lightly on his chest where her hand rested, and he paused. "Not the bed. My hair's wet."

His eyes shot wide and he gave a short laugh. "Are you joshin' me?"

"I have long, thick hair, and it's soaking wet. It'll get everything wet. I have to sleep in that bed." She toyed with one of his nipples, hard as a pebble. "So do you."

"All right, all right." His gaze darted to the rawhide sofa, the hardwood floor, then the table. He headed towards it and sat her on one end of it. With a sweep of his arm he sent the papers she had neatly stacked just minutes ago flying. She didn't care. Until his arm took aim at the beautiful antique table lamp.

She flung out her hand. "Not the lamp!"

He grabbed it and set it on the floor near some scattered papers then stood before her. He put his hands on her knees and spread her legs then leaned in to give her a long kiss. He drew away, raised his hands to her breasts, and cupped one in each hand. His thumbs teased her nipples. A gasp escaped her. He smiled. She smiled. He dipped his head to suck one hard peak, then the other. She moaned his name. He eased her back on the table where they had talked and eaten and drank beer, where she had dug a bullet out of his arm the night they met. His gaze traveled the length of her, his eyes devouring her, thrilling her.

"You're more beautiful than I ever imagined."

His husky words and the look in his eyes stimulated her more than his touch did. Anticipation made her body weep.

He slid his hands up her thighs then bent down to kiss her stomach. His hands and mouth traveled up to her breasts and stayed there.

She dug her fingernails in his back.

When she couldn't stand it anymore, she drew his face to hers for a kiss, her arms tight around him. His warm, lean body covered hers, and he slid inside her as if he belonged there. Had always belonged there.

Seth rose up slightly until their eyes met.

He started to move.

They watched each other in the evening light filling the room with a warm glow. She wrapped her legs around him and met his every thrust. Their gasps and grunts, and the scrape of the table legs on the floor filled the silence. His shadowed face filled her vision.

Until she squeezed her eyes shut and held on as he thrust harder and faster and rocked her world.

So this is how it feels with someone I love.

***

Hours later, Megan opened her eyes to darkness and stretched languidly in bed. She reached beside her. No Seth. She sat up and looked around the dark room. Relief flooded through her when she saw his shadowy figure sitting in a chair in front of one of the windows, looking out. She threw back the covers and climbed down from the bed. Her bare feet padded on the floor as she went to him.

She kissed the top of his head then wrapped her arms around his neck, her breasts pressing against his warm back.

"Can't sleep?" she asked softly near his ear.

"Just thinkin'."

"Did you get any sleep?"

"Dozed a bit. Mostly I watched you sleep." He kissed the back of her hand.

She rested her cheek against his clean-smelling hair. "How are you feeling?"

"I'm doin' all right. Don't you worry."

She didn't believe him. It had been hours since he last slept, and he'd had quite a workout since then.

After they had gotten off the table, they returned to the bathtub, which led to another bout of lovemaking. Luckily, no one cracked their head open. When her hair finally dried, they had gone to bed and made love again, slower, more thoroughly. They had used every inch of that big bed while enjoying every inch of each other. She'd fallen asleep in his arms, exhausted. He had to be near his limit of not coming apart.

"Seth, you should really get some—"

"Could there be a babe?" He looked over his shoulder at her.

She blinked in surprise. None of the other men she had been with had given a damn about consequences. His concern touched her deeply. "There *could* be but there's a ninety-something percent chance there won't."

"You take that pill I read about."

"Disappointed?" she ventured, curious.

"Relieved. I've been ponderin' how we'd raise a babe with you here and me there. Truth be told, I don't know if I'd want my child raised in your time. I don't think I could live here either. Even if I could leave this room, I don't want to live here."

"It's not all bad. You have an extremely limited view of it. Listening to me and looking out the windows and reading some newspapers don't give you the big picture. It's still a beautiful world. Just different."

He was shaking his head. "I still don't think I could live here. Sure, I'd like to go out into your world. I'd like to see what's become of my ranch. Go up in an airplane. Go to one of those movin' pictures you talk about. But I don't belong here." He paused. "It's hard knowin' what I know about everythin' that's ahead. Makes me wonder if I should bring any child into a world where so many terrible things are gonna happen."

"Terrible things happen all the time."

"But I *know* these things are comin'. Like that hurricane that's gonna destroy Galveston. How can I let all those people perish? I could warn them and save so many! Or that big ship that sinks in the Atlantic in 20 years or so. How can I not warn the captain about that iceberg? And the wars ... so many wars. If just one could be stopped ... There are times I wish with all my heart that I didn't know any of it. Drives me crazy, Megan. Keepin' it all to myself."

"You have to. You can't tell anyone."

"I know, I know." He rested his chin on her forearm looped around his neck. "It's an awful burden. I know so much." He heaved a heavy sigh. "And can't do a damn thing about any of it." After a moment, he said, "Promise me you goin' back to Illinois."

His subject change caught her off guard. "I can't. I—"

"Megan." He reached around and pulled her onto his lap. "You gotta leave. It pains me to say it but you gotta. That Barton fella is gonna cause trouble for you one way or the other." When she scoffed, Seth added, "I know his kind."

"Like his great-grandfather John Bingo?"

"I saw a resemblance. Something in his eyes. A meanness that goes to the bone. I can't protect you 'cause I'm not here, and if Barton hurts you because of me," his arms tightened around her, "why, it'd just-it'd just about kill me. Promise me you'll leave."

"I'm not promising you that. I already promised Donna, and I'm probably going to break that promise. I'm not going to break another one to you too. I take promises seriously."

"What's Donna got to do with this?"

Megan hesitated, then decided to tell him everything. "She talked me into giving a speech at a meeting. It's in Chicago. I won't be paid for it, but it's for a cause I believe in, and I'll make new connections, which could mean future work. So, I promised Donna I'd go. I told my boss at work I'm quitting. I told Mrs. Powell, the owner here, I'm leaving. I planned on flying home July ninth. Two weeks from tomorrow. Then the other day, Mrs. Powell told me an interesting story about this place." Megan related how Mrs. Powell had acquired the B&B.

Seth's eyes grew wider and wider as the story progressed, his growing shock evident in his questions. "Corrie invested money for a woman she never even knew? ... Mrs. Powell had to promise to save my door? ... The woman who started it all was named *what?*"

"Megan McClure," Megan repeated.

He asked incredulously, "Do you think she's *you?*"

"I don't know. Could be. Is that any more unbelievable than you coming here through that door?"

"Holy moly," he muttered, making her chuckle. "First that purple dress. I know Lottie made it, just not yet. Now this." He shook his head. "How would you go through? The pool in that water garden?"

"I guess so. Unless I happen to find another portal around here."

Seth sat back in the chair, the serious set of his face visible in the dimness. "You're pretty darn acceptin' of all this while I'm plumb flabbergasted."

She trailed the tip of her finger along his collarbone. "I was plumb flabbergasted too believe me, but now that I've had time to think about it, it doesn't seem that weird. There's something going on here that's bigger than the both of us, Seth. There's something special about you. And I'm curious as hell as to what it's all about. Aren't you? I can't leave now."

He ran a hand through his hair. "Something bigger than the both of us? What the devil does that mean?" He shifted his legs, jostling her. "All these years you've been sayin' I'm special and makin' me up to be some sort of hero or-or savior," anger tinged his voice, "and I'm tellin' you I'm neither one. Don't want to be either."

"You once said you wanted to end war. Change the world."

He snorted. "Yet you keep harpin' I can't change anything."

"I'm not harping." Megan sat up straight. "I'm just stating a fact."

"Well, none of it makes any damn sense!" He threw up his arm.

"Shh! Not so loud." She took a couple deep breaths. "What are we fighting about?"

"Hell, I don't know." He ran his hand up and down her back. "Guess I started gettin' mad when I realized you're not leavin'. What about Barton?"

"I won't have anything to do with him."

Seth shook his head. "He's trouble, Megan. I'm tellin' you."

"I'll go to work and come home. He won't bother me at either one. I have two weeks to figure things out." She could tell from his sour expression visible in the faint light from the streetlights outside that he didn't like her answer. "I won't have to worry about him when I'm back in your time." She tilted her head. "How do you think I'll fare back there?"

"Better than I would here." He played with a lock of her hair curled on her arm. "Would you be stayin'?"

"I guess it depends on what happens. What this is all about." She looked him in the eye. "And if I had a damn good reason to stay." She held her breath, waiting for his answer.

"Maybe you'll only be able to stay so long before you start feelin' like you're coming apart. Like me. Then what?"

Not the answer she had wanted. *Men!* "I guess I'll just have to play it by ear. Speaking of which, how are you feeling?"

"Awful. But it's different than before."

"How so?"

"It's not so much I feel physically weak but," he paused, pressed his lips together, "I'm feelin' weak inside. Not a bellyache or-or sick ... it's hard to explain. I feel all jittery and, I don't know, disconnected." He shrugged. "I don't know how else to explain it. Guess that's makin' me kinda ornery." He stroked her hair. "I gotta go soon."

She put her hand on the side of his face. "Come back to bed."

"I don't wanna go to sleep. I'm afraid I'll come apart and not wake up."

"Who said anything about sleeping?"

A ghost of a smile touched his mouth. "Damn, you're temptin', but I don't know if I'll be much good feelin' like I do."

"I'll do all the work." She slid off his lap and held out her hand. She could feel his eyes on her breasts. He put his hands on his knees and pushed himself to his feet, releasing a long-suffering sigh that sounded a bit exaggerated.

"I'm too weak to fight you off. I reckon I'll just have to let you have your way with me."

Megan smiled. A certain part of his anatomy belied his weakness.

He put his hand in hers.

Back in bed, they lay on their sides, kissing, touching, stroking.

Seth pulled away. "There's somethin' I have to confess. I lied to you."

"Oh?" She rose up on her elbow and propped her cheek on her palm.

"Remember a couple nights back when I was tellin' you 'bout the men who jumped me? And you said, *They left you for dead and you managed to make it up the stairs? To get help from Lottie?* You sounded surprised that I was goin' to Lottie for help."

"You needed serious medical attention. Lottie didn't seem a logical choice."

"I said I didn't remember any of it. I lied. I remember every bit of it. I knew I was dyin'. I wasn't lookin' for help. I was lookin' for a place to die. I dragged my bleedin' body up those stairs hopin' against hope that when I opened that door I'd be in your time and I'd see your beautiful face one more time before I died."

Her heart almost burst with emotion. If that wasn't a declaration of love, she didn't know what was. She opened her mouth, then bit back her own *I love you*. Instead of telling him, she would show him. She leaned over him and did just that.

When Megan woke, daylight filled the room. She patted the empty space beside her then sat up. Seth was gone. She wasn't surprised. Still ... Her gaze fell on a piece of paper on the nightstand. She snatched it up and read his scribbled words.

I told you we would make love often. I'll be watchin every waterin trough waitin for you. Hurry back to me.

Chapter 23

Hurry back to me.

Seth's words played over and over like a song stuck in her head while she got ready to face the day. The words accompanied her footsteps down the stairs. *Hurry. Back. To. Me. Hurry. Back. To. Me.*

Mrs. Powell stood outside her office, talking to a man holding a clipboard. She broke off their conversation to say, "Miss Megan, good morning. My, don't you look radiant." Mrs. Powell gestured to the man, who wore a gray shirt and trousers uniform. "This is Mr. Haywood, our plumber." Mrs. Powell said to him, "Miss McClure wrote the article I told you about."

He nodded to Megan. "Ma'am."

Megan nodded back. "More plumbing problems?"

Mrs. Powell clapped her hands like a little girl who had finally gotten a pony. "I'm having the whole system replaced so it will be in tiptop shape for the holidays." Her eyes sparkled. "Mr. Haywood is going to begin soon after you leave. You *are* still leaving on the ninth, right?"

Megan nodded. One way or the other, either to Chicago or to the nineteenth century, she was leaving. *Hurry back to me.*

"Not that I'm anxious for you to leave, Miss Megan," Mrs. Powell added. "I'm just glad to finally get this fixed."

"It's funny, you always talk about plumbing problems, yet I haven't had any trouble."

"That's because you're special." Mrs. Powell winked. She said to the plumber, "How long did you say this would take?"

Megan shook her head at Mrs. Powell's ridiculous words, *You're special,* and left on her errands. She cashed the check for the B&B article then took a bus to a used bookstore. She paused just inside and inhaled the comforting smell of musty paper and old books.

A man with a long, graying ponytail behind the counter laughed. "You'd be surprised how many folks do that. Anything I can help you find, ma'am?"

"World history books?"

"Near the back on the left just after American history."

After searching the shelves, she bought a book on world history from 1850 to 1950, replacing the book Seth took. She had a lot of reading to do.

The last stop was the Water Gardens. The place bustled with activity. Men and women in business attire, harried-looking women pushing strollers and yelling at toddlers, and teenagers smoking cigarettes crowded the walkways. More people sat on the concrete ledges, eating, talking, or reading. Screaming little kids played in the water to escape the heat of the summer afternoon. She joined the line of people walking down the big blocks to the bottom where she stared at the swirling water as spray misted her face.

She heard nothing, saw nothing.

She concentrated with all her might.

Nothing.

This has to be the portal, she thought as someone jostled her. *The voices. The visions. Now what? Do I come here day after day hoping I'll hit the right moment to go through? Like Seth does with his door? What the hell?*

***

Just before five o'clock, Megan approached the front entrance to The Tejas for her first shift since Sunday night, after which she had taken

Barton back to the B&B. It seemed a lifetime ago. So much had changed in a couple of days. *She* had changed. *Hurry back to me.*

Near the entrance, the manager stood talking to two police officers. One was Bubba, Bonnie's cousin. Joe waved Megan over. "You look like you should be on an island holding a drink with one of those little umbrellas in it."

Megan laughed. Her blouse had bright tropical flowers all over it.

"I'm glad you're not," Joe added, "because I'm glad you're back."

"It's good to be back." She smiled at the officers. "Hi, Bubba."

Bubba Newman was around her age. He had auburn hair and freckles. His six-foot build filled out his blue uniform just right. He wasn't handsome but had an affable face and manner that made him a favorite on his beat, and among the waitresses at work. They were all excited when he recently broke up with his girlfriend. His usual friendly demeanor seemed restrained when he replied, "Evening, Megan. This is Officer Clark. Officer Clark, Megan McClure."

She smiled at the dark-haired officer, whom she'd never seen before. He was slender, and a couple inches shorter than Bubba. He wore those mirrored sunglasses Megan found so annoying. He nodded to her.

"What's up, guys? You out here solving the problems of the world?"

Bubba said, "We'd like you to come down to the station with us, Megan."

She blinked. "W-what? Why?" She glanced at both officers then Joe.

Joe stepped closer to her. "Don't worry, it's just some routine questions, right?" He looked at Bubba.

"That's correct."

Joe said to Megan, "I wanted to meet you outside to save you from any ... unwanted attention inside. No one in there needs to know anything." He patted her shoulder. "You'll be back in no time. Right, fellas?"

"Of course," Bubba replied.

"We'll see about that," Officer Clark muttered.

Megan shot the officer a worried look, not liking the sound of that.

Minutes later, she sat in the back seat of a squad car for the first time in her life, completely baffled as to why she was there. The two officers in the front said little to each other. Every so often, the radio squawked. The car stopped at a red light.

Megan stared out the window. People in the car in the adjacent lane stared at her as if she was a wanted criminal. She slid down on the seat and tried to figure out what this was all about but came up blank.

Unless ... Barton.

He must have told his police buddies that she had never reported the gunshot wound of a man she had been harboring in her room. *Is that really a law?* She leaned forward to ask Bubba, then sat back, figuring the less she said the better. *How am I going to explain Seth to the police? What if they want to question him? But there's no proof he was here. Just Barton's word against mine. I'm a nobody. He probably has connections.* She gulped. *How am I going to get out of this? Damn you, Barton!*

After what seemed like an endless ride, the officers, one in front of her and one behind her, escorted Megan into the police station. They walked through the noisy, crowded hallway into a familiar office. Bubba gave her a reassuring smile as he closed the door behind them, muffling the noise in the hallway.

Detective Sullivan rose from behind his desk strewn with papers. "Good evening, Miss McClure. Thank you for coming. Please sit down." He gestured to a folding metal chair facing the desk.

He sat after she did, then shuffled through the mess of papers on his desk. He had his shirtsleeves rolled up, and there was a small red stain like spaghetti sauce on the front of his white shirt. A five o'clock shadow darkened the lower half of his face. Bubba and Officer Clark stood on either side behind her.

Megan gripped her purse on her lap to still her shaking hands. "Why am I here, Detective?"

"I want to ask you a few questions." He rifled through papers and manila envelopes.

"Do I need a lawyer?"

The detective met her gaze. "Do you think you need one?"

"I have no idea why I'm here. I haven't done anything wrong. You tell me."

"I just have some—"

"Questions. So you've said." She recalled cop shows she'd seen on TV. "Are you going to read me my rights?"

"There's no need for that. We're not arresting you." He picked up a manila envelope.

"Do I have to answer your questions?"

"No. Consider it a public service."

Since he put it that way ... "What do you want to know?"

Detective Sullivan held one end of the manila envelope and pulled out an 8x10 picture. He put it face up on the desk in front of Megan. "Do you recognize this man?"

She'd know that handsome face anywhere. "That's Barton Crone. Why? What has he said about me? He has no idea what—" she broke off, recalling her dad's advice concerning the police—*Never volunteer anything.* A flash of curiosity crossed the detective's face. "What about him, Detective?"

"How do you know Mr. Crone?"

"I waited on him one night in The Tejas."

"Was that the first time you met him?"

"Yes."

"You've been dating him about two months?"

She sat up a little straighter. "How do you know that?"

"Please answer the question, Miss McClure."

"About that, I guess. Why?"

"Are you two romantically involved?"

A blush heated her face. "No. It's nothing serious." She shifted on the hard chair. The air conditioner hummed as it cooled the room, but her armpits felt damp. *Didn't I put on deodorant?* "What's this all about?"

Detective Sullivan pulled out another picture and placed it on top of Barton's. "Would you please tell me what you're doing here?"

She stared in shock at a picture of herself in her lavender dress sitting on a bench, handing Jim the briefcase with the smiley face. "Why do you have a picture of me? Why is—?"

"Please answer the question."

She glared at the detective, who returned a placid, steady gaze. "I'm- I'm giving Barton's friend the briefcase he forgot."

"Where was Mr. Crone at the time?"

"Parking his car."

"Who is the man taking the briefcase?"

"Jim. I don't know his last name."

"This man?" Detective Sullivan showed her a close-up of Jim.

"Yes."

"What are you doing here?" Detective Sullivan put another picture in front of her. In it, she wore the yellow sundress and was handing Jim the briefcase through his car window.

"That was in the parking lot just before Barton and I went to a movie. I assume you know which movie."

The detective ignored her remark. "And in this one?" One by one, the detective dealt out pictures of her giving Jim his briefcase. After she had explained the last one, he asked, "At any time, did Mr. Crone force you to deliver the briefcase?"

"No."

"Did he pay you to do so?"

"No."

"Did you know what the briefcase contained any of those times you delivered it?"

"No."

"What do you think was in it?"

She shrugged. "Paperwork. Legal stuff. That's what I saw in it one day, the day of the movie, I think. It was full of papers. Why? What's this all about? Why is someone following me around taking pictures?" The very idea made her skin crawl.

Detective Sullivan sat back in his chair and laced his fingers below the spaghetti stain. "We have reason to believe that Mr. Barton Crone is involved in the production and distribution of methamphetamine. The briefcase in those pictures is probably full of meth."

She hit her fist on her thigh. "I *knew* it."

Officer Clark stepped closer on her left side. "So, you *did* know."

Her head jerked around to him. "Well, I didn't *know* it," she quickly clarified, not liking the accusation in his tone, nor the fact that he still had those sunglasses on. "But I had my suspicions."

"You're going to claim ignorance?"

Megan frowned at the man as a sick feeling uncurled in the pit of her stomach. *Ignorance of the law was no excuse* ran through her head. The clammy material of her sleeveless blouse stuck to her sweaty armpits. She took a deep breath to calm her pounding heart, which pounded even harder after the detective's next words.

"Officer Clark is with narcotics. He's been observing Mr. Crone for several months now."

"And, apparently, me."

Officer Clark crossed his arms. "Don't feel special. You're not his only mule."

Megan glared at her reflection in his glasses. "I was not his mule."

"Pictures don't lie," Officer Clark replied.

"Back off, Clark," Bubba growled.

Officer Clark already had her arrested, tried, and convicted.

"I didn't know. I had my suspicions something odd was going on. But I didn't know what. I thought it was paperwork." She imagined Clark rolling his eyes behind those mirrors. "*Probably* full of meth, as Detective Sullivan said. Those pictures don't prove a thing. There's no law against handing someone a briefcase, is there?"

Office Clark snorted derisively.

She stood. "I didn't come here to be accused of—"

"Please sit down, Miss McClure," Detective Sullivan said calmly, a touch of weariness in his voice. He glanced at the clock on the wall then scowled at Officer Clark. "We're just trying to sort things out here. Imagine my surprise the first time I met you. I agreed to an interview about methamphetamine, only to discover the writer was the woman in these pictures *probably* delivering the very same drug."

Megan remembered his look of recognition that day. She sat.

"I couldn't figure out your angle," the detective went on. "As far as I knew, you could be involved in organized criminal activity." He held up a hand when she opened her mouth to speak. "Yet you seemed sincere about your writing, your other articles I read were well written, and during our interview you appeared to know very little about the drug. I thought it might be an act. Then you wrote an excellent article about methamphetamine, which, by the way, I'm looking forward to seeing in this Sunday's paper. So, I went with my gut that says Mr. Crone duped you."

Megan breathed an inward sigh of relief at his conclusion. "He did. The only thing I'm guilty of is being an idiot."

Officer Clark snorted again.

"Sorry to disappoint you," she snapped. "And take off those glasses. How rude."

Officer Clark put his hands on his hips.

Bubba snickered.

Detective Sullivan said, "She's right, Clark. Take those things off."

The officer removed the sunglasses and put them in his shirt pocket. He shot Megan a nasty look.

"You're not an idiot, Miss McClure," the detective said. "Sometimes you can be too close to something to see all the facts. As to why you are here today ..." He sat forward, his hands clasped together on the desk. "Mr. Crone is a sly one. We're having a hard time catching him with the evidence, as these pictures show. He's very careful. You mentioned you've had suspicions about him. Could you elaborate on that?"

Megan told all she knew about Barton. When she mentioned the trailer in the country, Detective Sullivan asked, "Can you tell us about it?"

She described the dilapidated trailer with the big X made of duct tape on the broken window, the junk-filled yard, and the fence covered with spring-flowering vines. She added without thinking, "I think that's where he's cooking it."

The detective and Officer Clark exchanged a look while Megan felt like kicking herself. *Idiot! They already think I'm guilty!*

"Why do you suspect that?" the detective asked.

Megan hesitated.

"You're not in trouble," he said in a gentler tone. "I just want to know why you think that. If you have any proof that Mr. Crone is involved in methamphetamine production. We could use your help here."

He seemed sincere. It could be an act. She wondered if she was doing a public service or digging a deeper hole for herself. She decided to go with the truth. "During our interview you mentioned that meth had a sickening sweet smell. When I was sitting in Barton's car outside that trailer, I smelled something sickening sweet. I had no idea what it could be until you said that. Then I smelled it again." She told about finding Barton in the house with the kids shooting up and the following scene. She named the cross streets where the house was. "I meant to mention it to you, Detective Sullivan. I just hadn't gotten around to it yet."

Officer Clark made a scornful grunt that earned him an equally scornful glare from Megan.

The detective placed another picture on the desk. "Is this the house?"

"Yes. Jim supposedly lives there. I don't know who lives in that trailer in the country. Barton said it was the son of a builder." She shrugged. "That's all I know."

"Do you remember where that trailer is?" the detective asked.

She shook her head. "Out in the country somewhere. We went south on the freeway and turned west off at an exit for some small town." She bit her lower lip for a moment. "I think it began with an I."

"Itasca?" Bubba offered.

"I think so. Then we drove down country roads and frankly, I don't know where I was. We came back through Cleburne."

Detective Sullivan wrote notes on a yellow legal pad as she spoke.

Megan stared at the picture of Jim's house. "I don't get it."

"What?" the detective asked without looking up.

"Barton. He has a good job. Flexible schedule. Makes good money. Why risk it all selling drugs?"

"You mean his construction job?" Officer Clark asked.

"Construction?" Megan looked at the officer like he was crazy. "He's not in construction. He does land acquisitions for a developer."

Officer Clark laughed. "Crone lost that cushy job back in January when the economy started tanking." He smirked at Megan's surprise. "Fooled you there, too, didn't he? He had to find a way to continue his lifestyle. Pay for that flashy car. So, he became a drug dealer. He does some construction work just to keep up appearances, but his main occupation is selling meth. Jim's his partner. His girlfriend Tammy is involved too."

"Jim's girlfriend Tammy?" Megan asked with a sinking feeling.

"Barton's." Officer Clark grinned as if he enjoyed pointing out to Megan how stupid she was. "I believe we have a picture of her."

The detective pulled a picture out of the envelope. "Here it is."

Megan stared at the skinny blonde who had sneered, *You don't know anything.* She did now. Barton had a girlfriend. He didn't have a high-paying job. He was a meth dealer. He had lied about everything. He had used her. Her hands balled into fists. *Bastard!*

"I heard they've been together quite a while." Officer Clark threw more fuel on the fire he'd lit inside Megan.

She sat up straight, pushing the pictures away. "Why am I here, Detective? Besides to humiliate me."

"I never intended to humiliate you, Miss McClure. My apologies if you feel that way." The detective shot Officer Clark a frown then turned his attention back to Megan. "I was hoping you would be willing to help us in the matter of Mr. Crone."

She asked cautiously, "In what way?"

"We have reason to believe Mr. Crone has a major delivery scheduled during the next week or so. Probably around the July fourth weekend. Holidays always cause a spike in drug activity, especially when they fall on a weekend."

"So, Barton would make a bunch of money, right?"

The detective nodded.

"A few nights ago, he asked me where I would like to go if money was no object. The beach. The mountains. He said he'd heard of islands for sale in the Caribbean."

"Sounds like he's planning to make a run for it after the exchange." Officer Clark waved a hand at her. "And look at you. Wearing one of your island outfits."

Megan fought the urge to hit him. "You are an insufferable—"

"Officer Clark, wait outside, please." Detective Sullivan's voice rang with authority.

Officer Clark stepped forward. "Sir, I—"

"Now."

The officer spun around, glared at Megan, and left the room.

"My apologies, Miss McClure." The detective leaned forward, his elbows on the desk. "As I was saying, we believe Mr. Crone has a big exchange coming up, but our informant has been unable to find out the particulars. I was wondering if you've heard him mention anything ... suspicious."

Megan shook her head. "Just what he said about going somewhere." She chewed her lower lip. "Do you want me to spy on him? Like Officer Sunglasses?"

A slight smile played around the detective's mouth. "I can't ask you to do that, Miss McClure. Not legally."

"Legal or not, there are two problems with that, Detective. One, we broke up a couple of days ago. Had a nasty fight and it's over between us. And, two, I'm leaving in two weeks."

"Oh?" The detective raised his eyebrows. "Returning to Chicago?"

For lack of a better answer, Megan nodded. *Hurry back to me.* "Unless—you're not going to tell me I can't leave the area, are you?"

"You are free to go wherever and whenever you choose. And, since you two broke up—" The detective slumped back in his chair. "Well, that changes everything. It appears I've wasted your—"

"I'll do it."

The detective perked up. "Oh?"

"I'll pretend I want to get back with him."

Behind her, Bubba said softly, "It could be dangerous, Megan. Be sure before you volunteer."

Dangerous.

The word gave her pause. Barton had a temper. A meanness that goes to the bone, Seth had said. She thought about that day in Jim's house. How Barton had made her feel trapped and scared. With good reason, after what she'd just learned. She was lucky she got out of there unscathed. Another memory came flooding back. The day she didn't go on a picnic Barton had planned and Mrs. Powell had said, *I don't know what you said to him, but he looks mad enough to spit nails at a kitten.* He'd probably had another delivery lined up for her, but she had screwed up his plans. Probably cost him a lot of money.

If things turned bad, well, she may be short and slender, but she'd taken defensive tactics courses and, because of her size and sex, had the element of surprise on her side. She wouldn't be able to fight him, but she could deliver a quick kick somewhere or a well-placed fist in his Adam's apple then run like hell.

She looked at the detective. "I'd give my right arm to see that bastard behind bars. Barton probably won't want anything to do with me, but I'll see what I can find out and let you know."

***

"How long have you known about Barton?" Megan asked Bubba as he drove her back to work through the tail end of rush hour. She sat in the front seat since Officer Clark wasn't with them, to her relief.

"Not long. A couple days." Bubba glanced at her. "Swear to God, Megan. If I'd known before that, I would have warned you about him. When I found out I was gonna tell you at work, but Bonnie said you were home sick. I didn't want to bother you until you came back. Then Officer Clark showed up today, and here we are." He stopped at a red light and looked at her, his face serious. "You be careful around Barton, okay?"

"I will. I hope he shows up tonight."

She didn't see him that night. Or the next.

In the middle of her Friday night shift, Megan made a quick run to the restroom. Upon leaving it, she glanced at the men and women milling about in their jeans, boots, and cowboy hats while Eddie Rabbitt sang about loving a rainy night. She did a double take. *There he is.* She fluffed her hair and straightened her blouse. She sucked in her stomach, stuck out her chest, and headed towards Barton in a corner past the restrooms, elbowing her way through the crowd. He had his right side to her while talking to someone she couldn't see. He crossed his arms and shook his head. She drew closer, then stopped. He was talking to Julia.

Fired for not showing up for work last weekend, Julia had somehow talked her way back into her job. Maybe the manager felt sorry for her. Julia stared up at Barton with a pleading look in her eyes that looked huge in her pinched face framed by straggly brown hair. Her long-sleeved blouse hung loosely on her thin body. She said something, her hands flying around as she spoke. Barton shook his head again and turned away. Julia grabbed his arm. He spun back, knocking her hand off, then leaned down and stuck his face right in front of hers and said something that made her back away, her eyes wide, a thin hand on her throat. He straightened, pointed a finger at her, and said something that made her hang her head and wipe her eyes. He turned and walked in Megan's direction.

She ducked behind some people and watched Barton disappear into the crowd.

Julia leaned against the wall, looking miserable and frantic.

He's her dealer, Megan realized. Or used to be, because she was small potatoes, and he was moving on to bigger things. Like the deal Detective Sullivan had mentioned. Megan considered going to Julia, but hesitated. The girl was difficult to communicate with, and her problems were way out of Megan's realm of experiences. She decided the best way to help Julia and all the other Julia's was to bring Barton down. Megan headed back to work, determined to talk to him sometime that night.

Awhile later, Megan cleaned up a table on the edge of her area. She accidently bumped her elbow into the head of someone seated behind her who yelped, "Ow! Watch it!"

"Oh gee, I'm so sorry about-Lori?"

Twisted around on her chair, rubbing her head, Lori Rinsky's scowl turned into a look of surprise then quickly back to a scowl. "Be careful with that knobby elbow of yours. You damn near poked a hole in my head." Lori rubbed the spot again as if to prove it. Her blond hair hung in soft waves around her perfect face. She wore a colorful peasant blouse with a low neckline that exposed tanned shoulders with no tan lines. She looked sleek and healthy, almost radiant. Her blue-eyed gaze went to the tray of empty beer bottles and glasses Megan held. "You're still working here?"

Megan nodded, wishing it had been anyone else's head but Lori's.

Lori laughed. "Since I last saw you, I've been all over the place. A blues festival in Memphis. Fleetwood Mac concert in Green Bay. James Taylor at Champagne-Urbana. And of course, the big summer concert in Chicago. It's been a whirlwind. One party after another." She puffed out her red lips in a pout. "All the while, poor little you've been stuck here, shaking your ass for tips."

"The tips are great. And I've been having a wonderful time." *Hurry back to me.*

Lori arched an eyebrow. "Well, good for you." She glanced around as if looking for someone, then asked, "So you've given up writing?"

"Hardly." Megan laughed. "I've been writing my fingers to the bone. Just cashed a check for an article I wrote about the B&B. It'll be in this winter's *Travel Holiday*. Another two-part article will be in the local paper this Sunday and next Sunday."

Lori looked impressed. "My, you have been busy." She put her elbow on the back of her chair. "Are you going to move here or something?"

Megan shook her head. "I'm going home in two weeks. I'm giving a speech at a meeting in Chicago for the National Writers Union."

"You *are?*" Lori's eyes grew as big as dinner plates. "I read about that." Her expression turned pensive. "Maybe I should go too."

Megan didn't bother pointing out it was for freelancers. "I'd better get back to work. And you can get back to picking up a guy for tonight."

A comment like that might have insulted another girl. Lori laughed. "I'm way ahead of you. He's getting our drinks right now. We met last night at another bar. We went back to my hotel and he rang my bell last night and again this morning. I'm planning on an encore tonight."

"I suppose he or his daddy owns a ranch?"

"He's so good-looking and sexy I don't care what he owns. Ooh, there he is." She rose a little off her chair and waved her hand. "Over here, sweetie."

Megan turned to get a look at the sexy bell-ringer.

There stood Barton.

Chapter 24

Barton regarded Megan with cold eyes. The curve of his lips flattened into a rigid line. Animosity spewed from him like lava from a volcano.

Megan stiffened her spine and flashed a bright smile. "Hi, Barton. It's good to—"

"Here's your drink, sweetheart." Barton brushed past her as if she wasn't there and handed Lori a glass of red wine. The people sitting nearby clapped and yelled at some fancy moves out on the dance floor while the jukebox played *Dueling Banjos* from the movie *Deliverance*.

"Thanks, baby." Lori glanced from Barton to Megan. "You two know each other?"

Megan said, "We've been dat—"

"She served me drinks several times," Barton said loud enough to drown out Megan's reply. He pulled out a chair and sat. He put an arm around Lori's shoulders and drew her closer then glanced at Megan. "Don't you have work to do?"

The pure disdain in his look and voice made Megan take a step back and rethink her reconciliation plan. "I'll talk to you later, Lori."

Barton's gaze cut from Megan to Lori. "Y'all know each other?"

"We grew up together. Our mothers were close." Lori took a sip of wine.

He jerked away from Lori as if he'd touched a hot wire. "So ... you're old friends?"

"No," Megan and Lori answered at the same time, which made them echange a look and chuckle. Megan explained, "Like Lori said, we grew up together. She didn't say anything about us being friends. Right, Lori?"

"That's right. Now run along and shake your ass like a good little waitress." Lori made a shooing motion with the wine glass.

Megan gave Barton what she hoped was a pleading, heartbroken, I'm-so-sorry look then walked away.

Lori called after her, "Hey Megan, I meant to ask you, how's that handsome young cousin of yours—what's his name? Seth?"

Megan kept walking as if she hadn't heard Lori and felt Barton's eyes bore into her back. While she took orders and served drinks, she noticed Barton's serious expression as he and Lori talked. The longer Megan watched, the more it seemed Lori was doing most of the talking. He often glanced Megan's way. She had a sneaking suspicion he was questioning Lori about Seth, and her. She finally managed to grab a few minutes for a break and went out on the back steps. Moments later, Barton stepped outside.

It's show time.

He closed the door and stood beneath the overhead security light that left pools of shadows on his face. He crossed his arms on his chest, his stance tense and stiff. "You owe me an explanation. Just who the hell is Seth?"

"I'm glad you came out here. I've been wanting to talk to you and—"

"Is he your cousin?"

"No. Neither of my parents had any siblings."

"Why did you tell Lori he was?"

"Because Lori's a big-mouth idiot with her mind in the gutter." Megan shooed a mosquito away from her face. "She doesn't understand that men and women can just be friends. So, I said he was a cousin to shut her up."

"Is he your lover?"

Oh, I hope so. "He's my friend."

Barton uncrossed his arms and stuck one hand in his pants pocket. Crickets chirped out in the muggy darkness. "Lori says he's young, late teens. But that's impossible. He looked around my age."

"Lori sees what she wants to see. Although in her defense, his hair was shorter, and he didn't have a beard when she met him. Seth is a couple of years younger than you." *At least he was when he and Barton met.*

"Where was he hiding in your room?" He raised his free hand, palm up. "We both know he was in that room somewhere."

"No, he wasn't. The minute you left, Seth got dressed and left. He didn't want me to get into any trouble because of him."

"Left? He didn't come down the stairs or I would have seen him."

"Seth told me you were in Mrs. Powell's office. He snuck by and slipped out the front door." The lies flowed easily from her. *I'm getting better and better at it.* She leaned back against the metal railing and propped her elbows on it. Her breasts strained against the thin material of her blouse. They weren't as big as Lori's, but she'd never had any complaints. She could feel Barton's eyes on her.

He tilted his head. "I find it hard to believe I didn't hear him."

"Mrs. Powell said you came barging into her office, shouting. Maybe that's why you didn't hear him."

"How'd he get those injuries?"

Holy moly, he's interrogating me worse than Detective Sullivan did. "One of those beer bottle bashes that unfortunately included knives and guns and Seth being in the wrong place at the wrong time."

"Why'd he go to you and not the emergency room? Doesn't make any sense."

Megan snorted. "You're telling me. Freaked me out when he showed up like that. I tried to take him to a hospital, but he said he couldn't afford it. He was also worried that the hospital would report his injuries, like you said, and he didn't want that. So, he asked me for help." She held out her hands. "What was I supposed to do? Tell him no?"

"How did you two meet?"

"At the Laundromat. Really!" she added when Barton scoffed. "We started talking, then went and had a beer. We've been friends ever since."

"He lives near you?"

She shook her head. "He has a place southwest of town. The day we met, he was in Fort Worth on errands, and doing his laundry was one of them. We get together for lunch every now and then. He's a nice guy."

"What's his last name?"

"O'Connor."

"Seth O'Connor." Barton tilted his head. "Sounds familiar."

"You know a family named O'Connor?"

"No. But it still seems familiar."

The whine of a siren on a distant street filled a long moment of silence, then Barton asked, "So there's nothing going on between you two?"

"We're just friends."

He exhaled loudly, as if he'd been standing there with bated breath. *Or did he do that on purpose and want me to think that?* He was a much better actor than she was.

"Better friends than you and Lori, I take it," he said, eliciting a short laugh from Megan. "Quite a coincidence, isn't it?" he went on. "Me picking up her, of all people, last night."

"I'm not surprised. She's always been an easy lay."

Barton glanced away and grunted.

Megan added wistfully, "I can see why you'd choose her instead of me." She bowed her head and managed a few loud sniffles.

"I'd rather be with you." Barton stepped in front of her, blocking out the glare of the security light in her eyes as she raised her gaze to his. "I screwed up the other day. I know that. But finding that naked man in your bed made me see red. I've been mad as hell at you these past couple days. I felt betrayed and used and made a fool of."

Funny. That's how you make me feel.

"But even more," he paused, and looked away towards the darkened parking lot down the steps. The line of his shoulders, thrown in sharp relief by the light above him, tensed. In the dimness, she saw him close his eyes briefly. He seemed to be struggling with himself. His chest heaved as he released a deep breath, then he looked at her. "Even more, despite all that, I can't get you out of my mind, Megan. As much as I tried to hate you, *wanted* to hate you, I-I couldn't. I just couldn't." He paused. "I've missed you." He reached out his hand to her, then stopped, and dropped it back to his side. "I'm sorry for the other day. For what I said. How I behaved. For jumping to conclusions. I'm sorry. Can you forgive me?"

Megan hid her surprise—she had expected to be the one groveling for forgiveness. "Of course, I do, Barton. I'm sorry too for the whole situation. I've been hoping to talk to you, and explain—"

"There's nothing to explain." He pulled her against him and wrapped his arms around her. "God, you feel good." He rested his cheek on the top of her head. "I missed you so much," he whispered, his hand moving slowly up and down her back. "More than I thought possible."

He was a drug dealer, a liar, a womanizer, yet he held her tenderly, and sounded sincere as he said all the right things. He deserved an Oscar.

Unless ... Megan's heart skipped a beat. *He actually cares for me.*

She drew away. "Barton, I'm leaving here soon."

"I know." He stroked her hair. "Lori told me."

Of course, she did. "I've been meaning to tell you but then everything fell apart."

"Maybe there's still time for me to win your heart." He gave her a gentle kiss, then rested his forehead on hers, his arms looped around her. After a moment, he straightened. "I gotta come clean. I'm not—"

The door opened, and Lori stepped out. She stopped short in the doorway, the music twanging around her. "Well, what do we have here? Should I find another lover for the night?" She arched an eyebrow. "Or shall we have a threesome?"

Megan pursed her lips. Good old Lori had to show up just when he was about to come clean. Megan separated herself from Barton, who muttered something under his breath, and felt his hands fall from her waist. "We're just talking," she said.

"Sure, you are." Lori tilted her head. "So who will it be, Barton? Her or me?"

Megan didn't believe Barton really cared for her, and she didn't want to be with him that night or any night. Especially knowing he had slept with Lori. They deserved each other. There would be another time, some afternoon, to hear his revelation. She said softly, "Go with Lori."

His head jerked back. "What?"

"There's a saying I've heard here. You should dance with the one that brung ya. You two came here together, right?"

"Not really. I mentioned I might be here tonight. She said she might be here too. If we ran into each other—" He shrugged.

"You're buying her drinks and sitting together. That means you're together." Megan said to Lori, "He'll be right in. He's all yours. For tonight anyway."

"No threesome? Chicken." Lori grinned and went inside.

"Damn it, Megan." Barton ran a hand through his hair. "You and your scruples."

Megan put her hand on his chest. "How about we get together this weekend?"

Barton shook his head. "I'm busy all weekend."

"Going somewhere?" *Like a big drug deal?*

"No. I have work tomorrow. I'm spending Sunday with my family."

She smiled up at hm. "I'd like to meet your family."

"I'd like that too, but this wouldn't be a good time. It's ... a family thing. But we'll get together soon, I promise."

"I hope so. Maybe an afternoon picnic. Or a movie." She ran her hand lightly over his chest. "I care about you too, Barton."

"That's good to hear, darlin'." He took her in his arms again and kissed her with parted lips and a touch of tongues, then said gruffly before releasing her, "I'm gonna do my damndest to dissuade you from going back to Yankeeland."

He opened the door for her and followed her inside. When she lost him in the crowd, she rubbed the back of her hand across her mouth.

During her break, she dialed Detective Sullivan's home number. "Detective? This is Megan McClure." She cupped her hand around the mouthpiece and said softly, "Barton said he's working tomorrow, and has a family meeting on Sunday. I don't know if he means family or, you know, *family*. Anyway, I thought you could tell Officer Sunglasses. Give him something to spy."

"Thank you, Megan. Be safe." He hung up.

***

Bright sunshine beat down upon Megan as she stared into the swirling water in the heart of the Water Gardens. She wiped sweat off her brow and concentrated hard. She closed her eyes and recited *Om*, ignoring the snickers of someone standing beside her, and emptied her mind. She tossed in a handful of coins and made a wish. She waited, and watched, and listened, and hoped while the throng of people out and about on a sunny Saturday morning jostled her, and kids screeched and yelled, and water tumbled down the terraces. Her hands clenched at her sides. No voices. No visions. Nothing. The pool taunted her with its secret of the portal.

How does this work? What am I supposed to do? I can't keep coming here over and over. She looked up at a blue sky dotted with lacy clouds. *A little help please?*

She trudged up the big steps and left the Water Gardens. Her taxi still waited at the curb. *He'd better be after the big tip I promised him.* Inside the cab, she sat beside two bags of snacks and a few toiletries she had bought that morning and settled in for the ride back to the B&B.

Maybe the water wasn't the portal for her. Maybe it was somewhere in her room.

Back in the room, she put away her purchases, then went to one end of the farthest wall and ran her hands up and down all along it. She went all the way around the room, running her hands on the walls, high and low, even in the bathroom. No portal.

Hands on her hips, she looked around, disgusted. It seemed logical the portal would be in this room. She rolled her eyes. Logic had gone out the window the first night Seth ran through that door. Perhaps the portal was somewhere else in the house.

Megan left her room and glanced down the hallway then the stairs to make sure no one else was around because they would surely think she was crazy. Satisfied she was alone she ran her hands up and down the walls in the hallway. She went down the stairs, checking the walls, and feeling like a fool. She did the same on the ground floor, reaching as high as she could, then squatting down to feel along the baseboards. Voices came from the TV in the nearby sitting room.

"Can I help you, Miss Megan?"

Megan shot to her feet and spun around.

Mrs. Powell stood in the hallway outside her office.

"I-I lost a-a bracelet. I thought it might be down here." Megan wiped her hands on her shorts and straightened her tank top.

"Oh dear. I'll help you find it." Mrs. Powell came closer.

"Thanks, but I've already checked all around here." Megan shrugged. "No luck."

"What does it look like? I'll keep an eye out for it."

"It's-it's, um, gold. With three amethysts on it."

"I'll let you know if I or one of the girls find it."

"Thanks." Megan still had walls to check and made no move to leave.

"Is there anything else I can help you with?"

"No, thanks. I think I'll watch a little TV."

Mrs. Powell smiled and returned to her office.

Megan entered the room where a Mighty Mouse cartoon played on the screen. She changed the channel, found *American Bandstand,* and proceeded to check the walls around the room, bobbing her head to the music. The last wall behind the TV stretched before her when the show ended. Minutes later, the familiar theme song of *The Twilight Zone* and Rod Serling's distinctive voice came on.

"Oh good!" She stepped in front of the TV to see which episode it was. *My favorite!* She sat on the sofa to watch Burgess Meredith as a mild-mannered bank employee who just wanted time to read. At the end, he stood among stacks and stacks of books in a ruined world, holding his broken glasses, shouting, "That's not fair!" The title *Time Enough At Last* flashed on the screen at the end.

Megan went to check the last wall behind the TV.

After the commercials, the same theme song played again, and Rod Serling spoke. *Another one!* She ran over to see what one was on now. She put her hands on her hips. *How apropos.* She knew the episode by heart, but it had a completely new meaning for her now. The story was about a little girl and a dog lost in another dimension in the wall behind her bed and rescued by her father. During commercials, Megan finished searching for her own portal, but, unlike in *Little Girl Lost,* did not find one.

Megan rubbed her forehead, feeling a headache coming. *Now what?*

She snapped her fingers, and headed for the dining room, where she'd had the second vision. It seemed the next logical place to search.

Logical.

That word again. It made her pause in the doorway. It made her rub her forehead again. Nothing had been logical for so long.

Maybe I'm wasting my time. Maybe this is all for nothing. I need a sign. Megan looked up at the ceiling. *Give me a sign! Or-or I quit.* She put her hands on her hips. *Hear me? I quit!*

She tapped her foot, waiting.

No visions of the past. No clap of thunder. No bright light showing the way. Nothing.

She glared at the ceiling. *I swear I'll quit!*

Once again, *The Twilight Zone* music and Rod Serling's voice came from the TV. Her head snapped around at the familiar sounds. She headed back to the sofa and sat, slouching back, and crossed her legs.

The episode opened with a dark-haired young woman seated at a desk in a small apartment furnished with the basics—sofa, chair, coffee table, bookcases. The woman tapped on an adding machine, stopping frequently to write down figures in a ledger. An ashtray made of cut glass sat within easy reach.

A man suddenly appeared by the sofa. Wearing brown trousers, a dark shirt beneath a worn leather vest, a flat-brimmed black hat, and boots, he looked like a cowboy in a John Ford western. "Who are you?" he asked. "Where am I?"

The woman screamed, "Get out of here!" She grabbed the ashtray and threw it at the man. It flew right through him, hit the wall, and thudded on the floor. "You're-you're a ghost!"

"I am?" The man held out his hands, turning them over. "Last I knew I was standing in the middle of a street in Fort Worth. I don't remember anything after that." He raised a fear-filled face to the camera and cried, "What happened to me? What happened?"

Megan stared at the screen through narrowed eyes. She thought she had seen every *Twilight Zone* episode ever made, but she'd never seen this one. The young actor's face finally registered in her brain. She peered closer. *Robert Redford?*

Rod Serling stepped into the scene. Smoke curled up from the cigarette held between his fingers. "Meet a cowboy from the days of the Wild West named Seth O'Connor who—"

"*What?!*" Her feet hit the floor as Megan shot up straight on the sofa.

"—suddenly finds himself over one hundred years in the future, and, to his great dismay, one of the dearly departed. He has no memory of how or why he died. Nor any idea why he is in the future, which he finds not at all to his liking.

"It seems, despite all the innovations and conveniences that have made life easier, humanity hasn't yet learned to live without violence and war. He comes up with an idea. A preposterous, impossible idea. All he needs to make it happen is the help of Megan McClure—"

Oh. My. God. Megan had a white-knuckled grip on the armrest.

"—the woman he meets in *The Twilight Zone.*"

She watched in stunned disbelief while an extremely condensed version with many variations of her and Seth's experiences played out on the TV. The ghost returned to the room several times and became friends with the woman, played by Ann Blyth—*She's the best actress they could find?*—who lived alone and worked at a bank. She wore plain dresses that hit below the knees and had her dark hair in a pageboy.

She asked, "Where are you when you're not here?"

"Nowhere," he said. "Everything is dark and full of nothing. Except when I'm here with you."

She told him about life in her time, and they discussed things he read in newspapers and history books.

During one of his visits, he said, "I think I'm supposed to take you back to my time, so you can save me from dying."

The woman stared at him in wide-eyed surprise. "Why?"

"So I can change some things. Make the future different. Better. You can help me."

She laughed and lit a cigarette. "You can't change anything, or you'll change ... everything."

"Says who?" he asked.

A commercial came on for Wisk laundry detergent that got rid of ring around the collar.

Megan sat on the edge of the sofa and chewed a thumbnail. It wasn't a typical *Twilight Zone* episode. Anyone else would find it downright boring, with just the two characters talking. Megan, however, couldn't wait to see what happened next.

The show resumed with the woman pacing the room, wringing her hands. The ghost appeared and asked her what was wrong. She had discovered her boss was embezzling from the bank. He had denied it, of course, when she confronted him. That day she had received an anonymous threatening letter at her residence.

The ghost said, "You have to leave for your own safety. You should come back in time with me."

"How?" she asked.

"I'll take you."

"But how?" she asked again. "You're a ghost. We can't even touch."

"We can do it," he insisted. "Somehow it's possible. It's why I'm here, why I met you. It has to be."

"How can you even think that? Why would you think that?"

"Why else would I be here, in the future, if not to see how much it needs to change?"

"But you can't change it!" she shouted at him. "You can't!"

They argued about it and parted mad at each other.

Another commercial. A woman stood in an aisle of a grocery store, holding a package of Charmin Bathroom Tissue. Mr. Whipple hurried over and yanked the package out of her hands, saying, "Please don't squeeze the Charmin."

Megan ran up to her room to go to the bathroom. She made it back to the sofa just as the show came back on.

The woman sat at her desk, going over the figures in the ledger again, when someone knocked on the door. It was her boss, played by Edward G. Robinson. For several minutes, he acted friendly, then he got mad and mean. He ripped her ledger in two and pointed a gun at her.

The ghost appeared and held out his hand to her. "We'll save each other. Then worry about the future." Her boss stepped closer, yelling at her, the gun leveled on her chest. Shots rang out just as the woman put her hand in the ghost's hand, and they disappeared.

Rod Serling walked onscreen. "Change the future." He spread his hands. "Who hasn't wanted to do so? Maybe it has happened before. Time somehow resets itself. Or maybe it needs help to do so. Help from people like Seth and Megan. Did they accomplish it? Did she go back and save him? Or did the bullets hit their mark and make her a ghost, like him? If they did change the future, would we even know?" Smoke from his ever-present cigarette wafted around him. "How could we know? But it's possible. It's all possible, here, in *The Twilight Zone*."

He stepped closer, looked in the camera. "Maybe it's possible *outside* of *The Twilight Zone*."

The hair on the back of Megan's neck stood up. He was staring right at her when he said that. That's how it felt, anyway. He said those words to her.

The title flashed across the screen. *Time to Reset Time*. Written by Cordelia Pryor.

After several heart-thumping moments, Megan muttered, "Now *that's* what I call a sign."

She jumped up, made a beeline for the phone, and dialed Candace Huntington's number from memory. "Hello. This is Megan McClure. May I please speak to Mrs. Huntington?"

A woman's high-pitched laugh came over the phone. "She told me you would be calling, Mees Megan. As soon as that show on the TV ended, she say, 'Any meenute now, Rosy, that phone weel ring.'" The woman laughed again. "That lady. She know everytheen'."

Obviously. She knew I'd watch that show. But ... how?

"She saw *The Twilight Zone* episode?"

"Si. She weeshes you would come here Monday morning at eleven, por favor?"

"What's the address?" Megan wrote it down. "I'll be there Monday. Thank you." She hung up and pumped a fist. She would finally have answers.

***

"Great job on that methamphetamine article," the manager of The Tejas said to Megan when she showed up for work Sunday evening.

"You read it? Glad you liked it."

He laughed. "Didn't have any choice in reading it. Bonnie's been shoving it in everyone's face." He headed to his office.

She walked up to the bar and Bonnie announced, "Here's our famous writer."

"That's some damn good writing there, Megan," said a construction worker, one of the regulars.

Another regular, a truck driver, leaned forward on his chair. "I got a cousin messed up on that shit. He's worthless as a square tire." He pounded his fist on the bar. "Somethin's gotta be done about it."

Another one lifted his beer bottle in a toast. "Excellent writing. I'm going to save it to show it to my students."

A couple of other regulars added their compliments.

Megan grinned at her group of fans gathered at the bar. "Thanks for your kind words, everyone."

The jukebox started playing *Sunday Morning Coming Down* by Johnny Cash and the regulars started singing along and drinking their beers.

Bonnie put a mug of beer on Megan's tray. "We're celebrating after work. You, me, and the girls. We'll get something to eat, and who knows what else could happen."

"Sounds fun." Megan stashed her purse behind the bar. "Although this all seems a bit much over one measly little article."

Bonnie paused while drawing another draft and looked at Megan. "It's a big deal. Front page of the local section. That's pretty cool, girl." Bonnie put a perfect head on the beer. She added the mug to the others on the tray then wiped her hands on a towel.

Megan picked up the tray and went to work.

A couple of hours later, Julia came up to Megan. "HeyMegan. Iread thatarticle youwrote and Ireally likedit. It'sjust that ..." Julia looked away, rubbing her lips together, and wringing her hands.

Megan asked gently, "What is it, Julia? Something wrong?"

The younger girl scrunched her face. "Igot thisfriend. She ain'tdoin' sogood 'causeshe takesthat stuffand-and," her hands flew around as the words quickly tumbled out, "andshe really wants tostop." Julia met Megan's gaze. "Shereally wantsto butshe doesn't know how 'cause- causeit's hard todo. Sohard. You don't know howhard." Julia's voice shook, and she blinked a couple of times. "Iwas wonderin' ifmaybe you know whereshe could go get somehelp. Youknow, someone to talkto or- -or ... Idon't know, just ... help."

"I know someone I can ask. I'm sure he'll be able to help your friend."

"You thinkso?" Julia asked, wide-eyed.

Megan nodded. "He's a detective."

"A-a *cop?*" Julia took a step back, rubbing her hands up and down her arms. "Iain't talkin'to—Imean my *friend* ain'ttalkin' to nocop. Noway."

"Don't worry. I'll talk to him and find someone your friend should contact. No cops will be involved. All right?"

"Thankyou, Megan." Julia blinked several times. "You're thebest." She hurried away, wiping her eyes.

About an hour before closing time, Barton elbowed his way through the crowd to the bar.

"What's the matter with you?" Megan asked.

His hair was a mess, he needed a shave, and had dark circles under his eyes. Usually neatly dressed, he wore a wrinkled shirt and jeans that looked like they could use a wash. In fact, all of him could use a wash. She had never seen him so unkempt.

"Rough weekend." He said to Bonnie, "Whiskey. On the rocks."

Megan leaned against the bar. "Your family meeting didn't go well?"

"My what?" He looked at her, frowning.

"You said you had a family meeting today." It was a lie, she surmised, unless his family meeting included roughhousing in the dirt, because, from the looks of Barton, that's what he had been doing.

"Oh yeah, yeah. Thanks," he said to Bonnie when she set his drink on the bar. He picked it up and downed it then asked for another one. "Yeah. The meeting didn't go well. In fact, not a damn thing went right this weekend." He drank the second drink as fast as the first and asked for a third.

Bonnie gave him another.

He slammed his drink back then wiped his hand across his mouth.

Megan touched his arm. "What happened, Barton?"

He shrugged. "Nothing you need to worry your pretty head about." He gave her a weak smile. "Let's just say the whole weekend was a total bust." He covered her hand with his. "Can I take you home after work? It seems ages since we've seen each other."

"I'm sorry, I can't. I'm going out with Bonnie and her friends. We're celebrating the publication of my article in the paper today. Did you read it?"

"Yeah." Barton removed his hand from hers. "I read it." He raised one finger to Bonnie and pointed to his empty glass. He reached into his shirt pocket and pulled out a cigarette. He lit it and took a drag then blew the smoke upward to join the perpetual haze that hung throughout the bar.

After several moments of hearing Willie Nelson sing about an angel flying too close to the ground, Megan asked, "So what did you think?"

"About what?"

"My article."

"It was good." He picked up the drink Bonnie had given him and toasted Megan. "Good job." He lifted the glass to his lips then paused and lowered it. "What are you pissed about all of a sudden?"

She crossed her arms. "Is that all you have to say about it?"

He scowled. "I said good job. What more do you want? A medal?"

She turned away.

He grabbed her arm, stopping her. "Hey, hey, I'm sorry, Megan. It's been a crappy weekend. I don't mean to take it out on you."

"You're certainly in a surly mood."

"I know, I know. Family can be a pain in the ass sometimes. My folks read your article and said they can't wait to meet you. I was real proud of you, darlin', when I saw your name in the paper. Tell you what. We'll have our own celebration tomorrow. I'll take you somewhere nice for lunch. Maybe see a movie afterwards." He trailed his fingers up her bare arm.

She managed not to recoil from his touch. "I can't. Not tomorrow. I'm meeting someone."

"Oh." He removed his hand from her, reached for his glass and took a drink. He wrapped his hands around the glass and looked straight ahead. "You meeting him?"

Megan asked innocently, "Who?"

Barton looked at her. "Seth." He said the name as if it tasted like dirt in his mouth.

I wish. "No."

Barton raised an eyebrow, as if he didn't believe her.

"I'm meeting a woman from one of Fort Worth's oldest families. She's one hundred years old."

He still looked like he didn't believe her. "Well, have fun with the old lady." He downed his whiskey. "So, you're busy tonight and tomorrow. Think you can squeeze me in sometime?"

"What about Lori?"

"What about her?"

"Are you still seeing her?"

"Not since the other night when we were here. I dropped her off at her hotel and left."

Megan stared at him. "You're kidding."

He shook his head. "I never even got out of the car. You can ask her yourself next time you see her. She's back in Chicago for all I know."

"Holy moly. I don't think any man has ever turned her down."

Barton barked a harsh laugh. "Probably not. I did." He gazed into Megan's eyes. "Because of you."

"In that case, I'll try to find an hour or so to spend with you."

His expression darkened. "Gee, thanks." He stubbed his cigarette out with quick, jerky motions in the ashtray.

She nudged him with her elbow. "I'm kidding. Of course, we'll get together. I'd better get back to work."

"Guess I'll mosey over to the other side where some of my buddies are." He pulled Megan close and gave her a deep, long kiss. He tasted like an ashtray. When the kiss ended, he said in a husky voice close to her ear, "Pick a night for us, darlin'. At least one night, or all of them." He drew back so he could look her in the eye. "That's what I want. All your nights. Lori was just a roll in the sack to ease the ache you always leave me with." He kissed her forehead then reached into his pocket, pulled out a bill, and stuffed it into the tip jar. "See you soon, darlin'. Lookin' forward to our night." He winked then walked into the crowd.

It'll be a cold day in hell before we *spend a night together.*

***

At eleven Monday morning, Megan knocked on the door of a huge, white mansion on a bluff overlooking the Trinity River. Stately pillars adorned the wide porch bright with colorful pots of petunias and periwinkles and hanging baskets of draping ivy. White lace curtains covered the wide windows across the front of the house. A sloping, spacious lawn with islands of flowers and shrubbery spread out in every direction. Towering old trees provided shade from the hot sun.

An old woman wearing a print housedress opened the door. She had brown skin, dark brown eyes, and long black hair streaked with grey. She smiled. "Mees Megan? Come een, come een. I'm Rosalita."

"Hello, Rosilita. It's nice to finally meet you." Megan stepped inside and caught her breath at the majestic sight. A chandelier hung from the high ceiling of the foyer, and ornate, antique furniture filled the large, open room beyond flooded with sunlight from the many windows. A massive stone fireplace was in the center of one wall, with bookcases on either side of it. Potted houseplants added splashes of green among the dark furnishings and white walls. Exquisite figurines and expensive-looking knickknacks filled nooks and crannies and graced tabletops. A wide staircase with gleaming banisters led upstairs.

"Meesus Huntington ees waiting for you. Follow me, por favor."

Her heart pounding with anticipation, Megan followed the woman up the stairs to a room on the second floor. The door was open.

Rosalita said, "Meesus Huntington has been eell so please—"

"Is that her, Rosy?" a scratchy voice called from the room. "Send her in."

Rosalita ushered Megan into the room, saying, "I weel breeng your tea soon." She nodded to Megan and left.

Megan stared across the room at the tiny woman lying beneath the covers in a big bed. She had a head full of cotton-white hair, emerald eyes that shone as bright as Christmas lights, and a big smile. She held out thin, blue-veined hands. "Oh, Miss Megan, it's so good to see you again!"

Chapter 25

Megan stood rooted to the floor as the words *so good to see you again* ricocheted in her brain. "It's-it's true," she whispered. "It's all true."

Candace Huntington wriggled her outstretched fingers, as crooked and gnarled as branches on an old tree. "Come here, come here, so these old eyes can get a look at you."

Megan slowly crossed the floor. It was a large, sunny room, with rich, dark woodwork and gauzy white drapes on the tall windows. A pair of Chippendale chairs that faced each other sat before one of the windows with a marble-topped table between them. The table held a vase of pink roses, baby's breath, and pink hydrangeas. The sweet scents mingled with the smells of old age and bleach. An oval Oriental rug muffled her footsteps as she neared the bed where the old woman lay propped against a pile of pillows.

Candace's wrinkled hands reached out, grasped one of Megan's hands with surprising strength, and pulled her down to sit on the side of the bed. A pair of lively green eyes studied Megan as a breathy, high-pitched voice said, "You're as pretty as I remember, Miss Megan. That lavender sundress looks wonderful with your coloring."

Megan searched the old woman's face with its many grooves, lipstick-red lips, and a bright spot of rouge dotting each of her pale cheeks, hoping for, expecting some hint, some flash of recognition. But the woman was a stranger. Megan felt compelled to ask, knowing she was wasting her breath even as the words came out of her mouth, "Are you sure you have the right person, Mrs. Huntington?"

The old woman cackled. Her cold hands gripped Megan's. "With that black hair, those violet eyes, and that lovely face, why, I'd know you anywhere. Call me Candace. Or Candy. Like you used to. Did that purple dress fit you perfectly?"

Megan nodded.

"Just as certainly as the glass slipper fit Cinderella, eh?" Candace smiled a smile that made all the lines in her face curve up. "I've been waiting a long, long time to see you again."

Megan licked her dry lips and asked, "How-how long?"

"Ninety-one years."

"Ninety-one years," Megan repeated softly.

"I was nine when we met. My sister Corrie was twelve. That's us." Candace nodded to a framed picture next to a glass of water and several bottles of pills on the nightstand. Beside the nightstand was a matching bureau, its top lined with a dozen more picture frames, but Megan only had eyes for the sisters.

"May I?" Megan asked. At Candace's nod, Megan picked up the 8x10, black-and-white picture of two laughing young women in long light-colored dresses with frills on the bodices and bows and ruffles on the skirts. They both wore their hair in a big bun on top circled by a thick roll of hair. An open parasol one of the women held over her shoulder provided a backdrop. "You're both beautiful."

"The pretty Pryor girls they called us. That's me on the right. I was eighteen. She was twenty-one. We both had auburn hair and green eyes."

"Your sister wrote that *Twilight Zone* episode. How did she know I would see it that day? How did you?"

"You told us. You told us many, many things."

Megan replaced the picture frame then met the old woman's gaze. "I imagine you learned even more from that world history book Seth took back with him."

"We sure did." Candace's eyes twinkled. "We read it over and over again. It was our most prized possession. I still have it. In that bottom drawer." She nodded to the nightstand. "Go ahead."

Megan opened the bottom drawer and saw the familiar book with the unimaginative title *The History of the World Since 1900*. She picked it up. Mold and mildew gathered at the edges and corners and crept across the cover. A long crease, cracked and split in places and torn apart about an inch down from the top, ran the length of its spine, attesting to frequent use. She opened it and flipped through the pages. Many had underlined words or notations in the margins. A moldy smell wafted from the yellowed, dog-eared pages. She closed it and put it back in the drawer. "How did you end up with it?"

"You told us to go get it from Mr. Seth's room. We went there one stormy afternoon when no one else was out. Corrie stood outside and kept watch while I searched for the book. When I found it, I hid it under my coat and we ran home."

"I hope to God no one else ever saw it."

"No one did," Candace replied. "We kept it carefully hidden. We understood the consequences if it fell into the wrong hands."

Consequences. Megan stood and walked toward a wall that had a marble fireplace with an ornate iron grate. Carrara marble, she guessed. Expensive stuff. She caught a reflection of her pale face in a five-foot freestanding cheval mirror in one corner of the room. She spun around. "What about the consequences of *me*?"

"Come sit, Miss Megan." Candace patted the patchwork quilt of pink, yellow, and white squares that covered her up to the chest of her white nightgown. It had lace around the high-necked collar and long sleeves with lace around the wrists. "We have so much to talk about, and soon you'll know all you need to know."

Megan sat on the bed. That was an odd way to put it. *All you need to know.*

"Now. Where shall I begin?" Candace tilted her head.

"Tell me about Seth."

"Perhaps with *The Twilight Zone*," Candace went on as if Megan hadn't spoken. "I know it's your favorite television show."

Megan nodded. "I grew up watching it. I've seen every one of them at least a dozen times. Some of them I can recite almost word for word. But the episode that was on Saturday—I've never seen it before."

"Of course, you haven't." Candace giggled. "That was the only time it ever aired. That was part of the deal Corrie made with Mr. Serling. Oh my, how he despised that story!" She clapped a hand to her cheek. "He said it was amateurish and not at all suitable for his series. Poor Corrie struggled to write that story. Bless her heart. She worked with figures, not words. She most certainly wasn't a writer. Mr. Serling must have refused her dozens of times. But she was a persistent one, she was, dear Corrie." Candace's eyes took on a misty sheen as they settled on her sister's picture. "I do so miss her still," she said softly with a catch in her scratchy voice. She blinked and looked at Megan. "Where was I?"

"Rod Serling hated your sister's story."

"Oh yes, yes, he did. He refused to air it. Said it was trash."

"How did Corrie convince him?"

Candace chuckled. "She paid *him*, instead of the other way around. She offered him an exorbitant amount—she had more money than a body could spend in several lifetimes—and Mr. Serling was no fool. He took it and gladly agreed to only one airing of it on a specific date and time in the future. He even put it in his will. Corrie insisted. Smart girl. Especially since he died before the show would air."

"Why did Corrie choose that date and time?"

"You told her to, Miss Megan."

I told her. Megan let the words sink in. "Why then, specifically?"

"You told us that on that day at the time you were full of doubts and questioning everything, and on the verge of giving up. You said you needed a—what was the word you used?" Candace tapped her crooked pointer finger against her upper lip. "A sign." She held up the finger resembling a shepherd's crook. "That's what it was. You needed a sign."

Megan nodded. "That's all true."

"You also said to precede the story with two other specific episodes."

Two of my favorites, which would suck me right in to watching.

"Mr. Serling readily agreed to all of it. He even let Corrie choose the actors. She was beside herself when Bob Redford agreed to be in it. Such a nice young man. If I'd been younger—" She wiggled her eyebrows. One was drawn a bit higher than the other. "Corrie tried to get Elizabeth to play you, but she was shooting *Cleopatra* and couldn't—"

"Elizabeth?" Megan's eyes shot wide. "You mean ... *Liz Taylor?*"

Candace scrunched her face and made a big O with her lips. "Oh, how she hates to be called Liz. Hates it. She would have been perfect for the part, don't you agree? But Ann did a fine job, I must say."

"So your sister paid Rod Serling to produce a show that would only air once, on a certain day and time about 20 years in the future. You'd think he would have written a story about *that*." Megan crossed her legs. "Tell me about Seth O'Connor."

"Dear Mr. Seth." Candace said almost reverently. "He was one of the nicest, kindest men I've ever known. He was the town catch. I've seen the door in your room that he uses to visit you."

"You have?"

Candace nodded. "The first time was sometime in the '50s when the place was a boardinghouse for women and I was visiting a friend there. Years later, when it was empty, Corrie and I walked through the house pretending to be buyers. The whole place was falling down except for that door. It looked as strong and solid as it was when I was a child. I tried to open it that day. Oh, how I tried. I pressed my ear against it, hoping to hear ... something. There were a few times in my life I wished I could open it and go back to those days." Candace sighed. She leaned her head back on the pillow and closed her eye, lacing her gnarled fingers on her chest. Digits and knuckles stuck out in every direction.

While Candace dozed, Megan leaned sideways for a better look at the photos on the bureau. Two of them were of a young couple dressed in wedding finery. The same bride with a different groom. Candace, with two of her husbands. The other photos were of three different men, some with Candace and some without her. Megan leaned over further for a closer look at Candace's five husbands, and Candace herself, aging through the years.

"Quite a rogue's gallery, eh?"

Megan jerked back and sat up straight. She met Candace's alert green eyes. "They're all handsome men."

"They certainly were." Candace's gaze traveled slowly over the pictures. "I loved them all," she said softly. "I met the first two because of you. Thomas," she gestured to the first wedding picture, "was the first banker who handled Corrie's investments. A serious fella. We were so young. Monty, my second husband," she nodded to the other wedding picture, "was a lawyer at the law firm we used. He made me laugh." Her voice faded away as she gazed at his picture. She blinked a couple of times. "Where was I?"

"You were talking about your second husband Monty. He made you laugh."

"Oh yes, he was a prankster, but smart as a whip. He was big help to Corrie with all the legal malarkey. Just as Thomas was with the money. You made a wise decision, Miss Megan, when you put Corrie in charge of the money. She had a good head for it. Much better than me. She was the smart one. Because of her, that small amount of money you gave her grew substantially, as did our own investments. She did all the work. You gave her the hard part. I had it easy." She smiled. "All I had to do was live to be a hundred. Ah, here comes Rosy with our tea and cookies."

Rosalita walked in carrying a silver tray with a china tea set on it. She placed it on a small table in a corner, then carefully rolled it near the bed.

"Thank you, Rosy. Miss Megan will do the honors."

"Of course." Megan stood and got out of Rosalita's way as she helped Candace sit up a little straighter on the bed.

"Only two cookies, remember?" Rosalita said as she plumped up and rearranged the pillows behind Candace. "Doctor say you watch your sweets."

"Pshaw. Doctors." Candace leaned back, straightening the quilt with her bent fingers. "Worrying about sweets at my age. I'll eat what I damn well please."

Rosalita shook open a linen napkin and spread it over Candace's chest. "You want to go back to hospeetal? Then you eat all you want, stubborn lady." She straightened, and rolled her eyes at Megan, who hid a smile. Rosalita left the room.

"I sometimes wonder who is in charge around here." Candace shook her head, although a fond smile played around her mouth. "Would you pour, please, Miss Megan? There's no sugar or cream. The tea doesn't need it. Trust me."

Megan picked up the teapot. It had a picture of a pagoda surrounded by bamboo and delicate gold designs etched on both sides of the burgundy pot. The handle and spout were white, edged in gold. Megan filled the small matching cups and handed one to Candace. She held it with both hands, cupping it with her crippled fingers as she took a sip.

"Still a tad hot but so good. Lemongrass with honey. My favorite."

Megan sat on the side of the bed and tasted her tea. "Delicious. It's a beautiful tea set."

"Freddie bought it while we were in China. Downstairs is full of things from my travels."

"You've seen a lot in your lifetime."

"I traveled the world. Since I had so much time ahead of me, I decided why not? It seemed I was indestructible."

"You were." Megan set her teacup on the tray. "You survived two plane crashes, one train crash, and one fire. And that's just what I know of."

Candace chuckled. "There were many close calls, believe me. At first, when I was young, I was very careful about not hurting myself, or getting hurt, or putting myself in a position to get hurt, because I knew I had to live a long time to see you again." She took another sip of tea before continuing. "Then Thomas died when our house burned down, Monty died in a train crash, and both times, I should have died too." She shrugged. "After that, I decided that maybe, no matter what, I would survive until I was one hundred. So, I became a little reckless, took chances I shouldn't have, took risks. And did what I damn well pleased. Would you hand me one of those cookies, dear?"

Megan did so, noticing the familiar marking on the cookie. *Peanut butter*. She took a bite of one. It was as delicious as the tea.

"I'm sure it's happened to you too, Miss Megan."

"What has?" Megan took another bite, and almost choked on it at Candace's next words.

"Not dying when you probably should have. Are you all right, dear?"

Megan finished coughing and stared at the old woman for a long moment. "My parents died in a car accident," she said slowly. "I hardly had a scratch."

Candace nodded. "Is that the only time?" She nibbled her cookie.

Megan thought for a moment, and long-forgotten memories came flooding back. *Holy moly*. "When I was five, a tornado ripped our house apart. Mrs. Moore, an old lady who lived nearby was babysitting me that afternoon. We huddled in the basement and suddenly," Megan paused and swallowed hard, "suddenly it sounded like a train was barreling down on us. Next thing I knew, I was covered with boards and wood and-and stuff. I couldn't see anything but a jumble of ... stuff." She put her half-eaten cookie on the tray. "It was awful. I don't how long I was under there, shivering, scared, buried alive. Then I heard voices. It was night before they finally pulled me out of there. They found Mrs. Moore a few feet from me. She was dead. Everyone said I should have been dead too. All I had were a few cuts and bruises."

Candace made a clicking sound with her tongue. "How awful. You remember anything else?"

Megan looked down and brushed cookie crumbs off the front of her sundress. "I was a teen when I almost drowned. A bunch of us were swimming in an old quarry that had filled up with water. I dove in, hit my head on something underwater and blacked out. When I came to, I was lying on the grass. My friends were circled around me, staring down at me, and one of the guys was bent over me, repeating my name over and over. He'd been giving me mouth-to-mouth resuscitation. An ambulance came and hauled me to the hospital. I was fine. The doctors said I was lucky to be alive." Her gaze met Candace's. "I'd forgotten all about both of those."

"There were probably other times that you didn't realize you were ... at risk, shall we say. I imagine you are indestructible too." Candace patted her mouth with her napkin. "I had a wonderful life. I have you to thank for that."

"I had nothing to do with it. It was ... another Megan."

"You're wrong, Miss Megan. She is you and you are her. The same person only different. Variations on a theme, if you will."

Unconvinced, Megan picked up her teacup. "The whole reason for investing whatever money the other Megan gave you—"

"*You* gave us."

"—was to save the house, thereby saving the door, right?"

"Of course. If there's no door, Mr. Seth couldn't come through to meet you and you wouldn't know you have to go back."

Megan set down her cup and leaned forward. "Go back for what?"

"Oh, dear." Candace's lopsided eyebrows drew together. "This is the hard part. Corrie and I talked and argued often through the years about how much I should tell you."

"Everything! Tell me everything!"

"I don't think I should."

Megan straightened. "Isn't that why I'm here? To find out everything from you?"

Candace looked at Megan almost pityingly. "Only what you need to know. If you know it all, you may not want to do it. Or you'll do the same thing as before, make the same mistake, and nothing will change." She leaned forward slightly. "You have a choice, Miss Megan. You have many choices. The other time didn't work. Hopefully you will choose differently this time. But you must choose with your whole heart, of your own free will. You must be absolutely sure. You told me to tell you that."

Megan's shoulders slumped. "I-I don't understand."

"Open that top drawer." Candace nodded at the nightstand.

Megan did so. Inside lay an envelope, face down, yellowed with age. She picked it up and held it out to Candace.

"It's for you," Candace said.

Megan's heart leapt into her throat. "*Me?*"

"Read it, dear."

Megan looked at the envelope. It was handmade, a piece of paper folded into an envelope.

"I suppose I should have given it to you when you first arrived," Candace said, "but I wanted to chat with you a bit, get reacquainted, after all these years."

Megan turned it over. Her breath caught. Written across the front of it in her own familiar handwriting were the words *To Megan in 1981 from Megan in 1890.*

Chapter 26

Her hand shook. The penciled words on the yellowed envelope stared back at her from another century.

"Read it, dear," Candace repeated gently. "It will all be clear to you then."

"It's about time," Megan muttered. She slid her thumb under the flap and gently loosened it from the glob of flaking glue holding it together. She straightened out the flap and pulled out several sheets of paper. She unfolded them and wrinkled her nose from a musty smell wafting up. Her handwriting covered the papers, lightly browned at the edges from the passage of nine decades. She started reading.

> *Dear me,*
>
> *If you're reading this, maybe I finally did something right. I sure screwed up everything else. And I mean everything. I'm sure you find all this hard to believe. Me too! Still do, but it all really happened. I swear it did. I have so much to tell you and not much time. A few days at the most before I probably become too weak to write anymore. And then??? I don't know. Kind of scary. Scary—hell! I'm terrified! But I've accepted my fate. I deserve it. I probably deserve a lot worse for what I did. Or didn't do.*
>
> *I'm glad you've come this far and finally met Candy. Isn't she the sweetest? Wait until you meet her as a kid. She's a pistol, as Texans say. She and her sister found me in their pasture and hid me up here in their attic. No one else knows I'm here. Their parents just left for a few days. Abilene, I think.*
>
> *The servants or help or whatever they are never come up here, nor does the old aunt staying with the girls. The girls will care for me until, well, the end, however it may come. If I don't last long enough to tell you everything, Candy will.*
>
> *Knowing me/you, you probably want proof that you are me and I am you. In most ways anyway. I doubt we are identical, except maybe in looks, but probably not in our experiences and choices, especially as we grew older. It wouldn't make any sense if we were, because then we'd just keep making the same mistakes over and over. I'll tell you something only you/I would know.*

> *Something I've never told another soul, and I bet you didn't either if the same thing happened to you. When I was eight, a close male friend of the family put his hand in my underwear. Did something like that happen to you?*

Megan gasped. Her thumb crunched the side of the letter. *I was ten. It was Bob Rinsky on the Fourth of July. We were at their house for a picnic. I had on my swimsuit because Lori, and I and some other kids were running through the sprinkler. He and I went to the garage to get more lawn chairs. We were in the back corner of the garage and he rubbed his hands over my chest. I was just beginning to develop. I couldn't believe what was happening! I'd known him all my life! Suddenly, he was a monster. I slapped his hands away and told him if he ever touched me again I'd tell my parents. He never bothered me again.*

> *The man was Lori Rinsky's dad. It was the Fourth of July and we were sitting in the back yard watching fireworks that night. I was sitting on his lap just like I had since I was a baby. Only that night, he ran his hand up the inside of my thigh, up under the hem of my shorts, underneath my underpants, and touched me. Lori's mom, who was sitting in a chair beside us, leaned toward him, and he pulled his hand away. I jumped up and ran away, confused, scared. I've hated fireworks ever since. From then on, I avoided him. I avoided Lori too I'm ashamed to say. She and I had been playmates until then. But after that, I had a hard time facing her, as if I had done something wrong. It's only been during the last couple of days while I lie here fading away and with plenty of time to think about my life that I wondered for the first time if he had done the same or worse to Lori. Maybe he's part of the reason she was so wild in high school and earned the nickname Lay Down Lori. I don't know. But I've been feeling bad about how I treated her. Dropped her like a hot potato. I wonder what she might have suffered at the hands of her own father. The bastard.*

Oh God. Poor Lori, Megan thought for the first time in her life. *At least we never called her Lay Down Lori. I'm not impressed by fireworks. Is that a remnant of this other Megan? We were different ages when it happened and didn't have the same experiences. We're not the same. What does she mean by fading away?*

You want further proof about me/you? I don't have any relatives. No siblings, cousins, aunts, or uncles. Never knew any of my grandparents. Bet you don't have any relatives either. Mom and dad died in a car accident. It was my fault. Everyone said it wasn't, that's why it's called an accident. But I know better. It's just been in the last few days, with all this time to think, that I finally forgave myself for their deaths. I hope you can too. Don't wait until the end like I am. Do it now. Don't carry all that guilt and pain with you anymore. It serves no purpose and does no good. It doesn't change what happened. It only changes you. Forgive yourself. Want more proof? Knowing me, you probably do. The first boy I kissed was Jeff Thompson.

Megan started in surprise. *No, it wasn't! It was Todd Cummings. Jeff was the second.*

Gotcha! Jeff was second. Todd Cummings was the first. How's Donna? God, I miss her. What I'd give to see her again. She didn't marry Greg this time around, did she? He's not the one for her. I hope you're convinced by now. I am you and you are me. With variations, I'm sure. I'm a writer. Bet you are too. The last few years, I wrote movie and concert reviews for the Chicago Trib. Not a bad job. I got to see all the movies and go to a lot of concerts. But it got old. So, I jumped at the chance to go to Ft. Worth to cover the opening of The Tejas when the need arose. And one night a locked door in my room opened and in ran Seth, bleeding from a bullet wound and looking for his sister. He was something, wasn't he? Handsome, sure, but so much more. You know what I mean. Corrie and Candy talk about him like he was a rock star or something. Just about everybody in town liked him. They wanted him to be the city marshal. I guess they didn't realize he was a pacifist with a capital P. Although Gary Cooper pulled it off in High Noon. Seth hated war and violence and talked of changing the world. Maybe he could have changed things, especially with the knowledge he had about the future. Maybe somehow, he could have prevented a war. Any of them. WWI or II, the Korean War, Cuban War, Vietnam. Take your pick.

"Cuban War?" Megan muttered.

"You say something, Miss Megan?" Candace asked, her gaze moving from the window to Megan's face.

"She mentions the Cuban War."

Candace tilted her head. "We didn't go to war with Cuba. We came close. Was it the early 60s?"

Megan nodded. "President Kennedy and the Bay of Pigs."

"Yes, yes, that's it." Candace patted Megan's arm. "It appears you did some good after all. Somehow, because of you or something you did during that brief time back there, something changed that affected the future, and prevented one war in our time. Isn't that wonderful? Who knows what other changes, big or small, happened because of you?"

"Maybe all the changes weren't for the good."

Candace tipped her head the other way. "I don't recall you being such a gloomy Gus. Would you pour me some more tea, dear?"

Megan refilled Candace's teacup, then resumed reading.

> *Yeah, if anyone could, Seth could. And he would have. I know he would have. If I hadn't fucked up. If I wasn't a coward. If I had loved him more. There's the crux of my problem, and now the world's problem. Your world's problem. I didn't love him enough. Thought I did. The sex was wonderful. All those nights. Holy moly.*

All those nights? Megan glared at the words. *I only had one!*

> *But I didn't love him enough to do what needed to be done. To   . What the hell? The words I just wrote disappeared as fast as I wrote them. Just disappeared! Just as I was telling you how he   and I   . It did it again! I don't get it. I have a terrible headache and feel dizzy. I have to lie down and think about this.*

The sentences had started to run at a slant, the handwriting messy and cramped. When the letter resumed, the words were clearer, the strokes more even, as if the writer was less agitated and more in control.

> *I think I figured it out. After a nap and two pieces of delicious fried chicken the girls snuck up here for me I feel better. I just finished writing down everything that happened to me since I came back in time, and very little remains. The important words disappeared as fast as I wrote them, leaving only nonsense. Here, I'll write another sentence right now. You have to be sure you   his   he left on the   that   . See? All the important stuff is gone! It appears I can't tell you anything! And you really need to know what I just*

wrote above and disappeared for you to get back to his time. It's a vital part of the   . Shit! It seems Chaos—that's what I call whatever is in control of all this, I wonder what you call it?—wants you to do it on your own. No coaching from me. You go into it blind. Shit. This sucks. I received more information than that from the other Megan. Well, what do you know? Those words didn't disappear this time. I guess I can tell you about her.

Megan lowered the letter. *Tell you about her.* She reached for her cup and took a sip of warm tea. *Wish it had a shot of whiskey in it.* She glanced at Candace. The old woman rested her head against the pillows, her crippled hands clasped on her chest, her half-closed eyes fixed on the row of husbands on the bureau. Megan picked up the letter to read about *another* Megan.

Once upon a time, I was sitting on the side of Candy's bed, drinking lemongrass tea and eating peanut butter cookies, and reading a letter from long ago, just like you are. It was a letter from the Megan before me. Yes, you read that right. Turns out I'm not the first Megan to go through this. There's one before me, and one before her, and who knows how many more? I guess we're slow learners. We keep screwing up and just can't seem to get it right. Maybe you will. I hope so. I feel awful that I didn't. Just awful. When I saw Seth with those   in his   it tore me apart. Damn disappearing words. I guess I'll just keep writing and you'll have to make sense of the blank spots somehow. I'm sorry. I'm so sorry. I had no idea this would happen. It wasn't like that with me. I knew everything after reading it in the other Megan's letter. Every awful detail. Maybe that was a mistake. Maybe it'll be easier for you if you go in not knowing everything. Now I'll tell you about the other Megan.

She grew up very different from me, and hopefully from you. She was a wild one. Quit sophomore year in high school and ran away to hitchhike across the country. She relayed a few stories of her travels, none of them good. A lot of sex and drugs. It was late in her letter when she wrote that Lori's dad started molesting her when she was very young, which was why she finally ran away. She eventually returned home, made amends with mom and dad, got her GED, and somehow

> *got a job as a reporter for the Trib. She wrote greeting cards on the side, plus some porn. No shit. Greeting cards and porn. Her parents died the same way mine did. It seems mom and dad are expendable in every version of our stories. She didn't say how she ended up in Ft. Worth writing about The Tejas but everything happened about the same to her as it did to me, and probably you. She met Seth, got a job at a bar, some small place, sounded like a dump. I worked at a bar called The Wagon Wheel. There were drunken brawls almost every night. Beer bottle bashes I called them.*

Megan chuckled. *I still think it's a good title for a country western song. How eerie that this Megan used the same phrase.* She returned to the letter.

> *She got involved with a guy bootlegging alcohol and cigarettes. My guy was a beer truck driver who sold pot from his truck. A lot of pot, it turned out. I wonder what your bad guy does? You'll have to   him. Shit. She bought the purple dress at the sale in the church. Wrote the letter that ended up a historical document on the bank wall. Had a couple of visions of the past. I imagine you experienced all this too. I'm the one that added the Twilight Zone episode. I was packed up and ready to go home that Saturday, fed up with the mysteries and the bad guy making my life hell. I was downstairs, waiting for a cab, when I found that handful of old coins in my pocket. I'd forgotten all about them and was standing in the hallway, holding them on my palm, when the phone in the office rang. Startled, I dropped the coins. They scattered like cockroaches on the floor, rolling everywhere. Mrs. Powell came out of her office and said the call was for me. It was Rosalita, informing me that Candace Huntington wanted to see me. So, I stayed. While lying here, I decided to save you the hassle of packing and all that and ease your doubts. I wanted to give you the sign you would need at that moment. One I wish I'd had. I told Corrie about the Twilight Zone show and explained she needed to write a story that would convince you this was all really happening. I also told her to request certain episodes to air before it, and when to air them. You'd think Rod Serling would have written a story about that!*

Megan gasped. *That's what I said!* A soft snore came from Candace.

SETH'S DOOR

I guess it worked because here you are. Must have been a good story. I know I can depend on Corrie. She's a serious, levelheaded girl. Wise beyond her years. Candy is lively and adventurous. I'm wandering off the main topic--the other Megan. She went back to Seth's time, and on the night before the   she slept with Tim! Seth's best friend! Ballsy bitch! After everything was over, she—are you ready for this?—she came back through Seth's door. I have to stop now. I'm tired.

Megan flipped over the paper and continued reading.

I'm finally back. It was a bad morning. I could barely raise my head off the pillow much less sit up, hold a pencil, and think. Like I said, the other Megan came back through Seth's door. I could never open it in the room, bet you can't either. She said she ran up those stairs in Seth's time, it was dark and cold, just like he said. The door opened, and she was back in her room. The room, the whole place was in bad shape because when she was back here in this time she only gave Corrie $5 to invest! Whoopee! Not near enough money for it to do much good. She was more worried about saving her own hide and getting out of there. Frankly, I don't find that Megan very likeable. I'm not at all like her. Hope you're not either. Turns out she couldn't outfox the Heebee Jeebees. That's what she called Chaos. She wasn't back more than a couple of days when she started fading away. She found the portal again, returned to this time, and ended up here with the girls and did what she was supposed to do for the next Megan—me—before she faded away. I should tell you about fading away.

Remember Seth saying how he felt like he was coming apart if he was in the future too long? Something like that is happening to me. Although it feels more like I'm fading away little by little. I've been with the girls 4 days I think. I doubt I'll last much longer. It's not painful, just draining. I thought about going up those stairs and seeing if it's dark and cold and if I can open Seth's door and go home. But I'd just fade away there too. Besides, I have to set things in place for your turn. Because we Megans seem to have a mission, and I failed. So I'm going to stay and face the consequences,

and leave it up to Chaos. And you. Now it's up to you. I believe if you   . There they go again. Disappearing words. I'll reword it. I believe that if you do what you're supposed to do, you won't fade away. You'll stay back in this time and live a normal life. And if you live until just before your birthday in 1954, you'll know you got it right. That's my theory anyway. My hope. That's all I have left. Hope. For you. I don't know why this happens to you and me and all the other Megans. Why us? It's not like we're the brightest bulbs in the box, in fact we seem to be a bunch of duds. Why Seth? What's so special about him? He's just a man like any other man. But there must be some reason Chaos thinks he has to be   .
It seems time keeps resetting until something is changed. Now it's up to you. I guess you don't have to do any of it. You have a choice. Good old free will. You can walk away, live your life. Although how you could live with yourself after that I don't know. Don't you want to know why this is all happening? Isn't it driving you crazy not knowing? I know I ... Oh shit. I'm babbling. I need to concentrate. I guess if you choose not to do it, or choose to do it and don't succeed, there'll be another Megan, and another, and another, until we get it right. Mindboggling isn't it?

The handwriting turned sloppy. Letters and words ran together, making it harder to read. Megan rubbed her eyes and struggled on.

Maybe we Megans are stuck in the wrong time and just need to go home. Or maybe we need to be a better person and with each Megan we're improving. I know I'm an improvement over the other Megan, and she didn't write very highly about the one before her, who sounded like a timid little thing. Maybe you're the best of us. The one that will succeed. Or maybe it's all about Seth. He's the important one and we're just a bit player in the story. I'm rambling now. Oh hell, it's all crazy. I wish I knew why. Why? Why! But I'll never know. That pisses me off more than anything. I'll never know why. My fingers are cramping. I have to stop. I can barely keep my thoughts straight. My brain must look like Swiss cheese, parts of it fading away. I hope you can make some sense out of all this. It's raining outside. Sounds nice. I have a window open and can smell the rain. I'll miss that.

I've been crying. I'm scared. I look at my hand and I can almost see through it. I feel like the Wicked Witch of the West. I'm melting! I'm melting! Instead, I'm fading away. I don't want to die. Here. Alone. I'm sorry Chaos! I'm sorry Seth! I did love you! I did! I'm so very sorry! I don't want to die!

Watermarks smeared and blurred several of the penciled words. *From tears?* Riveted, Megan continued reading.

I just reread everything and almost crossed out the last paragraph. But I have no one else to talk to. I can't burden the girls with my despair. They're just children. I've already put a heavy load on them. They must think I'm crazy. I hope you don't go through this fading away. It's awful, knowing that soon I'll be—gone. Gone where? Is there a heaven for a repeating soul? Or is this my/our hell? Maybe I don't have a soul. Oh God what an awful thought. I'm going to start crying again.

I'm back. Don't know for how long. Everything's a struggle. Doubt I'll see another sunrise. I've left out so much. I thought I'd have more time! I forgot to tell you so much. Lottie. She's a tough cookie, rough around the edges, but I like her. She and Seth are devoted to each other. Tim. He'll help you. He saved me from the angry mob. Don't have sex with him! I like Susannah, not at first though. They all probably hate me now. I don't blame them. It's all my fault. Damn, it's hard to hold a pencil with fading-away-fingers. You can use Seth's door at least once for sure, to return to your present time. But not to go back to the 1800s. The portal. I have to tell you about the portal. It's in the   in your   . Shit. It's in the B&B. There! At least you know that much. The   are important. The "scattering cockroaches" are important. They'll show you the   . Damn it! You have to   Seth from   . You may have to the   for him. You may have to   yourself. You have to   Seth more than   life. You   to   him! You have to get it right! It's all up to you. Don't fuck it up. Please don't. You don't want to go through this, die like this, end like this.

Oh, the sunset. Reds, oranges, and pinks swirling across the darkening sky. A slice of moon like a lopsided smile. Texas has beautiful sunsets. I would have liked living here with Seth. I wish that for you with all my fading away heart. Lord I'm tired. I need to rest a bit. There's still so much I should tell you. Hope I have the strength. I like that lopsided smile hanging over me. Maybe it's a good sign. Hope. Faith. Love. You need all three.

Megan turned the paper over. It was blank. "That's it?" She looked at Candace, who opened her eyes.

Candace shrugged. "I never read it. Neither did Corrie."

"I can't believe that's it." Megan stared at the last words of the letter, then looked at Candace. "What happened to her? Did she ... fade away?"

"Like a patch of snow on a warm, sunny day."

Megan leaned forward, the bed squeaking beneath her. "Tell me everything. The other Megan said you would tell me everything."

"I thought you wrote it all down there." Candace nodded to the letter still clutched in Megan's hand.

"She tried to tell me, but words disappeared as she wrote them."

Candace's lopsided eyebrows shot up. "Words disappeared?"

Megan nodded.

"I've never heard of such a thing." The wrinkles around Candace's mouth deepened with the press of her lips. "That must mean there are things you don't want you to know. Hah! That's something no one else would say. You don't want you to know." She cackled as she reached for another cookie.

"Please don't think of her as me, or me as her. We had different experiences. We're not the same person."

"Oh, she's in there somewhere." Candace pointed her shepherd's crook finger at Megan and twirled it around.

"Wherever she is, she wanted you to tell me everything." Megan put the letter on the nightstand.

"That's impossible."

"But—"

"I don't know everything." Candace took a bite of her cookie. "I was nine."

Megan shoulders slumped. "But surely you know—"

"I'll tell you what I remember." Candace settled back on the pile of pillows. Her legs shifted beneath the covers. "Damn restless legs," she muttered. "It was a sunny spring day when my friend Annabelle came running up to our house with big news. Mr. Seth had a lady friend who had come to visit from up north. Corrie and I wanted to go see her right away, but mama wouldn't let us. She was packing for a business trip with papa that she didn't want to go on because she was going to miss the festivities that weekend. But papa insisted, and she griped to us all afternoon while packing. I remember she had on a peach-colored dress. She looked so pretty."

Candace's green eyes shimmered as she spoke of her mother.

"Mama was a beautiful woman. Not the smartest kernel on the cob, as my granddaddy used to say. She and papa finally left the following morning. Goodness gracious, we thought they'd never leave. Corrie and I hightailed it to the other side of town to get a gander at Mr. Seth's friend. And there you were." She smiled at Megan. "You were standing with Mr. Seth and Mr. Tim in front of the general store. Mr. Seth pulled my pigtails like he always did, and said you were visitin' from the big city of Chicago."

"Was I wearing the purple dress?"

"Oh no, not then. It was a blue dress with pearl buttons down the bodice and ruffles around the sleeves. I remember it like yesterday. It looked so pretty on you with your black hair. I said the color matched the—oh dear." Candace scrunched her lips together. "I don't think I should tell you that."

Megan quickly lowered the teacup she was about to drink from. "Tell me what?"

Candace went right on, "Corrie elbowed me and told me to shush. Mr. Seth looked mad, and I felt awful, because I'd never seen him so mad. Then you knelt beside me and talked real nice to me and got me to laughing. Corrie said something about wanting to have a picnic and you said that sounded fun. Mr. Seth said he'd come get us at our house later. But he didn't come. It was just you, carrying a picnic basket. You'd said you'd gotten lost a couple of times despite Mr. Seth's directions. You looked so hot and sweaty, even though it wasn't all that warm. Corrie and I took you to our favorite spot along the river. We sat there and ate while we talked." Candace picked up her teacup and held it in her crippled hands as she took a sip.

"What did I-I mean *she* talk about?"

"Well, we thought it was about life in the big city. Later, we realized you must have been talking about your time, in the future, because many of the things you said sounded fantastical. I made you a dandelion chain and you wore it the rest of the afternoon."

Candace reached out her shaking hand to replace the teacup on the silver tray. Tea jiggled in the cup. Megan leaned forward to take it from Candace and set it down.

"Thank you, dear. You asked us all sorts of questions about ourselves, and about Fort Worth and the people who lived here. It was a lovely day. It wasn't often an adult spent that much time or gave that much attention to us. That was back when children were seen and not heard, mind you. Not like young folks today." She shook her head. "All that raucous music. And the clothes they wear! Heavens above, what's the world coming to? Where was I?"

"You and Corrie were having a picnic with ... Megan."

"That's right. After the picnic, we didn't see you again until the next day, after the wedding."

"Whose wedding?" Megan's heart suddenly pounded with dread.

"It was Clyde Wheatley and Harriet Huntington, a cousin of my last husband. Oh, it was a grand affair. People came from miles around. There were tables laden with food. Cakes and pies galore. Lanterns strung all around. Bouquets of flowers everywhere. Mercy me, it was a sight. A lovely cool spring evening, perfect for the dance that night. Mama was fit to be tied when we told her how pretty everything was, and she missed it all. She was a beautiful woman, mama was." Candace's eyes took on a faraway look for a moment then she blinked and looked at Megan. "What was I saying?"

"About the dance that night."

"Ah yes. The dancing began, and you showed up in that purple dress. You dazzled everyone, especially when you danced with Mr. Seth."

"We-I mean they danced together?" *Is the vision I had of us dancing together the other Megan's memory?*

"You sure did. Miss Susannah didn't like that at all. She stood with her arms crossed, tapping her foot. And I don't mean to the music. She was really in a snit when you and Mr. Seth left the dance together."

"Then what happened?"

"Great-aunt Oleta made us go home to bed."

Megan sipped her tea. Candace's story had as many holes in it as the letter did.

"The next day, while we were getting ready for—well, for another celebration, Sarah arrived at the house. She helped in the kitchen. A nice girl. Not much older than my sister. She said the—the celebration was cancelled because—" Candace bit her lower lip and turned her head toward the window. After a moment, she said softly, "I didn't expect this." She glanced at Megan with watery eyes. "I didn't think I'd have to tell you this. I thought it would all be in your letter. And it's," Candace looked down at her hands, "it's hard to speak of what happened. Even after all these years ..."

"You don't have to," Megan said gently.

Candace lifted her gaze to Megan. "When we'd heard that *he* had died, we were all heartbroken. Simply heartbroken."

Megan had a good idea who *he* was. "Why don't you tell me how Megan ended up at your house? You found her in your pasture?"

"Yes, yes, I did." Candace brightened and sat straighter. "I'd gone out to see my pony the following evening after the funeral. She always made me feel better. I went for a ride and came upon a pile of purple. It was you, unconscious, wearing that purple dress. I raced back to get Corrie and we got you back to the house and upstairs to our room. Wouldn't have been possible if mama and papa had been home, but Great-aunt Oleta could barely hear or see and never knew you were there. You were in bad shape, Miss Megan. Bad shape." Candace slowly shook her head, her wrinkled brow furrowed.

"From the angry mob she mentioned in the letter? The mob Tim helped her escape from?"

"Angry mob?" The furrows deepened. "The mob. Hmmm. Yes, I remember Corrie mentioning that. She knew more about that than I did. She found out the next day that people were mad at you and blamed you and wanted you gone, one way or the other. I didn't know exactly what happened. Except it involved you and John Bingo. We never did like him."

Megan clenched her fist on her thigh. *I knew Bingo played a part in it.* The pieces of the puzzle were finally falling into place. "What do you mean I ... ah ... *she* was in bad shape?"

"Your face was smudged with dirt. Your hands were dirty and had cuts on the palms, from falling while running, you said later. Your hair was a straggly mess. When you came to, you started babbling and crying something fierce. Corrie sent me downstairs to get you something to eat and drink. When I got back to the room, you had calmed down. You looked so scared and helpless. Like a-a lost puppy. You asked us to help you. We couldn't say no. You were Mr. Seth's friend. And especially after what had recently happened."

Candace fidgeted with the blankets lying across her stomach.

"We took you up to the attic—no one ever went up there—and helped you change into one of mama's old nightgowns. You never left the attic again. You talked to us for hours, Corrie more than me. You said you'd come from the future to fix some mistake. Except you had failed. Your story was unlike anything we had ever heard before. It was like a bedtime story. We were fascinated by it, and you. Although I was a little frightened of you, especially as you became weaker and weaker and turned as pale as milk. You asked for another blanket because you were cold, even though it was awful warm in the attic.

"Then you asked for paper and a pencil. I remember you rallied a bit when you started writing that letter. You had more energy and appetite. For a day or so anyway. Then one evening we found you weeping. We could almost see through you. I swear to the Good Lord, see clear through you. Like the jellyfish I'd seen down at the coast. It scared me something fierce. We helped you put on your purple dress, you insisted, then you gave us both a long hug. The next morning, all we found was the dress, with that envelope on top of it, lying on the bed. You were gone. Just ... gone."

Holy moly. "What about the townspeople? Didn't they ask about her? Didn't they wonder what happened to her?"

Candace made a motion with her hand. "Oh, those busybodies in town had all sorts of ideas about you when you were nowhere to be found. Mercy me, the rumors flew. Some said you and John Bingo were in cahoots together. You both planned the whole thing and afterwards he set you up somewhere fancy as his mistress. Some said you hanged yourself with your petticoat out in the woods. Others said John Bingo took you somewhere isolated and kept you captive as his whore. He denied everything, of course. Funny thing is, after a time, people forgot about you."

Megan blinked in surprise. "What do you mean forgot?"

"Just what I said. They forgot all about you. Corrie and I couldn't understand it. *We* remembered you. But no one else did. Not Mr. Tim. Or Miss Susannah. Or Miss Lottie. No one. And there was no record of you anywhere, not in the newspapers or the town records or anything, even though there had been stories written about you, a visitor from far-off Chicago. Back then, anything and everything was news. We checked many times. It was as if you had never existed."

The words sent a chill over Megan, and she stifled a wild laugh. She apparently existed over and over and over. She gestured to the letter. "Do you want to read it?"

"Oh no, no." Candace held up her hand.

The shrill ring of a phone downstairs cut like a knife through the quiet house. Megan jumped at the sound.

"Won't be for me," Candace said. "Everyone I knew is dead. What were we saying?"

That is the saddest thing I've ever heard. Megan blinked away the sudden tears welling in her eyes. "I was wondering if you wanted to read the letter."

"No, that's not necessary."

"You devoted your whole life to waiting for me. You've earned it."

"Pshaw. As I said before, it was a wonderful life. What more could a body ask for?"

"I still wish I could, I don't know, repay you, thank you somehow."

"There's no need for that." Candace looked at the window a moment. Afternoon sunlight slanting through the glass highlighted the many lines on her face that mapped the length of her years. "Well, maybe—"

"What? Tell me."

"I've traveled the world. I've seen all the great cities. I've stood in the Vatican, and the Parthenon, and a witch doctor's hut in Africa. I walked in the Lord's steps in Jerusalem. Swam in the Dead Sea. Escaped from an anaconda in the Amazon. I saw the migration of the wildebeests and hunted lions on safari. I climbed the pyramids of Giza and Central America. I was one of the first Americans to see Machu Picchu in Peru. I danced at Stonehenge on the summer solstice. I saw the Northern Lights over a fjord in Norway."

Candace released a shaky sigh. "I met kings and queens and rubbed elbows with movie stars. I danced with Tyrone Power. Had dinner with Frank Sinatra. That evening with Ol' Blue Eyes was more exciting than meeting any of those kings and queens." She grinned and wiggled her mismatched eyebrows.

Megan chuckled. She leaned forward, enthralled by the tales.

"I had plenty of money, thanks to dear Corrie's investments. And clothes!" Candace's eyes sparkled as she clasped her hands to her chest. "Oh my, I had the most beautiful wardrobe. The height of fashion."

She turned her gaze to the row of husbands on the bureau.

"I've loved and been loved by five wonderful men. I've done it all, seen it all, had it all. Except one thing. The one thing I wanted more than anything in the whole world." Candace's bright gaze shifted to Megan. "I never had a child." Sadness etched her scratchy voice. "I had four miscarriages, and one stillborn. After the last miscarriage, in my forties, I accepted the fact that I would never bear a living child. I suppose it was too risky. Many women died in childbirth, and I knew I had a long life to live. So, I put it behind me. But the wanting, the aching wanting was always there." Candace leaned forward. "You say the Megan I knew when I was a child was another version of you?"

Megan nodded. "There are four of us that I know of, three before me."

Candace's lipstick-red lips formed an O as she breathed, "O-o-o-oh my." She placed a hand on her cheek. "I have lived four hundred years?"

Megan laughed. "I guess that's one way to look at it."

"No wonder I'm so tired!" Candace cackled. She repeated softly, "Four hundred years. My my. You said you and the other Megans had different experiences?"

"Yes. Different personalities too."

"Hmmm. Interesting. I wonder if *I* was different each time?" After a moment, she said, "Then all I ask, Miss Megan, is that you do whatever it is you are destined to do so that the next time, I can have a normal life. One with children."

Megan took Candace's hand. "I'll do my best. I promise." She glanced at the husbands. "Which one will be the father?"

"Joe. The last one. He was a childhood friend. My best friend. I was eleven the first time he asked me to marry him. He proposed many times after that. But he wanted to stay here. I knew I had a long life ahead of me and I didn't want to live all those years in one place. I wanted adventures. So, I left to see the world. After I'd seen it all, when I was growing old, I came home for good. Joe was still waiting. Oh, he had married and had children and a good life of his own, but we had always loved each other. He was a widower, I was a widow again, so we finally married. I loved all my husbands, but Joe," a radiant smile lit her face as she stared at his picture, "was the love of my life. If I have another life, I want to live it all with him and our children."

"You should tell me everything and I'll write your life story. It would be fascinating."

Candace chuckled. "I doubt there will be much time for that. Now that we've met, I probably won't live much longer. Goodness, Miss Megan, don't look so upset."

"But Candace—"

"Don't fret, dear. I'm very tired. I'm ready to go. Four hundred years, remember?" She squeezed Megan's hand. "I hope I've fulfilled my role. I hope I have helped you."

"You have."

"You know what you're supposed to do? What mistake you have to correct?"

"I believe so. John Bingo kills Seth, and I'm supposed to stop him." *And* not *sleep with Tim!*

***

In the taxi on the way back to the B&B, Megan reread the letter, and tried to fill in the holes with what she'd learned from Candace. One sentence in particular caught her attention.

When I saw Seth with those   in his   it tore me apart. She plugged in random but relevant words to see if any made sense. The taxi stopped at a red light. The left turn single blinked on the dashboard. Megan leaned forward, poised to tap the driver on the shoulder and tell him to turn right, the direction of the main library in Fort Worth. She drew her hand back and relaxed against the seat. She didn't need to read the gory details of Seth's death in the historical records. She knew all she needed to know. *When I saw Seth with those* bullet holes/bullet wounds/holes *in his* chest/stomach/head *it tore me apart.*

Inside the B&B, she went straight to the house phone and dialed Donna's work number.

"Donna? It's me. You busy?"

"Hey, Megs! Everything okay?"

"Yes. Do you have time to talk?"

"Sure. Just counting the minutes until I get out of here. What's up?"

"I spent this afternoon with Candace Huntington."

"Tell me everything. No. Wait. Hang up and I'll call you right back, so you don't have to pay for the call."

Megan hung up. Seconds later, the phone rang. She snatched up the hand piece.

Down the hall, Mrs. Powell stuck her head out of her office.

"It's for me, Mrs. Powell."

She waved and returned to her office.

Megan said into the phone, "Donna?"

"Tell me everything, Megs."

Megan did so, then read the letter.

The front door opened, and a middle-aged couple entered, talking and laughing as they walked by. Megan turned her back to them and spoke softer until they went upstairs. A long silence followed when she finished the letter.

"Donna? You still there?"

"Fucking mind-blowing," Donna muttered. "She even mentions me. Gives me goose bumps. How are you doing?"

"I'm all right."

"You sure? That's a whole bunch of heavy stuff."

"It's every-day-run-of-the-mill stuff for me anymore."

Donna barked a laugh, then her voice turned serious. "You want me to come down?"

"No. I'm fine."

A short pause. "You're not coming home next week, are you."

It was a statement, not a question. "How can I, Donna? I have a destiny to fulfill. Seth needs me. I love him."

A heavy sigh came over the phone. "Enough to somehow go back in time and risk your life for his?"

"All that and more. Whatever it takes. He's the important one. Besides, I made a deal with the universe."

"You're kidding. And frankly, I like the name Chaos. Seems more appropriate."

"I told the universe to do with me what it wants as long as Seth and I end up together. That's not asking too much, is it? It's fair, right?"

"Don't ask me. Ask stupid Chaos. Aw shit, Megs." Another heavy sigh. "Did you go to the library and check the records?"

"No. I know all I need to know."

"Oh boy," Donna muttered.

"What?"

"You need to read the historical records."

Megan's spine stiffened. "You sound like you know something. How could you?"

"Remember when I was down there? I left early the last day because I said I'd heard the traffic was bad. I lied. I left early to stop at the library on the way to the airport."

Megan's grip tightened on the phone. "What did you find out?"

"You know part of it. Bingo shot Seth in a gunfight. It's famous for being the last great gunfight on the streets of Fort Worth."

"Gee. What an honor."

"Megan." Donna paused.

Warning bells went off in Megan's head. *She never calls me Megan. Only Megs.*

"Seth died on his wedding day."

Chapter 27

LOCAL MAN KILLED IN GUNFIGHT

Blood once again stained the streets of Fort Worth today. Local saloon owner Seth O'Connor, age 30, was gunned down by prominent businessman John Bingo. Bad blood had simmered between the two men for years and finally boiled over when they faced each other on Main Street. The townspeople scattered. The two men exchanged insults. It is said a woman was involved, possibly Mr. O'Connor's sister, a long-time companion of Mr. Bingo. The two men stood poised to draw their weapons, watching each other.

Witnesses say something caught Mr. O'Connor's attention, no one could say exactly what, and in that instant Mr. Bingo shot Mr. O'Connor in the chest. He fell to the ground. His betrothed, schoolteacher Miss Susannah Mead, ran up screaming and dropped to her knees beside him. She gathered him into her arms, and there he died. It was to have been their wedding day.

Mr. O'Connor was born in 1860, in Albany, Georgia. He and his family moved to Fort Worth in 1868. He is survived by his sister, Charlotte. Mr. O'Connor was a respected, well-liked, long-time member of our fine community. A good man gunned down in his prime. When will the violence that taints our friendly town on this lovely prairie end?

Megan read the story dated April 13, 1890 in the *Fort Worth Gazette* then turned off the microfiche. She rose from the table, left the main library of Fort Worth, and headed to work.

***

Couples two-stepped around the floor to the music coming from the band on stage.

"Watch it!" hollered a young man.

Megan sprang back, jerking upright her tipped pitcher.

The man jumped up and shoved his chair back, barely missing a woman walking behind him. Two men sitting with him grabbed their beer mugs off the jostled table.

"I'm so sorry!" Megan grabbed a napkin off the table and dabbed the front of his wet shirt.

He knocked her hand away and scowled at her. "I just bought this damn shirt, lady." He looked down at himself. "Shit fire mother fuck."

"I'm very sorry. Here." Megan set the pitcher on the table. "It's on me."

His gaze hardened. "Half of it's on me."

"I'll bring you another pitcher—"

"Gee, thanks," he sneered.

"*Two* pitchers. I'm really very sorry."

He grumbled and sat down as she headed to the bar. She plopped on a stool, then dropped her head onto her crossed arms on the bar.

"I never took you for a Baptist," Bonnie said.

Megan raised her head. "What?"

Bonnie wiped a glass dry with a towel. "That's the fourth shirt you baptized tonight."

"Don't remind me." Megan lowered her head back to her arms. "At the rate I'm going, I won't make enough tonight to cover the alcohol I'm buying. And I won't drink a drop of it."

"Got a lot on your mind, I reckon, what with goin' home and all."

Megan kept her head down and closed her eyes. The only thing on her mind was Seth's death. It haunted her. She had known all along that he had died years ago but seeing it in black and white and knowing the details, the how and why, that he'd been shot in the chest and died in the street, had made it real. It felt like it had just happened. It messed with her head, squashed her spirit, and broke her heart. A tiny voice inside her reminded her that he was alive and well on the other side of the door in her room. Perhaps it was the voice of hope.

Hope. Faith. Love. You need all three, the other Megan had written.

I have love. Oh yes, I have love. I have hope. Faith? Well, two out of three ain't bad.

Bonnie said, "Think you can handle this order without performing another baptism?"

Megan stood, and picked up a tray with four mugs and three bottles of beer on it. She made a face at Bonnie, turned around, and rammed the tray into a big man's beer belly. Beer spilled all over the front of his shirt as the mugs fell over. The bottles crashed on the floor, followed by two mugs. The other two mugs rolled on the tray. People standing at the bar jumped out of the way.

The man with the beer-soaked shirt yelled, "What the hell!"

As Megan cleaned up the mess while Bonnie placated the man with free drinks, the manager walked up. He leaned an elbow on the bar. "Rough night, Megan?"

She wrung out a rag in the sink then draped it over the faucet. "I'm sorry, Joe. I'm all thumbs tonight, with two left feet."

"You want to leave early that's fine."

Her face heated up. She felt like a kid sent to the corner of the room for misbehaving. "Thanks. I will."

"Get those thumbs and feet under control. We have a big weekend ahead. I need you." He patted the bar, smiled at Bonnie, and moved on.

Bonnie leaned closer and said softly, "Gee, Megan. Tough break."

Megan shrugged. "I can't blame him. This place isn't making any money tonight with me here." She stepped behind the bar and grabbed her purse from a cabinet.

"What should I tell lover boy if he shows up?" Bonnie glanced around the bar area. "Actually, I'm kinda surprised Barton's not here."

"So am I. Tell him I went home, and I'll see him later this week."

During the taxi ride through empty streets to the B&B, Megan thought about the other Megan's letter. One part stuck in her mind. *The scattering cockroaches are important. They'll show you the   .*

The way? The portal? Darkened storefronts whizzed past the taxi window. *Time to check out the scattering cockroaches.*

Back in her room, she picked up the old coins from a shallow bowl on the dresser and tossed them on the floor. They rolled this way and that, scattering like—rolling coins. She tossed them in one corner, then another. None of the coins rolled anywhere in particular. She tried a couple of more places, until she realized they made lot of noise as they dropped and rolled on the wood floor. Maybe the noise bothered the people in the room below. She didn't need any more complaints about her. She put the coins back in the bowl and wondered how on earth she was supposed to find the portal.

The next morning, she called Detective Sullivan. "I'm sorry to say I haven't discovered anything about Barton. I've only seen him once. Sunday night. He was agitated, and I've never seen him so disheveled. He looked like he'd been rolling around in the dirt."

"Like he was roughed up?" the detective asked.

"Possibly. He didn't have any bruises or cuts or anything on his face, but something happened to him."

"Maybe his deal went south," the detective replied. "Keep me posted. You have my phone numbers. Call me any time. Even at home. *Any* time. And be careful."

"I will." She hung up, put his business card back in her wallet, then dialed Candace Huntington's number.

A couple of hours later, Megan was sitting in one of the Chippendale chairs facing the window, sipping lemongrass tea, and laughing at another tale of Candace's travels.

"I'm tickled you came to see me again, Miss Megan. I don't get many visitors these days." Candace sat in the matching chair, with a colorful quilt thrown over her lap. She lifted her face to the afternoon sun that made her scalp shine beneath the thinning crop of cottony hair. "It must be hot as blazes out there." Her crippled fingers pulled the edges of her robe closed over her nightgown. "I don't think you came here just to hear me rattle on about any old thing." Her sharp eyes met Megan's gaze. "You know about Mr. Seth."

Megan nodded. "I read about him in the library. I'd like to hear your version." She held up a hand when Candace started to speak. "I know you didn't witness it, and that you were only nine, and that it's hard for you to talk about it, but you know what really happened. You know the truth."

"The historical records don't mention you, do they?"

"Not a word. Please tell me."

Candace looked out the window where the neatly manicured lawn sloped down to the tree-shrouded street in the distance. A shaky sigh escaped her. She folded her hands together on her lap. "I reckon you need to know so you don't do the same thing again. Mind you," she tilted her head, "most of what I know Sarah told us. She was walking through town on the way to our house when she saw John Bingo at one end of the street and Mr. Seth at the other end. He was dressed for his wedding just hours away. Sarah said he looked so handsome. She'd always been sweet on him, just like many of the womenfolk were. No one else was on the street, although Sarah could see people peering out windows and huddling in doorways. Mr. Schwartz grabbed Sarah and pulled her inside his store where she crouched down beside a barrel of pickles and watched through a window. Mr. Seth and Bingo were hollering at each other. Sarah couldn't make out all the words, but she did hear your name."

"They were fighting over *me*? I mean *her*?"

Candace shrugged. "Sarah just said she heard your name amongst their shouting. No one had drawn a gun yet, but the tension was so thick in the air Sarah said a body could cut it with a butcher knife. Her papa was a butcher and she knew all about knives and knew how to use them. She could skin a rabbit quick as a blink. Why, one time—"

"What happened between Seth and Bingo?"

"What, dear?" Candace furrowed her brow, looking confused.

"You were telling me about the gunfight between Seth and Bingo," Megan patiently reminded Candace.

"Oh, yes, the gunfight." Candace tsked, shaking her head. "What a terrible, terrible day. The two men stood in the street exchanging insults. Sarah said she'd never seen Mr. Seth so mad. Then they got real quiet and just glared at each other, their hands poised over their guns. Sarah said she held her breath. She'd never seen a gunfight before. Me neither. I've seen a lot in my day but not an honest-to-God gunfight. Heavens no." A sudden smile curved the wrinkles in her face. "Did I ever tell you I once had dinner with Frank Sinatra?"

"Yes, you did. It must have been a wonderful evening." Megan propped her chin on her palm as she leaned her elbow on the armrest. "But you were telling me about the gunfight, remember?"

"Oh, that horrible gunfight. There they were, facing each other in the middle of the street, ready to shoot. Suddenly, *you*," Candace pointed a crooked finger at Megan, "darted out from somewhere shouting Mr. Seth's name. And Bingo shot Mr. Seth before he ever cleared leather."

Candace's gaze turned hard, and Megan saw a glimpse of the independent, formidable world-traveler the old woman had once been.

"He died because of *you,* Miss Megan. Because *you*—"

"Distracted him," Megan finished. She didn't bother correcting Candace's *you* with *her* or *she.* A difference of pronouns wouldn't dim the accusation in those green eyes.

"That instant Mr. Seth glanced at you was all Bingo needed to kill him."

Megan looked out the window. *They all probably hate me now. I don't blame them. It's all my fault,* the other Megan had written. *It certainly was,* Megan thought. "I wonder where she came running from? And why she did that?"

"It was a foolish thing to do. Absolutely foolish. Promise me you won't do that again."

"I won't. She must have been desperate. I wish she'd put all that in her letter." Megan reached for her teacup and took a sip. "What happened then?"

"You knelt beside Mr. Seth, and held his bleeding body in your arms, crying, while people gathered round. The doctor came but just shook his head. Mr. Seth died minutes later. Miss Susannah ran up screaming and shoved you away. She clasped Mr. Seth to her chest, sobbing, as his blood soaked her wedding dress. Then Miss Lottie showed up. When she saw Mr. Seth her face turned white, Sarah said. White as new-fallen snow. People told her what happened, and she lit into you, yelling and cursing and hitting you until someone pulled her off you. I wonder now if she instigated that mob you mentioned."

She's a tough cookie, rough around the edges, but I like her.

I like her? Holy moly! How could Megan write that about Lottie?

"The crowd grew," Candace said, "and pushed Sarah out of the way. She came to our house and told us the terrible news. Instead of Mr. Seth's wedding, the town prepared for his funeral. A sad, sad day."

"The funeral happened awful fast, didn't it? The next day?"

"That was Miss Lottie's wishes. She was never the same after that. None of Mr. Seth's friends were. His ranch hands tried to carry on without him but eventually John Bingo bought the spread. Then he bought Mr. Seth's saloon. Those days, Bingo was cock of the walk. Mr. Tim took to drinking. He must have finally accepted the fact that Miss Susannah wasn't ever going to marry him because he left town one day and never came back. Damn shame." Candace shook her head. "He surely loved Miss Susannah."

"What happened to her?"

"She taught school and helped at her papa's store. She never married. She died from a fever, in her fifties, I believe."

"And Lottie?"

"Poor Miss Lottie." Candace tsked. "Five, maybe six years after Mr. Seth died she hanged herself in her room."

Megan gasped. "In *my* room?"

"Why, yes, I suppose so." Candace raised her drawn-on eyebrows. "Do you ever feel her presence or spirit? See her ghost?"

"No. Nothing like that." Megan paused. "I wonder if *she* is the reason Seth is drawn to that room."

Candace placed her crippled fingers on Megan's arm. "It's you, Miss Megan. You're the only one who can change things and make it right."

A dry chuckle escaped Megan. "All those times I harped at Seth about not changing a thing. Now *I'm* the one that's supposed to change, apparently, everything." She blew out a breath, thinking of all the lives ruined by the other Megan's actions, overwhelmed by what lay ahead. Her gaze met Candace's. "Tell me about Seth. The Seth *you* knew. What was he like?"

Candace stared out the window, a distant look in her eyes. After a long pause, she said softly, "He was a friendly, cheerful man. Always nice to us young'uns. Most everybody liked him. But he had his faults too, mind you. Papa called Mr. Seth a dreamer. Said he was always looking so far ahead that he missed what was right in front of him. He also liked his liquor a little too much at times. Mama said he was a haunted man. I asked her if ghosts haunted him, but she'd just shake her head and tell me to get out from underfoot. Would you fetch that world history book from the bottom drawer?" Candace nodded at the nightstand.

Megan did so and sat back down in the Chippendale chair, holding the book.

"Take it with you. There's no need for anyone else to see it when I'm gone. Oh, don't look like that, Miss Megan." Candace patted Megan's arm. "I've had a wonderful life. I've so enjoyed our time together. But I'm very tired. I just want to sit here with the sun on my face and take a nap."

"And dream about Frank Sinatra?"

"Among others." Candace winked.

Megan stood and leaned over to hug Candace and kiss her wrinkled cheek. "Thank you so much for everything. Especially for waiting for me." Megan looked in the old woman's eyes. "I'll do it right this time. I promise. Next time around, you'll have your babies."

Candace's cold hands cupped Megan's face. "Do you love Mr. Seth?"

"More than anything."

"Then all will finally be the way it's supposed to be," Candace stated solemnly, then grinned. "Just think. The next time we see each other I'll be nine years old."

***

"Need a ride home?" Bonnie asked that night after closing time.

"No thanks," Megan replied. "You and Sam have fun."

"We're just gonna go somewhere and talk."

Megan laughed. "Talk, huh? Right."

Bonnie straightened the beer mugs and other glasses on the counter. "We talk a lot. About anything and everything. I think," she paused with one hand on a pitcher. "I think he's The One, Megan."

"You're in love with him?" Megan asked in surprise.

Bonnie nodded. "I think he feels the same way."

"I had no idea it was that serious." Megan smiled. "I'm so happy for you."

"I'm still gettin' used to it. I don't think I've ever felt this way." Bonnie furrowed her brow. "I wish you could be as happy."

"I will be. One day."

"Not with Barton, right?"

"No. Not Barton." *Hurry back to me.*

Bonnie put her hands on her hips and glanced around the dimly lit bar. "I think we're done here. You ready?"

"Just a sec." Megan went behind the bar and picked her purse up. She held it carefully, one hand grasping the strap, the other supporting the bottom.

Bonnie peered into the purse. "You got a bottle in there?"

Megan pulled the corked brown neck sticking out of the purse a little further out to show Bonnie. "An old whiskey bottle I saw in a thrift store today."

Bonnie's eyes widened. "You bought an old bottle? What for? We got tons of empties here."

"I like this one." Megan shoved the bottle back inside the purse. "It has character. Let's go. Sam's waiting for you."

The mention of Sam's name put a smile as wide as the Mississippi on Bonnie's face and she hurried out of the bar so fast Megan could hardly keep up.

On the cab ride to the B&B, she asked the driver to stop at the Water Gardens and wait for her, promising a big tip. She hurried through the dark on the concrete walkways beneath birds twittering in the trees. No one else was there at the late hour. She sat on a bench above the steps leading down to the terraced pool and by the light of the stars wrote a note on a piece of paper. A short message. Just three little words. The three most important words in the world. She signed it *MM* then stuck it inside the brown bottle and sealed it with the cork.

At the bottom of the steps, she glanced around to make sure no one was there to accuse of her littering, then tossed the bottle into the churning water. The bottle bobbed and swirled around and around then disappeared.

Gone where? Sunk to the bottom? Through the portal?

What are the odds that Seth will be the one to find it? Slim to none?

She looked up at the star-studded sky. *Please let him find it. So he'll know how I feel no matter what happens.* She scanned the pool once more but saw no bottle.

She climbed up the big block steps and sat on a bench. The expanse of white concrete between her and the steps stood out starkly in the darkness. Shadows from branches overhead softened the concrete edges and corners around the perimeter. The muffled roar of the water and the fluttering and chirping of birds were a welcome relief after the noise of the bar. A light breeze brushed her skin, easing the mugginess of the hot summer night. She put her elbows on the ledge behind her, leaned back, and stretched out her legs. With all that was going on—Seth, Barton, work, her impending trip back in time and all it entailed—it was nice to sit a moment and simply be.

The quiet serenity seeped into her. *I wish mom could see this place. She'd love it.*

Suddenly words from the other Megan's letter filled her mind. *It's just been in the last few days, with all this time to think, that I finally forgave myself for their deaths. I hope you can too. Don't wait until the end like I am. Do it now. Don't carry all that guilt and pain with you anymore. It serves no purpose and does no good. It doesn't change what happened. It only changes you. So forgive yourself.*

"She's right," Megan muttered. *I have important things to do, lives to save, lives to change. I don't need to haul all those bad feelings around with me like old luggage.*

She looked up at the sky. *I love you, Mom and Dad. I'm so sorry. I know you forgive me. You always did. You always would. And if you can forgive me ...*

Megan shot to her feet and hurried down the steps to the pool at the bottom. "I forgive myself. I forgive me." She thrust out her hands, fingers splayed, as if throwing another bottle into the water. One containing all the guilt, pain, loneliness, shame, and heartache that had shadowed her every moment since the night of the accident. She threw it all away into the water where it bobbed and swirled and disappeared into the depths.

A long exhale of relief escaped her, and a feeling of lightness filled her. All that old luggage was gone.

"Thanks, other Megan," she whispered. "You were right. Now all I have to do is find that portal."

She had nine days to do so.

Chapter 28

Barton smoothed hair off Megan's forehead and smiled down at her. "I'm glad we finally got together."

She had her head pillowed on his lap while he leaned back against a tree in the Fort Worth Botanic Gardens. A few yards away, a bed of perennials hosted butterflies and hummingbirds and buzzed with bees.

"Me too. It's been hectic at work the last couple of nights." She held up her hand to shade her eyes from the sunlight filtering through overhead leaves and glanced at her watch. *An hour and a half? That's all we've been here?* They had strolled around the gardens, then sat on a blanket beneath the tree and ate sandwiches, potato chips, a bunch of grapes, and drank from a thermos of iced tea, all courtesy of Barton. She should be looking for that portal, which still eluded her despite searching her room from top to bottom over and over the last couple of days. But Detective Sullivan was counting on her, so here she was. She trailed her finger down the front of Barton's shirt. "It's so peaceful here."

She no sooner said the words than a group of little kids ran out of the rose garden and raced across the sunlit grass, laughing and screaming all the way. Several women, one of them pushing a stroller, trailed behind the kids.

"You were saying?" Barton asked.

Megan laughed. "More peaceful than work. I'm glad we came. I imagine this place will be packed tomorrow. Do they shoot off fireworks here?"

"I don't know." He caught her hand in his and kissed her knuckles. "My family always goes to the lake on the fourth."

"Is that what you're doing tomorrow?"

He nodded.

"What lake?"

"Granbury. Want to come?" He linked his fingers with hers.

"Can't. Work." With her free hand, she scratched an itch on her thigh just below the hem of her shorts. Two motorcycles rumbled by on the road through the garden. "You going to the lake on Sunday too?"

"I have to work."

"On a holiday weekend? You sure have a strange job."

He chuckled. "Jim and I have to go over some papers."

"At your place?"

"My office. Wish I could see you sometime this weekend."

"You know where I'll be. Good old work. Sunday's my last day."

Barton's eyes searched her face. "I wish you weren't leaving."

She freed her hand from his and pushed herself up to sit facing him. "Don't start that again." She drew her knees up to her chest. "You know I have to go home sooner or later."

He ran his hand up her calf. "Stay. Just a little longer."

"I can't. Mrs. Powell is waiting for me to leave so the plumbing can be fixed."

"You can stay with me."

Her eyes widened.

"Why not? I have a spare room." He rested his hand on her knee. "You can have it. No strings attached."

What about Tammy? she almost asked. *Gonna kick her to the curb?* Maybe they didn't live together, but according to Officer Sunglasses, they were a long-time couple.

"I'll put a lock on the door," he offered when she didn't respond, "if that'll make you feel better."

Dappled sunlight danced over his coal-black hair. His gray t-shirt outlined his pectoral muscles and triceps. With those bright blue eyes and that movie star handsome face, he was a fine-looking man. *Too bad he's a lying, womanizing drug dealer. What a waste. What a fool.*

She swatted a bug off her arm. "You forget I have to give that talk in Chicago next Saturday." *I hope not. I have nothing prepared. Nothing!*

"Go give your talk, then come back." He put pressure on her knee as he scooted closer, shoving aside a copy of the newspaper he'd brought with him. "I have a better idea." He grinned. "I'll go with you."

She jerked back. *"What?"*

"It's perfect!" His grin widened. "You can show me the sights. I haven't been to Chicago in years. I can meet your friends. See where you grew up. It'll be great! We'll pack up your things and bring it all back here. What do you say, Megan?" He looked like an eager puppy, all but wagging his back end.

She dropped her gaze from his. She reached out to smooth the newspaper flat. "Barton, I don't think—oh no." A headline caught her eye. *Last Member of One of Fort Worth's Oldest Families Dies at 100.* She picked up the paper.

"What?"

"Candace Huntington died."

"Who?"

"The old woman I had lunch with earlier this week." Megan read the obituary and felt a burn in her eyes. A picture of Candace as a young woman accompanied the headline. "She died in her sleep Wednesday night." She handed the paper to Barton.

"Quite a looker. Five husbands?" He whistled. "Sounds like a Black Widow."

"It was all very tragic." Megan wiped sweat off her face, along with tears. "Her first husband died when their house burnt down. The second one died in a train wreck. One died of a fever in Cairo, and the last one of old age."

"That's only four." Barton handed her back the paper. "What about the fifth one?"

"That would be Freddie, the middle one. What I read in the library said he died of unknown causes. I meant to ask Candace about him but forgot. Now I'll never know. She was a remarkable woman."

"Sounds like she had quite a life."

You have no idea. "Darn it. The paper's torn right in the middle of the obit."

"I'll get you another copy."

Her gaze darted to Barton. "That's-that's very nice of you." *What a waste!* she thought again. At times, he was so thoughtful.

"Come here, darlin'," he said, his voice husky. "I'll show you nice." He put his arm around her, lowered her to the blanket, and kissed her.

Later, she might tell Donna how she endured 15, maybe 20 minutes of making out with Barton. How she suffered through it, doing her public service. In truth, he was a good kisser, and knew how to make a woman feel alive. *He's a good actor too,* she reminded herself while he nuzzled her neck and slipped his hand beneath her shirt to rest warm on her side. He sometimes almost convinced her that he really cared for her. *It's too bad he is who he is, and I love a dead cowboy. If things were different, I might have loved him.*

Megan tore her mouth from his and pushed him away. "I'm sorry, Barton, but it's too hot out here. I'm sweating like crazy." She sat up, wiping her hand across her brow as proof.

"Your room is air conditioned. We could go back there."

"I don't think Mrs. Powell would be too happy to see you."

"That bad huh?"

"Yeah." She looked at her watch. "I hate to be a wet blanket, but do you mind if we leave? This sun and heat drains me, and I have a long night ahead at work. Friday night on a holiday weekend, it'll be crazy."

Barton pressed his lips together and leaned back. His gaze swept over her, then he blew out a loud sigh. "All right. But will you at least think about what I said? You can stay with me as long as you like."

"I'll think about it."

Once on the road, he stopped at a convenience store and bought her another copy of the paper from a newspaper machine.

"You going to her funeral?" He shifted into first gear, then smoothly into second.

Megan had the paper opened to the obituary on her lap. She nodded. "It's Monday morning at eleven. I just remembered. Candace knew John Bingo."

Barton glanced away from the road. "No kiddin'? Well I'll be. She must have been just a kid. Damn, I wish I'd known that before she died. I would have liked to talk to her. I reckon she'd have a lot of stories about my great-grandfather. She say anything about him?"

"She described him as slick-haired and shifty-eyed." Seth's words, but Barton didn't know that.

Barton laughed.

Megan went on, "She said he was cock of the walk after the famous gunfight."

"She knew about that? It's part of our family lore. Did she see it?"

"No. But a girl that worked for her family saw the whole thing and told Candace, who was nine at the time." Megan listened to the now familiar hum of the engine as Barton shifted gears to stop at a four-way. "What do you know about the gunfight?"

"John Bingo had problems for a long time with some two-bit saloon owner, who was also the brother of John's favorite whore. Her name was Lottie. My granny would raise a stink whenever anyone mentioned *that woman,* as granny called Lottie. Granny never knew who her mama was. She was raised by a widow woman and all she knew was that her mama was a prostitute."

He laughed at Megan's surprise. "Yep, my great-granny was a whore. Supposedly in the same brothel this Lottie was. Granny always blamed *that woman* for keeping her father away from her and the other kids, even though they were all right here in Fort Worth. Guess John didn't visit very often although he seemed to care for them financially. She said they didn't have much, but they didn't go without either. She was the oldest of four kids, all with different mothers, all fathered by John." Barton accelerated across the intersection. "Anyway, one day, John and the whore's brother—I can't think of his name—had it out. Supposedly over a woman." Barton grinned. "Isn't it always over a woman? John shot the other guy dead. And that was the last great gunfight on the streets of Fort Worth. Quite a claim to fame, huh?"

Megan looked out the passenger side window, missing that two-bit saloon owner.

"My granny was one mean woman," Barton went on. "She had a rough time growin' up and I guess it made her mad at the world. She didn't take any crap from us kids." He gave a little laugh. "My sister was terrified of her. I adored her. She taught me a lot."

Like how to be mean?

Barton tapped his finger on the steering wheel. "Wish I could think of that guy's name. I've seen his gravestone."

A jolt shot through her. "You have?"

"I was riding my bike with my buddies one day. We were early teens maybe. We cut through Oakwood Cemetery, and the chain came off one kid's bike. While he was fixin' it, I wandered around, and happened upon a name I recognized. Seth!" Barton slapped the steering wheel. "That's it. Seth O'Connor." He looked at Megan, a look of puzzlement on his face. "Isn't that *your friend's* name?"

"Why, yes, it is. How odd." She glanced at the obituary. Candace's final resting place would be in Oakwood Cemetery.

Barton parked in front of the B&B. He killed the engine and turned to Megan. "So, are we going to Chicago next week?"

His direct words and gaze jerked her back to the present and caught her off guard. "I—I don't know. This is so sudden."

"It'll give us a chance to get to know each other better."

"How can you take off from work on such short notice, and for how long?"

"Don't worry about that. I hope I'll be quitting my job soon."

"You are? Why?"

Barton looked out the windshield a moment. His fingers drummed the steering wheel. "I have a big business deal brewing. If it pans out, I'll be kissing that job goodbye." His eyes met hers. "You and I could kiss all this goodbye and go somewhere else. Maybe to that secluded island somewhere."

"It must be one hell of a deal."

"It is. I'll tell you all about it while we're having dinner in the Sears Tower overlooking Lake Michigan. I'll tell you everything I've been wanting to tell you for some time now."

"Barton, I—"

"Okay, okay." He held up his hand. "I can see you're not too keen on my idea. How about this. Come to my place Monday evening. I'll make dinner. You can check out the spare room." He took her hand. "Maybe spend the night. Alone in your own room, if that's what you want." A slight smile curved his lips. "Although I hope not."

Damn, he's persistent! "I don't know what to say."

He leaned closer. "Say yes. Come to dinner. Spend the night with me. Whether we sleep together or not doesn't matter."

She raised her eyebrows. "It doesn't?"

He regarded her silently for a moment. "I have to confess that I can't remember the last time I waited this long to have sex with a woman. It's different with you, though, because—" he looked down at their joined hands then met her gaze "—because I've fallen in love with you, Megan."

Oh crap!

"And I'm willing to wait as long as it takes to win your heart. You're not just a roll in the sack." His free hand reached over to cup her face. "You're ... so much more." He gazed into her eyes. "I know you're not in love with me. Not yet anyway. Can you give me a chance? Come to my place Monday?"

I might get some information for Detective Sullivan. Even if it's after the big weekend deal, it might help. She smiled. "I'll come for dinner. We'll take it from there."

Joy lit his face. He leaned in for a quick kiss. "I'll pick you up—"

"I'll take a cab. That way you can concentrate on dinner."

"If that's what you want. Let me find something to write on." He bent over to open the glove box where he dug around and pulled out a piece of paper and a pen. He scribbled something on the paper and handed it to her. "Here's my address. I'll call you Monday to set a time. Although I'll probably see you at work this weekend."

Megan stuffed the paper in her wallet, next to Detective Sullivan's card.

Barton got out of the car and walked around to open her door and help her out. He took her in his arms, his chin resting on top of her head. "I love you, Megan. God, it feels good to finally say that." His embrace tightened briefly then he drew away. "I'll see you soon." He bent his head for one last kiss, then waited beside his car until she entered the B&B.

Megan went to the house phone and dialed the number at Candace Huntington's home, hoping to talk to Rosalita. The phone just rang and rang. Megan hung up then dialed a number at the police station. "Detective Sullivan? This is Megan. I have some more information for Officer Sunglas-I mean Officer Clark." She repeated everything Barton had said that might be connected to his alleged drug dealing.

For the rest of the night, during everything she did, and when she finally went to bed, in the back of her mind loomed the image of a gravestone with Seth's name chiseled on it.

***

The last great gunfight on the streets of Fort Worth took place in front of the Silver Slipper Saloon on April 13, 1890. Facing off was John Bingo (prominent business owner and City Council member) and Seth O'Connor (local saloon owner and long-time resident). Witnesses claim something distracted Mr. O'Connor and in that instant Mr. Bingo shot Mr. O'Connor. He died in the dusty street. Lawmen investigated the duel and declared it legal. Mr. Seth O'Connor was buried in Oakwood Cemetery. Mr. John Bingo went on to become one of Fort Worth's most successful businessmen. He died in 1907 while traveling back to his native state of Ohio, his first trip back east in 35 years.

Megan read the wood-framed, glass-covered notice outside The Silver Slipper Old Time Saloon on North Main Street. She didn't know how she had missed it. She had walked by that storefront many times during the last few months. All this time she had purposely avoided discovering the date and circumstances of Seth's death, and there it was, in broad daylight for all to see.

That notice has to go.

She turned her back on it and headed to work.

"Your last night, eh, Megan?" Officer Bubba stood beside his squad car outside The Tejas as she walked up. "Won't be the same without you. Bonnie's pretty tore up over you leaving."

"I'll miss her too." Megan paused beside Bubba. She wiped off sweat trickling down her neck from the late afternoon heat.

"She's also very proud of your article. So am I. You did a good job."

"Thanks. Although I couldn't have written it without her." The second part of her methamphetamine article was in that day's paper. "Speaking of Bonnie, what's your opinion of Sam?"

"I like him. I think he's good for her."

"I do too." She leaned closer and asked softly, "Any news about Barton you can share?"

"He wasn't at the lake yesterday like he said he'd be. He spent all day at that trailer in the country."

***

"There she is." Bonnie grinned. "We were just talking about you."

Megan eyed Bonnie and the group of regulars gathered at the bar. "No wonder my ears are burning. I thought it was from that hot sun."

A burly truck driver leaned toward her. "I just got back in town. What's this bullshit you're leaving us?" He put his hand on his chest. "Was it something I said?"

"Pro'bly, ya big dumb ox." A construction worker pointed his finger at the truck driver. "Always runnin' your head when you shouldn't be. All your fault our favorite gal is hightailin' it back across the Red River."

The group erupted into friendly insults blaming each other for Megan's leaving.

Soon they had Megan, Bonnie, and two other waitresses laughing.

A young man who taught high school said loudly, "I must commend Megan on the second half of her article in today's paper." He raised his glass to her. "Well done, Megan."

"You mean there's more?" one of the regulars asked.

"Sure is." Bonnie patted a stack of newspapers on top of the bar. "I just happen to have some copies."

The regulars snatched up the papers and started reading.

Megan and Bonnie smiled at each other over the men's bent heads.

"You wanna go out with me and the girls again tonight for a little while?" Bonnie asked.

"You bet," Megan replied.

On the jukebox, Hank Williams, Jr. sang *Texas Women*.

Joe walked up. "Y'all runnin' a library now?"

"They're reading the second part of Megan's article," Bonnie said. "Front page of the section again."

Joe chuckled. "I know. Good job, Megan. You're a hell of a writer. But if you ever come back to Fort Worth and need a job, you got one right here."

"Thank you, Joe. Kind of bittersweet." She glanced around the bar. "Last night and all. It's certainly been an experience." The hardest job she'd ever had.

"What are you doing Tuesday night?" Joe asked.

Megan shrugged. "Packing." *Looking for the portal—again.*

Joe leaned an elbow on the bar. "I'm having a combination employee appreciation and going away party for you on Tuesday night. Order some barbeque. Drink specials. It's usually a slow night and almost everybody's off. I thought it'd be a good time to get everyone together and show my thanks for all your hard work."

"Sounds good." Bonnie put a head on a beer. "We can get all gussied up."

"That's nice of you, Joe." Megan put her purse behind the bar. "I'll be here." *If I haven't found the portal yet.*

Some of the regulars had inclined their heads Joe's way.

Joe looked at the group. "Y'all clowns are invited too."

They cheered and raised their beers.

The truck driver shouted, "Next round is on me!"

***

Later in her shift, Megan saw Julia outside the restroom.

"Hey, Megan, I really liked your article."

"Thanks. You look pretty tonight." Julia's usually stringy, mousey brown hair was clean and brushed, her speech was normal, her eyes clear.

A shy smile crossed the younger woman's face. "I been makin' some changes. An' I need a change. I wanted to tell you goodbye."

"You're coming Tuesday night, right? We'll see each other then."

Julia shook her head. "I'm leavin' tomorrow. I'm fixin' to stay with my cousin for a few months in Galveston."

"Why?"

"I need to get away from-from things 'round here for a while."

She needs to get away from the meth.

"Thanks for havin' that woman from social services contact me. She's been a big help."

Megan hugged Julia. "I wish you all the best."

Julia drew away. "Megan? Barton ain't all he seems to be. He's-he's trouble."

"I know. Hopefully he'll soon be getting what he deserves."

Julia's eyes widened. "I hope so. You be careful 'round him."

***

"Last call!" Bonnie hollered.

Barton ran through the thinning crowd up to the bar.

"You made it just in time." Bonnie put away a clean glass and wiped her hands. "The usual?"

"Where's Megan?" he demanded.

"Right here."

Barton spun around.

"What's wrong?" Megan put her tray on the bar. He had a wild-eyed, frantic look. His hair stood up, as if he'd plowed his hand through it a hundred times.

He took her elbow and drew her aside. "I just-just needed to see you. Can I give you a ride home?"

"I'm going out with Bonnie and her friends."

"Again?" He shot a glare Bonnie's way. "You just went out with them the other night."

"And I'm going out with them again tonight." Megan sounded sharper than she had intended and softened her tone. "Sorry, but we already made plans. You look upset. What's the matter?"

He looked away. "Nothin'. Nothin' at all. Everything's just peachy." He practically spit out the last word.

Megan made another round of the tables, collecting empties, and saying goodnight to the customers. Many wished her well, and some of the regulars hugged her. The truck driver planted a sloppy kiss on her lips and promised her a dance Tuesday night.

Barton leaned back against the bar, smoking a cigarette, a scowl on his face.

The lights came on. People drifted towards the exit. The jukebox quit.

"Something going on Tuesday?" Barton asked Megan as she tossed empty bottles and trash into a trashcan.

"Joe's having a party for the employees. Barton, I'm sorry, but you have to leave so we can close."

He straightened up. "You sure I can't give you a ride?"

"Not tonight."

He pulled her against him, pressing her cheek to his shirt. It reeked of cigarettes. "I miss you, darlin'. Want to spend as much time with you as I can." He drew away. "You're coming for dinner tomorrow, right?" His tone had a hard edge.

"That's my plan."

"I'll call you in the afternoon." He kissed her then said softly in her ear, "I love you, darlin'. When I finally get you with me I may not want to let you go."

He released her and walked away, ignoring Bonnie's, "'Night, sugar." She looked at Megan. "What's his beef?"

"He misses me." Megan watched him leave. His parting words almost sounded like a threat.

**

A hot breeze stirred the petals of the flowers piled around the casket waiting to be lowered into the ground. "It was a beautiful funeral, Rosalita." Megan stood beside Candace's housekeeper in Oakwood Cemetery, the final resting place of many Fort Worth residents since its founding in 1879.

"I'm pleased you came, Meess Megan." Rosalita adjusted her veiled black hat. "Meessy enjoyed your veeseets so much."

"I did too. She was quite a woman. What will become of her house? Her things? Will you be all right?"

"She donated the house and antiques to the historeecal society. The rest weell be sold, the money geeven to chareeties. She very generous, Meessy was. Even to me." Rosalita wiped her eyes. "Most everyone who came today was from a chareety or group she supported."

There had been maybe 20 people at the funeral. Bankers. Lawyers. Business people. No family. No friends, except Megan and Rosalita. Megan's face felt tight from crying over an old woman she barely knew yet shared an incredible bond with. "Someone asked me if I was a great-granddaughter."

Rosalita waved her hand around the burial plot. "She should be surrounded by family. She should have had cheeldren. She would have been a good mama." Her voice broke on the last word.

You'll have your babies next time, Megan silently promised.

"She wanted me to geeve you sometheeng." Rosalita dug in her black beaded bag. "She spent her last day going through old papers and peectures. I heard her laughing and weeping. She even burned some theengs. That evening she gave me thees for you." Rosalita handed Megan a folded over piece of paper.

Megan unfolded an old, wrinkled, yellowed newspaper clipping. It pictured a smiling young man in front of a building, his raised hand pointing to the sign overhead proclaiming *The Panther Saloon*. She inhaled sharply. *I'd know that smile anywhere.* The caption read *Seth O'Connor celebrates the opening of his saloon.*

Fresh tears stung Megan's eyes as she stared at the grainy picture. *Thank you, Candace. How many times have I wished I had a picture of him? Bless you.*

"She write sometheeng on back."

Megan turned it over, read Candace's elegantly written message, and laughed.

Had I been older you might have had a fight on your hands for him.

After hugging Rosalita goodbye, Megan walked to the older section of the cemetery. She wandered among the weatherworn tombstones, many ornate crosses and statues, some just an old wooden board stuck upright in the earth, the names and dates eroded by the elements and time. A roadrunner darted across the path. It jumped up on the head of a concrete angel and perched briefly before hitting the ground running. The scent of new mown grass rose like a perfume in the heat of the day.

Megan stopped. Her breath caught somewhere between her lungs and her throat.

In the shade of a massive pecan tree, a flat, plain gravestone inches above the ground bore the chiseled name *Seth Jeremiah O'Connor*.

Heedless of her black dress and high heels, she knelt on the grass. Memories of him flooded her mind. The first night he ran into her room, a youth of seventeen. His wide grin when he drank his first cold beer.

His scowl as he stared at a plate of Mexican fast food and stated it didn't look like any Mexican food he'd ever seen. The look on his face as they made love in the moonlight. The way he said *Miss Megan*.

She traced his weathered name with the same finger that had traced his lips mere nights ago.

Jeremiah. I never knew that. March 10. Never knew his birthday either. She ran her finger along the dash that represented a life of 30 years. That dash said nothing about him. Not what kind of man he had been. Or that he had been a time-traveling cowboy. Or that he was the man she loved. Dead or alive. Here and now, or there and then, or anywhere, any time.

Her gaze moved to the date that had to be changed. April 13, 1890.

She pressed her hand to the cool grass covering his remains six feet under.

I'll change it. I promise. I'm coming, Seth. I'm coming!

***

Megan entered her room at the B&B. She went to the vanity, tossed Barton's picture into the trashcan, and propped Seth's picture next to the taped-up one of her. She looked around the room, muttering, "Time to find that damn portal."

Several unsuccessful hours later, she sat, dejected, at the table, eating tacos. Dust motes drifted in the evening light streaming through the windows. The air conditioner hummed softly.

She started to take another bite, then stopped. "Oh no. Barton." She had completely forgotten about dinner at his place. *I bet he's mad!* He had said he'd call in the afternoon, and he never did, as far as she knew. Maybe Mrs. Powell had been gone all day, and the phone downstairs had just rang and rang.

"Hopefully I'll never see him again," she muttered, and finished eating.

She studied the other Megan's letter, certain there was a clue she was missing. She stayed up late tossing old coins on the floor and feeling the walls, looking for the portal. She felt like banging her head against the wall in frustration.

The next morning, two days before her flight back to Chicago, she half-heartedly started to pack. She also packed a plain leather purse for a trip back to the past—just in case. Into it went her birth control pills, a toothbrush, a small notebook, a pencil, a pair of sunglasses, and as many tampons as she could stuff in it. Foolish, probably, to consider taking those things, but packing them made her feel like she was accomplishing *something* to go back in the past.

***

"We clean up pretty good, don't we?" Bonnie brushed her hair in front of the mirror in the restroom at work. She wore a summery yellow dress with spaghetti straps. Gold hoops dangled from her ears.

"We certainly do." Megan fluffed her curls. "Sam can't take his eyes off you."

"Barton's tongue would be hanging out if he saw you."

Megan smoothed her red dress over her hips. It had a full skirt that swished around her knees when she walked, a square neckline, and short sleeves. Her red shoes had T-straps and two-inch heels. She'd decided to put her problems aside for the night and go all out for the party at work. One way or the other, she was leaving soon.

"Where's Barton?" Bonnie asked. "Didn't you invite him?"

"Nope." She hadn't heard a word from Barton. "I want to have fun."

Bonnie laughed. "I'm gonna miss you and your shenanigans with that hunk." She sobered and the look in her eyes softened. "I'm gonna miss you."

"Oh no you don't. Don't start that now. We're having fun tonight, remember? It's party time." She linked her arm with Bonnie's and they walked out of the restroom.

Hours later, Megan plopped down on her chair, out of breath from dancing. She had a belly full of barbeque, and a nice beer buzz.

"Havin' fun?" Bonnie asked from across the table. She leaned against Sam, who had his arm around her.

"A blast. You?"

"She's smashed," Sam replied. "I'd better take her home."

Bonnie struggled to sit up straight. "But we're schupossed to give 'er a ride home," she slurred. Her eyelids drooped, and one of her earrings was missing.

"I'll take a cab," Megan replied. "Don't worry."

Sam stood and helped Bonnie up. She swayed then stumbled toward Megan, who got to her feet just as Bonnie threw her arms around her. "Tomorrow. Call me. We'll have lunch or-or schomething. Thish ishn't goodbye."

"I'll call. I love you, Bonnie." Megan looked at Sam. "Take care of her."

"I will." He grinned. "For a long time, I hope."

After they left, Megan partied until closing time. She called for a cab and hugged everyone goodbye. The hot muggy night wrapped around her like an oven mitt as she waited on the sidewalk for the cab. Insects gathered around the lights. A crescent moon hung above the trees. It looked like a lopsided smile, reminding her of the other Megan.

Maybe it is a sign.

Her spirits, already high from the dancing, fun, friends, and beer, soared. Maybe tonight she'd find the portal. She did a little dance while humming a Willie Nelson song.

Headlights bounced as a car pulled into the far side of the parking lot and came toward her.

She stepped to the curb, anxious to return to the B&B and find her way to Seth.

A red Corvette drove up and stopped.

Her spirits plunged. Her shoulders drooped. *Barton.*

Chapter 29

Barton left his car running and got out. He walked around the front of it, then stopped in the glare of the headlights and whistled. "I wish you'd showed up at my place last night wearing that."

"I'm sorry about last night." Megan took a step toward him. "After the funeral I—"

He held up a hand. "I don't need to hear your excuses."

"I feel awful about it, and—and want to explain. After the funeral, I started packing. Then took a nap. When I woke up, it was dark outside. I must have been exhausted. I'm sorry." She smiled. "I was looking forward to a home-cooked meal."

"I called the B&B several times. It just rang and rang." Barton put his hands in the pockets of his jeans. "Look, Megan. I knew it was a long shot. You and me. You're ready to go home. I get that. But I hoped you felt something for me." He shrugged. "I guess it wasn't meant to be."

She stepped to the edge of the curb. "I've enjoyed our time together. Thank you for taking me around and showing me the sights."

"I enjoyed it too. I just wish ..." He looked away and blew out a sigh. "Well, it doesn't matter now." His gaze returned to her. "Can I give you a ride to the B&B?"

She glanced at the street. "My cab should be here any minute."

"For old time's sake?"

Megan fiddled with her purse strap. She didn't want to ride anywhere with him. He might get his hopes up. He'd want to kiss her. She wanted to be done with him. Every instinct in her screamed, *Don't get in his car!*

Detective Sullivan came to mind. She had yet to give him any useful information. He was relying on her. He had believed her innocent despite incriminating evidence. She owed him for that.

If she wanted out of Barton's car, she'd open the door and bail out. She might get banged up—cuts, bruises, scrapes—but she'd survive because, supposedly, she was indestructible.

I hope.

Candace survived fires, plane crashes, an anaconda. What's a short car ride?

"All right. For old time's sake."

He grinned and walked over to open the passenger side door for her. She tossed her purse on the floorboard and climbed in. The hum of the engine almost drowned out the sound of a soft click after Barton shut the door.

Once behind the wheel, Barton drove off just as people came out of The Tejas and the taxi pulled in the far side of the parking lot. It occurred to Megan that no one knew she had left with him.

"Did you have fun tonight?" Barton shifted gears as he headed down a deserted street, taking a different route than usual.

"Tons. Danced almost every dance."

"The guys must have been lined up for you."

She laughed. "Hardly. I danced with the girls too. Bonnie and I took a spin around the floor. She got pretty drunk and her boyfriend took her home early." She bit her lower lip, realizing her mistake.

"Bonnie's boyfriend was there, huh? Were other boyfriends there? Or was I the only one not invited?"

"You've been so busy and—and upset lately. I didn't think—"

"About me. Obviously." He reached into his shirt pocket, pulled out a cigarette, and lit it. Smoke filled the car.

She tried to roll down the window.

"It won't open," Barton said.

"Then open yours." She waved smoke away.

He cracked his window and kept smoking. They came to I-35W. He turned north on it.

Megan looked at him. "The B&B is the other way. Where are you going?"

He accelerated and merged onto the freeway. "To see the Goat Man of Greer Island."

"*What?*" Megan shot up straight in the seat.

"I said I'd take you there. Remember?"

"This late? Dressed like *this*?"

"It's the perfect time. Everyone knows that monsters come out at night."

The Corvette sped up the freeway beneath a sea of stars surrounding the crescent moon. That lopsided smile suddenly looked like an evil caricature of the smiley face on Jim's briefcase.

"Turn around. Take me home."

He stubbed out his cigarette in the ashtray and kept on driving.

"Please, Barton."

"There's nowhere to turn around." He switched lanes to pass a semi.

Megan gripped the armrest as he jerked the car back to the right lane and accelerated. He stared ahead, his stern profile outlined by the headlights of vehicles heading south.

She hit his arm. "Damn it, Barton. Pull over."

The car swerved to the shoulder and came to a sudden stop. He put it in park, set the brake, then turned to her, resting his arm on the steering wheel. "Happy?"

She pushed the door handle. It didn't budge. The door was locked. She twisted around and pulled on the lock button. It wouldn't unlock. She glared at him. "Open the damn door."

"Can't."

"What do you mean can't?"

"I know a guy. He fixed it so once it's locked from the outside it can only be unlocked from the outside."

She remembered that soft click after he'd shut the door. "Then get out and open it."

He stared at her, his face hard as stone.

She tried the window again.

"I told you it won't open."

"Why not?"

"Same guy."

The blood drained from her face.

Barton went on, "It's amazing what people will do for a little bit of meth."

"So it's true."

"That I deal meth?" He nodded. "Want some?"

Megan shoved her shoulder against the door again and again.

"Won't do any good, darlin'."

"Don't you darlin' me." She yanked off one of her shoes and beat the two-inch heel on the window, trying to break the glass.

"Stop it, damn it." He grabbed her shoulder.

She turned and beat him with the heel. His head, face, anywhere.

He hollered and cursed, blocking her blows until he knocked her arm away. The shoe hit the floorboard.

Pain exploded in her brain when the back of his hand hit her face so hard her forehead and nose rammed the back of the seat. She gasped for air. Her ears rang. A metallic taste filled her mouth. The right side of her face throbbed. She touched it gingerly, then struggled to sit up, pushing hair out of her face. Her tongue found a cut on her upper lip. She stared at Barton through tears she couldn't control.

"You bastard." A bloody gash on his forehead gave her an absurd amount of satisfaction.

"You're not going anywhere. *Darlin'*. The only way out of the car is through me."

I guess that means while you're in my car you're at my mercy, he had said months ago when he learned she didn't own a car, or drive anymore, and had driven a stick shift only once years ago. The chill she remembered feeling then seemed tropical compared to the cold fear that gnawed her stomach and made her heart pound as loud as a hail of bombs. *This can't be happening!*

Headlights shown in the rear window and lit up the interior.

Barton looked in the rearview mirror. "Shit."

Megan craned her neck to look out the back window. A pickup pulled up behind them and stopped. A small sob of relief escaped her when a man got out of the truck and walked toward the Corvette.

Something hard and cold pressed against the side of her head.

She froze.

"Don't get any bright ideas. Or I'll blow a hole in that pretty head of yours."

Megan struggled to breath.

"You gonna behave?"

"Y—yes."

"Keep your mouth shut. And wipe that blood off your lip." Barton lowered the gun and held it beside him on the seat. He swiped his other forearm across the cut on his forehead.

She pressed herself against the door, and gently rubbed her knuckles across her split lip. Her face hurt. Her heart raced. *Would I survive a bullet in my head?* She rubbed goose bumps on her arms, knowing the answer. *Universe? Is this how my turn ends?*

Barton rolled down his window.

An old man bent down and peered inside. "Evenin', folks. Y'all doin' all right?"

"Just fine, sir," Barton replied. "Me and my gal are havin' a talk, is all."

"Thought y'all might be havin' car trouble or somethin' and figgered I better check on you."

"That's mighty neighborly of you."

"We gotta look out for each other, eh?" He tipped his head sideways and looked at Megan. "You doin' all right there, little lady?"

Barton kept the gun pointed at her.

"Yes." She cleared her throat before adding, "Just fine."

"Okie dokie then. Y'all have a good night."

"You too, sir." Barton waved his hand.

The old man straightened, patted the roof of the car then went back to his pickup.

Acid fear burned holes in her stomach as she watched him drive away.

"Now." Barton turned back to her. "Where were we?"

"Wh—why are you doing this?" She fought to keep her voice steady. Her mouth felt as dry as the Sahara. "What do you want from me?"

"Hmmm. What do I want." He draped his arm on the steering wheel again while his other hand held the gun steady on her. "For starters, I want you to pull down the top of your dress."

"What?"

"I said, pull down the top of your dress." He paused. "I won't ask again."

She worked up enough moisture to spit in his face.

A hard slap knocked her head to one side. More slaps followed, rocking her head from side to side, until she slumped in the seat, dazed and breathless, limp with pain. He ripped the neckline of her dress open and shoved her bra straps down her arms. Cold air from the air conditioner chilled her breasts as he freed them from her bra.

Her eyes fluttered open just in time to see Barton pick up his gun off his lap and point it at her again. She blinked tears from her eyes and pressed back against the seat. Her chest heaved with her quickened breathing. Blood trickled from the sides of her mouth. Cold sweat soaked her armpits. Her fuzzy brain struggled to find an escape from the monster beside her.

Barton flipped on the dome light.

The harsh brightness made her blink.

"You've been mighty stingy with those, darlin'. About time I get to see them."

She spit at him again.

He wiped his face with his sleeve. "You want it rough, keep it up." He gazed at her breasts. "Not very big, are they."

"Bigger than Tammy's," she snapped.

He laughed. "You got a point there. I guess your detective friend told you about her. Oh?" He tipped his head. "Surprised I know about that? Like I said, it's amazing what people will do for a little bit of meth. Even cops. Knowing an addict in the police department has come in mighty handy. That Mexican sings like a bird for me once a week. He recently told me all about your little visits with Detective Sullivan. I figured the first few were to get information for your article. Which, by the way," he waved the gun in her face, "fucked up my big deal the last two weekends. Got my guy to worrying about the exposure and the cops and he got cold feet."

"Pity."

"You're making the next delivery."

She drew in a sharp breath. "No, I'm not."

His ice-cold blue eyes bore into hers. "Oh yes you are."

An 18-wheeler rumbled by, making the car shake. Megan hardly noticed. She already shook like a leaf in a windstorm.

"Too bad you can't report that to the cops." His leaned closer and drew his left forefinger down a blue vein in her right breast. "Has Seth seen these?"

"Lots of times," she snarled. "And he'll see them a lot more."

"So you've been screwing him all along." Anger hardened his voice. "I thought so. You teasing little bitch." He twisted her nipple until a sob came from her. "Guess I can't trust you to give me blowjob, huh?"

Her fingers gripped the sides of the seat. "I'll bite it off."

He chuckled. "I wouldn't expect anything less from you. Maybe you'd rather suck on this." He pressed the gun against her lips. She refused to open them. "Maybe if I put it here," he pressed it against her temple, "you'll suck me off, knowing the first time I feel your teeth—bang! You just gotta hope your head bobbing doesn't jar my trigger finger." He grinned. "Makes it more exciting."

He's a sick man. "You said you loved me. How can you do this to me?"

He lowered the gun. His other hand pawed her breast. "You caught my eye that first night in The Tejas. Pretty. Personable. Intelligent. You were easy pickin's. A stranger, alone, far from home. The perfect one to make deliveries for me. Then I got to know you. You were completely different from any other girl I've dated. I fell in love."

"What about Tammy? Your long-time love?" *Maybe if I keep him talking, someone else will stop behind us.*

"Tammy." He snorted. "She's just a convenient piece of ass. Get this." He shifted in his seat and continued in a conversational tone he might use with his golf buddies, "She thinks you and I have been humping like rabbits so every time I go home after seeing you, she fucks my brains out. Guess it's her way of reclaiming me or some shit. Who knows what goes on in her pea brain. Boy howdy, she's been a wildcat lately. We've had the best sex ever, thanks to you. And every time," his fingers stroked her breast with feather-light touches, "I imagined it was with you. I wished it was you. I so wanted it to be you. I did love you, Megan. More than I ever loved any woman."

"Did? Past tense?"

"Yup. First, I find out you're a snitch for the cops. Pissed me off. I was ready to strangle you." His touch turned rough, painful. "Then my contact backed out at the last second. He did it again this Sunday. I was furious with you. But I had this problem." His hand left her breast to cup the side of her face.

She winced in pain from the pressure.

"I loved you. I've tried to tell you about the meth a couple of times, but something always interfered, or it wasn't the right time and place. I was going to tell you Monday night. I wanted to give you one more chance. All you had to do was come over to my place. I was going to tell you everything. Offer you everything. Once this deal goes through, I'll have plenty of money. We could've gone anywhere with no worries. Had the kind of life people dream of. But you never showed up." His fingers gripped her cheeks and squished them together, making her eyes tear. "You didn't even call. I knew then that I meant nothing to you. Never had. That's when I stopped loving you." He pushed her away and sat back. "It's amazing how quickly love can change to hate, disgust, loathing. I spent the rest of last night planning what I'll do with you."

Megan worked her jaw to loosen it up. Her face throbbed. Fear had gnawed her stomach hollow. *How can I get away? Unless ...* "Are—are you going to ... kill me?"

"Oh darlin', darlin'." He laughed as if she'd asked the funniest thing. "Hardly. I have plans for you. You have drugs to deliver. And surely you don't think I'm content with just playing with your titties, do you? Silly Yankee bitch. I've got just the place fixed up for you."

"Wh—where's that?"

"It's a surprise. Sit over there nice and quiet while I drive. You try to fuck with me or cause me to wreck the car or something I'll shoot you. I'll try to miss vital organs, but I can't promise anything." He aimed the gun at her knee. "Maybe I should shoot you in the knee cap to be on the safe side."

"No. No." She grabbed her knees. "I'll behave. I promise."

"Smart girl." He waved the gun. "Now, scoot over there in the corner. Good girl. Fold your hands on your lap where I can see them. That's good. On second thought, put those hands to use and play with your tits. Go ahead." He waved the gun again. "Don't be shy. I asked you to do it once before, remember? You didn't want to. Do it now." His voice hardened. "Or the knee cap goes. Yeah, like that. You got the idea. Rub your hands all over. Squeeze 'em. Yeah. Tease those nipples. Oh yeah, just like that. Good Yankee bitch." He lit a cigarette and smoked while he watched her. His eyes glinted in the dome light.

The smoke made her cough.

"Get used to it. There aren't any windows where you're goin'."

Cold sweat made her skin clammy. "You need help."

He leaned over and held the burning end of the cigarette inches from her face. "Shut up and keep rubbing."

She kept rubbing.

He sat back and finished smoking. He stubbed out the cigarette in the ashtray then grabbed her left breast.

Megan went still, her breath stuck in her throat.

"Don't just sit there. Play with the other one." His hand squeezed and pawed her. His breathing grew labored, the sound filling the silence. He shifted in his seat. It squeaked beneath him. The gun stayed steady on her, his other hand rough, pinching, hurting. A cruel smile twisted his mouth. "I got a hell of a hard on. A blow job would feel damn good right about now. You ready?"

She turned her head and stared out the window.

"Not there yet?" He twisted her nipple. "Soon you'll be begging to suck me off. We're gonna have so much fun."

He released her and sat back. He flipped off the dome light, then switched the gun to his other hand so he could put the car in gear. He hit the gas. After going through the gears, and steering with his left elbow, he switched the gun back to his right hand. "Keep playing with yourself, bitch."

He kept the gun on her and glanced at her often as the Corvette sped up the freeway.

Her hands did as he ordered. Tears trickled down her aching face as the dark cityscape swept past. *I have to get away. Think. Think.*

Soon the lights of Fort Worth lay far behind in the side view mirror. Darkness spread out all around except for the beam of the Corvette's headlights on the pavement and the lights of an occasional southbound car.

Barton hummed a Johnny Cash song.

Megan finally worked up the courage to ask, "Where are we going?"

"Well, I hope you're not disappointed but we're not going to see the Goat Man. Don't stop, darlin'. Keep those fingers busy. I'm enjoying the show. Although you could put a little more enthusiasm in it. I like gals with spunk." He gave her a pointed look. "Things will go a lot easier for you if you show some spunk."

"I have to go to the bathroom."

"Have to wait until we get to the farm."

"The farm?"

"Damn it. Didn't mean to tell you that. But it'll give you something to think about during the ride. A buddy of mine grew up on a farm up here. He lives in Iowa now. The farm is deserted. I check on it every now and then for him."

"You're going to keep me in the farmhouse?"

"Oh no, no." He laughed. "That place is a wreck. You're going in the root cellar."

Her hands stilled. Her heart raced erratically.

"There's a cot for you, and a bucket in the corner for your comfort." He grinned. "We're going to have a lot of fun down there, darlin'."

She stared at him, horrified. "You're insane."

His grin disappeared. "You'd better be nice to me. I'm all you're going to have in the world. Besides the cot and the bucket. And a pillow and blanket. Might get chilly down there." The car accelerated. The speedometer crossed 90.

I'll escape at the farm, before he drags me to the cellar.

"Here's what's going to happen, darlin'. Once I get you down there, I'm gonna shoot you full of meth. Not that shit you buy on the street. I'm talkin' primo. A big dose of it. Should give you one hell of an orgasm. That's what the girls say anyway. Personally, I rarely use the stuff. A snort every now and then but I've never injected it. That's where people fuck up, you know. They start selling it, then they start using it, and soon they're using up all the profits, and they're hooked. Fools." He shook his head. "Anyway, once you've had your little fun and you're all juiced up and horny, I'm gonna fuck you until it's running out your ears. When I'm done with you, I'll shoot you full of meth again and leave you there high, and horny, and alone." He scratched his chin. "I haven't decided yet if I'll leave you a light or not."

Raped for hours then left high, horny, and alone—in the dark? Bile surged up her throat. She gulped it back down. She felt light-headed. *I'll go mad down there.*

"I'll bring you some food the next day. Shoot you up again and fuck you good. Then shoot you up again and leave. That's what we're doing every day until the weekend. Sounds fun, doesn't it? I know you'll be happy to see me whenever I pop in. Happy to have some light too, huh? Yeah," he chuckled, "I bet you'll be giving me lots of blow jobs. On the weekend, I'll let you out of there to make the delivery. Don't worry. I'll be with you. You'll carry the meth. Might even let the guy fuck you if he lets me watch. Then back to the cellar you go. Where you'll wait for me. Of course, I'll have all that money. There'll come a time when I won't pop in anymore because I'm going away. You'll just sit there and wait and wait and wait." He glanced at her. "Kind of the way I did last night, waiting and waiting for you to come to dinner. Except you'll be waiting in the dark. Pitch black. Unless you're *really* nice to me."

Candace's voice echoed in Megan's mind. *Some said you and John Bingo were in cahoots together. You both planned the whole thing and afterwards he set you up somewhere fancy as his mistress. Some said you hanged yourself with your petticoat out in the woods. Others said Bingo took you somewhere isolated and kept you captive as his whore.*

Instead, his descendent is going to imprison me!

I'd rather be dead.

Then the cycle can start over. The next Megan can try to save Seth.

Seth.

A different kind of pain rocketed through her at the thought of failing Seth, of never seeing him again. She closed her eyes. *I love you.*

"Penny for your thoughts? Thinkin' about all the fun ahead?"

"I was thinking of Seth." She opened her eyes and looked at Barton. "And how very much I love him."

Barton's hand on the steering wheel clenched and unclenched as he stared straight ahead. He jerked out a cigarette from his pocket and stuck it in his mouth. He pulled out a lighter and held it to the cigarette tip. The flame from the lighter illuminated the angry set of his face. "I'll find his ass and take care of him."

Megan burst out laughing. "Good luck with that."

"What do you mean by that? What's so damn funny?"

"You wouldn't believe me if I told you."

"I'll find him and kill him," Barton snarled. "You're never gonna see him again. Get those hands busy or I'll smack you silly."

Never see him again.

The words crushed her spirit more than anything else Barton had said or done. She stared numbly ahead as the Corvette raced up the freeway. *Universe! Help me! God, help me. Seth.* She stifled a sob. *I'm sorry!*

Barton hummed another song, tapping his fingers on the steering wheel.

A line of semis sped past on the southbound side.

Out of the darkness, a tire rolled into the beam of the headlights and headed straight down the pavement toward the Corvette.

Megan sucked in a breath. *It's going to hit us head-on!* She gripped the armrest with both hands.

The tire rolled toward them so fast there wasn't time to scream *Look out!* or *Do you see that?* or anything.

The tire rolled closer and closer.

It's not supposed to end like this!

Chapter 30

The tire veered to its left.

Barton whipped the car to his left.

The tire loomed in her window, the top of the tire level with her head as it came in at a slight angle. Her fingers tightened on the armrest. The tire hit the car with a glancing blow and a cracking noise just behind her door. The impact jolted her sideways. The tire rolled off into the darkness.

Barton stopped the car on the left shoulder. He put the gear in neutral and pulled the brake, then ran his hand through his hair. "Jesus. That was close. Damn truck tire. I'm going to check the car." He pointed the gun at her. "Sit right there and behave. If you try to run, I'll shoot you."

"I'll behave." She cowered against the door. "Please don't hurt me."

He reached for the key in the ignition.

"Leave it on please," she begged. "The a/c. It's so hot."

He stared at her. "All right. Stay in the car." He got out of the car and left the door open, as if teasing her to run.

Megan muttered, "You bet I'm staying in the car." She shoved down the dress and bra straps to free her arms.

He walked around the front of the car. The metal of his gun glinted in the headlights beaming out across a grassy median revealing a slight dip separating the northbound and southbound lanes. He stopped just past her door and squatted down. She couldn't hear him through the window, but watching his lips, she guessed he said, "God damn it. Shit." He stood, lit a cigarette, and turned away, as if looking around for something, maybe the runaway tire.

Megan hiked up her dress and scrambled over the console. She had one shoe on and one shoe off. The hem of her dress caught on the stick shift. She yanked free and dropped onto the seat. She had to sit near the edge of it to reach the pedals and hold onto the steering wheel to keep herself there. "You can do this," she muttered. She had watched Barton enough times. She adjusted the rearview mirror and glanced at him just as he squatted down beside the car again. She eased down the parking brake, pushed in the clutch, and shoved the gearshift into first. Her bare foot pressed down the gas pedal. The car jerked forward.

"Hey!" Barton shot to his feet.

Megan gave it more gas. The car jerked forward again. In the side mirror, she saw Barton run around the back of the car. She rammed the gearshift into what she hoped was reverse and gassed it. The car jerked backwards and hit something with a thud. *Got him.* Barton landed belly down on the trunk. The right side of his face squashed against the back window. He looked surprised and pissed. She hit the brake, and he flew off the back of the car.

"You fucking bitch!"

She leaned over, grabbed the door handle, and slammed the door shut. She found first gear again. The car jerked forward. *Ease into it,* a teenaged friend had told her years ago the one time she drove a stick shift. "Easy to say when your life doesn't depend on it," she muttered, letting up a little on the gas. She pushed in the clutch, and ground into second.

In the side mirror, Barton struggled to his knees.

The car jerked forward. Megan gave it more gas and started across the grassy median. She hung onto the steering wheel while steering so she could reach the pedals. The car swerved from side to side. She concentrated on the pedals, the gearshift, the sound of the engine, the dip in the median, and Barton in the rearview mirror.

He stumbled, limping, after her.

The car bounced. The front of it scraped the ground in the dip. Megan eased up on the gas, praying the car wouldn't stall.

Pounding on the window made her jump.

"Stop the goddamn car!" The gun wavered in Barton's hand as he ran alongside the car.

She stomped the gas pedal. The tires chewed up the grass as the car climbed out of the dip and shot out onto the left shoulder of the southbound lanes. A semi with enough lights to rival a Christmas tree sped by, blowing its horn. Megan yanked the steering wheel to the left and slid back on the seat. Her feet slipped off the pedals. The engine sputtered. "Not now. Come on. Come on."

The car quit.

She gripped the steering wheel and pulled herself back to the edge of the seat, her feet reaching for the pedals.

The hot night air swept over her when her door suddenly opened.

"I'm warning … you," Barton panted. "Stop."

The round hole of his gun stared at her. Her feet found the pedals. Her hand turned the ignition key. The car roared to life. She found the gearshift and pushed it into first. The car lurched forward. The door bounced against Barton.

"Don't do it," he growled, his shadowed face furious.

She stuck out her tongue. She couldn't help it. He grabbed her arm and yanked. Instead of pulling away, she jabbed him with her elbow. He stumbled back, losing his grip on her. The car jerked out into the lane. She ground into second. The car accelerated. The engine revved. She steered into the passing lane.

A car whizzed by, laying on the horn.

She straightened the Corvette between the lane lines.

A shot rang out. Barton ran behind her.

She found third gear. Her hair blew around her face. She ignored it.

Another shot. A bullet hit the inside of the open door.

She released her right hand's death grip on the gearshift and grabbed the steering wheel. She leaned out into the hot wind and with her left hand yanked the door shut. Her hair settled down. The air conditioner chilled the heat away. Barton still chased her in the rearview mirror, the gun pointed at the car. *He loves this car. He won't shoot it—*

The back window shattered. Glass sprayed everywhere.

Megan screamed, ducking. The car swerved.

Another bullet plugged into the dashboard. She found fourth gear and made a smooth transition.

"I'll kill you," Barton yelled.

She floored it, flipped him the bird, and sped south on the dark highway, leaving Barton behind in the rearview mirror.

I'm driving. I'm driving! Oh my God. I'm driving.

She started to shake. Her breathing quickened until she gasped for air. The lights of oncoming cars in the northbound lanes appeared hazy and distorted. She choked back bile. The car swerved between the lines.

Don't think of that night. Concentrate on the road. Not the sound of the crash. Not mom and dad. Dead.

"Stop it." She clutched the steering wheel with shaking hands and gulped down air. "Just stop it. You're fine. You're doing great. You're driving!" The dark landscape flashed by. Maybe too fast. She eased up on the gas. She glanced in the rearview mirror. No sign of Barton. *He won't be far behind. He'll flag down a car, commandeer it, and come after me.* She sped up again.

Memories of all he'd done filled her mind. *He wanted to imprison me. Tried to kill me.* Her teeth chattered. She shivered uncontrollably. Strangled sobs escaped her. Tears rolled down her face. She couldn't stop shaking.

It's just shock. That's all. I'm fine. Drive.

She pulled herself together and drove toward the distant lights of Fort Worth. An occasional vehicle passed her, the sounds coming through the non-existent back window. The gas gauge hovered near half full. The cold air chilled her. She suddenly remembered she was half-naked, her clothes bunched around her waist. She didn't dare remove her hands from the steering wheel or her eyes from the road to fix her clothes, or to figure out how to turn off the air conditioner. She had a bigger problem.

Where am I going?

Logic told her the police station.

Another option was the portal in the Water Gardens. The might-be-there-might-not-be-there portal.

Her gut pointed her to the B&B. Her heart hoped Seth would be there, her hero.

If not, I'll find the portal. Surely, I'll find it now, when I need it. Surely.

Downtown neared. More traffic. Her back ached from perching on the edge of the seat. She didn't dare relax, or search for the button or lever or whatever moved the seat. The maze of the streets of Fort Worth spread out on her right. Panic gripped her. *Where's the B&B?* She knew the city by foot, bus, and cab. Not by driving. She exited the freeway and drove slowly, looking for familiar landmarks.

Seconds ticked by. Seconds that surely brought Barton closer.

She ran a red light. The next light had a pickup waiting. She pulled up behind it. The car sputtered. She gave it more gas. The car rocked forward. She slammed on the brakes just before hitting the pickup. Her hands shook. Her legs ached. Tears threatened. *I hate stick shift.* The light turned green. The car sputtered and jerked. She worked the pedals and the gearshift and finally managed to get going and headed down the dark streets. *Where's that B&B?* Minutes passed. She drove around and around.

Suddenly the big neon sombrero shone like a lighthouse beacon.

She sobbed with relief.

She stopped beside the curb beneath a streetlight and turned off the car. She slid back on the seat and rested her head on the headrest. Her shoulders relaxed. She breathed deeply, fighting tears. No time for those now. She straightened and pulled up her bra then her torn dress. She grabbed her purse and shoe, and climbed out, leaving the key in the ignition. She shoved her foot in the shoe then ran to the B&B, clutching the front of her dress together. Her hands shook and couldn't get the key in the lock. The key clinked on the ground. She scrambled to pick it up and jabbed it in the lock. Inside, she locked the door behind her.

She ran to the phone, dug in her purse, and pulled out a business card. She squinted to see the phone number in the glow of the gaslights on the walls then dialed. The phone rang. Megan glanced at the door, expecting Barton to crash it down any second. A groggy voice finally answered.

"Detective Sullivan? This is Megan McClure. Barton just tried to kill me. You heard me. He has a gun. I got away in his car. It's parked near the B&B. You can't miss it. It has bullet holes and a shattered rear window. He'll probably be here shortly, looking for me." She listened a moment. "Yes. Send as many police as you can. His big drug deal is this weekend. I don't know when or where or anything. I didn't stick around long enough to find out. One of your officers gives Barton information in exchange for meth. I don't know his name. He's Mexican. Wait here?" Megan laughed. "I'm not waiting here. I'm going somewhere Barton will never find me."

She hung up, dialed another number, and heard another groggy voice.

"Donna? It's me."

"Megs? What's the matter?" The sound of a yawn came over the phone. "What time is it?"

"Barton tried to kill me tonight."

"*What?* Are you all right?"

"I'm f-fine." Megan's voice shook. Everything was starting to catch up with her. She took a calming breath. "I got away in his car."

"You *drove?*"

"Listen. I don't have much time. He could be here any minute."

"I'm coming down there. Next flight."

"I'm leaving, Donna."

"You mean ... back in time? Did you find the portal?"

"Not yet. If I don't find it in the next few minutes I'm going to the one in the Water Gardens."

"You think it'll open or-or work?"

"It has to. Or I'm dead. He'll kill me first chance he gets." *Or worse.* Megan kept her eyes on the front door.

"Damn it, Megs. I'm coming down."

"I won't be here."

"You said you can come back through Seth's door at least once, didn't you?"

"That's what the other Megan said in her letter."

"Come back to let me know you're okay."

"Donna—"

"Promise me. I'll stay in that B&B until hell freezes over waiting for you."

"All right. All right. I promise. Okay?" Megan rubbed her throbbing forehead. "Listen. No one else needs to see my journals about Seth. They'll be in a manila envelope in a stack of papers and other envelopes on the vanity. I have to go. I love you, Donna." Megan bit back a sob. She cleared a lump out of her throat. "I'll never forget you."

"Oh Megs." Donna sniffled. "I love you too." Her voice cracked. "You'd better come back. This isn't goodbye. And for God's sake be careful."

"Thanks for being my dearest friend." Megan hung up, and took the stairs two at a time, wiping tears away.

Inside her room, she closed and locked the door. The light from the lamp on the nightstand left most of the room in shadows. *Please be here. Please be here.* Silence and an empty room greeted her. He wasn't there. *Just like a man. Never around when you need him.*

Megan turned on another light. She dropped her purse on the sofa and hurried to the nightstand. She picked up her journals, and stuffed them into a manila envelope, along with the letter from the other Megan. She stuck the envelope in the middle of a stack of paperwork on the vanity. She glanced in the mirror then did a double take.

"Holy moly."

She looked like a battered wife. Bruises covered her face, her right side more than her left. A thin strip of dried blood trailed from the right corner of her mouth down her chin. She hurried to the bathroom, and dabbed a wet washcloth on her face, wincing from the pain. It hadn't hurt until then. She eyed the shower longingly while taking two aspirins with a glass of water.

She left the bathroom, found the leather bag for her trip to the past, and opened it. She grabbed a handful of old coins and tossed them on the floor in each corner of the room. The coins rolled this way and that way with no direction or purpose. They rolled aimlessly. Over and over. She didn't care about the noise. When Barton got there, all hell was going to break loose.

"Come on come on," she muttered. She tossed coins in the corner near the armoire, where much of the dried blood of Seth's handprint had flaked away, leaving dark blotches on the wood.

She sat on her heels and stared at the armoire. The other Megan had said something, or maybe tried to say something about the armoire. *Some of the missing words?* She shot to her feet and ran to the envelope containing the letter.

She stopped in midstride and cocked her head. *Sirens?* She ran to the window. No squad car. The streetlight shone on Barton's car. She started to turn away. A car raced up and squealed to a stop behind the Corvette. Megan leaned closer to the window. A man jumped out of the car and ran to the Corvette. Her fingers gripped the windowsill.

Barton.

He bent to look inside his car then straightened. He beat his fists on the roof then tipped back his head. The streetlight bathed his upturned face as he looked at her window.

Megan darted back out of sight then slowly eased up for another look. He was gone.

He's coming.

Portal or no portal, I have to get out of here.

There was only one other way out of the room.

Megan grabbed one of the spindly-legged chairs. It looked fragile, but it had been made of heavy wood back when things were made to last. She held it high over her head with both hands and threw it at the window with all her might. The glass shattered. She ran to the window and looked down. A lazy breeze stirred the muggy night air. Lights in the room below her came on. Lights in the room above her came on. The chair had landed on one of the pointed tips of the iron fence surrounding the property. The tip protruded from the chair like a spear. The same way the broken tree had protruded spear-like from her father's dying body.

She let out a sob at the ghastly memory, tears burning her eyes.

Get it together. She dashed away tears and studied the layout below. The height. The distance. The obstacles.

I just have to jump far enough out to clear the fence. I can do it. Hell, I drove. A stick-shift. I can do this.

She ran back for the leather bag, and suddenly remembered what she'd wanted to do before Barton's arrival distracted her. *There's a clue in the other Megan's letter about the armoire. I know it.*

She found the manila envelope, yanked out the letter, and scanned it. Always before, she had studied the end of it for clues until she knew it by heart. Now she concentrated on the first pages.

"There it is. Has to be."

You have to   his   he left on the   that   .

She read it over, plugging *armoire* in the blank spaces. The only place it fit was after *the*. The rest of the sentence suddenly fell into place.

Noises came from downstairs.

She read aloud, "You have to be sure you touch, maybe, his blood he left on the armoire that first night."

Satisfied, grinning victoriously, Megan started to put the letter back into the envelope when several other sentences caught her eye.

Complete sentences that had not been complete before, the missing words somehow restored.

What she read made her breath catch in horror and turned her blood to ice.

Heavy footsteps pounded up the stairs. Loud voices argued.

The noise jerked Megan back to reality. No matter what the words said, she had to go. She crammed the letter into the envelope and shoved it back in the pile of papers. She snatched up more old coins and ran to the armoire. She put her hand over the remnants of Seth's bloody handprint, then tossed the coins on the floor. Several rolled aimlessly.

Two rolled towards one wall in the corner and disappeared.

She rubbed her eyes then picked up three coins, touched the armoire again, and rolled them toward the same spot.

They rolled right through the wall and were gone.

Megan dropped to her knees in the corner and put her hand on the bottom of the wall. Her hand went through it into freezer-like coldness.

This is it!

She felt around the wall with both hands and found an area of maybe two square feet of no wall.

Someone pounded on the door. "Megan, open up." More pounding. "Goddamn it, open the fucking door!"

Muffled voices came from the hallway. Loud curses. More pounding on the door. Sirens wailed in the distance, coming closer.

Megan gripped both sides of the portal and stuck her head through it. Black. Cold. Silent. Just like Seth had described climbing the stairs to his portal. She sat back on her heels, her heart hammering. *What if it doesn't lead to Seth's time? What if I end up in one million B. C? The future? What if—*

"I'm gonna kill you, bitch!" Barton hollered. Something heavy hit the door. People yelled. Another heavy hit on the door.

Hope, love, faith. You'll need all three, the other Megan had written.

Megan closed her eyes. For the second time that night, she prayed, *God. Help me.*

She took a deep breath, looked at the leather bag on the bed. *Birth control pills. Tampons. I wanted to take a shower. Change clothes. I look like hell.*

The door crashed open. "Where are you, bitch?" Barton stormed in.

Megan grabbed the edges of the portal, tucked her chin to her chest, and somersaulted through the wall.

Chapter 31

Oh God oh God oh God

Megan tumbled through a black, cold, silent void. No sense of up or down, right or left, falling, flying, anything. Only a vast expanse of nothing.

As she tumbled, the sentences she had just read in the other Megan's letter ran through her mind.

You have to   Seth from   . You may have to   the   for him. You may have to   yourself. You have to   Seth more than   life.

The somehow completed sentences followed.

You have to save Seth from dying. You may have to take the bullet for him. You may have to sacrifice yourself. You have to love Seth more than your own life.

Her mind reeled. *To save Seth, I might have to—*

Light burst around her, as if a door had opened to a bright sunny day. Her feet found solid footing. Dizzy, disoriented, blinded by the light, she stumbled on her two-inch heels. She fell forward and slid on her stomach, bumping down something that felt like steps, and landed face first in dirt.

—die.

"Grandpa's britches, did you see that?" a woman asked.

"Bet that hurt," another replied. "Who is it?"

"Dunno. I ain't never seen no dress like that."

"Lookit them shoes," a younger sounding woman said.

Megan raised her head, spitting dirt, and took a mental stock of injuries. Nothing seemed broken. Nothing hurt more than it had before going through the portal. She slowly pushed herself upright on one hip. She blew hair out of her face, and looked around, squinting in the sunshine.

A dirt street dotted with horse droppings and lined with wooden buildings and sidewalks on either side. Sun-bonneted women in long full skirts, and men in cowboy hats, old-fashioned clothes, and boots. Horses tied to hitching rails. Hardly a tree or anything green in sight. It all looked like a movie set for a Western. The only thing missing were tumbling tumbleweeds. A warm breeze carrying a mix of fresh, earthy, pungent smells stirred her hair. She leaned on one hand, shaded her eyes with the other, and looked up.

Three women wearing dingy white corsets and flouncy colorful skirts stood on the steps Megan had slid down and stared at her.

"I ain't never seen you before," one of them said. Dark-haired, stern-faced, she looked to be the oldest of the three. "Who the devil are you?"

"Yeah," a woman with long brassy hair chimed in. "Where'd you come from?"

"Where'd ya git them shoes?" a wide-eyed young blonde asked.

Megan asked her own question. "What year is this?"

"What year is this?" The brassy-haired one laughed. "I been asked many a strange thing—"

"One fella asked me t' spank him like his mama did." The blonde giggled.

"—but I ain't never been asked that."

"It's 1890," the oldest one replied. "What year'd you think it was?"

Am I dreaming? Dead? Is this real? It all seemed so confusing. Amazing. Impossible. "This *is* Fort Worth, right?"

The three women looked at each other.

The oldest one stepped onto the bottom step and glared at Megan. "You addled in the head? Askin' such silly questions. Did Matilda hire you? You gonna be—"

"Hello, ladies, may I be of assistance?" A husky man in a white shirt, black coat, shiny green vest, and black trousers walked up. He bent down and extended his hand to Megan. "Did you trip and fall, honey? Need some help?" he asked in a soft Texas drawl. He jerked back when she raised her face. "Oh my." He gently touched her cheek. Concern shone in his soft brown eyes. He had brown hair, a mustache, and beard, all cut short and neatly trimmed. "Who did this to you?"

Megan searched for a plausible reply.

"Lulu?" the man asked. "Who did this?"

"Dunno." The older woman crossed her arms. "Never seen her before."

"Me neither," the brassy-haired woman said. "We was sittin' on the porch when the door banged open, an' there she was, swayin' like that drunkard Willy Dee on a Saturday night. She fell an' slid on her belly down the steps."

The man stroked her cheek ever so lightly. "You a new girl?" His appreciative gaze drifted downward.

Megan realized she'd been sitting there with her torn dress hanging open. She clutched it shut with one hand on her chest. "Hardly."

A dimple appeared in the man's left cheek when he smiled. "Don't be shy, pretty lady. We're goin' to be very good friends. I promise I'll never treat you the way the previous fella did."

"He sure won't. Mr. Tim ain't nuthin' like that," the blonde said.

"Mr. Tim?" Megan grabbed the front of his shirt. "Seth's friend Tim?"

"Why, yes. You know Seth? Please don't wrinkle the shirt, honey." He pried her hand free and held it in his.

"I'm Megan."

He stared at her blankly.

"Megan. From-from ... *you* know."

"Uno?" one of the women asked. "That in Texas?"

Megan gave his hand a tug. "Megan. *Miss* Megan. Seth's friend from," she jerked her head to one side, "*you* know."

It took a whole minute. Then his blank stare exploded into wide-eyed shock. His jaw dropped. "*Miss Megan?*" He blinked. "*You're* Miss Megan? From—" he glanced at the other women, leaned closer, and whispered "—the future?"

She nodded vigorously.

He leaned back and studied her. He ran his free hand through his hair. "Holy moly," he breathed.

She grinned. "That's me."

"Does Seth know you're here?" he asked softly.

"I just got here minutes ago."

"Minutes ago." Wonder filled his voice.

"Can you help me up, Tim?"

He shook himself, as if coming out of a dream. "Of course. Up you go. Whoa there." He steadied her with a grip on her arm when she swayed on her feet. "You feelin' all right?"

She gave a shaky laugh as she clasped the front of her dress together and got her bearings. "It's been a long night."

His gaze went over her. "I reckon." He released his grip on her arm. "We should find—"

"Timothy. There you are." A woman walked up.

Tim's head snapped around. His whole face lit up.

"Sorry to interrupt but—" The woman looked at Megan and gasped, her hand to her mouth. "Oh, you poor thing. How awful. This must stop. Poor girl. Beaten up and abused by some wretched man." She touched Megan's shoulder. "Do you need the doctor? Help getting back to your room? Timothy, take the poor dear up to her room, please."

"Now, Sue—"

"The poor dear ain't got no room here, Miss Susannah," the brassy-haired woman said from where she and the other two ladies watched. "We don't know who she is."

Susannah. Megan eyed the other woman critically. She was maybe three inches taller than Megan was. She had whiskey-colored hair piled attractively on top of her head with soft tendrils framing an oval face. Intelligent brown eyes. Long lashes. Porcelain skin. A long tan dress with a cream-colored bodice, a high neckline, and long sleeves, all edged in lace, displayed an hourglass figure. She wasn't exactly pretty, Megan decided. The old-fashioned word *comely* came to mind. *Seth could have done worse. Although Tim calls her Sue. He lit up like Las Vegas at the sight of her.*

"Oh?" A look of surprise flittered across Susannah's face. "You're not one of the girls? I'm so sorry. Please forgive me for assuming—"

"Don't worry," Megan replied. "It's understandable."

Susannah tilted her head. "Have we met before? You seem familiar."

Which lifetime? "I don't believe so."

"You must have a twin. I never forget a face."

Tim said, "She recently arrived on the train from—" He broke off, a look of panic in the glance he sent Megan.

"Chicago," she finished for him.

"Oh my. Chicago. So far to come." Susannah gave Megan the once over. "Is that the latest fashion there? Hem all the way up to the knees? No petticoats?"

"Ah, in some places."

Susannah tsked. "Scandalous. Positively scandalous. What is the world coming to? Damn Yankees. Oh." She bit her lower lip. "I'm sorry. I meant no offense."

"None taken. Although the war *is* over."

"So it is. So it is. And someone accosted you on the train?"

Megan shrugged, and nodded.

"As she was gettin' off," Tim said, adding to the lies Megan hoped she'd remember to keep her story straight. "Stole her bags too."

"Mercy me." Susannah shook her head. "You must tell the Marshal. He'll do something about it. So, you have no clothes, and no money, I assume. I don't know where you would keep it in that dress. What will you do now?"

"I, um, I don't know."

Susannah took Megan's arm. "You can come home with me until you figure it out."

"Oh, no, I couldn't impose on you." Megan shot Tim a helpless look. The last place she wanted to go was to the home of Seth's bride-to-be. Besides, she was afraid that once she relaxed, she'd remember all that had happened—escaping Barton, tumbling blindly through the portal, the warning in the completed sentences—and she'd lose it, and fall apart. She couldn't do that in front of Susannah.

"Now, Sue." Tim stepped up. "I'm sure you have plenty to do, what with-with," he glanced at Megan, "the weekend comin' up. I'll take care of her."

"Nonsense." Susannah made a face at Tim. "She can't stay with you. She has no money for a room. Look at her. She's been through enough already. She's coming to my place. She can clean up. We'll do something with that hair. Find something in the store for her to wear. Although," she gave a silvery laugh, "it won't look like anything they're wearing in Chicago."

Megan touched her hair. "What's wrong with my hair?"

"Nothing. It's just a tad ... wild. Shall we?" Susannah linked her arm with Megan's.

Megan sent Tim a more urgent helpless look.

Tim held out his hands and shrugged.

"You're all coming Sunday, right?" Susannah asked the three ladies standing on the steps.

"We're invited?" the blonde asked in surprise. "I thought it was just Lottie."

"Of course, you're invited." Susannah beamed. "It will be the happiest day of my life and I want everyone to share it." She turned to Megan. "Sunday is my wedding day. I hope you will join us if you're still here."

Holy moly. That's the last place I want to go. "I, uh, I don't think I'll be there." Megan managed to add, "Congratulations."

"Thank you." Susannah's eyes sparkled. "I could not be happier."

Tim stared at the ground, the corners of his mouth drawn down.

Susannah led Megan away. "Come along now. You can tell me all about Chicago. I've never been there. I hope you have a chance to meet my betrothed before you leave. He's the—" her gaze moved beyond Megan, and a radiant smile transformed Susannah Mead and made her beautiful. "There he is." She waved her hand. "Seth!"

Megan spun around.

"Heavens above, where are my manners? I just realized we have never introduced ourselves. I'm Susannah Mead. And you are?"

"Megan McClure," Megan said over her shoulder. She thought she heard a gasp come from Susannah, but all her attention was riveted on Seth.

He stood with several men in front of a saloon not far down the street. He waved back. His hand froze in the middle of the wave. His eyes locked with Megan's where she waited with his best friend and his bride-to-be.

His long steps ate up the ground between them. He stopped in front of Megan, ignoring Susannah's greeting and Tim's presence.

"You're here." Awe filled his voice. His shocked gaze searched her face. His look hardened. He touched her bruised cheek the same way Tim had but it felt oh so different. "Barton?"

She nodded, drinking in the sight of him. New lines creased his face, bronzed from the sun except for the pale thin scar on his right cheek. Crow's feet from squinting in the sun radiated from the corners of his eyes. A trim mustache topped his wonderfully familiar lips. Everything within her wanted to be in his arms, but she made no move toward him. Not with Susannah watching.

His gaze swept down her ruined clothes. He pressed his lips together then said through gritted teeth, "I'll kill him next chance I get."

Sunlight flashed on the tin star pinned to his black vest.

"Marshal?" she asked in surprise. When he nodded, her heart overflowed with pride, respect, and love. She couldn't stop the smile that spread across her face. "Good for you."

Seth stood straighter, his shoulders squared, and the look in his eyes said he wanted to hold her too but not here, not now.

"You two know each other?" Susannah asked.

Seth's gaze never left Megan.

Megan, however, heard a sharp edge in Susannah's voice and saw confusion, surprise, and suspicion swirling like a hurricane in her eyes, which intensified when Seth replied, "We met years ago."

"In Chicago? When were you in Chicago, Seth?" Susannah's eyes narrowed. "I don't recall you ever going there."

"We met in Abilene," Seth answered.

"When you went on that trail drive? Why, heavens, that was ages ago." Susannah fixed her gaze on Megan. "You must have been in pigtails," she paused, then added, with that sharp edge once again in her voice, "Megan." Her gaze never wavered. "What were you doing in Kansas?"

Many children had surely cowered beneath that schoolteacher stare. It certainly made Megan uncomfortable. "I, um, I was there with-with my parents."

"You never mentioned why you are in Fort Worth now."

Seth stood beside Susannah with a panicked look on his face.

A young woman passing by smiled at Tim. "Lovely day, isn't it, Tim?"

"Not nearly as lovely as you, Emma," Tim replied in a soft drawl.

The woman covered a giggle with her hand and hurried on, her long calico skirt swishing around her ankles.

Susannah tsked.

Tim gave her his dimpled smile.

Susannah returned her gaze to Megan. "Well?"

"I'm writing a book."

"Oh? What about?"

"People I meet and places I see during my travels." Megan made it up as she went along. "I'm thinking of calling it *My Travels Through the West*."

"A writer. Interesting."

A look of relief came over Seth's face.

Tim winked at Megan.

"And you've come to Fort Worth because …?" Susannah raised her eyebrows.

"The train was passing through here. I thought I'd stop and see an old friend, spend a few days here. Maybe find something to write about. I didn't know your wedding was this weekend."

Susannah crossed her arms. "You and Seth have known each other for years. Yet he has never mentioned you. One would think that—"

"Susannah, I've been looking all over creation for you." A silver-haired woman waddled up. She was barely five feet tall, and round as a basketball. "I want to talk to you about flowers for the church on Sunday."

"Whatever you decide, Mrs. Woodson. You have impeccable taste." Susannah smiled at the older woman.

"Why, thank you, dear. My daughter wants you to stop by as soon as you can, so she can put the finishing touches on your dress."

"Tell her I'll be there shortly."

Mrs. Woodson turned to Seth. "Remember, Marshal, you can't see your bride's dress until the wedding." She shook her finger at him. "No peeking now."

Seth avoided looking at Megan. His face seemed red beneath the tan. "I won't, Mrs. Woodson."

She grinned. "It's going to be a glorious day. The wedding of the year. It's about time you two marry. I don't know what's taken you so long." She touched Susannah's arm. "You'll be a beautiful bride. Now don't forget to stop by my daughter's."

"I'll be there soon. And thank you for your kind words."

Mrs. Woodson said, "Good day, Marshal. Mr. Summerfield." Her gaze swept over Megan's scantily clad, bedraggled figure. She grunted, "Humph," and left.

An awkward silence fell after all the wedding talk.

Tim stared at the ground, his hands in his pockets.

Seth ran his finger around the collar of his shirt. Sweat beaded his forehead.

"It appears I have an appointment," Susannah said. "I'll take you home first, Megan. You can tell me how you and Seth met and kept in touch all these years, and—"

"What do you mean take her home?" Seth asked.

"I invited her to stay with me until—"

"She can go to Lottie's."

Susannah's eyes widened. "Lottie's?"

"She'll have somethin' in her sewin' room for Megan to wear."

"We have plenty of dresses in the store for her to choose from," Susannah replied.

Seth scowled at Susannah. "You got a problem with Megan goin' to my sister's?" he demanded in a voice tight with anger.

Susannah backed up a step. "Why-why no. I just thought she would be more—"

Seth turned away. "Come on, Megan." He took her arm.

"—comfortable in our spare room," Susannah finished saying to Seth's back. Her lips tightened, and faint lines creased her forehead. She glanced at Megan, at Seth's hand on Megan's arm, then at Seth. Her lips formed a thin line. She turned around and stalked away.

"Seth." Megan shook off his hand. "You were awful to her."

"Absolutely horrible," Tim added, his gaze on Susannah walking so fast down the street she kicked up dust in her wake.

"Well, hell, Megan, I—"

"Go after her right now and make amends. She has been nothing but nice to me."

"You just got here and—"

"Go. Now. And after you explain to her how we met and kept in touch all this time, fill me in so our stories match." She covered a yawn with her hand. "I'm too tired to come up with many more lies."

Seth studied her a moment. "Tim? Take her to Lottie, please. Ask her to find Megan some clothes." He touched her cheek in his old familiar way. "I'll be there as soon as I can." He went after Susannah.

Tim turned to Megan. "Good thing you got here just in time."

"For what?"

"To stop the weddin'." His tone implied, *What else?*

Megan shaded her eyes. She already missed her sunglasses. "Is that why you think I'm here?"

"Isn't it?"

"My life was in danger. I found the portal and went through it, not knowing when or where I was going. The fact that I ended up here and now is—" she searched for a word to explain it, but only one seemed appropriate "—a miracle."

"You don't care if they marry?" he asked in surprise. "Pardon my forwardness," he held up a hand, "but I feel like I know you after all these years."

"I feel the same way about you, although it's only been months for me. So, you won't mind me asking, why don't *you* stop the wedding?"

"Me?" He touched his chest.

"Don't give me that. I'm too tired for games. It's obvious you love her so don't waste your breath denying it. Have you ever asked her to marry you?"

He barked a harsh laugh. "Countless times." He looked down the street.

Seth had caught up with Susannah and caught her arm to stop her. He put his hands on his hips. Susannah pointed toward Megan. They argued. Seth took Susannah's arm. She jerked free and marched into a building bearing the sign *Mead's General Store*. Seth followed her.

"I was fourteen the first time. But she's only had eyes for Seth." Tim leveled her gaze on Megan. "And he loves you."

The words, even though second hand, sent a rush of joy through her veins, through her heart, right down to her soul. She asked softly, hopefully, "Does he?"

"Trust me. Is that reason enough for you to stop the weddin'? Or don't you love him?"

"I do," came her soft reply.

Enough to die for him. The sight of Seth's face, the look in his eyes when he saw her had obliterated any doubts or fears and sealed the deal for her. If she succeeded in saving him, and survived it, they could live happily ever after. If she saved him and died in the process, he would be sad, heartbroken, but Susannah would care for him, comfort him, and give him his passel of children. He wouldn't be alone.

Megan accepted her fate, regardless of the outcome. Stopping the wedding wasn't part of her current plan. Seth might need Susannah. Tim was on a need to know basis, and he didn't need to know all of that.

Two gray-haired women walked by, casting disapproving glances at Megan.

She tightened her grip on her ripped dress. "Tim, would you take me upstairs please?"

"Of course. This way." Tim gestured behind them.

Megan turned, and stared.

"What is it?" he asked.

"The house. I hadn't really noticed it until now."

Tim clasped his hands behind his back. "Does it look much different in your time?"

Megan took her first good look at the brothel that would one day be a B&B. "It doesn't have that big porch all along the front, just a few steps and a landing. I like the big porch. There are gardens and green grass all around the house. Very pretty. It's painted white and looks stately. How old is the building?"

"Twenty years or so, I think."

"It's over 100 years newer than the place I know. But with that dull gray paint, and no plants or flowers, just dirt all around, and those loose boards here and there, it looks much older, run-down, and ... sad. That unsightly appendage on the side of the house doesn't help either."

Boards nailed together formed a vertical triangle with the base on the ground stretching out from the house about 15 feet, and the third side angling up to the second floor. It took a moment for her to realize what she was looking at. "That's the stairway to Lottie's room. I never imagined it was enclosed."

"Keeps John Bingo out of the weather." Sarcasm tinged Tim's voice. He offered her his arm. At the entrance to the covered stairway, he suddenly stopped. "I want to apologize for the things I said earlier and for assumin' you were ... one of the girls."

She shaded her eyes. "The first time I met Seth he thought I was a whore. So did Susannah. And probably those two women just now. You too. What's with you people?"

Tim had a blank look. "I, um, well, I'm sorry, is all. I hate for us to get off on the wrong foot. I have to admit that Seth is right about one thing." He swept an admiring gaze over her. "You're one mighty fine lookin' woman. Shall we?" He gestured to the stairway. "It's kind of steep and not wide enough for two. Ladies first."

She started to climb. The boards on both sides and overhead not only blocked out the sun, leaving the stairway in dimness, but also cut off the breeze and encased the heat. Sweat formed on Megan's brow. A light shone at the top. Lottie's lantern that she kept burning day and night. Except when the door opened to the future.

"I'm a bit baffled as to why Seth insisted you come here," Tim said as they climbed. "It bein' Friday, the place'll get noisy once the ranch hands hit town."

Megan stopped so abruptly Tim bumped into her. "Friday?" She turned and looked down at him. "Today's Friday?"

"Yes. Why?"

"It should be Thursday. Last time it was Thursday."

"Last time?" Tim repeated.

Megan ignored him. *On Friday, I'm supposed to meet Candace and Cordelia, have a picnic with them, plant the seeds for our involvement. I've totally missed all of that. How will that affect the grand scheme of things? There's something else that's different. What was it?*

"When did Seth become the marshal?"

"Six months back maybe," Tim said.

The other Megan had written that the townspeople had wanted Seth to become the marshal. He never had.

But he was now.

"Some things are different this time," she muttered, stunned. The other Megan hadn't mentioned anything about that happening.

"This time? Last time? What are you talkin' about?"

"Nothing." She continued up the stairs. "What's Lottie like?"

For a moment, the only sound that came from Tim was breathing from the climb. "Hard as Texas clay. Tough as a ten-year drought."

"Sounds lovely," Megan said dryly.

"She's had a rough time. Always worryin' about Seth. He's her whole world. She's not too fond of most womenfolk, never has been. Even when we were young'uns she rarely played with the girls. Although she likes Sue, who is probably Lottie's only real friend. Lottie's always preferred associatin' with men. Mind you, that doesn't mean she *likes* them, but she'd rather be around them than women. I don't think she really likes anybody except a chosen few. Very few."

Lottie sounded worse by the minute. Megan wondered if she'd been better off going with Susannah. "She must like you. You grew up together."

Tim chuckled. "She tolerates me. Are you cold?"

"Are you nuts? I'm sweating like a pig."

"This is about where Seth said it turns colds when the door opens to your time. You don't feel anything?"

"No. The light's still on too."

"If it wasn't, would you go back to your time?"

As far as she knew, she had one chance to go back through that door. If, when, she used it, it would be for a damn good reason. "Hardly. I just got here."

They reached the top of the steps.

"Good. That means there's still time for you to stop the weddin'." He stepped in front of her. "Better let me go first." He knocked on the door. "Lottie? It's Tim." He paused. "Summerfield."

"My, my, do come in," a woman's husky voice called from inside.

Megan touched Tim's arm. "If you don't mind my asking, have you ever ... enjoyed her favors?"

"Lottie?" His eyes widened in his shadowed face. "Good Lord, no. Half the time I'm terrified of her." He opened the door.

Chapter 32

"Well, well, well," each *well* was drawn out dramatically, "it ain't often the esteemed Mr. Summerfield darkens my door," said a woman's voice, smoky as The Tejas on a Friday night, and sexy as a siren of yore. "You finally get up the nerve?"

Tim stepped into the room. "Lottie, there's someone I want you—"

"Who's that tart you're draggin' in behind ya?" The voice suddenly turned harsh.

Megan had a lot to do in a short amount of time, even less than she had anticipated. She didn't have time to be intimidated by anyone. She brushed past Tim and walked towards a woman rising from a loveseat halfway across the room that looked less than half the size of Megan's in 1981.

The room was narrower, minus the area that held the bed, dresser, and vanity in the future. Its portion of the outer wall had only two of the six tall windows. Dark, heavy curtains covered them, blocking out the sunlight. The air felt warm, the room stuffy, with an undercurrent of a sweet floral scent. Two oil lamps, one on a bureau along the back wall, the other on a small table beside the loveseat, provided the only light.

Clutching her torn dress closed with one hand, Megan extended her free hand. "Hello, I'm Megan McClure. It's so nice to finally meet you."

Lottie O'Connor was a tall, striking woman with auburn hair that hung in long riotous curls down to her elbows. She wore a lacy two-toned negligee, pale ivory in the front with long, flowing sleeves of rich, deep burgundy. The same burgundy lace graced either side of her torso, accentuating the dip of her waist and curve of her hips. Thin strands of burgundy ribbon dangled between her generous breasts, held high by some unseen means. They swelled gleaming white above layers of ivory lace lying low on the twin mounds. Her stern gaze went from Megan's face to her hand then back up. "Who in blazes are you?"

"Megan. Seth's friend from Chicago."

"Chicago." Lottie's red painted lips curled into a sneer.

"He's told me so much about you I feel like I know you." Megan flashed a friendly smile that gradually faded away beneath Lottie's hard glare. Megan lowered her hand.

"I ain't never heard of *you* so get out."

Tim took a couple steps into the room. "Megan just arrived in town."

"An' you bring her straight to me? Well, you can take her right outta here." Lottie pointed to the door. Burgundy lace dripped from her outstretched arm. "We don't need no more girls. Take her to one of the cribs down the street."

"She's not one of the girls," Tim explained.

Lottie snorted. "Looks it. An' looks like she didn't make the last fella happy."

"She was accosted by some men on the train. They roughed her up and took her bags. Seth asked me to ask you to fix her up with a dress. As you can see, she sorely needs one."

Lottie crossed her arms over her breasts and held her head at a haughty angle. "Ain't my problem."

She stood straight and regal. Delicate lace fell in elegant folds around her shapely form. Auburn curls draped her shoulders like a shawl. She might have been a courtesan in a royal court, or a goddess of mythology. In the future, she would have been a woman of importance, one to be reckoned with. Sunlight outside would lay bare the network of lines on her face, the gray threading her hair, the absence of bright-eyed youth. Here, in this darkened room hazy with smoke from the oil lamps casting their feeble light, she gave breath to the illusion of ageless beauty and raw sensuality. A vision of desire in ivory and burgundy lace.

Megan blurted, "You're one beautiful woman, Charlotte O'Connor."

Lottie's kohl-darkened eyes hardened. "Don't call me that."

"Charlotte? It's your name. Besides, you don't look like a Lottie."

"Tim. Take her away," Lottie demanded as imperiously as a queen. He stayed in the background, his hands in his trouser pockets.

"I'm going to call you Charlotte."

Lottie glared at Megan. "You will not."

"It fits you."

"I ain't gonna answer."

"Please help me. I have nothing to wear except this." Megan swept a hand down her torn, dirty dress. "Seth told me all about the beautiful clothes you sew. I'm sure whatever you can come up with will be lovely."

Lottie stared down her nose at Megan. "Just how does someone like *you*," disdain dripped like venom from her voice, "from *Chicago* know my brother?"

Megan began, "We met in Kansas years ago and—"

"While you two ladies get to know each other," Tim interrupted, "I'll see what's keeping Seth so long."

Megan caught his eye and mouthed *coward*.

He made a beeline for the door.

"Oh, no you don't." Lottie whirled towards him. "Timothy Josiah Summerfield, don't you *dare* leave this Yankee whore here."

He yanked open the door and shut it behind him with a resounding thud.

"Snake-bellied, snot-nosed, lily-livered poor excuse for a man," she yelled after him. "Ooo, that man." She spun back to Megan. "Get out."

"Now, Charlotte—"

Lottie towered over Megan. "I told you don't call me that."

"And all I'm asking for is for a little help here," Megan fired back, standing toe-to-toe with Lottie, craning her neck to glare up at the woman. "A dress. One damn dress. That's it. Would it kill you to help a fellow woman in a bad situation? I'm sure you've been in plenty of those yourself and know how it feels."

They locked eyes.

Lottie's nostrils flared. "I don't like you."

Megan gave a harsh laugh. "I'm not all that crazy about you either. Seth has always spoken so highly of you. He said you would help me." She stepped away, stretching her shoulders and neck, rubbing the kink in it. "I guess he doesn't know you as well as he thought he did. Thanks for nothing." Megan headed for the door.

"Why don't you fix your own damn clothes?"

Megan paused. "Because I don't sew. Besides, it's a rag, as far as I'm concerned." Full of bad memories.

Was it only hours ago I was drinking and dancing at The Tejas? Escaping from Barton? A wave of exhaustion washed over her. She hadn't slept since ... she was too tired to figure it out. She jumped when Lottie spoke from right behind her.

"What's that dress made of?"

"I don't know." Megan faced Lottie. "I got it in Chicago." She added, "Store-bought."

A spark of interest lit Lottie's eyes. She reached out to touch the dress, then paused. "Do ya mind?"

"Not at all." Megan smiled to herself, having discovered Lottie's weakness—fabric.

Lottie felt the material here and there. She rubbed it in between her fingers. Her brow furrowed. "I ain't never felt nothin' like that." She inspected the hem, the stitching, and exclaimed over the short length, as if she had just noticed what the dress really looked like.

"You gimme that, I'll fix one up for you."

"It's a deal."

Lottie nodded. She backed away and eyed Megan critically up and down. "I got somethin' won't take a lot of fixin' to fit you. Go sit on the divan. And take that off." Lottie crossed the room, opened the door that in 1981 led to the bathroom, and disappeared inside.

Megan was pretty sure it wasn't a bathroom. She quickly felt the back of the collar of the dress and found the tag. She yanked off the dress and tried to tear off the tag. It read *Made in California 100% polyester Machine wash cold.*

Lottie didn't need to see that.

Megan scanned the room, looking for something sharp. She had a hard time reconciling her room in 1981 with the small area Lottie lived in now. There were two stuffed velvet-covered chairs near a square dining table to the right of Seth's door. The door that led to the interior of the house was on the back wall near the bureau and the burning lamp. Along the wall in the front of the house stretched an Oriental screen with a picture of colorful birds, a pagoda amongst some trees, and a bridge spanning a small creek. The screen probably hid the bed, Megan surmised. Beyond it, in the back corner, stood a huge armoire with a frilly petticoat sticking out of the door. Small bottles and jars, a hairbrush, and other toiletries cluttered the top of a dressing table beneath a small oval mirror. But no scissors or knife in sight.

She started chewing where the tag attached to the dress. Mutterings came from Lottie in the small room. Megan gnawed faster. It felt looser. She tugged and pulled and chewed.

It broke free just as Lottie walked out of the other room, stretching out a measuring tape between her hands. "Damn thing got all tangled up somehow." She approached Megan.

Megan swallowed the tag. It stuck in her dry throat. She swallowed again, and again, then used her tongue to try to get the tag back out.

"What's the matter with you?" Lottie asked. "You got a funny look about you."

"May I ... have a drink of ... water please?" Megan croaked. The tag tickled her throat. She fought the urge to gag.

Lottie draped the measuring tape around her neck as she crossed the room, muttering, "The things I do for my brother." She opened a door in the front of the bureau, took out two glasses, and set them on top of the bureau. She took out a crystal decanter, pulled out the stopper, and splashed a generous amount of amber liquid in each glass. She came back, glasses in hand, and gave one to Megan.

Megan downed the drink in one gulp. It burned through her like flaming lighter fluid all the way down to her toes, making them curl. It hit her stomach with the force of a bomb and exploded in her brain. It made her eyes run like busted faucets. It left her gasping and coughing. "Oh, my G-God, wh-what was th-that?"

"You ain't never had whiskey before?"

"You c-call that wh-whiskey?" Megan coughed, wiping her eyes. At least the tag was gone. Probably incinerated.

"Ain't the best I got, but I sure ain't wastin' that on the likes of you." Lottie tossed back her drink and set the glass on the table. "Stand up so's I can measure you."

Megan remained on the loveseat, clutching the red dress to her front. "I'm sure whatever you have will fit me just fine."

Lottie planted her hands on her hips. "I ain't got all day to fritter away on you. Get up or get out."

Megan reluctantly put the dress aside and stood, wearing only her white cotton bra, lacy red bikini panties, and red T-strapped high heels.

Lottie's eyes grew as round as dinner plates as she stared at Megan. "What in blazes ... Where's your corset?"

"I don't have one."

"Chemise?"

"Nope."

"Petticoat?"

"Uh uh."

"Stockings? Garters?"

"Neither."

"My, my." Lottie shook her head. "Brazen little thing, ain't cha?"

"It's the latest fashion in Chicago. Very liberating."

"Hmmph. Stand straight. Hold your arms out." Lottie stretched the tape this way and that way and every other way and in no time had all the measurements. "'Bout what I figgered. Shouldn't take long to fix it up for you." She headed for the small room.

Footsteps sounded on the stairs outside.

Seth. Megan eagerly watched the door.

Lottie muttered, "That time already?" She paused in the middle of the room and struck a pose that emphasized her high big breasts.

The outside door opened, and a man walked in.

Megan snatched up the dress and clasped it in front of her.

"Get your skirt up, Lottie. I don't have much time." He loosened his black string tie with one finger and stuffed the tie in his trouser pocket.

Lottie said, "I got a guest."

"Guest?" He laughed harshly. He removed his black suit coat and gave it a shake. A crisp white shirt, and tight black trousers completed his wardrobe. "You don't have guests." He turned and tossed the coat on the loveseat. "You have custo—" His gaze landed on Megan standing there. "What do we have here?" He grinned and approached Megan. "A surprise for me?" He tilted his head and looked her over. "Lottie, old girl, you've outdone yourself this time." He glanced over his shoulder at Lottie, who had flinched when he said *old girl*. "And I didn't bring you anything. So sorry." His attention swung back to Megan. Beady blue eyes checked her over as if she was something for sale. "What a raven-haired sweet little piece of meat you are." He grabbed her chin and turned her head to one side.

She jerked free. "Don't touch me."

He smiled a cold smile that never reached his eyes. "I'll do whatever I please with you. From the looks of you, you don't obey very well. Or do you prefer being beat? I like gals that got a hankering for a good beating. What's this?" He snapped her left bra strap.

She smacked his hand away. "Keep your hands off me, you pig."

"Feisty, eh? What are you hiding under there?" He yanked the dress from her grip.

"Give me that!" She tried to get it back, but he held it up high as he stared at her jumping up and down in her scanty underwear.

"What the hell? Lottie, you see what she's wearing? Whooee, keep jumping, honey." He squeezed one of her breasts.

Megan shoved him away.

He stepped up and slapped her face, spinning her head to one side.

Megan saw red.

She slapped him back. Hard. The sound rang throughout the room, louder than Lottie's gasp.

Rage mottled his face. "You're going to regret that, bitch."

Megan clenched her fists. She pushed through gritted teeth, "Touch me again and I'll kick your balls up your throat."

Behind him, Lottie clapped a hand over her mouth, her eyes wide.

He looked momentarily stunned, then he threw back his head and laughed. "Mighty big talk for a slut. I can see why you're all beat up. You're the kind that asks for it, aren't you. Can't keep your mouth shut. Stupid little twit." He flung the dress on the floor. "You obviously don't know who I am."

Megan gave him a scathing once over. "Slicked-back hair. Shifty eyes. Acting like you're the big man in town. You must be that loser I've heard about named John Bingo."

Lottie's eyes widened even more.

A blank look flittered over his face. "Loser. *Los*er."

Megan added, "For such a bully, I thought you'd be bigger." He was five-ten maybe, slender, his broad chest and shoulders oddly out of proportion to the rest of his average-sized figure. He was nowhere near the size and height of his descendent Barton. Bingo had Barton's jet-black hair but lacked his movie star handsomeness due to a pocked-marked face and ordinary features. Although the eyes were the same. Deep blue and mean.

"Lottie? Where did you get this insolent wench?"

"She's from Chicago."

Bingo unbuttoned his shirt. "That explains it. Nothing good has come out of that cesspool." He went to Lottie, pulling his shirt out of his trousers. "Get on the table and spread your legs. All this excitement has worked up a powerful urge in me."

"John, let's use the bed." Lottie nodded to the Oriental scene.

"Get up there." Bingo raised his hand. "Or I'll—"

"Don't you dare hit her," Megan snarled, drawing Lottie's startled gaze before the hard look returned to her eyes.

"Shut up," he said over his shoulder. "Watch and learn. You're next." He shoved Lottie toward the table. She backed up and sat on top of it with little effort due to her height and leaned back on her elbows. Bingo grabbed her knees and pushed her long legs apart. His hands shoved the negligee up her naked white thighs. Lottie murmured something that made him laugh.

Next my ass. Megan glanced around for something to bash over his head.

A big brass spittoon sat on the floor past the end of the loveseat.

Hurried footsteps sounded on the stairs.

The door opened just as Megan snatched the spittoon and hefted it over her head.

"Sorry it took me so long—" Seth stopped in the doorway, the happy look on his face quickly dissolving as he stared at John Bingo standing between his sister's spread legs. One of Bingo's hands pawed Lottie's breast, while the other fumbled with the front of his trousers.

Seth's eyebrows shot up to his hairline when he saw Megan clad in only her underwear, holding the spittoon high.

She quickly put it back on the floor and made hand motions to Bingo and Lottie then shrugged.

Watching them, Lottie pressed her lips into a thin line. She locked eyes with Seth and jerked her head toward the door.

Bingo glanced over his shoulder. "Do you mind, Marshal? I'm about to poke your sister." He cocked a dark eyebrow. "Want to watch? No? Suit yourself." He returned his attention to Lottie.

A muscle bulged in Seth's cheek. "Get out, Bingo."

"Go to hell. I'm busy playing with your sister's tits. Nice, aren't they. You ever played with 'em?"

Seth crossed the floor in two strides. He grabbed Bingo's shoulder and jerked him around. "I said get out."

"Seth," Lottie cried.

Bingo shoved Seth away. He yanked his shirt straight, pulled down the cuffs. His trousers hung open in front beneath the shirttails. "You have overstepped your boundaries, O'Connor. You have no right to tell me to get out of here."

"You forget I'm the Marshal."

"And *you* forget that I pay for *all* of this." Bingo swept his hand around the room. "Including *her*." He jabbed his finger at Lottie, who had pushed herself off the table and stood beside it, her face tight with anger. "This is all mine. *She* is mine. Bought and paid for to do with as I please. You are trespassing. Marshal." Bingo buttoned up his shirt. "One would think you'd show me a little gratitude."

"Gratitude!" Seth had his hands balled into fists at his sides, and fury in his eyes.

"I took your sister out of the cribs and set her up here where she lives like a queen." Bingo stuffed his shirt into his trousers then buttoned the front. "Doesn't have to do a thing except keep me sated and fiddle around in her precious sewing room. All these years I've been taking care of her. I've spent a small fortune on her." He pulled out the string tie from his trouser pocket and put it on. "So yeah, a little gratitude isn't too much to ask. Instead, you keep harassing me. Fighting me every step of the way. Ridiculing my ideas for our fine city. Interrupting my afternoon poke with your dear sister. You keep it up and this can all disappear like *that*." He snapped his fingers. "And she'll be back in those cribs, with every man-jack crawling all over her like maggots on a dead critter."

He swiveled toward Lottie and his tone turned insulting. "If any of 'em will have her, old as she is. Take away her paints and powders, shove her out in the light, and we'll find a dried up old prune." He turned back to Seth. "So, you had better think twice before crossing me again. As it is," Bingo brushed something off his pristine shirtsleeve, "Lottie will pay the price for my interrupted pleasure today."

Seth took a step closer to Bingo. "You beat her and I'll—"

"Oh, I won't beat her. Maybe that one." Bingo nodded to Megan. "But not my old girl Lottie. No, I'll have to do something else."

Megan started to say something, but Seth stopped her with a quick shake of his head.

"Like what, Johnny?" Lottie sounded timid, almost afraid.

"I've been hearing a lot of complaints from Matilda about how she's losing so much money from not having that little room available. I know she can make a hell of lot more off a girl in there than the rent I pay her." He held out his hand, as if inspecting his nails. "Perhaps it's time I let her have it back."

Lottie hurried to Bingo and touched his arm. "Not my sewin' room, Johnny. Please."

"Now, Lottie," he patted her hand, "it's just a tiny room filled with doodads and frilly things."

"I'll do anythin' for you, Johnny. Anythin'."

"I know, old girl. Haven't you always? But Matilda—"

Lottie whirled to Seth. "Go. And take that Yankee whore with you."

"She's not a Yankee whore." Seth crossed his arms. "And we're not goin' anywhere."

"Seth. My sewin' room." Lottie's hard gaze turned pleading.

He stepped closer to her. "We'll leave if you come with us."

"What?" Lottie stared at her brother as if he'd sprouted horns.

"Come with us. Walk out of here. Leave all this behind."

An incredulous laugh erupted from Lottie. "And do *what?*"

"Yes, O'Connor." Bingo looked pityingly at Lottie. "What does a worn-out old whore do when no one wants her anymore?"

Seth ignored Bingo. "Anything but this, Lottie. Anything." Seth gripped her hands in both his. "I'll help you."

He spoke softly, his voice so sincere and pleading.

Megan's heart went out to him.

Not a crack appeared in Lottie's armored illusion. Her eyes locked with Seth's, she said, "Don't go, John. My brother's leavin'. Ain't cha, Seth?"

The corners of Seth's mouth turned down. "Ah, Lottie." He sighed the sigh of a too-often disappointed parent. Long-suffering and fed up. He released her hands and stepped back. "I'm still not leavin'."

Lottie snapped, "Damn it, Seth you better or I'll—"

"Don't worry, old girl, I'm going." Bingo walked to the loveseat.

Megan quickly moved out of his way to the other end of the loveseat.

He leered at her as he picked up his suit coat. He gave it a shake then shrugged into it. "Your brother spoiled the mood. Guess I'll go tell Matilda she can have that little room back."

Lottie glared at Seth with blame in her eyes.

Seth reached in his trouser pocket and pulled out a coin. "Here." He tossed the coin on the floor. It rolled a bit then fell over not far from the pointed tip of Bingo's shiny black boot. "There's your money back for today. You and Lottie are even. Don't go threat'n' her again about her sewin' room."

Bingo snickered. "If I were you, Marshal, I wouldn't go throwing money around. You're going to need every bit you can get your hands on to support the fair Susannah in the manner she deserves. Consider this a wedding gift." He pushed the coin towards Seth with the toe of his boot.

The hate between the two men felt as tangible as another presence in the room.

One side of Seth's upper lip curled. "Keep your gift."

"See?" Bingo raised his hand, palm up. "What did I tell you? No gratitude. Fine. If you insist." He picked up the coin and put it in his trouser pocket. "As they say, a fool and his money are soon parted. And you, Marshal, are a fool." He straightened his coat with a sharp tug on the bottom of it. "I'll do as I damn well please with Lottie and anything concerning her." He pointed at Megan. "I'm not through with you."

Seth took a step closer to Bingo. "Touch her and I'll kill you."

"Oh?" Bingo raised his eyebrows. He tilted his head and studied Seth a moment. A knowing look entered Bingo's eyes. "Ohhh. So, *you're* the reason the Yankee whore is here." He laughed. "Not even married yet and you're already arranging a poke on the side. Just in case the fair Susannah is a little too prim and proper for your tastes, eh? How prudent of you."

"Seth," Lottie hissed. "You ain't doin' that, are you?"

"Leave Susannah out of this," Seth growled, cutting a sharp look at Lottie. His high cheekbones stood out in sharp relief in the lantern light.

"You surprise me, O'Connor. I never imagined such foresight out of you." Bingo's insulting gaze swept over Megan. "I've never heard of a mail-order whore either. Wish I'd thought of that angle. One could make a fortune." He raised his hands to his hair and gently smoothed back each side.

Bingo didn't agree with Brylcreem's claim of *A little dab'll do ya*. Slicked back from all along his hairline from ear to ear, his hair shone with goo applied so thickly it looked like a helmet, impenetrable by rain, unmovable by wind. Megan wondered if Lottie ever tried to run her fingers through it. *Yuck.*

"You can have the slut, Marshal. Were I you," Bingo rubbed his hands together as he stared Megan in the eye, "I'd cut out that sharp tongue first thing."

Megan raised her chin and stared defiantly back at him, although she knew in her gut it wasn't over with him.

Lottie hurried to Bingo and touched his shoulder. "You comin' back later, Johnny?"

"I doubt it. I'm entertaining some men I hope to invest with."

"Bring 'em here," Lottie urged. "I'll entertain 'em like they never been entertained before."

"Oh, I don't know. There will be four of them. Plus, me."

She laughed gaily. "The more the merrier." She ran her hand down the front of Bingo's coat, then leaned close to him and said in a husky tone, "I can get a couple other girls to join us, if you think the men might like that."

Bingo smiled. "My lovely Lottie, I like the way you think." He kissed her cheek. He had to stretch a bit since he stood about an inch shorter than she was. "See you this evening." He headed for the door, then paused and turned back. "By the way, Marshal. You are mistaken. *I* will kill *you*."

The prophetic words sent a sheet of ice down Megan's spine. Her stomach twisted when Seth replied in a clear, firm voice, "Say when and where and we'll see who walks away."

Bingo laughed. "All in due time, Marshal. All in due time."

After Bingo left, Lottie turned on Seth. "What's the matter with you, boy? You tryin' to get me throwed out in the street? Get yourself killed? You fool."

Seth said, "I need to use your room."

"What for?"

"I need to talk to Megan, so I can find out who did that to her. It's my job, Lottie."

Lottie pushed past him and went to the dresser. "You got an office. Do it there. I gotta get ready for this evenin'." She picked up a brush and ran it through her hair.

"I have two men locked up. No privacy there. And she doesn't have anything to wear. Remember? You can fix her up somethin' while she and I talk."

Lottie slammed the brush on top of the dresser. The assortment of bottles and jars rattled and jumped. "If I hear one more word about that damn dress I'm gonna scream."

"Then just do it. And we'll leave."

She glowered at his reflection in the mirror. "All right, all right. Shouldn't take me long. Then you can get the hell out." She went into the little room.

"You not feelin' well?" Seth stepped closer to Megan. "You're awful pale."

"I'm just—overwhelmed."

He chuckled. "I know the feelin'." He reached for her hand, then lowered his hand back to his side when Lottie emerged from the sewing room carrying a dark blue dress. She stopped short, and eyed them suspiciously, standing so close together.

"I'll sew at the table while you two talk." Lottie started toward the table.

"I want to talk to Megan in private."

Lottie paused and pinned Seth with an icy stare. "I ain't leavin' you two here alone. It ain't fittin'."

Megan bit back a laugh at Lottie suddenly having morals.

"I'd like a little privacy, Lottie."

"Why? What you got to hide?" Her eyes widened. "You *did* bring that Yankee whore here an' now you wanna use my room to poke her." She threw the dress on the floor. "Get your own damn room."

"For God's sake, Lottie—"

"Seth had no idea I was coming here. I swear to it." Megan held up her right hand. "And I'm not a whore."

"Humph," came from Lottie.

"Megan and I are old friends. We need to talk. Please, just go, Lottie." Exasperation filled Seth's voice. "The sooner you get that dress done, the sooner we'll leave. So, it's up to you how long this takes." He crossed his arms. "You keep this up, we'll still be here when your *guests* show up. Johnny won't be very happy then."

Lottie pursed her lips then stalked over to the armoire. She opened one door and pulled out a lavender dressing gown with a wide lacy collar. She flung it at Megan. "Cover yourself. I'll be back in an hour. You better be done *talkin'* by then." She picked up the dress off the floor and went to the door leading to the interior of the house. She paused and glanced back at Seth. "Don't you forget you're marryin' Susannah on Sunday." Her gaze moved to Megan, who had put on the dressing gown. "I'll be in the next room. These walls are mighty thin."

The door no sooner closed behind Lottie and Seth pulled Megan into his arms. He kissed her hard then held her tight. "I can't believe you're here."

"I can't either." Her mouth sought his again, and they kissed long and greedily. She clung to the man for whom she had come through time. *He may be Susannah's come Sunday, until then ...*

He feathered kisses on her face and temple. "How did you get here? What happened with Barton?"

"Oh Seth, it was awful."

"Tell me everything."

Sitting on the loveseat, he held her while she told him about her last night in 1981. When she came to the part about escaping Barton, all the terror and fear came racing back. Her voice shook, and tears fell as the dam finally broke inside her. She cried in Seth's arms as she blubbered the rest of the story, ending with meeting Tim then Susannah. Seth stroked her hair, and let her tears soak his shirt, redolent with the familiar smells of horses and leather and that earthy scent that was only his. In his arms, she felt safe, cherished, home.

Chapter 33

Megan opened her eyes to a high ceiling that looked like it was made of tin. Confused, not knowing where she was, she glanced around, saw Seth, and remembered everything. He and Lottie sat across from each other at the table, deep in conversation. Their profiles showed the same nose and chin. Megan smiled, glad that they were talking amicably. Her fingers curled around the edge of a scratchy blanket smelling of floral perfume that covered her on the loveseat. She closed her eyes. The siblings' lowered voices droned on.

"—something Megan mentioned once."

Hearing her name, Megan's ears perked up although her eyes stayed closed.

"You mean it's *her* fault you became Marshal?"

"No, it's not her fault. Tarnation, Lottie, you keep twistin' things around to make it sound bad. She said something one time and it just stuck with me."

"What'd she say?"

"That I could be part of the solution not the problem. It made me think."

"So, you thought yourself right into bein' Marshal." A long, loud sigh followed. "That job'll get you killed."

"Appreciate your confidence in me, sister."

"You ain't no killer. Plain and simple."

"I'm not aimin' to kill anybody. Just tryin' to keep the peace."

"Won't be any peace you don't leave John alone. Don't give me that look. You know how mean he is."

"He's the rott'nest bastard on God's green earth." Seth growled the words. "Crooked, cheatin' brute. Piss poor excuse for a father too. Always dumpin' his bastards on the Widow Kemp like he does."

"I won't deny he ain't all those things, but he's good to the widow. He gives her plenty of money for those young'uns' upkeep. Those little ones are right fond of him. Heard tell they squeal like a litter of piglets ever' time he shows up."

"Litter's right. How many are there anyway?"

"Six. The two oldest are the widow's. The rest are Bingo's."

"From different mamas every one of 'em. They're all hellions."

Megan could picture Seth shaking his head. She realized one of those kids was Barton's grandmother. He'd said she was the oldest of four half-siblings fathered by John Bingo. *Wish I'd thought to ask her name.*

"Whores gotta do somethin' with their offspring," Lottie said matter-of-factly. "I reckon those four mamas are mighty grateful to John for findin' a decent home for their young'uns."

"He's a gen-u-ine saint," Seth drawled sarcastically.

After a pause, Lottie said, "That Yankee over there sure lit a fire in him."

"What happened?"

Lottie told Seth about Megan's interaction with Bingo. Seth chuckled a few times and said something under his breath even more times. He laughed when Lottie said, "Then she told him she'd kick his balls up his throat. I gotta say, I ain't seen many people stand up to John like that. She even told him not to hit me." Lottie paused. "I been in this town longer than I care to think of an' I can count on one hand the people who'd defend me. She did, and she don't know me from spit. Don't know why, but she did. She's made a powerful enemy, Seth. She ain't gonna be in town long, is she?"

"You'll have to ask her."

"I hope she don't plan on goin' to the weddin'."

Seth chuckled. "Actually, Susannah said she invited Megan."

"Oh Lordy. What're you gonna do with her in the meantime? She ain't stayin' here."

Moments passed before Seth replied, "I'll figure something out."

"You better stop that, boy." Lottie's voice turned sharp.

"What?"

"Starin' at her like she's the shiniest bauble you ever did see."

A chair scraped back, and boots stomped on the floor.

"Sit down," Lottie snapped.

"You don't understand." Seth's tone sounded harsh and strangled at the same time.

"What I understand is you asked Susannah for her hand in front of the whole town. 'Bout time, everyone said. Ever since, she's been happy as a bee in a meadow of wildflowers. She's waited a 'coon's age for you, although I don't rightly know why sometimes. Don't you go breakin' that sweet girl's heart over some Yankee gal who appears outta nowhere and none of us knows nothin' about."

"What I do with my life is none of your damn business." Ice encased Seth's voice.

Time to end this. Megan groaned and stretched her arms, opening her eyes.

"Well, look who's finally back among the livin'." Lottie scowled at Megan.

Smiling, Seth hurried over to her. "Feel better?"

"I'm sorry I fell asleep."

"You were plumb tuckered out." His warm gaze caressed her face. "Lottie has your dress ready."

"Oh, good." Megan flung back the blanket and swung her feet to the floor. The dressing gown fell open, exposing her legs. Seth stared as if he'd never seen them before. Aware of Lottie watching, Megan quickly stood, and shook the gown straight, then pulled the front closed over her breasts. "I'll change clothes and get out of your hair." She smiled at Lottie, whose scowl never changed.

"I'll leave you two to your women things and be back shortly." Seth nodded to Lottie and left.

Lottie went behind the Oriental screen. She emerged holding some sort of stiff contraption with dangling ties. "Put this on."

"I'm not wearing that."

"Every lady wears a corset."

"Not in Chicago."

Lottie's upper lip curled. "Maybe you should go back there."

"I could if I had something to wear."

Lottie grunted. She went behind the screen again and came out with a petticoat and a dress.

Megan put them on then looked at herself in the small oval mirror above the dresser. The dark blue dress had pearls buttons down the front, a high neck, and long, tight sleeves, all trimmed in ivory lace. The petticoat made the skirt puff out below her trim waist. It seemed awful warm clothing for spring, but it certainly covered her up, which may have been Lottie's intention. "It's lovely. Thank you. You have quite a talent."

"You can go now." Lottie went to the loveseat and folded the blanket Megan had used.

"One more thing. Do you have a pair of slippers I can borrow? Just until I get a pair of shoes from the General Store? These shoes are killing me."

Lottie straightened with a huff, stalked behind the screen again, and reappeared with a pair of slippers. "Now get out."

Megan took the slippers. "Thank you again, Charlotte." She headed for the door then paused when Lottie spoke.

"I don't know who you are or how exactly you know my brother but it's clear as a spring creek that he has feelin's for you. I don't want no trouble between him and Susannah over you."

Megan turned back to Lottie, who held the folded blanket against her chest, her face serious. "I'm not here to cause any trouble. I think the world of Seth. He's one of those rarities—a kind man. I think it'll help him be a good Marshal, don't you? I'm so proud of him. You must be too. I only want what makes him happy."

Lottie's face softened. Her voice sounded less gruff when she said, "Susannah makes him happy."

"I hope so." Everything inside Megan ached at the thought of Seth and Susannah together. *If he lives. If I die. If any of it even happens. If ... if ...* She repeated softly, "I truly hope so."

The door opened. There he was. Megan's heart skipped a beat.

Seth grinned, delight in his eyes. "You look beautiful. Thank you, Lottie." He glanced at his sister. "Think you got another dress Megan can wear to the dance tomorrow night?"

Lottie put her hands on her hips. "Another one?"

"What dance?" Megan asked.

"There's a barn raisin' tomorrow on the outskirts of town. There'll be a dance in the evenin'. You need another dress."

It had been a dance after a wedding in the other Megan's letter.

Lottie snapped, "Oh for—"

"Please, Lottie?" Seth asked.

"Boy, you're wearin' out your welcome right fast. I reckon I got one I can fix up for her." She glanced at Megan. "Come by later tomorrow afternoon." She paused, then added, "Megan."

Megan inclined her head in acknowledgement of the use of her first name. A small but promising step. "Thank you, Charlotte. I can't wait to see another one of your lovely creations." *I wonder if it'll be purple?*

Seth looked at Megan with one eyebrow raised. "Charlotte?"

"Go." Megan gave him a push and followed him out of the room. She held up the front the long dress and carefully descended the steps. The darkened enclosure felt like an oven turned up on high heat. *I already miss air conditioning.*

Halfway down Seth turned, caught her in his arms, and kissed her. They sank onto the steps and kept on kissing, their arms around each other. The heat, the sweat beading her forehead, the uncertainties, the possibilities of all that lay ahead suddenly receded into the background. All that matter was here and now, with him.

They would have few chances to kiss or touch or anything once they left the privacy of the stairway, Megan realized. After Sunday, they might never do any of it ever again. She deepened her kiss. His hand stroked her breast. *Oh God I want him. Just once more.* His labored breathing matched hers. *I've never done it on stairs,* crossed her mind. She ran her fingers through his coarse hair, then giggled against his mouth.

He broke away, and asked, his voice husky, "What's so funny?"

"I wonder if your sister ever tried to do this with Bingo." She toyed with his hair.

"Funny lookin', ain't it? I've never seen it move no matter how strong the wind blows."

Megan giggled again and rested her head on his chest. His arms encircled her, and she felt again that sense of being home. She sighed. "Your sister hates me." A soft laugh rumbled beneath her ear.

"She hates just about everybody. Don't take it personal. 'Sides, you called her Charlotte and she didn't skin you alive. That says a lot." He kissed the top of her head. "I've missed you, Miss Megan." That husky tone again.

She raised her face to his and met his gaze in the dimness. "I've missed hearing you call me that."

"My Miss Megan," he murmured. His mouth covered hers again, his hand caressed her breast, and Megan decided the stairs would be just fine.

The door at the bottom of the stairway opened.

Megan and Seth sprang apart as sunlight spilled up the first few steps and Tim poked his head inside. His eyes widened. "Oops. Sorry to interrupt." Grinning, he started to close the door.

"Damn it," Seth muttered, then said louder, "Hold up there, Tim. We're comin'." He gave Megan a quick kiss. "You ready to venture out into the Wild West?"

"Ye—" she started to say but quickly changed it to, "I reckon."

He laughed then put his hands on his knees and pushed himself up. He held out his hand to her. She pulled off her high heels, put on the slippers, then took his hand and stood. He touched her cheek, the look in his shadowed eyes a mixture of regret and confusion. She put her hand over his and held it there.

"I hate to nag but Sue's waiting on us," Tim called from below.

Megan asked, "Susannah?"

Seth shot a scowl over his shoulder at Tim, then took Megan's hand and kissed it before releasing it. "You're going to spend the night with her and her father."

Holy moly. This should be interesting.

"I'm sorry," Seth said. "But there's not a vacant room anywhere that's fit for you."

"It'll be fine." Megan smiled. "I like her."

Seth cocked his head, his eyes narrowed, his expression saying, *Women. Don't understand 'em.*

Megan kissed him once more, wondering if this was the last time, hoping it wasn't, knowing it should be. She reluctantly ended the kiss, and, clutching the shoes, hurried down the stairs to join Tim out in the sunshine. Seth followed behind her.

Tim gave her an appreciative once over. "I see Lottie worked her wonders again. You're as pretty as a bluebonnet, Miss Megan."

She smiled, glanced around, and recognized one of the whores still lingering around the porch. "What's that young blonde's name over there?"

"That's Daisy." Tim's dimple appeared. "Sweet, nimble Daisy."

"Daisy," Megan called, gesturing with her hand when the blonde turned around. "Come here, please."

Daisy put her hands on her hips. "What for?"

"Please?"

Daisy flounced down the steps and sauntered over, her hips swaying. She smiled at Seth and batted her eyes at Tim. She gave Megan a guarded look. "Wha'd ya want?"

"Here." Megan held out the red high heels.

Daisy's jaw dropped. She stared at the shoes with wide eyes. She licked her lips. "For ... me?" She glanced at Megan, who nodded. She took the shoes with both hands and held them as if they were made of fine glass. "I ain't never had nothin' so purty." Daisy lifted her startled gaze. "Thank ya kindly, ma'am. Thank ya." She hurried away, clutching the high heels to her chest as she joined the other whores. "Lookee what I got!"

"That was sweet of you, Megan." Seth smiled.

"She won't think they're so purty when her feet are killing her."

He chuckled. "I reckon you're hungry?"

"Starving. Where are we going to eat?" she asked, as if one of them would suggest McDonalds or Pizza Hut. She laughed to herself. Those days were over. Or yet to come, depending on how one looked at it.

A wagon rattled by drawn by two horses. Seth nodded to the man holding the reins. "At Susannah's."

"You're in for a treat. Sue's a mighty fine cook." Tim rubbed his hands together. "I can't wait. Shall we?"

"We're all eating there?" Megan shaded her eyes against the slanting sun. Late afternoon, maybe early evening, she had no idea what time it was. She'd lost her watch while coming through the portal.

Seth shrugged. "I thought it might be ... easier if we're all together."

It sounded like a terrible idea to Megan.

SETH'S DOOR

***

A couple hours later, Tim wiped his mouth with a linen napkin and placed it on his plate smeared with blotches of gravy. "Excellent meal, Sue. Appreciate you having me over."

"You know you will always be welcome in our home." The light from the gas sconces on the walls turned Susannah's hair to the rich, warm hue of top shelf whiskey. She looked across the table at Seth. "Isn't that right, Seth?" She paused, then repeated a bit sharper, "Seth?"

"Hmmm?" His attention snapped back to her from wherever it had been. "Oh yes, delicious, Susannah. As always."

"What I said was—" Susannah pressed her lips together then muttered, "Never mind." She stood and piled dirty plates on top of one another.

Megan gathered the silverware, heaving an inward sigh of relief that the longest, most awkward meal she had ever endured was over.

"Don't bother yourself with that," Susannah said.

"It'll go faster with the two of—"

"Please." Susannah held out her hand. "You are a guest."

Megan placed the silverware in Susannah's hand. "That was the best meal I've had in ages. Thank you. And thank you for letting me stay in your lovely home."

The small house reminded Megan of an antique store. They sat on matching floral upholstered chairs around a large claw-footed table made of dark wood. Nearby was sofa with a high back and elegant cream-colored cushions. A matching wingback chair sat beside a small table that held two books and an oil lamp. An upright piano stood along one wall. Bookcases lined another wall. Megan wondered how many classics she'd find on those shelves. Another wall had a fireplace built into it. A rocking chair sat in front of a window framing a dark night behind lace curtains. A door at the end of a hallway led to the back of Mr. Mead's general store.

"You're welcome." Susannah headed toward the kitchen with the dirty dishes.

As soon as she was out of earshot, Megan leaned over the table and said softly to Seth and Tim, "She knows something."

"What are you talking about?" Seth asked. "Knows what?"

"I don't know." Megan glanced at the kitchen doorway. "She's acting a lot different towards me than she did when we first met. She was warm and friendly then. She's hardly looked me in the eye this evening."

Tim rested his elbow on the table. "Now that you mention it, she has been a trifle cold towards you. But I don't know what she could possibly know or how she would have learned it. I don't think—we could have asked for prettier weather for the weekend," Tim smoothly changed the subject when Susannah returned. "Should be a perfect day for the barn raising tomorrow."

Susannah gathered bowls of leftover potatoes, carrots, gravy, and chunks of beef.

"'Course, it could snow tomorrow too." Tim crossed one leg over the other.

"In April?" Megan asked.

"Anything's possible during a Texas spring," Tim replied. "I reckon you get a lot of snow in your part of the country?"

"Several feet sometimes. The streets are impassable." Megan waited until Susannah had disappeared into the kitchen again then said softly, "I'm telling you, she knows something. She's acting weird. And you're acting like an ass." Megan gave Seth a pointed look.

He looked baffled. "What did I do?"

"She's brimming with excitement over her wedding day like any other woman. But every time she brings it up you ignore her or change the subject or look like you're off in La La Land."

After countless rebuffs, Susannah had stopped trying to engage Seth in conversation about their big day and had spent the latter part of the meal in silence, a sad look on her face.

Seth sat up straight. "We need to talk. We need to figure out—" He broke off when Susannah returned with a rustle of her tan dress.

"More coffee anyone?" Susannah rested a hand on Seth's shoulder. "Or would you gentlemen prefer whiskey?"

"Nothing for me, Sue. Got a long day tomorrow." Tim pushed his chair back and stood. He straightened his black coat then patted his stomach. "Thanks again for the meal and fine company." He nodded to Megan.

"Reckon I'll leave too. Gotta make my rounds," Seth said. Susannah removed her hand from his shoulder and stepped back as he stood. "Tell your father good night for me."

"I will. He's helping the new girl in the store or he would have been here. I'll walk out with you." Susannah smiled, linking her arm with his.

"I'd like to talk to Megan outside before I leave. If you don't mind."

Susannah's smile faded. "Of course." She removed her arm from his and clasped her hands together at her waist.

"Megan?" Seth gestured to the door.

She stood and went outside, feeling Susannah's eyes on her.

Out on the wide porch cloaked in darkness, Seth grabbed her hand, pulled her to the far end near a swing, and kissed her. It took all of Megan's will power and conviction of what lay ahead of her to tear her mouth from his.

"Seth, we have to stop this. You're getting married in two days."

He rested his forehead against hers. "Don't remind me." He ran his hands up her back, then drew away. "We have to find some time to talk, Megan. Serious talk. Soon."

She reached up and cupped the side of his beloved face. She hadn't the heart to tell him the one thing they probably didn't have was time.

"I knew about you and Susannah." She smiled sadly. "I wish I had gotten here sooner."

"I kept waitin' for you to show up."

"I didn't find the portal until tonight, or last night, or whenever it was." She lowered her hand to his chest. "So, you proposed to her in front of the whole town?"

"You heard that, huh? Wasn't the whole town."

"Tell me the story."

He leaned against the porch railing, holding her hand. "One day a month or so ago a couple of hogs got loose and were running around town, tearing things up. A bunch of us were tryin' to catch them, and not havin' much luck. Susannah came out of the schoolhouse with her arms full of books and one of those hogs ran right into her and knocked her down in the street. We'd had several days of rain and there was mud everywhere, and she landed in a big puddle of it. I ran to her to see if she was all right. She was covered in mud. Hair, dress, everything. She looked so surprised. Suddenly she started laughin'. She was laughin' so hard she couldn't stand. I tried to help her up, but her hand was all muddy and it slipped out of mine. I lost my footin' and fell flat on my backside beside her, splashin' more mud on her. She laughed even harder. I started laughin' too. There we sat, covered in mud, laughin' like a couple of loons."

He chuckled, shaking his head. "By then, quite a crowd had gathered 'round us, but all I saw was her muddy whiskey-colored hair and her sparklin' eyes. She looked prettier than I'd ever seen her ... and I've ... I've been so ... so lonely."

His admission came out softly, hesitantly, and caused a pang in Megan's heart. She squeezed his hand.

"An' the words popped out without me even knowin' it. *Marry me, Susannah.* Just like that. No sooner had I said it then I wished I could take it back. But she looked so happy. She threw her arms around me and we both fell back in the mud, and well, I couldn't ... I couldn't tell her it was a mistake. I just couldn't. She was so happy. She covered my face with kisses, giggling like a schoolgirl. And she's been happy ever since. Wasn't long I was startin' to feel happy too and lookin' forward to—to her and me ... being together. Now you're here." He lifted her hand and kissed the back of it. "And I don't know what to do. How to tell her the weddin's off."

"Don't do anything rash, Seth." He started to say something, but she hurried on, "We don't know how long I'll be here. How long before I—" she almost said *fade away* but quickly changed it to "—come apart."

"That might not happen to you."

"It might not. But we don't know for sure. You cancel your Sunday wedding, and I might be gone Monday. And maybe I can't come back. Maybe the portal won't open again. Where would that leave you?" She clasped his hand to her chest. "I don't want you to be lonely."

He made a sound between a grunt and a groan, pulled her to his chest. "Ah, Miss Megan," he stroked her hair. "What're we gonna do?"

"You're going to marry her." Megan paused to clear the emotion clogging her throat. The words were hard to say. "And have a passel of kids and live happily ever after." She drew back and raised her face to his. "And be the best damn marshal west of the Mississippi. Now kiss me once more before I go inside and send your bride-to-be out here."

When they finally came up for air, Megan broke free and hurried to the door, tugging her dress straight, and smoothing her hair. She paused, took a deep breath, and went inside.

Susannah looked up from where she and Tim sat at the table, cleaned of all evidence of their meal.

"Seth wants to tell you goodnight, Susannah."

Susannah jumped up.

"I'll give you two a few minutes." Tim stretched out his legs.

Susannah's face turned fire engine red as she hurried outside.

"Poor dear." Tim shook his head. "She's been waiting all evening for this private time with Seth, knowing she'll get some kisses." He cocked an eyebrow at Megan as she sat across from him. "Think he's going to disappoint her?"

"I have no idea what you're talking about."

"Of course, you do. You have that just-kissed look about you."

Megan clapped a hand to her cheek. "Do you think she noticed?"

A chuckle came from Tim. "Doubt it. For a smart woman, she's an innocent about many things between the sexes. Sure hate to see her get her heart broke." He grinned. "Good thing I'm here to pick up the pieces." He sat up and leaned forward. "When are you and Seth going to tell her? Better make it soon. Time's a wastin'."

Megan shot to her feet. "It's really none of your damn business."

Tim jerked back as if she'd slapped him.

She stalked across the carpeted floor and looked out a window at the shadowed forms of trees etched against the dark night. *What are they doing? Talking? Fighting? Kissing? I don't care. I can't care. I hope they're kissing.*

Liar, a little voice said in her head.

Shut up.

"I'm sorry." She faced Tim. "I didn't mean to snap at you. It's been a long day and a lot to take in."

"I understand. And you are right. It's just that—" His eyes widened in surprise when the door opened, and Susannah entered, her face pale, her eyes downcast. Tim caught Megan's attention and they shared a knowing look. No kisses for Susannah that night.

Seth stuck his head around the side of the door. "You ready, Tim?" His gaze rested briefly on Megan, the look in his eyes troubled and bewildered. Then he was gone.

Tim stood and tipped his head to Megan. "Until tomorrow, Miss Megan." On his way out, he paused beside Susannah, and kissed her on the cheek. "Have I ever told you what a beautiful woman you are?"

Susannah rolled her eyes. "How many times have you said *that* to a female today?"

"All those other times were just a rehearsal for saying it to you."

Her cheeks turned a becoming pink and she gave a little laugh as she swatted Tim's arm. He winked at Megan then left, closing the door behind him.

"He's certainly crazy about you," Megan said.

Susannah tilted her head. "Crazy?"

"Smitten. He's certainly smitten with you."

Susannah went to the door and locked it. "Crazy might be more fitting. Woman crazy to be precise." She reached up and turned off the closest gas sconce.

"He's male. What do you expect?"

Susannah walked around the room extinguishing all the lights until only two candles burned on either end of the fireplace mantel. "Some restraint."

Megan laughed.

"He's a terrible flirt," Susannah said sternly. "Not a woman passes by he doesn't toss some flowery comment to."

"He's a charmer. I'm sure most of those women know he's full of baloney." Megan bit her lower lip. *When did that phase come into use?* She shrugged it off. She'd go nuts if she stopped to analyze everything she said before saying it.

Susannah looked puzzled. "What is ... full of baloney?"

"It means nonsense."

"You certainly have an odd way of saying some things. Although he *is* full of nonsense." Susannah went to the fireplace and picked up one of the candles. "I'm well aware of Timothy's feelings for me. It matters not one whit." Candlestick holder in hand, she turned and looked Megan in the eye. "I'm in love with Seth. Two days from now I will be made his wife. Two nights from now he will make me his."

Megan heard possessiveness, even a challenge in the other woman's voice, and there was a flash of defiance in her eyes. *She knows something. What? How?*

Susannah handed Megan the candle then took the other one from the mantel for herself. "If you'll follow me please I'll show you to your room." One hand cupping the dancing flame, Susannah went to the corner of the room and ascended a staircase leading upstairs.

Megan climbed the steep, narrow stairway, holding her skirt up with one hand, the candle with the other. Stairs creaked beneath her feet. They came to a narrow hallway. Shadows leapt up the walls.

"Father's room is at that end." Susannah pointed down the hallway. "He should be coming up soon. Mine is here in the middle. Yours is down here." They turned right and went to the door at the other end. "It's more of a storage area. I hope you'll be comfortable." She opened the door and stepped aside for Megan to enter.

Holding her candle high, Megan glanced around. Several trunks lined one wall. A metal dressmaking form stood in a corner near a chest of drawers. A huge armoire filled another corner. Beneath a window was a narrow bed covered with a patchwork quilt. She went further into the room. Susannah followed.

"If I had had more time—"

"This is fine." Megan put the candleholder on a table beside the bed, and in the candlelight, she saw what darkness and shadows had hidden. On top of the quilt was a hairbrush, washcloth, towel, bar of soap, and a white silk nightgown. "Oh Susannah. How thoughtful of you. Thank you so much."

"I know you have nothing of your own. If there is anything else you need, please let me know." Susannah glanced around. "Well, I'll leave you to settle in. There's water in the washbowl, and more in the pitcher. The necessary is out behind the house," she pointed in the direction, "and there's a chamber pot under the bed. There are extra blankets in the corner if you get chilly. Good night." She started to turn away.

"What's on the agenda for tomorrow?" Megan covered a yawn. She could barely keep her eyes open. The narrow bed looked like the next best thing to heaven.

"The barn raising. I'll be up and gone early. You may do as you wish."

"Can I go with you? I've never been to a barn raising."

A look of surprise flittered across Susannah's face. "You may join me if you're up before daylight. Good night."

She crossed the floor then paused in the doorway. Her free hand gripped the doorknob. She bowed her head. She seemed to be battling some inner demon. Her narrow shoulders heaved with a ragged breath Megan heard across the room.

When Susannah spoke, her words were low, harsh, and agonized.

They hit Megan like a punch in the stomach.

"I knew you would come one day. I hoped. I prayed. I wished on countless stars that I would never lay eyes on you." Susannah whirled around so fast the flame on her candle went horizontal. Her face looked unnaturally red in the candlelight that made the tears in her eyes shine. Her hand balled into a fist at her side, she cried, "Why couldn't you have just stayed away?"

Shock and surprise left Megan speechless.

Susannah pressed her fist to her mouth, her eyes wide. "I'm sorry," she gasped. "That was perfectly dreadful of me. I'm so sorry." She bolted out the door.

"Wait!" Megan ran after Susannah, who stopped at the top of the stairs and clung to the railing as if for support, keeping her back to

Megan. "I don't know what you're talking about." Megan stepped closer. "Why are you so angry with me? I've never seen you before today."

Susannah turned around. Her eyes glittered like shards of ice in the faint glow of the candlelight. "I knew I recognized you from somewhere, but it wasn't until you told me your name that I remembered where. Then in front of our store Seth called you Miss Megan and I—I—" She hung her head.

Baffled, Megan urged, "You what?"

Susannah's words came out soft but forceful. "I hated you."

The vehemence in her voice made Megan catch her breath in surprise. "But—but why?"

"Because," Susannah raised her head, "I believe you are Seth's Miss Megan."

Megan tried to hide her shock. "Susannah, you're talking in riddles. Please tell me what you think you know."

From downstairs came the chimes of a clock numbering the ninth hour before Susannah spoke. She kept a one-handed grip on the railing. "Several years ago, a fever swept through town, and Seth took terrible sick. Lottie tended to him night and day. I sometimes sat with him to let her rest. One night, the worst night, he was delirious and mumbled something over and over. I listened closely, trying to make out his words. I finally determined that it sounded like Miss Megan, which made no sense because I didn't know anyone by that name and had never heard it before. He started thrashing, shouting, *I can't get the door open. I keep trying but it won't open. Miss Megan. Miss Megan. I'm trying. I'm trying. But I can't get to you.* He shouted it over and over, wild with delirium." She lowered her gaze to the railing where her fingernail picked at the wood. "It was a terrible night. I remember it like yesterday. He was so sick. So ... tortured. Over a woman I'd never heard of."

Megan bit her lower lip, jealous to the core because Susannah was the one who had cared for Seth, who had shared countless meals, and evenings, and dances with him. Who had a history of years with him. At the same time, Megan felt a strong urge to thank Susannah for all she had done for Seth during those years. Instead, Megan asked, "Did you ask Seth about it?"

"I never got a chance. When he recovered from the fever, he returned to his ranch and I didn't see him for several months. I put it all from my mind. Until a year or so later. I was sewing up a rip in one of his shirts and found something in one of the pockets. It was a square piece of very thick paper stiffer than a playing card. A material I'd never seen before. It was a picture of a young woman. A colored picture of all things. I had no idea who she was. She wore a bright yellow top that had thin straps over the shoulders and a low rounded neckline. Absolutely scandalous. Her arms and shoulders bare, her chest exposed." Susannah clicked her tongue. "She had her black hair pulled back, so I couldn't tell how long it was."

I wore blue jean shorts, a yellow tank top, and had a ponytail that day, Megan remembered.

Susannah's gaze never wavered from Megan. "It was your hair that threw me. I didn't recognize you with those long curls." She paused and seemed to be waiting for some response or explanation.

She needs to know the truth. She deserves to know.

Fighting a battle of *Should I, or shouldn't I?* Megan kept her mouth shut.

After a long silence, Susannah continued, "There was a name written in Seth's handwriting on the back. Miss Megan McClure. The words Miss Megan hit me like a hundred-pound sack of sugar. I wondered if this was the same woman of his delirium. Then I noticed the document on the wall beside her. I know that document. Everyone knows the story about the Widow McClure returning the stolen money. I had seen her letter with my own eyes more than once on the wall of the bank in Cleburne. But the wall in the picture didn't look like the wall in the bank. And the letter looked yellowed and old. None of it made sense. Why was that oddly dressed woman standing beside that letter that had the same signature name as the name on the picture? Finally, I put it back in the pocket, and never mentioned it."

"Why not?"

Susannah looked down at her hands. "I was afraid. I didn't want to know if there was another woman somewhere else. And as long as no one with that named arrived in town." She shrugged. Her gaze rose to Megan's. "Did you write that letter?"

Megan hesitated then nodded.

"Are you the Widow McClure?"

Megan made a face. "Not really."

Susannah crossed her arms. "Either you are, or you aren't."

"It's ... it's complicated." Megan felt backed into a corner. *Tell her.*

"Are you Seth's Miss Megan?"

"You'll have to ask him."

"It's obvious he cares for you."

"Susannah—"

Susannah held up her hand. "There's no point in denying it. I saw you two this morning. He only had eyes for you. I remember verbatim your first conversation. He said, his voice full of wonderment, *You're here.* He touched your cheek, and asked, *Barton?* I don't know who Barton is. You nodded. *I'll kill him next chance I get,* he said, and sounded like he meant it. You said, *Marshal? Good for you.* In that moment he looked prouder than I have ever seen him." A pained look crossed her face. "You two said more to each other in those dozen words than he and I say in a year's worth of conversations."

She released a shaky sigh. "I should have known it was too good to be true when he asked me to marry him. I had a feeling he instantly regretted his spontaneity, but I took advantage of the chance and said yes. The closer the wedding came, the more I began to believe it would actually happen. It's less than two days away. So close." She motioned to Megan. "And here you are. Just in time to ruin my happiness." She laughed humorlessly, bitterly. "And to think I liked you when we met."

"Susannah, I'm not here to take Seth away from you. I swear it." At the other woman's dubious expression, Megan threw caution to the wind and said, "I'm here to save his life."

"Save his—what are you talking about?" Susannah stepped closer. "Who *are* you?"

Chapter 34

"You did *what?*" Seth stared at Megan as if she'd just said she had swam across the Atlantic. Tim stood beside Seth and looked just as shocked. The three of them stood on the boardwalk outside The Panther, Seth's saloon. Behind the bat wing doors, someone whistled a merry tune, and the smell of freshly baked bread came from the bakery next door.

Megan turned her back to the mid-morning sun. "I told Susannah about me. Where I'm from, how you and I met, everything. We were up pretty late."

A look of horror on his face, Seth repeated, "*Everything?*"

"Well, not *every*thing. Mainly the time traveling aspect."

The tin star pinned to his brown leather vest glinted in the sunlight as Seth removed his black hat and ran his hand through his hair. "Good God, Megan." He settled his hat back on his head, and asked in a tense voice, "Are you plumb out of your mind?"

"The poor woman thought she was going crazy. I know what that feels like. There are moments I still wonder if I'm nuts and locked up somewhere and this is all a delusion."

The hard look in Seth's eyes briefly softened. The ends of the red bandana around his neck fluttered in the warm spring breeze. Two men riding by on horses called a greeting to him, and he nodded in response.

Megan brushed a wind-blown curl off her face. "Susannah took it remarkably well. I think she believes me." She frowned at Tim when he snickered. "You believed Seth when he told you, right?"

Tim barked a laugh. "Honestly? Not one whit." At Seth's look of surprise, Tim said, "I believed that *you* believed it wholeheartedly. I just went along with it. I'll admit I was worried about you, making up those fanciful tales. Until we went up those stairs to Lottie's that time. You disappeared through a brick wall I knew didn't exist, but it did at that moment. I could hear you faintly on the other side. I started believing.

Then yesterday I met the mysterious Miss Megan in the flesh and—" he held out his hands "—I'm a bona fide believer." He chuckled. "Poor Sue. She probably thinks you're crazy as a loon, Miss Megan."

"Sure wish you hadn't told her," Seth growled. "That was a dumb thing to do."

Dumb! Megan put her hands on her hips. "It's your own damn fault. If you hadn't brought that picture back here she wouldn't have seen it and none of this would have happened."

"Oh, no you don't." Seth wiggled his finger in front of her face. "Don't you go blamin' this on me. You're the one who told her."

She swatted his finger away. "And I told *you* not to take anything back but noooo, you just had to. Like that history book. God only knows who's seen that."

"No one has seen it," Seth shot back.

"Yeah, right." Megan rolled her eyes. "The same way no one saw that picture. You showed it to Tim. Then Mr. Toby. Then your girlfriend saw it. You might as well have published it in the paper."

Seth's nostrils flared. "Don't call her that."

"Pardon me. Your betrothed."

"Megan," he growled.

"How about your future wife."

"Now, now, you two lovebirds—"

"Shut up, Tim," Seth and Megan said at the same time.

Tim took a step back, holding up one hand. "All right. All right. I'm just trying to help." His gaze moved beyond Seth and Megan. His dimpled smile appeared. "Good morning, ladies."

Megan expected to see a bevy of beauties. Instead, two young girls jumped up on the boardwalk from the street. Red hair. Green eyes.

"The pretty Pryor girls," Megan murmured, causing both Seth and Tim to glance at her in surprise.

"'Mornin', Mr. Tim, Marshal. Miss." The oldest girl smiled shyly. She had her hair parted neatly down the middle and hanging in two long braids.

The younger girl walked up to Megan, tilted back a headful of long curly red hair, and said, "Howdy. I'm Candy and that's my sister Corrie. You must be Mr. Seth's lady friend from Chicago. We heard you was in town and couldn't wait to meet you."

"Candy, hush," Corrie whispered.

Candy pushed out her lower lip. "Why? You were the first one out the door after mama and papa left and ran all the way here, hoping to see the new lady in town."

Her face red, Corrie muttered, "You talk too much."

Megan smiled at the two girls who seemed as different as night and day. Corrie wore a high-necked gray-and-pink striped dress, pristine white stockings, and black leather shoes. She had a serious, studious look about her. Candy wore a red plaid dress that had a big red stain on the front, and her white stockings had smudges of dirt and a small hole in one knee. Her shoes resembled moccasins. Her eyes sparkled with the same vitality and mischievousness of the elderly Candace. "It's nice to meet you, Candy and Corrie. I'm Miss Megan."

"I never met anyone from Chicago." Candy clasped her hands behind her back. "Is that on the ocean? I never seen an ocean. We read about them in school. Someday I'm gonna see 'em all. That's a pretty dress, Miss Megan. The color matches the bruises on your face. Ow!" Candy rubbed her side where her sister had jabbed her with her elbow and frowned at Corrie. "What'd you do that for?"

"You shouldn't say things like that, Candy," Corrie snapped. "It's not proper."

Candy's mouth formed an O. Her wide eyes darted from Megan to Seth and widened even more.

Corrie elbowed me and told me to shush. Mr. Seth looked mad, and I felt awful, because I'd never seen him so mad, the elderly Candace had said just a week or so ago. Megan glanced at Seth. He did look very mad. Probably from their argument, not from the bruises on her face.

"I—I'm sorry." Candy's face scrunched up. "I didn't mean nuthin'." Her lower lip trembled.

Megan knelt in front of the little girl. "It's all right. At least it's a pretty blue."

A smile lit Candy's face. "It'll be a different color tomorrow. I skinned my knee the other day," she pointed to the hole in her stocking, "and the bruise is green and yellow now. Maybe your bruises will turn those colors too."

"If they do I'll have to find a matching green or yellow dress, won't I?"

The little girl giggled, and Megan rubbed the top of her curly-haired head. "We'll talk later, all right? Maybe go on a picnic one day soon."

Candy clapped her hands. "Hear that, Corrie? Miss Megan's gonna take us on a picnic. I'll show you my favorite place by the river."

"I'd love to see it." Megan stood. "But right now, I have a barn raising to get to. I was going to go with Susannah," she said to Seth and Tim, "but she was gone when I got up."

"We're fixin' to go there too," Candy said, and Corrie nodded.

"How far is it?" Megan asked.

"A few miles out of town. Y'all can ride in the wagon with me," Tim offered. "I just came from there to pick up a couple of barrels to take back. Guess now I know why Sue acted so strangely toward me." He gave Megan a pointed look before saying, "You ladies wait right here while I load the barrels then I'll pick y'all up." He walked away, his boots clicking on the boardwalk.

"I'll help you." Without a glance at Megan, Seth joined Tim.

"What history book?" Tim ask Seth, who just shook his head.

Fifteen minutes later, the wagon rattled down the rutted street heading out of town with Seth and Tim on the seat, Tim holding the reins. Seth's white-and-brown speckled horse, tied to the back of the wagon, trailed behind. Megan sat on a crate between the two barrels secured to either side of the front of the wagon. The crate jumped and jostled and hurt her butt. She didn't complain. Seth had insisted she sit up front. She wanted to sit in back and chat with the girls. They had argued about it until Seth threw up his hands, told her to do what she wanted, and climbed up on the seat.

Megan turned her attention from his stiff shoulders and straight back, and asked the girls sitting on the floor of the wagon, "What's your favorite subject in school?"

"Playing with my friends." Candy stretched out her legs and wiggled her feet.

"That's not a subject." Corrie made a face. "I like numbers."

While the little girls chattered, Megan listened with one ear and responded as necessary while she recalled how Candace had described meeting the other Megan. One of the men had pulled one of the girls' braids. That hadn't happened. They had met in front of the general store, not Seth's saloon. They were all going to a wedding the next day, not a barn raising today. So many things were different. Small things, granted, but still ... Megan held on to the crate with both hands as the wagon bounced over bumps. *If small things are different, could big things be different too? Will nothing happen tomorrow except Seth and Susannah's wedding? Then what? Do I stay here, hanging around in case the need arises for me to swoop in and save him? Stay here while he and his bride live together, start their life together? Me watching them from afar? If I'm not here to save him, why am I here? Where do I fit in? What's the point?*

The landscape passing by suddenly registered in her brain, and she stared, entranced, at springtime in 1890 Texas. A palette of color spread in all directions. Wildflowers of yellow, red, violet, orange, blue, every shade imaginable dotted the verdant spring grass rippling in the breeze. Pink and white flowering trees mingled with greening trees and shrubs bursting with blooms and new leaves in every shade of green. Countless twittering and chirping birds as colorful as the wildflowers darted among the branches and flew up into the bright blue sky. A pair of roadrunners raced across the grass. Squirrels dashed up tree trunks and scurried from limb to limb. Everything looked fresh and new. Like the Garden of Eden.

She noticed what was missing—utility poles and power lines, the drone of an airplane, the rumble of traffic, concrete, litter, any sign of human habitation, except for the rutted road they traveled on.

The people in that time didn't have indoor plumbing or fast food or tampons, but they had all this.

The wagon topped a rise. She gasped. "How beautiful."

It looked as if the sky had come down to cover the rolling terrain in a carpet of blue. She had never seen anything like it.

"Bluebonnets," Seth said over his shoulder.

"They're gorgeous." Megan studied his profile as he looked at the bluebonnets. They weren't near as gorgeous as he was. They had so little time left together. She reached over the front of the wagon and touched his arm.

He twisted around on his seat to look at her.

"I'm sorry. I hate it when we argue."

"I'm sorry too. I wish you hadn't told her but," he shrugged, "what's done is done. We'll just have to see what happens."

"It'll be fine."

Seth gave her a skeptical look then faced front again.

She touched his arm again. "What's your horse's name?"

"Chevy," he said over his shoulder, and grinned when she laughed.

"Hang on," Tim hollered as the horses pulled the wagon across a rushing creek.

Candy scooted up, grabbed Megan's hand, and held on. She squealed when water splashed on her. "I have a pet horny toad. His name is Bob. You wanna meet him sometime?"

Megan smiled. "I'd love to. I've never seen a horny toad." She wiped drops of water off her face with the back of her free hand.

Candy's jaw dropped. "You *haven't?* Oh, he's the bestest." She prattled on about Bob until the wagon pulled up to a homestead bustling with people.

There was a log house, a garden with neat lines of green sprouts protected by a fence made of crisscrossed logs, a horse stall and corral with several horses prancing around, and almost half of the framework of a barn. Several long tables, one laden with pots, pans, and big bowls, were set up on the hard-packed dirt yard. The smell of roasting meat made Megan's stomach growl.

"Looks like they've gotten a lot done." Tim secured the reins as Seth jumped down.

"There's Miss Susannah." Corrie rose, brushed dirt off her dress, then climbed out of the wagon.

Candy stood up and waved her hand like a flag flapping in a gale. "Hi, Miss Susannah!" Tim lifted her out and set her on the ground. She ran towards Susannah, who had left a group of women gathered by a table and headed to the wagon.

The sounds of hammering and voices came from the men working on the barn like an organized colony of ants. Men hurried back and forth, carrying lumber, poles, and tools. A few children helped with the building but most of them ran around playing on the far side of the house. Several barking dogs ran with the kids.

Seth took Megan's hand and helped her down. As she shook her dress and brushed it off, he said, "I don't know what to say to her."

"I doubt she'll say much around all these people." She fussed with her wind-blown hair. "How do I look?"

"Beautiful."

"You have to stop looking at me like that."

"It's the only way I know how to look at you."

"It's not how you were looking at me when you called me dumb."

"I didn't call you dumb. I said it was a dumb thing to do. And it was." He reached for her hand. "But I understand why you did it."

She took a step back. "There she is."

Susannah walked up, holding Candy's hand. "Hello, Corrie. Don't you look pretty. I believe Elizabeth and Mary are looking for you two."

"Oh goody! See ya later, Miss Megan." Candy and Corrie ran off.

Susannah watched after them a moment, her hands folded at the waist of her gray dress. It had a white collar and white cuffs on the elbow-length sleeves. She looked at Tim, stroking the head of one of the horses. "Timothy, would you please take the barrels to the far table?"

"Sure thing."

"Thank you." Her cool gaze swept right over Seth to settle on Megan. "I have a place for you in the serving line if you want to help."

"Of course."

"Come along then." Susannah turned and started walking away.

Megan fell into step beside her.

"Susannah, wait," Seth said.

She kept walking. She waved a hand, and said over her shoulder, "Not now. Dinner will be served shortly." She said to Megan, "Somehow I ended up in charge of organizing the meal." She brushed back tendrils that had escaped her coiled hair. "I've had a very busy morning." She walked fast.

Megan stepped up her pace. "I wish you had wakened me when you got up. I would have helped you."

A wagon with a load of lumber rattled by. The grizzle-haired driver raised his hat to them.

"I needed to be alone," Susannah said after the wagon and its noise had moved on. "I had a lot to think about."

"Susannah—"

She held up that hand again. "Not now. I must make sure all these people are fed. I do have questions, however." She gave Megan a direct look. "Many questions."

"Ask away."

"Later. Right now, let me introduce you to some of the women."

They drew abreast with several women by the table with the pots and pans on it. The women's ages ranged from late-teens to wrinkle-faced grandmothers. Many of them wore aprons over their nice dresses and most had on a sunbonnet.

"Ladies," Susannah announced, "this is Miss Megan McClure who is visiting from Chicago."

That caused a twitter among the women, although Megan was sure news of her arrival had already spread like an epidemic through the town.

"Megan, this is Beulah Hornsby," Susannah said, "the wife of our blacksmith. This is Corabelle Twinsky. Her husband is Amos Twinsky, the lawyer. Here's Mabel Bahr, the baker's wife." Susannah continued naming everyone in the group.

The names and faces were a blur to Megan. She tried to remember that Beulah Hornsby had dark chin hairs on her double chin, and that Mabel Bahr was a large woman with a thick German accent, and that the wife of a saloon owner had sleek black hair and slanted, exotic dark eyes. Megan smiled and nodded to each one and hoped there wasn't a test on everyone's name later. Some of the women asked questions about Chicago, and Megan answered as best she could, mentally kicking herself for not reading up on Chicago's history. She sighed with relief when Susannah motioned her to a spot near the middle of the table.

"You'll be dishing out the beans. Don't scrimp. We have plenty." Susannah clapped her hands. "Ladies, are we ready?"

The women hurried to their assigned spots. The preacher's wife took her place on Megan's left to dish out potatoes. Corabelle Twinsky stood on Megan's right, in charge of the corn bread. Someone rang a dinner bell, and all work on the barn ceased. Men climbed down from the framework, those on the ground dropped what they were doing, and they all headed to a water pump to wash up before lining up for food.

The next couple of hours passed in a parade of faces and tin plates held out for a dipperful of beans. Megan's face soon hurt from smiling. She caught glimpses of Seth mingling in the crowd and shared a smile with him when she dumped beans on his plate. After the men had been served, the children lined up. Finally, the line ended, and the women took their turn to eat.

Mrs. Hornsby dabbed her mouth with a handkerchief. "Between today's meal and tomorrow's after the wedding, there should be plenty left over to provide a few meals for you and the Marshal, Susannah. We all know you two will have better things to do besides cook." She gave a sly smile, and a twitter ran through the group.

Susannah blushed, but kept eating, her eyes on her plate. Several more suggestive comments followed about her upcoming nuptials to Seth and their wedding night.

Megan watched in admiration as Susannah handled the kidding with grace and tolerance, despite all she had learned the night before, and her suspicions about Megan and Seth's relationship.

She should be giddy and happy, joining in the laughter, the excited bride-to-be. And she would be, except for me. I'm ruining her wedding.

Megan set her plate down, her appetite suddenly gone. She blinked back sudden tears, feeling awful for what she was doing to Susannah, knowing how she would feel if the situation was reversed. She scanned the crowd, looking for Seth. He stood with several men drinking and talking near a barrel of whiskey. He must have said something funny because the men laughed and one of them gave Seth a good-natured slap on the back. Just then, he glanced her way, and their eyes met. He smiled that smile that was just for her. Her heart swelled with love.

If I have to ruin her wedding in order to save his life, so be it. No matter whom he marries.

***

Hours later, Megan knocked on Lottie's door.

"Come in," Lottie's husky voice called.

Megan entered, and found Lottie in a pale pink negligee and her show-my-big-boobs pose.

"You," Lottie snarled. She resumed her normal posture. "What do you want?"

"I was wondering if you had that other dress ready for me for tonight."

"Depends."

"On what?"

"Are you gonna need another dress for my brother's weddin' tomorrow?"

"No. I'm not going."

Surprise and relief flashed in Lottie's eyes before she went to her sewing room.

Megan stepped further into the stuffy, gloomy room. "What would have happened if I'd said yes?"

"Guess you'll never know." Lottie reappeared, holding up a dress.

Megan caught her breath.

The purple dress. In all its new glory.

The silk had a sheen to it that made the color shine like a polished amethyst. The cream-colored lace was crisp and clean. The darker skirt was a deep, rich hue that made the purple stand out that much more.

"It's absolutely beautiful," Megan said as she took it from Lottie. "Thank you, Charlotte."

"Oughta go good with those purple eyes of yours."

"Violet."

Lottie made a rude sound. "There's a petticoat, too. Get dressed and get out."

Minutes later, Megan checked herself in the mirror over the dresser.

"Perfect fit," Lottie muttered. "That don't happen often." A frown creased her brow.

Seeing Lottie stare so intensely at the dress, Megan asked, "What is it?"

"Nothin." Lottie gave Megan a critical once over. "What're you gonna do with your hair?"

Megan shrugged. "Brush it."

Lottie pulled a stool over. "Sit down. I'll fix it for you."

In a matter of minutes, Lottie had many of Megan's curls artfully arranged, pinned on top of her head, and trailing down, emphasizing her neck. Soft tendrils framed her face.

Megan hardly recognized herself.

"Like it?" Lottie asked.

"Holy moly, yes. Thank you, Charlotte." Megan grinned. "I feel like Cinderella."

Lottie turned away. "Time for you to go. I gotta get myself ready for tonight. You ain't the only one gonna be dancin' at the ball."

Megan stood. "Thank you again for everything."

"How you gittin' there?"

"In Tim's wagon. He brought several of us back to change clothes."

"Gonna be chilly tonight. You gotta coat?"

"No."

Lottie opened her armoire and took out a dark hooded cloak. She handed it to Megan.

Impulsively, she hugged Lottie, who stood stiff-armed, then left.

***

A thin line of fiery red painted the western horizon as darkness covered the land. The new barn stood bathed in the light of lanterns strung around the hard-packed yard. People wandered around in the barn, in and out of the house, and congregated in the yard. It looked like every adult from town was there. Not many little children but plenty of teenagers and preteens. The women wore their finest dresses, their hair piled high in fancy hairdos. The men wore everything from black coats and trousers to denims and clean shirts. Most of the men gathered around barrels of whiskey off to one side. Several fiddle players stood together, tuning and playing their instruments. Seth wasn't anywhere in sight.

Tim helped Megan down from the wagon. When she removed her cloak, Tim took it and put it on the wagon seat. He let out a low whistle. "Mercy me, Miss Megan. You're gonna turn all the men's heads and turn all the women green with envy. Shall we?"

She placed her hand on his offered arm as they headed to the yard. More stars than she had ever seen sparkled like glitter against the black sky. She asked the one question she'd wanted to ask the whole ride there but couldn't due to the other women riding along. "Tell me the truth, Tim. If Seth happened to be in a gunfight, would he ... win?"

Tim looked at her. "What kind of question is that?"

"Just answer me please. Would he?"

After a pause, Tim replied, "He has a good eye, and a steady hand. But ..." He met Megan's gaze in the gathering dimness. "He's not fast enough. Most any man he'll be up against will probably be faster." He shrugged. "Let's hope it never comes to that."

A cold chill swept over her. She shivered, despite a warm southern breeze.

"Cold?" Tim asked. "I can go back and get your cloak."

"No thanks. I'm fine."

"Why did you ask that? About Seth?"

"No reason. Just ... curious."

He stopped walking. "Is this about the future? Is that how he—"

"Stop." She held up her hand. "Don't ask me questions about the future. I can't tell you."

"Miss Megan—"

She turned away. "Please. Just drop it."

He was silent a moment, then said softly, "It must be hard. Knowing all those things and not being able to do anything about any of it. It tortures Seth. Says he's had nightmares about some of the things to come. He feels helpless. One night years back we got blubbering drunk and he said he wished he'd never learned any of it. Wished he could reach into his head and tear all that knowledge right out. It's changed him. The way he thinks. The way he views the future. That passel of kids he always talked about having since we were kids ourselves is the last thing he wants now, I think."

Megan covered her face with her hands. "Oh God, I've ruined him. I should have never let him read those books. Those newspapers."

Tim's warm hand settled on her shoulder. "I reckon I over spoke. I'm sorry. Seth'll skin me alive if he finds out I told you all that."

"There you are, Timothy. I've been looking—Megan? What's the matter?"

At the sound of Susannah's voice, Megan straightened, brushing hair off her face.

The lanterns swayed gently in the wind, casting their light upon Susannah dressed in a form-fitting pale blue dress with lace around the neckline and down the center of the bodice. Her hair was piled high on her head in a tight, neat coil. Her gaze took in Tim removing his hand from Megan's shoulder. A small crease appeared on Susannah's smooth brow.

"Evenin', Sue." Tim smiled at her. "My, my, aren't you lovely, my dear."

"Thank you." She demurely dropped her gaze from his and turned to Megan. "What a gorgeous dress."

"Thank you. Charlotte made it."

Susannah tilted her head. "Charlotte?"

"Lottie. She's quite handy with a needle."

"That she is. I'm sorry to interrupt you two but—"

"We were discussing the curse of knowing the future," Tim said casually, as if he'd said they were discussing the weather. He brushed something off the sleeve of his crisp white shirt. He also wore a brown leather vest and brown trousers. A band with tiger-eye agates on it circled the crown of his brown hat.

Susannah blinked. "Oh. Well. Umm."

"Personally, I find it fascinating," Tim said. "I'd like to know more about your time, Miss Megan."

Megan stared at him through narrowed eyes. He was starting to annoy her. "I know what happens to you two. Do you want to know your fates?"

Susannah took a step back. She clapped a hand to her cheek. "Oh, heavens, no. No," she added more forcefully.

"What about you, Tim? You don't want to know? You still think it's so fascinating?" Sarcasm tinged Megan's voice.

"I do. Just nothing personal. I don't need to know that. I reckon we all end up the same. Dead." Tim turned to Susannah. "You said you were looking for me. What do you need?"

"Some tree stumps need to be moved near the tables."

"For seats. Of course. I'm your man, my dear. Shall we?" He offered his arm to her. Susannah hesitated, then placed her hand on his arm. "Miss Megan?" He held out his other arm. When she took it, he grinned. "I hope this is how I die. A beauty on each arm."

"I declare, Timothy, you are ... full of baloney."

Megan leaned forward and glanced at Susannah, who had a slight smile when their gazes met. *I like that woman more and more.*

Tim laughed as he escorted them across the yard. Nearing a group of women by the dessert table, he looked around. "I don't see Seth anywhere."

"He went to town hours ago," Susannah replied. "He said he'd return when he could."

***

When the musicians started playing, Tim took Megan's hand and pulled her, protesting, onto the hard-packed dirt that served as the dance floor and spun off with her in a polka. She muddled through several dances with him, learning different steps, until she relaxed and began to enjoy herself.

Tim spun her around then pulled her close. "Thank you for loving my friend." His soft brown eyes gazed into hers. "I believe he has loved you since he was seventeen."

Touched by his words, she replied, "I believe that I have loved him too since he was seventeen." She shared a smile with her love's best friend.

"Maybe you should be tellin' him that."

"Maybe I will."

One man after the other lined up to dance with her. She felt like the belle of the ball. She drank apple cider, then added a splash of Tim's whiskey to the cider and danced some more.

Exhausted from dancing, Megan sat on a stump and ate a piece of berry pie. Not the best combination with whiskey-spiked cider but she was hungry. Her attention on the dancers, marveling at their grace and fancy steps, she frowned when a man stepped in her line of vision and said, "I believe the next dance is mine."

She looked up at John Bingo's beady blue eyes. "No thanks."

"Come now. You danced with all the cowboys and hicks. Why don't you try a real man?"

Megan laughed. "That sure isn't a pipsqueak like you."

Rage colored his face. "You little—"

"Move aside, loser." She motioned him away. "You're blocking my view."

He leaned down until his face was inches from hers, his eyes boring into hers. He said in a soft but steel-edged voice, "You just keep digging your grave deeper, you uppity little slut. You won't be so mouthy by time I'm done with you." He straightened, adjusted his black coat with a quick tug, turned on his heel, and stalked away.

"Asshole," Megan muttered, then turned her attention back to the dancers. Her gaze strayed to Bingo as he joined several other men, all scruffy looking.

Tim walked up to her, a glass of whiskey in his hand. "Having fun?"

She nodded. "Never thought I'd attend an actual barn-raising. Is that Bingo's gang he's with?" She jutted her chin in Bingo's direction.

"Yup. Stay clear of them 'cause one's meaner than the next. The big one with the bushy beard is Jethro Seller, Bingo's right-hand man. He supposedly does most of Bingo's dirty work." Tim's gaze searched the crowd, then he grinned. "Excuse me. I'm fixin' to dance with a sweet little blonde." He sauntered off, running a hand over his hair.

When Megan couldn't resist Nature's call a minute longer, she went to the outhouse. It was such an ordeal in her beautiful dress, she vowed to go somewhere out in the bushes next time. On her way back, she ran into Daisy, who gushed her thanks again for the red high heels, twirling around to show them off. Lottie stood near a whiskey barrel with several other women who looked like fellow prostitutes from their painted faces and scanty attire.

Megan drew Lottie to one side. "I want to thank you again for the dress, Charlotte. I've had many compliments on it."

Lottie slugged down a glass of whiskey, then wiped her mouth with the back of her hand. She wore a fire engine red dress overlaid with black lace. Short, puffy sleeves circled her lily-white upper arms. The low neckline strained to contain her high, full breasts. Her long auburn curls were gathered on top of her head and cascaded down her back.

"Funny thin' 'bout that dress." There was a slight slur to her words. "First time I picked up that purple silk I knew I was gonna make a dress outta it. Knew the size, length, everythin'. I had a picture of it in my head. Only thin' I didn't know was who it was for." She stepped to the barrel and refilled her glass from the spigot. "Not many would look good in that color. 'Specially 'mong these old biddies. I made it anyway an' put it aside months ago an' forgot 'bout it. Then lo an' behold, here comes my brother's little Yankee friend with the perfect colorin'. Black hair. Purple eyes."

"Violet."

"Violet," Lottie sneered, "an' needin' a dress. I hardly made any changes on it afore I give it to you. Fit perfectly. That just don't happen." Lottie took a drink, her kohl-darkened eyes staring at Megan over the rim of the glass.

Megan shrugged, and the alcohol she'd had made her say, "Maybe we knew each other in another life and you knew I would need a dress."

"Think you're funny, don't cha. There's somethin' 'bout you. Dunno what. Somethin' ... strange. I'm gonna keep my eye on you, missy."

***

The music ended. Megan thanked her partner, a young cowhand from a nearby ranch, and headed back to her whiskey-spiked cider.

Seth stood across the crowded yard.

Her heart took wing. Wanting to run, she walked as normally as possible toward him. He started towards her. The crowd parted like the Red Sea. They met in the middle and smiled.

"Look at you, wearing a purple dress."

"I was wondering if you were going to be here."

"Got here fast as I could. Good thing, too, seein's how you're dancin' with every fella in the county."

"You've been watching?"

"Uh huh. Prettiest gal on the dance floor."

"All those dances were just rehearsals for dancing with you."

"Hmmm. That sounds like something Tim would say."

"Actually, it is."

They laughed. It seemed as if they were the only two in the world.

He looked impossibly handsome in tight black trousers, a long-sleeved white shirt, and a black vest that hugged his trim torso and bore the tin star. His black hat had a band of beaded turquoise circling the crown.

The strains of a waltz came from the fiddlers. Seth said, "I reckon this is our dance."

He took her right hand, slipped his other arm around her waist, and waltzed away with her. They glided across the hard-packed dirt as if they had danced together all their lives. Her dress belled with each spin.

She felt lighter than air, graceful as a gazelle. Countless stars glittered like diamonds overhead, and the light from the lanterns limned the cheekbones and jaw line of his beloved face as he smiled down at her.

"Is it like your vision of us dancin'?"

His warm hand clasped hers. His strong arm circled her. She smiled. "Better."

Because it was real.

They danced another waltz, and another, circling, spinning, gliding, oblivious of everything and everyone else.

Seth maneuvered Megan out into the darkness, away from curious eyes, and kissed her.

She called upon all her inner strength to push him away. "Don't. You're marrying Susannah tomorrow." Susannah had watched them dance with a sad look on her face. Megan squirmed out of Seth's arms and took a step back.

"No, I'm not. I'm gonna tell her tonight."

"Seth. Don't."

He held out his hands. "How can I marry her when it's your face I see when I close my eyes? How can I marry her when it's your voice I hear on the night wind?" He took a step towards her. "How can I marry her when it's you I want in my life, my home, my bed?" He touched her cheek. "When it's you I love so very much."

Megan's heart beat as fast as a hummingbird's wings. The sweet scent of spring-blooming clematis perfumed the night, and she knew that forever after that scent would remind her of this moment.

"I know you love me too." Seth lowered his hand. "I found your note."

"You found the bottle?"

He nodded. "In a watering trough on Rusk Street."

"The Water Gardens really *is* a portal."

"Don't go changin' the subject. You wrote *I love you* on it. Do you?"

His gaze pinned hers through the starlit night. He stood tense and still.

Megan clasped his hand in hers. "I love you so very much too."

Seth pulled her close and held her tight. "Now you see why I can't possibly marry Susannah tomorrow?"

Megan wanted the moment to last forever but knew it would not. Could not. Should not. She closed her eyes, imprinting the moment in her memory to savor later. The feel of him. The smell of him. The love he offered. She blinked back tears and drew away from him. "It changes nothing. You have to marry her in case I don't—" She bit back the words.

"Megan. You know something about me. That's it, isn't it? You finally read about me somewhere and found out what happens to me, and it scares you. Is that it?" He cupped her cheek with his big hand. "Tell me what you're frettin' over. Please."

She shook off his hand and backed away. "I can't." She would end up telling him everything. Ruining everything. She had to get away from him. She could think of only one method of escape. She ran.

"Megan! You'll get lost out there," Seth called.

She hiked up her skirt and kept on running into the night. The sound of him calling her name faded away. Dark shadows loomed on her left. She realized it was the woods. The wagons were on the other side of it. She ran into the trees. Branches and brambles tore at her hair, snagged her clothes. She went down a small ravine, scrambled up the other side, paused to catch her breath, then took off again. The trees and brush thinned. She plowed into someone. They both went sprawling.

"What the hell—? Miss Megan? That you?"

Megan rolled onto her side, spitting leaves out of her mouth. She squinted through the darkness at a familiar figure rising to his feet. "Tim?"

"What are you doing out here? Give me your hand." Tim helped her up.

She brushed dirt and leaves off her dress, hoping she hadn't ruined it during her mad dash. "What are you doing here?"

"Relieving myself. You?"

"I was with Seth. He told me he loved me. I told him I loved him."

"That's wonderful." Tim sounded thrilled.

"It's awful." A sob escaped her. She felt like sitting down and having a good cry. "Please take me back to town, Tim. Please."

He brushed the front of his vest, then swiped a hand across each knee as he regarded her silently for a moment. "What about Seth?"

"Just take me back." It dawned on her that if she was gone, Seth and Bingo couldn't have a confrontation over her. She couldn't think of any reason Seth would challenge anyone to a gunfight, except to defend her so-called honor.

Tim walked beside her to the wagon. In the distance, the dance was in full swing, the floor crowded with couples. Seth wasn't anywhere in sight. Tim helped her into the wagon then walked around the horses and fussed with them. Fiddle music, whoops and hollers filled the night air. Tim walked to the back of the wagon. Megan put on the cloak and pulled the hood over her hair. She tapped her foot impatiently, wanting to be gone. One of the horses shook its head. Tim finally reappeared and climbed onto the wagon seat, the wagon dipping and creaking. He picked up the reins, made a clicking sound, and the horses started off. He'd put on a coat and kept the collar turned up against the wind.

Megan stared straight ahead, not seeing any of the darkened landscape pass by. She didn't feel like talking, and was relieved Tim seemed to feel the same way. He sat quietly on the seat.

As they entered the town and passed darkened stores, a deep voice asked quietly, "What are you afraid of, Megan?"

Her gaze snapped to her companion. "What are you doing here?"

Seth pushed down the coat collar, turned his head, and smiled. "Just seein' my gal safely back to town."

"Oh, for Pete's sake." She stared ahead, disgusted. Seth must have changed places with Tim when Tim went to the back of the wagon. "We're not sleeping together, if that's what you're hoping for."

"I don't recollect gettin' much sleep that night."

I will not think of that night. It'll make me weak. I need to be strong.

"You didn't answer my question. What are you afraid of?"

She lifted her chin. "I'm not afraid of anything."

A sigh came from him. They rode down the street in silence. He stopped in front of a three-story brick building. Above the door were the words, in big bold letters, *FORT WORTH JAIL*. The courthouse was across the street.

"I have to get something from my office. Then I'll take you to Susannah's." Seth climbed down from the wagon. He started to walk away then paused and looked up at her. "You want to see the inside of a real jail in the Wild West?"

Megan glanced around the dark, empty street, and felt very exposed. "Sure." Seth helped her down, then unlocked the door to the jail and let her in.

He lit a lantern on a desk as wide as a twin bed and shuffled through a stack of papers. "I shouldn't be long. Look around if you want. Not that there's much to see."

Behind the desk was a swivel chair with a cracked leather seat. A washbasin, pitcher, and several glasses were on a wooden stand beneath a window. A dozen or so wanted posters were tacked on the wall near the door. Megan skimmed them but didn't recognize any of the names. In one corner of the room stood a wood-burning stove with a coffee pot on top. A brass coat rack, a bookcase full of books, and two wood-slatted chairs completed the furnishings. Four jail cells lined the back of the room. Weird shadows from the lantern light danced around the emptiness. She paused outside a cell and stuck her head inside. A cot, blankets, and a slop bucket. She stepped into the cell and glanced around then walked to the small window in the back wall. She stood on tiptoe and looked through the bars at the dark night beyond.

The cell door clanged shut behind her.

Chapter 35

Megan spun around as Seth turned the key in the cell door lock. The click of the lock sounded as loud as a crack of thunder in the quiet room. "Is this part of the two-dollar tour?" She looked around as she walked across the cell toward him. "Not very comfy. Kind of creepy actually."

She glanced at the pile of papers on his desk. "If you're done, I'm ready to go."

"I'm not done yet. An' you're not goin' anywhere." Seth dropped the key into the pocket of his vest.

Her gaze narrowed. "Let me out of here."

"Not until we have a little talk an' clear some things up."

"We can do that just as easily somewhere else."

"No one'll bother us here. An' you can't run away."

She grabbed the bars. "Let me out damn it."

"Let's talk. Then we'll see."

"We'll see?" she pushed through gritted teeth.

He removed his hat and tossed it on the desk behind him. He filled a glass with water from the pitcher and took the glass to her. "Here."

"I don't want any damn water." She pushed his hand away. "I want out of here."

He bent down, reached through the bars, and set the glass on the floor. He stood, pulled over a chair and sat, facing her. The light from the lantern touched the right side of his face and left the other side in shadows. "Let's get a couple things straight. I love you an' you love me."

She crossed her arms. "Not at the moment."

"Understandable." He nodded. "Let's just say we love each other an' leave it at that. Then there's Susannah. She's no fool. Far from it. She knows something has changed between her an' me since you showed up yesterday."

Was it only yesterday?

"An' she knows you an' I have feelings for each other. I've been wantin' to tell her I can't marry her but for some reason you don't want me to. Which isn't fair to her an' is makin' me look like the hind end of a horse." He leaned forward, his expression serious. "I care for her. Not the same way she cares for me, but I do care for her. I'm not at all happy about treating her so callously."

"I know," Megan said softly. She put her hand on one of the bars. "I'm sorry. But ..." She bit her lip. She didn't want to reveal too much.

He rested his elbows on his knees and clasped his hands together. He looked down. "I reckon you know plenty about me by now. You knew I married Susannah. You knew Corrie an' Candy are called the pretty Pryor girls. An' I'm sure," he raised his head and met her gaze, "you know how, an' where, an' when I die."

He said it so matter-of-factly a chill ran through Megan.

"I reckon it's in a gunfight," he added.

She let out an indignant huff.

Seth chuckled. "Did you really think Tim wouldn't tell me about your conversation?" He sat up straight and crossed a knee with a booted foot. "I reckon it's sometime soon too. I got a naggin' suspicion you plan on doin' somethin' foolish like try an' stop it. Which we both know you're not supposed to do because then you'd be changin' history, somethin' you've told me over an' over an' over I can't do." He tilted his head. "You wouldn't be thinkin' any of those things now, would you?"

She crossed her arms again and lifted her chin. "I'm not saying a word until you let me out of here."

He stared at her until the silence grew loud in the room. "Well then." He put his foot on the floor and stood. "I reckon you'll feel more like talkin' in the mornin'."

She grabbed the bars and watched in disbelief as he walked to the desk and picked up his hat. "Where do you think you're going? Let me out of here!"

"I'm goin' back to the dance to tell Susannah the weddin's off." He settled his hat on his head. "An' I'm gonna do my job an' make sure everyone keeps the peace."

"Seth, don't tell her that. Please don't."

He eyed her curiously. "That's one thing I can't figure out. Why you're so all-fired determined I marry her. But I'm not. An' that's that." He headed for the door.

"You can't just leave me here!"

"You'll be fine," he said over his shoulder. "I'll know right where you're at an' won't be worryin' about you. I'll leave the lantern. There's two blankets if you get cold."

"Damn it, Seth. Let me out!"

He paused with one hand on the doorknob and looked at her. "I'm leavin' you here for your own good. I love you." He shut the door on her string of curses.

**

Megan removed her cloak, then yanked a hairpin out of her hairdo and tried to pick the lock. She dropped that hairpin, then another one, then another one, all falling out of her reach. She bent a couple and soon ran out of hairpins. Her hair hung long and loose, her beautiful hairdo ruined. She shook every bar in the cell trying to find a loose one. When she shook the last sturdy, stubborn bar, she hit it with the palm of her hand. "Damn you, Seth."

She sat on the cot and tried to lay down, but her dress and petticoat belled out so much in front she instead leaned back against the wall. She had no idea what time it was or how long she had been there, or what had had happened to Seth. Time dragged by and the unending silence grated on her nerves. Her mind whirled with different scenarios of Seth's break-up with Susannah, and the possible consequences. *What will happen tomorrow?* She caught her breath. *This could be my last night alive. What an awful way to spend it.* Her pulse quickened when she realized she had set nothing in place for the next Megan—no money for Mrs. Powell to inherit, no bonding with the Pryor girls to ensure their care of her, no idea where they even lived if she needed to find them, nothing.

She put her head in her hands. *I haven't done anything right. I failed.* She fought back tears. *Did any of the other Megans end up in jail? Probably not. Just stupid me.* She pounded her fist on the cot.

Time crawled by. Occasional sounds came from outside. Muffled voices. The whinny of a horse. More silence. The last night of her life crept along at a snail's pace.

The door to the jail opened. Quick footsteps sounded on the wood floor.

Megan sat up. "It's about time. Let me out of he—Susannah?"

"Mercy me. I didn't believe Timothy when he said Seth had you locked up in here." Susannah hurried across the floor, pushing the hood of her black cloak off her coiled hair that looked a bit straggly after the long day. "When I didn't find you at home I realized he might be telling the truth."

Megan bolted off the cot and ran to the bars. "Where's Seth? What happened?"

"Remember last night when you were telling me all about you? You never explained what you meant when you said you were here to save Seth's life. We fell asleep, remember? Tell me now what you meant." Susannah stepped closer to the cell. "Quickly. Tell me how he ... dies."

Red cheeks. An intense look in her eyes. A nervous twisting of her hands. Something had Susannah worked up and compelled Megan to answer without hesitation. "He died on April 13, 1890, in a gunfight with John Bingo. It was at noon, on his wedding day. He died in your arms."

Susannah's face paled in the lantern light. She took a step back and put her hand on her chest. "Sweet Mother of Jesus."

"I saw his grave. I read the plaque on the building where it happened in front of. It's famous as the last great gunfight on the streets of Fort Worth."

"His g-grave. A-a plaque. F-famous." Susannah sank onto the chair Seth had sat in earlier. She closed her eyes and rubbed her hand across her forehead.

"You're not going to faint, are you? I can't help you if you hit your head or something."

"No, no." Susannah waved her other hand. She drew in a shaky breath then opened her eyes. "You're serious. This is all true. You are honest to God, swear on a Bible speaking the truth."

"I swear on a whole stack of Bibles." Megan held up her right hand. "I swear on my parents' grave. On Seth's grave. I'd swear on yours too, but I never thought to look for it in Oakwood Cemetery."

Susannah's face had blanched at the mention of her grave. Her eyes widened. "That's the name of our cemetery."

Megan nodded. "One and the same. It's still in use in 1981. I knelt on Seth's grave and vowed to change what had happened."

A crease appeared in Susannah's brow. "Assuming this is all true, how do you plan on saving his life?"

"The easiest way is to prevent Seth and Bingo from having any confrontation. That way there's no reason for any of it to happen."

"Oh, dear Lord." Susannah bowed her head. Her next words came out in a strangled whisper. "It's too late for that."

Megan grabbed the bars. "What happened?"

"Seth returned to the dance." Susannah raised her head, her eyes unnaturally bright. "He said he wanted to talk to me. We walked off a bit for privacy and met up with John Bingo and a couple of his men." She stood and paced back and forth in front of the cell. "He was quite inebriated and insulted Seth the way he usually does. He is a most unpleasant man. Always has been. He said some unflattering things about you. Some quite vulgar. Seth, sober as the Pope mind you, had a few unpleasant things to say to Bingo and soon they were in an intense argument. Bingo said they should just get this over with and settle it once and for all. And Seth agreed!" She threw up a hand.

"Oh no." Megan rested her forehead against the bars. Her shoulders slumped in defeat. That foolish man had said himself that he suspected he died in a gunfight—soon—then he goes and stages his own death.

"I pleaded with him not to. He unpinned his star and threw it on the ground. I picked it up and tried to give it back to him, but he didn't want it. He sent me away as if I were a child."

"At least he didn't lock you up. Did you go away?"

"He thought I did but I hid behind a tree. I heard Bingo say they'll meet at noon on Main Street. Seth said he didn't want Bingo's blood on the fine streets of Fort Worth and suggested somewhere else, less public, and earlier in the day. They decided on an hour after dawn."

More differences and changes. Megan wondered if circumstances had changed with every previous Megan. Maybe it didn't matter as long as she attained the ultimate goal—Seth alive at the end of the day.

Susannah whirled around and went to Seth's desk. She yanked open drawers and pawed through them. "He must have another key somewhere." She opened another drawer and dug around. "Ah ha." She held up a key and hurried over to the cell.

Seconds later the door to Megan's cell swung open. She grabbed her cloak and stepped out. "Where are Seth and Bingo meeting?"

"What are you going to do?" Susannah wrung her hands.

"I'm going to stop them."

"How?"

"I haven't figured that out yet." Megan put on her cloak. "What time is it?"

"It's a couple of hours until dawn."

"Where will they be?"

"I'll take you there." Susannah went to the door.

"Susannah, you don't need—"

"It's dark. You'll get lost. It's easier to show you." Susannah pulled her hood over her head. "Come along."

Outside, Megan closed the jail door and followed Susannah down the boardwalk. They moved quickly past the closed, dark stores. The cool night wind brushed Megan's face. She wrinkled her nose, detecting a curious potpourri of spring blooms and cow manure. A dog barked in the distance. They turned a corner and hurried down a dark street, their cloaks billowing around them. Clouds scurried across a waning moon.

"We should have gotten Tim," Megan said between heavy breaths. Susannah kept a fast pace.

"He's probably with Seth."

"Tim knew about all of this?"

"I ran into him when I left Seth. Timothy offered to give me a ride home, but first I sat him down and asked him some questions about you and what all he knew. Then I told him what happened with Seth. Timothy left without a by your leave and I haven't seen him since. I assume he went in search of Seth."

"How did you get back to town?"

"I rode with a family who lives on the other side of town then walked the rest of the way."

They kept to the alley and crossed a street, then two more. Minutes later, they left the buildings behind and followed a trail of wagon ruts. An ocean of stars twinkled overhead. Knee-high grasses and the shadowy forms of scrub brush rose around them. A long dark shape lay nearby. Susannah went to it, brushed her hand around, and sat down.

"Rest a bit. We have a ways yet to go."

Megan realized it was a log and sat, holding her dress and petticoat down with her elbows. "Where are we going?"

"A clearing near the river. It's where the men sometimes go for this sort of thing." Disgust filled Susannah's voice. "Settle their differences, as they say."

"Settle their differences?" Megan regarded Susannah in disbelief. "This isn't a fistfight, where both walk away. This is a gunfight that will end in someone's death."

"I know." Susannah's tone said, *What do you think I am, an idiot?*

"I thought gunfights took place on the main street in broad daylight, in front of witnesses so there isn't any foul play. Not out in the middle of nowhere with no one else around."

"I don't know where you got the idea that gunfights only take place in town. Many do, of course, probably most, but they can happen anytime, anywhere. As for witnesses, Timothy will be there, and Bingo will have a man with him. The deputy will be there too to make sure it's fair. He's a good man. No friend of Bingo's."

"Have you seen a gunfight before?"

Susannah pulled her feet in. "There have been many opportunities, but I refuse to participate. I stay inside and find something else to do besides watch one man kill another."

From a tree above them, something took flight with a great rush of wings.

Megan jumped. "What was that?"

"An owl." Susannah clasped her hands together on her lap and sat prim and proper. "I guess the conversation is making you a tad jumpy."

After a moment, Megan asked, "You and Seth never talked earlier?"

"No. But I'm sure he was going to tell me there will be no wedding. At least not his and mine."

Megan looked down at her hands. "I'm sorry, Susannah." She looked at Susannah. "I truly am."

Susannah pushed back her hood and tilted her face up to the night sky. "I may not know much about what goes on between a man and a woman, but I do know one thing. You don't choose love. Love chooses you. And somehow," she turned her head and met Megan's gaze in the darkness, "love transcended time and chose you for Seth, and him for you." Her voice thickened. "I don't understand how or why. I most certainly am not pleased with this turn of events. But I love Seth enough that I want only his happiness. He loves you. So be it."

"He does love you, you know. In his own way."

"I also know that he has never looked at me the way he looks at you. I do not want to be his second choice."

After a moment, Megan replied softly, "Tim looks at you that way."

Susannah tilted her head to the sky again. "But I don't love him that way."

"Maybe you would if you give him a chance. See him from a different perspective." *As I have Seth.* When she'd discovered he was the Marshal she'd never felt prouder of him or respected him more. And had fallen in love with him all over again. All day, she had watched him move easily among the crowd, talking, laughing, slapping men on the back, charming the women, paying patient attention to the children. He was a natural people person. He had finally found his calling—public service. She had seen a new side of him. Although he had a funny way of keeping the peace. *Ends up in a gunfight. Foolish prideful man.*

"Timothy." Susannah gave an unladylike snort. "He's so ... I don't know."

Megan swatted something off her cheek. She wasn't at all proud about offering Tim as a consolation prize to Susannah. But if Seth was out of the picture, for whatever reason, Susannah and Tim might find happiness together. Megan decided to give Susannah something else to think about. "Would you rather die a spinster from a fever in your fifties?"

Susannah jerked back as if slapped. "Is that how—?" She held up a hand. "Don't tell me." She faced forward, pulling her cloak tighter about her as if suddenly cold. Something rustled a nearby bush and made a chirping sound. She stood, pulling her hood over her head, and said in a sharp tone, "Come along."

They hurried down the rutted road. The air smelled fresh and fertile, rich with the promise of greening spring. A symphony of bird calls swelled as night slowly eased away and a faint pink hue outlined the horizon. At one point, Susannah went left into the grass. Megan followed, grateful the grass wasn't wet with dew to ruin her dress.

Two grazing deer lifted their heads and stared at them a moment then bounded away. Stars slowly faded away like disappearing ink.

"It's not far now," Susannah said softly.

They skirted a grove of trees.

Susannah stopped. "Rest a moment. We'll have to be very quiet from here on."

"How far is it?"

"Up yonder just a bit. The river is beyond these trees. The clearing is up ahead. We can wait in the trees for the men to arrive."

"You go back, Susannah. I'll go on alone."

Susannah had been looking behind them. She whirled around and stared wide-eyed at Megan. "I'm not leaving you here alone."

"Please, Susannah. This is something I must do. My ... my destiny." Megan cleared a lump in her throat before adding, "I don't want you to get hurt."

"Why on earth would I get hurt?" Susannah drew in a sharp breath. "Megan. What exactly are you planning to do?"

"I told you last night. I'm here to save his life."

"But how? Are you going to try to reason with them?" Susannah laughed humorlessly. "You don't know John Bingo. He's despicable. There is no reasoning with that man. And Seth," she shook her head, "he's so consumed with hatred for Bingo he loses every iota of reason. I can't think of any way to stop them. Tell me your plan."

"Please go back, Susannah. You don't need to be involved."

Another unladylike laugh, short and harsh, came from Susannah. "I welcomed you into my home. I set you free and led you here. I am still, in all truth, Seth's betrothed. I love him and don't want to see him killed any more than you do. I don't think I can be much more *involved*."

Without a word, Megan walked off in the direction Susannah had indicated, staying close to the tree line. Hurried footsteps came up behind her.

"Megan, stop. You're going the wrong way."

"But you pointed—"

"You need to cut through the trees. See? You need me." Susannah wore a smug look as she brushed past Megan and led the way into the trees following a deer trail. They walked as quietly as possible through tangled brush and snagging branches that resembled weirdly twisted limbs in the lingering shadows.

The trees thinned to a clearing bordered on three sides by forest. On the fourth side, a river rushed loudly in its spring fullness.

Susannah stopped several yards from the tree line. She said softly, "Now we wait." She pulled her cloak tight around her, leaned against a tree, and gazed at the clearing.

Megan stood beside another tree, her hands clasped together over her hammering heart. She prayed the men wouldn't show up and this wouldn't be the day Seth, or she, would die.

Have mercy on Seth. On me.

"Susannah, I have one thing to ask of you."

"I'm not leaving."

"I noticed." Megan raised her gaze to the brightening sky. She swallowed hard before speaking. "Promise me you'll take care of Seth if … if anything happens to me."

Seconds spun out. Susannah drew in a sharp breath. "You're not thinking of—of saving Seth by sacrificing yourself, are you?" She grabbed Megan's arm. "Megan. Tell me that's not your big plan."

"Susannah, please—"

The sound of snapping twigs and a rustling in the bushes behind them made them jump.

A familiar voice said, "I don't know what the hell y'all think you're doin' here but you're both goin' back the way you come."

Chapter 36

Lottie shoved branches aside with one hand and stepped out of the bushes. "Did ya hear me? Git on back to town."

Megan crossed her arms. "I'm not going anywhere."

Susannah crossed hers too. "I'm not either."

"Now you listen here, you two." Anger flashed in Lottie's eyes. She stepped closer, holding a branch back with her left hand while keeping her right hand beneath her olive-green cloak. "You don't need to be here. If Seth sees either one of you, he'll lose his concentration. You need to go."

Susannah asked, "What if Seth sees you?"

"He ain't gonna."

Megan pushed off the hood of her cape. "What's your plan?"

"Why would I tell you?" Lottie looked down her nose at Megan.

"Because I love him too and don't want to see him die."

Lottie stepped forward, releasing the branch behind her. It snapped back like a whip. Her eyes narrowed, and her nostrils flared as if fire would shoot from them. "I knew there was somethin' goin' on between you two. You damn Yankee wh—"

"Lottie." Susannah placed her hand on Lottie's arm. "We all love Seth. We want to help. What can we do?"

"Leave."

"But what can *you* possibly do?" Susannah persisted.

"You'll find out later." Lottie glanced toward the clearing then back to the two women. "Now git on back before the men git here. Please, Susannah. You don't need to be around to see this. Take her with you." She jutted her chin at Megan then started to turn away. She stopped when Megan spoke.

"I know what your plan is."

"Oh, you do, do you," Lottie sneered with disdain in her eyes.

Megan stood her ground. "You said Seth wouldn't see you. That means you'll be behind him. You wore that green cloak to blend in with the trees so none of the other men will see you either. Tim said Seth had a steady hand and a good aim, but he wasn't fast enough to beat another man. I'm sure you know that too. When Seth and Bingo are facing each other, poised to draw, you'll be hiding in the trees behind Seth with that gun you have underneath your cloak, and you don't have to worry about being fast enough. *You're* going to shoot Bingo."

Susannah gasped, clasping her hands to her chest. "Sweet Mother of God, is *that* what you're going to do, Lottie? *Murder* John Bingo?"

Lottie pressed her lips into a thin line, a defiant look in her eyes. "Call it what you want. I'm gonna do whatever I gotta do to save my brother. One of 'em's gonna die and it ain't gonna be Seth."

"I think it's brilliant." Megan smiled at the surprised look on Lottie's face. If Lottie's plan succeeded, it would solve Megan's problem, and all would be well without her or Seth dying. "Come on, Susannah. Let's leave Charlotte to her—"

The sound of male voices and approaching horses filtered through the trees.

"Quiet!" Lottie ordered softly. She crouched in the brush. Susannah and Megan followed suit. Megan pulled her hood over her head.

Seth and Tim emerged from the woods far to the left of the women and rode their horses into the clearing. Two other men followed.

"The first man, the young one, is Deputy Culpepper," Susannah whispered to Megan. He had a thick brown mustache, and a tin star on his leather vest. "The man with the tall black hat is the undertaker, Mr. Kitching." He had a white beard, wore black trousers, and a long black coat.

The men dismounted. The undertaker took the horses, tied them to trees at the edge of the clearing, and stayed there.

Seth removed his coat and handed it to Tim. Deputy Culpepper stood nearby.

"Maybe he won't come." Tim's voice carried clearly to the women hiding in the woods several yards away.

"He'll come." Seth drew out his gun from its holster, opened the cylinder and spun it, then closed it. He slid the gun back into the holster, then adjusted his gun belt lower on his hips. The vest he wore over his blue shirt looked different without the tin star pinned to it. He withdrew some folded papers from his trouser pocket and handed them to Tim.

Tim stepped closer to Seth and talked quietly to him. Seth shook his head. Tim made several gestures with his hand. Seth turned away and walked to the middle of the clearing. His hand resting on the butt of his gun, he pushed his hat back and lifted his face to the morning sunlight slanting over the treetops.

Watching him with her heart in her throat, a thousand thoughts raced through Megan's mind. *What is he thinking, feeling right now? How does a man prepare himself for his possible death? What are those papers? Last will and testament? Letters? To me? Lottie? Susannah? Every fiber in my being wants to go to him. But I mustn't. I can't. I can't ruin it again, the way it's been ruined before, over and over and over.*

Love, hope, faith. You'll need all three, the other Megan had written. Megan folded her hands, bowed her head, and closed her eyes.

Please God, have mercy on him. Guide Lottie's hand. Hold it steady.

Is it murder? What is this gunfight? This stupid gunfight. Isn't it just another name for murder?

The pounding of hooves came from the woods on the other side of the clearing.

Megan opened her eyes. Susannah had tears running down her pale face as she stared in the direction of the noise. Megan took Susannah's hand.

Susannah gripped Megan's hand tightly in return.

John Bingo rode a big black horse into the clearing, followed by another man. They reined in their horses. The other man dismounted. He looked maybe twenty, clean-shaven and baby-faced.

Bingo wore a white shirt, and black from his hat to his boots. "Good morning, gentlemen. I see we're all here." He dismounted with a spring in his step and turned to Seth with a grin. "It's a beautiful day to die, don't you think, O'Connor?"

"Guess you'll find out real soon."

Bingo threw back his head and laughed. "I believe there will be moments in the future when I'll actually miss you."

Lottie whispered, "Somethin' ain't right."

"What could possibly be right about any of this?" Susannah sobbed. She wiped her free hand across her cheeks.

"What do you mean, Charlotte?" Megan shifted positions, easing a cramp in her leg from squatting so long. Her heart raced with the knowledge that it would all be over soon, one way or the other.

"That's Tommy Clausen with John. Tommy's just a kid. New to the gang. What the hell's he doin' here? Should be one of the other men."

Lottie shook her head. "Somethin' ain't right." Her gaze went to the woods Bingo had come from.

Deputy Culpepper approached Seth and Bingo. "You men ready?"

Seth nodded.

"You bet I am." Bingo removed his coat and hat and tossed them to Tommy.

"You both know how this works," the deputy said. "You go to opposite ends of the clearing. I'll be in the middle, on the side. Mr. Summerfield and Tommy will be with me. After I shoot my gun in the air, the rest is up to you two. Take as long as you want. Mr. Bingo, you go over there." The deputy pointed to the side of the clearing on the women's right. "Marshal—I mean Mr. O'Connor, you go to the other end."

Seth turned, only to turn back when the deputy said, "Mr. O'Connor? Good luck." Deputy Culpepper held out his hand.

Seth shook it. He turned to Tim. They clapped each other on the shoulders, shook hands, then looked at each other for a long moment. If any words passed between them, the women were too far away to hear. Seth headed to his side.

"I think I'm going to be ill." Susannah's whispered voice quivered. Her hand tightened on Megan's.

Megan felt Susannah shaking.

"Trust Charlotte," Megan reassured Susannah. "Have faith."

"I gotta git behind him." Lottie rose up a bit, took a couple steps, and tripped over something, making her yelp as she landed on her side, her skirt and cloak tangled around her legs. She froze.

"Someone's in the woods over here." Tommy Clausen's young voice carried clearly to the women.

"Oh, dear Lord," Susannah murmured, squeezing Megan's hand in a death grip.

Bingo spun around. "Deputy? You want to check those trees?"

"What's going on?" Seth's voice came nearer.

"It appears we have an audience," Bingo replied. "Probably some young'uns come to watch the excitement."

Deputy Culpepper walked to the edge of the clearing.

Lottie stayed where she was, as still as a log. Megan and Susannah crouched as low as possible among the branches and brush. A small, hairy black spider crawled up Megan's arm. She bit her lower lip, afraid to make any motion to brush it off. Twigs snapped beneath approaching footsteps. She tore her gaze from the spider and looked up just as the branches above her parted. Deputy Culpepper's head appeared. His eyes widened in shock.

"What the devil are you ladies doin' in there?"

Megan yanked her hand free from Susannah's grip and brushed off the spider while Lottie replied, "Why, we was enjoyin' a sunrise picnic breakfast when you fellas showed up. What'd ya think we was doin'?" She waved her left hand. "Give me hand up, will ya, Nancy?"

"It's Yancy." The deputy stepped closer and helped her stand just as Bingo walked up.

"Lottie? I wasn't expecting to find *you* hiding in the woods."

Tim's head popped up behind Bingo's. "Sue?" Tim pushed past Bingo and went to help Susannah to her feet. "Are you all right?"

"Of course." She shook out her dress and cloak then smoothed them down with her hands.

"Is it the Tolar boys?" Seth asked as he walked up and joined the group. "Those boys are always—Megan?" His eyes grew as round as Frisbees when she rose to her feet from the leaf-littered forest floor. He exploded. "How in the hell did you get out of your cell an' what the hell are y'all doin' here?" His angry gaze swept over Lottie, then Susannah, and paused. "You surprise me most of all, bein' involved in this."

Susannah lifted her chin. "I set Megan free."

A muscle twitched in Seth's clenched jaw.

Tim held Susannah's arm as she stepped carefully out of the woods into the clearing. Lottie shook off Bingo's arm, took the Deputy's, and followed Tim and Susannah. Megan left the woods last, brushing off her clothes, feeling Seth's angry glare follow her.

"I'm surprised you're not getting ready for your wedding day, Miss Susannah," Bingo said.

She gave a humorless laugh. "I believe most of us here know there won't be a wedding for me today."

"Whaddaya mean?" Lottie demanded. Her angry gaze darted from Susannah to Seth to Megan.

Tim grinned as if he'd just won the Publisher's Clearinghouse grand prize.

Seth had gone still as a statue.

Deputy Culpepper removed his hat and scratched his head. "I didn't know that."

Megan resisted the urge to cower beneath Lottie's deadly glare. *At least she's keeping that gun hidden behind her skirt, and not pointed at me. Hopefully.*

Bingo wore a smug smile. "You are as smart as you are lovely, Miss Susannah. Because you are correct. It's hard to have a wedding when the groom is in the care of the undertaker. Let's get this over with, shall we?" He walked towards his assigned spot.

"Don't you dare hurt my brother, John Bingo," Lottie called.

"Keep out of this, Lottie," Seth pushed through gritted teeth. "You women need to go."

Bingo stopped and slowly turned around. "Why, Lottie, old girl, you know I have to kill your brother. Otherwise, he'll kill me. You don't want that, do you? Who would take care of you? Who would give you the kind of life you deserve? And I know you don't want to deprive our sweet little girl of her papa, now do you?"

All color drained from Lottie's face. "Johnny, don't ..." Her voice sounded strangled, small.

Bingo continued, "It's bad enough she doesn't even know you're her mama, and—"

"*What?*" Seth stared from Bingo to Lottie. "You have a *daughter*? I'm an ... *uncle*?"

Lottie bowed her head.

"Well, well, well." Bingo laughed, looking cocky and pleased with himself. "She never told you, O'Connor? Never said a word about our daughter? Shame on you, Lottie. What a bad sister you are."

Seth had eyes only for Lottie. "When?"

"You were on that trail drive." Lottie kept her gaze down. "Twelve years ago. Her name is Amelia.

"After granny," Seth said softly, his face full of wonderment and hurt.

"She goes by Melly," Bingo added.

"Melly?" Seth asked Lottie, "The oldest girl at the Widow Kemp's?"

Her head still bowed, Lottie nodded.

Barton said his granny was the oldest of Bingo's kids in the care of a widow. If Melly is Charlotte's daughter, then Seth is Barton's great-great-uncle! Megan's mind reeled at the realization.

Seth removed his hat, raked his hand through his hair, and settled the hat back on his head. "I can't believe, all these years, you never told me."

"I'm sorry," Lottie whispered. She slowly raised her kohl-darkened eyes to Seth. "I'm so sorry." Her once-fancy hairdo was a tangled mess, and in the morning sunlight the wrinkles on her cheeks, forehead, and around her lips showed as clearly as highways on a roadmap.

Megan felt a surge of pity for Lottie. A woman old before her time, worn out and worn down by the hardships of a life full of bad decisions, desperate decisions, and too little kindness.

Seth stared at his sister, his expression hard, unforgiving. His gaze cut to Tim. "Did you know?"

"Nope."

Seth looked at his bride-to-be-or-not-to-be.

"I didn't know until a few years ago." Susannah stepped closer to Seth, reaching out her hand as if to touch his arm, then paused, and slowly withdrew it. "Melly tries hard in school. She's bright and—"

"She's mean as a rattler," Seth interrupted in a flat, cold voice. "She picks on the little kids. More than once, I've seen her kick that old dog that sleeps behind the barber's shop. A couple months back, I caught her lighting a cat's tail on fire. I gave her what-for an' she cussed me out like a drunken cowhand on a Saturday night. She dresses like a street urchin. She's filthy, an' her hair's a rat's nest." Fury flashed in his eyes as his gaze moved from Lottie to Bingo. "She's not being raised the way my niece, or any child, should be."

"I agree, O'Connor." Bingo flicked something off the front of his shirt, a smirk on his face as he glanced at Seth, who had jerked back slightly at Bingo's words. "She's getting too old to be a tomboy. I'm going to have her cleaned up, get her some fine new clothes. Why, underneath all that grime I bet she's prettier than her mama was. I have plans for my little Melly."

Seth's eyes narrowed. "Like what?"

"Nothing you need to worry about." Bingo grinned. "Since you won't be around anymore." He rubbed his hands together. "Why don't we get this over with?"

"What kinda plans, Johnny?" Lottie's voice trembled.

"None of your business." Bingo sent her a dismissive glance before turning away. "Come on, O'Connor. I have a busy day ahead."

Megan could almost see smoke coming out of Seth's ears as he watched Bingo strut over to the deputy and Tommy. She hoped Seth wasn't letting Bingo's comments get under his skin and undermine his confidence. She didn't know what all this meant for Lottie's plan. Or her own, half-baked as it was.

"Tim?" Seth turned to his best friend. "Would you please escort the ladies home?"

Tim frowned. "I think I should stay here."

Seth shook his head. "Get them out of—"

"We'll leave," Megan quickly said, not wanting Seth to be without Tim's moral support.

"We will?" Susannah's eyebrows shot upward.

"Yes. We will." Megan took Susannah by the arm and started leading her into the woods. "We won't go far," Megan whispered to Susannah, then said louder, "Come on, Lottie. Lottie?" Megan and Susannah stopped when Lottie stayed where she was.

"What plans, Johnny?" Lottie demanded in a louder voice.

Bingo had his back to her and waved as he stood with the other men.

"If you two are ready," Deputy Culpepper said, "go to your side."

Bingo walked to one end of the clearing.

Seth handed his hat to Tim, then said, "Not until the women leave."

"We're leaving," Megan reassured him. "Don't worry. We're leaving."

His gaze, cold and distant, met hers, and for an instant, the look in his eyes softened.

Is this the last time I'll gaze into your eyes? Hazel flecked with green. They caught my heart that first night you crossed time to change ... everything. Including yourself. And me. She ached to touch him, hold him, kiss him. Just once more. But she could only mouth, *I love you.*

He nodded, glanced at Susannah, then Lottie. He turned abruptly, shoulders squared, and headed to the other end of the clearing.

Her vision blurry, her insides cold and hollow, Megan watched the man she loved walk away into history to become weathered words chiseled on a gravestone, etched on a plaque.

Or not.

"Come on, Lottie," Megan urged. "You have to get behind him. Come on." She pulled Lottie's arm. "Hurry up."

Lottie shook free and took a few steps in Bingo's direction. "John Bingo, I asked you a question." Her voice rang loud and clear.

Bingo stopped and turned around, as did Seth.

"What is it, woman?" Bingo demanded.

"What are your plans for Amelia?"

"Why, I'm going to send her back east to a fancy boarding school. Make a lady out of her."

"Don't you lie to me." Lottie shoved her cloak aside and raised her right arm, pointing her gun at Bingo.

"Oh my God," Susannah moaned, gripping a branch.

"Oh shit," Megan said at the same time. She moved to the edge of the clearing, not far from Tim, who stood slack-jawed, shading his eyes with one hand. Beside him, Tommy waited, his slender body tense as a strung bow, his young face flushed.

"Lottie!" Seth ran back, stopping a couple yards from his sister. "Put that gun down."

"You heard him, Miss Lottie." Deputy Culpepper went to stand near Seth. "Put it down."

"Y'all shut up an' stay outta this." Lottie kept her gun on Bingo. Her hand never wavered. "Tell me the truth, John. What are your plans for Amelia?"

He stepped closer to her. "Why do you suddenly care?"

"I've always cared. I'm her mama."

A harsh laugh came from Bingo. "A piss poor one, old girl."

"You bastard. You wouldn't let me be a mother. You took her away, an' told me to leave her alone. No tellin' what you told her about me."

"I've told her nothing." Bingo spread his hands wide. "She has no idea you are her mother. She just knows her mother is a whore."

Lottie held her gun steady on Bingo. Her cloak rippled in the wind.

"Give me the gun, Lottie," Seth said with a pleading tone in his voice.

"Listen to your brother." Bingo slowly moved forward a couple steps. His helmet of hair had the sheen of an oil slick. "For once he's right."

"Shut up, Seth," Lottie snapped. "An' you don't you come any closer, you slime-suckin' snake." She cocked the gun and held it with both hands.

Bingo stopped. "Lottie, Lottie."

"You're gonna make her a whore, ain't cha? You're gonna set her up in her own room an' sell her just like she's any other gal."

Standing on the edge of the woods beside Tim, Susannah covered her mouth. "Dear God. Not that."

"Sick bastard," Megan muttered.

Out in the clearing, Seth had a look of horror and disbelief on his face. His hand gripped the butt of his holstered gun.

"You're wrong, Lottie. She's not like any other gal. Melly is young, pretty, fresh. I'm a business man." Bingo shrugged. "I'll make a fortune off her first time."

"Your own daughter." Lottie's voice shook, but not her hands. "Your own flesh and blood."

"How about I split her first time with you. Just think of all the paints and powders and frilly doo dads you could buy with that money."

"I don't want your damn money. I want you toes up six feet under."

A shot rang out.

Megan jumped.

Lottie grabbed her left arm. "Son of a bitch!" She dropped her gun.

Another shot fired.

Someone shouted, "Bingo!"

For an instant, Megan felt like she was playing games at a church picnic. Then she gasped.

Bingo stood with a look of surprise on his pockmarked face, his hands clasped to his chest where a red stain spread across his crisp white shirt. He stumbled forward two, three steps then fell to his knees. "Lottie ... old girl ..." Blood trickled out of the side of his mouth. He toppled sideways to the grass.

Tommy ran and dropped to his knees beside Bingo's body. Deputy Culpepper knelt, too. The undertaker joined them.

Seth, Tim, and Susannah ran to Lottie.

Megan followed more slowly, stunned by the turn of events.

"Some son of a bitch shot me!" Ashen-faced, Lottie had her right hand clasped to her left upper arm.

"Let me see." Seth pried her bloodied hand off her arm.

"It was Tommy," Tim said.

"You tiny dick bastard!" Lottie twisted around to shout at Tommy.

"Hold still," Seth barked. "The bullet just grazed you. We'll wrap it up—"

"Here." Susannah held up a strip of linen she'd torn off the bottom of her petticoat.

"—an' have the doc look at it."

Tommy scrambled to his feet and ran over, pushing Tim aside to get to Lottie. "You were gonna shoot him. I had to stop you. You shot him anyway!"

"I didn't shoot him," Lottie yelled back. "I dropped my gun and it shot him."

"Be still, Lottie." Susannah wrapped the linen around Lottie's arm.

Tommy shook his finger in Lottie's face. "Only place you're goin' is to jail for murderin' Johnny."

"You snot-nosed turd." Lottie slapped his hand away. "Go to hell."

"Quiet, both of you," Seth ordered when Deputy Culpepper joined them. Seth asked, "Bingo?"

The deputy shook his head.

A moment of silence followed.

Susannah voiced what most were probably thinking, "I can't believe John Bingo is dead."

"Good riddance," Lottie added with a sharp, smug tone in her voice.

"Murderin' whore!" Tommy lunged at her, his face blotchy with rage.

Tim yanked Tommy back by his collar. "Watch your mouth, boy. No one murdered anyone."

"It was an accident," Seth replied as he secured the end of the linen. "Lottie dropped the gun an' it discharged."

Tommy fought and twisted to be free. "She said she wanted him toes up! Y'all heard her. Then she shot him!"

Seth turned to his deputy. "Handle this, will you?"

Deputy Culpepper nodded.

Seth walked over to Bingo's body.

Susannah looked at Megan. "It's over." Susannah grinned. "It's all over."

It's over. Megan looked at Seth, standing over Bingo. *We're both alive.* Her shoulders sagged with relief. *Neither of us had to die.* Gratitude and joy overwhelmed her. *Thank you, universe. Thank you, God. Thank y—*

Something glinted in the woods, like sunlight on metal.

Megan stared at the spot. Fear squeezed her heart.

She could almost hear Bingo's instructions to one of his goons. *If something happens to me, kill O'Connor.*

She ran.

She ran faster than she ever had before. Her feet barely touched the grass as she raced towards Seth, screaming his name. She shoved him out of the way as a shot exploded from the woods.

White-hot pain sliced through Megan.

She screamed. Her knees buckled. She crumpled on the cool grass like a rag doll.

"Megan!"

Shouts, screams. More gunshots.

Shocked faces hovered above her. Gentle hands ran over her pain-wracked body.

"Megan. Oh God Megan. Why did you do that?"

The blue sky swam in her vision. Then Seth's anguished face blocked all else. "Don't you die on me. Please don't die."

She struggled to keep her eyes open against threatening blackness. Her limbs felt like dead weight. Something warm pooled beneath her. Pain swamped her.

People gathered around, and poked and prodded and wrapped parts of her up. Blood reddened their hands.

"It was Jethro Seller," the deputy said. "He's dead."

"We gotta get her to town," Tim said. "I can't stop the bleeding."

"Use my petticoat. Quick." Lottie's voice shook.

"Shot through like that she ain't gonna make it," the undertaker declared.

Megan stared into Susannah's eyes.

Take care of him. Give him children. Love him. For me.

Susannah buried her face in her bloodied hands and turned away.

"Tim, get Chevy. Hurry." Seth brushed hair off Megan's cheek. "Stay with me, love. Please." He kissed her forehead, whispered hoarsely, "Don't leave me. I don't want to live without you. I need you. I love you. Tim," he shouted. "Where's my goddamn horse!"

Megan struggled to draw a ragged breath. Lord it hurt. Everything hurt. She moaned in agony.

"Easy, love. Easy." Tears rolled down Seth's face. He stroked her hair over and over. "I love you. Don't leave me. Please don't leave me. Not after all we've been through. We crossed through time for each other. Don't you dare die." His voice broke. "My brave, beautiful Megan."

She focused her blurry eyes on his beloved face. She tried to lift her hand to touch it, but it took too great an effort. Her hand fell limply on the ground.

Seth took her hand and pressed it to his lips. His tears wet her skin.

She longed to hear him call her *Miss Megan* one more time. She felt life ebbing with each slowing beat of her heart. Gathering the last of her fleeting strength she croaked, "Do ... great ... things ... my ... love ..."

Her task completed, her destiny fulfilled, Megan McClure closed her eyes and gave in to the blackness.

Chapter 37

"When do you think she'll wake up?"

"It's only been two days since her surgery. Give her time. With the trauma she's had, the best thing for her right now is sleep. You should go home and get some rest yourself. I'll let you know if she wakes up."

"I'm not leaving."

"There's no one else who could sit with her? Her folks?"

"They're both dead. She's my best friend. I'm staying"

Voices came and went. An irritating beeping sound went on and on and on. Sharp objects pierced her flesh. Pain, like the voices, came and went, then came again.

Oblivion, quiet, peaceful, pain-free, beckoned her, tempted her.

Not yet. Seth ... Seth ...

***

Megan opened her eyes, blinking from bright lights overhead. Machines surrounded her. Tubes snaked from them that somehow connected to her beneath a white blanket.

"You're awake!" A young woman wearing a white nurse's uniform smiled as she leaned over Megan.

"I'm back?" Megan whispered. Her gaze swept the hospital room. TV mounted on the wall. Nightstand beside her bed with a table lamp and a box of tissues on it. One cushioned armchair, and one straight-backed wooden chair. An airplane far away in the sky framed by the window. Definitely not 1890.

"You certainly are. About time too. How do you feel, Miss McClure?"

"You know my name? How?"

"Your friend who brought you in. She's barely left your side." The nurse put her hand on Megan's forehead. "How are you feeling?"

Megan thought a moment, her brain slow, fuzzy. She wiggled her toes. Moved her legs, fingers, hands, and arms. All her limbs worked. The only pain centered on her torso, wrapped in bandages like a mummy. "Tired. Weak." She frowned. "Confused."

"Understandable." The nurse removed her hand and straightened. "You've been through a lot. The doctor—oh, here's your friend."

Donna walked into the room and dropped a can of pop. "Megs!" She ran to the bed. "You're awake! Oh Megs. Thank God." She leaned down then jerked back. "I want to hug you but I'm afraid to. All those tubes."

Megan blinked back tears. "Go ahead and hug me."

Donna wrapped her arms around Megan's neck, and pressed her cheek to Megan's cheek.

"I thought I'd never see you again," Megan whispered, breathing in Donna's favorite perfume *Charlie*.

"I told you I'd be here until you came back. Never expected you to show up like this."

"How long have I been here?"

"Four days."

"Holy moly. How did I get here?"

Donna drew back and glanced at the nurse standing near the door writing on a chart. "You don't remember?"

Megan shook her head.

"I'll give y'all a chance to talk." The nurse picked up the can of pop off the floor and handed it to Donna. "I'm glad you hadn't opened it yet. Better wait a bit before you do." She hung the chart on the end of Megan's bed. "I'll be back in a few minutes."

After she left, Donna said, "Seth brought you."

"He did?" Megan's eyes widened. "That's right. According to the other Megan, I had one chance to go back through that door. I guess being carried through counts. Tell me all of it."

Donna sat on the side of the bed and put the pop on the nightstand. She looked relaxed and casual in a pair of jeans and a sleeve-less white shirt. "The other evening, I was sitting in my room, or your room." She tsked and waved her hand. "The room at the B&B when suddenly Seth's door banged open and in ran a cowboy dripping blood on the hardwood floor."

That's how he came in that first night.

"He asked, *Donna?* and held out his arms, sobbing, *Help her. She's dying.* He was holding you. You were the one bleeding all over the floor. I ran downstairs and called for an ambulance, then waited with him in the room, both of us pressing towels to your wounds to stop the blood while he told me what happened. How you sacrificed yourself for him." Donna covered Megan's hand with her own on top of the covers. "You really did it? What you were supposed to do?"

"Yeah. Got the bullet hole to prove it." Megan smiled weakly.

"Two holes, actually."

"What?" Megan sat up suddenly, then winched at the pain, and quickly lay back.

"Take it easy. The bullet went in your right side and out the left."

"I had no idea. All I felt was pain when I was hit."

"You're lucky the bullet went through you instead of staying inside you for evidence or you'd have some explaining to do."

"What happened with Seth? Quick, before the nurse comes back."

"He hid when the paramedics arrived and took you away. He said he was going to stay until he heard how you were. When you came through surgery okay, I went back and told him. I took him some tacos and we talked while he ate. I found out he didn't know about the other Megans."

"I didn't have time to tell him any of that. I was only there two days."

A frown creased Donna's forehead. "He said the same thing and that's something I don't understand. Here, in this time, you were gone five days."

"Five!" Megan gasped. Time seemed to have a sense of humor.

"I gave Seth the other Megan's letter to read, plus your last journal."

"Now he knows everything." Megan covered a yawn.

"You don't mind, do you?"

"I'm glad he knows. Maybe he understands better now and won't be mad at me for what I did."

"Mad at you?" Donna laughed. "That man's crazy in love with you. I really like him. I can't wait to tell him you're finally awake."

"He's still here?"

Donna nodded. "He doesn't—"

The nurse walked in. "Hate to break this up, y'all, but my patient needs to rest." She smiled at Donna. "You should go home and rest too."

***

Doctor Jeffries straightened, looping his stethoscope around his neck. "Everything sounds and looks good. Your wounds are healing nicely." He stuck his hands in the pockets of his white coat. He was middle aged, with salt-and-pepper hair and kind eyes. "You're recovering remarkably well, considering the shape you were in."

"Does that mean I can leave soon?" Megan sat up, ready to go. Seth waited for her at the B&B. Nothing else mattered.

"Not for a few more days." At her sound of protest, he said sternly, "You shouldn't rush it, Megan." He regarded her silently for a moment. "I don't know if you're aware of the gravity of your injuries. You were seconds from bleeding to death when you got here. You needed ten units of blood. Luckily, the bullet didn't hit anything vital as it passed through your body, but it was still a huge shock to your system. Your heart stopped twice while you were on the operating table. Frankly—and I don't say this lightly—it's a miracle you're alive, much less doing as well as you appear to be. I want you to stay a few more days so I can keep an eye on you just to be safe. All right?"

I died twice on the operating table? A miracle I'm alive? Numb with shock, Megan sank back on the pillows. She nodded.

"Excellent. I'll check on you tomorrow." He started to leave and paused at the door. "The police want to talk to you. Do you feel well enough?"

"Of course."

"Don't overdo it. I'll send them in." The doctor left.

She sat up a little straighter, wincing. She straightened the top of her hospital gown then touched her hair. *Yuck!* She tried to fluff it up, make it presentable. The tubes swayed like suspension bridges with her movements. They stilled when the door opened, and she lowered her arms.

Detective Sullivan walked in followed by Officer Bubba, who went to Megan and gave her a quick, careful hug.

"How's Bonnie?" she asked when he stepped back.

"Chompin' at the bit to come see you."

"I'd love to see her."

"I'll tell her." He went to stand by the door.

"Hello, Detective."

Detective Sullivan smiled. "Good to see you, Megan. The doctor says you're recovering well. I'm glad to hear it. Very glad. I'd like to ask you a few questions if you feel up to it."

"Of course. But first, what happened to Barton?"

The detective unbuttoned his suit coat then sat in the straight-backed chair near the foot of her bed. "He's been in jail since the night you ... disappeared. The owner of the B&B filed charges against him. Destruction of private property. Trespassing. Disturbing the peace. Maybe we can get some more against him with your help." He took a small notebook and a pen from his breast pocket. "Can you tell me what happened the night of Tuesday, July seventh?"

Megan told him everything. He made notes and said little. She ended with, "I threw a chair through a window. When Barton broke down the door, I jumped."

Detective Sullivan finished writing, then waited, his pen poised. He glanced up over the rim of his glasses. "Then?"

"I woke up here today."

His eyebrows drew together. "You don't remember anything that happened to you since the night you jumped out of the window to escape Barton Crone until today?"

"Not a thing." Megan shrugged.

"No idea how or why or where you were shot or who shot you?"

She shook her head. "Maybe I hit my head or something when I jumped out of the window. I don't remember anything after that."

Detective Sullivan put his policemen's stare on her, his eyes boring into hers as if the truth was written on the back of her eyeballs.

Megan stared right back at him. Even if he could see the truth there, he wouldn't believe it because it was so unbelievable.

He pressed his lips together then flipped through a couple pages in his notebook. "That night with Mr. Crone you had on a red dress." He glanced at her. "Correct?"

"Yes."

"Yet you showed up five days later in an old-fashioned purple dress."

"I don't remember. I woke up today in this." She tugged the collar of her hospital gown.

"According to your friend Miss Bonnie Hudson the dress fit the description of a purple dress you bought at a church sale and wore at The Tejas for Chisholm Trail Days. Miss Hudson said it was hanging on the back of the bathroom door the time she was in your room. Is that correct?"

"Yes. I have a purple dress, and as far as I know, it's still hanging on the door. At least it was two—I mean five days ago. See?" She gave a little laugh. "I didn't even know how long I was ... gone. I've," she bit her lower lip, "I've lost five days. Five whole days." She sank back against the pillow, the back of her hand on her forehead. "I'm sorry, Detective. But it just hit me. Five days gone. Just ... gone." She hoped she looked properly devastated.

The detective cleared his throat. "I'm sorry, Megan. I know this is hard on you. It's—"

Donna walked in. "Oh." She stopped. "Sorry. I'll come back later."

"No, stay," Megan insisted.

The detective stood. "Yes, Miss Miller. Please join us." He gestured to the cushioned chair.

"Well, if you're sure." Donna sat down beside the nightstand. She flashed Bubba a big smile. "Hello, Officer Newman."

He nodded. "Miss Miller."

Detective Sullivan sat in his chair again and looked at his notebook. "May I ask you some questions, Miss Miller?"

"Sure." Donna crossed her legs.

"Was the purple dress hanging on the bathroom door when you arrived on Wednesday, July eighth?"

"Yes."

"Has it been there ever since?"

Donna glanced at Megan. "Um, no."

Megan raised her eyebrows.

Donna shrugged.

Detective Sullivan asked, "When did you notice it was gone?"

"I think it was the third morning."

"When did you see it next?"

"When I returned to the B&B four nights ago and found Megan lying on the floor in the room."

"She was wearing the purple dress?"

"Yes."

"Megan, do you have any idea of how you went from wearing one dress to wearing another that somehow disappeared from your room three days after you disappeared?" the detective asked.

"No."

Detective Sullivan stared at her a moment through his dark-rimmed glasses. His gaze shifted to Donna. "Do you have anything more to add, Miss Miller?"

"No, sir. It's all a mystery to me. I'm just glad she's back." Donna smiled at Megan.

The detective put his notebook and pen back in his pocket. He placed his palms on the top of his thighs and pushed himself up. "You must be tired, Megan, so we'll leave now. Please let me know if you remember anything. Anything at all. Amnesia is often temporary. I'm sure you'd like to know who shot you, and why. They might come back to finish the job so be careful."

"I will. Just so Barton stays locked up."

"You can charge him with attempted kidnapping and assault. Maybe we can add drug charges with your testimony. I'm going to assign an officer to you."

"Oh no, no." Megan repeated more emphatically, "No. Thank you, Detective, but that won't be necessary."

Detective Sullivan clasped his hands behind his back. "Somewhere out there is someone who tried to kill you. It might be someone who read your methamphetamine article and didn't like your views." He paced a couple of steps. "It might be someone involved in Mr. Crone's drug deals. His partner. One of his customers. The person he had his big deal with." He turned and paced back to where he'd started. "Or maybe one of those young men from that meth house you stumbled into." He shrugged. "It might be some nut who had nothing better to do at the moment." He stepped closer to Megan, his gaze boring into hers. "Whoever it is most likely knows you're alive. All he or she has to do is read the newspaper or watch the evening news. You're also a prime witness against Mr. Crone. I wouldn't be doing my job if I left you unprotected. An officer will be outside the front door of the B&B at all times. Your landlady has already agreed. There will also be an officer outside this door until you leave."

"But Detective—"

He held up a hand. "It's for your own good. And I'll sleep better at night." A slight smile touched his mouth.

Megan saw no way out of it. She forced out a gracious, "Thank you."

Detective Sullivan put his hand on her shoulder. "I'm glad you're all right, young lady. You take care of yourself and I'll come see you again in a few days." He nodded to Donna, and started to leave, then paused at the door. "One more thing, Megan. That night when you called to tell me you had escaped from Mr. Crone, I asked you to remain at the B&B. You replied that you were going somewhere Barton would never find you. Where specifically did you mean?"

"Hmmm." Megan frowned and stared off thoughtfully. "I don't remember much of that conversation, Detective. I was so terrified and freaked out. I really don't know what I meant. Except I had to get away from him any way possible. He would have killed me. There's no doubt in my mind that he would have killed me. I'm sorry." She covered a yawn. "I wish I could be more help."

"Maybe it will come back to you along with your other memories. Get some rest."

After he left, Bubba said, "Get well, Megan. I'll tell Bonnie to stop by." He grinned at Donna. "I'll call you later, sugar bear." He winked and left the room.

Donna blushed and ducked her head.

Megan's mouth fell open. "Sugar bear? You and Bubba? How long was I gone?"

Donna's blush climbed to the roots of her brown hair. "He's been so nice."

"Spill it."

"I thought you were tired."

"Not too tired to hear this."

"Good. Because I've been dying to tell you." Donna scooted the chair closer to the bed. "The first day I got here, the detective and Bubba had been there that night and all day investigating the room and talking to Mrs. Powell and the other guests. I was a basket case. Worried sick about you. But I couldn't tell them the truth. All I could do was watch them do their work and know it was all for nothing. When they left, Detective Sullivan said he'd send an officer to stay with me in case you came back. Bubba offered to return after his shift and stay with me. He brought pizza and beer."

"Smart guy."

"I know, right?" Donna laughed. She flipped back her hair. "We talked the night away. I fell asleep beside him on the sofa and woke up in my bed. He had carried me there." Donna slapped her hand to her cheek. "I was mortified. Him carrying my fat ass to bed. Poor guy could have thrown out his back or gotten a hernia."

Megan scoffed, "You don't have a fat ass. You've lost weight. You look good." Her eyes widened. "Holy moly, you're in love with him."

A giggle escaped Donna. "I am. With a freckle-faced redhead named Bubba of all things." She laughed. Then her brown eyes turned serious. "He's the nicest man I've ever met, Megs. Decent. Funny. Caring. Good listener."

"Was he in that bed with you when you woke up?"

"He was on the sofa." Donna made a face. "Nosy."

They laughed and reached out to hold hands.

"It happened, Megs. Just like you said."

"What did?"

"The first time he kissed me, my knees went weak."

"I'm so happy for you, Donna."

"I'm so glad you're back, and alive."

"Me too. I would have died back there if Seth hadn't brought me here."

"Megs." Donna paused. "The operating table wasn't the only place your heart stopped. Seth said you were dead by the time he got you on his horse. He said your heart beat briefly when he got to the house—maybe from the jarring ride, I don't know. But you had died again by the time he ran up the stairs. He didn't feel your heart beat again until he came through the door."

"I felt myself dying," Megan said slowly. "I felt life leaving."

Donna squeezed her hand. "How awful."

"Actually, it was ... peaceful. But something was missing."

"Seth?"

Megan smiled. "Seth." She scrunched her forehead. "Seth's door. That's why I came back to life and why I'm healing so quickly. He said after he went through the door he healed faster than normal. I guess it worked for me too. You never told me how you explained my sudden appearance to the police."

"Oh that." Donna waved her hand. "I told them I came home, and found you lying on the floor bleeding to death. I didn't know where you had been, or come from, or how you'd gotten in or anything. You're the mystery woman, Megs. Front page news."

"Holy moly. I don't want that." She yawned, covering her mouth with her hand.

"I should let you get some sleep. Want me to stay?"

"Go have fun with Bubba. Is Seth still here?"

Donna nodded. "But he doesn't know how much longer he can stay. He said he doesn't feel well, and he doesn't look well either."

"He's been here too long and he's coming apart. Tell him to go back to his time and come back here soon because I'll be out of here soon."

"And you'll be going back with him?" Donna asked softly, sadly.

Megan nodded. "Somehow, some way. I love him."

"I know. I'll tell him for you. Now get some sleep and I'll see you tomorrow." Donna kissed Megan on the forehead. "Love you." She headed for the door.

Megan sang out, "Love you too, sugar bear."

Donna flipped the bird as she walked out of the room.

***

Detective Sullivan knocked lightly on the open door of the hospital room. "Mornin', Megan. Mind if I come in?"

"Of course not." Megan sat in a wheelchair with a bag on her lap that held rolls of gauze and a box of sterile pads for new dressing, and a bottle of pain pills from the hospital pharmacy. On a nearby table were a vase of roses, baby's breath, and white lilies from the gang at work, a vase of yellow roses from Bonnie and Sam, and a potted philodendron. "Thanks for the plant."

The detective nodded. He took a few steps into the room, glancing at the various machines behind her now quiet. "You look a sight better than you did the other day."

"I feel better too. It's nice to finally wear my own clothes." She had on her yellow sundress since the bandages around her middle were too bulky for shorts or jeans.

"I'm glad I caught you before you're discharged. I didn't want to bother you at the B&B."

"I'm ready to get out of here. I'm just waiting on Donna."

The detective put his hands in his trouser pockets. He wore a brown plaid suit coat over a white shirt. "If you feel up to it, I'd like you to come down to my office in a few days and give your statement concerning Mr. Crone."

"Absolutely. When?"

"Say, Friday, about noon?"

"What day is today?"

"Tuesday." The detective frowned. "Is Friday too soon?"

"Oh no, no." Megan waved her hand. "Friday is fine. I—I just have a hard time keeping track of the days in here. They've all run together."

"You've been here nine days."

She blew out a breath. "It seems like forever."

"Your doctor says your recovery is nothing short of miraculous. I've seen my share of gunshot victims, and I have to agree."

"Good genes, I guess."

Donna walked into the room. "Hey, Megs."

"It's about time." Megan smiled.

"I take it you're ready to blow this Popsicle stand? Brace yourself. It's hot as Hades out there." Donna plucked the dampened V-neck of her pink tank top from her skin and fanned it against her chest. Sweat beaded her forehead. "Hi, Detective Sullivan."

"Miss Miller." He nodded.

"The detective wants to see me Friday at noon," Megan said to Donna. "Can you drive me to the police station?"

"You bet. Anything to keep Barton behind bars."

"Miss Miller." Detective Sullivan pinned his shrewd eyes on Donna's face. "I have one more question about that purple dress. Where is it?"

Donna shrugged. "I don't know. Last time I saw it was when they took Megan away in the ambulance. Ask the paramedics."

"They said she still had it on, partially anyway, when they wheeled her into the emergency room."

Donna walked to the table and picked up the big vase of flowers. "The doctors might know." She buried her nose in a lily before handing the vase to Megan.

"They said it was stuffed in a plastic bag and put aside for evidence. No one can find it."

Megan sat up straighter in the wheelchair to hold the vase steady on her lap. "Someone lost it? Damn it. I love that dress." Her voice shook with indignation.

"It probably doesn't have any connection to Mr. Crone, but it might have provided a clue as to who shot you." Detective Sullivan paused while a gurney with squeaky wheels rolled by in the hallway. "We'll search the hospital again and find that someone simply misplaced it, I hope. We're doing our best to discover who the shooter was."

"I hope you do. It's freaky, knowing someone who shot me is out there walking around." Megan shivered.

"You still don't remember anything? Anything at all?" the detective asked.

She kept her face blank beneath his probing gaze. She had escaped Barton. Stood up to Lottie, and John Bingo, and taken a bullet for the man she loved. She had traveled through time. Died several times.

In comparison, Detective Sullivan was small potatoes.

She shook her head. "I keep trying." She lifted her shoulders in a helpless shrug. "I wish I could."

"Give it time." He reached up to adjust his glasses. "Well, I reckon y'all are anxious to leave. I'll see you Friday, Megan. Get plenty of rest. Don't overdo it." He nodded and left.

A nurse walked in. She flashed a smile, showing teeth as white as her uniform, a striking contrast against her ebony skin. "Miss McClure, you ready to go?"

"I certainly am," Megan replied.

Donna picked up the philodendron and the vase of yellow roses. "I'm parked out front."

She led the way. The nurse pushed the wheelchair down the hallway to the elevator, then out the front doors of the hospital.

Megan blinked several times from the blinding sunlight, lowering her head to avoid the glare. Mugginess enveloped her. Sweat formed on her forehead in the few minutes it took them to reach Donna's rented car. The nurse helped Megan into the front seat on the passenger side while Donna put the plant, flowers, and bag of medical sundries on the floor of the back seat and got in on her side, shutting the door.

Safe in the privacy of the car, Megan said, "Detective Sullivan would have a stroke if he knew you took that dress."

"Let's hope he never finds out, or I'm in hot water." Donna started the car. The air conditioner blew hot air. She rolled down the window.

"Deny everything. I don't want you in trouble because of me."

"They shouldn't be so careless with evidence. I mean, the bag was sitting there, just sitting there in the corner while everyone in the room focused on you. It was a madhouse. Snatching it up was a piece of cake. You want to go anywhere special? Or straight to the B&B?"

"The cemetery."

Donna shifted out of Park. She rolled up the window and drove away from the hospital.

"I hope that woman can fix the dress," Megan said. "What's her name?"

"Mrs. Jeter. She's a wiz, according to Mrs. Powell. She does sewing for other women in their church. We should hear from her any day about repairing it. I figure you're going to need it back there. Back *then,* actually." Kim Carnes started singing *Bette Davis Eyes* on the radio. "Oooh. I *love* this song." Donna turned up the volume and sang along in a rich alto. She bobbed her head and tapped her fingers on the steering wheel.

The time and temperature sign on a bank flashed 100 degrees. A reporter on the news the night before had mentioned the previous summer of 1980 when Texas had had a record of 69 consecutive days of 100 degrees or more. It was so hot, people had fried eggs on the sidewalk or on the hood of their cars, Megan had heard from some of the regulars at work. She had wondered then, and now, if it was true or just another tall Texas tale. *What would an egg fried on the sidewalk taste like, and would I even want to eat that?* She rolled down the window, lifted her face, and closed her eyes. The hot wind tangled her hair, and the blazing sun warmed her skin like a moist hot towel in a beauty salon. Nine days in a hospital was nine days way too many.

Twenty minutes later, she and Donna stood in the dappled shade of the old pecan tree and stared at Seth's gravestone.

"I can't believe it broke right there." Donna crossed her arms. "How weird is that?"

A big chunk of the granite had broken off the bottom right hand corner, leaving a jagged diagonal edge just past the dash, cutting off his death date.

Megan bent down, wincing, and laid a yellow rose on his gravestone. *Coincidence? I doubt it.*

Donna kicked the grass and looked around on the ground. She searched as far as the next grave where arching branches of wild red roses fragranced the muggy air with a heavy, musky scent that swirled lazily around the tombstones. A roadrunner ran by, and the rattle of cicadas broke the eternal silence of the graveyard. Donna, her gaze on the ground, made a slow circular search of the area then returned to Seth's grave. "I don't see that piece anywhere."

Megan turned away. "Let's go. I want to check somewhere else." On the way out, she paused at Candace Huntington's grave. It looked the same. "I did it," Megan whispered. "Thanks for your help." She touched the headstone. "You were quite a kid."

They got back in the car, and Donna drove off. A ballad by the Carpenters came on the radio, and Donna sang along.

The lyrics caused a sharp pain in Megan's heart as real as the bullet that had ripped through her body. Threatening tears burned her eyes. *Hurry back to me,* she silently prayed. *Oh please, hurry back.*

Donna stopped outside The Silver Slipper Old Time Saloon. A bench stretched along the front of the brick wall that once had a plaque about the last great gunfight on the streets of Fort Worth on April 13, 1890.

"You sure this is the place, Megs? I don't see a plaque."

"Because it didn't happen now. I just wanted to be sure."

Donna pulled away from the curb. "Do you want to check the records at the library?"

"Yes, but ... all those stairs." Megan rubbed a shaky hand across her forehead.

"I'll run in. I know where to look. Shouldn't take long."

Megan looked at Donna. "Thanks for all you've done—and are still doing—for me."

"You'd do the same for me."

George Harrison started singing *All Those Years Ago*. Donna and Megan joined in.

After another song and a commercial, Donna parked outside the main library, and left the car running. "I'll be right back."

Top of the hour news came on the radio. Something about an infestation of Mediterranean fruit flies in California. The forecast predicted more hot weather in the days ahead. Megan drummed her fingers on the door, her eyes trained on the front steps of the library. Minutes crawled by. The news ended, and the DJ rattled on about a traffic snarl in Dallas. She shifted positions, grimacing with pain at the movement. The medications were wearing off.

"Finally," she muttered as Donna exited the library and hurried down the stairs. "Well?" Megan asked before Donna had barely sat behind the wheel.

Donna slammed the door and adjusted an air vent, so it blew right on her face. "The bottom floor is temporarily closed due to some busted pipes. I couldn't find out anything. Sorry." She smiled sympathetically.

Megan's shoulders slumped. Then her gaze narrowed. "Did anyone say when the pipes burst?"

"I think the woman said nine days ago."

"The same day I returned." Megan gave a humorless laugh. "Imagine that. It seems I'm not supposed to find out what happened to Seth. Let's go to the B&B."

Donna accelerated into the traffic. "Damn Texans drive like they're nuts."

Megan propped her elbow on the car door, put her chin on her knuckles. A commercial about some hospital in Dallas came on the radio. "How am I ever going to pay that hospital bill? They saved my life. I feel obligated ... but I don't have that kind of money."

"Give a donation." Donna slowed to turn a corner. Air from the vents blew strands of her brown hair. "John Peter Smith is an old hospital so give it a big donation when you're back there. It'll ease your conscience and help out the hospital."

"Holy moly, that's a good idea. You're so smart, sugar bear."

Donna rolled her eyes. "Stop it."

At the B&B, Donna helped Megan out of the car and took her arm to help her inside.

"I'm not an invalid," Megan grumbled despite her waning strength.

"Shut up and enjoy some pampering."

They nodded to the police officer outside the house.

"Welcome back, Miss McClure. You need anything, I'm here."

"Thank you, Officer."

As they climbed the couple of steps to the front door, Megan said, "The house looked better with the wide porch."

"Maybe you can do something about that when you go back."

"Hmmm. Maybe I can."

Inside the B&B, Mrs. Powell stood outside her office talking to an elderly man. When she saw Megan, she hurried down the hallway and gathered Megan in a gentle embrace. "Oh, Miss Megan, it's so good to see you." Mrs. Powell drew back, her eyes searching Megan's face. "You poor dear. Bless your heart. I'm so glad you're back."

"Thanks. Good to be back. I'm sorry about breaking the window."

Mrs. Powell chuckled and chided gently, "Lord a mercy, dear, don't you give that another thought. You let me know if you need anything. Anything at all." She glanced at Donna. "Either of you."

"We will." Megan realized it was a good sign that Mrs. Powell still had the B&B. *It means I'll be going back to set everything in place for Mrs. Powell to get the B&B in the first place in case another Megan comes along.*

Mrs. Powell opened her mouth, then shut it and pursed her lips. She stared at Megan with an intense look in her eyes.

"Is there something else you wanted to tell me, Mrs. Powell?"

"I reckon it can wait." Mrs. Powell smiled. "You look tuckered out. We'll chat another day."

Megan leaned heavily on Donna as they slowly walked to the stairs. Megan paused at the bottom and looked up. The stairway seemed as challenging as climbing Mount Everest.

"Ready?" Donna asked.

Megan took a deep breath and blew it out. "Okay." She gripped the banister gleaming a rich molasses brown in the meager sunlight that stretched down the hallway, her other arm held tightly by Donna. Their steps halting, they climbed the stairs.

Donna said, "I can't wait to find out what that was all about. Might explain why Mrs. Powell acted so strangely the other day."

"Strange in what way?"

"She came back from somewhere, cornered me in the TV room, and started asking me a ton of questions. How long have you and I known each other? Where did we grow up? How big was your family? What were your parents like?" They reached the second floor, paused so Megan could catch her breath, then turned right. "Stuff like that. It was a regular third degree. But in a nice way." They stopped outside their room. Donna unlocked the door. "Home sweet home."

In a way, it did feel like coming home as Megan walked in and looked around the familiar room. *Funny. The last time I was here, it was Lottie's room.* It gave her an odd sensation, a tingle on her skin. Then and now. Past and present. Same place, only different. *Same me ... only different?* Her gaze automatically went to Seth's door. "When did Seth leave?"

"Three days ago. He said he'll be back the first chance he gets."

"God only knows how long that will be. How old he'll be." Megan glanced at the vanity and dresser. "Where's that small leather purse? Last I know it was on the bed."

"I think I know which one you mean." Donna walked over to the vanity, opened the top drawer, and took out the purse. She handed it to Megan, who opened it and dug through the contents. Several tampons fell on the floor. "The police didn't know what to make of what you had in there. All those tampons had them scratching their heads."

Megan scraped up a few old coins off the bottom of the purse and hobbled as fast as her injuries and the pain allowed to the armoire. She touched what remained of Seth's dried blood, bent down, and scattered the coins on the floor in the corner. They rolled around. Some ran into the walls. Not through the walls.

"Damn it." She straightened with a groan, holding her side. "I don't know what I was thinking. Why I expected it to be open. That would be too easy."

Donna took Megan's arm. "Get in bed."

With Donna's help, Megan shuffled across the room, exhausted, and swamped by waves of pain.

"Oops. I moved your stool." Donna grabbed the stool from the corner and put it beside the bed, then pulled back the covers. "There you go, shorty."

Clutching Donna's arm, Megan stepped on the stool, and climbed on the high bed. She lay down with a wince and a shaky sigh. "Thanks," she murmured as Donna pulled up the covers. Megan turned on her side. Despite the 100-degree temperature outside, the comforting warmth of the blanket seeped into her tired, injured body.

"I'll go get the rest of the stuff out of the car. You look like you need a pain pill."

Megan managed a wan smile. "Drugs. I need drugs." She snuggled under the blanket. Her gaze traveled slowly around the room until it landed on a stack of her paperwork on the floor near the dresser. On top of the stack was a folder with NWU in bold letters on it.

"Oh *shit*." She pushed herself up on her elbow. "Shit shit *shit*."

Donna stopped at the door and glanced over her shoulder. "What's the matter?"

"The conference. The National Writers Union conference. I forgot all about it." Megan sank back down on the bed. "My name is mud."

"Don't worry. I found their number and called and told them you had a bad case of laryngitis and you were terribly sorry, but you couldn't make it. They were very understanding."

"Donna, you're the absolute best."

"I know. Go to sleep. You're very pale."

As the door closed behind her, Megan thought, *I've missed her so much.* Her eyes welled up. *I'm going to miss her forever.*

**

The next morning, Donna said, "I'm going downstairs to get some coffee."

"And plenty of sugar." Megan burrowed under the covers.

Donna returned with a tray bearing three cups, a coffee pot, cream and sugar, and a surprise.

"Bonnie!" Grinning, Megan sat up in bed and held out her arms.

Bonnie ran across the room, holding a white bag in one hand, her blonde ponytail swinging. She bent down and gave Megan a light, quick hug. "I'm so glad you're okay. You had me worried sick. I hope that bastard Barton burns in hell." Bonnie sat on the side of the bed. "I'm sorry I didn't come see you in the hospital, but I hate those places. 'Sides, every time I was in one I didn't want no one comin' by and gawkin' at me while I'm lookin' my worst and feelin' like crap."

"I'm glad you're here now. Thanks for the roses." They filled the tall blue vase on the nightstand. The same vase Megan had threatened to bash over Seth's head that first night.

Bonnie opened the bag. "I brought somethin' even better today. Donuts and éclairs. I was hopin' y'all had coffee here."

"Coming right up." Donna set the tray on the table and started filling the cups.

Megan got out of bed and she and Bonnie sat at the table. They dug in the donut bag, then passed it to Donna as she sat across from Megan.

"How's Sam?" Megan took a bite of a powdered donut.

"Wonderful. Penny and me are movin' in with him. He's real good to her." Bonnie picked up an éclair.

"I'm so happy for you. For all of you." Megan brushed powder off the front of her t-shirt. The air conditioner kicked on and hummed quietly. "Are you still working at The Tejas?"

"For now. Sam said I can quit and go to school fulltime so I'm fixin' to do that. Hey, I got a postcard from Julia. She's still down on the coast an' lovin' it. She's waitressin' in a restaurant and going to hairstylin' school. Sounds like she's gettin' her shit together."

"Good for her." Megan blew on her coffee. "What gossip do you have from work?"

Bonnie regaled Megan and Donna with tales from behind the bar while they had their fill of sweets and drained the coffee pot twice. Megan told Bonnie about the terrifying night with Barton, then her amnesia. The three of them talked the hours away.

When Bonnie had to leave, she and Megan hugged. "You take care of yourself and I'll see you soon. I'll tell everyone at work you said hi."

"Thanks for being such a good friend." Megan swallowed a lump in her throat as she and Bonnie separated.

"That's the only kind to be, ain't it? I'll tell Bubba hey for you, Donna. I ain't seen him this cow-eyed over a gal in a month of Sundays." Bonnie grinned.

Donna blushed.

"'Bye, Bonnie." Sudden tears filled Megan's eyes as her friend walked out the door. *I wonder if I'll ever see her again.*

Donna groaned, holding her stomach. "I can't believe I ate so many donuts."

Megan closed the door and leaned back against it. "You and Bonnie get along okay?"

"She's great. But I wish she hadn't brought those damn donuts."

Megan smiled fondly at her best friend. *You'll need a friend when I'm gone.*

Chapter 38

Megan paused at the top of the steps outside the Fort Worth Police Department. The July sun blazed like a fireball in the clear blue sky. She put on her sunglasses. Tiny beads of sweat dampened her forehead.

"Another scorcher. Man, this is getting old." Donna stepped closer to Megan to get out of the way of two men in business suits and ties hurrying up the steps, part of the steady stream of people going in and out of the police station. "Did everything go well?" Donna opened her shoulder bag and dug around in it.

"I guess so. Detective Sullivan recorded everything I had to say about Barton. They arrested Tammy and she's spilling her guts. The police busted the trailer in the country and caught the guy while he was cooking a batch. He's in jail. Jim is too. They're charged with organized criminal activity."

"That's great. Did they lock up that briefcase too?" Donna pulled out her sunglasses from her bag and slipped them on.

"Detective Sullivan had me identify that damn thing. God, I hate that smiley face."

"You showed it who's boss."

"I did more than that. I stuck my tongue out at it as I walked out of the detective's office."

Donna broke out in her full-throated laugh.

Megan laughed too. "I'm glad that's over." She held her long hair off the back of her neck for a moment to feel the slight breeze.

"Except for the court date when you have to testify."

"The detective said he'd let me know when. What if I'm already gone by then?"

"You gave an affidavit of your testimony, right?"

Megan nodded.

"Then you're covered in case you can't make it for some reason. Of course, the courts want you to be there but if you can't, they have your testimony, and Barton will get what he deserves." Donna linked her arm with Megan's as they slowly descended the stairs. "We should celebrate. You hungry? Bubba told me about a place called Kincaid's. Supposed to have the best burgers in town. Sound good?"

"Let's go."

A couple of hours later, their bellies full, Donna helped Megan out of the car and they walked up to the B&B.

"I haven't seen that cop before," Donna said. "Must be the weekend guy."

A short, swarthy Mexican in a police uniform stood on the sidewalk in front of the B&B in the shade of a crape myrtle adorned with vibrant pink blooms.

"Hello, Officer—" Megan glanced at his name tag "—Hernandez."

"Ladies." He nodded.

"You need some water or tea or anything, let us know," Donna offered as she and Megan climbed the front steps. "Don't want you passing out from the heat."

"Thank you, ma'am."

Blessed coolness welcomed them inside the B&B as the door closed behind them. Megan paused to rest up for the climb to her room. "When is Bubba on duty out there?"

"From eleven tonight until seven in the morning." Donna removed her sunglasses, stuffed them in her purse, then lifted her hair off the back of her neck. "God, that a/c feels good."

"You going to take him some tea during the wee hours? Step outside wearing something sexy?" Megan teased as she took off her sunglasses.

Donna gave Megan a nudge. "Smart ass. He'll be on duty. Nothing sexy will be going on. Not even any kissing."

Megan raised her eyebrows. "None?"

"Well, maybe a little."

They grinned at each other then walked slowly down the hallway. As they passed the office, Mrs. Powell looked at them from behind her desk and called out, "Miss Megan, Mrs. Jeter is here to see you."

"That's the woman who fixed your dress." Donna's voice rose with excitement.

They entered the office. Megan stopped in surprise. "Mrs. Jeter?"

A woman with short gray hair and a friendly smile rose from a chair in front of the desk. "I figured it was you. I never forget a dress."

Donna asked, "You two know each other?"

"This is the woman from the sale where I bought my dress," Megan explained. "Mrs. Jeter, meet my friend, Donna."

Mrs. Jeter nodded. "Hello, Donna."

"Ah, the sewing expert." Donna grinned. "Nice to meet you."

A silvery laugh came from Mrs. Jeter. She looked crisp and cool in a blue and white striped seersucker pantsuit and a thin white blouse beneath the jacket. "I wouldn't call myself an expert, but I think Megan will be pleased with the results." From the chair beside her, she picked up the purple dress, holding it high by the hook of a hanger.

Megan caught her breath. She stepped closer and held out one side of the dress, spreading the skirt wide. The purple, rich and vibrant in the sunlight streaming in a window, made a striking contrast with the darker godets the color of Concord grape wine. The dress looked fresh and clean, almost like new. "Holy moly. It looks fabulous."

"I'll say." Donna held out the other side of the dress. "How did you get out all the blood?"

"That was a challenge." Mrs. Jeter smoothed the cream-colored lace attached to one of the puffy sleeves. "I had to dab the areas with cold salt water. Took hours of dabbing. Fortunately, some ladies from my sewing circle helped. We ended up cleaning the whole dress that way. Then we patched it. We cleaned the petticoat that way too."

Megan looked closer at the dress. "I can't even tell where the bullet holes were." A shudder ran through her at the memory of white-hot pain slicing her in half.

"Sit down." Donna took Megan's arm and helped ease her into the chair where the dress had been. "You look awful."

Megan took a steadying breath. She looked at Mrs. Jeter. "How did you repair those holes so well?"

"We took excess material from the hem and seams. Luckily, we found enough. The exit hole was so big and ragged it had me worried. It turned out rather well, don't you think?"

"It's beautiful. Thank you. Tell your friends I thank them too."

"I found something interesting while searching for excess material." Mrs. Jeter draped the dress over her chair and picked up the hem. She turned it over and slowly passed the edge through her hands. "Here it is." She held up a section of hem for Megan to see. "Someone's initials. COC." Mrs. Jeter pointed to them. "It must be the dressmaker. I've never seen any initials sewn onto old clothing. Isn't that fascinating?"

"Name brand clothing in the 1800s. Who'd have thought?" Megan smiled. She wondered what had happened with Charlotte and Amelia. *What's going on back there? What's Seth doing? Hurry back to me, my love!*

"Melba." Mrs. Powell tapped her pen on the desktop cluttered with invoices, bills, and other papers, and a vase of zinnias on one corner. "Tell Miss Megan the *really* fascinating story about that dress."

"I'm fixin' to, Florence. Don't rush me."

"I'll hold that," Donna picked up the dress, "so you can sit down."

"Thank you, dear." Mrs. Jeter sat down, facing Megan. "A group of us were at Emma's, one of the ladies in my sewing circle, dabbing away on the dress while we chatted. Out of the blue, Emma's great-aunt Bertha said, *I remember this dress.* We didn't believe her at first, I mean, the woman is older than Moses, and her memory—"

"How old?" Megan sat straight and tense on the chair.

"Ninety-eight."

Megan and Donna exchanged startled glances. Great-Aunt Bertha would have been seven when Megan was back there.

"And her memory isn't the best," Mrs. Jeter continued. "She surprised us, though, as she told her story as if it had happened yesterday. When she was just a young'un, she and her family rode in their wagon from Weatherford to Fort Worth for a barn raising at her kinfolks. That evening, she and her siblings and cousins watched the couples dancing to the fiddlers. One of the women wore a purple dress. *This* purple dress. She was pretty, with black hair, Bertha said, and her dress swayed like a bell as she spun around the floor. Every eye there was watching when the handsome marshal and the pretty lady danced together. The marshal's wedding was the next day and Bertha's family was going to that too. No one missed a gathering of any kind back then,

Bertha said, whether they knew the people of not. She thought he was marrying the pretty lady until her cousins told her the bride was another woman, the school teacher. But the wedding never happened. Bertha never did learn why, and her family returned to Weatherford the next day." Mrs. Jeter paused. "Bertha said the name of the pretty lady in the purple dress was Miss Megan." She tilted her head. "Isn't that the oddest thing you ever heard?"

Silence hung in the room for a moment. The long leaves of a tall schefflera in a corner next to a filing cabinet trembled in the currents from the air conditioner.

Someone's still alive that saw me back then. She remembers it the way it happened this time, not the way Candace did. Megan's hands gripped either side of the seat of her chair. *Holy moly. Did I change anything by being there? Would I know?*

"That's ... quite a story," she managed to say.

"Yes, it is," Mrs. Powell agreed.

Something in her tone drew Megan's attention. Their gazes locked. *She knows something.*

"Well." Mrs. Jeter stood. "I really must be going."

Megan stood too. "What do I owe you?"

"Oh, my dear." Mrs. Jeter patted Megan's arm. "Don't worry about it."

"But you did a wonderful job. All the time you spent on it—"

"Pshaw." Mrs. Jeter waved a hand. "Working on a garment so old was ... an honor. Fun." She grinned. "You just enjoy it. I imagine you look beautiful in it. Just like that pretty lady in Bertha's story."

Megan gave Mrs. Jeter a quick hug. "Thank you so much for all you did."

"My pleasure. Try not to get any more bullet holes in it. I'm glad you've recovered from your ordeal. I'm fixin' to do a little searching in the historical records to see if I can find out who COC is. I'll let you know if I learn anything."

"I'll walk you out, Melba." Mrs. Powell rose from her chair and came around the desk. Mrs. Jeter nodded to Donna and left the office with Mrs. Powell.

Donna shifted the dress from one arm to the other. "Must have freaked you out, hearing that Great-Aunt Bertha remembered you."

"It makes sense, though," Megan replied. "Candace died before I went back in time. Bertha didn't. Their memories are different because it happened differently for each of them. Would you take the dress and petticoat upstairs for me? I want to talk to Mrs. Powell."

Donna left just as Mrs. Powell returned.

"Is there something you wanted, Miss Megan?"

"Actually, I have a feeling there's something you want to tell me."

Mrs. Powell clasped her hands at the waist of her mustard yellow dress. "What's it like back then?"

Her directness startled Megan. "Back when?"

"Before the turn of the century in Fort Worth."

"I-I'm not sure what you mean."

"I had lunch with an old school chum not long ago. Ruth Ann Cuffee. I went to Cleburne to meet her at the bank where she works. While waiting for her, I looked at the old documents on the wall. One of them is a letter from a widow named Megan McClure. Ruth Ann told me the story. Including the part about how Megan wasn't even a name back then. I looked closer at that letter and recognized the handwriting. That's *your* signature, Miss Megan. I've seen it enough times to know it. *You* wrote that letter."

Megan kept her lips sealed, wondering what to tell or not tell, or just say nothing at all. She didn't flinch beneath Mrs. Powell's schoolteacher stare.

"It wasn't another woman, or a long-lost ancestor named Megan McClure who gave Cordelia Pryor that money to invest for my eventual ownership of this building. It was *you* back in 1886."

"Not 1886. It was 1890," Megan blurted. She clamped her mouth shut. *Shit!*

Mrs. Powell's eyes lit up. "You know the year." Her words came out breathless, excited. "Except for the lawyer, no one else knows it. Not even my husband. It *was* you." She stepped closer. "Did you go through that door? Is that why it had to be saved? For you to go back? Are you going back again? Can you help me?"

Megan's eyes widened. "Help you?"

Mrs. Powell abruptly turned away and walked behind the desk. She collapsed in her chair, put her elbows on the desk, and dropped her head in her hands. "I'm sorry, Miss Megan. I shouldn't be badgering you so. I just ..." She released a shaky sigh.

What the hell? "What's the matter, Mrs. Powell?"

"Everything."

Megan sat in a chair. "Tell me."

After several moments, Mrs. Powell raised her head. "I received an offer for the B&B. A very generous offer. A developer wants to tear it down and build apartments."

"Holy moly. What does your husband say?"

"Oh, he's all for it." Mrs. Powell waved her hand, making a face. "He complains all the time about all the work he does around here. Says this isn't how he planned on spending his retirement. He was a CPA for 30 years, and does the books here, but other than that, he just wants to play golf and go fishing. Not patch a hole in a wall or change a light fixture or deal with the plumbing. Those damn pipes." She shook her head.

"I thought you hired a plumber to replace the system?"

Mrs. Powell rolled her eyes. "The more that fella looked, the more problems he found besides the plumbing. Rotten boards. Faulty wiring.

Termites. His list gets longer and longer, the cost higher and higher. I considered raising the room rates, but I don't feel right doing that, and it wouldn't be enough anyway. My husband said he's fixin' to look for a house beside a golf course. I know he's not happy, and I don't blame him. He worked hard all his life and deserves his free time. But the very idea of leaving here, well, it just breaks my heart." She blinked telltale moisture from her eyes. "He knows how I love this place. We're both sentimental about it. We met at the little Mexican restaurant across the street."

"The place with the sombrero? Tell me the story. I love how-we-met stories." Megan leaned her elbow on the desk and propped her chin on her knuckles.

"I was eating lunch there one summer afternoon, staring at this place and wondering how I could buy it. The restaurant was crowded, and I heard this deep voice ask if I would share my table. I looked up, and there's this handsome man smiling down at me. Lord a mercy, what a smile. And those eyes of his. My, my." A dreamy smile lit her face. "There were a few other empty seats, but he chose my table. I was so flattered and flustered. He sat down and said he liked my hair. I wore it longer back then, and it was still brown, with a nice natural wave." She waved her hand over one side of her hair to demonstrate. "We talked until the manager gave us dirty looks for tying up the table, so we left and went for a walk. He asked if I liked music. I said yes. That evening we went to the symphony. I was a widow. He was divorced. We were married six months later."

"What a great story." Megan grinned.

"He knew from the get-go how I felt about this place and was as happy as I was when I finally ended up with it. We moved in shortly after we were married. Our years together have been wonderful. I never thought I'd fall in love again. I don't want to lose him over this house. But," Mrs. Powell heaved a long sigh while her gaze traveled around her office, "I don't want to lose this house either. I may not even be in business when your article comes out in *Travel Holiday*, and I'm mighty upset about that too. All your hard work and that wonderful publicity for nothing." Her shoulders sagged, and she suddenly looked older than her years.

"You asked if I could help you." Megan clasped her hands together on the desktop. "What did you mean?"

A rosy tint colored the fine wrinkles on Mrs. Powell's cheeks. "It was a crazy thought I had after seeing that signature in the bank. It looks so much like yours I'd swear it is yours, and it would explain so much. Who left me the money. Why I had to keep that door. Where you went those five days then suddenly appeared with gunshot wounds. It all pointed to one thing. Time travel."

The words hung in the air.

"Time travel." Megan kept her voice neutral, her face blank. Inside, her stomach churned like one of the blenders Bonnie used to mix drinks at work. *Tell her or not?*

Mrs. Powell nodded. The blush on her cheeks deepened. "If you go back I was hoping you could, well ... leave me more money." She gazed intently at Megan, as if looking for a sign of affirmation, then gave a weak smile. "Preposterous, I know. I guess I read too many science fiction novels and romances." She dropped her head in her hands again. "You must think I'm nuttier than a grove of pecan trees. Lord knows I've wondered myself if I'm crazy for even thinking such a thing, much less asking you such a question. Shows you how desperate I am."

Megan knew how awful it felt to think you're crazy. She stared at Mrs. Powell's bent head with silver waves cut in that short hairstyle older women seemed to favor. *She's treated me like family, not a customer. She loves this house. It's part of her love story, part of her. I can give her this.*

"I didn't go back through that door."

Mrs. Powell's head snapped up, her eyes wide, lips slightly parted.

"It never opened for me," Megan continued. "I found another portal just as Barton broke down the other door."

"And you went back in time to 1890," Mrs. Powell whispered.

Megan nodded.

"Holy Mother of God." Another whisper. "Are you," Mrs. Powell glanced at the open door and empty hallway, then leaned over the desk and whispered even softer, "from another time?"

Megan smiled. "No. I'm from a small town in rural Illinois. There's nothing special about me. I don't know any more than you do why it happened to me. The whole experience has been very ... bizarre."

"Are you going back?"

"I hope so. If I can figure out how to get there."

"Is there a fella?"

Megan laughed. "Isn't there always?"

Mrs. Powell laughed too. "The Marshal from Bertha's story? You're the pretty lady in the purple dress?"

Megan nodded. "He's the one who uses that door. The only one as far as I know."

"That's how you met him? Oh, my word." Mrs. Powell rocked back in her chair, clapping a hand to her cheek. "He's the man Mr. Crone claimed you had in your room. He wasn't lying."

"For once, Barton wasn't lying. But how could I tell you or anyone the truth? You'd think I was ... nuttier than a grove of pecan trees."

Mrs. Powell grinned. Then they both laughed.

"I hope you find your way back to your fella, Miss Megan."

"Me too. Did you know this house used to have a wide front porch?"

"Why, yes it did. I saw a picture of it from the forties. I liked it with the porch."

"I do too. Don't sell the B&B. When I go back, I'll see what I can do about getting you more money, so you won't be in this predicament. I promise."

A huge smile spread across Mrs. Powell's face as tears brightened her eyes. She stood and came around the desk. She took Megan's hands and drew her to her feet into an embrace. "I've wanted for so long to say this to the woman who gave me this house. Thank you, my dear, for all you've done. Thank you from the bottom of my heart." She released Megan and stepped back. "Maybe one afternoon you could tell me a bit about life back then."

"I will. Now, if you'll excuse me, I'm going to go upstairs and read up on life around the turn of the century."

Megan started for the door, and paused when she heard Mrs. Powell mutter, "This is all so impossible."

Megan turned back to Mrs. Powell. "My dad told me something once. When I was little, we'd often lay on the lounges outside and look up at the night sky. He taught me the constellations and knew when all the meteor showers were. One night I asked him if all those stars were going to fall on us. He said it could happen, but it probably won't. I asked, Does that mean yes or no? He said it's possible but not probable. Then he said something that stuck with me and eventually led me to write about strange and unusual things that seem to defy explanation. He said, Remember that nothing is impossible. Improbable maybe but not impossible. Imagine the possibilities." Megan smiled at the memory. "Think of that, Mrs. Powell. All the possibilities that just might happen. That's what happened to me. One of those infinite possibilities that, improbable as it may be, really happened."

***

Evening sunshine poured through the tall windows and spilled across the floor, turning the wood a rich brown the color of coffee. Beyond the windows, haze draped the skyline of Fort Worth. The purple dress once again hung on the back of the bathroom door.

"So, you're going to invest more money for her?" Donna reached for another piece of pizza from the box sitting in the middle of the rawhide sofa.

"Somewhere along the way I'm going to buy the house and fix it up before she gets it." Megan sat cross-legged on the other end of the sofa. She wiped tomato sauce off her hand with a napkin. "I'll still have Cordelia invest the money if she wants to. I hope so. She did such a great job. Plus, I'm going to set up a separate bequest for perpetual upkeep and maintenance of the property."

"I take it you're not worried anymore about changing history."

Megan shrugged. "I already did when I saved Seth's life. That seems to be the purpose of all this, so the future is bound to change. For the better, with any luck, and a whole bunch of prior knowledge. Maybe it's already changed, and we don't realize it."

Donna ate a piece of pizza with a thoughtful look on her face. After a drink from a can of beer, she asked, "How will you know you're doing what Chaos wants you to do? What if you end up doing something with terrible consequences?"

"What if I do something wrong? I don't know. Maybe another Megan will fix it. Regardless, I'll die before my birthday, February 1, 1954. Then the next Megan McClure will be born, with hopes and dreams and experiences all her own. And her own Seth to find."

Donna looked at Megan with shocked eyes. "And she'll go through all of this all over again? We all will? Holy crap. It could go on forever, over and over."

Megan feigned a hurt look. "Have some faith in me that I'll break the cycle and the next Megan will live a normal life in the current time-period."

Donna laughed. "Listen to you. Talking about faith. Now that's a miracle."

"I'm learning."

Donna gestured to the pizza. "Last piece. Want it? No? Good." She picked it up, then stared at it a moment. "Do you think I'll remember you?" Her solemn gaze met Megan's.

"I don't know. I hope so." *Don't cry,* she scolded herself. *Not yet. Time for that when we part but not yet.*

"Me too." Donna ate the last piece of pizza then downed her beer. She brushed crumbs off the sofa into the pizza box and closed the lid. After throwing it in the trash can, she went into the bathroom. Minutes later, she came out, brushing her hair. "You have to leave me a sign. Something I'll recognize. I don't know what. Maybe something in this room. Think about it while I'm out with Bubba."

***

The old house creaked and groaned in the late-night heat and humidity. The lock on the door clicked, and a strip of light from the hallway briefly split the darkness as the door opened and closed. Soft footsteps crossed the floor.

"I'm awake. You can stop tiptoeing." Megan switched on the light beside the bed, blinking in the sudden glare. "Have fun?"

Donna grinned as she neared the bed, dropping her purse on the floor. Her eyes sparkled in the dim light. Her cheeks had a rosy glow. "We walked to a park and sat on the swings. I can't remember the last time I played on the swings like a kid. We got ice cream cones, found a picnic table, and talked the hours away. Oh Megs, I'm nuts about that guy. How was your night?"

"Nothing like that. But I did come up with a sign for you."

"Let me get ready for bed first." She changed into her nightclothes and was in and out of the bathroom in no time. She climbed onto the big bed and slipped under the covers. "Okay, what is it?"

"An actual sign. A brass plaque over Seth's door that says, what else, *Seth's Door*. You see that, you'll know I was here and everything worked out. Life was good."

Donna nodded. "That'll work. I better see it."

"You will." Megan switched off the light and lay down. Headlights from the street below flashed like a strobe light around the room. She asked, her voice low, hesitant, "Donna? What if Seth doesn't come back?"

"Don't be ridiculous. He'll come back."

"What if he can't. I mean, I did what I was supposed to do. Maybe it's over. He's there. I'm here. That's that. His door is closed forever."

"He loves you. He'll come for you. Have faith."

Megan sighed. "I hope so."

After a moment of silence, Donna said, "Maybe I'll read about you in the history books. Who knows what you'll do? What your kids and grandkids will do? Maybe one of them will discover the cure for cancer or be the first man to walk on the moon."

"I'm all for the cancer cure, but Neil Armstrong will always and forever be known as the first man to walk on the moon and those kids of mine better not change that. I'll have to be sure to impress that upon them. Some things just shouldn't be fucked with."

Donna laughed her full-throated laugh. "You and your hero worship of Neil Armstrong. You're so weird."

Megan smiled sadly in the darkness. *I'll miss that laugh.* She said softly, "I'm naming our first daughter after you."

Donna caught her breath. "Oh, Megs." Her voice shook.

"Don't cry. Not now." Megan reached across the covers and gripped her best friend's hand. "Not yet."

***

After going to a packed Sunday matinee of *Raiders of the Lost Ark*, Megan and Donna stopped by a grocery store. They stocked up on snacks and drinks, and Donna bought more shampoo and conditioner. They loaded the bags in the car and drove to the B&B. They talked about the movie. They both loved it.

As they walked up to the front door of the B&B, their arms loaded with grocery bags, Megan glanced around. "I wonder where Officer Hernandez is? He's usually out front."

"Bubba doesn't like him. Said he's strange, a loner. Never hangs out with the other cops. I got the door. Go on in."

"He should be here. It's his job. Very unprofessional."

Megan stepped inside. She shifted her hold on the bags and walked down the dimly lit hallway past the empty office. She trudged up the stairs, feeling the bags slip, along with her strength. Her grip tightened. Donna breezed up the stairs and headed for their room on the second floor. Megan shuffled up behind as Donna braced her grocery bags on her knee against the wall and stuck the key in the lock.

"Hurry up. I'm going to drop these."

"I am. I am." Donna hefted the bags and pushed open the door with her butt. She took three steps into the room, and stopped in her tracks, still as a statue.

"Move." Megan pushed past Donna and hurried into the room. She froze. Her heart stopped. The grocery bags clunked to the floor at her feet. The bottle of shampoo and a can of Pringles rolled towards the sofa. Cold fear shot into her soul.

Barton stood near the bathroom with a gun pointed across the room at Seth.

Chapter 39

His hands raised high, Seth stood about a yard away from the open door exposing the brick wall. His black hat shadowed his face but didn't hide the taut set of his mouth or the muscle that jumped in his cheek when Barton spoke.

"Howdy, darlin'. Miss me? Shut and lock the door."

The hate in those blue eyes she'd once found attractive sent a sheet of ice down Megan's spine. She closed the door and turned the lock. The click punctuated the tension in the room.

Her hand trembled. *One of us might die in this room.* The thought shook her to her core. She kept her back to Barton, not wanting him to see her fear. She rested her hand on the door and closed her eyes, gathering her strength. Her palm pressed against the sturdy wood. Perhaps the fortitude of the old house would seep into her.

"I don't have all day, darlin'."

Megan took a deep breath. She opened her eyes, and went to stand next to Donna, who still clutched two grocery bags. Donna's freckles stood out like brown connect-the-dots on her pale face, her stance tense and rigid as a flagpole.

Barton's cold gaze swept over Donna. "Who the fuck are you?"

Megan's foot nudged the can of Pringles aside as she stepped in front of her friend. "Let her go. She has nothing to do with this."

"Too bad for her. Put the bags on the sofa and move near him." He motioned with his gun toward Seth. "Both of you. Put your hands up and keep 'em up."

"Let the women go," Seth said as Megan and Donna obeyed Barton's order. "This is between you and me."

A harsh laugh came from Barton. "This is between that black-haired bitch and me. You're a bonus I hadn't counted on. You two stop right there."

Megan and Donna stopped near the table, a few feet from Seth.

Megan looked at him. Their gazes met. The shifting emotions in his hazel eyes seared her heart. Relief that she was well and healthy, love vaster than the Texas sky, and fear for her and Donna.

She tore her gaze from Seth, aware of Barton watching them, his finger on the trigger. She lifted her chin. "How did you escape from jail and get past the officer outside?"

"He owes me."

Megan caught her breath. "Hernandez is your snitch. Did he help you escape?"

Barton raised one dark eyebrow. "Now isn't it possible I was found innocent and set free?"

"Hardly. You have a rap sheet as long as the Mississippi. Besides, if you had been freed, you wouldn't be going around looking like that." His black hair looked oily and stringy, as if he'd worked in a greasy spoon diner all day. His face sported a couple days' worth of five o'clock shadows. A gray t-shirt, long and baggy, swallowed his large frame, and the legs of his blue jeans stopped several inches above a pair of white boating shoes. *He stole those clothes. Probably off a clothesline.*

Where did he get the gun? Hernandez? Seth? She glanced at Seth. A snug tan shirt and tight brown trousers clad his tall, lean figure. His chest bore the tin star. His holster was empty.

Seth wouldn't have given up his gun without a fight, but neither man's face had any bruises or split lips. Barton must have been waiting for her. Then Seth walked in, expecting to find her, not Barton. Caught by surprise, Seth relinquished his gun. Her gaze narrowed. That meant Barton had two guns, the other hidden somewhere beneath the baggy t-shirt.

"I was so anxious to see you, darlin', I didn't have time to get all spiffed up. I was just asking your boyfriend here where the hell he came from. That door opened," Barton pointed at it, "and he stepped out of that brick wall like it wasn't even there." Barton turned his hateful glare on Seth. "Just how the hell did you come through that wall, Sheriff? There's no—"

"It's Marshal," Seth corrected.

"Marshal Dillon, eh? From *Gunsmoke?*" Barton grinned at Megan and Donna. His grin turned into a scowl when they remained grim and silent.

Seth replied, "Marshal O'Connor."

A furrow creased Barton's brow. He cocked his head. "O'Connor. Seth ... O'Connor." He said it slowly, as if the name sounded familiar to him, but he couldn't quite place it. His face scrunched up, he stared hard at Seth.

Megan wondered if Barton's memories of what had been, such as seeing Seth's name on a gravestone and the tale of the gunfight with Bingo, were gone, since, now, it had never happened the way it had in another time.

Barton straightened and puffed out his chest. He took a step toward Seth, the gun aimed at his head. "You're leadin' us outta here, Marshal. Get moving."

"How?"

"Through that brick wall you came through, that's how."

"I don't see a brick wall."

Barton took another step closer. "You're gonna see a bullet if you don't get going."

"I see a stairway that goes down to the street—"

"Now you're talkin'. I've heard some of these old houses have secret stairways and hidden passages. Let's go."

"—in 1890."

"That an address? I don't give a shit about addresses."

"The year," Seth paused, then said slowly and distinctly, "eighteen hundred and ninety. That's where I'm from."

Barton leaned back a bit, his head tipped to one side. "What the fuck are you talkin' about?"

"I came through that door from the past."

Annoyance flashed in Barton's eyes. "You're telling me you live in the year 1890 on the other side of those bricks. And that doorway is a—a gateway to the past."

Seth nodded.

Barton barked a laugh. "Yeah, and I'm the Man in the Moon."

"My sister Lottie lives in this room in a brothel," Seth said. "She's a prostitute. She had a daughter with John Bingo. Her name was Amelia."

"You probably knew her as Granny Melly," Megan added.

"Granny Melly—what the—?"

"Barton," Megan said. "Seth is your great-great-uncle."

Barton stared at her then at Seth.

The air conditioner turned off and ticked a moment or two. Light from the late afternoon sun stretched across the wood floor almost to Barton's feet.

He threw back his head and laughed. "Boy, you two are somethin' else." He shook his head. "You can sure come up with some doozies. I guess you're Annie Oakley," he said to Donna, "my long-lost second cousin once removed, huh?"

"Ah sure am," she drawled in a poor imitation of a Texan. "Gimme a gun and I'll show ya some tricks."

"Just my luck. Another smartass."

A knock sounded on the hallway door.

Megan jumped.

Barton cut his gaze to her. "You expectin' anyone?"

She shook her head.

"Get rid of 'em." He grabbed Donna's arm and yanked her to him.

She yelped then clamped her mouth shut when he held the muzzle of his gun to her temple.

"Not a peep out of you. Hear me? You." Barton looked at Seth. "Get in that corner." Barton jerked his head in the direction. "Say a word, make a wrong move, this bitch dies. Keep your hands where I can see 'em."

Seth crossed the room to the corner near the armoire.

Barton pulled Donna behind the open bathroom door. "Make it short and sweet," he hissed to Megan. "Don't get any bright ideas. Act normal. Or else."

Megan glanced at Donna's terrified face, then at Seth, his jaw set, his raised hands clenched into fists. She went to the door, wiping her clammy hands on her shorts. She took a deep breath. Her stomach churned and rolled. *I hope I don't puke.* She unlocked the door and opened it just enough to see out.

The young woman who helped in the office on weekends had her hand poised to knock again. "Oh, Miss McClure, I'm glad you're in." She lowered her arm. "I wanted to catch y'all as soon as you walked in, but I reckon I missed you. Mary said she saw y'all from the kitchen. The cops called here for you not long ago. I wrote it all down." She handed Megan a piece of paper. "I'll keep a lookout for the bastard."

"Thank you." Megan closed and locked the door then glanced at the note.

Barton stepped out from behind the bathroom door, pulling Donna with him. "What's it say?"

Megan cleared her throat then read, "*Detective Sullivan called. Some guy named Barton escaped from jail. He may be coming to the B&B!!!! Cops be here soon.*" She lowered the paper.

"That it?" Barton demanded.

She bit her lower lip, hating to give him a warning.

He shoved the gun under Donna's chin, forcing her head back. Her eyes widened even more as anger flashed in his. "Is it?"

"The girl wrote down the time of the call. About ten minutes ago."

Barton shoved Donna away.

She stumbled a few steps and fell, hitting her head on the end of the bed with a loud clunk. She crumpled to the floor.

"Donna!" Megan ran across the room.

"You son of a bitch," Seth spit out.

"Stop right there, O'Connor." Barton caught Megan by the arm.

"Let go!"

He pulled her to him, her back against his front, and clamped his rock-hard arm around her.

She struggled to be free, then stiffened when the cold muzzle of his gun pressed against her temple.

"Slut. You're gonna pay for fuckin' up my life."

"Take your filthy hands off her," Seth growled.

"What're you gonna do about it, *Uncle?*"

Seth replied in a flat, cold voice, "Kill you. Slowly. Painfully." His tone turned lethal. "The Comanche way."

Barton laughed, the sound filled with scorn. "Now is that any way to talk to your kin? What you're gonna do is lead us out the way you came. Move it."

"But Donna!" Megan squirmed and wiggled to be free. "I have to help—"

"Fuck her." Barton tightened his hold on her. "Come on, Marshal." Barton jerked his head toward the open door. "Lead the way."

Seth shrugged. "There's nowhere to lead you."

"Through that brick wall," Barton snapped.

"You can't go through it."

"Why the fuck not? You did."

"Because it's a damn brick wall to you." Exasperation filled Seth's voice. "Are you dimwitted or somethin'?"

"It can't be a real brick wall, or you couldn't have come through it. It must be a fake wall, or wallpaper, or something."

"It's a real brick wall," Seth insisted. "Megan can't go through it. No one from your time can."

"She can't?" Barton removed the gun from her forehead and his arm from around her. His hand gripped her shoulder.

Megan sighed with relief when he lowered the gun. The tension in her eased. She replied, "No, I can't."

"Let's see."

A hard shove sent her flying into the brick wall. She slammed into it face first. Pain exploded like a sunburst followed by a spray of stars. Someone called her name. She rocked backwards, felt another hard shove, and hit the wall again. The wind knocked out of her, her knees buckled. She collapsed into a puddle on the floor, gasping for air.

"Megan!" Seth cried.

"Don't you move another inch, Marshal."

"You lily-livered bastard. Only a coward hurts a woman."

"Think you can take me, Uncle Marshal?"

"Put down that gun and we'll find out," Seth ground out.

"Too bad we don't have time right now."

"Sounds like somethin' a coward would say."

"Fuck you, O'Connor."

Megan shook her head. Something wet and warm dampened her throbbing forehead. She touched it gingerly. Her fingers came away bloody. She felt her nose. No blood. Her forehead must have taken the brunt of the blow and prevented a broken nose. Wincing from aches and pains up and down her body, she slowly pushed herself up on one arm. *Where the hell are the cops? Why is Seth arguing with Barton? Egging him on?* She blinked the blur from her eyes then looked at the men. And realized what Seth was doing.

"I'm ashamed of you, nephew. Refusing to act like a man. Come on." Seth lowered his fists into a fighting stance. He stood near the sofa. "Let's settle this." He danced around a little, backing up a few steps. "Like men do. If you're man enough to quit hiding behind that gun."

"As much as I'd like to kick your ass," Barton walked a few feet away from Megan and stopped with his back to her, "it won't be happening here or now."

He's drawing Barton away from me. He's stalling, waiting for the cops. Where are they?

A low moan came from the other side of the bed.

Donna.

Megan didn't want to stand and draw attention to herself while the men insulted each other so she crawled across the floor and around the end of the bed to where Donna struggled to sit up.

"Megs, you're bleeding," Donna whispered. "Your forehead."

"It's nothing. How are you?"

"I'll live." She rubbed her head while glancing at the men. "What are they doing?"

"Seth is stalling."

"Where are the cops?"

"Donut shop?"

"That's not funny. Bubba hates it when people say that. Oh shit." Donna spoke even softer, "He's coming this way."

Barton had backed up until he was about a yard away from them. "Quit your bullshit and get your hands up, Marshal. We're gettin' outta here."

He was so close. Megan looked at Donna and mouthed, *Let's get him.*

Donna nodded, her eyes huge in her pale face, her jaw set.

Megan glanced around for a weapon. She pantomimed her plans to Donna.

Donna pantomimed her part.

They nodded.

Megan held up one finger, then two. After the third, she scrambled on all fours to the nightstand and grabbed the tall blue vase. She sprang up, ran to Barton, and smashed it against the back of his head.

Donna gave him a swift kick to the back of his right knee.

"Mother fucker!" Barton's knee collapsed. He leaned to his right as his upper body swayed back, his legs spread wide.

Seth kicked Barton in the groin.

Barton howled. The gun clattered on the floor as he cupped his groin with both hands.

"Good shot!" Donna pumped her fist in the air.

Megan muttered, "Kick the bastard again."

Barton folded in half and fell, gasping and groaning as he curled into a fetal position, his hands between his legs.

Seth grabbed the gun and clubbed Barton in the head. Barton went limp and silent. Seth flipped open the chamber and emptied the bullets onto his palm. He stuffed them in his trouser pocket. "You two all right?" He glanced at Donna then Megan, his gaze lingering on her forehead. He stuck the empty gun in his other pocket.

"We're fine." Megan nudged Barton's side with the toe of her sandal when she really wanted to kick him, hit him, beat him again, and again, and again. "What are we going to do about him?"

"Leave him for the law." Seth bent down, reached underneath the back of Barton's t-shirt, and pulled out the other gun stuck in the waist of his jeans. He straightened, checked the gun over then slipped it into the holster strapped to his thigh. He checked Barton's pockets and found spare bullets he stuffed in his trouser pocket with the other bullets.

"Didn't I hear you say something about killing him in the Comanche way? You're not going to do that?" Donna sounded disappointed. She rubbed her head again. A big purple bruise blossomed on her left thigh just below the hem of her shorts.

She always did bruise easily. Megan wanted to kick Barton again for hurting her friend.

His hands on his hips, Seth stared at Barton. "As much as he deserves it, he *is* my great-great-nephew. That's the only thing savin' his worthless hide." He pushed his hat back with his fingertip and smiled at Megan and Donna. "You ladies will do to ride the river with."

Donna tilted her head. "What on earth does that mean?"

"It means you're capable, a good partner. It was a sayin' of high praise among the mountain men."

"Why, thank you, Marshal," Donna drawled, batting her eyes.

Seth laughed. His gaze rested on Megan. "You've had a hankerin' to bash that vase over someone's head ever since I met you."

Megan smiled. "You're lucky it wasn't you that first night."

The look in his eyes turned serious. "The luckiest night of my life." He took her in his arms and kissed her, taking his time as if all they had was time.

His lips finally left hers, and he said against her hair, his voice husky, "I'm glad you're alive and well."

She kissed the side of his neck, breathing in his scent, reveling in his strong embrace. Love and joy and hope and forever rushed through her limbs like a great river in the fullness of spring, powerful and mighty and breathtaking. Her overflowing heart made her voice shake. "I'm so glad you're here."

"I got plumb tired of waitin' on you." With gentle fingers he brushed a lock of hair off her forehead. "When he hurt you—"

"He'll never hurt me again."

The muscles of his face tightened. He said in a flat, final tone, "No one will ever hurt you again as long as I draw breath."

Sirens wailed in the distance.

Donna said, "I hate to break up you lovebirds, but you two need to get out of here."

Megan put her hand on Seth's chest. "Go back. I'll meet you there."

His eyes searched hers. "How're you gettin' back?"

"The portal in the corner. It worked the last time I needed to escape. Let's see if it does this time." Megan hurried to the vanity and yanked open the bottom drawer. She grabbed a handful of old coins from the leather purse and ran to the armoire. A dozen or so small flakes of dried blood still clung to the edge. Afraid she'd knock off the fragile bits, she barely touched them with her palm, then bent down and scattered the coins on the floor. They rolled here and there. Several hit the walls in the corner and fell flat. "Fuck."

"It's not working?" Donna asked.

Megan shot up straight. "The dress." She spun around. "I need the dress. That's why it won't open." She ran across the room, tearing off her tank top and tossing it on the bed.

From the back of the bathroom door, Donna grabbed the petticoat and gave it a shake.

More sirens wailed, coming closer.

Megan pulled off her shorts and kicked them aside then glanced at Seth. "It'll work. I know it will. You need to go."

He shook his head. "I'm not leavin' until I know you can."

"Seth—" The heated look in his eyes stopped her. His gaze traveled over her in her bra, bikini panties, and the bandages around her waist.

He frowned. "You sure you're all healed?"

"Fit as a fiddle." Megan stepped into the frilly, hooped petticoat Donna held out then helped pull up and adjust. "Go. Before the cops get here and start asking questions." Megan held up her arms while Donna slipped the purple dress over her head and pulled it down. The silk dress shimmered like an amethyst in the sunlight slanting low through the windows.

A moan came from Barton.

Seth whipped out his gun and clubbed Barton in the head again. He holstered his gun and turned to Megan. "I don't want to leave."

"You have to." Megan stared at him in exasperation while Donna adjusted the bodice then straightened the skirt. The sirens grew louder. Megan flung her hand at the windows. "The cops!"

"What if you can't find your portal? What if I can't come back for weeks? Months? Years? Maybe never again? I never know when ... if I can come here. Megan," his voice turned harsh with anguish, "I can't leave you. What if—"

"What if, what if, my ass." Donna put her hands on her hips. "Do you really think you two went through all of ... *this—*" she made a circle with her hand as if encompassing the universe "—for nothing? Have a little faith. Go back. Megan will be right behind you." She looked at Barton motionless on the floor and heaved a sigh. "I'll deal with this mess somehow."

"It'll be fine, Seth. Come here and kiss me then go."

Doubt in his eyes, his expression somber, Seth came over and kissed her.

Megan clung to him a moment, hoping she was right and they would be together again in mere minutes. *Don't screw me over now, universe.*

He drew away. "I'll be waitin' for you." He turned to Donna and tipped his hat. "Thank you for everythin', Miss Donna."

"Come here, you big lug." She held out her arms. Chuckling, he stepped into her embrace. "You'd better take care of her. Or else."

"Yes, ma'am." Seth released Donna and stepped back. His eyes met Megan's. "I love you. Don't dally."

"I love you too. Get out of here."

Seth turned and headed for his door.

Donna went behind Megan and buttoned up the dress from the bottom. "Oh man, all these damn buttons will take forever."

Megan glanced over her shoulder at Donna. "Just do a few of them." She looked at Seth again, hoping to catch a glimpse of him before he left through the door.

He stood still as a statue in front of the open door, not making one move to go through it while the sirens grew louder and louder.

"Holy moly, what are you waiting for?" she asked, exasperated. "Go."

"I can't."

"Damn it, Seth, we just went through this. You have to g—"

"There's a brick wall."

"*What?*" Megan picked up her skirts and ran to the brick wall, heedless of Donna saying, "Shit, Megs, you almost made me tear that button off."

Megan stopped beside Seth. "You see it too?"

He nodded, his stunned eyes wide. He placed his hand on the bricks. He hit them. Hit them again. "Christ A'mighty, what's goin' on? I'm trapped here."

Megan grabbed his hand. "You're coming with me through my portal." She led him to the armoire.

"Megs."

Donna's strangled voice brought Megan abruptly around.

Tears shone in her best friend's eyes. "Oh, Megs, I'm going to miss you."

"I'm going to miss you too."

Then they were hugging and crying and promising never ever to forget the other.

Until Donna pushed Megan away, saying gruffly, "Go. Sounds like the cops are coming down the street." She kissed Megan's cheek. "Go with God. Make me proud." She backed away, a tremulous smile on her tear-stained face.

Seth put his arm around Megan. "You need those coins?"

Megan nodded, wiping her eyes.

Seth bent down, picked up the coins off the floor, and handed them to Megan.

She glanced at Donna one more time, and tried to smile, but her lips quivered too much to make the corners curve upward. Fresh tears threatened, blurring her already blurred vision. *I need to get my shit together.* Megan wiped tears away with the back of her hand then ran a finger under her runny nose. She took a deep breath then touched her palm to the dried blood on the edge of the armoire. She leaned down and scattered the coins on the floor in the corner.

Seth reached over and gripped her hand as the coins rolled around.

None of them went through the wall.

Not the next time either. Or the next.

"It must be me." Seth released her hand and backed up. "Try it now."

It made no difference. Nothing did.

Sirens wailed outside.

Donna ran to a window. "The cops just pulled up. One car so far." She faced Megan and Seth. "What are we going to do?"

"Do?" Megan laughed harshly. "There's nothing to do. We're stuck here." She looked at Barton conked out on the floor and imagined the tales he'd tell of all that had happened, all he'd heard. She looked at Donna, her promising career possibly already ruined by her prolonged, unplanned absence from her job. She looked at Seth, a man from the past with no proof of identity, or even existence, trapped in a room with a scene like this. *What will the cops do to him? Want him to leave a room he can't leave? How to explain all this?* She thought of her own hopes and dreams of a future with Seth in the past now dashed to pieces against that brick wall.

More sirens came from outside.

"Another squad car pulled up." Donna wrung her hands.

"Holy moly. We're screwed."

Chapter 40

Donna looked out the window again. "You need to hide, Seth."

"I'm not hidin'. There's nowhere to hide in here anyway."

Megan shook her head. "This is bad. Real bad." Her eyes met Seth's. "I'm so sorry you're mixed up in this mess."

"It's not your fault. Blame that no-good kin of mine."

Donna had her forehead pressed against the window as she peered down outside. "That's weird. I don't think any of the cops have come in yet." She hurried across the room to the door.

"Where are you going?" Megan asked.

"Checking the hall below." Donna unlocked the door, pulled it open, and stepped out to look over the handrail.

Megan went to peer out the window. She pressed her cheek against the cool glass. Two squad cars, lights flashing, parked beside the curb. Curious onlookers milled about and gathered on the sidewalks and street corner, some of them pointing at the B&B. Two cops stood around, as if waiting for something or someone. One of them glanced up at the window. Megan jerked back, and instantly chided herself for acting guilty. *I'm a victim. All three of us are. Barton terrorized us. How are we going to explain this? Explain Seth?* She rested her forehead against the glass, closed her eyes, and wished a simple click of her heels would whisk her and Seth back to the past. *Donna too. Why not?*

"Megan, the brick wall's gone." Surprise and confusion laced Seth's voice.

She spun around. "Good. Go back and I'll—"

"Not that wall. *That* one." Seth pointed to the hallway door.

Her breath caught in her throat. Her next words came out in a rush. "What do you see?"

"Gas lights on the wall. Flowered carpet on the floor. Miss Donna standing beside the handrail."

"Holy moly, you can see out the hallway door." She ran to Seth and clutched his arm, grinning up at his stunned face. "Maybe you can leave the room."

"Let's find out." He dropped a kiss on her lips then straightened, adjusting his hat. "For luck." He smiled, then faced the door, and reached it in three long strides.

"What's all the noise about?" Donna stood just outside the room.

"Watch." Megan clasped her hands together under her chin. She knew it would work. It suddenly made sense.

Seth walked through the doorway and out into the hall. He turned around. "Your time is very confusin'." He held out his hands in a helpless gesture. "I don't understand any of this."

Donna said, "At least you're not trapped in there anymore."

Lifting her skirt, Megan joined Seth and Donna in the hall. "I have a theory. That door on the outside wall is Seth's portal. The portal in the corner is mine. The one in the Water Gardens—" she looked at Seth "—is ours."

He frowned. "Why do you think that?"

"Yours suddenly closed to you. Mine won't open for me. We know there's a portal in the Water Gardens." Megan shrugged. "Why else would it be there?"

"Maybe there are more," Donna added.

"It's the only other one I know of so that's where we're going."

Seth lifted his hat and ran his other hand through his hair before replacing the hat. "We have to jump in the water and climb out of a watering trough?"

"Sounds fun, doesn't it?" Megan smiled.

"I'll drive." Donna pulled her car keys out of a front pocket of her shorts. "Is there anything you're forgetting in the room?" she asked Megan. "You'd better take one last look around."

Megan turned to walk into the room.

Seth said, "Take a looksee at your fella and make sure he's still out."

She glanced over her shoulder. "Quit calling him th—" She saw Seth's grin and tossed her head, smiling to herself as she walked to Barton and checked him over. He was out cold. She straightened, and realized this could, should be the last time she'd see the room as it was now. Her gaze slowly traveled around it.

The vanity with the yellowed newspaper clipping of Seth in front of his saloon that Candace had given her, and beside it, the taped-together picture of herself, both propped against the mirror. The table where she had dug the bullet out of Seth's arm, and ate pizza and tacos and drank beer with him and made love with him the first time. The rawhide sofa where they had sat and talked so many times. The armoire stained with the last flakes of his dried blood. The mysterious door that had brought him to her. The six tall windows framing the courthouse and Fort Worth skyline on the horizon.

Megan walked across the gleaming wood floor to look out one of those windows one last time. The two cops stood on the corner as another car pulled up. A man in plain clothes got out of the driver's side and shut the door. He adjusted his glasses then tucked the back of his shirt in his trousers as he walked around the front of the car to join the officers.

Megan looked closer. Detective Sullivan.

She turned to leave but paused to look at the room one last time.

It had become home and given her a future she could never have imagined, a love so great it filled her to overflowing, a chance to do what Seth once wished—change the world.

Her throat tightened as she said a silent goodbye.

The pipes rattled from a toilet flushing upstairs, and boards creaked in the floors and walls. The old house seemed to sigh, as if it knew it had done its part, its job done.

Megan smiled at the fanciful idea, and whispered, "Thank you." She walked across the floor, past Barton, out into the hallway, and shut the door behind her.

Seth and Donna had moved away from the rail to stand against the wall. Voices came from below. Megan peeked down. Mrs. Powell and the weekend office girl stood outside the TV room, looking toward the front door.

"Got everything you need?" Donna asked softly.

Megan took Seth's hand. "I certainly do." She smiled at Seth, then glanced at Donna. "But we can't just walk out of here. The cops—"

"I have it figured out." Donna whispered to Seth, "You're Barton's partner. You double-crossed him and knocked him out. You're taking us two as hostages. At gunpoint. Get out your gun. The other one too. Then—"

"I'm not pointin' a gun at you ladies," Seth whispered back, his voice indignant. "I only take it out when forced to."

"It's the only way we'll get out of here," Donna insisted. "We'll go to my car, and I'll haul ass to the Water Gardens where you guys can jump into the portal."

Megan nodded. "I like it." She tugged Seth's hand. "Let's go."

He wouldn't budge. "It's not safe."

"Oh pul-leeze." Donna rolled her eyes. "I live in Chicago. People run around with guns shooting people every day. Unload it if it makes you feel better."

"What good is an unloaded gun?"

"Oh, my God." Donna rubbed her forehead. She glanced at Megan and raised her eyebrows.

Megan remembered his youthful dislike of guns. "Seth, it's not far to the car. I doubt you'll accidently shoot one of us during that time."

He released her hand and crossed his arms, his stance rigid. "A gun should only be drawn as a last resort."

"This *is* our last resort." She put her hand on his arm. "The police will ask you questions that you can't answer. And when Barton starts talking." She shrugged.

"I know, I know." His eyes searched hers for a moment. The tension in the set of his shoulders eased. "All right," he said on a sigh. He drew his gun out of its holster then reached behind him and pulled out Barton's empty gun. "Let's get this over with."

"Get up here with me, Megs." Donna waved Megan forward. "Seth, stick the guns in our backs and we'll go down the stairs, and out the door. Once outside, just keep walking. Ready?"

Megan nodded. Her heart raced. Her mouth felt as dry as Death Valley. She wondered if they were crazy for thinking they could pull off such a stunt. The thought of the police grilling Seth made crazy the logical choice. She shot a sympathetic look over her shoulder at Seth with a gun pointed at her back. "This is a hell of an introduction to our time."

He smiled. "Just think of the tales we'll have to tell our young'uns."

"Hands up," Donna ordered. "Let's go."

Donna and Megan, hands raised, walked down the hallway then descended the stairs with Seth behind them.

"You need to act gruff and mean," Donna said over her shoulder to Seth. "Boss us around. Tell us to hurry up. Give one of us a shove every so often. You're a bad ass criminal desperate to escape."

"Christ A'mighty."

Megan bit back a grin at Seth's mutter. When they reached the main floor, she plastered a terrified look on her face when Mrs. Powell and the girl looked at the three of them.

"Miss Megan?" Mrs. Powell's gaze swept over the trio. Her eyes widened with alarm. "What on earth?"

"Stay back, Mrs. Powell," Megan warned, her voice rushed and high-pitched with panic. "He's Barton's partner but he knocked Barton out cold upstairs. He has a gun."

"Two guns," Donna whispered.

"Two guns," Megan quickly added.

"Holy Mother of God." Mrs. Powell backed up, her hand pressed flat beneath the top button of her white blouse.

The weekend girl darted into the TV room and shut the door.

"Keep movin', you two," Seth ordered. He poked his guns in their backs.

Heavy footsteps pounded on the second-floor landing.

Donna looked back. She gasped. "Barton!"

Seth and Megan whirled around.

Mrs. Powell covered her mouth with her hand and backed up against the wall.

Barton flew down the stairs. He had a snarl on his face and murder in his eyes. Four steps from the bottom, he let out a savage cry and launched himself through the air, his upper body leaning forward, his hands made into fists.

Megan backed up so fast her feet tangled in her dress. She stumbled but quickly righted herself, yelling, "Shoot him, Seth! Shoot him!"

Instead of shooting anyone, Seth shoved Donna out of the way just before Barton slammed into him and they both crashed to the floor. Seth's hat and the two guns went flying. Barton's fists flew when he scrambled upright, straddled Seth and started pummeling him.

Seth fought back, blocking blows, and landing his own. The two men thrashed and struggled. Their grunting and the sounds of flesh hitting flesh filled the hallway. Blood and saliva flew.

Megan and Donna looked frantically around the sparsely furnished hall, searching for the guns. A long, narrow bureau stretched along the wall behind Megan. She ran to look beneath it.

"Under the phone!" Mrs. Powell pointed down the hallway at the house telephone on its stand. On the floor beneath it lay a gun.

Megan hiked up her skirts and ran to snatch up the gun then raced back to the men. She gripped the gun by the barrel and stood ready to club Barton's head. She started to swing. His head jerked backwards from one of Seth's punches. She took aim again, and his head whipped to one side to avoid Seth's next blow. *Hold still, asshole!* She tensed for another try.

Barton's arm suddenly shot out and whacked her healing wound. She stumbled sideways, gasping, and fell. The fall knocked the wind out of her and the gun out of her grip. It landed with a thud somewhere behind her. She shook her head and struggled to push herself up off the floor, ignoring the stabbing pain in her side.

Across the hall, Mrs. Powell stood plastered against the wall, her eyes wide, her mouth an O.

Donna ran up to the brawling men, holding the other gun by its barrel. She stood poised to use is it then jumped back when the men rolled toward her.

Seth managed to end up on top and proceeded to beat Barton until he finally lay still. Seth crawled off Barton and sat on the floor, his shoulders heaving with his rapid, harsh breathing. He drew one leg up and bent a knee to rest his forehead on.

Donna bent over Barton and peeled back his eyelid. "He's out cold. I'll go find that other gun." She hurried down the hallway.

Megan scrambled over to Seth. "Are you okay?" She caught her breath as he slowly raised his head. "Holy moly, your face."

"It's fine. Don't worry." He licked blood off his lip. "You all right?"

"It's *fine?*" Blood oozed from a cut over his left eyebrow and several smaller cuts on his cheeks. Bruises colored any skin not covered with blood. He had a split lip.

Seth touched his forehead. "I reckon it looks worse than it is." He nodded to Barton, whose slack face was just as bruised and bloody. "He's a scrapper I'll give the boy that."

The pride in his voice made Megan shake her head in amazement. And made her realize how deeply he felt about family relations. He wouldn't shoot Barton because, good or bad, he was kin. "Boy," she scoffed. "He's about the same age as you." She rose stiffly to her feet, holding a hand to her side where Barton's arm had slammed into her. "Can you get up? We need to go."

"'Course I can." Seth pushed himself up off the floor, grunting with the effort, and stood with the slowness of an old man. He swayed a little.

Megan grabbed his arm. "Whoa there, cowboy. Don't pass out on me now."

He straightened his shoulders and shook off her hand. "I'm right as rain." He tugged his shirt cuffs down and tucked his shirt back in his trousers as if to look as presentable as a beaten man could.

"You better be." Megan knew his head had to be pounding. At least the cuts had stopped bleeding. "I don't want to have to drag you to the car."

"Me neither." Donna returned from down the hall and gave Seth his hat. She waited while he settled it gently on his head then gave him both guns. He slid his gun back in its holster and stuck the other in the small of his back.

Mrs. Powell joined them. "Here." She gave Megan a wet washcloth, and Seth a bag of frozen peas. "For the swelling." She looked him in the eye. "I take it you're not Mr. Crone's partner."

"No, ma'am. An' thank you." He pressed the peas against his swelling eye.

Megan dabbed her forehead with the washcloth. "This is Seth—"

"Ma'am." Seth tipped his hat.

"—he's from—from the past."

"I knew it." Mrs. Powell grinned. "He's the Marshal from Great Aunt Bertha's story. He's your fella." She nudged Megan. "You found yourself a good one there, dear. A sight better than that one." She jutted her chin towards Barton.

"Don't I know." Megan glanced at the front door, expecting the cops to bust it down any second. "Mrs. Powell, we need to get out of here without drawing the attention of the police. Can you help us please?"

"I can't believe they didn't hear the commotion. Use the kitchen door. The parking lot is nearby." Mrs. Powell glanced at Barton. "What about him?"

"Give us a few minutes head start then let the cops in to collect him."

"He'll tell them about y'all." Mrs. Powell glanced at the Donna, Seth, then Megan. "He'll tell them all about this fight, how I witnessed it."

"Tell them the truth." Megan shrugged. "We ran out the back."

"We better hurry. Follow me." Mrs. Powell led the way to a door next to the office.

Loud knocks pounded the front door. "Police. Open up."

Mrs. Powell paused and stuck her head in the TV room. "Don't open that door," she said to the girl hiding in there. "I'll answer it in a minute or so. You stay here." She shut the door and hurried on, saying, "Quick now."

They entered the kitchen, skirted a big rectangular table in the middle of the floor, and hurried past a stove where steam rose from a whistling teakettle. Mrs. Powell turned off the burner as she passed. She led them by an upright freezer then went to a door beneath an *Exit* sign. She said over her shoulder, "Y'all wait here while I take a looksee for any police around." She opened the door then stepped outside and out of sight.

Seconds later, she reappeared in the doorway. "There's one officer on the corner but if you can get around the bushes and stay low, you should be fine. Come on."

Megan, Donna, and Seth hurried outside. The sun rode low in the western sky smeared with white clouds as gauzy as a wedding veil. A slight breeze stirred the glossy leaves of a row of big bushes on the right.

Mrs. Powell pointed to the bushes. "The parking lot is on the other side of those Photinias. I'll stall the police as long as I can." She looked at Megan. "You're not coming back, are you?"

Megan shook her head. "There's this fella ..."

A silvery laugh came from Mrs. Powell. "Isn't there always?" She swept an appreciative gaze over Seth. "Don't blame you a bit, dear." She drew Megan into an embrace. "I wish you all the happiness in the world, Miss Megan."

Tears burned Megan's eyes as she hugged the older woman. "Thank you for all your help, Mrs. Powell. For ... everything."

"You've certainly made things interesting around here." Mrs. Powell chuckled. "And thank you for giving me this beautiful old house." When they separated, she said to Seth, "You take care of her, you hear, young man?"

"I intend to, ma'am." He reached behind him and drew out Barton's gun. "I reckon you best take this. It's empty."

Mrs. Powell slipped her hand beneath the hem of her blouse and took the gun with her cloth-covered hand.

"These too." Seth placed a handful of bullets in Mrs. Powell's other hand.

She put them in a pocket of her skirt.

"One more thing, Mrs. Powell," Megan said. "Tell Detective Sullivan that Officer Hernandez is Barton's snitch in the police department."

"That nice young officer?" Mrs. Powell tsked. "I'll tell him. Now git."

Donna led the way down the row of bushes. As Megan rounded the last one, she turned to wave at Mrs. Powell.

She waved back, wiped her eyes, and went inside, pulling the door shut behind her.

The finality of that closing door suddenly struck Megan with the reality of what she was about to do. Close the door on the only world she'd ever known. Her heartbeat did triple time and her palms turned clammy. Spending two days in 1890 didn't amount to a hill of beans compared to a lifetime of living in the past.

"Stay down and get around here!"

Donna's whispered command jolted Megan back to their plight. She ran around the bush and crouched beside Seth. Donna knelt on his right. The parking lot with about a dozen cars was in front of them. Two cars blocked them from the view from the sidewalk where an officer walked by, his head turned toward the parking lot.

Seth held the frozen peas on his eye. "You all right?"

She looked at him, her reason for everything. She smiled. "I'm ready to leave."

"Me too." He wrinkled his nose, making a face. "Smells funny here."

She bit back a laugh. "What does it—?"

"You two listen up," Donna whispered. "The cop is busy talking to that old man. The cops know my car and right now, he's not watching it. Stay low and run to the car."

Megan rose up a little and saw the cop down on the corner talking to a little old man holding the leashes of two panting Pomeranians. The cop had his back to the parking lot, where a van parked next to Donna's rental car blocked his view of the car. The two vehicles were parked in the second row nearest the road, isolated from the other vehicles closer to the buildings.

"Let's go." Donna crouched down and ran between the cars.

Megan took Seth's hand and pointed with her other one. "We're running to that white car and getting in the back seat."

A frown creased his brow. "The what?"

"Just stick with me." She crouched down, checked to make sure Seth did too, and they ran between the cars then sprinted across the open lot to Donna's car where Donna already sat in the driver's seat. Megan yanked open the back door and climbed inside, struggling with her wide skirt and petticoat, then Seth got in behind her. He didn't duck far enough as he sat down and knocked off his hat. He tried to catch it and fumbled with it as if it were a football until he dropped it on the ground. He bent down, grabbed his hat, and settled it on his head as he straightened on the back seat.

Megan reached across him and pulled the door shut, making sure not to slam it. "Don't be nervous."

He lifted his chin. "I'm not." Despite his words, his face seemed pale beneath the bruises.

She looked out her window, so he wouldn't see her smile.

Donna started the car. "I've often wondered what it would be like to drive the get-away car." She pulled out of the parking lot and turned right, the opposite way of the cop.

Megan watched out the rear window. "He's running after us. He stopped. He's on his radio now." She swayed against the back seat as Donna stomped on the gas.

Donna sped down the street. "They'll be looking for us in no time. Hang on." She whipped the car around a corner, tires squealing.

Seth had a white-knuckled grip on the back of the driver's seat. He stared around Donna's head as she drove miles above the speed limit. Cars whizzed by going the other way.

Megan put her hand on his arm, rigid as an iron bar. "You okay?"

"Lordy, this is fast." He jumped, and his head snapped around when an 18-wheeler pulled out from a side street. He leaned toward the middle of the seat when it looked as if the behemoth was going to run right into his side of the car. The metal grill on the front of the truck loomed in the window like large, shiny teeth before the truck fell back and rumbled along behind the car.

Seth blew out a breath.

"Sit back and relax." Megan tugged on his arm until he slowly lowered both arms, then pushed him back against the seat. "It's a short ride. Enjoy the scenery. Where's your ice pack?"

"Guess I dropped it." He glanced back at the semi, looking nervous.

To distract him, she asked, "How much time has passed since you left me here?"

"Two weeks."

"You're kidding. It's been two weeks for me too."

He looked at her. "You mean the same amount of time passed for both of us? That never happened before."

"Maybe it's a good sign," Donna added from the front of the car. "I wonder what happened when the cops found Barton?"

Megan snorted. "I hope he rots in prison." She said to Seth, "How is everyone? Anything happen between your sister and Amelia?"

"Lottie moved out of the brothel."

"She *did?*" Megan couldn't have been more surprised than if he'd said Lottie now lived on the moon.

Seth nodded. "I found her a small place on the outskirts of town. She says she has enough money saved up to get by for a spell. She's wantin' to meet Amelia, but I reckon she's scared. She hardly ever leaves her house."

"A lot of big changes for her. Do the townspeople treat her well?"

He shook his head, a sad set to his mouth.

"Give them time. And ... Susannah?"

He must have noticed her hesitation. He put his hand over hers where it rested on her thigh. "She's fine. Don't worry. We had a long talk and parted as friends."

"Oh good. I really like her."

"She likes you too. Makes it easier on all of us." He smiled and leaned over to kiss her. When they parted, he touched a finger to his split lip.

"Hurt? I'm sorry."

"It was worth it. I'd wink but my winkin' eye hurts."

Megan laughed. *God, I've missed him.* "How's Tim?"

"Oh, you know Tim." Seth chuckled, shaking his head. "He's goin' out of his way to be sweet to Susannah, but he's got enough sense to not go sniffin' 'round her like a hound dog huntin' a scent."

"Sounds like he's giving her some space."

"Yeah. That's a right good way to say it. Givin' her some space. I reckon he'll whittle down her resistance. They'll make a fine couple."

"Yes, they will."

The car stopped at a red light beside a bank.

Seth craned his neck as he looked out his window. "Boy howdy, that's a tall buildin'. Looks a lot taller than they did from your window."

"It's a nice city. Clean, friendly, booming." Megan squeezed his hand. "One you'll help build into this, or something even better."

"Been thinkin' on that." His gaze met hers. "I want to run for office."

"You mean, like, the mayor?" Megan grinned. "That's wonderful. You'll be a great mayor."

"I'd vote for you," Donna said as she drove across the intersection.

"I reckon I'll start with mayor, but I got my eye on the governor's mansion."

"*Governor.*" Megan started in surprise. "Holy moly. Governor O'Connor." The words rolled off her tongue. "Has a nice ring to it."

The car bumped over some railroad tracks so hard and fast Seth grabbed the back of Donna's seat with both hands and held on.

"Sorry, guys." Donna glanced at them in the rearview mirror. "I was so engrossed in your conversation I wasn't paying attention. Governor, huh? Cool."

Seth unclenched his hands from the back of the seat and leaned back. "How 'bout Governor and Mrs. O'Connor." He took Megan's hand again, the look in his eyes hopeful. "If you'll have me."

Megan's heart took wing. A smile spread across her face that stretched from ear to ear. "Oh, I'll have you all right." She trailed her fingertip down the front of his shirt. "Over, and over, and over."

"I certainly hope so." He pulled her close and kissed her as if his lip didn't hurt at all.

Sniffles came from the front seat. "Oh Megs, congrats!" Donna laughed. "He proposed to you in a car in 1981. I'd love to hear you tell your kids *that* story."

Sirens wailed behind them.

The sound jerked Megan and Seth apart. They looked out the back window.

A squad car raced after them, lights flashing.

"Hang on." Donna whipped into an alley and tore down it to the next street. She made a couple quick turns, throwing Megan and Seth from side to side, then slowed down. "Maybe I lost them for a few minutes. It's not far now."

Megan settled back against the seat, her hand still in Seth's death grip. She tugged him back beside her. "How are you enjoying your first ride in a car?"

"I'm never gonna get in one ever again."

He said it so firmly and passionately, his expression so serious, Megan burst out laughing.

"Hey," Donna yelled from the front. "I take offense at that."

Megan, still chuckling, leaned forward to pat Donna's shoulder. "You're doing great." She sat back and said to Seth, "I bet you do. You'll be a car nut like most men are. Although, you think this was a rough ride, just wait until you're in those early cars. Like the Model T. You saw the pictures in the history book."

Seth nodded. "Those contraptions didn't look at all like these here in your time. And the roads were terrible. Rutted and muddy." His eyes lit up with an excitement reflected in his voice. "We need better roads.

Maybe I can do something about that as mayor. For sure as governor." He grinned at Megan, his bruised and battered face full of joy. "Just think of all the things we can do together."

That enthusiasm and desire to help people. He reminds me of Dad, Megan realized. Not a bad thing. Not at all. She replied softly, "Imagine the possibilities."

Seth angled his head to one side. "I like that. It'll be my slogan. I can see the banners now." He held up his free hand, fingers splayed, palm out, and swept it across the air before him. "Imagine the possibilities. It's perfect."

Donna swung the car around a corner and jerked to a stop. "We're here." She glanced around and turned off the car. "I don't see any cops anywhere." She opened her door, got out, and looked around. She shut her door and beckoned to them through the window.

Seth climbed out then took Megan's hand and helped her out. Her dress belled around her when she straightened. "This is where Hell's Half Acre used to be," she said to Seth.

His jaw dropped as he looked around at the concrete and greenery, the tall buildings of sun-bathed glass in the distance. They had parked on Houston Street, almost empty of cars on a hot Sunday evening. "You're joshin' me."

She held up her right hand. "Swear to God."

Sirens echoed off the walls of the Convention Center.

"Come on," Donna urged.

Hand in hand, Megan and Seth ran beside Donna into the Water Gardens. Birds twittered among the leafy branches etched across the face of the lowering sun in the western sky. People moved aside or stopped to look at Megan in her old-fashioned dress and Seth with his battered face, tin star pinned to his shirt, and a gun strapped to his thigh as they hurried by. Several people aimed a camera at them.

Maybe they think we're dressed up for a play or something, Megan thought.

The trio passed the top of the wall of water around the Quiet Pool, Megan tugging at Seth, who slowed to look around. They ran by the Aerating Pool where little kids played in the fairyland-like sprays, then ran out into the Central Square. Dozens of people milled about in the heat of the summer evening, many taking or posing for pictures. More people sat or lounged on the concrete ledges, and kids ran around playing. A dog chased a Frisbee sailing through the air.

Donna, Megan, and Seth ran to the Active Pool and started down the big blocks of concrete, brushing past people climbing up from the pool at the bottom. Water roared as it flowed down the surrounding terraces where shadows slowly crept up.

Megan and Seth passed Donna and reached the bottom just as another couple started back up. No one else gathered at the pool.

Seth glanced around. "Never seen nothin' like this. Miss Donna's not comin' down?"

Megan spun around.

Donna had stopped six steps above. She waved at them.

Megan picked up her skirts and ran back up the big blocks. "Come with us."

Donna shook her head. "I can't. That's your destiny." Tears glistened in her eyes. "Not mine."

"I know. I just—" Tears stung Megan's eyes. There was so much yet so little to say. They had been saying goodbye the past two weeks. Last pizza. Last movie.

Donna wrapped her arms around Megan.

Megan held tight to her best friend. *Last hug.* "I'll never forget you," Megan choked out, her voice thick with sorrow, muffled against the front of Donna's blouse, damp from the spray.

"Friends to the ends, right?" Donna's voice shook.

Megan nodded, then drew back. "I love you, Donna."

"I love you too, Megs." Donna smiled through her tears. "Now go join your man and make me proud."

"Police!" an officer shouted from the top of the terrace. "Stop where you are." He and another officer ran down the steps, their guns drawn.

People climbing up the blocks moved out of the officers' way and hurried to the top where curious onlookers gathered.

Donna gave Megan a shove. "Go. Hurry."

Megan whirled around and ran down to Seth. When she reached him, she turned and shouted over the roar of the water, "Be happy, sugar bear."

"Thank you, Miss Donna," Seth hollered.

Donna waved with one hand, wiped her eyes with the other.

The police officers reached Donna. One stopped behind her.

The other officer continued down to the bottom.

Seth took Megan's hand. "You ready?"

"Hold tight. I don't want to get separated when we jump in. We might end up in different time periods for all I know."

"Don't worry. I've got you." His hand tightened on hers. "I'll never let you go."

Something warm and wonderful surged through Megan. He had finally said them, the words he'd said that night of the dance in her first vision. It meant something to her, she wasn't sure why. Maybe an affirmation that she had done well, that all was as it should be. She thought of all that had led her to this moment. A door to the past, the interfering universe, even her love of *The Twilight Zone.* She thought of the Megans who had come before her. *I did it. I damn well did it.*

"You two raise your hands," a police officer ordered as he stopped on the block above them. "Don't try any funny stuff."

Seth looked at her with eyes full of joy and passion and the promise of forever. "I love you, Miss Megan."

"I love you too, you wonderful cowboy. Let's see what good things we can do together."

Hand in hand, they jumped off the ledge into history.

Chapter 41

Donna ran down to the bottom and searched the water where Megan and Seth had jumped in. No bubbles. No sign of them. *Did they make it? Did they—?* Someone touched her shoulder. She jumped.

"Fancy meetin' you here, sugar bear."

"Bubba?" Donna started in surprise at the sight of his smiling freckled face. "What are you doing here?" She glanced around. *Where are the other cops? Why isn't anyone shouting that two people jumped into the water?* She brushed damp hair out of her eyes and scanned the top of the terrace that seconds ago had been lined with people. *What happened to all the onlookers? Everyone acts as if nothing happened.*

The thought shook her to the core.

Because it didn't happen. Not now.

That quick, between one heartbeat and the next, time must have reset itself to whatever changes Megan had caused.

"—and I stopped to see if I could find you."

Donna realized Bubba was talking and gave her head a shake. "I'm sorry, Bubba. What did you say?"

He shifted from one foot to the other. He had his thumbs hooked on his jeans' pockets. The front of his blue shirt had a small splotch of ketchup near a middle button. "I said I just finished eatin' lunch and was drivin' home to get ready for work when I spied your car. I stopped to see if I could find you to say howdy. And give you some sugar." He leaned in and gave her a quick kiss, then drew away and looked at her closely. "You were studyin' that water awful closely. Drop something?"

"No, no. I was just—just looking."

"You here alone?"

"I was with Megs. But she's ... gone now."

Bubba tilted his head. "Who?"

"Megan. From The Tejas. Your cousin Bonnie's friend."

He shrugged. "'Fraid I don't know who you're talkin' about."

"But—" Donna stopped, confused, then wondered if Megan had been erased from his memory since she had not lived in the current present. She had probably been erased from everyone's memory. *Except mine.*

Her heart skipped a beat. *Will I forget her?*

She had a sudden urge to return to the B&B. "I'm sorry, but I really need to go."

He glanced at his watch. "Me too. Gotta be at work soon. I'll walk out with you. I parked behind your car." He took her hand and they climbed up the big blocks to the top then walked across the Central Square. The lowering sun sent long shadows across the expanse of concrete beneath their feet. "Wanna do something tomorrow?"

"Mondays aren't your usual day off."

"It is this week 'cause Tuesday we're protectin' the President."

"The President is coming to Fort Worth?"

"Well, former President. And he'll be in Dallas actually, attendin' a meetin' about puttin' a museum somewhere near Dealey Plaza. A bunch of us are goin' to help out in Dallas."

Donna stopped in her tracks, making Bubba stop too. "Wait a minute. Are you talking about JFK?"

"Excuse us, folks." Bubba nodded to an older couple who almost ran into them when they stopped so suddenly. He tugged Donna aside to let the couple pass. "Yeah. He's been here a time or two since that November day. It's always a big hoopla. Especially if Jackie's with him. Last I heard she'll be here too." His light blue eyes peered closely at Donna. "You all right? You look like you've seen a ghost."

Kennedy didn't die. Her mind reeled. *You did it, Megs. By God, somehow you changed things. Big things.* She grinned at Bubba. "I'm fine." She squeezed his hand. "Let's go." She couldn't stop smiling. Kennedy lived. The country had been spared those awful days, that ripping apart of its soul. She felt like skipping.

"I really admire that man," Bubba said.

He must have been a great President.

"Everythin' he went through. Learnin' how to walk and talk again and everythin' else. Took him a long time to recover." He looked at Donna. "You ever wonder how things might be if he'd been able to finish his term? Maybe serve another?"

It took a moment for Bubba's words to sink in as Donna walked beside him. *Kennedy is an invalid.* Her smile slumped. *He was never President again.* Her steps slowed. She took a deep breath to compose herself. *Maybe some things are not supposed to be changed.* She pressed her lips together. *The rules according to Chaos.* Aware of Bubba watching her, she forced a bright smile and matched her steps to his. "Sure, I do. Guess we'll never know."

As they passed the wall of water, Donna asked, "Did you eat with some other officers today?"

Bubba nodded.

"Did you guys hear anything about what happened to Barton back at the B&B?"

Bubba looked at her. "Barton who?"

"Barton Crone."

Furrows creased his brow, and a look of surprise crossed his face. "You mean the City Manager? What was he doin' at the B&B?"

Donna came to an abrupt halt. "City Manager? Barton Crone?" She rubbed her forehead with her free hand. This new world was full of surprises. JFK was alive but an invalid; Barton worked for the city. *I wonder if he's changed. Or embezzling money.*

"Yeah." Bubba eyed her curiously. "How do you know him?"

"I—I don't. I must have the—the wrong name. Forget I said anything."

Bubba placed his fingertip beneath her chin and raised her head until their eyes met. "You sure you're feelin' okay, Donna?"

She managed a weak smile. "It must be the heat. It's been so hot."

"I reckon you're not used to it yet. Being a Yankee and all." He squeezed her hand. They walked on beneath birds twittering in the trees.

They exited the Water Gardens and stopped beside her rental car. Bubba leaned back against it and drew Donna close, linking his arms around her waist. "What do you want to do tomorrow? I don't care what it is as long as we're together."

"I feel the same way. Surprise me."

He nuzzled her nose with his. "I'm glad you came to Fort Worth."

"Me too." Later, she had to find out from him what reason she'd given for visiting Texas. *Do I still have the same job? I need to call mom and dad. Maybe they didn't get divorced. Maybe—*

Bubba kissed her, and her thoughts trailed off. Her knees went weak. She clung to his tall, lanky frame, glad their relationship hadn't been one of the changes in the new world she was about to discover. The kiss ended far too soon.

He leaned his forehead against hers. "I sure do like you, Donna."

"I sure do like you too."

"I'll pick you up about 11. We'll have lunch and take it from there." He kissed her once more then took her hand. They walked around to the driver's side where he opened the door for her, then shut it behind her after she got in.

Donna started the car and waved to him. She headed for the B&B, remembering the wild ride from there with Megan and Seth in the back seat and the cops in pursuit. Except it had never happened now. *What else has never happened, or has now happened? I feel like a fish out of water, a stranger in a strange land whose history I have to learn.*

Vibrant shades of orange and purple streaked across the evening sky, and a slight breeze stirred the leaves on the trees lining the street. Her gaze narrowed, and she slowed down, looking at all the trees along the street, and in the yards and parks. There seemed to be more of them, and many of them were tall, some massive, obviously older trees. She'd driven the same streets enough times to notice the difference. Donna didn't see any other major changes in the city until the B&B came into sight.

She stopped in front and stared. It had a wide front porch painted white and the sign in the yard read *Miss Megan's Bed & Breakfast.*

"Holy crap, Megs," she breathed. "Look at that."

Minutes later, Donna paused inside the front door of the B&B. No evidence of Barton or his fight with Seth remained in the hallway. Her head didn't hurt anymore either, she realized. She heard Mrs. Powell talking to someone in the office as she passed by and ran upstairs to her room.

When she opened the door, her gaze went to the door on the outer wall. It had a small plaque above it. She stepped closer and saw etched in brass the words *Seth's Door.*

"You remembered," Donna muttered. "You were fine, and all was well." She wiped a tear from her eye. "God, I already miss you. What am I going to do without you?" She heaved a long sigh. "Maybe I'd be better off if I did forget you."

She searched the room and discovered no evidence of Megan remained. All her things were gone. Even Seth's dried blood on the corner of the armoire. It was as if she never was.

But she had been, and Donna planned an early morning visit to the library.

Then she laughed. A wealth of information lived right downstairs.

Donna left her room and shut the door. A brass plaque above it she hadn't noticed before caught her eye in the mellow glow of the gaslights. *Miss Megan's Room.*

A chill ran over her skin.

She checked the door to the next room. *Miss Charlotte's Room.*

The next one, *Miss Susannah's Room.*

Donna caught her breath when she read the plaque above the last room on that floor. *Miss Donna's Room.*

She swallowed a lump in her throat and hurried downstairs.

"Mrs. Powell?" Donna stuck her head inside the office and saw Mrs. Powell still had company. "Oh. Sorry. I didn't know you were busy."

"Nonsense, dear." Mrs. Powell waved her hand from her chair behind the desk. "Come in. Come in. This is my niece Jolene." She nodded to a pretty girl with long blonde hair sitting in a chair beside the desk. Her yellow blouse and white shorts contrasted attractively with her dark tan. She had one long leg crossed over the other. "She's leaving in a few days for her senior year in college and we're just having a chat. Everything all right, Miss Donna?"

"Everything's fine. I was wondering about this Miss Megan the B&B and my room are named for. If you have a moment."

Jolene laughed as she swung her sandaled foot. "You'll be sorry. Aunt Flo can talk for a month of Sundays about her favorite person."

"Oh, stop it." Mrs. Powell tsked.

"You can." Jolene looked at Donna. "She really can."

"I wouldn't have this house if not for her. That's why I named it after her."

Donna stepped further into the room. "Who was she?" It felt weird to ask that about her best friend whom she knew better than anyone else. Had known, anyway.

"A mystery." Mrs. Powell folded her hands together on top of the desk. "Miss Megan McClure showed up in town one day in 1890 and claimed to be from Chicago, but no one ever knew for sure. She wasn't one for talking about her past. Then again, Texas was settled by people leaving behind a life somewhere else. She might have been one of them. She and the marshal, a man named Seth O'Connor, fell in love right off the bat even though he was already engaged to a woman named Susannah Mead. Her name is above a door on your floor too."

Donna nodded. "I saw it."

"There was bad blood between the marshal and another fella named John Bingo and on the marshal's wedding day the two men met out in the woods somewhere. There was gunfire, and witnesses said John Bingo died and Miss Megan had been hit. Shot clean through, mortally wounded. The marshal high-tailed it to town with Miss Megan in his arms, and suddenly, she was gone. Not dead." Mrs. Powell held up one hand. "Just ... gone. No one in town saw her anywhere or knew where she was. Except the marshal, and he never said a word about her. He and Miss Susannah called off the wedding. Late one evening a couple weeks later, an eyewitness claimed he saw the marshal and Miss Megan, wearing a fancy purple dress, climb out of a watering trough on Rusk Street."

Jolene giggled. "That's my favorite part." Her foot swung faster as she listened with her chin on the palm of her hand, her elbow propped on the armchair.

Mrs. Powell smiled then went on, "The witness was a drunkard named Willie Dee and no one took him seriously. Exactly where Miss Megan was during those couple weeks remains a mystery to this day. Anyway, she and the marshal married soon after that, and eventually had six children."

Donna caught her breath. *Six! I bet she was a great mom.*

"Four boys and two girls. There's a room on your floor named for the oldest girl, Donna. The other room is named for Miss Charlotte, the marshal's sister. She, Miss Susannah, and Miss Megan were very close."

Donna's smile faltered upon hearing that room wasn't named for her. But Megan had named her daughter after her. That meant more to her than an old room.

"Anyway, the marshal ran for mayor of Fort Worth during the late 1890s and was elected for two terms. Some years later, he was elected governor and served two terms. That's a photograph of them." Mrs. Powell nodded to the wall behind Donna.

Donna spun around and saw Megan and Seth.

"It's a copy of the first colored photo of them," Mrs. Powell said. "Colored photography was in its infancy then."

A large framed photo, maybe two feet by three feet, showed Megan from the waist up. She sat with her hands folded on her lap and a slight smile as she stared serenely out at the world. Her off-shouldered, plum-colored dress had a low neckline with a small black bow at her cleavage. Tight sleeves over-laid with cream-colored lace ended just past her elbows. She had her black hair piled up in luxuriant curls atop her head with tendrils falling over her forehead, temples, and neck. A gem the size of a walnut and the same color as the dress hung from a black choker around her neck.

Behind her, tall and lean, with his right hand on her bare shoulder, stood Seth. He wore black trousers, a black coat, and a dark-striped waistcoat over a white shirt with a high collar, and a white bow tie. His short, sandy hair had a touch of red in it, the way it did when the light hit it just so, and the tips of his thin mustache curled up slightly. He gazed down at Megan with the kind of look every woman wished her man had when he looked at her.

Tears burned Donna's eyes as she stared at her friend—older, more mature, a wife and mother, first lady of Texas. Time traveler.

"I always thought she looked a little like Liz Taylor," Jolene said behind Donna. "That black hair. Those purple eyes."

"Violet," Donna muttered.

"Violet," Mrs. Powell said at the same time. She and Jolene laughed, then Mrs. Powell explained, "Miss Megan always corrected people when they said she had purple eyes. She preferred violet. She often wore purple when they entertained. They were the height of society for years. They traveled Europe before World War Two broke out."

"It sounds like they had quite a life," Donna said softly.

"It wasn't without tragedy." Mrs. Powell sighed. "Their youngest son drowned in the Trinity when he was ten. Terrible thing. Just terrible." She clicked her tongue. "Miss Charlotte died in a train wreck in the thirties. Mr. Seth took her death hard."

"Was he," Donna cleared a lump in her throat before continuing, "a good mayor and governor?"

"Oh my, yes," Mrs. Powell said. "He did many good things. Planted lots of trees. Improved the roads and sidewalks. Fought for building requirements. He supported many causes, like women's right to vote, child labor laws, clean water. People called him a dreamer, and, mercy me, he had some wild ideas for that era, but he was a dreamer who actually tried, and did, make things happen. She had a lot to do with it, I'm sure. She wrote many articles and editorials for the paper."

"She also wrote about other stuff," Jolene added. "Like those weird lights in Marfa in west Texas."

Donna smiled, glad that Megs had continued writing. She turned back to Mrs. Powell. "Why did you say it's because of her that you have this house?"

"You might as well sit down," Jolene nodded to the chair beside her, "if you're gonna hear Aunt Flo's favorite Miss Megan story."

"Thanks." Donna pulled out the chair and sat.

Mrs. Powell said, "She and Mr. Seth returned to Fort Worth before the war began and lived on the west side of town. This house was falling apart when they bought it. She fixed it up and offered free housing to any service men that needed a place to stay for however long. She put those names above the rooms on the second and third floors. I believe they're all the women she loved most in the world." Mrs. Powell smiled as if she knew a secret. "It's been a boarding house ever since. I loved this old place the minute I saw it. I knew I could never afford it on a teacher's salary if it ever came up for sale, but it never did. One day in 1974, a lawyer called me out of the blue and asked me to meet with him. When I did, he handed me the deed to this house, free and clear."

"Wow." Donna didn't have to feign surprise. The story was different this time.

"Isn't that cool?" Jolene chimed in. "It gets even better."

"Heavens, yes. I not only got the house but there was a separate bequest for perpetual upkeep and maintenance of the property."

"How wonderful." Donna smiled, remembering her conversation with Megan about Mrs. Powell and the house.

Mrs. Powell raised her hands. "A Godsend. How could I *not* name it after her?" She gave a little laugh. "I still don't know how or why or—or anything. Why, by then, she'd been dead for 20 years." She shrugged. "Guess I'll never know why she did all that for a complete stranger, but I'm so grateful."

Dead.

Donna knew Megan couldn't still be alive. Still, hearing that word brought a rush of tears to her eyes and she quickly glanced away, blinking rapidly.

"I can't believe you haven't shown her the book yet, Aunt Flo."

"What book?" Donna looked from Jolene to Mrs. Powell.

Jolene reached behind her to grab a book off the bookcase along the wall. She held it out to Donna, who took it and read the title.

The Life and Times of Megan McClure O'Connor

"There's been many books written about her but that's the best one, in my opinion," Mrs. Powell said. "You can read it if you're interested."

"I'd love to." Donna flashed a tremulous smile. She ran a hand over the name embossed on the leather cover. "She sounds like a fascinating person."

A girl about Jolene's age rushed into the office. "Sorry it took so long. That place was packed, and it took forever." She stopped when she saw Donna. "Oh. Sorry to interrupt." She had shoulder-length auburn hair, wore shorts and a tank top, and held a Styrofoam tray holding three drinks and a white paper bag.

"Gimme those tacos." Jolene reached for the bag and dug around in it. "I'm starving."

"You're not interrupting, dear." Mrs. Powell nodded to Donna. "This is Miss Donna, one of my guests."

"Howdy." The girl smiled at Donna as she passed around the drinks. "I'm Tiffany Huntington, Jolene's friend. Want a taco? There's plenty."

"No, thanks. Here. Take my chair." Donna rose and stepped aside.

Tiffany sat down. "Thanks. Sure you don't want a one?"

"Positive. Did you say Huntington?"

Tiffany nodded as she took a taco from Jolene and peeled off the wrapper.

"Any relation to Candace Huntington?" Donna asked.

"She was my great-grandmother. She died recently. You knew her?"

Donna shook her head. "No. I've heard about her is all. One of Fort Worth's oldest families, I was told. I'm sorry for your loss."

"Thanks." Tiffany took a bite of her taco then dabbed her mouth with a napkin. "She was a hundred, you know. The best granny in the world."

"She must have had an interesting life, living that long." Donna paused. "Maybe even traveled the world."

Tiffany laughed. "Not Granny. She was a homebody if there ever was one. She rarely even left Fort Worth. I can probably count on one hand the times I know of that she went as far as Dallas." A fond smile lit the girl's face. "She used to say she must have lived before and already seen everything because she had no desire to do so now. All she ever wanted was to have her kids around her."

"Big family?"

"Seven kids, nineteen grandchildren, and twenty-eight great-grand kids. So far." Tiffany nodded to the book in Donna's hands. "Reading up on Miss Megan? She and Granny were good friends."

Jolene took another taco out of the bag. "Tell her your favorite Miss Megan story, Tiff." When Tiffany scoffed, Jolene said, "Come on. She knows mine, about the watering trough. Aunt Flo told her about getting the house. Tell her yours."

"Well, it has more to do with one of Miss Megan's grandsons. It's in the book."

"I'd love to hear it."

Tiffany took a sip of her drink before speaking. "Her grandson Adam O'Connor was an astronaut and part of the Apollo 11 crew. He was the initial commander of the flight and would be the first man to walk on the moon. But he turned it down."

"Can you believe that?" Jolene leaned forward, her eyes big. "Turned down the chance to be the first man on the moon." She sat back, shaking her head. "Unbelievable."

Donna chuckled. "It is hard to believe. Did he say why he did that?"

"Oh yeah." Tiffany rolled her eyes. "He made no bones about it. He said that when he told his grandmother he wanted to be an astronaut and maybe someday walk on the moon, she told him that Neil Armstrong and only Neil Armstrong should be the first man to walk on the moon."

"How odd." Donna played along, knowing full well Neil Armstrong had been Megan's personal hero. "Did she know him?"

"Nope. Said she'd never met him—mind you, this was in the early 1950s when she told Adam all this, and Apollo 11 was years away—but she insisted a man named Armstrong was the man for the job and Adam better not interfere when the time came. So, he didn't."

"That's quite a sacrifice he made for his grandmother."

Mrs. Powell gathered up empty wrappers off her desk. "He did get to the moon." She stuffed the trash into the bag. "But most people don't remember him because he was the third man to walk on it. You don't remember him, right?" She glanced at Donna, who shook her head. "See? Being first is what counts."

There had only been three crewmembers, two of them walked on the moon, Donna remembered. Before, anyway. She blew out a breath. So much to relearn.

Jolene sipped on her drink as she gazed at the picture behind Donna. "Wasn't the first time she seemed to know what was going to happen. Funny how she knew stuff like that." She sucked on the straw. "Maybe she was a time traveler."

A soft gasp escaped Donna. Her hands had a death grip on the book. *Is she serious?* Jolene didn't look serious, though, as she sat there, swinging her foot, her young face open and innocent.

Tiffany giggled. "You're nuts."

"It would explain a lot." Jolene grinned. "But it is nuts."

Donna happened to glance at Mrs. Powell, then did a double take. *Did she wink at me?* Donna stared hard at Mrs. Powell. The woman had the same open, innocent look as her niece. It must have been a trick from the overhead light. Either that or ...

Donna squared her shoulders. "I should leave you to your visit." She nodded to the girls. "Nice to meet you. Thanks for the history lesson." She held up the book. "And for loaning me this. I'll return it soon."

"No hurry, dear." Mrs. Powell smiled. "Have a nice night."

On her way out, Donna looked at the couple in the photo. She paused in the doorway. "How did they die?"

"Mr. Seth died in a car accident," Mrs. Powell said. "He had a tendency to drive too fast. A fan belt or something broke on the car, and he crashed. He was in his late eighties. Miss Megan died in her sleep in January 1954, just shy of turning ninety-one. They had a long, good life together and their legendary love is part of our Texas lore."

Donna gazed at her friends, frozen in time, together then and now and forever, and a certain peace flowed through her. Clutching the book to her chest, she said goodnight, left the office, and started up the stairs. She passed the second landing and continued to the third floor, where she'd never been.

She went left in the dim light thrown by the gaslights on the wall and stopped at the first room to read the plaque. *Miss Candace's Room*. The plaque above the last room on that side read *Miss Cordelia's Room*. The pretty Pryor girls.

Donna backtracked to the two rooms on the other side. The next plaque said *Miss Amelia's Room*. Charlotte's daughter. Megan and Seth probably took the girl in and raised her with their children. Maybe Charlotte lived with them too. It was all probably in the book.

Donna moved on to the last door. She saw the name and clapped a hand over her mouth. Laughter bubbled up along with tears. The brass plaque glimmered in the flickering gaslights and the words upon it shimmered in her blurred vision.

Sugar Bear's Room.

She laughed, wiping tears away. Mrs. Powell's words came back to her.

I believe they're all the women she loved most in the world.

Donna tucked those words away in her heart.

She returned to her room and locked the door behind her. The lamp beside the bed cast a circle of light across the bedspread and over the floor. Outside the tall windows, the skyline of Fort Worth etched the black sky. She kicked off her sandals, crossed the room, and climbed on the bed. Sitting cross-legged, she held the book a moment, savoring the anticipation of reading the life story of her best friend.

The old house creaked and groaned. The familiar sounds made Donna smile. She remembered a time when she had found the place creepy. It had grown on her, the old house full of history and mystery where love had blossomed and flourished between two people with a destiny to reset time to something else, something, hopefully, better.

Across the room, beyond the reach of the light, the faint outline of Seth's door stood out among the shadows.

Donna wondered if it would ever open again.

ACKNOWLEDGMENTS

Thank you to the members, past and present, of my writing critique group NMSAWCG, without whose help this story would never have been written: Gay Downs, T'Keyah Adams, Bill Nash, Lynda Lotman, Linda Webb, Jason Charles, and Kristen Duke. To Gay Downs who helped me with formatting. To Bill Nash who gave me advice about self-publishing.

Thank you to those who read my story and gave suggestions: my sister Kathleen (Augsburg) Luczynski, my friends Betsy (Jaeger) Lawson, Kisha White-Farrar, and Roberta Meyers.

Thank you to friends who gave me advice and input on other issues: Chris and Michelle Bilardi, Debi Dreyer, Connie Driskell, Sandy Lenox, Carol Leszczynski, and Tracy Manning. To Bev Olin who helped me with describing, cleaning, and repairing the purple dress.

Special thanks to the priests, lay teachers, and especially the nuns who provided me with an excellent education at the Catholic schools I attended: St. Irene's in Warrenville, IL, Holy Cross in Batavia, IL, and Aurora Central Catholic High in Aurora, IL.

Love and gratitude to my late mother, Dorothy Augsburg, who instilled in me the love of the written word.

Finally, my gratitude to you, the readers, who took the time to read about Seth and Megan's love story.

ABOUT THE AUTHOR

Linda L. (Augsburg) Carlow grew up in Batavia, IL, a small town 40 miles west of Chicago. She moved to Fort Worth in 1980 where she met and fell in love with a tall, dark, and handsome Texan. They live in Alvarado, Texas, with a lovable German Shepherd and two demanding cats. Linda enjoys reading, writing, gardening, traveling, especially road trips, and laughing with her friends. She believes in the old Girl Scouts' motto: Make new friends but keep the old. One is silver, the other gold.

Follow Linda at www.facebook.com/lindacarlow-author

DISCUSSION QUESTIONS

1) Suggest a different title for the book.
2) What would you do if you mistakenly entered a meth house?
3) If you have watched *The Twilight Zone,* which episodes do you remember? Which is your favorite? Why?
4) What other time travel stories have you read?
5) If you could only take one small handbag with you to the past, what items would you put in it?
6) Have you ever had déjà vu? Do you think it means you lived a past life?
7) If you have ever been a waitress in a bar, what was the best part of the job? The worst?
8) If you could have a conversation with a 100-year-old person, what questions would you ask?
9) Given the chance, would you travel back in time? Which era or year? Why?
10) Which modern convenience would you miss the most? Why?
11) Which major event in history would you like to change? Why?
12) What was your experience the first time you drove a stick shift?
13) If you didn't have a car, how else could you get around where you live?
14) If your best friend told you she/he had met a time traveler, what would be your reaction?
15) What do you think would be Seth's reaction to music from the seventies and early eighties? His reaction to TV?
16) Discuss Megan's comment: "We may have more conveniences and gadgets in our time, but when you get right down to it, we really haven't come all that far from the cave."
17) How did the language of each character portray his or her personality?
18) Try to identify which character said these words:
    - Holy moly.
    - I can't let you just walk out of here.
    - If you know it all, you may not want to do it.
    - What is ... full of baloney?
    - You look mighty fetchin' in that dress.
    - All those other times were just a rehearsal for saying it to you.
    - I don't like you.

The Reader's Mark

___ ___ ___ ___ ___
___ ___ ___ ___ ___
___ ___ ___ ___ ___

Made in the USA
Lexington, KY
11 December 2019